Phillip Davis
1698 Coventry Rd
Cleveland Hts 18, Ohio

THE ENEMY CAMP

Books by Jerome Weidman

NOVELS

I Can Get It for You Wholesale
What's in It for Me?
I'll Never Go There Any More
The Lights Around the Shore
Too Early to Tell
The Price Is Right
The Hand of the Hunter
Give Me Your Love
The Third Angel
Your Daughter Iris
The Enemy Camp

SHORT STORIES

The Horse That Could Whistle "Dixie"
The Captain's Tiger
A Dime a Throw

ESSAYS AND TRAVEL

Letter of Credit
Traveler's Cheque

THE ENEMY CAMP

A NOVEL BY

JEROME WEIDMAN

RANDOM HOUSE · NEW YORK

FIFTH PRINTING

© *Copyright, 1958, by Jerome Weidman*

All rights reserved under International and Pan-American Copyright Conventions. Published in New York by Random House, Inc., and simultaneously in Toronto, Canada, by Random House of Canada, Limited.

Library of Congress Catalog Card Number: 58-5258

DESIGNED BY PHILIP GRUSHKIN

Manufactured in the United States of America

For Peggy

"Let us add another story, closely connected with this theme, which Seneca relates in one of his Epistles. 'You know,' he says, writing to Lucilius, 'that Harpaste, my wife's fool, was left on my hands as a hereditary charge, for I have a natural aversion to these monsters; and if I have a mind to laugh at a fool, I need not seek him far, I can laugh at myself. This fool has suddenly lost her sight. I am telling you a strange but true story. She is not aware that she is blind, and constantly urges her keeper to take her out, because she says my house is dark. What we laugh at in her I pray you to believe happens to every one of us; no one knows himself to be avaricious or covetous. The blind at least call for a guide, while we go astray of our own accord. I am not ambitious, we say, but in Rome one cannot live otherwise; I am not a spendthrift, but the city requires a great outlay; it is not my fault if I am choleric, if I have not yet settled upon a definite course of life; it is the fault of youth. Let us not seek our disease outside of ourselves, it is within us, it is implanted in our bowels. And the mere fact that we do not perceive ourselves to be sick makes our cure more difficult.' "

Not to Counterfeit Sickness
MONTAIGNE, Essays, II, xxv

"Never lose your enthusiasm, always keep cool, and the world is yours."

DANIEL SHAW, Commencement Address, UCLA,
June 11, 1949

I

I

1

If it was trouble you were after, Miss Akst was your girl.

"She can type a letter like nobody's business, and the way she handles a switchboard, Alexander Graham Bell himself would be proud of her," Mr. Farkas, her former boss, had said when George Hurst had called him up four years ago to get a line on Miss Akst's ability and character before he hired her. "But if you ask her to send down to the drug store for a container of coffee, I warn you, Mr. Hurst, when she brings it into your office Miss Akst will make you feel they sweetened it not with sugar but with a couple of teaspoons of ground glass."

George Hurst's wife Mary, who had majored in psychology at Bennington, had a more colorful explanation for his secretary's state of mind.

"Miss Akst's attitude toward life," said Mary, "is exactly the same as the attitude of the Lewis and Clark expedition toward the Indian tribes they met along the way: there's always a chance that they're friendly, but until they prove it, it's better to remember that you're in imminent danger of being scalped."

It occurred to George, as the sudden explosion of sound upstairs caused the razor to leap nervously up the side of his jaw, that he was in somewhat similar danger himself. He dabbed hastily at the small red stain that began promptly to ooze out of the lather on his cheek, turned off the hot water tap, stepped to the bathroom door, and shouted up the back stairs, "You want me?"

"Didn't you hear the phone?" Mary called.

"I had the water running."

"It's Miss Akst. She wants to talk to you."

Astonished, George glanced back across his shoulder at the wrist watch he had placed on the edge of the basin before he started to shave. "Now?" he said. "For God's sake, Mary, it's twelve minutes after seven!"

"It's what?"

"Twelve minutes after seven."

"Oh, Lord, that means the clock in our bedroom is on the blink again. It shows seven-thirty."

Mary's father, who had made his money as an industrial engineer in Philadelphia, had lost too much of it in the 1929 market crash to leave anything for his children that could be described as more than tokens of his affection. But Mary, who had inherited his good looks, had also managed to acquire her father's passion for accuracy. An electric clock that was out of order could spoil her day.

"If you bring it downstairs with you when the kids are dressed and put it on my briefcase in the study, I'll drop it off at Ashorn's on my way to the train," George said. "But what in God's name is Miss Akst calling about at this hour of the morning?"

"I don't know, darling. She's your secretary, not mine. Will you please pick up the kitchen phone and talk to her? I'm trying to get Win dug out from under all these frying pans."

During the summer months the two Hurst boys, of whom Winston, aged six, was the oldest, attended the Danville Y.M.C.A. day camp. On this day the Braves at Camp Shawmut were scheduled to have a cook-out. This meant that the six-year-olds, instead of eating the customary sandwich lunch they brought from home every day, would be allowed, under the supervision of a counselor, to roast hot dogs and fry hamburgers at a communal fire. Hot-dog eaters, according to the schedule, were to bring nothing but their raw material. Hamburger consumers, however, were required to bring, in addition to the meat, their own frying pans.

Win, who loved food more than he loved his parents, was determined to have both. He had completed all his preparations the night before by taking up to his room, and piling on a chair beside his bed where he could get at them without delay first thing in the morning, a frying pan, a spatula, a tin drinking cup, a bread knife, a barbecue fork, a small portable grill, and a mess kit that Mary had found in an army and navy store in Norwalk.

George Hurst always woke up at least a half hour before anybody else in the house stirred and, because he didn't want to disturb Mary and the children, always came downstairs to shower and shave in what the builder of the house had intended to be the maid's bathroom. George had not yet seen, therefore, what had happened upstairs in Win's room when his oldest son woke up and, surrounded by all those cooking utensils, the process of getting dressed got under way. But George could imagine.

"Tell Miss Akst to hold on," he called up the back stairs to his wife. "I'll be right with her."

He stepped back into the bathroom, snatched a towel, glanced hastily into the mirror, saw that the red stain was spreading down the lather in two tiny rivulets, and pressed a corner of the towel against the cut as he hurried out of the bathroom and across the kitchen toward the phone. He did it with a feeling of annoyance that he knew was unreasonable.

Unlike most commuters, George Hurst did not find the process of getting to work every morning the hysterical sprint against time that it was painted by comic-strip artists and television playwrights. He was a methodical person, with a neat and orderly mind. His neat and orderly mind told him that, if you started early enough, there was no need even to hurry, much less to sprint, and George liked to start early. He enjoyed the hours just after dawn and the small chores with which he filled them: putting on the coffee; taking in the newspapers and the milk; letting out the dog; bringing up from the freezer in the cellar the package of horsemeat that, late in the afternoon, would be d'Artagnan's thawed-out meal; pouring Mary's first cup of coffee; tiptoeing upstairs with it and nudging her awake as he set the cup on the small table between their beds; then coming downstairs again for his shave and his shower.

"It gives me a chance to come awake slowly, without any jolts," George had once explained to Mary. "And to do some thinking."

"What do you think about?"

"Nothing much," George had said. "Business mostly. I plan my day."

The plan for this one, which included lunch with Nick Perrini, one of George Hurst's oldest clients, had been jogging along smoothly, taking the sort of solid shape in George's mind that he always aimed at, when Miss Akst's unexpected phone call had come crashing in. George made an effort to conceal his annoyance as he reached for the phone.

It stood on the counter under the cupboard in which Mary kept cereals and canned goods. George picked up the phone and moved with it around the side of the cupboard toward the place where, under the magnetic knife rack, the Hurst family's part-time maid, Carolina, had hung the small mirror she had won two years ago at the Danbury Fair.

"Hello," George said. "Miss Akst?"

"Yes, hi, Mr. Hurst. Listen." There was a click in the earpiece. Miss Akst's voice, tense with sudden suspicion, demanded sharply, "What was that?"

"My wife," George said. "Hanging up the upstairs extension."

"Oh," said Miss Akst. Traces of disbelief as well as disappointment lingered unmistakably in her voice. Wire tappers, George recalled, had been very much in the news lately. "Listen, Mr. Hurst," Miss Akst said. "I hope you don't mind my calling you like this? This early, I mean?"

"No, of course I don't mind," George said. "It's just that—" He paused and, dipping down so he could see the damaged side of his face more clearly in Carolina's mirror, shifted the corner of the towel with which he was applying pressure to the shaving cut. "Miss Akst," he said. "Where are you calling from?"

"My home, of course," his secretary said. "Where *would* I be calling from at this hour of the morning?"

If she were physically attractive and ten or fifteen years younger instead of, like her boss, pushing forty, George could have thought of any number of romantic replies. As it was, his only thought was to remove at once even the most fragmentary implication of insult from the mind of the best secretary he'd ever had. "All I meant," George said, "I mean it's so damn early—"

"Not to a girl who has to come all the way from Bushwick Avenue to open an office on Forty-second Street by nine o'clock," Miss Akst said. "I get up a quarter to seven every day of my life. Listen, Mr. Hurst."

He wished as always that, instead of urging him to do so, she would get to whatever it was she wanted him to listen to. "I'm listening," George said.

"Do you know a Mr. Kashkin?"

"A Mr. Who?"

"Kashkin," Miss Akst said. "K, a, s, h, k, i, n?"

The simple syllables and innocent letters, crackling across the long-distance wire from Brooklyn to Connecticut, had a curious effect. In George Hurst's mind, at any rate. It was as though a bell had been struck. All at once, three decades after he had first known him, George could see clearly the blacksmith whose forge used to glow so brightly across the street from Aunt Tessie's tailor shop on Fourth Street, near the East River, where George had grown up. The blacksmith's name had been Kashkewitz. Doodoo Kashkewitz had been in George Hurst's class at P.S. 188. He had not thought of Doodoo for thirty years. It seemed funny to be thinking of him now.

"Kashkin?" George said. "No, I don't think I know anybody by that name."

"That's what he said."

"What?"

"That's what Mr. Kashkin said," Miss Akst said. "He said you wouldn't know him."

"Is that what you called to tell me?"

"For heaven's sake, Mr. Hurst. Of course not. What do you think I am?"

George wished she wouldn't tempt him like that. "Who is Mr. Kashkin?" he said.

"I don't know," Miss Akst said. "That's what makes me suspicious."

George moved away from Carolina's mirror, carrying the phone with him out into the middle of the kitchen, where he could see the electric clock over the refrigerator. It showed a quarter after seven. There was still plenty of time, since he rarely caught anything earlier than the 9:14 into New York. But d'Artagnan's ear was bad again and, in addition to getting the kids to camp and picking up Carolina at the Center and leaving the faulty electric clock at Ashorn's, George had promised Mary that, on his way to the train, he would drop off the dog at the vet. Until a couple of minutes ago it had looked as though all this could be accomplished with ease. Now that Miss Akst was on the phone, however, George was not so sure. His secretary's lust for trouble was followed closely in her affections by a passion for talking about it. She could go on, if not forever, certainly long enough to make a man miss his train.

"Miss Akst," George said. "How did you stumble into this Mr. Kashkin?"

"Who stumbled?" she said. "Last night, a few minutes after

you left to catch the five-twenty-five, he called up and introduced himself and asked for you. I told him you were gone for the day and was there anything I could do for him. He said no, he wanted to talk to you personally. I said okay, if he'd leave a number I'd have you call him back tomorrow, because after all, who knows, maybe he's a new client or something. You never can tell with these calls that come out of the blue. And this Mr. Kashkin, first he said okay, never mind you calling him back, don't bother, he'd give you another ring himself in the morning, and what time did you get into the office? I said around ten-thirty, depending on whether the train wasn't late or something, but say a quarter to eleven, or certainly by eleven o'clock he could be sure to get you in, and I thought that was that, when all of a sudden, instead of hanging up, this Mr. Kashkin he starts asking me these questions."

"What questions?"

There was a pause at the other end of the wire. George couldn't imagine its cause. He had never found Miss Akst to be hesitant in documenting her suspicions about the imminence of disaster.

"Well," she said finally. "He wanted to know what sort of person you are."

"What sort of person I am?"

"That's what this Mr. Kashkin asked," Miss Akst said.

Suddenly, and with a small sense of shock, George found himself trying to answer the question. He knew his address and the date of his birth and the names of his children and the color of his eyes, all the facts and figures that went into the blank spaces on a questionnaire. But the picture of which these facts and figures were a part, the picture that he had always assumed was as familiar to him and indelible as his own name, seemed all at once to have faded away, leaving nothing but an unrecognizable smudge. It was like those simple, commonplace words, used every day for years and without thought, that suddenly and for no apparent reason lose their meaning. So that hearing someone say shoe or ask for coffee becomes as strange an experience as overhearing a conversation in Hindustani.

Somewhat shaken, George moved back quickly with the phone, toward Carolina's mirror under the magnetic knife rack. Staring into the small oval, he saw the familiar and as yet uncombed black hair, the lather that had not yet been scraped away, the strong and fairly handsome features, the razor nick that had temporarily marred one cheek, the fine dark eyes that Aunt Tessie had loved and, years later, Mary had found disturbingly attractive.

They were all there, all the familiar pieces George Hurst had been looking at every morning of his life, certainly every morning since he started to shave. They were all there, and they were all familiar, and yet the face they added up to was not. It was, inexplicably and somewhat frighteningly, the face of a stranger.

"Well—" George said, and he tried to sound casual. He wasn't sure that he succeeded. All at once he wanted very much to hear Miss Akst's reply. "What did you tell Mr. Kashkin?"

"What *should* I tell a man who asks what sort of person you are?" Miss Akst said. "I told him you were an accountant, for my money one of the best in the field, and you were a swell boss to work for—"

"Thanks," George said. He had intended it as a humorous interjection, to relieve the odd tension he had suddenly felt building up on the telephone wire that separated him from Miss Akst. But his small joke failed. Miss Akst did not laugh. She merely paused. So that George had to prod her again. "What else did you tell him?"

"Well, he repeated he was more interested in what you were like as a person, not as an accountant," Miss Akst said. "So I told him you were a commuter, and you lived out in Danville, which is between Norwalk and Westport, one hour from Grand Central, and you were married, and you had two little boys, Winston six and a half and James five, and—"

Miss Akst's voice ground to another halt. George had the feeling that he must help her.

"I don't see anything particularly alarming about a man asking questions like that," he said. "Those things are pretty normal."

"It wasn't those questions," Miss Akst said. "It was the next one."

"What was the next one?"

"This Mr. Kashkin, Mr. Hurst, he asked if Mrs. Hurst, he wanted to know if your wife, if she was Jewish."

The mystery of Miss Akst's hesitation vanished along with the odd tension that had built up on the telephone wire.

"I see," George said.

He did not think he was an exception to the fairly general rule that no man is a hero to his valet or his secretary. But George had learned with the years that Miss Akst tended to regard him as a creature molded from clay somewhat finer than that which had been poured into the making of most men. He was, in Miss Akst's spinsterish, devoted eyes, that most desirable of creatures: a nice Jewish boy.

Except for one puzzling flaw.

Miss Akst's cultural roots were sunk in Bushwick Avenue and the bosom of a large, warm, complicated, closely knit orthodox Jewish family. She found it impossible to understand how a nice Jewish boy could marry anybody but a nice Jewish girl.

"What did you tell Mr. Kashkin?" George said.

"What should I tell him?" Miss Akst said. "First, I mean my first instinct, I wanted to say it's none of your business whether Mr. Hurst's wife is Jewish or not. But then I figured no. First of all, in case this Mr. Kashkin is a client, potentially I mean, this is a way to make friends and influence people? By telling him first crack out of the box mind your own business? And second, after all, it's something to be ashamed of?"

It would have been difficult for a stranger to tell whether Miss Akst had asked a question or uttered a statement of fact. George, however, was no stranger. He knew that Miss Akst's voice had come to another abrupt halt because she most certainly did consider it something to be ashamed of, and she was horrified because, after four cautious years, she was now afraid she had at last inadvertently revealed her true feelings on the subject. Secretaries as good as Miss Akst did not grow on trees. George did not want her to quit because she had accidentally embarrassed herself. The time had come to get Miss Akst off the hook.

"How did Mr. Kashkin react?" George said.

"To what, Mr. Hurst?"

"Your portrait of what I'm like as a person?"

"He said you sounded like just the man he was looking for, and tomorrow morning, that's today already of course, he said tomorrow morning when you came in the office, he'd be there waiting for you."

"I see," George said, although he didn't. "Did Mr. Kashkin say why I sounded like just the man he was looking for?"

"No, he didn't, Mr. Hurst, and that's exactly why I'm calling. After he hung up and I closed the office and I went home and I had my supper and my mother and I we watched *I Love Lucy*, all that time, Mr. Hurst, you won't believe it, but all that time my mind was going around and around, worrying about it. Not big worrying. I don't mean I kept thinking about it. I mean it was sort of in the back of my mind, you might say. Like a little, oh, an itch maybe, Mr. Hurst. You know?"

"Yes, of course," George said.

The way, even as he was listening to Miss Akst, in the back of his own mind there was that small, puzzled, nagging sound which kept repeating over and over again variations of Mr. Kashkin's question: *What sort of person is George Hurst?*

"I won't go so far as to say it kept me awake," Miss Akst said. "But it was in the back of my mind all night, Mr. Hurst, I can tell you that. Sort of bothering me, you might say. And a little while ago, when I got up, there it was, still bothering me. I can't exactly say what it is that bothers me about it, Mr. Hurst, but a few minutes ago, while I was in the shower, all of a sudden I got this picture in my mind."

George winced. The pictures Miss Akst got in her mind, he had learned, could very often serve as illustrations for Dante's *Inferno*. "What picture?" he said.

"I got this picture in my mind of you around say a quarter to eleven this morning, Mr. Hurst. You're coming into the office from the train. You don't suspect anything. You open the door. You walk in carrying your briefcase and your newspaper. And bango, sitting in the reception room, there's this Mr. Kashkin. Without warning, I mean. You know what I mean, Mr. Hurst?"

"Well," George said.

"Exactly," Miss Akst said. "So I thought to myself no, this I won't let happen, and I decided to call you up and warn you. Because it's like my mother always says, Mr. Hurst. Forewarned is forearmed. You know?"

"I certainly do," George said. "Thanks a lot, Miss Akst."

"That's all right, Mr. Hurst. You catching the nine-fourteen?"

"Yes."

"Are you sure you don't know anybody named Kashkin?"

"Positive."

"That's funny," Miss Akst said slowly. "I could have sworn—" She sighed and said, "Oh, well, I'll see you around a quarter to eleven, Mr. Hurst."

George had replaced the receiver and started back across the kitchen toward the bathroom before he realized that he had neglected to ask Miss Akst what she wanted him to be forewarned against and to what it was she could have sworn.

"George?"

He paused at the bathroom door to look up the back stairs. "Yes?"

"Jimmy's casting rod," Mary called. "Have you seen it?"

"Wait a minute."

George went back across the kitchen to the room in which Carolina would have slept if the Hursts had been able to afford a full-time, live-in maid. Since Carolina worked for the Hursts only on Thursdays and Fridays, the room had been converted into a play-room for Win and Jimmy. The conversion had been accomplished with a second-hand studio couch, a home-made bookcase, and a battered television set that Mr. Karp, who owned the Danville Music Shop, had taken as a trade-in from a customer and then sold to George for fifty dollars.

These three main items in the room were surrounded and held together, the way bricks are surrounded and held in a wall, by a crude but effective mortar composed of crumpled comic books; incompleted, finished, and partially demolished model airplanes; bits and pieces of two Erector sets; damp swimming trunks; wadded dirty towels; four baseball bats; a catcher's mitt; a bushel of bubble-gum wrappers; the entrails of a teddy bear; a torn butterfly net; four miraculously intact badminton rackets; several dozen items that even the toy manufacturers from whose plants they had come could no longer have identified with any degree of certainty; and the two frayed wicker chairs in which the rulers of this untidy domain sat while they ate their breakfast and watched television.

Leaning against the bookcase, between d'Artagnan's water dish and Win's leather camera bag, was Jimmy's casting rod. George checked it quickly to make sure the reel was in working order, then went back across the kitchen to the foot of the back stairs.

"Mary?"

"Yes?"

"It's down in the playroom."

"What is?"

"Jimmy's casting rod."

"Oh, that. Yes. All right, darling, thanks." Mary's voice died away as she turned to convey to Jimmy the reassuring news that his career as a fisherman was not about to be cut short, and George turned back into the bathroom. Mary's voice stopped him. "Oh, George?"

"Yes?"

"What did Miss Akst want?"

"Some question about the Perrini balance sheet," he said. "I'm lunching with Nick Perrini today, and she was afraid I might overlook it."

"Couldn't you train her to wait until you came into the office?"

"You know Miss Akst."

"That poor troubled girl," Mary said. "The way she keeps hunting for floods, pestilence, and hangnails. Honestly."

George didn't answer. He didn't have to. Mary's voice had sunk once more into the pool of complicated noises that were the regular morning accompaniment to the job of getting Win and Jimmy on their feet. It wasn't until he had turned on the hot-water tap and moistened the lather that had gone dry on his face while he'd been talking with Miss Akst, that George had his second shock of the morning.

Why, he was suddenly asking himself as he stood there, razor poised, staring at himself in the mirror, why hadn't he told Mary the truth about Miss Akst's call? Why had he lied about it?

He was still trying to think of an answer when, having finished his shave, smeared the small nick with styptic powder, and stepped out of the shower, it was time for what Mary called the Hurst Family's Daily Double.

Mary had learned many things while growing up in Philadelphia and studying at Bennington that were still a puzzle to George. The language of the race track was not one of them. Mary had no idea what a daily double was. But she did have a painter's eye and a musician's ear. They told her instinctively that the phrase "daily double" was the perfect description in sound, no matter how inaccurate it might be technically, for what happened every morning in the Hurst house when George turned off the shower taps in the downstairs bathroom.

"All right, kids," Mary always said in a loud, clear voice. "The old man is on his way up."

Winston and James never failed to respond with a series of protests about the fact that they were only partially dressed.

"You can finish downstairs," Mary said. "Come on, now, get going."

They always did, down the front stairs, carrying their shoes and socks, while George, carrying his pajamas and robe, went up the back stairs. This reversal of positions was always accomplished without either party to the scene catching sight of the other, so that it was not until he came downstairs again, fully dressed, that George had his first chance of the day to catch a glimpse of his family all in a group.

On this morning, as on hundreds of others that had preceded it, the sight gave him a funny little feeling in his heart. On this morning, as on hundreds of others that had preceded it, he had to stop for a moment at the far end of the kitchen. Not exactly to collect himself. After all, in approximately sixteen hours he would be forty years old, and he had known these three people for a long time. But George Hurst always did need that moment to adjust himself to the reality of their existence. He couldn't believe, until he lived through the moment of adjustment, that they really belonged to him.

"How did I do it?" an inner voice always demanded. "How did I get a wife like this and kids like these? How did it happen?"

In her early twenties, when George Hurst had met her, Mary Sherrod had been breath-taking. Not just what was known in her parents' circle as a great beauty and in her own set as a knockout. She had been literally breath-taking. And not only to George. When he thought about some of the men from under whose noses he had snatched her, he experienced not pride but an intensification of the feeling of disbelief. He couldn't have done it. It was impossible. Yet he had. Somehow or other he had managed to swing it. There she was, every morning, in her early thirties still a knockout and to him still a little breath-taking, to prove that he had done it. And there to underscore the proof were the children, with his height and Mary's features, giving every indication already that they were well on their way to being knockouts themselves. The evidence refused to be anything less than incontrovertible. George Hurst may not have known how he had done it, but it was obvious that he had.

"Hi, darling," Mary called from the stove. "The boys are having eggs. How about you?"

"I don't know," George said, and he started across the kitchen toward her. The moment was over. Once again, as on all those hundreds of preceding mornings, he had adjusted to the incredible fact that Mary and Win and Jimmy belonged to him. He stopped at the stove, kissed the top of Mary's blond head, and tried to peer at what she was stirring slowly in the frying pan. He said, "What kind?"

"Scrambled."

"Uh-oh," George said. "Not for me, thanks."

Ever since Aunt Tessie had first made them for him down on East Fourth Street, scrambled eggs had been one of his favorite dishes. Then came the war, during which George was stationed in England, where powdered eggs had been to the table in his mess as Rodgers is to Hammerstein. As a result, four years after V-E Day, even hearing the word scrambled was still enough to give George Hurst a slight feeling of queasiness.

"Now, really," Mary said. "Don't you think it's high time you stopped all this nonsense about scrambled eggs?"

"I do," George said. "It's my stomach that doesn't."

"I could make you some oatmeal?"

"No, you go right ahead with the kids' stuff. I'll find something."

He took a strip of bacon from the neat row draining on a paper towel near the frying pan and munched it as he went to the table at the far end of the room. It was set for two. Picking up the electric percolator, George leaned across to peer into the playroom. "Hi, men," he said.

Neither Jimmy nor Win replied. They were sitting in their wicker chairs, breakfast trays on their laps, sipping orange juice and staring transfixed at the television screen.

"I wouldn't try to elicit any response," Mary said from the stove. "It's an old Krazy Kat cartoon."

"They look like they're watching Lindbergh come in at Le Bourget."

"These kids never even heard of Lindbergh," Mary said. She scraped golden mounds of scrambled egg from the frying pan into two plates, set the pan in the sink, and picked up the plates. "I could boil one for you?"

"No, thanks," George said. He filled his cup, set the percolator back in place, and sat down at the table. "I don't believe it."

"Believe what?" Mary said, coming across with the plates.

"That they never heard of Lindbergh."

"Okay, watch," Mary said. She went into the playroom. She put a plate of scrambled eggs on the tray in front of each of her sons, then clapped her hands sharply. "Hey, you two!"

Nothing happened. George, watching from the table in the kitchen, took a sip of coffee. It was, as always, good coffee. But, as always, it didn't taste right. Aunt Tessie had believed that coffee, along with tea, whiskey, and opium, was an invention of the devil. She'd never had coffee in the house. George had been almost eighteen before he realized it was considered proper by some people to drink anything but milk with their meals. He had tried to emulate them, but without success.

It was not until he married Mary, and he learned how much she enjoyed that first morning cup of coffee in bed, that he had tried again. He wanted to share all her experiences. So George had started, in those early years of their married life, to bring two cups of coffee into their bedroom every morning. For several months he had even managed, sitting on his own bed and chatting with Mary, to drink his coffee. But he didn't really like it, and after a while he had stopped doing it.

The explanation he had given Mary was that he found it impossible to enjoy eating or drinking anything until he had shaved and showered and was fully dressed. The truth of the matter was that he found it impossible to enjoy coffee under any circumstances. The undoubtedly silly belief that it was a vice, which Aunt Tessie had implanted in the mind of a child, refused to yield to the dictates of either an adult intelligence or a now fairly sophisticated palate. George Hurst still disliked coffee.

Nevertheless, for a dozen years he had pretended otherwise. At least with Mary. He never ordered coffee in restaurants when he was alone or lunching with clients in New York. In some way that he did not quite understand, however, he would have felt disloyal to Mary if he did not drink at least one cup with his breakfast and, more important, go through the pretense of enjoying it.

He took another sip and smacked his lips to simulate delicate appreciation as he watched Mary, in the playroom, pick up a disemboweled electric locomotive and one of the baseball bats and begin to beat them together. For several moments the hideous clatter accomplished nothing. Then, slowly, like a strip of adhesive tape being peeled from a finger, Win's glance came away from the television screen.

He had a fresh, round face, wide blue eyes, and Mary's blond hair. Nothing his mother was doing was half so outlandish as the antics of Krazy Kat on the small screen, but Win stared at Mary as though she had said something deliberately insulting to Tim Keogh, the athletic instructor at Camp Shawmut who currently occupied in the Hurst boys' private pantheon of heroes a position not unlike that occupied by Abraham Lincoln among America's political figures.

"For Pete's sake, Ma," Win said. "You nuts?"

Before Mary could reply, Jimmy's glance, too, came peeling away from the television screen. He was small and compact, with a lean, handsomely shaped head and his father's dark eyes and black hair. He was not volatile, like Win. Jimmy was patient and methodical, like his father, with a surprisingly complete replica of George's own neat and methodical mind.

"Ma," Jimmy said in a pained but elaborately calm voice, "I am trying very hard to listen to a program."

"And I," said Mary, "am trying very hard to get your attention."

"For what?" Win said.

"I want to ask you a question."

"Will you please ask it, Ma?" Jimmy said. "Before we miss any more of this program?"

"Did you ever hear of Lindbergh?"

"Who?" Win said.

George leaned further across the table, toward the playroom door. He was aware of a sudden and unreasonable sense of anxiety. "Charles A. Lindbergh," he said.

Win and Jimmy turned from their mother to look at George. "Who?" Win said again.

"Charles A. Lindbergh," George repeated in a loud, clear voice. He tried not to sound tense. "Charles Augustus Lindbergh?"

A faint frown appeared on Jimmy's neat little face. Win, running his tongue along the rim of his orange-juice glass to capture the last drops, suddenly started to smile. He put down the glass and nudged Jimmy. "Dad's joking," Win said.

"I am not," George said sharply. According to Gesell and Ilg, whose books Mary kept within easy reach on the clothes hamper in the upstairs bathroom, in much the same way that early settlers in hostile Indian territory used to keep their flintlocks handy when they were ploughing, six was the age of contrariness. George was willing to take the good doctors' word for it. His own memory told him, however, that if, at six or any other age, he had talked to Aunt Tessie the way his sons were allowed to talk to him and Mary, his rear end would have been walloped until he couldn't sit. George had never walloped either of his children. It seemed, he thought now, that the least Win could do to repay him was remember Lindbergh. Enunciating even more clearly, George said, "Charles Augustus Lindbergh?"

"Sure you're joking," Win said. "It's a joke, Dad, and you know it." He nudged Jimmy again. "It's just a joke."

"A fine time to make jokes," Jimmy said. "When we're in the middle of a program."

"While you're at it," Mary said, "I want you to get into the middle of your scrambled eggs, please. Both of you."

"Okay, okay, okay," Win said, picking up his fork. "For Pete's sake."

A moment later, shoveling scrambled egg into his mouth, he had been reclaimed by Krazy Kat. Jimmy didn't even bother to reply to his mother. Mary waited just long enough to make sure that he, too, in spite of his absorption in Krazy Kat, was forking up scrambled eggs. Then she came out into the kitchen, sat down at the table facing George, and poured herself a cup of coffee.

"You and your Charles Augustus Lindbergh," she said. "How about some cornflakes?"

"All right, sure, thanks," George said. He felt a little hurt, and a little cheated, as though he had been let down by someone on whose loyalty he had come to believe he had a right to depend. He shook his head as Mary stood up, went to the cupboard, took down the box of cornflakes, and brought it back to the table. "If they didn't know who Suzanne Lenglen was, all right," George said, trying for a light tone, as though it were a joke. "Or Zachary Landsdowne. But Lindbergh, for God's sake!"

"Zachary Landsdowne?" Mary said. "Who was he?"

George stopped pouring cornflakes into his bowl. He forgot all about the light tone. "You mean to say you don't know who Zachary Landsdowne was?"

"Skip that *My God, How Did I Ever Land in This Nest of Idiots* look," Mary said. "I do mean to say I don't know who Zachary Landsdowne was. You want some cream with that?"

"No, this milk is fine," George said. "He was the commander of the *Shenandoah*."

Behind the uplifted coffee cup Mary's face did that extraordinary thing it always did when her mind, constantly on the alert for new facts, found one. Her face seemed to glow. "The *ill-fated Shenandoah!*"

George began to feel better. "See?" he said. "You do remember."

"I remember the headlines, anyway," Mary said, smearing butter on the corner of a scrap of toast. "That's still no reason why these television-reared kids behind me should remember Lindbergh. Every generation has its own heroes. Suppose, when you were a child, your mother had asked you if you remembered Ulysses S. Grant?"

That was one thing about Bennington girls, thought George, who had come to know quite a few of Mary's classmates: they knew how to argue.

"She couldn't very well have asked that," he said. "Since I never had a mother."

Mary made an impatient gesture with the scrap of toast. "Biologically speaking everybody had a mother," she said. "You know what I mean."

He certainly did. George had been adopted at the age of three, and removed from the Henry Isaacs Orphan Asylum on Houston Street to her tailor shop on Fourth Street, by the woman he had come to know as Aunt Tessie.

"I don't think Aunt Tessie ever heard of Ulysses S. Grant," George said. "In fact, I'm sure of it."

"Well, I'm sure of this," Mary said. "Not knowing who Lindbergh is won't prove to be a stumbling block to Win or Jimmy on the road to their first million."

"I didn't say it would," George said. "I merely said—"

"What Miss Akst would have said," Mary said. "If they don't know who Lindbergh is, it shows they're in a bad school, and if they're in a bad school, it means they're receiving no instructions in how to fly a DC-7, so that when they happen to be up in one, and the pilot drops dead of a heart attack while the plane is twenty thousand feet over the Continental Divide, neither Win nor Jimmy will be equipped to leap to the controls. Result: holocaust. Cause? They were not taught who Lindbergh is."

Mary smiled at him across her coffe cup, waiting for his laugh. It didn't come. Not because she didn't deserve it. As breakfast table humor went, George felt that Mary's bit had been pretty good. The trouble was that he couldn't bring himself to laugh. By mentioning

Miss Akst, Mary had suddenly thrust him back into the uneasy mental state that had descended on him when, a quarter of an hour ago, he had been talking to his secretary on the phone.

"Listen," George said. "Do we know anybody named Kashkin?"

"Haskin?"

"No, Kashkin. K, a, s, h, k, i, n."

Mary peered thoughtfully out at the grape arbor as she nibbled her toast. "There's that Mrs. Bashlin in the League of Women Voters," she said. "The one who wears all those bracelets made of sea shells and wants to run for First Selectman."

"No," George said. "Her husband is the advertising man. I see him on the train all the time."

"Well, there's Henry Praskin."

"Who's he?"

"Mr. Karp's son-in-law. The red-headed man, the young one. He works in the Music Shop. He delivered the boys' television set and was here for hours installing it. You've talked to him a thousand times."

"That guy, no," George said. "I'm not talking about local people out here in Danville."

"You mean someone we knew in New York?" Mary said. "Before we moved out here?"

"I don't know," George said. "I guess so."

Mary looked puzzled. "You guess so?"

George poured more milk over his cornflakes. He did it very carefully. "If I knew," he said, "I wouldn't be asking, would I?"

"I don't know exactly what you're asking."

It occurred to George that he didn't really know himself. "I'm asking if we know anybody named Kashkin."

"But why?"

"Miss Akst mentioned him on the phone."

Mary's face cleared. "Oh, it's something to do with the Perrini Brothers balance sheet," she said. "Your lunch date with Nick Perrini today?"

"Well, yes," George said uncomfortably. "It's sort of connected with the Perrini balance sheet."

"Then why don't you say so, instead of being so mysterious about it?" Mary said. "Let me think, now."

She stared out the kitchen window, scowling slightly at the grape arbor in the back yard. It had been planted many years ago by an

Italian family that had lived in the house long before the war. The succeeding owner, from whom George and Mary had bought the house, had told them that he had always meant to cut it down because, even though the blue Concords were nice to have, especially if you liked grape jelly, the truth of the matter was that, what with the cost of spraying and pruning, it was much cheaper to buy your jelly at the grocer's and, besides, during the summer, when the leaves were out, the arbor tended to block the sunlight from the kitchen window.

All this was true enough, yet George and Mary had not cut down the grape arbor. Every year they meant to make grape jelly, and every year, when they didn't get around to it, they agreed it was silly to waste money on spraying and pruning something they did not use, and every year they decided to cut the arbor down. But they hadn't, and George knew they never would. Not because Mary said she couldn't bear to cut it down because it reminded her of the grape arbor they used to have back of the house in Bala Cynwyd in which she had been born and raised. On that score George knew, if he insisted, Mary would give way. He had never insisted, however. He had never told Mary why, either. Not that he had wanted to keep anything from her. It was just one of those things you felt but never got around to putting into words. When he had been a boy, every year, in the early fall, pushcart peddlers used to show up on East Fourth Street with baskets of grapes. Aunt Tessie always bought four baskets, with which she and George made the Passover wine for the following year.

There was quite a gap between Bala Cynwyd on the Philadelphia Main Line and East Fourth Street on New York's Lower East Side. It seemed to George that the grape arbor in the back yard of the house in Danville narrowed the gap considerably. It was something he and Mary had in common. He didn't exactly know how to put it into words that wouldn't have sounded a little silly, so he had never mentioned it to Mary. But he had never stopped feeling it, and he felt it now as, across the breakfast table, he watched Mary scowling out at the arbor, trying to find in the massed green leaves some clue to the question he had asked.

"Kashkin," Mary muttered. "Kashkin, Kashkin, Kashkin."

"There's an Alvin Kashkin in my tepee, Ma."

Mary turned to look into the playroom. George stopped spooning up cornflakes.

"What happened to Krazy Kat?" Mary said.

"Aah, it's that creep selling Naturo now," Win said. He pointed his fork at the television screen. The rich, round, depraved tones of the commercial came pouring into the kitchen. Win made a disrespectful noise in the direction of the set and said, "Alvin Kashkin is in my tepee, Ma."

"Are you sure?" Mary said.

"Positive," Win said.

"Is he a new kid in town?" George said. "I mean, do you know him from school, too, or just camp?"

"Just camp," Win said. "I think his family came out here for the summer. From New York."

Jimmy, who had been following the announcer's account of Naturo's many virtues, suddenly tore his glance from the screen. "Who you talking about?" he demanded.

"Can't you hear?" Win said. "Alvin Kashkin. In my tepee. With those white sneakers that have the red line around the bottom."

Jimmy's neat little features arranged themselves in a look of disgust. "Him, for Pete's sake."

"Yeah, him," Win said. "What about him, you're so wise?"

"The kid with the fiberglas rod?" Jimmy said. "And the red and blue Jitterbug?"

Jimmy's passions, though few, were total. When he embraced a hobby it became, for the duration of his enslavement, a way of life. He had fallen in love with fishing only the week before, when school had ended and camp had started. It was in terms of fishing and fishing tackle that he now judged and identified people.

"Yeah," Win said. "So what?"

"So this what," Jimmy said. "That kid's name ain't Alvin Kashkin."

"Isn't," Mary said.

"Isn't," Jimmy said.

"You're so wise," Win said, "all right, what is it?"

"Alvin Kingston," Jimmy said.

"You're crazy," Win said.

"You're crazy yourself," Jimmy said.

"All right, boys," Mary said. "Back to Krazy Kat."

"He's finished," Win said. "Now it's this creep with the commercial."

"Let's have some more work on those eggs," Mary said. "Come on, it's getting late."

The phone rang. George reached across to the counter and took the receiver. "Hello?"

"Is Winston there?"

"Yes," George said. "Just a moment."

He held the phone out toward his oldest son. "For you, Win."

The round face lit up. Win was as gregarious as a ward-heeling politician. Half the calls that came into the Hurst house were for him. To George this seemed only proper since, when he and Mary had decided to move out to Danville after the war, the theory on which they had based their decision had been built around their then infant son.

They had been married during the war while Mary, who had graduated from Bennington a couple of years before Pearl Harbor, was still studying art and George was home on leave. The small apartment they took on West Twelfth Street, just off Fifth Avenue, had been more than adequate for a young couple one half of which was in London most of the time and the other half of which was working at the Academy on Fifty-seventh Street five days a week. By the end of the war, during which George had managed to wangle missions that brought him back to New York several times, the apartment on West Twelfth Street was far from adequate: George and Mary were no longer a couple. They had become a trio, and a second baby was on the way.

"I don't want to sound like a nagging wife," Mary had said one day when she came home from her regular weekly checkup by the obstetrician. "But don't you think this little love nest is beginning to seem a trifle crowded?"

"I was just thinking the same thing myself," said George. "I'll call Nick Perrini in the morning and ask him if he can help find us a larger apartment. Nick has a lot of friends in real estate."

"Instead of moving to a larger apartment," Mary said, "I've been thinking maybe we ought to move out to the country."

"You mean you want to turn me into a commuter?"

"Just because you were born and raised and lived all your life on Manhattan Island does not mean that to attempt any other way of life is the equivalent of signing a suicide pact. My own father commuted from Bala Cynwyd to his office in Philadelphia for almost thirty years before he died, and there was nothing wrong with Winston Sherrod the First."

"Nothing that could be fixed by moving his home and his office to the same location, no."

"Let's not start that. You know Father was really very fond of you, deep down."

"Deep down where?"

"Deep down where we all keep the store of quirks and prejudices that we have absolutely nothing to do with accumulating. They're handed to us at birth, and they get underscored and intensified by the kind of lives we are forced by our elders to lead before we have anything to say about the kind of life we want to lead. Instead of taking pot shots at him, I think you really should take your hat off to Daddy for the way he adjusted to our marriage. After all, you were quite a blow to him."

"That remark hangs up a new record in the Putting Things Mildly Sweepstakes," George said. "I suppose if he'd dropped dead when you told him you were going to marry me, instead of just screaming his beautifully groomed head off, you would have expected me to call on the district attorney and plead with him to indict me for murder."

"No, I wouldn't, but I'd expect you to be grown-up and adult about it."

Bennington girls, George had noticed, always expected you to be grown-up and adult about it, no matter what "it" was.

"There are a couple of things I don't want to be grown-up and adult about," George said. "One of them is the memory of your father. He hated my guts from the minute he heard about me, and he hated them worse after we met, and if I live to be a hundred I'll feel exactly the same way about him."

"That's very childish."

It was also very satisfying. "I can't help that."

"Of course you can. All you have to do is make an effort."

"That's one effort I don't want to make."

Mary had looked at him quickly, with an odd little expression on her face. It was as though she had been hurrying along a familiar corridor and all at once she had caught a glimpse, through a window the existence of which she had never suspected, into an unpleasantly furnished room the contents of which were somehow offensive to her.

As soon as he saw that expression on her face, George regretted his words. He had spoken without thought, out of a depth of feeling he had not himself suspected. It was a feeling, he saw in that unguarded moment of revelation, he could not ask Mary to share. Not because she was pregnant, and he didn't want to distress her. Nor even because he loved her, and he couldn't bear to see her hurt. It was simply that his reasons for hating her father could never be Mary's reasons. She could fall in love with a man named George Hurst. She could marry him. She could live with him. She could even think she thought like him. But she could never hate like him. To be able to do that you had to be born a Hurst.

George had been careful during the years that followed not to give Mary any more glimpses through that unsuspected window into that unpleasant room. The years of practice had made him skillful as well as careful, so that keeping the window shut had become fairly automatic, something that required almost no effort at all. On that day of revelation, however, so soon after their wedding, he had not yet learned the necessity for being careful, and he had not yet had the practice that later made him skillful. On that day during the third year of their marriage he had been shaken by the discovery that there were things he would never be able to tell her. So much so that, for several long, uncomfortable moments, he could think of nothing to say.

Mary recovered first. "You said there are a couple of things you don't want to be grown-up and adult about," she said quietly. "What's the other one?"

"Becoming a commuter," George said, glad to get back to a safe subject. "I thought you liked New York?"

"I adore it," Mary said. "Or rather I did when I was, you know, a girl. But now I'm a mother, and I'm about to become a mother again, and I've had almost a full year of baby-carriaging Win over to Washington Square for a daily dose of sun and air, and frankly it doesn't strike me as being the best or most sensible way to do it. In Bala Cynwyd sun and air were not a project. In Bala Cynwyd sun and air were something everybody had all the time because they were all around you, and you may think I'm old-fashioned, but I still think that's the best way, and I'd like our kids to have it that way. Commuting isn't all that bad, darling. Really it isn't."

"Assuming it isn't," George said. "Where would I be commuting to?"

"There are dozens of places out on Long Island and Connecticut and up in Westchester, all perfectly nice and all within our price range. It's just a matter of shopping around."

"You mean we're going to start spending our week ends driving all over the map from one town to another trying to find—?"

"No, because for our special situation I think there's really only one place."

"Our special situation?"

Mary looked at him through a small, puzzled scowl. "Darling," she said finally, "our children are half Jewish."

"Oh," George said.

It was not the most appropriate comment, but it was all he could manage at the moment. Again he had been taken by surprise, and this seemed so odd that he was astonished. How could he possibly be surprised by a thing like that? It was preposterous for Mary to have to remind him of what she called their special situation.

"If we stayed on here in New York," Mary said, "I don't suppose it would be much of a problem. Anti-Semitism in a big city can usually be diluted, or you can usually insulate yourself against it. All you have to do is move in the right circles. I don't exactly know what they are in New York, but I'm sure as the children grow older we'd find out. Commuting towns, though, they're different. It's infuriating maybe, but at least it's not surprising. You always know where you stand with a commuting town long before you get there, or even try to get there. In our special situation, for example, if we tried to settle in Darien, anything that happened to us, well, don't get sore, but we'd deserve it. Darien is that kind of town, and they're not only not ashamed of it, they want everybody to know how they feel, so people like us won't make the mistake of trying to settle there. In Danville, however, it wouldn't happen."

"Danville?" George said.

"Where Eileen Bucknell lives," Mary said.

Eileen Bucknell had been raised three houses down from Mary in Bala Cynwyd and had gone to Bennington with her. After graduation they went on together to the Academy on Fifty-seventh Street, where Mary enrolled in several fine arts courses and Eileen settled down to become a fashion designer. Less than a year after she came to the Academy, Eileen married her teacher, a talented Hungarian refugee named Milton Schneider. Soon after Carlotta, their first and only child was born, Eileen and Milton gave up their apartment on Bank Street and moved out to Danville.

"How do they like it?" George asked.

"They're crazy about it," Mary said. "I talked to Eileen on the phone this afternoon, just before I went to see Dr. Stern for my checkup. They've been there almost a year now, and Eileen says they like it better every day. So far as Milton is concerned, it's not a bad commute at all. Fifty minutes from Grand Central, and it gives him a chance not only to read the papers, but also to get some work done. Eileen says you'd be surprised how much Milton gets done during those two train trips every day."

"Milton is a Hungarian," George said. "Aunt Tessie used to say—"

"Is there any subject under the sun on which Aunt Tessie did not at one time or another utter the definitive observation?"

"I don't think she ever said anything about commuting," George said. "But she sure polished off Hungarians. Aunt Tessie used to say a Hungarian is the kind of person who will come into a restaurant without a penny in his pocket, walk over to your table, sit down without an invitation, and not only will he calmly order the most expensive dishes on the menu and have them put on your check, but he will insist that the violinist come over and play in his ear while he eats."

"You know darn well Milton Schneider is not like that at all," Mary said. "He's a sweet, meek, shy, mousy little man who—"

"He's a Hungarian," George said. "Underneath that sweet, meek, shy, mousy exterior—"

"There is now a happy commuter. But the main reason Milton is happy, Eileen says, is not because of the amount of work he gets done on the train. It's because of the kind of community Danville is. It's not one of these stuffy suburban towns, full of fake Tudor houses and restricted areas. Danville is full of artists and writers and actors and advertising men, the kind of people who don't have any special feelings about Jews or religion or that kind of thing. There are a lot of mixed marriages in Danville, just like ours and Eileen's and Milton's, and the people are all friendly and pleasant, but the main thing, Eileen says, is that there is absolutely no anti-Semitism."

"Honey bunch," George said. "There is anti-Semitism on the Ross Ice Shelf."

"Where is that?"

"Near the South Pole. Admiral Byrd discovered it."

"You and your childhood heroes," Mary said. "Well, there may be anti-Semitism on the Ross Ice Shelf, but according to Eileen there isn't any in Danville. Which brings me to my main point. I'm not neurotic about anti-Semitism. But I'm not so sure that I'll be able to say the same for our kids."

"Why not?"

"They're going to be different from you and me," Mary said. "You can kid me all you want about Bennington and my psychology courses, but I did learn enough from them to appreciate that Win and Jimmy are going to need a special break. Just as Eileen's and Milton's daughter Carlotta is going to need it. Eileen says in Danville she's getting it. I'd like our children to get it, too."

"What kind of break?"

"The break of not being considered freaks by the rest of the community. I want Win and Jimmy to grow up on an equal footing with all the other children in their neighborhood, regardless of race, color, creed, or previous condition of servitude, exactly as it says in the Constitution. I don't want people whispering about them behind their backs. I don't want them to be taught to cower in corners because they're different from other people. I don't want them cut out of things. I don't want people not inviting them to parties or letting them go to a certain dancing school or— Oh, you know. God damn it, you can laugh at me if you want to for using a silly word, but what I want, I want my kids to be popular."

George had not laughed at her. He, too, wanted his kids to be popular. So they had moved to Danville and now, four years later, there were times when he and Mary couldn't get to the phone. Holding it out now toward Win, watching his oldest son clamber out of the wicker chair and, with eyes alight, come hurrying eagerly across the littered playroom into the kitchen, George felt it was all worth it.

Win snatched the phone and, with the back of his hand, wiped bits of scrambled egg away from his lips. "Hi," he said into the mouthpiece. "Who's this?" He listened for a while, nodding happily and twisting the telephone cord with his free hand. "I'll ask my mother," he said finally. "Wait a minute." He turned to Mary at the table. "It's Dickie Stiefel," Win said. "He wants to know could I bring some hard-boiled eggs along for the cook-out?"

"Eggs *for* hard-boiling?" Mary said. "Or eggs already hard-boiled?"

"Wait a minute," Win said, and then, into the phone, "Eggs to hard-boil in camp, Dickie, or hard-boiled already here at home?" He listened for a moment or two, then turned back to Mary. "Dickie says already hard-boiled here, Ma."

"Does Dickie realize that you already have in your lunch box six hamburgers and six hot dogs?" Mary said. "Not counting a dozen rolls and a bottle of ketchup and a jar of mustard and a jar of pickles?"

"I know, Ma, but gee whiz," Win said. "It's just hard-boiled eggs."

"It's also, if you'll take a look at that clock, almost eight o'clock on the button exactly," Mary said. "If Daddy's going to get you to camp and do all his other chores and still make his nine-fourteen train, you'll all have to leave the house in a few minutes. There's no time now to hard-boil eggs. I'm sorry, Win."

Win nodded brightly. He was rarely disgruntled or even depressed by a rebuff. Not because, at his still fairly tender age, he had already developed reservoirs of stoicism on which he drew in times of disaster. Win's cheery disposition, even in the face of a setback, was due to his peculiar conception of a setback: complete cessation of activity.

If, after being told he could not have hard-boiled eggs, he had been prevented from telling it to somebody else, he might very easily have burst into tears. Since the continued flow of movement and conversation had not been interrupted, however, he was perfectly happy. Some, indeed most, people lust after success. Winston Hurst, at the age of six and a half, craved only action.

"You see, Dickie, it's like this," he said into the phone. "After he drops me and Jimmy off at camp and before he can catch the nine-fourteen, my dad, he's got to pick up Carolina at the Center on account of today is Friday, and then he's got to drop off d'Artagnan at the vet because that dopey poodle, his ear is bum again—"

"Don't omit Ashorn's," George said as he poured the glass of milk with which he always finished his breakfast. "I wouldn't want the Stiefel family to have any gaps in their chart of my morning movements."

"Wait a minute, Dickie," said Win into the phone. "What did you say, Dad?"

"The electric clock in our bedroom is on the blink," Mary said. "Dad's going to drop it off at Ashorn's on his way to the train."

"Oh," Win said happily and, into the phone, "There's this other thing, too, Dickie. The clock up in my mother's and father's bedroom is on the blink, so my dad, he has to drop it off at Ashorn's on his way to the train, and all those things, Dickie, Carolina at the Center and d'Artagnan to Dr. Rettig and the clock to Ashorn's, we have to leave for camp right away. So there's no time to hard-boil any eggs, Dickie. See what I mean?"

Dickie probably did. All the Stiefels were quick.

"Ask Dickie," George said, "why *he* can't bring the hard-boiled eggs?"

"George!" Mary said.

But she was too late.

"My father wants to know," Win was saying cheerily into the phone, "why *you* can't bring the hard-boiled eggs?"

"Hey!" George said. "I didn't say you should say *I* said—!"

"Serves you right," Mary said and, to her oldest son, "Win, will you please—?"

Win made a shushing motion with his free hand, bobbing his head up and down as he listened hard. Finally his face cleared. "Hold it, Dickie," he said and, to his parents, "Dickie says he can't bring the hard-boiled eggs because his mother is giving a big dinner party tonight and there's already about eleventeen people working like crazy in the kitchen. They even gave him his breakfast on a tray up in his room. That's where Dickie is calling from. He says his mother is so busy with the party, she even—"

"Oh, my God," George said.

His wife and son stared at him. "Now, what?" Mary said.

"Is the Stiefel party tonight?" George said.

"Yes, of course," Mary said.

"You mean the big one? The party Polly is giving for that Hollywood woman?"

"Ella K. Mason, yes," Mary said. "I don't know why you're making all this fuss, darling. Polly Stiefel always gives a big party during the Fourth of July week end, and the guest of honor is always one of her weird theatre or Hollywood friends, and we're always invited, and you've known all about this one for weeks. Why are you all of a sudden having kittens now?"

"Because there's a Dandypops meeting at the school tonight."

"Oh, my God," Mary said.

"You see?" George said.

"No, I don't. You and those darned Dandypops."

"Easy, Ma," Jimmy said, coming in from the playroom with his tray. "Don't blow your cork."

"That's right," George said. He winked at his youngest son

"Hold it, Dickie!" Win said tensely into the phone. "There's something happening that might—"

"No, it won't," Mary said firmly. "The hard-boiled egg question has been settled, and will you and Dickie please stop this marathon telephone conversation? We're trying to straighten out a—"

"I can't just hang up on him." Win's round face was the picture of slightly pained but revoltingly sweet reasonableness. "It isn't polite, Ma."

"Darn right," George said.

Mary gave him a murderous look. George smirked innocently, winked at both his sons, and took a long swallow of milk.

"Do you have to attend this Dandypops meeting?" Mary said.

"Did MacArthur have to attend the signing of the Japanese surrender on board the *Missouri?*"

"Your relationship to the Dandypops isn't exactly the same as MacArthur's relationship to the Japs. Couldn't you skip it just this once?"

"I don't see how," George said. "I'm on the Food Committee, and the purpose of the meeting is to make some last-minute changes in the plans for tomorrow's clambake, and as you well know, my sweet, one of the reasons the Danville Elementary School is such a fine institution is because the parents take such a keen interest in its activities, and the keenest interest they take is through the fathers' club known as the Dandypops, and the things the Dandypops do during the year for their sons and daughters at Danville Elementary all depend on money, and the bulk of our money for all these good deeds is raised at our annual Fourth of July clambake, so that asking me to—"

"George Hurst, if you don't shut up," Mary said, "I will crown you."

"Go ahead, Ma," Jimmy said.

"Hold it, Dickie," Win said into the phone. "Just one more minute!"

D'Artagnan came loping into the kitchen, paused in front of the electric stove, stared mournfully at all four members of the Hurst family, then moved toward the table and put his woolly head in George's lap.

"See?" George said. "D'Artagnan loves me."

"D'Artagnan doesn't keep a date book that you mess up behind his back," Mary said. "What time is this Dandypops meeting?"

"Hoxter Monahan wants us all to be there at seven sharp," George said. "And you know Hoxter."

"I am happy to say that I *don't* know Hoxter," Mary said. "Except by sight, and that's quite enough for me, thank you. When do you think this Dandypops meeting will be over?"

"I don't know," George said. "But I imagine it'll be going on for some time, because Porky Haenigson said since most of us will be going to it direct from the train, he'd have sandwiches and coffee sent in from his restaurant."

"How thoughtful of him," Mary said.

"I got an idea," Jimmy said. "Why doesn't Dad go over to the Dandypops meeting tonight right from the train, and Mom, you can go over to the Stiefels, and then when Dad's meeting is finished, why can't he join you at the Stiefels?"

"Why not?" George said.

Mary gave Jimmy a kiss. "You are a very sensible young man," she said, "and when you grow up and get married, I'm sure you won't make dates for the same nights on which your wife has accepted a dinner invitation." Mary stood up. "All right, men," she said. "Time to go."

George moved d'Artagnan's head from his lap, finished his milk, and stood up.

"Hey, wait, you mean it's all settled?" Win said. He sounded disappointed.

"Every square inch of it," Mary said.

"But what about the hard-boiled eggs, Ma?"

"In view of what I have already packed into your lunch box, I think you and Dickie Stiefel will probably be able to live through the day without hard-boiled eggs."

"Come on," George called, moving out of the kitchen toward his briefcase in the study. "Let's get going."

The reminder of action drove the look of disappointment from Win's face. "I have to hang up, Dickie," he said into the phone. "We're on our way."

2

Camp Shawmut sprawled shapelessly, like a ladleful of spilled pancake batter, across a dozen rocky acres on the west bank of the Danville River. It was a fifteen-minute run by car from the Hurst house on Queen's Court Road.

"Okay, Dad," Win said as George guided the car into the leafy tunnel beyond the entrance gate. "If you grab hold of the frying pan and the mess kit and the bag with the meat, I think I can handle the rest."

"Which would you rather carry?" Jimmy said. "My bait box or my lunch?"

"What are you using today?" George said. "Live bait?"

"No," Jimmy said. "Worms are no darn good for steelies. I brought only my lures."

"In that case, I'll take a chance on carrying your bait box," George said. "If I arrive in the office smelling of worms, Miss Akst will make me take off my coat so she can send it out to be dry cleaned, and then I'll be late for my lunch date with Nick Perrini."

"She will?" Win said, his eyes wide with surprise and delight. And then, "Aah, you're kidding!"

"You wouldn't think so," George said, "if you knew Miss Akst."

"Dad," Jimmy said. "Worms have no smell."

"Live worms, no. But some of those worms you've had in that bait box this last week were not alive."

The car came bumping out of the leafy tunnel. George maneuvered it across the scrap of stubby meadow that served as Camp Shawmut's parking area and stopped at the far end.

"Easy with that bag, now, Dad," Win said. "The pickles and the mustard and the ketchup, that stuff's all in glass, you know."

"If I break anything," George said, "I promise to replace it."

"A fat lot of good that'll do me for my cook-out," Win said.

"Don't break my bait box, either," Jimmy said. "Mr. Monahan over The Sport Emporium, he said that's the last one he had, and there's no chance of getting any more of those plastic ones till Labor Day."

George eased himself out of the car with Jimmy's bait box and Win's frying pan in one hand, holding the mess kit in his other hand, and clutching in his teeth the paper sack containing the raw materials with which Win hoped to keep himself from starving before he got back to Queen's Court Road late that afternoon for his pre-dinner snack. D'Artagnan, on the rear seat, growled nervously.

"Nobody's running out on you," George said to the dog, mumbling the words around the paper sack. "I'll be right back."

George shoved the car door shut with his hip, shifted the paper sack from his teeth to the bend of his arm, and hurried to catch up with Win and Jimmy. They had started down the long flight of stone steps that led from the parking area to the camp buildings on the river bank. When he reached the top step, George saw Tim Keogh crossing from the camp office to the canoe racks where the athletic director kept his Buddy Board. Win and Jimmy saw him at the same time.

"Hi, Tim!" Jimmy yelled.

"Hi, Tim!" Win yelled.

"Hi, boys," the wiry little Irishman called. He waited for George at the foot of the stone steps. "You going to be at that Dandypops meeting tonight, Mr. Hurst?"

"Unless the New York, New Haven and Hartford goes out of business."

"Ought to be some fireworks," Tim Keogh said. "Hoxter Monahan's cooking up some new plan for the clambake."

"At this late date?" George said. "My God, Tim, it's tomorrow night."

Tim Keogh shook his head. "You know Hoxter."

George did. Everybody in Danville knew the peppery proprietor of The Sports Emporium. But it wasn't Hoxter Monahan or his capacity for converting a Dandypops meeting into a free-for-all that was suddenly occupying George Hurst's thoughts. To his considerable surprise, as in the golden morning sunlight he stared at the Camp Shawmut athletic director, George Hurst found himself thinking about Doodoo Kashkewitz. It was the second time in an hour that, after thirty years, the long forgotten blacksmith's son with whom George had attended P.S. 188 had suddenly become a vivid figure in his mind's eye.

Doodoo had been crazy about physical culture. Every morning, when George came out of Aunt Tessie's tailor shop on his way to fetch the breakfast ingredients from Mr. Forman's grocery store, the first sight that greeted him was Doodoo Kashkewitz chinning himself on the bar that ran across the top of the arched double-doored entrance to his father's blacksmith shop.

Doodoo had been a small boy. His muscles, however, had been impressively disproportionate to his size. There was something about the disproportion, George could see now, that was true of Tim Keogh. A little man like Tim, no more than an inch or two better than five feet, with an almost emaciated body that seemed to have been put together out of lengths of rope, had no business making his career as a director of athletics. The fact that he was a good one didn't change the fact that he looked wrong for the role. Just as Doodoo Kashkewitz's bulging muscles had always looked wrong on the skinny body he could hoist up and down with such astonishing ease on the bar over the doors of his father's smithy on East Fourth Street.

Why, George wondered, during all the time he had known Tim Keogh here in Danville, had he never before been struck by the athletic director's resemblance to Doodoo Kashkewitz? George didn't have to ask himself why, having been struck by it now, he found the recollection disturbing. Once again he was struggling with the uneasy feeling that had assailed him when Miss Akst had advised him on the phone that the mysterious Mr. Kashkin had told her George Hurst sounded like just the man he was looking for.

"Hey, Tim!"

The athletic director turned. So did George. Win had come up to relieve his father of the frying pan, the mess kit, and the bag containing the raw materials for the cook-out.

Tim Keogh laughed. "Boy," he said, "you're really going to eat."

"It's not all for me," Win said. "I brought a hot dog and hamburger for you."

"Thanks."

"You're welcome," Win said, and then, with a glance at George, "Listen, Tim, we got an Alvin Kashkin in my tepee?"

Tim Keogh's brow furrowed. "Alvin Kashkin?"

"The kid with the fiberglas rod," Jimmy called from the other side of the canoe rack, where he was carefully inspecting the contents of his lure box. "He's got a red and blue Jitterbug, and his name ain't Kashkin."

"Isn't," George said.

"Isn't," Jimmy said. "But his name is Kingston. Alvin Kingston."

Win turned to his hero. "Which is it?" he said. "Kashkin, Tim, or Kingston?"

George found himself waiting for the athletic director's answer.

"Kingston? Kingston? Kashkin? Kashkin?" Tim Keogh scratched his head and then shook it. "Darned if I know." He smiled apologetically at George. "All these kids, so many of them, I get to know them all by their first names, there isn't a one I don't know by his first name, but the last names, sometimes I—" Tim Keogh paused and snapped his fingers. "Hold it a minute." He stepped across to the Buddy Board hanging on the canoe rack. He ran his finger down the list of typewritten names that were paired for swimming safety.

"Yeah," Keogh said, looking up. "Here it is." His finger poked at the list. "Kingston," he said. "Alvin Kingston."

"See?" Jimmy said. "What did I say?"

"Aah, you big—" Win stopped and shot a quick glance at Tim Keogh. There was a lot of talk at Camp Shawmut about good sportsmanship. Win swallowed his rage at Jimmy and turned to his father. "I'm sorry, Dad."

So was George. Now he wouldn't be able to learn anything about Mr. Kashkin until he got to the office. George touched Win's shoulder lightly. "Don't be sorry," he said. "Just don't eat all those hamburgers and hot dogs by yourself. You catch any steelies, Jimmy, we'll have them for lunch tomorrow. So long, men. I have to run."

"So long," Tim Keogh said. "See you tonight at the Dandypops, Mr. Hurst."

"Yes," George said. "And let's try to sit on Hoxter Monahan."

Tim Keogh laughed. All the way back down Hill Tower Road toward the center of Danville, George wished he could do the same. A good laugh, Aunt Tessie used to say, is better than a good laxative. But George didn't feel like laughing and, because he knew this was due to Miss Akst's phone call, George felt like a fool.

"Mr. Kashkin probably is nothing more to worry about than a salesman with a new approach," George said aloud as he swung the car left, out of Hill Tower onto the Post Road, "who will try to sell you a set of the Britannica or Canadian mining stocks. So why don't you just relax and forget about him until you get to the office?" D'Artagnan growled worriedly on the rear seat. "Not you, boy," George said. "I'm talking to myself. You just relax, too. As soon as I drop this clock at Ashorn's and pick up Carolina, we'll have Dr. Rettig take a look at your ear and put you back in shape."

The Post Road, which ran through the center of Danville, bellied out across the street from the State Police Barracks to form a small shopping center with a paved parking court known as Scheuer Square. This was appropriate enough, since Scheuer's Department Store, The Danville Hardware Company, The Lobster Pot, and the Danville Professional Building, which dominated the square, were all owned by members of the Scheuer family. By nine-thirty it would be impossible to find a parking place in Scheuer Square. At this hour, however, when most Danville commuters were still shaving and their wives were still brewing coffee and only a few hard-working shopkeepers like Mr. Ashorn had put their keys into their front locks, it wasn't even necessary to obey the curb sign that read in bright yellow letters: "Angle Parking Only." George pulled up parallel with the curb, reached across to give d'Artagnan a reassuring pat, took the electric clock from the seat beside him, and climbed out of the car.

"So early in the morning you have already jewelry trouble?"

George grinned at Mr. Ashorn. The round-shouldered old man was on the sidewalk, grinding down the blue and white awning over his front window.

"Not jewelry trouble," George said. "Clock trouble." He held up the electric clock.

Mr. Ashorn gave it a contemptuous glance. "Clocks," he said in disgust. "Everything they call clocks today."

He went right on grinding the awning handle. George might have been a passer-by who had called out an insult. There was nothing in Mr. Ashorn's manner to indicate that he had just been approached by one of the few people in Danville who traded with him out of preference. Nobody else in town went near Mr. Ashorn's shop unless The Jewelry Mart on Main Street was closed or its stock proved inadequate. George didn't blame them. Mr. Ashorn was easily the most unattractive man in Fairfield County, and he had a personality to match his appearance. He was short, fat, round-shouldered, and bald. His thick lips drooped in a permanent sneer. His deep-set eyes burned with hatred for everybody and everything. He seemed incapable of speaking a kind or friendly word. George did not blame people for staying away from the old man's shop. But George didn't blame Mr. Ashorn, either. George understood about ugliness. He had learned it from living with Aunt Tessie on East Fourth Street.

"It wasn't that she was homely," George once said in trying to explain Aunt Tessie to Mary. "There are thousands of homely people who get along perfectly well with their fellows, and are even loved by a few. After all, as you probably learned in some course or other at Bennington, if only people who are beautiful or handsome could function successfully, society would come grinding to a halt pretty damn fast. You can't run things only with movie queens sitting around looking sexy. You've got to have some hewers of wood and drawers of water. The thing about Aunt Tessie, who could hew wood and draw water better than anybody on East Fourth Street, was that she got people's backs up. I never could figure out if it was because she was ugly or because, as a result of being ugly, she was always slicing away at people with her razor-edged tongue the minute they came within range. Sort of getting her licks in first, you might say, before they had a chance to make cracks about her appearance or laugh at her.

"I remember the first time I saw her. When she came to look me over at the Henry Isaacs Orphan Asylum. They never told you that someone was looking you over for adoption. They didn't want the kids to be disappointed if they were turned down. Just the same, I knew why Aunt Tessie had come, of course. We all did. And all of us, every one of those kids in that asylum, we would have done anything to make a good impression so we would be taken out of there. Even so, that first time I saw Aunt Tessie, I was, well, not exactly scared, but sort of shocked. She didn't look the way ordinary homely or non-beautiful people looked. There was a sort of fierceness about her homeliness, as though she were making a point of it, wanting you not to miss it, sort of.

"She was small and thin, with black hair pulled tight at the back of her head, and a long thin face, with bright black eyes that seemed to burn right through you, and no lips. Absolutely no lips. It was as though somebody had just put a nick in her face to serve as her mouth. She was wearing the sort of dress I learned later she always wore. A kind of shiny black alpaca, or something like alpaca, with a tight little collar and long sleeves that ended in tight little black cuffs. She reminded me of a black cigar. I don't know why. I was only three, and I don't think I'd ever seen a cigar, but that's what she reminded me of. A tightly rolled black cigar. And she shocked me. I mean that. I had a feeling I wanted to turn and run. Until she smiled, and then I knew it was all right. She had the most wonderful smile I've ever seen. It was as though somebody had put a match to that cigar and it had started to glow.

"The trouble was that Aunt Tessie glowed for very few people. I was one of them. That's why I stopped being shocked and started to love her almost as soon as she took me home to those two small rooms in back of the tailor shop on East Fourth Street. When she was with me, she wasn't ugly. With the rest of the world, though, they never saw her any differently than I'd seen her during those first moments in the Henry Isaacs Orphan Asylum. That's why she had such a tough time making a living. People hated to bring her their dresses and suits to alter or mend or press or dry clean. They'd carry their clothes to tailors as far west as Avenue B to avoid her. Only when they were in a hurry or a jam would they come to Aunt Tessie. She knew that, and she let them know she knew it, so that they hated her even worse. I suppose it's a little like the chicken and the egg. Which came first? Aunt Tessie hating everybody because people couldn't conceal the fact that they thought she was ugly? Or everybody hating Aunt Tessie because she cut them to pieces with her tongue because she could see they thought she was ugly? I don't know. All I know is that everybody on East Fourth Street wished to God she would move away, and the more they wished it, the more determined Aunt Tessie was to stay. She stayed."

So did Mr. Ashorn. The old jeweler had no way of knowing, of course, why George Hurst preferred his shop to The Jewelry Mart. Even if George had told him, George doubted that it would have caused Mr. Ashorn to be more polite to him. You had to love someone and know you were loved in return, the way Aunt Tessie had loved George and known he loved her, before you could forget that fate in her indifferent cruelty had marked you with the touch of the monster.

"What's the matter with it?" Mr. Ashorn said. "This piece of junk?"

"At twelve minutes after seven this morning my wife said it showed seven-thirty," George said. "And it can't be a piece of junk, Mr. Ashorn, because you sold it to me."

"I'm in business to sell clocks," Mr. Ashorn said. "A person comes in and he says he wants one of these things, it's not my business to tell him it's not a clock. There was a time, once, a clock it had springs, wheels, things inside that they moved and worked and you knew why it told you it's time to get up and go to the office. But now? These things?" The old man looked at the clock as though he expected it to bite. "An empty tin can with inside it goes through it a thing called electric." He jerked his head toward the open door. "Come inside a minute."

"I can't," George said. "I've got a train to catch."

"I said come inside."

Mr. Ashorn disappeared into the store. George was annoyed by the peremptory tone of the old man's voice. He was aware, however, that he could not disregard it. You couldn't be the only person in town who didn't mind Mr. Ashorn's insulting manner and then, at odd moments, choose to mind it. Having embraced a cause,

George was stuck with it. He followed the old man into the shop.

"When it comes to fountain pens," Mr. Ashorn said as he went behind the counter, "you like a Waterman?"

"Mr. Ashorn, this is no time to try to sell me a fountain pen," George said. "I've still got a couple of stops to make before I catch the nine-fourteen and it's already—"

"Who is trying to sell you something?" Mr. Ashorn said. "I asked a question. You like a Waterman?"

"As a matter of fact," George said, "I happen to prefer a Parker."

"This is what I told her."

"Told who?"

"Your wife. She came in yesterday with the children, they said on Saturday it's your birthday, the boys with their own money they saved up, they want to buy you a surprise present a fountain pen, so what's the best kind? Your father, I said, I know he likes a Parker, and I start showing them my whole line Parkers, but the big boy, the one that what's his name?"

"Win," George said.

"That's the one. With the blond hair. He said no, no Parker. He saw in a magazine a picture for the new Waterman, instead just plain ink it has a thing a cartridge with ink you put in, and this he wants for your birthday. The other boy, the smaller one—"

"Jimmy," George said.

Mr. Ashorn nodded. "He saw the picture, too, and by him it has to be a Waterman also. So I turned to Mrs. Hurst, I said Mrs. Hurst, a surprise for Mr. Hurst's birthday is good only if he gets what he likes, and I tell you Mr. Hurst he likes a Parker. But she said no. She said if the boys they want to buy you a Waterman, it's their own money, they saved it up from their allowance, then they should get you a Waterman." Mr. Ashorn shrugged. "It's your birthday, Mr. Hurst, and it's your surprise, and with whichever fountain pen you get, it'll be you and not me that does the writing. But I thought so long as you dropped in, and I have a chance to warn you—"

"No, that's all right," George said, suddenly moved. Not so much by the fact that Win and Jimmy should want to spend their savings on a birthday surprise for him. They had done that before, and George had more or less expected them to do it again this year. What had moved him was that Mary, who felt about Mr. Ashorn the way everybody else in Danville did, should nevertheless have brought the boys to the old man's shop to choose the gift for their father. It was a gesture of loyalty to her husband about which, but for Mr. Ashorn's violation of Mary's confidence, George would not have known. That made it doubly precious. He said, "As a matter of fact, I'd like to have a Waterman."

Mr. Ashorn's sneering lips twisted in disgust. "So all right, if that's what you want," he said with a shrug. "Only please don't tell Mrs. Hurst or the boys I told you. A surprise they want, a surprise let them have. The only reason I told you, I felt you ought to have a chance to decide what—"

"I know, and thanks a lot," George said. In the mirror on the wall behind Mr. Ashorn's counter he saw the bus from Norwalk pulling into the crescent in front of the State Police Barracks across the street. "I've really got to run now, Mr. Ashorn."

"You run, you'll fall," the old man said. "Try walking, and live a little."

George went out, slipped into the car, and swung it around to the north exit from Scheuer Square. He waited for a break in the Post Road traffic, shot through, turned left, and pulled up behind the Norwalk bus just as Carolina stepped out of it.

She was carrying her large red patent-leather purse and mopping her neck with a wad of paper towels. Catching sight of George, her broad black face exploded in a grin of astonished delight, she waved the wadded toweling wildly, and heaved her heavy body toward him in a loping, eager half-run. A stranger might have thought she had just recognized in the passing crowd a beloved brother from whom she had been separated since childhood. George, who had been picking Carolina up at this bus stop twice a week for almost five years, never ceased to marvel at the enthusiasm she continued to hurl into their meetings.

"Morning, Mr. Hurst," she gasped as she reached the car. "You ever see anything like this heat?"

As a matter of fact, George had. Many times. Usually in late May or early September. If there was anything unusual about the heat, it was the fact that it was hardly that. For the first day of July the weather was surprisingly cool. And George knew Carolina knew it. But the knowledge was something she didn't dare admit. Just as Miss Akst's life was a constant quest for disaster, so Carolina managed to get through her days by endlessly trying to throw dust in the eyes of fate.

When she was healthy or solvent, she was afraid to say so.
God might hear her, think she was bragging, and send her a head
cold or a large electric bill just to teach her a lesson. It was safer to
pretend she already had a head cold or was saddled with debts. The
same was true of the weather. Carolina hated heat and lived in
terror of cold. When the winters were mild, therefore, even though
her eyes glowed with gratitude, she complained loudly that the icy
winds were cutting her to the marrow. And on the coolest July
first in George Hurst's memory, Carolina wanted to know if he
had ever seen anything like this heat.

"It's not too bad," George said. "If it doesn't get any worse
than this all summer, I won't complain."

He opened the car door. Sliding in beside him on the front seat,
Carolina paused to give d'Artagnan a pat.

"Morning, Donyin," she said. George had once tried to explain
to her the derivation of the poodle's name. But the creations of the
elder Dumas, plus the elements of French pronunciation, had proved
beyond Carolina's grasp. It had seemed simpler to let her continue
thinking the dog's name was Donyin. "How's his ear, Mr. Hurst?"

"Not too good, I don't think," George said. He started the car
and eased it out into the Post Road traffic. "I'm going to drop him
off at Dr. Rettig's on our way back to the house."

"Poor Donyin," Carolina said. "I bet that pain in his ear it's
all on account of the heat. Don't you worry, Mr. Hurst. This heat'll
get lots worse. We gonna see some bad days this summer. Real bad
ones. Wouldn't surprise me we get a couple this week end. July
fourth, that's always a bad day."

"Not according to the orators who will be rising to say a few
words from coast to coast."

"Beg pardon, Mr. Hurst?"

"Nothing," George said, and he made a great pretense of peering through the windshield at the traffic ahead. He didn't want
Carolina to see his sudden embarrassment. He knew it was silly to
make these strained efforts at light conversation. Why didn't he
just sit there in silence and drive? Carolina was not a client he was
trying to impress. Or a neighbor in front of whom he did not want
to appear an inept tongue-tied clod. Carolina was a part-time maid.
She was paid for the services she rendered. There was no necessity
for George, who paid her, to entertain her as well. "I was just
making a joke, Carolina," he said. "About the politicians who make
all those Fourth of July speeches."

There may have been no necessity for him to entertain her. But George could never free himself from the compulsion to make the effort. He wanted Carolina to think he was as important a figure in the world as some of the other people she worked for. George Hurst was ashamed of the compulsion. But he was honest enough, at least with himself, to recognize its existence, and to understand its motivation: he was secretly ashamed of the fact that he could not afford to provide his wife with a full-time, live-in maid.

Aside from the Stiefels, who were either rich or pretended to be and certainly acted as though they were, no family in the Danville circle to which George and Mary Hurst belonged had a full-time, live-in maid. Not even the Schneiders, who served as George's secret yardstick in these matters because Eileen Schneider, nee Bucknell, had grown up in Bala Cynwyd and had gone to Bennington with Mary. Just the same George had never been able to shake off the uneasy feeling that, in failing to provide Mary with a full-time maid, he had somehow failed in the obligations he had assumed when he had married a Sherrod of Philadelphia. Worse than that, he sensed that Carolina felt it, and worst of all, he could not prevent himself from acting on the preposterous conviction that, by making small jokes with her, Carolina would somehow come to believe that the Hursts preferred her services two days a week to the convenience of a full-time maid, not because they couldn't afford the latter, but because Mr. Hurst was a democratic eccentric who hated to run with the herd.

"Come on, d'Artagnan, this is it," George said as he swung the car from the Post Road into Dr. Rettig's driveway. The poodle clambered down out of the car like a veteran of the War Between the States descending from the taxi that has brought him to the Bethesda Naval Hospital for his annual checkup. George said, "I'll be out in a minute, Carolina."

The odds were against this. Not because what was wrong with d'Artagnan's ear required lengthy explanations or because George had any desire to make them. It was merely that Mervyn Rettig, who was generally considered to be the best veterinary in Danville, was a man of passion.

"Come on in!" he called through the screen door in answer to the chimes George had set off by pulling the small bronze poodle on the jamb. "Make yourself at home."

George came in, but he made no attempt to make himself at home. Even d'Artagnan, who was by nature better equipped to do so, indicated clearly that making himself at home in Dr. Rettig's quarters was something he preferred not to try.

The house was an old salt box that Dr. Rettig had remodeled by putting up bright red shutters with green poodles painted on them and converting the kitchen into a surgery. Between the front door and the surgery, in what had originally been a small entrance hall, there were two straight-back chairs and a stack of old magazines to indicate that this area now served as a waiting room. A small room behind the surgery served as Dr. Rettig's office. What served as the cleaner and disinfectant that gave the entire house its stupefying odor neither George nor, he suspected, the U. S. Army's Chemical Warfare Branch could have divined. The smell caused the back of his throat to ache and made d'Artagnan cower against the screen door for a breath of fresh air. Dr. Rettig didn't seem to mind it. He was standing beside his desk in the office, talking on the telephone. He beckoned George into the surgery as he talked.

"No, I didn't say that," Dr. Rettig said. "What I said, Mrs. Schneider, was this: when you're mating dogs, it's always better to do it in a place that's familiar to them, especially to the male, who has to do the work. For that reason I would prefer to have this done at the Stiefel house, since hers is the male and yours is the bitch. Unfortunately, Mrs. Stiefel says it can't be done at her house today because she's giving a party tonight and the whole place is in an uproar, which is why I suggest we postpone the thing until tomorrow. I beg your pardon?" Dr. Rettig's voice rose a full octave. "Mrs. Schneider," he said, "I'm just quoting what Mrs. Stiefel told me on the phone ten minutes ago."

He paused, rolled his eyes to the ceiling, and put his free hand to his forehead in a gesture of despair. Then he shrugged and beckoned George further into the surgery.

"Is that Mrs. Milton Schneider?" George asked in a whisper as he came in. "From Powder Horn Hill?"

Dr. Rettig put the mouthpiece against his shoulder. "Yes," he hissed. "*Your* friend!"

She wasn't exactly that. The intimacy between Eileen Bucknell and Mary Sherrod that had started twenty-five years ago in Bala Cynwyd had continued to the present day in Danville. The intimacy between George and Eileen, however, or even between George and Eileen's husband Milton, had never reached a point where it could properly be described as that. George had always found this puzzling.

He liked Milton and Eileen. He had every reason to believe they liked him. He and Mary had come to Danville originally because the Schneiders lived there. And the fact that both marriages were mixed should have been, in theory at any rate, an additional factor in solidifying a relationship that had begun between two of its four members so many years ago. In practice, however, it didn't work out that way.

The two families saw each other frequently. But George was aware that the only ones who really enjoyed the meetings were Eileen and Mary. The husbands, George sensed, were always a little on guard with one another. At any rate, he was. When the two couples met at a party, George had noticed, Eileen and Mary made for each other like happy conspirators. He and Milton, however, after the greetings were out of the way, made for different corners of the room. It wasn't that they disliked each other. It seemed to George they both acted instinctively. It was as though they had managed to pass through the carefully guarded front door of a club from which because of their race they were barred and, thinking they were undetected and seeing no reason why they shouldn't be able to carry off the evening successfully, it suddenly occurred to them, on finding they were not the only ones who had pulled off the trick, that there was less chance of giving one another away if they mixed with the crowd and avoided each other's company.

"Give her my best," George said.

"Here, you do it," Dr. Rettig said, pressing the mouthpiece against his shoulder. "I've given her as much of my best as I can spare in one day. Another second of this, and I'll be a stark, staring, raving lunatic." Before George could protest or duck, the vet had seized his arm, and was saying into the phone, "Hold it a second, Mrs. Schneider. Somebody here wants to talk to you."

George took the phone and had a moment of total frustration. What in God's name did you say to your wife's old school chum from the office of a veterinary twenty minutes before you caught the 9:14?

"Hi," George said.

"Hi?" Eileen said. "Hi, who?"

Then, after a pause, she emitted the loud whooping scream of delight that was as indelibly associated with her personality as the red tunic is associated with the Royal Northwest Mounted Police. Eileen was not a pretty girl. Her talent as a fashion designer was small. Her reputation in professional circles, while respectable, was far from distinguished. And for many years since her family's affluent days in Bala Cynwyd she had lacked the distinction of money. She was determined, however, not to be mistaken for just another face in the crowd. Eileen Schneider prided herself on standing out from the herd. It seemed to George that her pride was justified. Nobody could be mistaken for just another member of the herd who made the simple act of greeting sound like one of the air-raid sirens with which George had lived for so long in war-time London.

"Am I going off my rocker?" Eileen said. "Or is that the voice of George Hurst I hear at the other end of this phone?"

"How are you, Eileen?"

"Never mind that. Here I am in the middle of a conversation with Dr. Rettig about mating my darling Peppy with Polly Stiefel's neurotic Bismarck, and all of a sudden I find myself talking to you. Elucidate, George. Elucidate."

Eileen's notions about humor had been gleaned from Dickens, whose works her father had read aloud to his children when they were still too small to defend themselves.

"I'm on my way to the nine-fourteen, believe it or not, but d'Artagnan's ear is bad again, so Mary asked me to drop him off at Dr. Rettig's on my way to the train, which I was in the middle of doing—"

"When you got caught in a revolving door," Eileen said. "I know. It happens in this damn town all the time. Milton says life in Fairfield County is exactly like life in Hungary before the Revolution."

"In what way?"

"How should I know? I come from Philadelphia. When you see Milton at the Stiefels tonight you can ask him."

"Are you going to be there?"

"George, dear, the only person who isn't going to be there is Albert Schweitzer, and if I know Polly Stiefel it isn't because she didn't send the old boy an invitation. Listen, George."

"I've got exactly eighteen minutes to run Carolina back to the house and then get to the nine-fourteen."

"I don't care. Peppy's in heat and we've had this date for her to be mated with Bismarck. The date was set up weeks ago, and it was all arranged, and now, just because Polly is busy with her party, that damned violinist refuses to co-operate."

"Who?"

"Mervyn Rettig."

"Oh," George said. He turned with the phone to look into the surgery. Dr. Rettig had lifted d'Artagnan up on the table and was carefully probing the poodle's ear with a cotton-tipped swab. It had never occurred to George that the veterinary looked like a violinist. Now that Eileen had mentioned it, however, George saw what she meant. Dr. Rettig was short and plump, with full, moist lips, bushy hair, large, liquid dark eyes, and the sort of soft, rounded Middle European chin that was somehow associated in George Hurst's mind with serious music. He said into the phone, "How can I help you, Eileen?"

"You can convince that fool Rettig that it's not going to kill either my Peppy or that damned Bismarck if the mating takes place in Rettig's office rather than in Polly's house."

"Why can't you just wait until tomorrow, after Polly's party is out of the way?"

"Because I've lost track of Peppy's days, and for all I know tomorrow she may not be in heat any more, that's why. Now will you please stop being difficult, George, and talk to Mervyn Rettig?"

"All right," George said. "I'll talk to him. See you tonight, Eileen."

"What time will you be there?"

"I'm not sure. Mary's going on ahead alone and I'll join her later. I have to go to a Dandypops meeting at the school first."

"So does Milton. He's going direct from the train and then he's meeting me at the Stiefels. Would you mind giving him a lift, George?"

"Of course not."

"Wonderful. Thanks. I think what I'll do, I'll call Mary and she and I can go over together."

"That's a good idea."

"See you tonight, George, and please talk to Rettig."

"I will."

George hung up. Dr. Rettig turned from d'Artagnan, holding the soiled cotton-tipped probe aloft as though it were a dart he was about to hurl at a target on the other side of the room.

"You don't have to tell me," the vet said. "She wants you to use your influence with me so I will call Mrs. Stiefel and have her bring Bismarck down here so Mrs. Schneider can bring Peppy down, too, and the mating can take place here."

"Well, yes," George said. "Sort of."

Dr. Rettig turned his large, liquid eyes to the heavens. "Women," he said. "My God."

"What's wrong with the plan?" George said, coming into the surgery. "I mean, as long as today is the day you agreed on, and the Stiefel house is out because of the party?"

"Nothing is wrong with the plan," said Dr. Rettig. "Or maybe I should put it this way, Mr. Hurst. Nothing would be wrong with the plan if it applied to a couple of poodles. But Mrs. Schneider's Peppy and Mrs. Stiefel's Bismarck both happen to be Weimaraners, and for my money, Mr. Hurst, you can have them. Those dogs have absolutely no brains. They lack completely the capacity to adapt to a new situation. Bismarck can't even have a bowel movement when he's away from his own home, Mr. Hurst, so how the hell can the dumb dog be expected to mount a bitch in a strange place? Ooop, that one hurt, didn't it?" He rubbed the cringing d'Artagnan's nose with a gesture of apology for the pain he had caused the dog. "You know what I think, Mr. Hurst? I think you'd better leave d'Artagnan with me for a couple of days. How about you give me a ring on, say, Monday?"

"Monday is the Fourth of July," George said. "Will you be open?"

"No, but my man will be here."

"Well, I may still be tied up all day cleaning up after the Dandypops clambake, so if I don't get a chance to call on Monday, will Tuesday be all right?"

"Why not?" said Dr. Rettig.

Why not indeed, George thought as he walked back to the car. At three dollars a day Dr. Rettig could hardly object to having a guest so well mannered as d'Artagnan.

"This clock," Carolina said, pointing to the dashboard as George slid into the car. "Is it right, Mr. Hurst?"

"Clocks in automobiles are never right," George said. He glanced at his wrist watch and pressed the starter. "But it's okay, Carolina. I still have fourteen minutes."

Three of them were spent in getting back to Queen's Court Road and making the U-turn on the parking court at the end of the driveway so that, when Carolina got out to go into the house, the car would be headed in the right direction for the run to the railroad station.

"You watch out for that heat, now," Carolina said. "Heat like this, Mr. Hurst, a place like that New York, you could really fry."

"I'll try to keep cool," George said.

He pulled the door shut, waved to Carolina, and stepped on the gas. At the same moment, above the controlled explosion of the motor, he heard his name called. George shifted his toe to the brake and turned. He saw Carolina moving up the walk toward the front door, out of which Mary had just stepped.

"George!" Mary called again.

He pulled the hand brake, disengaged the gear, and slid across the seat to the opposite window. "What's wrong?"

"I don't know," Mary said, coming down the walk toward the driveway. "At least it doesn't sound wrong to me. But you know Miss Akst."

George didn't like the way the smooth, rhythmic beat of his heart seemed to falter for an instant. "Miss Akst?" he said. "What about Miss Akst?"

"She called back," Mary said. "A few minutes after you drove off with Win and Jimmy."

"What did she want?"

"There was something she'd forgotten to tell you when she called earlier. She'd forgotten to tell you that Mr. Kashkin is from Albany."

George felt somewhat the way he occasionally did at a party when somebody accosted him with a clever remark to which the speaker clearly expected an obvious reply that would enable him to make the witty retort for which his first remark had been merely a setup. George couldn't think of the obvious reply. During the past twenty minutes, ever since he had left Win and Jimmy with Tim Keogh at Camp Shawmut, George had managed to keep penned up in a far corner of his mind his completely unreasonable reactions to Miss Akst's puzzling phone call about the mysterious Mr. Kashkin. Now the pen in the corner of his mind seemed to have burst open. Once again he was being assailed by an uneasiness that, because it made no sense, was beginning to make him angry.

"When I get to the office," he said, "I think I'd better point out to Miss Akst that long-distance phone calls cost money."

Mary looked at him curiously. "You mean the call is not important?"

"Not fifty cents' worth," George said. "Or whatever the long-distance rate is from Bushwick Avenue to Queen's Court Road."

"That's odd," Mary said. "Miss Akst seemed to feel it was very important. When I told her you'd already gone, she sounded quite upset. Then, when I told her I could still catch you because you'd be dropping Carolina off just before you went to the train, she asked me please to make sure I did catch you."

"Well, you caught me," George said. "Now I'd better get hopping if I expect to catch my train."

He slid across the seat toward the wheel, but Mary did not take her hand from the door of the car.

"George," she said. "Who is this Mr. Kashkin?"

"Damned if I know," George said, and then he remembered what he had told Mary when he'd hung up on Miss Akst, and he felt his face flush. Not so much for the lie that was almost an hour old and that he still did not know why he had told, but for the new one he was being forced, as a result, to invent. "He's got something to do with the Perrini Brothers balance sheet, which involves a matter of New York State taxes, and so I suppose Miss Akst feels the fact that Mr. Kashkin comes from Albany, where the New York State Tax Department has its central office, is in some way very important. When you're dealing with a mind like Miss Akst's, there's no point in playing guessing games."

"No, I suppose not," Mary said. "Well, have a good day." She blew him a kiss as she turned from the car. "See you tonight at the Stiefels'."

"I'll be driving over with Milton Schneider from the Dandy-pops meeting."

"When did you arrange that?"

"A couple of minutes ago at Dr. Rettig's. Don't ask me to explain how. Just call Eileen. She said she wants to go to the Stiefels with you."

George put the car in gear, stepped on the gas, and once again, above the roar of the motor, he heard someone calling. He tapped the brake, shoved in the clutch, and leaned across the front seat for another look. He saw that Mary, who had started up the walk toward the house, had stopped halfway. Carolina was standing in the front door, holding the screen door open.

"—on the telephone," George heard her call to Mary. "And she say it's important!"

Starting to move more quickly up the walk, Mary called back

across her shoulder toward the car, "Hold it a second, darling. This may be Miss Akst again."

George waited tensely. A few moments later, when Mary came back out of the house, she looked more puzzled than ever. "Guess what?" she said.

"Not with eight minutes before train time," George said. "Was it Miss Akst?"

"No, Polly Stiefel. Checking up to make sure we were coming tonight."

George didn't blame his wife for sounding astonished. They had known the Stiefels for almost three years, ever since Polly and Hume had moved out to Danville from New York. But the two families were not really very close. As a hostess, Polly leaned toward quantity rather than quality, so that a guest who accepted one of her invitations and then, finding it impossible to attend, called up later to apologize, was usually embarrassed to discover that Polly had not even noticed his absence. There may have been people whose presence Polly and Hume Stiefel valued so highly that Polly would make an extra effort to insure their attendance at one of her parties. George knew he and Mary were not in that category. Staring at the expression on his wife's face, he could see Mary knew it, too. What George could not see, and what he could not mention to Mary, was why he should have the sudden feeling that there was some connection between Miss Akst's two puzzling phone calls from Brooklyn and this even more puzzling call from Polly Stiefel.

"I guess we're beginning to arrive in this town socially," George said. "Who would ever have thought Polly Stiefel would double check to make sure an accountant showed up at one of her parties?"

"I'm not so sure it's because you're an accountant."

George gave his wife a sharp glance. "How do you mean?"

Mary was frowning. "I don't belong to the Let's-Hate-Polly group in this town," she said. "Most of the girls in Danville who make up that group joined it because Polly Stiefel is pretty and she's got money and she has all those interesting big name friends from Broadway and Hollywood, and these other dames are plain jealous. But just because I'm not jealous of Polly and I won't join that group of catty tearer-downers, it doesn't mean I'm starting a movement to have her canonized. She's a pretty cold little fish, Mrs. Polly Stiefel is. Cold and calculating. She took us up for the same reason she took up everybody else in this town who isn't a café society big shot.

Because she's thorough, and she doesn't like to overlook any possibilities, however small. That's the level on which we exist for her, and calling up like this in the morning to make sure we're coming to her party tonight doesn't check with that level."

"Meaning what?"

"I don't know," Mary said. "Not for sure, anyway. But it smells to me like Polly wants something from us."

"If she does," George said, "I can't figure why she doesn't ask for it. So far as I've been able to see, she always does. I've never known her to beat around the bush."

"If my hunch is right, then whatever it is, she'll ask for it tonight, don't worry," Mary said. "Meantime, darling, you better head for that train."

One of the advantages of living on Queen's Court Road was that it was within walking distance of the Danville station. Before the Hursts became a two-car family, George used to walk it every morning in fifteen or twenty minutes, depending on the weather. Now that he drove, it rarely took him more than five minutes. During the hot months the trip usually took a little longer because Danville was a popular summer resort with well-to-do New Yorkers, and from the middle of June to the middle of September the approaches to the railroad station were choked with Cadillacs at train time.

Year-round residents, however, had their own little short cuts, as well as their special parking places, so that even though George had left his house at six minutes after nine, and traffic down Railroad Avenue was moving at a crawl, he was on the platform at nine-twelve.

George walked through the crowd, his eyes fixed on the Railway Express luggage cart at the far end of the platform against which he always leaned while he waited for the train. He was aware as he moved that men were nodding to him, and George nodded back, but he was careful not to catch anybody's eye. He had learned during his years as a commuter that the conversation most people made on station platforms while waiting for the morning train was hardly the sort of thing Boswell would have cared to attribute to Samuel Johnson. The trick was to meet the minimum requisites of politeness without actually getting involved with anybody.

He had a bad moment just before he reached the luggage cart. The Railway Express man, who usually did not stir until he heard the rumble of the approaching train, decided for some reason to shove the loaded cart a foot or two closer to the platform edge. This caused several women, who were industriously reading their newspapers, to shift position. As a result, George was forced to alter his gait and, as he stepped swiftly aside to avoid Ceil Scheuer, whose husband owned the Danville Hardware Company, he found himself face to face with Polly Stiefel.

"Hey," George said. "What are you doing here?"

"I'm going into New York to pick up my guest of honor for tonight, Ella Mason."

"No, I mean didn't you just talk to Mary on the phone? No more than six or seven minutes ago?"

"Of course I did," Polly said. "I'd been wanting to call Mary all day yesterday, but I was going so fast and hard I never got near a phone, so when I got to the station a few minutes early this morning, and I saw the booth back there in the waiting room, I said here's my chance and I took it. I'm awfully glad that you're coming tonight, George."

He was sure she was. There were people in Danville who said Polly Stiefel was an insincere little bitch, and even Mary, who was fair-minded to a point where she could be annoying, had said only a few minutes ago that Polly was a cold fish, cold and calculating. But insincerity is not like arthritis or flat feet or any other physical infirmity that the sufferer can neither control nor get relief from. Even an insincere person could be, if it suited his or her book, temporarily sincere. About certain things, at any rate. And there was no doubt in George Hurst's mind that Polly Stiefel was completely sincere when she said she was glad he was coming to her party tonight. That was what bothered him.

"I'm glad you invited us," he said. "I'm going to be a little late because I have to stop in at a Dandypops meeting at the school first, but Mary will go on ahead and I'll join her later."

"Oh, grand," Polly said. "It will be such fun to see Mary again."

This was the point at which conviction fled. Not because Polly and Mary didn't get on together. It was simply that George knew Polly Stiefel couldn't possibly find it fun to see any woman again. Men were her speed. She was the sort of woman Aunt Tessie would have described as "busy." Even when Polly Stiefel was sitting down, some part of her was in motion. There was something a little coy and old-fashioned about all this movement, as though she were a Ziegfeld chorus girl who had stopped learning anything new about the art of coquetry when she stopped growing older in 1929.

Polly's red hair was done in a manner that had been known, when George was a boy, as shingled. She had a neat little figure and she kept pace with the newest fashions in clothes, but George always had the feeling that she belonged in a cloche hat and a dress with a waistline down around her hips. Polly may have felt this herself. At any rate, late at night, when things got gay at her own parties, she frequently broke into a fairly abandoned Charleston that male guests, new to the Stiefel household, sometimes misunderstood. This was unfortunate. Polly worked hard at being sexy, but she was not wanton. George could not recall hearing so much as a whisper of scandal about Polly and Hume Stiefel during all their three years in Danville.

This was surprising, because Hume Stiefel was a stuffy, elderly, dull-witted manufacturer of bathing suits, who was constantly flying off to visit his firm's factories in California, leaving Polly alone in the big house on Hawthorn Hill. Alone, that is, with their son Dickie, the two maids, and the endless stream of guests who poured through night after night. Most of these, aside from neighbors like George and Mary, were in some way connected with the theatre and Hollywood.

Since these two worlds were all that Polly Stiefel really cared for, George could not understand why she had moved out to Danville. It was true that there were in Fairfield County a great many representatives of the theatrical and motion picture worlds, but it was not the center of either. Feeling as Polly Stiefel did about Broadway and Hollywood and coming to Danville to indulge this passion was, George felt, a good deal like being crazy about ships and settling on the shores of the lake in Central Park. You could probably see plenty of rowboats but the odds were pretty heavily against your catching many glimpses of the *Queen Mary*.

Running swiftly in his mind through all these facts about Polly as he stood facing her on the Danville railroad platform, George was uncomfortably aware that he had missed the one fact that was making her so important to him at this moment. As the platform began to tremble beneath his feet, and the commuters around him raised their heads from their newspapers and began to peer up the track toward the approaching train, George made a last desperate effort. He thrust his mind back to the first disturbing moment of the morning, the moment when Miss Akst's voice had come to him on the phone, then ran quickly through the events that had followed, touching briefly on Tim Keogh and Carolina and Mr. Ashorn and Dr. Rettig and then, all at once, as the train roared in, he had it.

"Hey," George said. "Hey, Polly!"

"What?" she shouted, ducking her head against the rush of air and dust raised by the train. "I can't hear you!"

"Something I just remembered!" George bellowed, leaning down to her ear. He had just remembered the feeling he'd had while talking to Mary in the car on his own driveway, the feeling that there was some connection between Miss Akst's two puzzling phone calls from Brooklyn and the even more puzzling call from Polly Stiefel. "Albany!" George roared. "Didn't you once tell me you came from Albany?"

"Yes, I was born there!" Polly shouted back at him. "What about it?"

"A man named Kashkin!" George yelled. "Do you know anybody named Kashkin?"

"Who?" Polly screamed, and then, as people around her turned to stare, she laughed and lowered her voice. The train had stopped. "Now say that again," Polly said as she moved with George across the platform, toward the train. "In a normal voice."

"I was just asking if you knew anybody named Kashkin," George said. "K, a, s, h, k, i, n?"

"The slot-machine Kashkin?" Polly asked. "Or the Albany Kashkin?"

George gave her a quick glance. Polly was waving her white-gloved hand at some man further down the platform. She seemed to have forgotten all about George. "Is there any difference?" he said.

Polly turned back to him. "What?" she said.

"Is there any difference between the slot-machine Kashkin and the Albany Kashkin?"

"The slot-machine Kashkin is just a gangster," Polly said. "Some sort of big shot in the rackets that have to do with trucking dresses and bathing suits and that sort of thing. I've heard Hume mention him lots of times, and in no complimentary terms, believe me." She stopped. They had reached the train step. She waited daintily for George to give her his hand. He put it on her elbow. Polly smiled radiantly, as though she had just been presented with two or three pounds of emeralds, and said, "Thank you, George."

"What about the other one?" he said, heaving her up the step with a short, firm thrust. "The Albany Kashkin?"

Polly turned, as he started up into the train after her, to look down on him from the top step.

"The slot-machine Kashkin, the gangster, he's bad enough," she said. "But the other one, the Albany Kashkin." Polly threw up both hands as though she were going to slap a volley ball. "*That* guy," she said. "Oh, brother!"

3

George Hurst's suite in the Tarleton Tower on Forty-second Street consisted of three rooms: his private office, a reception room, and a smaller office between these two in which Miss Akst worked. It was possible to enter all three rooms from the hall, but the doors to George's room and Miss Akst's room were kept locked, so that visitors had to enter through the reception room. George never came in through the reception room. He always let himself directly into his own office with his key. This morning, when he came in, he found Miss Akst waiting for him.

"He's here." She made it sound as though the place was being raided by the vice squad.

"All right," George said, trying to sound casual. He didn't want Miss Akst to know how unreasonably apprehensive he was about this meeting with Mr. Kashkin. "I'll see him in a minute." George put his briefcase on the desk, snapped it open, and pulled out the Perrini Brothers balance sheet, on which he had worked late the night before. "How are you fixed for time, Miss Akst?"

"I'm pretty well caught up," she said. "Why?"

"I'm going downtown later to have lunch with Nick Perrini. I'd like to have this typed so I can take it with me, if that's possible?"

"Why shouldn't it be possible? I'm all of a sudden a cripple?" Miss Akst took the handwritten sheets of analysis paper from George and nodded toward the reception room. "This Mr. Kashkin," she said. "You got my message, I left it with Mrs. Hurst, that he's from Albany?"

"Yes, I got that."

"Did it help?"

George hesitated. All the way in on the train he had been turning over in his mind the things Polly Stiefel had told him about Mr. Kashkin. "I don't know," he said. "What made you think it would?"

Miss Akst scowled. "I'm not exactly sure. It's just Albany, sort of. The sound of it. Who comes from Albany? *To* Albany, yes. That's different. It's the capital of the state. People are always going to Albany. To see the governor, to do something in the legislature, things like that. You say Albany, it means sort of politics. You know? But *from* Albany? Who ever heard of anybody coming from Albany?"

"I had an uncle who did," George said. "He lived up there for forty years."

Miss Akst looked at him as though he had announced that from now on he intended to commute to and from Danville by bicycle. "Is that the truth?" she said.

For all practical purposes it was. Uncle Zisha had been Aunt Tessie's brother.

"Cross my heart," George said. "He was in the soda bottling business."

"Well, this Mr. Kashkin, he doesn't look like he's in any soda bottling business."

"How can you tell?"

Miss Akst beckoned George with her forefinger. Even though it made him feel silly, he followed his secretary out into her office and peered with her through the small window over her desk that looked out into the reception room. On one of the three chairs near the water cooler sat a squat, barrel-chested, middle-aged man with thinning gray hair. He wore a dark suit and rimless octagon-shaped glasses. His pearl-gray hat rested on the chair beside him. If Mr. Kashkin was aware that he was being scrutinized through the small window, he gave no sign. He continued imperturbably to read his morning paper, and it was this imperturbability that caused George to see clearly what Miss Akst had meant when she said Mr. Kashkin did not look as though he was in the soda bottling business. Mr. Kashkin looked like those men whose photographs appeared every day in the financial section of the *New York Times* over stories announcing changes in the chairmanship of corporation boards.

"All the time I was growing up in Albany," Polly Stiefel had said on the train, "the Kashkins were nothing. By that I mean they were just another family on the block. Mr. Kashkin was a house painter with a flock of kids and the usual worries about making both ends meet, and then all of a sudden this brother Maurice showed up. Where from? Only God and maybe the F.B.I. can tell, although I must say that's a little unfair. I don't actually know anything crooked about Maurice Kashkin and I have no right to imply anything of the kind. It's just that it was sort of funny. There was this house painter, just one jump ahead of the sheriff, and then all of a sudden there was his brother, dropping in out of the blue, you might say, and from then on the Kashkins stopped being nothing and became quite a lot. They moved into a brand-new big house and they bought two cars and they started snooting everybody they'd known in the old days."

Polly had paused to look thoughtfully out the train window, and then she had chuckled.

"I didn't exactly blame them for that," she said. "If you're poor, as I was when I was a kid, and then you put your hands on some money, as I did when I married Hume, you go a little haywire. It's only natural, and my analyst tells me I'm probably still a little haywire. But not Maurice Kashkin. There was nothing haywire about him. He was the quiet type, and at first nobody could figure out why he'd come to Albany, but then people started seeing him going in and out of the governor's mansion at all sorts of hours, and everybody stopped trying to figure it out. I mean everybody immediately assumed Maurice Kashkin was some sort of political big shot, and he'd come to Albany because he was close to this new governor who'd just been elected, and he'd settled down with his housepainter brother because Maurice wasn't married himself and he wanted to have a respectable front. I haven't been back to Albany for years, so I don't really know if the Kashkins are still up there; and if Maurice Kashkin is still a political big shot, it's all behind the scenes, because I haven't heard his name mentioned in a long time. But this much I can tell you: wherever he is, and whatever he's doing, it's big."

Looking out at Mr. Kashkin through the small window over Miss Akst's desk, George was inclined to agree. There was something about Mr. Kashkin's posture that suggested power and wealth.

"If it turns out that this boy actually is in the soda bottling business," George said, "I can tell you one thing."

"What's that?" Miss Akst said.

"He doesn't make anything smaller than gallon-size jugs." George stepped away from the window and started toward his own office. "Why don't you bring him in?"

A few moments later she did so.

"Mr. Hurst, this is Mr. Kashkin."

Miss Akst pulled the door shut, and George stood up to take his visitor's hand.

"How do you do, Mr. Kashkin?"

"Glad to meet you, Mr. Hurst. I guess I owe you an apology for busting in on you this way, and if that's so, okay, I apologize. Most people, they want to see a man, they call up for an appointment or they write him a letter. But all that does, it gives the man you want to see a chance to say no, and frankly, Mr. Hurst, I didn't want to take any chances on your saying no."

"Why should I do that?" George said.

"Maybe you'll be able to answer that better than I can after I tell you why I'm here," Mr. Kashkin said. "Mind if I sit down?"

"Of course not," George said.

He waited until Mr. Kashkin was settled in the chair facing the desk before he sat down himself, and then George saw that Mr. Kashkin was far from settled. First the short, thick-set man adjusted his trousers across the knees so that the creases would not be damaged by the act of sitting. Then he put his newspaper on the floor beside the chair. Mr. Kashkin's portly figure and his slow, deliberate, fussy manner gave George the impression that he was watching a pastry chef put the finishing touches to a wedding cake.

"Okay, then," Mr. Kashkin said finally, but apparently it wasn't. Not yet, anyway. From the top left-hand pocket of his expensively tailored dark vest he pulled a gold cigar case, snapped it open, and held it out across the desk. "Cigar, Mr. Hurst?"

"No, thank you."

"Mind if I do?"

"Of course not."

Mr. Kashkin selected a cigar, replaced the case in his pocket, performed a small surgical operation on the end of the cigar with a gadget plucked from another pocket, and brought the cigar to life with a golden lighter from a third pocket. George did not smoke cigars, but he had learned something about their cost from a number of clients who tried regularly to list on their tax returns the amount they spent on cigars as a deductible business item. He guessed, from the smell of Mr. Kashkin's cigar, that if his visitor had come to see him about a tax problem, it was undoubtedly in the upper brackets.

"Okay, then," Mr. Kashkin said again, and this time he seemed to mean it. "Now I'll tell you, Mr. Hurst, why I came to see you." Mr. Kashkin took the cigar from his mouth. "What I've come to see you about, Mr. Hurst," he said. "I've come to see you about a man named Daniel Shaw."

For a long, long moment, during which it seemed to George he could hear nothing but the suddenly exaggerated beating of his own heart, his mind seemed capable of only one thought: *How had Miss Akst known?*

During the four years that she had been working for him, George had never said a word to her about his past. They had never discussed his private life. He had never uttered Danny Shaw's name in her presence. And yet, as soon as Mr. Kashkin had called up the night before, he had made Miss Akst uncomfortable. Something had warned her that this was no ordinary caller. Why hadn't it, whatever "it" was, warned George? All morning, from the moment Miss Akst had spoken to him on the phone at home, he had been uneasy about Mr. Kashkin's visit and he had been raking through his mind for some reason to explain his uneasiness. How could he possibly have overlooked the only reason that required no explanation?

"I beg your pardon?" George said. But this didn't sound right even in his own ears. He made an effort and managed to pull himself together. "I don't think I quite got that name?"

"I think you did," Mr. Kashkin said.

George put both hands on the desk, palms down, and leaned forward. "Look," he said.

"I will," Mr. Kashkin said. "As soon as you start pointing to something interesting, Mr. Hurst. In the meantime there's nothing to get flustered about. There's just that simple statement I made: I've come to see you about Daniel Shaw."

"All right, you've made your simple statement," George said. "Now I'll have to ask you to leave."

"Why?"

"I'm busy."

"I'm sure you can think up a better reason than that, Mr. Hurst."

"I don't know anything about anybody named Daniel Shaw."

"We think different, Mr. Hurst."

"Who is we?"

"The people I represent," Mr. Kashkin said. "We think you

know more about Danny Shaw than anybody alive in this country today."

"I can't help what you and the people you represent think," George said. "I don't know anything about anybody named Daniel Shaw. Good-bye, Mr. Kashkin."

George stood up. Mr. Kashkin didn't move. He squinted at George through the smoke of his cigar as though he were sighting a gun.

"Mr. Hurst," he said, "I came all the way down from Albany to see you. Don't send me back without listening to what I have to say."

"I'm not interested in what you have to say."

"I think you are," Mr. Kashkin said. "Anyway, you should be. Because if I don't say it to you, Mr. Hurst, I'll just have to say it to somebody else, and while I wouldn't like to do that, I think you'd like it even less." Mr. Kashkin took a long pull on the cigar. The cloud of smoke, when he blew it out, was so large and thick that for a moment or two Mr. Kashkin's head vanished from view. When it reappeared, George saw that Mr. Kashkin looked troubled. He said, very quietly, "Sit down, Mr. Hurst."

George sat down.

"The people I represent are a group of citizens, Mr. Hurst, who are very interested in a new phase of Daniel Shaw's career," Mr. Kashkin said. "It is not as yet generally known, and the general public will not be allowed to know it until all the spadework has been done behind the scenes, but Daniel Shaw has developed certain political ambitions."

"What does he want to be now?" George said. "The first Jewish President of the United States?"

As soon as the words were out, George regretted them. The bitterness in his voice was so obvious that he could feel his face grow hot.

Mr. Kashkin looked thoughtfully at the end of his cigar. "I see you do know Daniel Shaw," he said, and he paused, as though waiting for another denial.

George, who was cursing himself inwardly, decided the most sensible thing at the moment was to keep his mouth shut.

Mr. Kashkin looked up from the cigar and nodded, as though he understood what was going through George's mind and approved his decision. "The exact nature of Daniel Shaw's political ambitions are unimportant at the moment," he said. "Although when the proper moment comes, I will be glad to tell you what they are. At this moment, Mr. Hurst, I would like to stick to my reason for coming to see you, and it is this: while we, the people I represent, are interested in Daniel Shaw's political ambitions, before we commit ourselves to helping him achieve them we want to make sure that achieving them is not impossible."

Mr. Kashkin leaned across and, with a delicate flick of the smallest of his beautifully manicured fingernails, he splashed a half inch of almost pure white ash into the tray on George's desk. "In plain English, Mr. Hurst, we don't want to be caught with our pants down. We don't want to back Mr. Shaw and then find out, in the middle of a campaign, when a lot of time and money has been spent, that there's something about our candidate that makes it impossible for him to win."

Mr. Kashkin paused again. Staring at his visitor in silence, it occurred to George that he was trying to look as imperturbable as Mr. Kashkin had looked a few minutes ago when Miss Akst and George had peered out at him in the reception room. George hoped, as he tried to control his breathing and throttle down the beating of his heart, that he was being as successful as Mr. Kashkin in achieving the outward appearance of imperturbability.

"So far as we can see, and we've done enough investigating to be able to see pretty far, Mr. Hurst, there's only one thing about Danny Shaw that could kick up the kind of trouble that might make it impossible for him to win." This time, when Mr. Kashkin paused, he looked directly at George. "That potential trouble comes in two words, Mr. Hurst," he said. "His wife."

Mr. Kashkin waited. George let him wait. If he could not control what was happening to his heart, he could still control what he did with his tongue. George held it.

"Daniel Shaw was married in 1932," Mr. Kashkin said. "Ten years later, in 1942, his wife disappeared. Daniel Shaw claims she is dead."

George moved slightly in his chair. It gave him a small feeling of relief, like easing the lace of a tight shoe. "How can a dead woman cause a political candidate any trouble?" he said.

"If in the middle of the campaign," Mr. Kashkin said, "it turns out she's not dead and there are certain things about her that might make her, well, let's say certain things that might make her somewhat less than the ideal wife for a political candidate to have."

"Don't you take Mr. Shaw's word about the death of his own wife?"

"We can't, Mr. Hurst."

"Why not?"

"Mr. Shaw doesn't know where his wife is buried."

George put his hands on the desk again. "Now, look," he said.

Mr. Kashkin held up the cigar as though it were a pointer. "No, please," he said gently. "Let's not get started on that again. Let's keep our voices low, Mr. Hurst, and let's stick to facts. Mr. Shaw doesn't know where his wife is buried because he has no actual proof that she's dead. He didn't bury her. He didn't see her die. One day, when he came home, she was not there. That's all. She just wasn't there. She'd disappeared."

"Didn't he make any effort to find her?"

"He says he did, Mr. Hurst."

"But you don't believe him?"

"Mr. Hurst, when a woman is involved it's hard to know how much of what any man says you can believe or not believe. Especially when the man has political ambitions and there's something mysterious about the woman. Since I'm being completely frank with you, Mr. Hurst, I'll tell you this: Danny Shaw says he did make an effort to find his wife, but curiously enough we can find no record that the police of this city were ever asked to trace the wife of Daniel Shaw. We haven't told him that yet. We didn't want to confront him with what might be described as discrepancies until I'd had a chance to talk with you. What do you make of it, Mr. Hurst?"

"Maybe Mr. Shaw didn't want her found?"

Again George wished he could recall his words. He had uttered them too quickly.

Mr. Kashkin was nodding. "That seems likely," he said. "Doesn't it?" George didn't answer. Mr. Kashkin leaned forward and splashed more ash into the tray on the desk. "Why do you suppose he didn't, Mr. Hurst?"

"Why do you suppose I would know?"

Mr. Kashkin reached into his breast pocket and pulled out what looked like a business letter. He unfolded it slowly, studied the page for a few moments, lifted a slip of paper that was clipped to the top, allowed the slip to fall back, then looked up.

"We've done a little investigating," he said. "According to our investigators, at the time Mrs. Shaw disappeared, she was not living with her husband. She was living in an apartment on East Forty-eighth Street. At the time of her disappearance, Mrs. Shaw was three months behind in her rent on this apartment. When she disappeared, the landlord naturally thought that was the end of it. According to our investigators, however, he was wrong."

Mr. Kashkin tapped the letter with the side of his cigar, the way an orchestra conductor might tap the edge of his lectern to attract the attention of his musicians.

"A few days after Mrs. Shaw disappeared, a man showed up, let himself into the apartment with a key, and started to pack Mrs. Shaw's clothes and other personal effects. He had a couple of suit-cases filled up, and he was working on the third, when the landlord walked in on him. According to the landlord, who still remembers the whole thing, the man didn't even wait to be told that he wouldn't be allowed to take away Mrs. Shaw's clothes and other personal effects until her back rent was paid. According to the landlord, this man stopped packing long enough to pull out his checkbook and write a check to cover Mrs. Shaw's arrears in full."

Mr. Kashkin paused and set the cigar between his teeth the way a man at a desk might set a fountain pen into its holder to free his hands for further action. Using both hands, Mr. Kashkin freed the slip of paper from the clip that held it to the letter, leaned forward again, and placed the slip of paper beside the ash tray on George's desk. The slip of paper was a photostat of a canceled check, drawn on the National City Bank of New York in the sum of $180.00. Mr. Kashkin's thumb and forefinger, spanning the width of the check, held it flat on George's green blotter. The forefinger covered part of the neatly written date, so that only "June 12, 1——" was visible. Nothing covered the signature. The small, firm, slightly faded letters spelled out "George Hurst."

For several long moments, while the muted noises of Forty-second Street, twenty-one floors below, suddenly seemed to swell and fill the room as though it were a cage in which a flock of birds had gone wild, Mr. Kashkin and George remained motionless, lean-ing toward each other across the desk, staring down at the slip of paper with faded ink, like a couple of chess players in a painting. Finally, with a small sigh, Mr. Kashkin leaned back. His hand, com-ing away from the desk, brought the check away with it.

"Now, then," he said quietly, addressing the check as, very care-fully, he slipped it back under the clip at the top of the letter. "Let me make a couple of things clear, Mr. Hurst. First, we have reason to believe that Daniel Shaw is telling the truth when he says he believes his wife is dead. Second, we don't really care whether she is dead or not. Do I make myself clear?"

George drew a deep breath. "I think you can probably do better than that."

Mr. Kashkin nodded. "Put it this way," he said. "We, that's the people I represent and myself, Mr. Hurst, we don't want to pry into anybody's private affairs. All we want to do is make sure if we decide to back Daniel Shaw, nothing is going to come along behind us and hit us a wallop back of the ear when we're not looking."

"How can I help you make sure of that?"

"You can tell us if Mrs. Shaw is dead, and you can fill us in on what it is or was about her that could maybe prove embarrassing to a candidate like Daniel Shaw in the middle of a campaign. That's what you can tell us, Mr. Hurst."

"Suppose I can't?"

"When you say can't, Mr. Hurst, do you mean won't?"

"Suppose I do?"

Mr. Kashkin shook his head slowly as he blew a stream of smoke at the letter in his hand. "In that case," he said regretfully, "I'm afraid our investigators, who were told to pause when they got as far as you, will be told to resume digging." He refolded the letter and replaced it in his breast pocket. "I served with the army of occupation in Germany after the First World War," Mr. Kashkin said. "A lot of men, I remember, they were always digging around on some of the big battlefields for souvenirs to send home. Every now and then, in the process of digging, one of these souvenir hunters would hit something he hadn't counted on finding, and there would be a hell of a bang." Mr. Kashkin moved his head to bring it out from behind a cloud of cigar smoke. "You're a married man, Mr. Hurst," he said. "You have a wife, children, a home, a position in your community and in your profession. I'm sure all that is very precious to you." Mr. Kashkin sighed. "Digging is a nasty business, Mr. Hurst," he said quietly. "We'd like to stop doing any more of it before somebody gets hurt."

George stood up and went to the window. Looking down on Bryant Park, he tried quickly to sort out the emotions that were flailing around inside him, out of control, like so many rubber hoses that had been severed while under full pressure. It was a hopeless task, and George knew it. There wasn't much chance that something he had been unable to straighten out with himself for thirty years would be solved in as many seconds. A boy carrying a large package stepped off the curb in front of the Public Library and, for a few moments, George forced himself to watch the boy's darting progress as he cut across Forty-second Street through the moving traffic toward the other curb. Then the boy moved out of George's angle of vision, and he was forced once more to contemplate the problem Mr. Kashkin, a total stranger, had brought unexpectedly into this room. It looked insoluble.

"Mr. Hurst."

George turned. Miss Akst had come in. "Yes?"

"The Perrini Brothers balance sheet," she said. "It's typed."

"Thanks," George said.

She walked across the room, giving Mr. Kashkin a cold look, and placed the balance sheets on George's desk. On her way back to the door she kept her icy glance on Mr. Kashkin. He seemed completely unaware of her hostility. Mr. Kashkin was watching George.

"I'm sorry," George said as he crossed to his desk. "I can't tell you anything now."

"You mean you want to think it over?" Mr. Kashkin said.

George picked up the Perrini Brothers balance sheets and jogged them gently into alignment. "I've got to go downtown to a meeting with a client," he said. "I can't tell you anything now."

Mr. Kashkin took off his glasses, pursed his lips, and scowled as he massaged his eyeballs with the thumb and forefinger of his free hand. "When will you be able to tell me?" he said.

George hesitated. He knew he was not handling this right. He also knew, however, that there was no really right way for it to be handled. What had happened was inevitable. From the very beginning he had known in his heart that it was bound to come. The only thing that had been unpredictable was the form it would take. If it hadn't been Mr. Kashkin, sooner or later it would have been somebody else. Very little was to be gained by stalling. Yet that very little suddenly seemed the only thing that mattered.

"Today is Friday," George said. "I won't be able to tell you anything until after the week end."

"It's going to be a long week end," Mr. Kashkin said. "Monday is the Fourth of July."

"I know," George said. "I won't be able to tell you anything until Tuesday."

"Why not? What difference does it make whether you tell me now or Tuesday?"

"I don't want to argue about it," George said. "I won't be able to tell you anything until Tuesday. I'd like to let it go at that."

"I don't want to argue about it, either, Mr. Hurst, but I think I'm as busy a man as you are. I came all the way down from Albany for only one purpose: to see you. I have nothing else to do here in New York. I don't like to hang around for three whole days, doing nothing, waiting for you to tell me something I don't see why you can't tell me right now."

"I said Tuesday, Mr. Kashkin. Take it or leave it."

Mr. Kashkin pursed his lips and stared at the end of his cigar. "What time Tuesday?" he said finally.

"I don't know yet. It depends on a number of factors." George opened his briefcase and slipped the Perrini Brothers balance sheets into it. "Where are you staying?"

"The Waldorf."

"I'll ring you at the Waldorf sometime Tuesday."

"You sure you couldn't make it sooner than that?"

"No, I'm sorry," George said. "That's the best I can do."

4

When George first met them, in 1931, there had been five Perrini brothers. Now there was only one. But Nick Perrini still kept the firm's old name, Perrini Brothers, and he still operated on the top floor of the old loft building on Astor Place in which his father had started the family business soon after the old man came to this country from Naples.

The building was half a block from the Astor Place station of the Lexington Avenue subway. Every time George walked that short distance he was reminded of his first meeting with the Perrini Brothers. Today he would have preferred not to be reminded. George wanted time to think through the problem Mr. Kashkin had dropped in his lap. But he didn't see how he could break his date with Nick

Perrini. When Nick had called up the day before and had asked George to lunch with him, Nick had said he wanted to see George about something very important. Therefore, even though his mind was struggling with the problem of Mr. Kashkin, the moment George came out of the subway and started across Astor Place, he was once again intensely aware of that first encounter.

It had been one of those February days in 1931 that people who had lived through the depression were always talking about, but those who had lived through it in New York hated to remember. Less than two hours before he came up out of the subway into Astor Place, George had landed a job with Malvin Gewirtz & Company, certified public accountants, on Thirty-fourth Street. And now, on the way to his first assignment accompanied by a superior, George was still a little shaken by his luck.

People who landed jobs in 1931 in New York were looked upon somewhat like sweepstakes winners. If they had any brains, they looked upon themselves that way, too. What bothered George was that Mr. Rapf, the superior to whom he had been assigned, seemed to look upon it as a joke.

"How old you say you are?" Mr. Rapf said as they dodged traffic on the way across Astor Place.

George hadn't said anything. Not about his age, anyway. He had the uneasy feeling, though, that all the way down in the subway from Thirty-fourth Street he had been running off at the mouth. This feeling was caused by the way Mr. Rapf had been looking at him from the moment they met: out of the corner of his eye, with a sort of turned inward smile, as though there was something about George that reminded Mr. Rapf of an old joke and he couldn't make up his mind whether to let anybody else in on it or not.

"I'm twenty-one," George said.

"Uh-huh," said Mr. Rapf. He was a tall, slightly stooped man with buck teeth which he attempted to conceal by keeping his lips thrust out to cover them. All this did was make him look as though he was trying to whistle. "You can tell me the truth about your age, kid," he said. "I'm not Mr. Brodsky."

Mr. Brodsky, who had hired George, was one of the two partners in Malvin Gewirtz & Company. Mr. Brodsky had explained that the company's staff of forty-two men, which was sent out of the Thirty-fourth Street office every morning in teams of two and three to audit the books and records of clients in various parts of the city, was broken down into three categories: seniors, semi-seniors, and juniors. The seniors, as their designation implied, were the elite corps of the staff. They were all middle-aged men. In fact, some of them looked pretty ancient to George. At least forty. Maybe even older. They received the highest salaries and, on the Gewirtz staff of forty-two, there were only six of them. Mr. Rapf, who was the oldest of the six, was also, according to Mr. Brodsky, the best man to break in a new employee. George was grateful for being turned over to the company's best man. It sort of underlined the unexpected break of landing the job in the first place. But he wished Mr. Rapf would ditch that funny grin and stop poking around for information about George's private life.

"It's the truth," George said. "I'm twenty-one."

What else could he say? Mr. Brodsky had laid it on the line at the beginning of the interview: it was a policy of Malvin Gewirtz & Company not to hire anybody under the age of twenty-one.

"I see," Mr. Rapf said through that turned-in smile. "Where do you live, kid?"

"University Place."

"Hey, so down here on Astor Place we're practically in your own back yard?"

"Sort of."

"You know where we're going?"

"Mr. Brodsky said a firm called Perrini Brothers. For the regular audit."

"That's right. You got any idea what Perrini Brothers manufactures?"

"No," George said. "What?"

Mr. Rapf didn't seem to hear the question. He was in the grip of that secret joke again. As he dodged a truck and hopped up onto the curb, the smile on the senior's face spread out so far that his buck teeth came into full view. "When's your birthday?" he said.

"July," George said.

"So it's now February, that means you'll be twenty-one in five months," Mr. Rapf said with a chuckle. "Not now twenty-one but in five months twenty-one. Right?"

"That's right," George said. "July second I'll be—"

He stopped as though he'd been hit. For several moments, as he stared at the man who had trapped him, George could feel the tips of his fingers grow icy. He couldn't believe, deep down in his heart, that anybody would be son of a bitch enough to get a guy fired from a brand-new job just because he'd lied a little about his age. But George had learned during the past terrifying weeks of job hunting that what you believed deep down in your heart didn't count for very much these days. Queer things were going on in February of 1931.

"Not even twenty-one years old yet," Mr. Rapf said through another chuckle. "And they ship him down to Perrini Brothers." For a few steps, as they moved along the sidewalk, the secret joke seemed to take full possession of the senior. His tall, slightly stooped figure shook with silent laughter. "A kid of twenty, for Christ's sake," he said. "They send him to Perrini Brothers."

Then, all at once, Mr. Rapf seemed to become aware of George's face. The senior's buck teeth vanished as the smile disappeared. "You don't have to worry, kid. I won't squeal to Brodsky you're not twenty-one."

Oddly enough, George believed him. "Thanks."

"Forget it," Mr. Rapf said and then, as they turned into the entrance to a loft building, he was suddenly chuckling again. "Where did you go to school, kid?"

"Franklin Pierce High."

"You were a good student?"

"Pretty good."

"You figure you got a good education there at this Franklin Pierce High?"

"I suppose so."

George wondered what the hell Mr. Rapf was getting at.

"Today here at Perrini Brothers," the senior said, "I guarantee you'll get a better education."

There was nobody in the lobby of the loft building. George, who couldn't figure out what Mr. Rapf was talking about, couldn't figure out this lobby, either. It seemed to be a combination of a freight entrance and a front entrance. There was a tenants' directory on the wall, neatly framed in glass, and the elevator doors were painted bright red. But along one wall there were two rows of loaded ash cans, apparently waiting to be picked up.

Mr. Rapf pressed the elevator button, looked to right and left, and then leaned close to George. "Listen, kid, you a virgin?"

"What?" It sounded stupid, and George knew it, but he couldn't think of anything else to say.

"Women," Mr. Rapf said. "Broads. You ever been banged?"

Before George could think of an answer, he didn't have to make one. The elevator door crashed open. Mr. Rapf, taking George's arm and guiding him into the car, suddenly began to chuckle so hard that the elevator operator, an old man in a dirty coat, looked at him in surprise.

"Perrini Brothers," Mr. Rapf said. "The postgraduate course after Franklin Pierce High School!"

By the time the elevator reached the nineteenth floor, he seemed to have forgotten the joke, whatever it was. In fact, by the time George followed Mr. Rapf out of the elevator into the premises of Perrini Brothers, the best senior on the staff of Malvin Gewirtz & Company had become once again the figure of buck-toothed dignity to whom Mr. Brodsky had introduced George an hour ago in the office on Thirty-fourth Street.

George followed the suddenly solemn Mr. Rapf across a cluttered storage area, through a battered metal door on which was lettered "No Admittance," and into a small office. It was about ten feet square and had been constructed by partitioning off one corner of the loft. Through the glass in the partitions George could see out onto the loft floor where forty or fifty girls were bent busily over their work. He could not make out what kind of work they were doing but he could see they were doing it at large round tables.

A dark woman with a mustache and a sour face looked up from behind a desk in the far corner of the office. "Hello, Mr. Rapf," she said. "You're late."

"Good morning, Miss Yeager," Mr. Rapf said. "I was delayed because we added a new member to our staff today. Miss Yeager, this is Malvin Gewirtz & Company's newest junior, George Hurst."

"How do you do?" George said.

Miss Yeager didn't answer. At first George thought she hadn't heard him. Then he saw that Miss Yeager was not looking at him. She seemed embarrassed about something. She even seemed to find it difficult to meet Mr. Rapf's glance. She was scowling down at her desk when she addressed the senior. "Is he a Gilly?" she said. "Or a Lit?"

Mr. Rapf turned to George. "You a Gilly?" he said. "Or a Lit?"

"My Aunt Tessie was born in Austria," George said. "But her family came from Hungary before that."

"What does that make him?" Mr. Rapf said to Miss Yeager. "A Galitzianer by proxy?"

"As long as it doesn't make him a Litvak," Miss Yeager said, "I don't care. I got enough trouble running a decent set of books in this place without Malvin Gewirtz sending any Litvaks down once a month to check up on me."

Mr. Rapf laughed heartily. George smiled nervously. Miss Yeager looked even more embarrassed. She kept her eyes fixed on the books and records that she helped Mr. Rapf take from the safe and spread out on another desk. Even after George and Mr. Rapf were seated at this desk, facing each other across the ledgers, Miss Yeager refused to look at them. She sat at her own desk, making entries in the cash payments book, pretending she was alone in the office. George wondered, as Mr. Rapf explained how the audit was conducted, what was going on. First Mr. Rapf and his private joke. Now this horse-faced old battleax and her mysterious embarrassment. It certainly was a screwy setup.

"If you pay a little attention, kid," Mr. Rapf said, "I think you'll get the hang of this quicker."

"Sorry," George said.

He brought his glance quickly back to the ledgers. There really wasn't very much to get the hang of. Mr. Rapf, who sat with his back to the glass partition, would call off a figure from the cash receipts book and next to it make a small inverted check mark with a fountain pen filled with red ink. George would find the figure in the accounts receivable ledger, call it out to Mr. Rapf, and next to it make the same sort of check mark with the red-ink fountain pen Mr. Brodsky's secretary had given him when he was hired. There was probably a good deal more to an audit than that. At the moment, however, that was all Mr. Rapf had asked George to get the hang of. As a result, he had plenty of time for sneaking looks across Mr. Rapf's head, through the glass partitions, out onto the loft floor. There were sixty-four girls on that loft floor. George had counted them.

He knew also that there were eight of the large round tables, and eight girls sat at each one. Because of what they were doing and the way they were dressed, all these girls looked alike. They were small and dark, apparently Italian, and they all wore black alpaca smocks. The tables reminded George of newsreel shots that showed tea tasters at work. Not that these girls were tasting anything or had anything resembling tea cups in front of them. At regular intervals one of the five Perrini brothers would come through the swinging doors at the far side of the loft, carrying a huge basket on his shoulder. From the puffs of steam that escaped into the loft when these doors were opened, George guessed that behind them lay the manufacturing end of the Perrini Brothers business. The brother carrying the basket would come up to one of the tables and, across the heads of the seated girls, would dump the contents of the basket into the center of the table, and the girls would pack the contents into small boxes.

"You want to watch your pen, kid."

George brought his glance back quickly to Mr. Rapf. "Beg pardon?"

Mr. Rapf nodded to the ledger page in front of George. "Your pen's scratching, kid. You don't want to mess up the client's ledger with a lot of red-ink blots."

George looked at the ledger page and then at the point of his fountain pen. He didn't see any blots. He didn't see that the pen was scratching, either. All he saw was that Mr. Rapf seemed to be once again in the grip of his secret joke.

"Go on out there on that loft floor," Mr. Rapf said. "Ask one of those girls to give you a couple of those pen wipers."

"Is that what they make here?" George said. "Pen wipers?"

"Yeah, go ahead," Mr. Rapf said. "Get a couple for me, too. Step on it, will you, kid?"

George jumped up. He felt a little embarrassed about walking out into the loft among all those strange girls. But he wasn't nearly so embarrassed as Miss Yeager. The bookkeeper's dark face was suddenly much darker as she shot an angry glance at Mr. Rapf. The senior pretended not to see it. He was smiling that turned-in smile again.

"Step on it, kid," Mr. Rapf said again. "We got an audit to finish."

"Yes, sir," George said.

He pushed through the door in the partitions. At once he became aware of something he had missed while in the office: the girls at the round tables were chattering away at each other in Italian. George became aware of it because, as soon as he stepped out onto the loft floor, the chattering stopped. He wanted to stop, too. But he couldn't. He was caught between the eyes of Mr. Rapf and Miss Yeager in the office behind him, and the sixty-four watching girls on the loft floor in front of him. Nuts, George thought angrily. If Mr. Rapf wants some pen wipers I'll just damn well get him some pen wipers, that's all. He started directly for the table nearest him, moving more quickly than he really wanted to move.

A moment later George saw what the girls were packing into the small boxes, and it was as though he'd stepped off a curb and the gutter proved to be a couple of feet down. George actually stumbled.

The sixty-four girls giggled. The sound was like a sudden shower. A moment before there had been silence. Now there was all that giggling. George recovered his balance and, while he could feel his face begin to burn, tried to decide what to do. He couldn't go back into the office. Not right away. He had to have a little time to steel himself for Mr. Rapf's derision. And he couldn't do anything so stupid as to ask these girls for pen wipers.

So George just stood there, understanding at last Mr. Rapf's private joke and the reason for Miss Yeager's embarrassment, watching the giggling little Italian girls at work. Then George saw the doors at the other side of the loft and he snapped out of it. He started forward, moving right through the giggling girls, until he reached the washroom.

He was standing at the window when Mr. Rapf came in behind him. George didn't turn, but he knew it was Mr. Rapf. He could tell by the senior's chuckle. He could also tell that Mr. Rapf was warming up to some sort of smart remark. George suddenly found himself trying desperately to figure out what it was going to be. He didn't want to look like any more of a dumb kid than he already did. He wanted to have an answer ready for Mr. Rapf's remark. He had to.

"For Christ's sake," Mr. Rapf said. "What are you looking at so hard out of that window?"

"The river," George said.

"What's so special about the river?" Mr. Rapf said.

"We're so high up here," George said, "I can see the place where I was born."

He hadn't planned the words. He hadn't ever known they were in his mind. They took him by surprise. But the funny thing was that they seemed to take Mr. Rapf by surprise, too. They made the senior forget all about his private little joke.

"No kidding?" Mr. Rapf said. He came up beside George. "Where?"

George showed him, and from then on, whenever he came to Perrini Brothers, George always made it a point to go into the washroom and take a look through that window. He did it all during the time he worked for Malvin Gewirtz & Company. And then, when George went into practice for himself and Nick Perrini took his account away from Malvin Gewirtz & Company and Perrini Brothers became George's first client, George did not stop doing it.

Even today, almost nineteen years later, with most of his mind concentrated on the problem Mr. Kashkin had thrown at him up on Forty-second Street, George was aware as he came out of the elevator and pushed through the door marked "No Admittance" into the Perrini Brothers office, that before he left the premises he would pay a visit to the washroom and take a look out of that window.

"Good morning," Miss Yeager said. "Nick's been asking for you."

By now she must have been somewhere in her fifties, perhaps even in her sixties, but George could see no change in Miss Yeager. She still wore the same sour expression that had impressed him on that first day in 1931, and she still had the same dark mustache, and she was still too embarrassed by the product the Perrini Brothers manufactured to meet anybody's glance. Occasionally, when George showed up for the monthly audit, their conversation would shift from the company's books and records to other matters, and then Miss Yeager would reveal the same preoccupation with whether people were Gillys or Lits. For Miss Yeager at any rate, time seemed to have stood still.

"I've got the balance sheet," George said. "Where is he?"

"Out in the factory," Miss Yeager said. "He said the minute you came in, Nick said I should come get him. He's very anxious to see you."

She hurried out of the office, across the loft floor, toward the doors that opened into the factory. Watching her move in and out among the large round tables, it occurred to George that the small, dark girls in the black alpaca smocks hadn't changed, either.

They were different, of course. They were not the same girls who had sat there in 1931. But they looked the same. Even Nick Perrini, when he came through the factory doors with Miss Yeager and started back across the loft floor toward the office, looked the same.

For a couple of moments, as he watched Nick dump across the heads of the girls onto one of the tables a bushel of the garter belts that George had once thought were pen wipers, he was struck by the astonishing thought that nothing had changed. That it was still 1931, and he was still five months short of his twenty-first birthday, and he had just come into this office with Mr. Rapf, and he had never even heard of a man named Maurice Kashkin. Then the door opened, and Nick Perrini came in with Miss Yeager, and George drew a deep breath.

It was not 1931, and he was not five months short of his twenty-first birthday, and he never would be again. In less than a dozen hours he would be forty, and Mr. Kashkin was at the Waldorf, and he would be there on Tuesday, waiting for his answer, and while he waited George Hurst's whole life, the structure he had built with Mary during the past eight years, the life that only this morning, four short hours ago, had been jogging along pleasantly from Queen's Court Road to Camp Shawmut, touching Win and his cook-out and Jimmy and his casting rod and Tim Keogh and Mr. Ashorn and Carolina and Dr. Rettig and the commuters waiting on the Danville platform for the 9:14—all that had suddenly come to a halt. On the edge of a precipice. And there was no turning back. It was silly to pretend Mr. Kashkin did not exist. Or was not at the Waldorf, waiting. By Tuesday morning George would have to call him with an answer. There was no other way out.

"Hi, George," Nick Perrini said.

"Hello, Nick."

"How's the family?"

"Fine," George said. "Yours?"

"Can't complain," Nick said. He paused, caught his lower lip in his teeth, sent a worried glance at Miss Yeager, then looked back at George. "It's all the same to you," he said, "why don't we go right out and eat?"

"Whatever you say," George said, looking more closely at his client. Something was certainly bothering Nick. Or was it merely that George, on edge himself because of his meeting with Mr. Kashkin, was seeing nervousness where it did not exist? "I'll take my briefcase along," he said. "We can discuss the balance sheet while we're eating."

"Sure, sure," Nick said. This time there was no mistaking the impatience in his voice. "You want to wash your hands, George?"

"No, I'm all right."

"Let's go, then." Nick took his jacket from the coat tree near Miss Yeager's desk, tucked it under his arm as though it were a swagger stick, and started rolling down the turned-up sleeves of his shirt as he moved toward the door. "You want me for anything, Miss Yeager, we'll be at Resnick's."

"All right, Mr. Perrini."

Following Nick out to the elevator, George was suddenly aware of the other man's silence. Nick was a short, stout man, almost exactly George Hurst's age, with thick black eyebrows that met across the bridge of his nose, and, as a rule, a pleasant smile. He was not smiling now. While they waited for the elevator, and Nick finished rolling down his shirt sleeves and slipped into his coat, he scowled down at his toes. George was surprised at Nick's mood. He was, as a rule, an outgoing, optimistic man. Even business worries rarely depressed him. George knew that Nick had been concerned about the balance sheet because he wanted to renew the loan he had made from his bank in January, and the bank was certain to ask for his figures, but it was not like Nick to be all that upset by a problem that was, after all, far from crucial.

"I suppose you're wondering about the balance sheet," George said, reaching for the zipper on his briefcase. It helped take his mind from the problem of Mr. Kashkin to concern himself with the problem of Nick Perrini. "Well, I think you'll be pleasantly surprised, Nick. The figures show—"

"When we get to Resnick's, when we get to Resnick's," Nick said with an impatient wave of his hand. George blinked at him. If he was so worried by what the figures might show that he had asked George to come all the way downtown to discuss them, why would he want to postpone hearing the news? Then, as the elevator door opened and they stepped in, Nick suddenly said, "How are things out in Danville?"

"Pretty good," George said, trying not to show his surprise. Even though he had known Nick Perrini for nineteen years, aside from asking each other perfunctorily when they met how their families were faring, they never discussed personal matters. "How are things out in Woodmere?"

"Pretty good," Nick said, but the words had nothing to do with the look on his face. He was watching George with a curious expression. "Getting much heat out there?"

"Not so far," George said. "As a matter of fact, it's pretty cool for the first of July."

"Big week end coming up?"

"Oh, you know."

"Lots of parties and that stuff?" Nick said. "On account of the Fourth of July?"

"Quite a few, I guess," George said, wondering what Nick was driving at. "Mostly it's stuff for the kids, though."

"How do you mean?" Nick demanded with sudden interest. "For the kids?"

"We have this club at the school," George said. "All the fathers of the kids. And once a year, around the Fourth of July, we give this big clambake down on the beach, with fireworks and all, and we charge admission and, well, whatever profit we make on the deal, it goes toward buying things for the school. Baseball bats, basketballs, that sort of thing."

"Sounds like a nice town to live in."

"Well," George said. There was suddenly a small, tight feeling in his chest. He was thinking of Mr. Kashkin up at the Waldorf, waiting. "Yes, it is a nice town."

"A young couple, they just get married," Nick Perrini said, "it must be a swell place to—"

The elevator gate, slamming open, obliterated the rest of his observation. Walking out into the street at Nick's side, George did not feel like asking him to repeat. Besides, Nick seemed to have forgotten George's presence. He strode along, scowling at the sidewalk, as though he were alone. Even when they reached Resnick's, and started through the long, narrow restaurant toward Nick's favorite table, he still seemed unaware of his surroundings. This was so unusual that George knew Nick Perrini was really troubled.

"Today you're not alone," the waiter said to Nick when he and George were settled at the table. Nick didn't answer, and the waiter looked at George. "When he wakes up, you can tell Mr. Perrini we don't put it on the check here if a customer says a few words."

George smiled and made a small sound, not unlike a grunt. It was designed to indicate that he appreciated the waiter's remark but, at the same time, was not in a mood to embark on a conversation. He had been here before. Resnick's waiters were all alike: bald, emaciated, pasty-faced, ageless men in spotted black coats who looked consumptive and sounded irascible. This one set thick tumblers of water on the chipped white marble table top in front of George and Nick, handed them copies of the smudged, typewritten menu, and stood back to watch them with an expression of challenging contempt.

"How about you, Nick?" George said, looking up from his menu. "See anything you like?"

"What?" Nick Perrini said, and then, "Oh." He dropped the menu and looked up at the waiter. "You got any bean soup today?"

"All the years you been coming here, you remember yet one day we didn't have bean soup?"

"Make it bean soup, then, a hot pastrami sandwich, and a bottle of beer," Nick said. "How about you, George?"

"I'll have the same," George said. "Except you can skip the bean soup, and instead of the beer I'll have iced tea."

The waiter gathered the menus, nodded toward George, and addressed Nick. "Next time you bring along Milton Berle to lunch, Mr. Perrini, you'll please give us a little notice in advance so we can have the photographers ready." He turned to George. "Why don't you try a little chopped chicken liver to start?"

"Thanks," George said. "Not today."

"What's the matter with today? For chopped chicken liver there has to be special days?"

"I just don't feel like it," George said. "All I want is the sandwich and some iced tea."

"So while Mr. Perrini, here, he's eating his bean soup, what'll you be doing?"

"I'll watch him."

"And how do you think this will make Mr. Perrini feel?" the waiter said. "He's eating his bean soup, trying to enjoy it, and across the table a man is sitting watching?"

"George," Nick Perrini said. "Why don't you take the chopped chicken liver?"

"I don't want any."

"I know that," Nick said. "But take it anyway and just let it stand there in front of you. Otherwise we'll never get rid of this guy."

"All right," George said to the waiter. "Bring me some chopped chicken liver."

"Favors here in Resnick's we're not looking for," the waiter said haughtily. "Just to look at and not to eat, our chopped chicken liver we don't serve."

He walked away. George looked at Nick, to see if it was necessary to make the effort of joining him in a laugh, and saw that Nick was scratching small squares on the marble table top with a fork and scowling at his handiwork. The time had obviously come to put him out of his misery.

"Look, Nick," George said as he opened his briefcase and pulled out the balance sheet. "I know you've been worrying about this, so I might as well tell you right at the start that there's nothing to be upset about. As a matter of fact, just the opposite. Your accounts receivable are down eight thousand from the figure at the end of last year, when the bank made the loan, but your inventory is up nine and your cash position is up four, with no substantial changes at all on your liability side, which means your net worth as of today, or rather as of yesterday, since this balance sheet is dated June thirtieth, your net worth is five thousand better than it was when the bank made the loan. Now, I'm not the bank, of course, so I can't say for certain, but judging by past experience, yours as well as mine, I'd say all you have to do is take this balance sheet over to the bank and show it to them, and they'll renew the loan without any—"

"I know, I know, I know," Nick Perrini said. He dropped the fork, seized his tumbler, and took a long swallow of water. "I don't give a damn about the balance sheet, George!"

"But yesterday, when you called up and asked me to lunch, you said it was very important."

"Yeah," Nick said. "There's something I want to ask you about." He scowled at the tumbler and began to scrape the beads of sweat down its side with his forefinger. "It's something personal."

George looked from Nick to the balance sheet and then back at Nick. "You mean it has nothing to do with this?"

Nick reached across, took the balance sheet, and put it beside his paper napkin. "Forget this damn balance sheet," he said. "I know the bank'll renew the loan. That's not what I'm worried about. What I'm worried about—"

His words stopped. The waiter had arrived with the bean soup. He set down the bowl in front of Nick, and gave George a disdainful glance. "Don't spoil it for him by licking your lips every time he sticks the spoon in his mouth," he said. "Just close your eyes and think about that chopped chicken liver you didn't feel like having today."

The waiter went away. Nick Perrini picked up his spoon, put it into his soup, lifted the spoon halfway to his mouth, then put it back in the bowl. There was something about the combination of movements that George suddenly found familiar. It was as though a bell had been struck somewhere in his mind. He found himself listening for the echoes.

"George," Nick said in a troubled voice. "You know my daughter Violetta?"

"Violetta?" George said. "Of course I know Violetta."

What he meant was that he knew about Violetta. Just as he knew about Nick's three other children. From casual remarks George and Nick had exchanged about their families through the years. George had never met Nick's wife or Nick's children, but he knew that Violetta, the oldest, was a sophomore at Barnard and her father's pride and joy.

"Well, my Violetta," Nick said. "She wants to get married."

"My God," George said. "It seems only yesterday you were handing out the cigars."

Nick nodded. The worried look had deepened on his plump, good-looking face. "That's right," he said. "She's just a kid. Not even nineteen yet. But she wants to get married."

"Well, Nick, you were married yourself before you were nineteen, so I don't see what—"

"Sure, that part of it, that doesn't bother me," Nick said. "We Italians, you know, we believe in early marriage, anyway. The only thing is—" Nick paused and the worried look seemed to rearrange itself on his face. "The only thing is, George, the boy she wants to marry—" Nick paused again, and he took another swallow of water, and he looked anxiously at George as he said, "My Violetta, George, she wants to marry a Jewish boy."

"Oh," George said.

All at once he could hear the echoes. All at once George knew why the combination of movements, as Nick Perrini had started to spoon up his soup, had seemed familiar. All at once George was no longer in a greasy little restaurant off Astor Place where the waiters treated you with contempt if you didn't order the chopped chicken liver. All at once it was as though seven and a half years had been erased, and the war was still on, and George was home briefly on one of his missions from London, and he was walking up Fifth Avenue to have lunch with Mary's father at the old man's club.

"It isn't really Father's club," Mary had explained. "I mean he's a member all right, but he doesn't use it very often. It's just a place father belongs to so that, when he comes up to New York from

Philadelphia on business, he can take people there. People he wants to impress. Clients, I mean."

"Why would he want to impress me?" George said. "I should think it would be the other way around."

"Darling, I don't understand you," Mary said. "When I first told you father would scream at the news that I planned to marry you, you said let him scream his head off, you didn't give a damn what he said, screamed, thought, or did. Now you tell me you want to impress him."

Even then, before they were married, George had been touched by her forthrightness. Touched and disconcerted.

"I didn't say I wanted to impress him," George said. "I said if anybody was interested in doing any impressing at this lunch meeting, it should be me impressing him. That's the tradition, anyway. Young man goes to see father of girl he wants to marry. Father is naturally suspicious. Young man is just as naturally anxious to please. That's all I meant."

Mary gave him a long look. "Are you really anxious to please Father?"

George hesitated, and then he took her in his arms, and he held her very close. "God damn him, yes."

"Then I don't care whether you do or you don't," Mary whispered. They remained like that, quiet and motionless, for several long moments. Then she stirred in his arms, and she kissed him lightly, and she said, "But I wish you would try, darling. For my sake."

"All right," George had said. "For you I'll try."

Walking up Fifth Avenue in the noon sunlight, he reminded himself of his promise. It really wasn't much to do for someone you loved. And George was pretty sure he could do it. He just wished Mr. Sherrod had not suggested his club as the meeting place. It would only make George's task of pleasing Mary's father more difficult. George had never been inside a club. His notions about them had been gleaned from reading English novels. They were part of a way of life that had no reality for him. He was inclined to be shy, and he had a tendency to be intimidated by new places and people. He did not want to be intimidated by Mr. Sherrod or his club. Knowing that he might be, however, made George uncomfortable. He was afraid that, to counteract his discomfort, he might become truculent. And George did not want to be truculent with

Mary's father. He wanted to be relaxed and friendly and get the meeting out of the way without incident. He would have had fewer doubts that this could be accomplished if Mr. Sherrod had suggested that they meet in a restaurant. George knew how to handle himself in restaurants.

He was pleasantly surprised, therefore, when he reached the address Mr. Sherrod had given him, to find that there was nothing intimidating about the building in front of which he had stopped. It was just off Fifth Avenue, and it reminded George of the Hamilton Fish Park branch of the New York Public Library to which Aunt Tessie had taken him at the age of seven for his first borrower's card. The building was made of the same brown sandstone and, like the library he remembered so clearly, it looked old and dirty. There was no sign outside. Just the street number on the glass door in gold leaf that was flaking away. Over the door, however, on two staffs that jutted out over the sidewalk like the horns of an ibex, hung two flags. One was blue, but it hung so limply that, if it bore any markings, George could not read them. The other was an American flag, and George wondered if it had hung there always or if it had been put up since Pearl Harbor. The pole seemed much brighter and newer than the one from which the blue flag dangled.

There was nothing bright or new about the lobby. It was lined with discolored marble that had once been white. George thought it looked a good deal like the men's washroom in Grand Central, and he began to feel less apprehensive. Aside from the smell, there was nothing intimidating about the men's washroom in Grand Central. At one side, behind a tall desk, stood a little old man in a blue coat with some sort of insignia embroidered on the lapels. He looked up expectantly when George came in from the street.

"Mr. Sherrod?" George said. "Mr. Winston Sherrod?"

The old man looked down at a chart to which were clipped many slips of paper. "Yes, sir," he said. "Lieutenant Hurst?"

"That's right."

"Mr. Sherrod is in the bar, sir," the little old man said. "One flight up and turn to your right."

"Thank you."

"Wouldn't you care to check your hat, Lieutenant?"

"Oh," George said, and he could feel his face flush. He hadn't noticed the checkroom door just beyond the little old man's desk. "I guess I'd better," he said. "Thanks."

George checked his hat, telling himself it was silly to feel flustered over such a small thing, and besides, the fact that he had not noticed the checkroom could not be held against Mary's father. Nevertheless, George did hold it against him. It was just the sort of thing that would not have happened, he told himself as he went up the white marble stairs and turned right, if Mr. Sherrod had asked George to meet him at a restaurant. Everybody knew where the checkroom was in a restaurant. There was no chance to make a fool of yourself by walking to your table carrying your hat. George reached a massive mahogany door, pushed it open, and stopped short. He was staring at a man naked to the waist, suspenders looped down around his knees, standing in front of a basin and shaving. He stared back at George in the mirror over the basin.

"Sorry," George said hastily. "I was looking for the bar."

"Down the end of the corridor," the man said. "You can't miss it, Lieutenant."

George backed out and closed the door. He stood there for several moments, making an effort, but it was too late. There was nothing he could say to himself that would wash away his ridiculous but yet very real embarrassment. All he could do, as he turned and started down the corridor, was hope that none of it would show when he came into the bar.

This proved to be a long, high-ceilinged room paneled in gleaming mahogany. The brass lighting fixtures resembled clusters of fruit. They had either been converted from gas to electricity or had been designed to look that way. Several stuffed animal heads stared down from the walls and, behind the bar, hung a murky painting of a Rubens-like nude in an elaborately carved gold frame. The bar stretched the entire length of the room and had a highly polished brass foot rest. Between the bar and the opposite wall the floor space was dotted with round dark tables surrounded by armchairs upholstered in red leather. The atmosphere was a trifle self-consciously Gay Nineties Masculine. George had the feeling that he was expected to pick out Diamond Jim Brady and Stanford White among the men who crowded the room.

They stood all along the bar and sat at the tables in small groups. Every table was occupied, but George had no trouble picking out Mr. Sherrod. Neither did Mary's father have any difficulty identifying George. She had quite obviously described him to Mr. Sherrod as carefully as she had described Mr. Sherrod to George. As soon as George came in the door and paused on the threshold, Mr. Sherrod stood up and came toward him.

"Lieutenant Hurst?"

"Yes, sir," George said. "Mr. Sherrod?"

"That's right." He took George's hand, gave it a single, firm, brisk shake, and dropped it. "I've managed to save a corner table," he said. "It's not an easy thing to do, as you can see from this crowd, but I told Samuel we wanted to be alone, and he swung it. Don't ask me how. Samuel has been here ever since I can remember, and he runs the bar the way Pershing used to run the A.E.F. Come along, won't you?"

"Yes, sir."

George liked the fact that Mr. Sherrod had not said he was glad to see him. He could have done so without giving the conventional phrase any special meaning. The fact that he had omitted it could only have been deliberate. It showed that Mr. Sherrod was not inclined toward the small hypocrisies with which most people smoothed their daily paths. George saw that Mary's forthrightness, which he admired, was honestly come by. As they threaded their way across the room, moving around the many tables, George kept watching Mr. Sherrod out of the corner of his eye. It was easy to see where Mary had picked up the ingredient that made her a knockout. It wasn't merely that Mr. Sherrod was good-looking. Any man with his tall, spare figure, his white, beautifully groomed hair, and his strong, sharply chiseled features would have been good-looking. Goodlooking and, after a casual glance, forgotten. What drew the eye back for a second glance, just as people always turned for a second glance at Mary, was Mr. Sherrod's indefinable air of distinction. It made him look slightly unreal. He might have been not a human being but a drawing by James Montgomery Flagg.

"Here we are," he said. He touched the back of one of the red leather chairs. George moved toward it and waited. When Mr. Sherrod saw why George was waiting, he nodded to indicate his appreciation of the gesture and said, "Thank you." He sat down and then George sat down. Mr. Sherrod touched the stem of the glass in front of him and said, "I'm having a martini. Will that be all right for you?"

It would have been perfect. A martini was just what George

wanted at the moment. It would have eased the embarrassment he had suffered on the way to the bar. The fact that Mr. Sherrod had suggested it, however, made it impossible for him to accept. George knew this was foolish. But he couldn't help himself.

"Nothing for me," he said. "Thanks."

Mr. Sherrod's eyebrows went up. "I hadn't been told you're a teetotaler."

George noted that Mr. Sherrod did not mention the name of the only person who could have told him: Mary.

"I'm not," George said. "I just don't think I'll have anything right now."

"Because you're in uniform?"

George could feel his face grow warm. There were quite a few men in uniform in the room. They were all drinking. Mr. Sherrod's remark seemed to imply that George was being a trifle stuffy.

"No," he said. "I just don't feel like a drink right now."

"That's because you're young," Mr. Sherrod said. "When you reach my age, a bit of alcohol at midday becomes almost a necessity." He took a sip from his glass. "How are things in London?"

This remark could not be held against him. Everybody wanted to know how things were in London.

"Not bad," George said. "All things considered."

"What sort of things?"

"The doodle bugs or buzz bombs," George said. "They're a pretty constant factor. Some people say they're not as bad as the blitz, and some people say they're worse. I don't really know since I didn't get shipped to London until long after the blitz. My station is out in a place called Brondesbury. That's sort of like, oh, if where we are here on Forty-fourth Street just off Fifth were to be considered the equivalent of, say, Piccadilly Circus, then Brondesbury would be about, let's say, Ninety-sixth Street and Broadway. That's not very far out. It's almost the center of town. And while I don't think any of us on the station likes the buzz bombs very much, I've noticed these last few weeks that the men in my mess hardly ever mention them. It's sort of like the traffic noises outside this club. In a more aggravated form, of course. You learn to live with them."

Mr. Sherrod drained his glass. "Do you mind if I have another one of these?"

George could feel his face flush again. He had not meant to talk at such length. It was just that, for a moment, he had forgotten to whom he was talking. It hadn't occurred to him that Mr. Sherrod was not listening.

"No, of course not," George said.

"Sure you won't have one with me?"

"Positive."

Mr. Sherrod raised his hand in a gesture of casual elegance. He might have been Aladdin rubbing his lamp. A dignified, elderly Negro in a white coat materialized at his elbow. "Sir?" he said.

"Another one of these, Samuel, please."

"Yes, sir, Mr. Sherrod." Samuel disappeared with the empty glass.

Mr. Sherrod delicately stroked his slightly stringy throat with the tip of his forefinger as he stared at George. "When are you going back to London?" he said finally.

"I'll know definitely after I come back from Washington," George said. "I'm going down tomorrow morning for a day or two of conferences. They never tell you anything definite in advance, but my guess is that I'll be going back in a couple of weeks at most."

"That's not very long, is it?"

"No, sir."

"Do you feel—?" Mr. Sherrod did not complete the question. Samuel had arrived with the fresh martini. He set it down and pulled a pad from the pocket of his white coat. "Would you like to have lunch here in the bar, Mr. Sherrod?"

"I don't know," Mr. Sherrod said. "It depends on the lieutenant. Would you like to lunch here or would you prefer to go up to the dining room?"

"It doesn't matter," George said.

"The food is exactly same," Mr. Sherrod said. "The only difference is that if you have lunch here in the bar you can't have dessert. I don't know why. It's just a rule of the club."

"It's the kitchen, sir," Samuel said. "The desserts don't come from the—"

"I don't want to hear the explanation," Mr. Sherrod said. "Samuel makes it to me every time I come, and every time he makes it I can't remember what he said. If you don't care about dessert, why don't we have our lunch right here? It's so much simpler."

"All right," George said.

Samuel put the pad on the table in front of Mr. Sherrod and handed him a pencil. Mr. Sherrod took a sip of his martini and wrote

his name across the top of the pad. "What would you like?" he said
to George. "The bean soup is very good."

"All right," George said.

"Two bean soups," Mr. Sherrod said as he wrote it on the pad.
"And what would you like to follow? They make an absolutely wonderful ham and cheese sandwich?"

"All right," George said.

"Two aitch and see aitch sandwiches," Mr. Sherrod said, writing
it down. "And coffee?"

"No, milk for me, please," George said.

"One milk and one coffee," Mr. Sherrod said as he wrote.
"There you are, Samuel." He handed the pad and the pencil to the
waiter.

"Thank you, sir."

Samuel went away. Mr. Sherrod took a long sip from his glass.
George was sorry he had refused a drink. He didn't know exactly
what it was he was doing wrong, but he sensed that he was not
handling this right. He had promised Mary he would try to please
her father. It had not occurred to him that this was a good deal like
promising to be cordial to a refrigerator. Nothing Mr. Sherrod had
said could be construed as insulting. Even his gestures, as he raised
and lowered his glass, were outwardly innocent to the point of
banality. There was something about his movements, however, just
as there was something about the tone of his voice, that indicated
clearly how he felt. Mr. Sherrod felt, and it was plain he wanted
George to know he felt, as though he was lunching with Samuel.

"For such a brief visit," he said suddenly, "I understand you've
made some rather long-range plans."

George wondered if everybody in Bala Cynwyd talked like that.

"Yes, sir," he said.

"Don't you think it would be wiser to wait a bit?"

"No, sir," George said.

A faint flush rose to Mr. Sherrod's cheeks. Oddly enough, it
didn't make George feel better. He didn't want to score over this
man. He just wanted to have the lunch done with, and get the hell
out of here.

"Many people make all sorts of hasty decisions during a war,
decisions that they regret later," Mr. Sherrod said. "You're going to
be overseas for the duration, anyway. Don't you think it fair, even
if you don't think it wise, to the other party concerned to postpone

your decision until you're both sure the war has nothing to do with it?"

"No, sir," George said.

The flush grew deeper on Mr. Sherrod's handsome face. "Why not?" he said.

"I may not live through the war," George said.

For the first time Mr. Sherrod's handsome face lost its look of distinction. A mean little smile, in which only the lips were involved, was suddenly disfiguring it.

"Oh, come now," he said. "You're not in the trenches or whatever they call the trenches in this war. You're in a cushy rear echelon Intelligence job in the heart of London. You're in no more danger than Samuel, here, or any of the other waiters in this club."

"Last week, just before I flew home," George said, "two of the waiters in my mess were killed by a buzz bomb."

Mr. Sherrod's faintly crimson cheeks grew bright red. Samuel appeared with a tray, set down the two bowls of soup, and went away. Mr. Sherrod picked up his spoon, put it into his soup, lifted the spoon halfway to his mouth, then put it back in the bowl.

"Look here," he said, and there was a sudden rasp in his voice. "It's all very well for you youngsters to thumb your noses selfishly at the rest of the world, but the rest of the world has a way of catching up with you and having the last laugh. Do you realize what some of the consequences will be if you and Mary persist in going through with this decision of yours?"

"We love each other," George said.

Mr. Sherrod made an impatient gesture. "That's no answer to what I'm talking about."

"What are you talking about, Mr. Sherrod?"

The older man's lips grew thin. "You know damn well what I'm talking about," he snapped. "If you have children, and I assume you will, do you realize, to take an example at random, that they won't be permitted to stay at certain hotels in Florida?"

George began to feel a little better. Everything became so much simpler when they got down to cases. Because their cases were always the same, no matter where they came from, Hitler's Chancellery or Bala Cynwyd.

"I wouldn't want my children to go anywhere their father can't go," George said.

Mr. Sherrod flushed again. "Mary won't be able to go, either."

"I wouldn't want my wife to go anywhere I can't go," George said.

Mr. Sherrod seemed to lose control. He jerked sideways in his chair, as though some inner support on which his balance depended had given way. He slapped the table with his hand.

"All right, if you want to keep the discussion tied to that preposterous issue," he said, "I'd like to point something out to you. Up to now, all of her life, Mary has been able to go to those hotels. Now, by marrying you, she won't be able to go to them. Do you want to deprive her of something she previously enjoyed?"

"Maybe Mary feels she's getting something just as good or even better in exchange," George said.

Mr. Sherrod stared at him for several moments. During the silence the inner support that had given way seemed to mend itself. At any rate, Mr. Sherrod again sat up straight in his chair. He dipped up a spoonful of bean soup, swallowed it, and then stared thoughtfully into the bowl. George could feel his heart begin to hammer wildly. He didn't know how it had happened, but he knew from the older man's simple gesture that it was all over. George had won.

"I'm not going to wish you luck," Mr. Sherrod said finally, in a low voice.

"I'm glad of that," George said. "If you did, I'd have one more reason to hate you: for being a liar."

A flicker of something not unlike admiration raced across the older man's face. "Damn you," he said bitterly. "Why the hell couldn't you be born right?"

Almost eight years later, in a greasy little restaurant off Astor Place where the waiters treated you with contempt if you didn't order the chopped chicken liver, George Hurst could still hear the echoes of that bitterness. Except that now they did not come to him from the voice of an industrial engineer named Winston Sherrod who lived on the Philadelphia Main Line. Now they came to him from the voice of a garter belt manufacturer named Nick Perrini who lived in Woodmere. The sounds, however, were identical.

"Is he a nice boy?" George said.

"Oh, sure," Nick said. "Violetta brought him up the house, introduced him, all that. He's in medical school. Wants to be a doctor. Comes from a good family, plenty of money. That's not the point."

"No," George said. "Of course not."

Nick Perrini's face flushed. Exactly the way, eight years ago, Winston Sherrod's face had flushed.

"Look, George," Nick said. "Don't get me wrong."

"Is there any chance of that?"

Nick glared down into his soup bowl.

"All you Jews, for Christ's sake," he said sullenly. "Always so God-damn sensitive."

"I'm sorry," George said, and he was. He was getting things mixed up. His feelings about the problem Mr. Kashkin had dropped in his lap had nothing to do with the problem Nick's daughter Violetta had dropped in her father's lap. "I didn't mean to sound sensitive," George said. "What is it you wanted to ask me?"

Nick made a helpless gesture with his spoon. "She gets married to this boy," he said. "She goes away to live with him, with all those other Jews, his family and all. Violetta doesn't know anything about Jews. You're the only Jew I know, George, that's married to a gentile. You're the only one I can ask."

"Ask what?" George said.

"What'll it be like for my Violetta?" Nick Perrini said worriedly. "Living with all those Jews?"

All at once George could feel that funny little thing in his heart. The thing he felt every morning when he came downstairs into the kitchen out in Danville and he caught his first glimpse of the day of Mary and Win and Jimmy, all in a group.

"I can't tell you what it will be like for Violetta living with all those Jews," George said. "But I can tell you what it'll be like for that boy living with all you Italians."

Nick Perrini stared at George in surprise. A completely new thought had obviously been thrust into his mind. He took several moments to adjust to it.

"Okay, tell me," Nick said finally. "What'll it be like for that Jewish boy, living with all us Italians?"

George hesitated. Not out of respect for Nick Perrini's feelings. George hesitated because he was suddenly uncomfortable about his own. They had sneaked up on him without warning. He had not meant to bring his thoughts to this point. He did not want to say to Nick that the boy who married Violetta didn't know it, but he was embarking on a lifelong masquerade. As long as he lived, certainly as long as he loved Violetta and remained married to her, that boy

would be doing things that, deep down in his heart, he did not want
to do.

He would drink coffee even though he loathed the taste. He
would name his son after Violetta's father even though he might
hate Nick Perrini. He would be secretly ashamed if he could not
provide her with a full-time maid. He would cling desperately to
ridiculous symbols like a grape arbor in the back yard because it
gave him something in common with the girl he loved. He would do
all these things, plus a thousand more which added up to the answer
to Nick Perrini's question that George Hurst suddenly did not want
to answer.

But Mr. Kashkin, a total stranger who had elbowed his way
rudely and without warning into George Hurst's life, was waiting at
the Waldorf. George would have to give him an answer. The answer
Nick Perrini wanted was inextricably intertwined with it. George
could no more refuse to give one answer now than, on Tuesday morning, he would be able to refuse to give the other. The moment of
truth had arrived.

"I'll tell you what it's going to be like for that boy," George
said. "No matter how much Violetta loves him, and no matter how
much he loves her, and no matter how nice you are to him, Nick,"
George said quietly, "all his life, deep down inside, that boy will
feel like Joe Louis at a white dinner."

5

There were a number of things on George's desk that Miss Akst
had said required his attention that afternoon. Miss Akst had a
tendency to think about papers accumulating on a desk in much
the same way that a householder on the banks of the Mississippi
might think about flood waters creeping up to the front door. George
had promised her, therefore, that as soon as he finished lunch with
Nick Perrini he would come back to the office and clean up the
backlog. After he left Resnick's and said good-bye to Nick, however,
the thought of facing his trouble-hungry secretary and the papers on
his desk suddenly seemed unbearable.

The question Nick Perrini had asked had unexpectedly complicated the problem raised by Mr. Kashkin's visit. It was almost as though the two things had been planned to take place one on the heels of the other. What had seemed no more than an uncomfortable coincidence suddenly gave George the feeling that unseen forces were at work, driving him toward a destination he did not want to face.

He stopped short and looked around. He had reached the Astor Place subway station. A taxi was parked at the curb. George walked up to it, opened the door, and climbed in.

"Take me up to Fifty-seventh Street," he said. "The Seventh Avenue corner."

"Carnegie Hall?" the driver said.

"Yes," George said. "Carnegie Hall."

Even as he said it, George thought what a peculiar place for a retired schoolteacher to live. Not that Miss Corcoran actually lived in Carnegie Hall. Her apartment house was several doors down the street. And living on Fifty-seventh Street probably did not seem as peculiar to Miss Corcoran as it did to George. In fact, he was pretty sure the old lady didn't think it was peculiar at all.

When George had first met her in P.S. 188 more than thirty years ago, Miss Corcoran had been one of those strange people who showed up regularly from the completely incomprehensible world identified in George's mind as Uptown. Every morning she entered his life by arriving in the school building on the corner of Lewis and Houston Streets, and every afternoon she vanished from his life as completely as a puff of smoke dispersed by a gust of wind. At that time George had never set foot north of Fourteenth Street or west of Avenue A. He couldn't imagine what the world looked like beyond those boundaries. He assumed some sort of life went on out there, but it had no reality for him. It was in his mind not unlike those huge white areas on the classroom wall map of the world that were marked "Unexplored."

Many years later, when he ran into Miss Corcoran and learned she had retired and was living on Fifty-seventh Street and he started dropping in on her once or twice a year, George realized that in those early days, when she was his teacher in P.S. 188, he had thought of her as being like the sleeping princess in the story Miss Corcoran was so fond of reading to the class. Not *exactly* like, because Miss Corcoran was a humpbacked little woman with thick glasses who looked about as much like a princess as Doodoo Kashkewitz looked like a prince. To a boy of nine, however, Miss Corcoran's daily departures for the unexplored world known as Uptown was a little like the deep sleep into which the princess fell in the story. Once she left the world George knew, the world bounded by Avenue A, Fourteenth Street, and the East River, Miss Corcoran ceased to be the living creature she had been all day. She passed into a suspended state, like the deep sleep of the princess in the story. The only difference was that the princess was awakened after a long time by the kiss of the handsome prince who found her, but Miss Corcoran was brought to life every morning by the necessity for showing up in P.S. 188 to teach arithmetic and spelling to George and his classmates.

"This all right, buddy?"

The taxi had stopped in front of Carnegie Hall.

"Yes, thanks," George said. "This is fine."

He got out, paid the driver, and walked across the street to the drug store. He bought a box of peanut brittle and came back to the south side of the street. The entrance to Miss Corcoran's apartment house was high and narrow. There were gargoyles and signs of the zodiac carved into the sandstone surrounding the door, which was sandwiched between a dress shoppe and a costume jeweler. The elevator operator, a very old man in a frayed plum-colored uniform, was dozing on a bench that ran along one wall of the small dingy lobby.

George shook him awake. "Is Miss Corcoran in?"

The old man yawned and scratched his head. "Miss Corcoran, now. I think so. Yes. Let's go up and see."

He followed George into the elevator, which looked like a cage. As it swayed upward slowly, George peered out through the black metal bars at the passing floors and wondered, as he always did, who lived on them. He had never seen anybody in this apartment house except Miss Corcoran and the elevator man. The cage came to a shuddering halt. George stepped out and knocked on Miss Corcoran's door. Somewhere behind it there was a small, delicate flurry of movement.

"She's in," the elevator man said. "You caught her in the middle of making tea, I guess."

It was not a brilliant guess. Miss Corcoran was always in the middle of making tea. He slammed the gate shut and the elevator started down. Miss Corcoran's door opened. The little old lady

stared out blankly for a moment or two before her face crinkled in
a quick, pleased smile of recognition.

"Why, George, what a pleasant surprise," she said. "I've just
been thinking about you."

"Really?" George said, startled. "Why?"

"Surely you don't expect me to tell you while you're standing
out in the hall." Miss Corcoran laughed. "I was just making a cup
of tea and I want you to have one with me."

"I think maybe I won't, thanks just the same. It's sort of hot
for tea."

"Nonsense. Hot tea is the best thing in the world for your system in this weather. Come in, George."

He followed her into the small, crowded living room that looked
out on Fifty-seventh Street.

"I brought you something." George held out the box of peanut
brittle. "For your sweet tooth."

Miss Corcoran laughed again. "It's the one tooth in my head
that doesn't need nourishment. But you're a dear to remember what
an old woman is fond of. Thank you, George. Now you sit down and
make yourself comfortable while I go fetch the tea, and then you
can tell me why you came."

"No special reason. I just happened to be passing by, and I
realized I hadn't seen you for months, so I thought I'd run up for a
few minutes."

Miss Corcoran, on her way out to the kitchen, paused in the
doorway to turn and give George a quick, sharp glance. She had
always been a small woman, but age seemed to have shriveled her,
so that now she was positively tiny. With her snow-white hair, thick
glasses, and misshapen back, which caused her to hold one shoulder
higher than the other and walk in a sort of delicate, hopping little
skip, she looked a good deal like a sparrow with an injured wing.
People wanted instinctively to pick her up and stroke her. But George
could never forget Miss Corcoran as he had first seen her, standing
in front of a classroom packed with forty boys and girls, a crippled
but curiously imposing figure, holding a ruler as though it were a
mace of office, sweeping the room with her cool glance to see where
the noise was coming from. She had not been known as a murderer,
the word by which the boys of P.S. 188 identified a tough teacher,
but Miss Corcoran had not been known as a pushover, either. What
she had lacked in brawn she had supplied with the strength of her

personality. This was still true of her. At least for George. The years had reduced her to the appearance of a gentle freak, but for George Hurst her most innocent remark and most casual glance still carried with it the weight of an authority he did not dare challenge. In Miss Corcoran's presence he was always, at least to some extent, nine years old.

"If you came up for just a few minutes," she said, "I'd better hurry that tea along."

She went out into the kitchen. George looked around the room. The furnishings were nondescript and shabby. He ran his finger along the edge of a table. Not to see how good a housekeeper Miss Corcoran was. He wanted to see if she could still afford the cleaning woman who used to come in twice a week when George first began to visit this apartment. His finger came away black with dust. George was not surprised. He had no accurate idea about the size of Miss Corcoran's retirement pension. But he did know that the sum had been fixed long before the postwar inflationary rise in prices, and George knew enough about real estate values from handling the affairs of Nick Perrini and other clients to realize that, even on this shabby little apartment in a run-down building that obviously couldn't hold out much longer against the encroachments of commerce which were squeezing it from all sides, Miss Corcoran's rent couldn't be very low. Her income, whatever it was, would almost certainly have gone further if she lived in a less central neighborhood. George was standing at the window, looking down into the clanging bustle of Fifty-seventh Street, when Miss Corcoran came in with the tea tray.

"Thank you," she said as George took the tray from her and set it on the small table in front of the frayed couch. "What were you doing at the window?"

"Listening to all the noise," George said. "And wondering."

"About what?"

"How you happened to choose this place to live in."

Miss Corcoran gave him another of her quick glances as she held out a full cup. "You don't mean live in, George. You mean retire to, don't you?"

"Yes, I guess I do mean that."

"Where would you have me retire to?"

"I don't know," George said. It was a subject that had never crossed his mind before. Crossing it now, the subject left a trail that looked remarkably like those insurance company advertisements which urged people to invest in annuities so that the autumn of their lives might be free from financial cares and jammed full of golf, tarpon fishing, and round-the-world cruises. Somehow, he couldn't quite fit Miss Corcoran into that picture. "I merely thought that Fifty-seventh Street is pretty noisy," George said. "And I imagine it's pretty expensive, too."

"It is," Miss Corcoran said. "Much too expensive." She took a sip of tea. "But it depends on what you want. I'm sure I can get a nice little apartment out in Queens or in Brooklyn or up in the Bronx for half what I pay here, and I'd be surrounded by trees and flowers and I'd be awakened by the singing of birds and the sunshine would pour in all day and it would all be just lovely."

Miss Corcoran paused, and her narrow, twisted little shoulders dipped in a sharp movement that George knew was meant to be a shrug.

"It would all be just lovely, and I would die of boredom in a month," she said. "From the age of twenty-three, when I received my permanent appointment, until I reached sixty-five, when they made me retire, I spent from eight to ten hours every weekday of my life, not counting summers, of course, in P.S. 188 on Houston Street. Since I retired I've done quite a bit of reading of a kind I never had the time to get around to when I was teaching, and I gather from what I've read that places like Houston Street are considered underprivileged areas. Full of disease, filth, malnutrition and several other things, all calculated to turn your stomach or worse. Well, maybe they were. I wouldn't know. All I know is that Houston Street never turned *my* stomach. All I know is that I was there for forty-two years, and while there were times when the dirt did seem to get a bit out of hand, and there were other times when some unpleasant and even ugly things happened, those times didn't seem to matter. What mattered was how you felt. All the time I was down there, every minute of those forty-two years," Miss Corcoran said, "I felt alive."

The little old lady paused again, and she turned toward the open window. Through it came the roar of motors and the honking of automobile horns and the confused noises of a busy thoroughfare in the afternoon of a business day.

"After I retired," Miss Corcoran said, "I tried it for a while. It was just before the war, and I have this married sister, and they own this house in New Canaan. Her husband is in the oil business, and they dragged him down to Washington as a lubrications expert, so that he was gone from Monday morning to Friday night, and my sister said why don't you come and live with me, there's plenty of room in the house. So I did."

Miss Corcoran's shriveled little face squeezed itself into a smile.

"It almost killed me," she said. "The quiet, I mean. There were all sorts of noises, of course. Birds singing and frogs croaking and the trees rustling in the breeze, but they weren't the right kind of noises. Not for me. I began to get restless and I lost my appetite and my sister insisted on taking me to her doctor. He was a terribly nice man in Stamford, and he prescribed a tonic and suggested I take a nap every afternoon. Well, I tried that, too. For two or three weeks. At the end of that time I was just a bundle of nerves. I decided I would do some prescribing for myself. Because you see, I'd been doing quite a bit of thinking, and by this time I knew what was wrong with me." Miss Corcoran smiled again. "I missed the noises of Houston Street."

She set down her cup.

"If you've lived with something for a long time, and you've been happy with it, you can't cut it out of your life and expect to continue to be happy," Miss Corcoran said. "I couldn't go back to Houston Street. There's no place down there for a retired school-teacher to live, as you know, and besides they were already beginning to tear most of it down for that East River Drive, so I decided to find a place that was like it." The little old lady chuckled as she nodded toward the window. "All those elegant dress shoppes and jewelry stores and art galleries on this street, and Carnegie Hall on the corner, I suppose they'd have a fit if I told them I moved here because it reminded me of Houston Street, but I did."

She paused and she picked up her teacup and she took a sip and she cocked her head to one side. So did George. Listening to the roar of motors and the honking of automobile horns and the confusion of other noises that rose from Fifty-seventh Street, he suddenly understood what Miss Corcoran meant. The similarity was not readily apparent. The individual pieces did not look or sound alike. In Miss Corcoran's day most of the traffic on Houston Street had still been horse-drawn, and the cries of pushcart peddlers were not quite the same as the shouts of taxi drivers, and the whistle of a tug on the river was different from the screech of brakes. But if you disregarded the individual pieces, if you listened as Miss Corcoran listened and as George was listening now, you understood what she meant about the similarity between the Houston Street of thirty years ago and Fifty-seventh Street of today.

"You always had a neat mind, George, even all the way back there in P.S. 188, so now that I've told you why I retired to Fifty-seventh Street, I know what your mind is worrying about next," Miss Corcoran said. "You don't have to worry, George. After I pay the rent, my pension still leaves me enough for the rest of my very few and fairly simple wants." She smiled. "Am I right? Isn't that what you've been worrying about?"

George smiled back at her and took a sip of tea. Thanks to Aunt Tessie's training, he didn't like tea any better than he liked coffee. But he couldn't hurt Miss Corcoran's feelings any more than he could hurt his wife Mary's.

"That's right," he said. "I've often worried about whether your pension was adequate."

Miss Corcoran chuckled. "Now that I've put your mind at ease on that score," the little old lady said, "is there anything else I can do for you?"

"You can tell me what you meant when you opened the door a few minutes ago and you said you'd just been thinking about me."

Miss Corcoran again set down her cup. She stood up, walked to a cluttered secretary at the far side of the room, picked up an envelope, and brought it to George. "Read that," she said.

George took the envelope. It had a thick, expensive feel. On the back flap, in engraved type, was printed: *The Nook, Roxbury Drive, Beverly Hills, California.* Miss Corcoran's name and address had been typed on a machine with a green ribbon. Above the address, scrawled in a handwriting that looked vaguely familiar, was written: *"Air Mail Special Delivery! ! ! !"* George opened the envelope and pulled out two sheets of paper. They were covered in single space with the same green typewriting. George read:

Dear Miss Corcoran:

I can just imagine the surprise you will experience on perusing this letter, since it is being written by someone you have not seen for at least thirty years and perhaps even longer. It is even possible that you will not remember me, although I must say, without being conceited, that it is just possible you have run across my name in the newspapers every now and then.

You may even have seen me on the cover of Time *magazine* last year, when I bought the Champlain Hotel in Chicago and thus became the proprietor of the largest privately owned chain of hotels in America, but if you did not connect the face on the cover of Time *magazine* with your old pupil in P.S. 188 I do not blame you one little bit. Many of my friends say it was not a very good likeness. But I say, and I'm sure you will agree with me, it is better to have a bad likeness on the cover of Time *magazine* than not to have any likeness on the cover of Time *magazine* at all.

I do not want to sound as though this letter is a puff from a press agent, which it is not, I assure you, but I have just learned that Worldweek *magazine* is going to run a cover story on me in its July 4th issue, which will be on the stands the day after tomorrow, or the day on which you should be reading this letter, if Uncle Sam is still in there pitching and delivering the mails on schedule, which I think he is. I do not mention this Worldweek *magazine* cover story because I want to sound conceited. It is merely that I understand from some friends who have seen advance copies that it is a pretty good take out, all things considered, and in case you missed the Time *magazine* story and you should want to catch up on the career of one of your old pupils, why, this is your chance.

You don't have to read the whole story, of course, although I'm sure you will find it interesting if only because of our past association, just as I would find it interesting to read through a cover story in Worldweek *magazine* or Time *magazine* based on your career as a teacher, because of our past association. Which, when you come to think of it, is not a bad idea.

I know what a modest person you are, so I am sure your first reaction will be to think I am kidding an old lady, and I hope you won't take offense at my calling you an old lady. I am sure you are young in spirit, and in your mind you are probably even younger than I, because that's the kind of vital, full of ginger, peppy sort of person I remember you as. But we are all getting on. I will be forty years old myself in just a few days, and even though I don't feel it, I am all of a sudden conscious of age, which is why I referred to you as an old lady, since my secretary, in addition to finding me your address, also found out and informed me that you retired from P.S. 188 just before the war in 1941 at the age of sixty-five.

*I know you are still alive though, and as I said, full of vitality
and pep and ginger, as anybody who remembers you from P.S. 188
would certainly expect you to be, regardless of your age in years.
Which is why I think a cover story on you for one of the big news
magazines would be an excellent idea.*

Why not?

*Do all the cover stories have to be devoted to industrial tycoons
and foreign statesmen and guys who run the mile in four minutes
or discover a cure for vertigo? Why not a cover story in* Time *magazine or* Worldweek *magazine about a schoolteacher? A woman who
devoted her whole life to implanting and instilling and inculcating
in men like me the important rules of morals and conduct by which
we have lived our lives and achieved whatever success we have
achieved?*

*I know you are a modest person, and I'm sure your first instinct
is to pooh-pooh this whole suggestion, or you may even think I am
some sort of wise guy who gets his kicks out of pulling an old lady's
leg.*

I am not.

*I am a guy who has achieved whatever he has achieved by acting
on his hunches, purely and simply and no matter what anybody
else says to the contrary, and my hunches tell me this is a great idea
that* Time *magazine or* Worldweek *magazine will go for like a
ton of bricks once it is presented to them properly, and I will see to
that. I am not without influence in certain quarters, as you may have
gathered if you've followed my career at all, and I give you my word
here and now that I am getting my people onto this at once and
without any waste of time. So if any researchers from* Time *magazine or* Worldweek *magazine should start calling you up for facts
about yourself, you will know whom to thank.*

*Not that I expect or want thanks. When I consider how im-
portant an influence you have been on my career, there is almost
nothing I can do for you that is too much. But enough of that. I
don't want to start sounding sloppy. I just wanted you to know how
I feel. After all these years, it has given me quite a bang to be able
to have this long talk with you via letter, so to speak.*

*I hope this finds you well, and with all the best, I am your old
and devoted pupil*

Daniel Shaw

*P.S. One of the reasons you may not have been able to follow
my career in the papers is that in those days back in P.S. 188 when
I was in your class my name was Schorr.*
*P.P.S. In case anybody should get in touch with you and ask for
information about me in the days when I was your pupil, I am sure
you will be giving them exactly the same kind of honest, up-beat facts
about the kind of kid I was as I will be giving those researchers from
Time magazine and Worldweek magazine when they come to me
for facts about you.*

For quite a while after he finished reading the letter, George
continued to keep his eyes fixed on the green typewritten lines. He
didn't feel ready to look up and face Miss Corcoran. No wonder the
handwriting in which the words *"Air Mail Special Delivery! ! ! !"*
were scrawled on the envelope had seemed familiar. It was like the
moment in his office that morning when Mr. Kashkin had first
announced why he had come to see George. His stunned mind had
seemed capable of only one thought: How had Miss Akst known,
merely from looking at him, that Mr. Kashkin was not an ordinary
visitor?

Now, as George stared at the green typewritten lines, his mind
couldn't seem to get beyond another thought. It was the thought
that had struck him on the sidewalk as he was walking from his
lunch with Nick Perrini to the Astor Place subway station, a feeling
that unseen forces were at work, driving him relentlessly in a direction he did not want to take.

Finally, George cleared his throat and looked up. "What is there
about this letter to make you think about me?"

Miss Corcoran's eyebrows rose in surprise above her thick glasses.
"Why, because you and he were such friends," she said. "You and
Danny and that girl whose father owned the doll factory. Dora
Dienst."

It was George's turn to look surprised. "You remember her?"
he said.

The little old lady chuckled. "There isn't anything I don't remember about my pupils," she said. "Look."

Miss Corcoran set down her teacup, pushed the tray aside, and
started drawing imaginary lines on the table with her bony, waxlike,
liver-spotted forefinger.

"Here's the East River," she said. "And this is Lewis Street running parallel to it. Then here, crossing Lewis Street at right angles, is Fourth Street. And here, at the point where Fourth crossed Lewis, on the, let me see, yes, on the northwest corner, we have this large tenement house. On the street floor there are stores. One of them, to the right of the stoop as you stand facing the house, that one belongs to your Aunt Tessie. She has her tailor shop there and you and she live in the two rooms behind the store. On the other side of the stoop, facing Fourth Street just as your Aunt Tessie's shop faced it, we have this store in which Mr. Dienst and his family lived and put hair on the heads of dolls. I can close my eyes," Miss Corcoran said, and she did. "I can close my eyes," she repeated, "and smell that hot glue they used to smear on the heads of the dolls to make the hair stick, and I can see Dora coming out of the store, carrying her schoolbooks. And across the street, facing your Aunt Tessie's shop, I can see Mr. Kashkewitz's blacksmith shop, and I can see his son, the one who was crazy about physical culture, David his name was, but I think you boys called him Doodoo. I can see him chinning himself on the bar across those double doors, and I can see—"

Miss Corcoran paused and opened her eyes.

"My, she was pretty," the tiny, shriveled old lady said in a tone of wonder. "Little Dora Dienst. With that pointed little face and her black hair all done up in braids. Like one of those dolls in her father's store. A Chinese doll. I wonder whatever happened to her?"

George didn't answer. Even if he had known what to say, the words wouldn't have come. It was a good deal like the way he used to feel in London when the buzz bombs were coming over and, all at once, one of them would cut out directly overhead. There was a tightness in his chest, and a sudden frozen feeling of paralysis. All you could do was wait.

"I used to think she was the prettiest little girl I ever saw," Miss Corcoran said. "Little Dora Dienst." The old lady shook her head. "That's what made me think of you when I read this letter." She reached across and took the typewritten pages from George. "It came special delivery just a little while ago. I didn't quite understand it, but as soon as I saw who it was from, I thought of you."

Miss Corcoran moved her twisted little body on the couch as though she wanted to adjust herself physically as well as mentally to the recollection.

"Because you were all such good friends," she said. "The three of you. Danny Schorr and you and Dora Dienst. The moment I finished reading this letter, and I saw the signature, it all came back to me, and I found myself thinking: *I wonder if George Hurst is—?*" The little old lady paused. "Then the doorbell rang, and there you were."

Miss Corcoran paused again. Behind the thick lenses her eyes were suddenly alight with the blaze of memory.

"George," she said. "George, do you remember Armistice Day?"

George nodded. To himself as well as to Miss Corcoran. At last he knew why, reacting to the panic that had seized him on the sidewalk in front of the Astor Place subway station, he had jumped into the taxi and told the driver to take him to Fifty-seventh Street. It was the destination toward which he had been heading all day, from the moment Miss Akst had interrupted his shave with her puzzling phone call. He had come back to the beginning.

"Yes," George said. "I remember."

II

6

What he remembered most vividly, what loomed up in George Hurst's mind as one of the landmarks of his youth, was the feeling with which he awoke on that day.

Somebody was going to die.

He could feel it so strongly, from the moment he opened his eyes he was so totally saturated with the knowledge of death's presence, standing right there at his elbow, waiting impatiently for some sort of signal, that George found himself holding his breath. It was as though the name of the person who had been chosen was about to be announced aloud, and George was afraid that his own breathing might drown out the crucial syllables. Then he heard the tapping on the window, and George came fully awake.

Only one thing could cause that tapping. Danny was sending him a message. But Danny would not be sending a message at this hour of the morning unless something unusual was up. Unless it was something real big Danny would wait until he and George met, as they did every morning at eight o'clock, in Forman's grocery store.

George twisted over on the narrow bed and reached for the window. Behind him, out in the kitchen, he could hear Aunt Tessie shoveling coal into the stove. George pulled up the window slowly. He didn't want to make any noise. Aunt Tessie didn't like this system he and Danny Schorr had worked out for sending messages. Aunt Tessie didn't like anything that caused drafts. From drafts you caught colds, and from colds you got pneumonia, and once he got pneumonia what was a person's life worth?

George poked his hand out into the cold November air. He grabbed the tin can dangling from the length of clothesline and dragged the can into the room. He bent back the jagged top, pulled out the folded piece of paper, smoothed away the creases, and read Danny's penciled lettering:

*"Meet me in Forman's right away! Don't wait! !
Very important! ! ! Hurry up! ! ! !"*

George could feel the excitement begin to take hold. Boy, that Danny! He was always cooking up something! George pushed the can back out through the open window. He yanked the clothesline twice. This was the signal to Danny that his message had been received. Then George leaned across the bed and pressed his face flat against the window to watch the can start on its way back up to Danny.

He couldn't watch very long. The small room in which George slept faced the back yard around which the tenement was built. Through the barred window he could see all the way up to the roof on the south and west walls of the yard. This meant he could see the windows of about half the forty-eight families who lived eight to a floor on the six floors of the big gray stone house. But George couldn't see Danny's windows. Danny Schorr and his father lived on the fifth floor, directly above Aunt Tessie's tailor shop. The tin can disappeared.

"George!"

He banged the window shut. "What?"

"Never mind with the what!" Aunt Tessie called from the kitchen. "In November, Mr. Danny Schorr he has for you one of his crazy messages, let him climb downstairs on his own two feet to deliver it, or it could wait a few minutes till he sees you in Forman's or in school. In November is no time to open windows!"

"Okay," George said, trying to sound as though he didn't know from nothing. "I'm getting dressed."

He reached for his clean jumper. It was spread out on the foot of the bed. Aunt Tessie, who slept in the kitchen, always ironed a fresh jumper for him as soon as she got up. She brought it into George's room before he was awake.

"George! The shoes and stockings first!"

Aunt Tessie wasn't afraid of anybody in the whole world. There was nobody on two feet from Delancey Street all the way up to

Fourteenth who could make her turn and run. But she was scared stiff by the common cold.

"Okay," George said. "I forgot."

"People who forget and they stand around by open windows in November with naked feet, those people they're carrying out to the cemeteries in Brooklyn every day like flies!" Aunt Tessie said. George heard her rap hard on the wooden table. "God forbid," she said. "It shouldn't happen in this house."

George grabbed the buttonhook from the nail in the wall over his bed, fastened his shoes, and hurried toward the kitchen.

"The sweater!" Aunt Tessie said.

"I'm not washed yet."

"In November you wash in the sweater, please!"

"Okay, okay."

George ran back to the chair near his bed and grabbed the sweater. Pulling it over his jumper, George came into the kitchen. It was the larger of the two rooms. Aunt Tessie's bed, next to the sink, was already made. She was on her knees in front of the stove, blowing life into the coals she'd banked the night before.

"Watch the sleeves!" she said as George bent over the sink. "With Mrs. Gordon's Rachel it started with wet sleeves!"

Mrs. Gordon owned the candy stand on the Lewis Street side of the building. Her daughter Rachel had died of flu the week before.

"If I didn't put the sweater on until after I washed," George said, "I wouldn't get it wet."

"If you wouldn't give me an argument over every least little thing," Aunt Tessie said, "I would live longer." She got to her feet. "What did Mr. Danny Schorr have so extra special this morning? From General Pershing a message? Or maybe yet President Wilson?"

"Nothing special," George said. He shoved the sweater sleeves up over his elbows and turned on the faucet in the sink. It was made of cast iron. It smelled of stale vegetables and toothpaste. It was their only bathroom. "Danny just says I should meet him in Forman's."

"So how is it you can stand there in front of the sink on both feet?" she said. "A message from Mr. Danny Schorr and you're not jumping up in the air already like a bird to fly where he wants you?"

There were times when George wondered how anybody as smart as Aunt Tessie could be so dumb about Danny.

"When I get to Forman's," George said, "I'll find out what he wants."

"What Mr. Danny Schorr wants I don't care," Aunt Tessie said. "What I care is you shouldn't catch pneumonia because you're in such a hurry to see him you haven't got time to dry off the water from washing."

"I'm dry, I'm dry."

"By Mr. Danny Schorr, maybe. By me, no."

She took the towel and tackled George's face as though it was a dirty window.

"Okay, okay, okay! Pretty soon I won't have any skin left."

"When that happens you can ask Danny Schorr, he knows everything better than the whole world, you can ask him how to grow some more. Hey, Mister Hurry Up. In what are you going to bring the milk back in, in what? Your open hands?"

George came back. He grabbed the tin pitcher from the nail in the wall over the stove and took the twenty-five-cent piece from Aunt Tessie. He ducked through the beaded portieres and came out into the store. He hurried past the pressing machine and broke into a trot near the cutting table. He was running when he reached the rocking chair in the front window where Aunt Tessie sat and worked all day because that was where the light was best. George unhooked the chain bolt and turned the big key and pulled open the door.

On the threshold the wind from the river hit him in the throat. George gasped. Jesus, it was cold. Across the street Doodoo Kashkewitz was chinning himself on the long metal bar that ran across the top of the open door of the blacksmith shop. What a schmohawk this Doodoo was. The middle of November, and the big schlom was chinning himself in his underwear.

"Hello, stupid," Doodoo said.

"Up yours," George said.

"You're looking for your wise guy boy friend," Doodoo said, "I can tell you where he went."

"When I want to know anything from a dope," George said, "I'll come running to you."

He saw the lump of spit coming, and ducked. George grabbed half an orange from the garbage can on the sidewalk next to the stoop and let it go. It caught Doodoo in the chest with a wet plopping smack.

"You son of a bitch," Doodoo said, but he didn't drop from the chinning bar. George knew he wouldn't. When it came to chinning, this Doodoo was a regular bug. He never quit till he finished the thirty or forty pull-ups or whatever it was he felt he had to do every morning. "I'll fix you good," he said. "You wait, you little bastard."

"I'll wait," George said, starting up the street fast. "And when you catch me, you better duck." He wasn't afraid of Doodoo Kashkewitz. He wasn't afraid of anybody Danny Schorr wasn't afraid of. And muscles or no muscles, Danny could kick the tail off Doodoo Kashkewitz with one hand tied behind him. If he wasn't in such a hurry to meet Danny, George would have thought up something real good to let Doodoo have before he beat it. Instead, he just said again, "Up yours."

Forman's was in the tenement on the other side of the empty lot halfway between Lewis Street and Avenue D. Aunt Tessie hated the joint. She said it was the worst grocery store from here to Delancey Street. She said Mr. Forman sold stale rolls, and when he put a lump of butter on the scale and he said it was half a pound, you could be sure he was hiding a stone somewhere behind it. Aunt Tessie told anybody who would listen that Mr. Forman was a crook. Maybe he was. But George knew Aunt Tessie didn't hate Mr. Forman because he sold stale rolls or because he was a crook. Aunt Tessie hated Mr. Forman because he was a Hungarian and he made jokes behind her back about how ugly she was.

George didn't like Mr. Forman, either. George didn't like any bastard who made jokes about Aunt Tessie. But the main reason George didn't like this particular bastard was that Mr. Forman made his jokes about Aunt Tessie in front of George, and George didn't know what to do or say when it happened. If there had been any other grocery on the block, George knew he wouldn't even have had to ask Aunt Tessie if he could go somewhere else for the breakfast rolls and milk. She would have made him go there. But there was no other grocery on Fourth Street between Lewis and Avenue D. So every morning George went to Forman's, and every morning he wished Mr. Forman would drop dead. The black-bearded Hungarian never did, though, and George could see as he came into the grocery store on this morning that Mr. Forman, the son of a bitch, was still very much alive.

He was a tall, thin man. His beard was clipped to a point and he wore a black Homburg hat while he waited on customers. The morning talk in Forman's was always loud. This morning it seemed louder than usual.

George wondered, as he pushed his way around the crowd, moving along the cracked white marble counter on which Mr. Forman kept the lox and smoked white fish, what all the excitement was about. Then George reached the roll bin, where Danny Schorr always waited for him, and he stopped short. Danny was not there.

"They could say what they want about how it was General Pershing, but by me, if you ask me what it was, what it was it was somebody told the Kaiser if he wins and he comes over here, he has to marry Tessie Hurst, and that's what scared him, not General Pershing."

A roar of laughter swept through the store. George could feel everybody turn and look at him. He didn't care. George was wondering about Danny. Danny's message had said George should meet him in Forman's right away. Danny was never late.

"Listen, everybody, you should excuse me," Mr. Forman said. There was a mean little twinkle in his eye. In one hand the grocer was holding a paper bag in which he'd been putting a customer's rolls and, with his other hand, he was tugging his beard. When Mr. Forman tugged his beard it was a signal that he was about to let go with a real hot one. "You know how it is by me in my store," he said. "First come, first served. Always, and with no exceptions. But on a morning like this, she did for us more even than General Pershing, I think we should show Tessie Hurst a little respect. That we appreciate what she did to the Kaiser. No?" Mr. Forman looked around with a smile. "So I'll make today an exception, and I want nobody should complain, please, I'll take care of Tessie Hurst first." The customers laughed. Mr. Forman leaned forward across the counter and said, "What would you like today, George?"

I'd like to jab you in the zudick with a broken seltzer bottle, George thought, but he said, "A quart and a half milk."

He pretended as he handed over his tin pitcher that he didn't know everybody in the store was grinning at him. He didn't have time for Mr. Forman now. He had to find Danny. But some day, when he and Danny did have the time, they would figure out a way to take care of Mr. Forman. To pay him back for all the jokes he made about Aunt Tessie. Figuring out ways to pay people back, that was something Danny was good at. If Mr. Forman had any brains he'd watch his step. But Hungarians, Aunt Tessie said, they didn't have any brains. All they had was chutzbah.

George leaned down into the big bin and started squeezing rolls. He usually squeezed a dozen or more until he found the three that were just right. But there was no time for that today. George took the first three rolls he touched and put them on the counter. Mr. Forman emptied the quart dipper into George's tin pitcher, dropped the dipper back into the big milk can behind the counter, filled the half-quart dipper, and emptied it into the pitcher. Then he put the cover on the pitcher and set it down on the counter. The grocer started to smile again, winding himself up for another joke.

"That's all," George said.

Mr. Forman's eyebrows went up. He pushed the fedora back a little on his forehead as he looked out, across George's head, at the other customers.

"That's all?" Mr. Forman said. "On a day like this, when even General Pershing he's having a little something extra for a celebration, by Tessie Hurst it's just plain rolls and milk like every day in the year and that's all?"

Everybody laughed. Everybody but George. You big Putz Face, he thought. You great big Hungarian Putz Face.

"That's all," George said.

He put the twenty-five-cent piece on the counter. Mr. Forman chuckled as he dropped the rolls into a bag and gave George his change. The grocer was still chuckling, and his customers were still chuckling with him, when George pushed his way out into the street. On the sidewalk, holding the milk pitcher and the bag of rolls, he stopped. A coal wagon had come up from the dock and stopped in front of the blacksmith shop. Doodoo, still wearing nothing above the waist but his underwear, was helping the driver take the horse out of the shafts. Watching them, George suddenly remembered what Doodoo had said to him a few minutes ago.

"You're looking for your wise guy boy friend, I can tell you where he went."

The words had meant nothing a few minutes ago, because a few minutes ago George thought Danny was waiting at the roll bin in Forman's.

George ran down the block. "Hey, Doodoo!"

The blacksmith's son stopped tugging on a harness strap. "Look who's here," he said to the driver. "Kid Schmutz in person." He turned to George. "What's on your mind, stupid?"

"You seen Danny? You know where he went?"

"The same place you can go."

The wagon driver laughed. The horse jerked his head up and made a whistling noise. Doodoo picked up the orange with which

George had hit him a few minutes ago, and belted it across the street. George ducked. The orange slammed against Mr. Dienst's window on the other side of the stoop from Aunt Tessie's shop. The heavy sheet of plate glass rumbled.

The door opened. Dora Dienst came out. "Doodoo Kashkewitz," she yelled, "I saw you!"

"Aah, shut up!"

"My father will come out and give you a shut up!"

"Tell him to come on, and I'll give him something back!"

The wagon driver laughed again. With Doodoo's help he backed the horse into the blacksmith shop.

"The little bum," Dora said. "He almost broke the window." She came around to the front of her father's doll store and scraped the scraps of orange pulp from the glass. She had to stand on her toes to do it. Her braids shook as she worked. "What's the matter with you?" she said irritably to George. "Why do you fight with a bum like that?"

"Who was fighting? All I did, I asked him if he saw Danny."

"Why do you have to ask a dope like him?"

"Who else should I ask? Danny sends me a message I should meet him in Forman's, and I should hurry up because it's important, but when I get to Forman's he's not there."

"That's a reason for fighting with a bum like Doodoo Kashkewitz?"

"Forget it," George said. When Dora made up her mind to hear only what she wanted to hear, that was all she was going to hear, no matter what. Telling her more was a waste of time, and George didn't have any time to waste. He had to find Danny. "How about you?" he said. "You seen Danny?"

"Not this morning."

A sudden crash of glass made them both turn. Somebody had thrown a whiskey bottle out into the gutter. George looked quickly up toward the windows above Gerrity's saloon. The red brick building was on the northeast corner of the intersection between Lewis and Fourth, diagonally across the street from the tenement in which George and Dora and Danny lived. George didn't know what went on in Gerrity's. He'd never been inside the place. All George knew was that in the red brick building lived a bunch of crazos, the only people of their kind he'd ever seen, and he didn't see them very often. Mike Gerrity, the big, red-faced Irishman who owned the saloon, was supposed to have a wife and kids, but they never came out on the street. Mike himself came out only once in a while, usually when one of his customers had taken a little too much and had to be taught a lesson. Mike's customers were tough. Teaching them lessons indoors was rough on the furniture. They worked for Forrester Lumber and O'Brien Coal, the two companies that occupied the Fourth Street dock area. Some of them drove the lumber and coal wagons. Others lived on the barges that brought the lumber and coal up the river to the storage yards on the Fourth Street dock. Some worked in the yards. All of them hung out in Gerrity's. They never mixed with the people of Fourth Street. The people of Fourth Street never mixed with them. Even Doodoo Kashkewitz and his father, who took care of the horses for both companies, had never been inside Gerrity's saloon.

The day Aunt Tessie brought George from the Henry Isaacs Orphan Asylum to Fourth Street, when she was showing him around the place that was now to be his home, he'd pointed questioningly to the red brick building across the street.

Aunt Tessie had put her arms around him as though to protect him from somebody who was about to let him have it. "Shkutzim!" she'd said. "Gentiles!"

George had never heard the word before. But he understood right away what Aunt Tessie meant. He didn't need any translators. All he needed was the sound of Aunt Tessie's voice. This, she was saying, is the home of the enemy. Stay away. George didn't have to be told twice. He soon became used to hearing whispered stories about the crazy things that went on inside the house of the shkutzim. Just the same, throwing a whiskey bottle out into the street at eight in the morning was a surprise.

"Those shkutzim," Dora said. "They've been going crazy all night."

"I better take in the rolls and milk before Aunt Tessie gets sore."

"We had prunes last night," Dora said. "You?"

"Sure," George said.

Ever since the collection box had been set up on the sidewalk outside P.S. 188, he had hounded Aunt Tessie into serving prunes almost every night.

"Could I have your pits?" Dora said.

That was Dora for you. Not even a please. Just plain could I have your pits. If he gave them to her, where would that leave him? Every morning, at ten-thirty, Miss Corcoran marched the class out into the street so her pupils could deposit in the collection box the prune pits they'd brought from home. Miss Corcoran said the prune pits were used for making gas masks. George didn't believe her, of course. Anybody with half a brain in his head could see it was a lie. Prune pits and gas masks. What a lot of crap. But he assumed Miss Corcoran had some special reason for making believe the pits were used for gas masks. People from uptown had all sorts of reasons for doing things that didn't make any sense to George. He'd learned it was foolish to try and figure them out. But he liked Miss Corcoran. He wanted her to like him. She'd praised him several times for the number of pits he'd brought to school. George had eaten more prunes last night than he really wanted, just so he could have an impressive contribution to make this morning. If he gave his pits to Dora, he would have to march out empty-handed to the collection box at ten-thirty.

"If you want to be a mizzo," Dora said coldly, "okay, never mind."

"Who's a mizzo?" George said, thinking fast. Then he had an idea. "If you want them, you can have them."

"You mean it?"

"Sure."

"How many?"

"I don't know. I didn't count them."

This was a lie. He'd counted them twice. But Dora didn't have to know that. He would divide his thirty-six pits in half, give her one bunch, and keep the other bunch for himself.

"Gee, George, thanks."

"It's okay," he said. "If you see Danny—"

"I'll tell him you're inside," Dora said. "Don't worry, George."

But he did worry. That was why, instead of going into the store, George went up the stoop and climbed quickly to the fifth floor. He knocked on Danny's door. There was no answer. Mr. Schorr was a house painter. He kept his cans and brushes downstairs, in the cellar, but his overalls and work shirts hung from a row of nails on the inside of the apartment door. They made the whole fifth floor stink of turpentine. George could always tell by the strength of the stink whether Mr. Schorr was home or not. The stink was good and strong now. This was surprising. Mr. Schorr usually went off to work at seven o'clock. George knocked again. The door opened.

"Well, for God's sake, look," Mr. Schorr said, peering out into the dim hallway. "It's George. Hello, George. Come on in, George."

"I can't." George wondered why Mr. Schorr was home, and why he was wearing a regular suit instead of his working clothes, and then he saw that Mr. Schorr was holding a bottle of beer. "I just want to talk to Danny a minute."

"You want to talk to Danny a minute or even a second," Mr. Schorr said, "I think maybe you better get some salt and shake it on his tail like he was a bird."

Mr. Schorr liked his own joke. He laughed, then put the bottle to his mouth and took a long swig of beer, after which he belched.

"Please," George said. "I just want to talk to Danny."

"So first you'll have to find him." Mr. Schorr laughed again. "And don't forget the salt."

"Danny's not home?"

"Home? Who is home on a day like this?" Mr. Schorr lifted the bottle as though it was a candle. "Tell your Aunt Tessie she should open the Passover wine. Today it won't kill her. Tell her she should drink a little to General Pershing!"

"If you see Danny—"

"See Danny?" Mr. Schorr said. "George, I can't even hardly see *you* any more." Mr. Schorr laughed until he gasped for breath. "By eleven o'clock, George, and this is a promise, you should believe me, I won't be able to see anything!"

He slammed the door. George turned and ran down the stairs. God damn it. Everybody knew Mr. Schorr was a lush. But why the hell did he have to start guzzling so early in the morning on this particular day? When George was trying to find out what had happened to Danny?

"Mr. Forman he made you go outside to milk the cows?" Aunt Tessie said. "Or maybe to bake the rolls?"

"The store was crowded," George said. He sat down in front of his bowl of oatmeal. "Everybody talking and talking."

"Talking about what?"

"Something funny is happening today."

Aunt Tessie cut open a roll and smeared both halves with butter. "If by funny you mean crooked," she said, "I'm not surprised. What else should be happening in a grocery store it's owned by a crook? Don't shovel in the oatmeal so fast. A stomach God gave you, not a garbage pail. Here." She put the buttered roll beside his plate. "With each spoon oatmeal, a bite of roll, please."

George bit into the roll. "I don't mean only in Forman's," he said. "Mr. Schorr, too. He didn't go to work yet. He's still home and he's wearing a regular suit and he's already drinking beer."

"How do you know?"

"I went upstairs to find Danny."

"He wasn't in Forman's?"

"No."

"So no wonder you look like you lost maybe an arm or a leg, God forbid." Aunt Tessie poured a glass of milk and set it in front of George. "Don't worry," she said. "Mr. Danny Schorr, your great big prize package, he won't run away. A servant like you, to dance on his every least little wish, this nobody is so stupid to turn his back on it. You'll answer me maybe one question, please?" George worked away at his oatmeal. He knew what was coming. "You could please tell me, just for a favor, you could tell me what you see in that Danny Schorr?"

"He's my friend," George said.

"Better friends than this the world doesn't make? A little gangster like that? Always across the street there by the shkutzim? This is the best friend you can find?" George didn't answer. When Aunt Tessie got started on Danny the best thing to do was shut up and let her run out of words. "Wait, wait," she said. "You just wait and see. Trouble he'll get you into yet, that Danny, it'll take you a whole lifetime to climb out. With the milk a bite of roll, please!"

George didn't want the roll. He wanted to get going and find Danny. But he knew he didn't have a chance of getting out until he finished everything Aunt Tessie put in front of him. He got it down as fast as he could, then went to the shelf near the stove. The small paper sack was gone.

"What happened to my pits?"

"A few minutes before you came back with the rolls and milk, Dora came in and she said you told her she could have the pits from yesterday's supper. This is true or not?"

"Well," George said. "Sort of."

"Sort of today, sort of tomorrow," Aunt Tessie said. "You said she could have them or you didn't?"

George knew he didn't have a right to be sore. But he was. Dora was always in such a damn hurry. Why couldn't she wait until he gave them to her? Now he'd never have a chance to divide the pits in half. Now he'd have to go to school empty-handed.

"I asked a question," Aunt Tessie said. "You said Dora could have the pits or you didn't say it?"

"Sure I said it," George said. "But I didn't mean—"

"So next time you're dealing with Dora Dienst, when you don't mean, say that too. You told her she could have them, you should have known she wouldn't waste any time coming to get them. You know Dora long enough. One bite of roll is left here, please!"

George took the last bite of roll and Aunt Tessie kissed him. He grabbed his schoolbooks and ran. On the stoop he paused. Something really big was happening with the shkutzim. A lot more bottles had been thrown out of Gerrity's windows. The gutter in front of the saloon was covered with broken glass. From all the way across the street George could hear drunken voices singing.

He ran down the stoop and turned into the doll store. Mr. Dienst, wearing his short black leather apron, was stirring the glue pot on the stove. In the back of the store Mrs. Dienst, fat and asthmatic, was breathing noisily as she tended the oven in which the artificial hair, rolled tightly on sticks, was baked into curls. Frannie and Ida, the two older Dienst daughters, were already seated at the work bench, smearing the naked doll heads with glue and combing out over the sticky mess the tight little curls that became neat golden wigs. Everything looked and smelled and felt the way it did every morning when George came in to pick up Dora, and yet everything was different, the way it had been different in Forman's. George couldn't understand why.

"Dora ready?" he said.

"Dora's gone," Frannie said.

"She went to school already?"

"Where do you expect her to go?" Ida said. "Canarsie?"

"Hang a lock on the big mouth," Mrs. Dienst called from the back of the store. "The boy asks a plain question, give him a plain answer."

Ida stuck out her tongue at her mother and then, turning back to George, she crossed her eyes in the look of a simpering idiot. "Yeth, deah!" she said. "Your thweetheart hath gone to thkool alweady! Ith that plain enough for an anther?"

George moved backwards toward the door. He wouldn't have admitted it to anybody, but he was scared of Ida Dienst. You never knew what she was going to do or say. Frannie was okay. Frannie was fat and nice and stupid, like her mother. But Ida was nuts. Aunt Tessie said the trouble with Ida Dienst was that instead of being glad to help her mother and father make a living in the doll store, the way any decent girl with a little brains would be happy to do, Ida Dienst's head was stuffed like a kishke with crazy ideas about becoming an actress.

"Don't listen to her," Mrs. Dienst said. "Dora said she couldn't wait for you this morning, George. She wanted to get to school in a hurry."

"Okay," George said. "Thanks."

As he came out into the street, another bottle crashed down into the gutter from Gerrity's saloon. The noise made George jump. Somebody across the street laughed. You shkutz bastard, George said under his breath as he turned the corner into Lewis Street. Mrs. Gordon was standing on a ladder, nailing up strips of red, white, and blue bunting on her candy stand. George was surprised to see her. Ever since Mrs. Gordon's daughter Rachel had died the week before, the candy stand had been closed.

"Hello, George."

"Hello, Mrs. Gordon. You seen Danny?"

"No, but I saw Dora. A few minutes ago. She must be already in the school."

George wanted to ask her what the red, white, and blue stuff was for, but decided not to take a chance. If it had something to do with Rachel's death, Mrs. Gordon might start crying again. Some people cried quietly, or they turned away, or they went into a room and closed the door before the waterworks started. Not Mrs. Gordon. She cried loud and wet and all over the joint. George stepped on it.

At the Third Street corner he saw Old Man Saydl limping across the gutter. He was starting on his daily round. George did what all the kids on Fourth Street did when they laid eyes on the beggar: he spit into his left palm, touched the saliva with his right thumb, punched the wet blob home with a smack of his fist, and muttered the lines that were supposed to bring good luck:

> *I see Old Man Saydl,*
> *Old Man Saydl sees me.*
> *God bless Old Man Saydl,*
> *God Bless me."*

George was halfway across the gutter before he remembered the feeling with which he had come awake. He stopped short, startled by the opportunity fate had just thrown in his path. If there was any connection between the feeling that somebody was going to die and Danny's mysterious message to meet him in Forman's, here was the only sure way to stop whatever was going to happen. George turned, his heart hammering with sudden excitement, and ran after Old Man Saydl.

Catching up with him was no problem. The crippled old man moved like an animal with a broken back. He shoved one foot forward a few inches and stopped. He balanced himself with the cane made from an old broomstick while his whole body shook. After a few seconds, when he'd got his wind back, the old man dragged his other foot up to the first one. He then took another rest before repeating the whole business. It took him a quarter of an hour, sometimes more, to move a single block. This didn't hurt his business. The more slowly a beggar moved, the more he collected. Especially a beggar like Old Man Saydl.

He looked like a scarecrow that somebody had started to make by throwing a bundle of dirty brown rags at a pair of crossed sticks and then had forgotten to do anything more about it. From these rags, in the place where other people had a face, hung long white wisps of beard. From somewhere behind this beard came a low, whining moan that made George think of the way he felt when some kid in school scraped his fingernails down the blackboard.

Day after day, winter and summer, he moved through the neighborhood like a trickle of spilled mud, inching his way forward, staring at the ground, rattling his tin cup, collecting a slow but endless stream of pennies. Nobody knew where he came from in the morning or where he went at night. Some people believed he had a fortune hidden away in a secret place. Every kid on Fourth Street believed that it was possible to save somebody's life by touching him.

George had never touched Old Man Saydl. He'd never wanted to save anybody's life before. All of a sudden, though, he was thinking of that feeling he'd had when he woke up, the feeling that somebody was going to die, and George knew what he was going to do. He came up behind the old man, hesitated for a moment and then, as the beggar dragged his crippled leg up into position and paused to rest on his cane, George reached out and touched the shaking bundle of dirty rags.

"Okay," he muttered to himself. "Okay." He turned and ran. "Now it's okay."

But it wasn't. In the school yard, combing back and forth through the crowd several times, he still had not found Danny. All he found was the funny feeling that something was different, as though the boys and girls shouting and playing in the school yard had been infected by the same excitement that had touched the people in Forman's and the shkutzim in Gerrity's.

"Hey, George."

He turned, and his heart jumped with relief. All the way over at the other side of the yard, near the door from Lewis Street, he could make out the skinny figure in the torn gray sweater. George shoved his way toward it.

"For Christ's sake," he said. "You send a guy a message, and then you don't show."

"I started downstairs right after I pulled the can back," Danny said. "I'm halfway up the block to Forman's when I get the whistle from Mike Gerrity."

"Oh," George said.

What else was there to say? Danny's relationship with Mike Gerrity and the shkutzim who hung around Mike's saloon was the only thing that bothered George about his best friend. It bothered a lot of other people on Fourth Street, too. Some of them told Mr. Schorr it didn't look right for his son, a nice Jewish boy like Danny, to be seen going in and out of the enemy camp across the street. From things like this no good could come. Jews belonged with Jews, and shkutzim belonged with shkutzim.

Mr. Schorr had asked these people if they were all of a sudden going to make him a Rockefeller. Unless they were, maybe they'd better think of a little something with brains behind it before they opened their mouths and started talking. Money was money. When it came to paying for a quart of milk or half a dozen rolls, did Mr. Forman ask where the nickel came from? If Danny could make a few cents by running errands, who cared whether he ran them for Mrs. Gordon or for Mike Gerrity? The things from which no good came, Mr. Schorr said, were not because a nice Jewish boy had a few shkutzim for friends. The things from which no good came, Mr. Schorr said, were long noses that stuck themselves like spoons into pots that they didn't put on the stove in the first place.

After that nobody said anything to Mr. Schorr or to Danny.

Not even George. But everybody thought about it, including George. And people talked about it among themselves, including George and Aunt Tessie. What Aunt Tessie had to say about it you could hear all the way over on Avenue B.

"Mike never asks me to do anything for him until sometimes lunch hour or mostly after school," Danny said. "So when he gives me the whistle, and it's not even eight o'clock yet, I know right away something is up. I run back to the saloon and Mike hands me five bucks and he says I should beat it over to Cheap Haber's right away and buy him an American flag."

"What's the matter with the flag he's got in the window?"

"He says that's for Mike Junior because he's in the army, but this one he sends me for, it's a big one. Like we have here in school for Assembly."

"What's he want a flag that big for?"

"How the hell should I know? Mike tells me go get something, I go get it." Danny pulled a dime from his pocket. "He gives me this."

"For yourself?"

"No, I should split it up with the whole school. Where's your head, dope? Sure for myself." Danny flipped the coin high in the air, caught it on his tongue, spit it into his hand, and winked at George as he shoved the dime into his pocket. "I just get back a couple minutes ago. That's why I miss you in Forman's. But that's okay. What I sent the message for, boy, I want you to listen." Danny's bright, restless eyes darted across the yard like the beam of a flashlight. The smile twisted slightly on his thin face. He leaned close to George. "Today we do it."

"Do what?"

"Christ! Do what he asks!"

The look of disgust, which was one of Danny's specialties and took a little time to work up, was interrupted by the bell. The noise in the yard disappeared like a nickel dropped through a sidewalk grating. A thousand boys and girls froze in their tracks like so many statues. A moment later the bell rang again. The statues started shuffling in all directions, arranging themselves in a series of long, straight lines. The scuffing of shoes on the cement floor was the only sound. You got caught talking in the school yard after the second bell, and you got sent on a little visit to the office of Mr. Dunn, the principal, a real murderer.

"Stay behind me," Danny whispered. "I'll give you the layout on the way up."

George nodded and followed Danny to the line in front of the card lettered "5B-1." The third bell rang. The yard could have been a mass of molten wax that had been dipped suddenly in ice water. George stood up stiff and straight, the way he'd been taught on his first day in P.S. 188, chin and belly sucked in, eyes front, hands flat against the seams of his pants. Mr. Dunn mounted the small platform at the front of the yard.

"Boys and girls," he said. "It is not for me to tell anybody how to celebrate this day toward which we have all looked forward for so long with so much hope. Every one of you has in one way or another been touched by the terrible struggle in which our great country has been engaged. Even those families that have not sent a son or a brother or a father or a cousin to the fighting front have made their sacrifices in their own way. I am proud of the contributions you have made. P.S. 188 ranks near the top in prune pit collections and war savings stamps throughout the city. I know you will not mar that record by your conduct during the small celebration that we have prepared as P.S. 188's small contribution to the festivities that will sweep across the country today." Mr. Dunn turned to the left. "Miss Gillin?"

The white-haired old lady who taught the Crazy Class stepped up on the platform beside the principal. He whispered something in her ear. The old lady nodded. Mr. Dunn stepped down. Miss Gillin raised her ruler.

"*Uh-oh say can you see?*" she sang in a high, unsteady treble. "Ready, boys and girls?"

The ruler came down. The whole yard broke into "The Star-Spangled Banner." Danny Schorr took a short step backward. George took a short step forward. Under cover of the singing their heads came close together.

"We're getting Old Man Saydl's bundle today," Danny said. "Can you hear me?"

George didn't answer. He couldn't. Not for a few moments. For a few moments he could hardly breathe. Getting Old Man Saydl's bundle was something Danny had been talking about for weeks. George had never believed he really meant it.

"Can you hear me?"

George snapped out of it. *"What so proud-ly we hailed,"* he roared, and then whispered to Danny, "I can hear."

"I got it figured how he moves," Danny said out of the corner of his mouth. "I been watching him for weeks. It looks crazy, like he don't know where he's going, but that's a lot of bull. The old putz he knows all right. He's smarter than you think. Every morning when we're on the way to school he's on his way up Third, going toward Avenue D."

"That's right," George said, and then he bellowed, *"Whose broad stripes and bright stars."*

"What you say?" Danny said.

"I said that's right," George said. "That he's on his way up Third when we're on the way to school."

"You been watching him, too?" Danny sounded suspicious.

"Not watching," George said. "I just happened to see him to-day when I crossed Third on my way to school. I—" George stopped. Danny was funny. He didn't believe all the things everybody else believed. He might laugh if George told him why he'd run after the crippled beggar and touched Old Man Saydl. George sang loudly, *"Gave proof through the night."*

"After he hits Avenue D he works over to Fourth and then heads up toward Avenue B," Danny said. "Watching him like that for a while, I noticed something. You ever see Old Man Saydl during lunch hour?"

"No."

"Me neither," Danny said. "A few days ago, though, Mike Gerrity sends me over to Woolworth's on Avenue B for some spoons. It's during lunch hour, and I'm coming back with the spoons, when bango, what do I see? Right there on the corner of Seventh and Avenue B, right by the park, I see Old Man Saydl, and he's heading back to Avenue C. I don't think about it for a while. I'm in a hurry to get the spoons to Mike and get back to school. When I do, all of a sudden I remember I never see the old putz *after* school. See what I mean?"

George shook his head. He could see only one side of Danny's face. It twisted irritably.

"Jesus, you're dumb," he said. "If he's on Seventh and Avenue B around lunch time, and he's heading back to Avenue C, where does he disappear?"

"Oh," George said.

"Yeah, oh. So what we're doing today, you and me, boy, we're beating it up to Seventh and Avenue B when lunch time comes, and we're not coming back the rest of the day. We're following Old Man Saydl till we find out where he disappears. You know why?"

George nodded. "Because if we find out where he disappears, we also find out where—"

"Right," Danny said, and the side of his face twisted in the quick, knowing grin. "We also find out where he hides all those bundles of pennies!"

"Jesus," George said. What a brain Danny had. The singing took on a warning note. George joined in and bellowed, "*And the home—of—the—brave!*"

Miss Gillin stepped down from the platform. Mr. Dunn waved his hand. The fourth bell rang. The lines of boys and girls began to march toward the staircases. Danny came close to George at the first bend on the way up, between the yard and the second floor.

"When the lunch bell rings, you beat it right out of school and up to the Avenue B and Seventh Street corner," Danny whispered. "I'll meet you there. I don't want anybody to see us leaving the school together."

"Okay," George said.

Every morning, when the class filed into her room, Miss Corcoran was seated at her desk up front, correcting papers that had been turned in the day before or working out the problems for future tests. Today, however, it was different. Just as it had been different in Forman's and downstairs in the yard. Today Miss Corcoran was standing in front of a large cardboard box near the radiator. She was pulling from the box small tin drums, paper horns to which were attached red, white, and blue streamers, and wooden noisemakers. She smiled to herself as she sorted these out and arranged them in rows on the window sill back of the radiator. After he hung his hat and coat in the class closet, George went to the cupboard near Miss Corcoran's private closet for the sponge and basin. It was his turn to wash the blackboard.

"Not today, George," Miss Corcoran said. "We won't bother about the blackboard today."

George shoved the basin back into the cupboard and went back to his seat. If she didn't want the blackboard washed, that was okay with him. His mind was full of Danny Schorr's plan. He sat there, thinking about it, and watching Miss Corcoran.

"Before I distribute these," she said, "I think it would be a good idea if I wrote out on the blackboard the words of the two or three songs that we're going to play."

She turned her narrow, twisted back and began to write. She started on the left blackboard, where she wrote all the words of "Over There." On the middle board she wrote the words of "K-K-K-Katy." And on the board at the right she wrote the words of "Pack Up Your Troubles."

"Now, then," she said, turning back to face the class. "If the Number Ones will come up, please?"

The Number Ones were the kids who sat in the first seat of each row. They stood up and followed Miss Corcoran to the window.

"Suppose we alternate drums with horns," she said, taking them down from the window sill and handing them to the Number Ones. "A drum to the first pupil, a horn to the second, a drum to the third, and so on. Is that clear?"

The Number Ones nodded and began to move up the aisles, dropping drums and horns on the desks. George got a drum. It was about the same size as the pot in which Aunt Tessie cooked oatmeal. A pair of drumsticks were tied to it.

"I don't expect us to sound like a symphony orchestra," Miss Corcoran said. "But I think if we practice for—" She looked at her tiny gold wrist watch. "Well, we have almost an hour, and if we really practice, I don't see why we shouldn't at least learn to keep time. Now, then, children, ready?"

For almost an hour the boys and girls in Miss Corcoran's class accompanied her on their tin drums and paper horns while she sang "Over There," "K-K-K-Katy," and "Pack Up Your Troubles." It was good and noisy, but George didn't mind. He was thinking about the best and quickest way to get from the school to the corner of Seventh and Avenue B after the lunch bell rang.

"Very well, children. I think that will do."

George stopped beating his drum and looked up at Miss Corcoran. She must have received some sort of signal. Her eyes were shining behind her thick glasses like greased marbles. Her cheeks were flushed.

"We're ready!" she said. "Indian file, please!"

George followed the rest of the class to the side of the room, where they shoved and poked themselves into a single line. The way Miss Corcoran watched them, she looked like somebody was about to hand her a great big present. She opened the door and peered out into the hall. George, who was in the middle of the line, could hear noises down the corridor.

Miss Corcoran waved to someone, then pulled her head in. "All right, children!" Her voice cracked with excitement. "Let's go!"

She stepped out into the hall. The class followed. When George came through the door he saw that Miss Leopolstadt's class also had drums and horns. They fell in behind Miss Corcoran's class, forming a crooked snake some seventy or eighty kids long.

"Ready?" Miss Corcoran called from up front.

"Ready!" Miss Leopolstadt called from the back.

"All right, children!" Miss Corcoran said. She looked and sounded happy, but there were tears in her eyes. Miss Corcoran brought the ruler down sharply. *"Over there,"* she sang shrilly. *"Over there! Send the word, send the word, over there!"*

George banged away at his tin drum. So did the other kids. At the same time the horn blowers tore into the song. With Miss Corcoran in the lead, singing her head off, the noisy line began to move. Down the hall the door of Mr. Mussaius' 3B-1 class opened. Mr. Mussaius stuck his white head out, grinned, waved, and stepped aside. Miss Corcoran, singing so hard that the veins stood out on her skinny neck like spaghetti, led the long line into Mr. Mussaius' room. Banging their tin drums and blowing their paper horns, the line of marchers circled the room while Mr. Mussaius' class screamed and cheered. When she came back to the door, Miss Corcoran led the line out of Mr. Mussaius' room and down the hall to Mrs. Goldfarb's class. Here the same performance was repeated.

It was repeated again and again, in every classroom on the third floor. Then Miss Corcoran led the line of drummers and horn blowers down to the second floor. They had covered about half the classrooms on the second floor when, without warning, the school bell began to ring.

Three blasts. Pause. Three more blasts. Pause. And another three.

"Boys and girls!" Miss Corcoran yelled. "Your attention, please!"

George stood up straight, the way he stood in the yard when the third bell rang. Everybody on the line, he could see, was doing the same. It was suddenly dead quiet in the hall. George twisted to look down the line. Danny pushed his head out of the line. He winked at George. George winked back. As soon as this was over they'd go after Old Man Saydl. George looked up at the clock on the wall. The minute hand was just a tiny hairline after twelve and the hour hand stood at eleven. The minute hand moved. The bell exploded. A single, long blast.

Miss Corcoran's body seemed to melt. "That minute of silence," she said in a shaking voice, "is in memory of the brave men who will not come back." Then she raised the ruler over her head, smiled happily, and cried, "Ready?"

"Ready!" Miss Leopolstadt called.

"*K-K-K-Katy,*" Miss Corcoran sang. "*Beautiful Katy. You're the only g-g-g-girl that I adore.*"

George walloped his drum. The other kids went back to doing their stuff. The line moved forward. It continued to move, through the rest of the classrooms on the second floor, then up to the fourth. The line was circling Mr. Cartright's 6B-1 class on the fifth floor, and George was helping them bang out "Pack Up Your Troubles," when he suddenly realized he was hungry.

As soon as the line got back out in the hall, he looked up at the clock on the wall. Astonished, George saw that it showed ten minutes after twelve. He looked quickly up the line, toward Miss Corcoran. She was singing away, shaking her head and waving the ruler. George glanced back at Miss Leopolstadt. She was singing like crazy.

George worked his way out of the line and inched up beside Danny. "What about the lunch bell? You hear it?"

Danny scowled and shook his head. "God damn," he said. "The one day I want to get out twelve sharp, they go and end the lousy war on me!"

For a moment or two George did not grasp what Danny meant. Then, when he did, and the puzzling events of the morning took on meaning, he was suddenly engulfed by the celebration of which he had been an unwitting part. For several moments he was in the grip of the excitement that held Miss Corcoran and Miss Leopolstadt. Then George saw Danny's face, and the excitement disappeared. The war, which had not done very much to change the course of life in the two rooms behind Aunt Tessie's shop, was all at once an unexpected monkey wrench in the machinery of the most exciting plan Danny had ever cooked up. Why did they have to end the war today? Why couldn't they have done it the day before? Or waited until tomorrow?

"We gotta be up at Seventh and Avenue B by a quarter after

twelve," Danny said. "How the helliwee do that if we're still here with this damn *K-K-K-Katy?*"

"It ought to be over soon," George said.

But it wasn't. Miss Corcoran and Miss Leopolstadt kept their classes on the march, beating the drums, singing, and blowing horns, until the line had visited every classroom in the school. By the time Miss Corcoran led them back into their own room on the second floor, George had forgotten all about how hungry he was. He was thinking about Danny. When Danny got sore it was no fun for anybody, and George could tell, as Miss Corcoran turned to face her class, that Danny was boiling.

"Children, that was simply lovely," the teacher said. "I want to thank each and every one of you for helping make this day memorable. I'm sure you're all very hungry, because it's long past your lunch hour, but I'm also sure you don't really mind being hungry for a little while because this day is one that none of us will ever forget. Besides, Mr. Dunn has asked me to tell you that you don't have to come back this afternoon. School is dismissed for the day!"

Out in the hall George tried to get close to Danny. He wanted to ask if they were to stick to the plan. But Danny was shoving his way down the hall, pushing people aside like a swimmer doing the breast stroke. George figured from this that Danny still didn't want them to be seen leaving the school together, which meant in turn that he was to stick to the original plan. That was okay with George. Danny was boss.

Somebody called to George as he came out on the sidewalk through the Houston Street entrance, but he didn't stop to find out who it was. He moved up the street toward Avenue D. The crazy feeling that had boiled up inside the school seemed to be spilling over into the street. People who should have been in their stores waiting on customers, or away at work in their shops, were out on the sidewalk, laughing and shouting and, in many cases, singing.

On the corner of Third and Avenue D the owner of the chicken store, Mrs. Shumansky, was dancing a jig with two soldiers. George didn't even pause for a second look. He had to get to Seventh and Avenue B. Besides, everybody was nuts today, so why should Mrs. Shumansky be any different? George turned right and headed up toward Fourth. Halfway there he was trapped by a bunch of girls wearing sailor hats who formed a laughing circle around him and sang "Oh, How I Hate to Get Up in the Morning." George battled his way clear and decided he could probably make better time by heading west on Fourth. He did, for about half a block. Then a parade of coal wagons turned into Fourth from Avenue C, and George was shoved up against the stoop of a tenement. The coal wagons were decorated with red, white, and blue bunting, like Mrs. Gordon's candy stand, and jammed with soldiers holding beer bottles. They pounded each other on the back and yelled at the people in the street.

"Hey, kid!" one soldier yelled. "Catch!"

He tossed the beer bottle. George reached out instinctively and caught it. A cheer went up.

"Tell the Kaiser where to stick it!" a soldier yelled.

A roar of laughter swept up Fourth Street. George dropped the bottle, squeezed past a woman and a soldier locked in a tight kiss, and started shoving his way toward Avenue C. On the Fourth Street corner a soldier was crouched on the curb, in front of Sheffield's, holding a whiskey bottle and vomiting between his knees into the gutter. Just beyond Fourth Street, as George passed Cheap Haber's, Mr. Forman came out of the stationery store. He had two small American flags stuck into the ribbon around his black fedora and a larger flag in his hand.

"George, they're going to hang the Kaiser!" the grocer said. "Go get your Aunt Tessie! The Kaiser he'll take one look at her, it'll give him a squeeze here by the heart, they won't have to bother hanging him!"

"Drop dead," George said as he ran past.

He began to feel better. He'd been wanting to say that for a long time. At Fourth Street George paused to take a quick look around. Avenue C looked bad. Soldiers were moving in and out among the pushcarts, grabbing vegetables and throwing them at each other. Far down the avenue, beyond Sixth Street, a crowd was gathering and moving toward him. George decided not to take a chance. He turned west, up Fourth Street, and ran right into the arms of Danny's father.

"George!" Mr. Schorr screamed, waving a bottle over his head. "George, look, I can still see!"

A woman came up with an American flag which, without warning, she used as a club and smashed the bottle from his hand. Mr.

Schorr started to laugh so hard the spit ran out of his mouth and down his chin. George ducked around him and ran.

"Three more blocks," he panted when he paused for breath on the Avenue B corner. "Three more blocks."

They turned out to be the worst. The Avenue B trolley car, which had been stalled at the Fifth Street corner, seemed to be on fire. By the time he reached the fringes of the crowd gathered around it, George saw that the car must have been stuffed with fireworks which looked like they'd been touched off by accident. Nobody was in the car, but bits of flame and sparks of colored fire kept shooting out the windows in all directions. People screamed and ducked and ran away and then ran back, laughing and squealing, as though they couldn't make up their minds whether or not they wanted to be burned. George squirmed past a man wearing a Prussian helmet, ducked his head, and ran. On the Seventh Street corner he saw Dora Dienst. She was standing on one of the green benches at the entrance to the park, peering across the heads of the crowd.

George ran up to her. "What the hell you doing here?"

"Waiting for you," Dora said. "What took you so long? I've been here ten minutes."

"I got trapped on Fourth Street. There's a whole bunch of coal wagons with soldiers. They're throwing bottles and there's people dancing and—" George paused and looked at her sharply. "What do you mean you're waiting for me?"

"You don't have to look so wise. I know what you're after. Danny told me. The only thing is, he says it's too late to catch Old Man Saydl up here. On account of how we were kept in late in school, Old Man Saydl passed here already."

"You saw him?"

"If I saw him, I wouldn't be standing around here waiting for you, would I? If I saw him, I'd be trailing him, like you and Danny were supposed to do."

"What am I supposed to do now?"

"I don't know. All Danny said, he said beat it up to Seventh and Avenue B, grab George, and bring him back to Gerrity's." Dora took his arm. "Come on, Danny's in a hurry."

"Okay, okay, quit pulling," George said. Not because Dora actually was pulling. It was just there were times when Dora got pretty wise. She didn't have to think she knew everything. "How did you find out about this?" George said as he moved down Seventh Street with Dora. "When did Danny tell you?"

"Right after Miss Corcoran dismissed us. I tried to catch you because I counted up the prune pits you gave me—"

"I didn't give you. You went and took them."

"You said I could have them."

"I said I'd *give* them to you."

"You said I could *have* them, so I went in and told Aunt Tessie and she said sure, if you said I could have them."

"I said I'd *give* them."

"What's the diff?"

"If you don't understand, I'm not gonna tell you."

"There *is* no difference. *That's* what I understand. Except in school, when Miss Corcoran was teaching us the songs, before the marching started, I counted them, and when I saw there was thirty-six, I thought it was too much. I mean it was enough pits for two people, so I thought I'd give you back half and we'd both have something to put in the collection box when Miss Corcoran took us out. Except she didn't take us out today, so when she dismissed the class I tried to catch up with you, but you disappeared, so I caught up with Danny and I told him, and he said never mind the prune pits, something bigger was happening, and he told me." Dora looked at George out of the corner of her eye. "You want half the pits back?"

"We'll see tomorrow. When it's time for going out to the collection box."

"Danny says there won't be any more collections. Danny says they won't need any more gas masks."

"Then forget it. I don't want the pits back."

"You're not sore?"

"Why should I be sore?"

"Because I went in and asked Aunt Tessie to give me the pits."

"I'm not sore."

"Then here." Dora pulled something from the pocket of her coat. "I stopped in the store before I came up here to wait for you," she said. "Ma gave me two rolls. I saved one for you."

George didn't realize, until he bit into it, how hungry he was. The roll tasted wonderful. It was soft and chewy and there was a thick layer of butter in the middle. George finished it quickly and was wondering how to get hold of another one, when he and Dora came around the corner into Lewis Street and they saw Danny. He was standing on the sidewalk in front of Gerrity's. Not exactly standing. Danny never did that. He was sort of jigging, the way he always did when he had to wait, kicking his heels against the curb, poking his hands in and out of his pockets, and peering up and down the street.

As soon as he saw George and Dora he came running toward them. "Where the hell you been?"

"We came as fast as we could," George said. "It ain't easy. The crowd, boy, I'm telling you, it's—"

"Nuts to the crowd," Danny said. "Come on."

He ran across the street toward the tenement in which they all lived. George and Dora followed him through the stoop door between Aunt Tessie's shop and Mr. Dienst's doll factory, and up the six flights of stone steps to the roof.

Leaning against the ledge that faced the river, Danny pointed down toward Gerrity's. "He's in there."

"Who?" George said.

"Who do you think, schmuck?"

"Old Man Saydl?" Dora asked.

"Who else are we trailing today?" Danny said. "General Pershing?"

"You don't have to be so snotty," Dora said.

"You don't have to be so dumb," Danny said.

George wondered what Old Man Saydl was doing in the shkutzim's saloon, but he figured he'd rather keep on wondering than have Danny call him a schmuck again. When Danny got excited he didn't care what he said. Even to his best friends. George squinted down across Gerrity's roof toward the barges tied up at the dock. Between the back of the saloon and the edge of the river the neat lumber stacks in the Forest looked like great big lumps of sugar arranged in rows.

"You can call me dumb if you want," Dora said. "But I don't understand what Old Man Saydl is doing in Gerrity's."

"In Gerrity's?" Danny turned to look at her. "Who said anything about Gerrity's?"

"You did," Dora said. She pulled George's sleeve. "Didn't he just say Old Man Saydl is in there?"

"For Christ's sake," Danny said before George could open his face. "If the old bastard was in Gerrity's, would I need any help to trail him? I said he's down *there!*" Danny pointed toward the lumber yard beyond the saloon. "In the Forest."

"Oh," Dora said, and she leaned further across the ledge. "How do you know?"

"I got eyes in my head," Danny said.

Suddenly he laughed, and he poked Dora and George with his elbows. George stopped worrying about being called a schmuck again. When Danny laughed like that, when Danny felt good, everything was okay. And one thing was sure: Danny was feeling good again.

"I knew it," Danny said, grinning happily. "I knew he'd show up in the Forest. I figured he had to."

"Why did he have to?" Dora said.

That was Dora for you, George thought. Never willing to let well enough alone. Danny was feeling good, so she has to go asking questions.

"Look at it yourself, for Christ's sake," Danny said. "Every day, around lunch time, he's up there on Seventh and Avenue B. Every day, by three o'clock when we get out of school, he's disappeared. Where does he go? First I thought the way to find out is trail him. Miss Corcoran and her God-damn parade, she loused that up. By the time we get out of school, Old Man Saydl he's disappeared again, and first I figured the hell with it, we'll trail him tomorrow. But then I figure no. I start thinking." Danny tapped his forehead with a forefinger. "How come, I says to myself, an old guy like that, he moves so slow, creeping along like a snake with a busted back, how come he's moving down Seventh Street, everybody can see him, and all of a sudden he disappears?" Danny laughed. "Because he don't *stay* on Seventh Street, that's why! And a guy who don't stay on Seventh Street, he can only go one place." Danny pointed toward the river. "But we know Old Man Saydl he don't go into the river, because every morning he shows up again, and he don't look wet to me." Danny laughed again. "So instead of the river, when he hits the end of Seventh Street, it stands to reason Old Man Saydl he's gotta go some place else." Danny nodded down toward the Forest. "That's where he goes."

George wondered about that. The Forest was so close, how come nobody had ever seen Old Man Saydl sneaking into the place before today? But George let it go at wondering. He wasn't taking any chances on getting Danny sore by asking questions.

"If that's where he hides his pennies," Dora said. "If he's been sneaking in there every day, how come nobody ever saw him doing it before today?"

George gave Dora a dirty look. Why couldn't she keep her trap shut? Then he shot a quick glance at Danny. He saw with surprise that Danny was grinning.

"Because before today nobody ever had the brains to figure it out," Danny said. "Today a guy with brains came along and figured it out. Me. And today I saw him creep in from the back on Fifth Street. With my own eyes I saw him. You satisfied?"

Dora began to tug the end of one of her pigtails. "You say you saw him with your own eyes, okay, you saw him with your own eyes," she said. "But that doesn't mean we got the money yet. The Forest is a big place. How do we know where he hides his pennies when he gets in there?"

Danny's grin grew wider. "That's what we're gonna find out," he said. "Come on."

He led them back down to the street. A straw figure of the Kaiser was hanging from the bar across Mr. Kashkewitz's blacksmith shop. Half a dozen drunken soldiers were standing around with bottles in their hands, spitting mouthfuls of beer at the straw figure and laughing so hard every few seconds they had to double up and grab their guts. George kept his head down as he followed Danny and Dora across Lewis Street to the dock. He didn't want Aunt Tessie to see him and call him back. Mr. Dienst did see him, and then the doll manufacturer saw Dora, and he called to her from the doorway of the doll factory, but Dora paid no attention to her father. She kept right on going. George wasn't surprised. Dora talked back to Danny, and every once in a while she said she was sick and tired of the way he bossed everybody around, but George knew that was a lot of bull. When Danny cooked something up, if he left her out Dora got sore as hell. Dora wanted to be in on everything. Danny stopped outside the gate that separated Forrester Box & Lumber from O'Brien Coal. He looked back toward Lewis, then down toward the barges. Nobody was watching.

"Now listen, both of you," he said. "There's three ways into the Forest. This gate here. The back way on Fifth Street. And up across the coal yard from the river. If we come in from all three sides, we got him surrounded. All we have to do is keep our eyes open and move quiet, without any noise, so the old man won't know we're in there with him, and pretty soon one of us'll spot him.

Whichever one it is, we just keep our traps shut and our eyes open, and when the old man finishes shoving his pennies in the hiding place and he beats it, the dough is ours. Okay?"

Dora nodded.

"Okay," George said.

"Dora, you go in this way, by the gate," Danny said. "George, you take the river side, and me, I'll cover the back from Fifth Street. Okay?"

Dora nodded again.

"Okay," George said again.

"Then shake a leg," Danny said. "And remember: no noise."

Dora ducked under the gate and disappeared. Danny headed back toward Lewis Street for the long circle around the block to the Fifth Street gate. George moved down toward the river. He was surprised, when he reached the first barge, to see that it looked deserted. He'd come into the Forest from the river side many times, but always it had been necessary to kid the bargemen or their wives into thinking he was just mooching along, with nothing special on his mind, and then, when they weren't looking, make a run for it. Moving along, George saw that there was nobody on the second barge, either. That was damn funny. If the men were gone, okay. George could understand that. Half the time, when they were supposed to be working, the bargemen were up at Gerrity's, guzzling beer. But their wives were always on the barges, washing clothes or peeling potatoes. George wondered if the wives were over on Avenue D, celebrating the end of the war, and then he figured the hell with it. He had to get up into the Forest.

He slipped past the loading chute, dipped down in a crouch for the run past the gate just in case somebody was watching from the office, then slid into the coal yard. Keeping his head down, he ran around the great black hill of coal, edged past the office, and made for the fence. He was out in the clear now, but even if he was spotted it wouldn't have made any difference. George had been over that fence too often to worry about anybody catching up with him now. Nobody did.

He made it in two jumps, dropped down on the other side, remained like that in a crouched position for a few moments, then straightened up and started working his way slowly up toward the side of the Forest that ended against Gerrity's back yard. He did what Danny had ordered. He kept his ears open.

Halfway down a narrow alley between two stacks of lumber that stuck up over his head almost as high as Mr. Kashkewitz's blacksmith shop, George suddenly stopped. He'd been listening for the sound of Old Man Saydl dragging himself along. George knew that sound. He'd been hearing it for years. But he'd always heard it on a sidewalk. Here, on the spongy mixture of dirt and sawdust that formed the floor of the Forest, George knew the sound would be different. Just the same, George was pretty sure he would recognize it. His ears had been ready to catch it.

What they had caught instead was a series of sounds that were completely unrecognizable.

George flattened himself against the lumber stack on his left. Slowly, breathing through his mouth to make as little noise as possible, he edged forward. At the end of the stack he stopped and listened. The sounds were louder. George poked his head carefully around the corner of the stack. Nothing.

George scratched his head. This particular alley ran the whole length of the Forest, from the coal-yard fence all the way up to Gerrity's back yard. It was as empty as Forman's grocery on Yom Kippur. But the sounds were all over the place. Where were they coming from?

There was only one way to find out.

George reached for the board over his head and started up the lumber stack. It was like climbing a ladder, except that you had to be careful about splinters. When he got to the top, he crawled out flat on his belly, hugging the top boards. Near the far edge he started to come up on one knee for a better look, and then stopped.

"Jesus," he said aloud and then, more quietly, "Jesus Christ on a raft!"

His first thought was: where did they come from? Then he was too busy trying to count them. A moment later he realized how dumb that was. What difference did it make how many there were? The important thing was to warn Danny.

George edged his way back to the other side of the lumber stack, climbed down, and ran back the way he had come, toward the river. He went over the fence, skinned past the barges, turned into Fourth Street, and headed for Lewis. Halfway to the corner he stopped short. A lot could happen before he got to Danny. Before he got to Danny it might even be too late. Somebody had to keep an eye on what—

George turned, slipped under the gate, and started after Dora. He caught up with her in an alley that ran at right angles to the one along which he'd been working his way up from the river.

"What are you doing here?" she said.

"Pipe down," George said. "Come on."

He started up the nearest lumber stack. It was higher than the one he'd climbed at the other side of the Forest. He didn't bother to look back until he got to the top. Then he reached down and gave Dora a hand. They lay flat on their bellies and worked their way toward the edge. When they reached it, George pointed down.

He heard Dora catch her breath, and then she said the same thing he'd been thinking. "Where did they come from?"

"I don't know," George said. "But I know this: they're after the same thing we're after. I gotta tell Danny. You stay up here and keep an eye on them."

"Okay," Dora said.

She took the end of one of her pigtails in her teeth and started to chew it nervously, but her eyes were shining with excitement.

"Don't do anything until Danny and I come back," George said.

"Don't talk so much," Dora said. "Go get Danny. Quick."

George climbed down, ran back to the Fourth Street gate, slipped under, and hurried up toward Lewis. The drunken soldiers were no longer spitting beer at the Kaiser in front of Mr. Kashkewitz's blacksmith shop. George wasn't surprised. Beer cost money. He ran up Lewis to Fifth, turned down toward the river, stopped at the row of lumber stacks that guarded the back entrance to the Forest, and climbed the nearest one. It was not very high, and there was no time for any more climbing. George drew a deep breath and jumped.

A moment after he hit the sawdust, Danny came running out of the nearest alley. "What the hell's the matter with you?" he hissed. "You trying to screw up everything?"

"Ssssshhh!" George said. He grabbed Danny's sleeve, dragged him into the alley on his left, and started up the side of the tallest stack.

Danny shook his sleeve free. "Listen, schmuck," he said.

"No," George said, grabbing for his sleeve again. "Come on, Danny. I gotta show you something."

Danny hesitated, scowling hard, then followed. At the top he did the same thing Dora had done. Danny caught his breath. "The son of a bitch," he said slowly. "The dirty rotten little son of a bitch."

George turned back to look. It was like watching a movie, except that the screen was on the ground instead of on a wall. At the far end of the alley Old Man Saydl was inching along, dragging his broken body slowly in the sawdust, heading for his hiding place. He thought he was all alone in the Forest. But he wasn't. He was completely surrounded. The soldiers were coming at him in three groups, from three different directions. Some of them were still carrying beer bottles. All of them were hugging the walls of the alleys. They reminded George of Indians sneaking up on a wagon train in one of Miss Corcoran's story books.

Then George recognized the little guy with the muscles leading the middle column. "It's Doodoo!" he said.

"The son of a bitch," Danny said again, and then he shoved himself up from the board on which they were lying. "Okay," Danny said, and for a moment George didn't realize Danny was not talking to him. "Okay, you bastard," Danny said softly. "You asked for it." He started down the stack.

"Where you going?" George said. Danny didn't answer. George said, "Want me to come with you?"

"Stay up there," Danny said. "Keep an eye on them."

His head disappeared below the edge of the stack. George turned back to the soldiers. He was surprised at how quietly they were moving. With all that beer inside them, George would have thought they'd be yelling blue murder. He didn't know how long he'd been watching, when all of a sudden he heard something at the other side of the Forest. George squirmed around on his belly and looked up toward Lewis Street. Something funny seemed to be happening in Gerrity's back yard. A moment later George saw what it was. The shkutzim were piling out of the saloon, running toward the fence that separated Gerrity's from the Forest. George could see Danny in the lead and, behind him, the big, red-headed figure of Mike Gerrity.

George saw them go over the fence and come down the long alley between the lumber stacks, yelling as they came. Just as Doodoo Kashkewitz and the soldiers turned to face them, George saw Danny's father. Mr. Schorr was running with the shkutzim, waving a beer bottle and yelling. He stopped behind Danny and Mike

Gerrity. The shkutzim bunched up in a ball back of them. The soldiers did the same behind Doodoo Kashkewitz.

Looking down on them from the top of the lumber stack, George was reminded of a couple of ant hills he'd once kicked in Tompkins Square Park. There was a lot of crawling and squirming and pushing, but the two groups remained separated by a narrow open space. Danny stepped out of his group, into this open space. The way he did it made George's breath come faster. Danny did it as though he was General Pershing or somebody.

"Okay, Doodoo," Danny said. "Take your friends and get the hell out of here."

Doodoo wet his lips with his tongue. "Who's gonna make us?"

"Me and *my* friends."

Danny jerked his thumb at the shkutzim behind him. Doodoo gave them a quick look. Then he glanced at the soldiers crowding up against him. George had the feeling Doodoo was counting, to see who had more men. From the top of the lumber stack, where George lay on his belly, it wasn't necessary to count. There were almost twice as many shkutzim as soldiers.

"Anybody's getting the hell out of here," a soldier yelled suddenly, "it ain't gonna be us!"

"Come on!" another soldier yelled. "Let's get these bastards!"

They started forward. George, who was watching Doodoo, saw something funny. Doodoo didn't start forward with them. Doodoo seemed to be leaning back, as though he were a dam and the soldiers were a river and he was trying to keep the water from breaking through. For a moment or two George didn't understand what was funny about it. Then he saw Doodoo stagger, as though the dam was beginning to go, and he realized what made it look funny. A split second before he heard Doodoo's voice, just from the look on his face, George knew Doodoo Kashkewitz was scared.

"You rotten bastard!" Doodoo screamed at Danny, the words choking in his throat. "You dirty stinking shkutz lover! Why the hell don't you fight with your own people?"

Mike Gerrity hitched up his pants. "Okay, boys!" he said to the shkutzim across his shoulder. "Let's shovel the garbage out of this lumber yard!"

He moved forward. Danny moved with him. So did Danny's father. George saw it clearly because George was watching Danny. That's why George didn't see the drunken soldiers who came up with the plank and shoved it into the side of the lumber stack behind the shkutzim.

George didn't know anything about it until the stack began to rock and he heard Dora scream. Then he remembered that he'd left her as a lookout at the other side of the Forest, on top of a lumber stack. Quickly George pushed himself back to the edge of his own stack and started down. But it was too late. A great many people were suddenly screaming. But it was only Dora's voice George heard.

"*Help me, George!*" she screamed as the stack started to go. "*George, help me!*" she screamed. "*Help me!*"

7

"Go ahead!" Uncle Zisha said. "Don't be bashful! Smell the air! Breathe it in! Up here in Albany it's not like in New York! Up here for fresh air there's no charge!"

He sucked in a deep, noisy breath. George tried to do the same. It wasn't easy. Uncle Zisha was moving across the railroad station like a greyhound in the newsreels. His long, loping strides pulled him forward so fast that George had to trot to keep up with him.

"In New York, on that verkockte Fourth Street," Uncle Zisha said, "it smells like this?"

George didn't know whether Uncle Zisha expected an answer. The big man in the long overcoat was steaming toward the street doors as though he were trying to win a race.

"I asked a question!" His voice reminded George of the barge horns on the river back home when the fog closed in from Brooklyn. "Air like this you ever smelled?"

George, who had just stepped out of the train from New York, made another stab at sampling the air. The only other railroad station he'd ever been in was Grand Central. The air in this station smelled just about the same.

"No," George said.

"No what?" Uncle Zisha said.

"I never smelled air like this," George said.

The big man paused in his gallop toward the street. He turned to look down at the boy beside him. The large, broad, handsome face broke in a sudden, unexpected smile. Uncle Zisha put out his hand. He touched George's shoulder. It was like receiving without warning the weight of one of Mr. Forman's butter tubs. George staggered.

"You bet your life!" Uncle Zisha said. "This is America you're smelling!" He kicked open the door to the street. He held it wide with George's suitcase and gestured with his free hand. He looked like Balboa discovering the Pacific in the picture over Miss Corcoran's desk. "Go on!" Uncle Zisha cried. "Take a look! For the first time in your life you're seeing a piece of America! Take a good look!"

George took a good look. He saw a row of yellow taxis and a long black Buick touring car parked in front of a diner, a grocery store, an ice-cream parlor, and a shoe-shine stand. He had a feeling of disappointment. If the taxis and the Buick had been parked in front of Mr. Kashkewitz's blacksmith shop on East Fourth Street, the scene would have been the same. Uncle Zisha's letters, from which Aunt Tessie had been reading aloud for years, had led George to expect something more of Albany.

"Here you'll begin to understand why people come to this country from garbage pails like Austria! Here you'll begin to live! Come on!"

Uncle Zisha grabbed George's hand. He dragged him across the street. They stopped in front of the Buick. Uncle Zisha tossed George's suitcase into the back.

George blinked. "It's yours?" he said.

He knew from what Aunt Tessie had told him that Uncle Zisha was rich. It had never occurred to him, however, that Aunt Tessie's brother owned a car. Nobody on Fourth Street owned a car. Not even Mike Gerrity, who was the richest man on the block.

"If it wasn't mine, would I put your satchel in it?" George could see that Uncle Zisha was getting a kick out of George's surprise. The big man opened the door. "Jump in. There's no charge. You're now with Zisha Hurst. Everything is going to be all right."

George gave him a quick look. It had not occurred to him until this moment that Aunt Tessie must have told Uncle Zisha in one of her letters all about what had happened in the Forest on Armistice Day. But George couldn't read anything in the big man's face. Uncle Zisha was walking around the front of the car. He

opened the door on the far side and climbed in behind the wheel.
George opened the other door and slipped in beside him.

"You like this car?" Uncle Zisha said.

It started with a roar and a jerk, as though it had been kicked
from the curb by a giant foot. George's head snapped back against
the black leather seat. He managed to nod.

Uncle Zisha chuckled. "It's the biggest model. They had it
standing there in the window on Pearl Street. I was walking to the
bank and I stopped to take a look, and the minute I saw it I said
to myself this they made for Zisha Hurst, special! So I went in and
I bought it. You ever had a ride in a car like this before?"

"I've never been in a car before," George said.

Uncle Zisha clapped his hand to his forehead as though he was
trying to kill a fly. "What kind of a head have I got, a thing like
this I shouldn't know? Where on that verkockte Fourth Street would
a person get rides in cars?" He laughed. "So today it's for you a whole
bunch first things! First time in Albany! First time to meet Zisha
Hurst! And first time in a car!" He laughed again. "Wait, wait!
There's more yet, too! Wait till you see the house! Wait till you
see the factory! Wait till you see Mrs. Gerstenberger!"

He drove the way Art Acord rode his horse in *The Oregon
Trail*, the weekly movie serial George and Danny Schorr and Dora
Dienst had followed for almost a year at the American Theatre on
Third Street. Uncle Zisha sent the car forward in a roaring burst
of speed that carried them anywhere from ten feet to half a block.
Then, as somebody stepped down from the curb or another car
appeared up ahead, he slammed on the brakes. The car, like Art
Acord's horse when suddenly reined in, seemed to rear up on its
hind legs and come to a shuddering halt. The pedestrian or other
driver screamed and yelled. Uncle Zisha roared with laughter as he
poked and kicked at the controls of the stalled car to get it started
again. When he wasn't laughing, he was pouring out in his loud,
booming voice a running commentary in which the modest, neat
little frame houses along the tree-shaded streets through which they
were driving were described in terms so glowing that they would
have been a trifle excessive if they had been applied to the Taj
Mahal.

George heard very little of it. A few minutes after they pulled
away from the railroad station the palms of his hands had suddenly
begun to sweat and the terrible, familiar sick feeling came bubbling

up in his stomach. Without warning, the way it had been happening over and over again for weeks, he found himself back in the Forest, remembering Dora on top of the lumber stack where he had left her, watching with horror as the stack began to go, seeing Mr. Schorr's drunken face peering up at him from among the drunken soldiers who had followed Doodoo Kashkewitz into the Forest, and hearing Dora's terrified screams for help.

George knew he was swallowing hard and fast, because he had discovered this was the only way he could keep the sick feeling from bubbling over. But George did not know he had closed his eyes tight until somebody tapped him on the shoulder and, with a jump, he opened them.

For a moment, for a split second of agonized embarrassment, he thought he saw Uncle Zisha watching him with a troubled frown. Then the moment was gone. It was possible that it had never even existed. Because Uncle Zisha's big, handsome face was once again broken up into the small, crinkly pieces of his shining smile as he gestured toward the house in front of which he had stopped the car.

"This is where Zisha Hurst lives," he said proudly. "A little bit different from two egg boxes in back of a store on Fourth Street, no?"

George had never seen a house like this, except in the movies and in newspaper and magazine pictures. Unlike the huge gray tenements made of brick on East Fourth Street, this house was made of wood. It was very white, so white that it hurt your eyes a little to look at it in the bright sunlight, and it had green shutters with small crescents cut into the tops and bottoms. The street was steep, and there were houses on both sides. The houses were separated from one another by trees and gardens. Uncle Zisha's house seemed more separated than any of the others because Uncle Zisha's house sat on the very top of the hill. It wasn't much bigger than some of the other houses, but it seemed to tower over them the way Uncle Zisha had towered over everybody in the railroad station. There was a driveway at one side that led to Uncle Zisha's factory behind the house. The driveway was spanned by a curved wooden arch across which was printed in large black and gold letters: "Hurst Soda Bottling Works, Inc."

"We better go in," Uncle Zisha said. "Mrs. Gerstenberger is looking out at us from behind the curtain. If we keep her waiting another minute, she could maybe bust, and when Mrs. Gerstenberger busts, believe me, it'll make a splash you could hear all the way down in New York."

She was a short, round, timid German woman with a face like a basketball on which somebody had stuck a gray wig and painted small, inadequate features. It was impossible to tell whether nature, or her years as Uncle Zisha's housekeeper, had twisted those features into the troubled look that was as permanent a part of Mrs. Gerstenberger as her spotless blue and white checked apron. It was the look of a woman who, while trying hard to concentrate on what was happening in her immediate presence, could not help listening nervously for the sound of something about to fall in another part of the house.

"This is my nephew George," Uncle Zisha said when she opened the door for them. "My sister Tessie said we should take good care of him."

Mrs. Gerstenberger beamed shyly at George and touched his head with one of her round, red, pudgy hands. She did it hesitantly, as though he were a piece of china that she wanted to make sure was in its proper place on a shelf but which she was afraid might crack under her clumsy touch.

"Ve'll try," she said in a thin, squeaky voice that seemed hopelessly inadequate for supporting so heavy a German accent. "Ve'll to our pest vid heem."

The process started almost at once, with the midday meal. It was served in a dining room as large as Aunt Tessie's shop. On two of the walls hung large, beautifully framed pictures of a handsome, dignified man with white hair and eyes so sad that they brought a lump to George's throat. Both pictures were identical. The door from the living room was propped open by a small yellow canvas sack about the size of a watermelon. It was lumpy and shapeless, as though filled with potatoes, and fastened at the top with a drawstring as thick as a clothesline. George and Uncle Zisha sat at opposite ends of a table that could have been brought into the room in which he slept on Fourth Street only by taking the table apart in the street, carrying it through the store, piece by piece, and then reassembling it indoors. Every inch of it, he soon saw, was necessary to accommodate Mrs. Gerstenberger's notion of a decent meal.

"Eat, eat!" she squeaked in a pleading whisper as she stared worriedly at the bowl of soup he had been unable to touch and pushed the platter of rye bread closer to him. "Your uncle set if py the time you ko home to New Yuk you're not ten pounts heffier, he'll trow me out in the stritt!"

George forced himself to take a mouthful of soup and wondered why she was whispering. Then he glanced at Uncle Zisha, and George saw that eating was a serious business in this green and white house on Westerlo Street. The big man at the other end of the table ate in silence, leaning low over his plate, breathing heavily as he stoked himself with short, economical thrusts of his loaded fork or spoon. Uncle Zisha at table reminded George of shkutzim he had seen on the Fourth Street dock, shoveling coal by hand from the moored barges into the waiting wagons on days when the loading crane was out of order.

Please, God, please don't let me get sick right here at the table, George prayed deep down inside his head, behind the place from which he forced himself to watch Uncle Zisha work his way through two bowls of thick bean soup, a slab of roast veal with potato pancakes, red cabbage, and green peas, a platter of rye bread, a lump of rice pudding as big as a grapefruit, half an apple pie, and a plate of stewed prunes and apricots. Occasionally, when his mouth was too full to accommodate more, or while he waited for Mrs. Gerstenberger to refill his plate, Uncle Zisha would wink at George or make an encouraging gesture with his fork, urging George to dig in more heartily. Not a word was spoken, however, until Uncle Zisha had finished his third cup of black coffee.

"Judge Brandeis," he said, nodding toward the beautifully framed pictures on the walls. "The greatest American in the whole world since Abraham Lincoln."

He waited, as though he expected George to say something, but George couldn't think what. A puzzled look appeared on Uncle Zisha's face.

"Judge Brandeis," he said again, and he waited once more. The puzzled look changed to disbelief. "George," Uncle Zisha said. "You never heard of Judge Brandeis?"

"No."

For a moment, the only moment since George had first set eyes on the big, handsome, friendly face, it reflected anger.

"That verkockte Fourth Street!" Uncle Zisha said bitterly. "That —that—!"

The bitterness and the anger went as quickly as they had come.

"So all right," Uncle Zisha said as he pushed himself back from the table and then up out of his chair, doing it in two series of slow, deliberate movements executed with all the care and precision of a tug warping a liner into her mooring. "So all right," Uncle Zisha said with a smile when he finally stood erect. "That's another first thing for you here in Albany! To know there is such a person like Judge Brandeis!"

With a slight wave of his hand, as though he were departing for a short journey on which he would not be gone long enough to justify a more elaborate or even spoken farewell, the big man moved heavily across the dining room, through the door propped open by the yellow canvas sack, and disappeared into the living room. George, after hesitating for a moment, stood up and started to follow.

Mrs. Gerstenberger caught him at the door. "No, no!" she squeaked in a terrified hiss. "It's the lunch!"

Astonished, George stepped aside. Mrs. Gerstenberger hurried into the living room. From the doorway George watched Uncle Zisha lower his great big body, now distended by the huge meal, onto a brown leather couch with a headrest at one end. He undid his belt and the top button of his pants, sighed contentedly, and sent a single, admiring glance up at the picture of Judge Brandeis that hung over the couch. It was another copy of the two pictures in the dining room. Then Uncle Zisha closed his eyes. Mrs. Gerstenberger came up swiftly with a large red silk handkerchief, spread it over Uncle Zisha's face, tiptoed to the window, drew down the shade, and then, with a finger to her lips, she came back to George in the doorway.

"Effry tay," she said as she led George away from the living room, "efter he eats, for one hour it's the lunch."

Years later George realized why Uncle Zisha's siesta was called the lunch. It was Mrs. Gerstenberger's way of pronouncing the word by which she and Uncle Zisha identified the piece of brown leather furniture on which he took his midday rest: a lounge.

On that first day in the house on Westerlo Street, however, as Mrs. Gerstenberger took him upstairs to show him his room, George realized only that his palms were beginning to sweat again, and the sick, bubbly feeling had started to churn once more in his stomach.

"You petter take a lunch, too," Mrs. Gerstenberger said when they came into the sunny little room on the second floor where George's suitcase lay on a chair near the bed. "Your uncle, ven he vakes op, he's like a steam injin! A person could vear out chust from votching heem!"

George didn't answer. He couldn't. "If she doesn't get out," he thought desperately, "I'll puke right here, in front of her." The thought of this humiliation made the bubbly feeling in his stomach get worse. "Please, God, no," he prayed. "Please, God, don't let me puke. Please, God, get her the hell out of here fast."

"Ve'll unpack the tinks fum the setchel later," Mrs. Gerstenberger said. "Fum New Yuk it's a lunk trip. A little lunch you could use, no?"

George nodded. He didn't trust himself to speak. "Go!" he screamed inside his head. "Go!" And then, somewhat incredibly, she was gone. George stood there, staring at the closed door, listening to her tiptoeing heavily down the hall toward the stairs, trying not to relive again the horror of those moments when the lumber stack started to go and Dora began to scream—and then he stopped trying. It didn't do any good. It hadn't done any good for weeks. He stepped quickly to the basin in the corner of the room and was sick.

George remained there for a long time, resting his forehead against the cool white enamel of the basin, wondering stupidly how long it would be before he could forget. He guessed he never would. Aunt Tessie disagreed. Aunt Tessie thought all he needed was a change of scene. That was why she had gone to Miss Corcoran and asked if she could take George out of school for a couple of weeks. Miss Corcoran thought it was a good idea. She and Aunt Tessie had felt that all George needed to forget what had happened on Armistice Day was to get away from Fourth Street for a while. But George knew better. George knew what Aunt Tessie may have suspected but couldn't really know. George knew about the nightmares, and the times during the day when the nightmares closed in on him in broad daylight. George could see the twisted, broken body of Danny's father, and he could hear Dora whimpering, and he could feel the weight of the board that had killed Mr. Schorr and smashed Dora's arm and fallen across George's legs but, by some miracle, had done no more than bruise his ankles.

Leaning on the basin in this strange house on Westerlo Street, George wished he was back on Fourth Street. At least there, when the nightmare struck, he could give in to the horror. On Fourth Street he didn't have to worry about being caught vomiting by two

strange people like Uncle Zisha and Mrs. Gerstenberger. All at once
he was so sorry he had come to Albany that he started to cry. He
cried with his mouth open, so the sobs would make less noise, and
his forehead bounced up and down on the cool enamel. He cried
because he was afraid and he was lonely and he didn't understand
this strange brother of Aunt Tessie's who talked so loud and ate
so much and laughed so hard. After a while the sobs stopped.
George straightened up and, by running the hot and cold water for
a few minutes, he managed to clean up the basin. He was brushing
his teeth when a sound outside brought him to the window.

His room looked down on a large, square, paved yard into which
the driveway that ran along the side of the house opened. The far
side of the yard ended against a loading platform at one end of a
long two-story gray building that was obviously Uncle Zisha's factory. A large truck was backed up to the loading platform. What
had brought George to the window was the noise two men in leather
aprons were making as they stacked the truck with cases of bottled
soda that came pouring slowly out of the factory on a narrow metal
treadmill.

George watched the men for a while, and then realized all at
once that his stomach was all right. He turned back to the room.
He saw for the first time that, over the bed, there was a picture of
Judge Brandeis. It was less formal than the pictures in the dining
room and the living room downstairs. This picture had been cut
from a newspaper. It showed Judge Brandeis on the platform of
a railroad station, smiling at several people who had come either
to greet him or to to say farewell. George wondered what it was with
Uncle Zisha and this Judge Brandeis. He was surprised that Aunt
Tessie had not mentioned it.

"George!"

He jumped nervously, then went to the door and opened it.
"Yes?"

"Come on!" Uncle Zisha shouted. "It's time to take a look at
the factory!"

The heart of it was a row of machines into which men in rubber
aprons at one end fed long rows of empty, freshly washed bottles.
They came out at the other end, full of different-colored liquids.
Other men slapped labels on the bottles as they went by, and still
others shoved the bottles into wooden cases. These were dumped
on the metal treadmill that carried them out to the loading plat-

form, where they went either directly into waiting trucks, like the one George had seen from his bedroom window, or into storage sheds at the other side of the paved yard.

All of it was interesting, especially the machines that filled the bottles, but what George found most interesting was Uncle Zisha. He moved about among the machines and the men who tended them the way he had moved across the railroad station with George's suitcase: in long, loping, sure-footed strides, bellowing orders above the roar of the machines, never pausing for a backward look to see if his orders were being carried out, a towering, self-confident figure that seemed, somehow, to dwarf even the huge machines.

"So all right," Uncle Zisha said, stopping suddenly and turning on George. "Which part do you like best?"

"I don't know," George said. "It's all so—so—"

Uncle Zisha laughed. "Come on," he said. "I'll show you the part Zisha Hurst likes best."

He led George around the machines to the office at one side. The bookkeeper, an old man with a green eye shade, was clearing a wooden table near his desk. Through the open door George saw that the yard was suddenly full of trucks. The drivers were coming into the office, chatting, lighting cigarettes, and calling greetings to the bookkeeper and Uncle Zisha as they formed a crude line in front of the table. When the bookkeeper was ready, the first driver handed over a batch of slips. The bookkeeper added them up on a machine at his elbow. Then, after the bookkeeper called out a total, the driver pulled a roll of money from his pocket and began counting it out on the table. When the sum agreed with the bookkeeper's total, he shoved the money across the table toward Uncle Zisha, who sorted it out according to denomination.

"The collections," he said to George with a grin. "This is the part Zisha Hurst likes best."

He laughed. The bookkeeper and the drivers laughed with him. By the time the last man had turned in his collections, some of the piles of money in front of Uncle Zisha were as high as Miss Corcoran's dictionary.

"On Fourth Street," Uncle Zisha said as he strapped rubber bands around the bundles of bills, "you ever saw money like this?"

He laughed again as he shoved the bundles of money into a canvas bag, poured in all the coins except the pennies, and locked the bag away in a wall safe. The pennies were swept into a paper

bag which Uncle Zisha handed to George. "You carry it," he said.
"It feels good to carry money. Such a feeling every person should
learn."

Out in the yard, where all the trucks were now parked for the
night, Uncle Zisha stopped in front of a pile of cases full of empty
bottles. He looked through them quickly, found one he wanted, and
pulled it out.

"You see this?" he said, holding the bottle toward George.
"See what it says on the side? Not Hurst Bottling Works. It says
Star Bottling Works. This Star, soda he makes it taste like ink,
but there's all kinds dopes in the world, and some of them like
to drink ink, so Star sells a few bottles here in Albany, too. Me, I
give my customers the bottles for nothing. They want to give them
back? All right, thank you, Zisha Hurst takes them, and I fill them
up again. They don't want to give them back? All right again, keep
them, it's a present from Zisha Hurst, you're welcome. But this Star,
he shivers so hard he should get his bottles back, his customers they
have to give him a deposit, a nickel on every bottle, and when they
give back the bottle, he gives them back the nickel. Some of those
nickel bottles, they come back to me by mistake, like this one."
Uncle Zisha held it up for George to see again, then dropped
it into the case.

"You like the way that money feels in your hand?" He tapped
the paper bag full of pennies. George nodded. He had never held
so much money at one time. There must have been six or seven
hundred pennies in the bag. "So all right," Uncle Zisha said. "Remember what I just told you about these Star bottles, and tomorrow
I'll show you how you can start getting rich yourself, just like Zisha
Hurst!" He laughed and put his hand around George's shoulders.
"But first let's go see what Mrs. Gerstenberger has for us to eat."

This proved to be a roast turkey with dumplings. Before they
sat down to it, however, Uncle Zisha opened the drawstring of the
yellow canvas sack that served as a door stop in the dining room.
The sack was full of pennies.

"Go ahead," Uncle Zisha said, and he laughed when he saw
the expression on George's face. He tapped the paper sack George
had carried across from the factory. "Dump them in!"

After dinner, which like the midday meal was eaten in complete silence, Mrs. Gerstenberger cleared the table and removed
the cloth. Uncle Zisha hoisted the yellow canvas sack up onto the

table, opened the drawstring, and poured. The pennies came spilling out on the polished mahogany like a flood of dirty honey. From a drawer in the sideboard Uncle Zisha brought a stack of small pink bank wrappers.

"What you do at night on Fourth Street, I don't know," Uncle Zisha said with a grin. "But up here in America, we count money! You sit over there, I'll sit here, and you do like I do."

Deftly, using his long, thick fingers as a rake, he showed George how to slide five pennies at a time out of the spilled mass of coins. When he had fifty bunched together in a small pile, Uncle Zisha stacked them in a tiny column, took the column between thumb and forefinger, placed it on its side on one of the pink wrappers, and rolled the paper neatly around the coins. He crimped the wrapper at both ends to seal the tube, tapped the ends sharply on the table to make the creases hold, set the fifty-cent roll of pennies aside, and started on another.

After a few minutes, during which he spilled several stacks while trying to place them on their sides, George got the hang of it. Soon he was working almost as quickly as Uncle Zisha. When she finished the dishes, Mrs. Gerstenberger came in and joined them. She did it without a word, placing her chair carefully several feet down the long table from the place where George and Uncle Zisha sat facing each other. It was as though either she or Uncle Zisha, or perhaps both of them, did not want the relationship of employer and employee to be blurred even in this group activity. The separation had no effect, however, on the warm team feeling that filled the room. They were working, George felt, in a common cause. He had not felt so good for a long time. He was so absorbed by the work that he did not notice when Uncle Zisha started to talk. After he did notice, several minutes went by before George realized Uncle Zisha was telling about his early days in America.

"Tessie came over first because she was older," the big man said. "When she got off the ship there on Ellis Island, where does she go, where? To Fourth Street. And why? Because on Fourth Street there was living a lot of other Austrians. She didn't know them. In Austria she never met them. The names she never even heard before, not once. But because they're Austrians, and because they live on Fourth Street, so my sister Tessie, she, too, she has to go live on Fourth Street! If God forbid Tessie she came from Poland, so now she'd be living on that *verkockte Ninth* Street there in New York, because Polacks the minute they got off the ship, right away they go where other Polacks go. Or if worse yet Tessie she came God forbid from Russia, now she'd be living on Seventh Street, because Russians they're like sheep, too. The minute they get off the ship, quick, like a wild animal was chasing them, they run to the same place where other Russians are living!"

Uncle Zisha tapped down the creases of a tube of pennies and placed it on the growing pile in the middle of the table.

"But me, no!" he said firmly. "Like a sheep, to go where other sheep go, just because it's easy? Not Zisha Hurst!" His powerful fingers began to rake out the pennies for a new stack. "The fourth year she's here in America, when Tessie sends me the money I should come, Zisha Hurst is ready to go, believe me! Four years the army took already out of my life, and to go again another four years to clean up after horses and eat brown bread with onions for Franz Josef, this is a bargain? No, thank you! Not for Zisha Hurst! I took the money Tessie sent me, and I bought a ticket, and to Franz Josef and to Austria it's good-bye Charlie! Zisha Hurst is going to America!"

He paused, and he looked up at the picture of Judge Brandeis on the wall, and his large face broke into the small crinkly pieces of his extraordinary smile.

"Tessie was waiting for me," Uncle Zisha said. "A greenhorn, a baby, not yet twenty-one years old, I get off from the ship in America, and there's my older sister, my Tessie, she's waiting!" He shook his head slowly. "To have somebody waiting, when you get off from a ship or a train, in the whole world there's only a few things like that, and those few things I'm not sure they're nicer!"

He paused again. George wondered guiltily if Uncle Zisha was drawing a parallel between his arrival in America all those years ago and George's arrival in Albany that morning.

"My sister Tessie, from the ship, she brings Zisha Hurst home," Uncle Zisha said. "I take one look at what my sister Tessie she calls home, and right away I think here in America Tessie she's become a joker. This is a home? Two holes in the wall? In back, there, by a store where she presses pants? On a street with ash cans standing on the sidewalk? With garbage pails right there under your nose instead of fresh air? With houses made of stone they stretch up into the sky like a ladder? With people living on top of each other in little holes like shirts in bureau drawers? With a street that it ends in a dock, there, with lumber and coal wagons? This is a home, Zisha Hurst says to his sister Tessie? This is my home, she says. Stop with the jokes, Zisha Hurst says. Show me where you live, he says. You're looking at it, Tessie says. Zisha Hurst takes another look at that Fourth Street outside, and he says no!"

Uncle Zisha slapped his hand down on the table, hard. The pool of pennies shivered and spread wider across the polished mahogany.

"Not for Zisha Hurst!" he said. "To live on that verkockte Fourth Street, for this Zisha Hurst didn't eat herring and black bread twenty-eight days in the bottom of a ship! For this Zisha Hurst didn't leave Austria! From America Zisha Hurst expected something better!"

He paused once more, and his booming voice dropped to a low roar as he chuckled.

"And from America Zisha Hurst *got* something better! Tessie said I was crazy. She said I'd get killed. She said I was a greenhorn, I couldn't speak yet a word English, I wouldn't know what to ask or where to go or how to do! She was right! A greenhorn I was! A word English I couldn't speak! What to ask or where to go or how to do, I didn't know! But I was in America! That's all Zisha Hurst had to know!"

He laughed happily and, for a while, Uncle Zisha stared across George's head at the picture of Judge Brandeis on the wall. George could tell that the big man at the other side of the table was no longer there. Uncle Zisha had returned to a glowing moment in the past.

"I walked away from Fourth Street," he said finally. "On my own two feet, the greenhorn feet he brought from Austria, Zisha Hurst walked away from Fourth Street! By the time I stopped walking, two months later, I knew one thing for sure: a mistake I didn't make! From New York here to Albany this morning in a train you came in a few hours. Thirty-five years ago the same trip it took Zisha Hurst two months. But what a two months! Every day, pure gold! Every person he met, a doll! Every piece bread he ate, sponge cake! Every place he slept, a palace! Every job he took, a pleasure! This was America! This was what Zisha Hurst came to see and get!"

Uncle Zisha laughed as he swept his large hand out in a gesture that took in the room, the house, the factory outside, the mound of pennies on the table.

"And he got it!" he said. "Zisha Hurst got what he came for." He laughed again. "It didn't come in a minute. Even in America the only things that they come to you in a minute, it's better they should stay away! Zisha Hurst had to work, and he worked hard, and there was nights, believe me, plenty of them, when he wondered sometimes where the next day he'd get his breakfast. But one thing he never had to wonder, because this is America, one thing Zisha Hurst never had to wonder was *if* he'd get breakfast! From the day he came to America, Zisha Hurst always ate good!"

He was eating again when George came downstairs the next morning. Not until Mrs. Gerstenberger had set a large bowl of oatmeal in front of him did George realize that, for the first time since Armistice Day, he had slept soundly through a whole night, without waking up out of the familiar nightmare wet with sweat.

George sat quite still, waiting tensely for the terror to come creeping back, but it didn't. After several moments, very cautiously, he picked up his spoon. He took a tentative mouthful of oatmeal, and had a moment of astonishment. It tasted good! He took another mouthful. It tasted even better. George dipped hungrily over the bowl. When he looked up again, he saw both Uncle Zisha and Mrs. Gerstenberger watching him with pleased smiles.

"Those ten pounds," Uncle Zisha said to his housekeeper. "It looks like maybe to stick them on him we won't have so much trouble!"

Mrs. Gerstenberger giggled shyly and brought George another bowl of oatmeal.

After breakfast he drove to the bank with Uncle Zisha to make the deposit that had been locked away in the safe the night before. Then they returned to the factory yard, where Uncle Zisha proved he had not been joking when he'd said the night before that he would show George how to get rich out of Star bottles.

Every morning after that, when they came back from the bank and Uncle Zisha disappeared into the factory to spend the morning bellowing orders, George tackled the cases of empties that the drivers had unloaded and stacked in the storage shed the night before.

He combed through the cases carefully, hunting for Star bottles that had been returned by mistake to the Hurst factory. Every morning he found anywhere from five or six to a couple of dozen. If there were too many to carry, George loaded them into a small handcart Uncle Zisha had said he could use, and trundled them out of the yard and down Westerlo Street to Dougherty's Ice Cream Parlor at the foot of the hill.

Even though Dougherty's was so close to the Hurst Soda Bottling Works, Mrs. Dougherty bought her soda pop from Star, which used only deposit bottles. By pretending, as Uncle Zisha had instructed him, to be a customer who was returning empty bottles on which he had paid a deposit, George was able to get from Mrs. Dougherty a nickel each for the empties he combed out of the cases in the factory yard. At the end of his first week in Albany, when George had accumulated almost five dollars, Mrs. Dougherty became difficult.

"Twelve bottles," she said, staring suspiciously at the row of bottles George had placed on the marble counter. "All cream soda. I don't remember nobody buying no twelve bottles of cream soda."

Uncle Zisha had prepared George for this contingency.

"They're not all from my house," he said. "Our neighbors said as long as I was going down to Dougherty's, they asked I should take down their empties, too."

"What neighbors?"

"Mrs. Cushing and Mrs. Teilheit."

Uncle Zisha's briefing had been thorough.

"Where do you live, boy?"

George jerked his thumb across his shoulder, trying for the touch of casual authority he found so impressive in Uncle Zisha. "South Pearl Street."

"South Pearl, and you come all the way over here to Westerlo for cream soda?" Mrs. Dougherty said. "What's the matter with Grainger's?"

"Grainger's? They sell only that lousy Hurst soda," George said with a straight face. "Up at our house, we like Star. Mrs. Cushing and Mrs. Teilheit, too."

"Well," Mrs. Dougherty said, "all right, but now look. I can't keep taking all these empties. I'm not saying they didn't come from here. All I'm saying, I'll tell you what." She gave him a sharp glance. George, who knew he was tall for his age, knew also that Mrs. Dougherty was trying to figure how smart or stupid he was. "I'll give you half in cash, and half in trade." She nodded toward the row of bottles on the counter. "Twelve bottles, a nickel apiece, that's sixty cents. I'll give you thirty cents in cash, and the rest you take in trade. How about it?"

It was George's first contact with the theory about half a loaf. "Okay," he said.

He took the three dimes and hesitated for some time over the candy racks before he chose three ten-cent Oh Henrys. He ate one on the way back up the hill. The ten-cent Oh Henry in those days was as big as a small salami. By the time George reached the house, the other two did not feel very attractive in his pocket. In fact, George felt like throwing them away. He would have done just that if Mrs. Gerstenberger had not opened the front door at that moment to shake out her dust mop. George went upstairs, added the three dimes to his other savings in the Prince Albert tobacco tin that served as his safe, and put the two Oh Henrys in his bureau drawer.

By the end of his second week in Albany, when the time came for him to leave, George had piled up $7.95 in the tobacco tin and thirty-seven Oh Henrys in his bureau drawer. He packed them all carefully under his jumpers in the bottom of his suitcase.

The box lunch Mrs. Gerstenberger packed for him to eat on the train weighed almost as much as the suitcase. At the front door, which Mrs. Gerstenberger was holding open so George could follow Uncle Zisha out to the Buick, the housekeeper reached out and did that funny thing she had done on the day George arrived in Albany. She brushed the top of his head with her round, red, pudgy hand, doing it hesitantly, as though, knowing her clumsy movements might shatter something priceless and fragile, she nevertheless could not resist touching it. George ducked, and then stopped short. Great big tears were rolling down the fat German woman's cheeks.

Staring at her in astonishment, George suddenly felt the way he did when Miss Corcoran called on him in class for an answer to a problem he had not realized, until he got up on his feet, he did not understand. In his mind he was suddenly clawing desperately back through all the facts, hoping by rearranging them to find the answer he had missed in his first attempt.

All at once he could see himself as he had been two weeks ago, an awkward visitor from another world, living with a terror that woke him in the night and closed down on him without warning during the day, completely absorbed by the problem of preventing these strangers into whose hands Aunt Tessie had committed him from learning his humiliating secret.

For two weeks he had spent his days going to the bank with Uncle Zisha, combing the empties in the factory yard for Star bottles, accumulating a small fortune in coins and a hoard of Oh Henrys, watching Uncle Zisha eat his enormous meals, listening to him praise the still unidentified Judge Brandeis, helping him count pennies out of the yellow canvas sack that propped open the dining-room door and roll them into tubes of fifty.

Somewhere in the background of that busy time the shy, red-faced German woman had moved on her large but surprisingly quiet feet, bringing in food, making beds, helping to roll pennies, washing clothes. George had accepted her as he had accepted Uncle Zisha's furniture, something to be used while he was a guest in Uncle Zisha's world. But George had never given her a thought, except when he wanted something, and he had never spoken to her, except to ask for what he wanted. He had always thanked her, because Aunt Tessie had taught him to be polite, but it had been an empty cere-mony, like brushing your teeth, something you did automatically, without thought. It had never occurred to George that he had meant any more to Mrs. Gerstenberger than she had meant to him, that he was anything more to her than another piece of furniture, as it were, that it was part of her job to dust and keep tidy.

If she had not been standing in the doorway right now, he would have left the house without saying good-bye to her. But she *was* standing in the doorway, and she *wasn't* acting like a piece of furni-ture. She was crying her eyes out, making no effort to keep her round, shapeless body from shaking with sobs, and all at once there was a strange feeling in George's chest. He didn't like it, because it was painful, and he didn't understand it. He stared at Mrs. Gersten-berger helplessly, swallowing hard, and she stared back at him through her tears.

"Hey, George!"

He turned. It was Uncle Zisha, calling from the Buick.

"I'm coming!"

He turned back to Mrs. Gerstenberger and, with a quick, awk-ward, hesitant gesture, not unlike the way she had patted the top of his head, George touched her hand, turned again, and ran out of the house.

For several minutes after the car jerked away from the front of the house, Uncle Zisha was silent. Then, soon after he turned into Pearl Street, he uttered a loud grunt. "Say!" he said. "Take a look!"

George looked. Uncle Zisha was pulling the car up to the curb in front of a store with a long plate-glass window in which a beautiful red car was on display.

"Come on," Uncle Zisha said, getting out of the Buick. George followed him into the store. A salesman came out of the back, his eyebrows arched inquiringly. Uncle Zisha pointed to the car in the window. "It's for sale?"

The salesman's eyebrows came down. "Why, yes," he said. "Certainly."

"How much?" Uncle Zisha said.

The salesman pulled a piece of paper from his pocket, consulted it, and then mentioned a figure. Uncle Zisha unbuttoned his long black overcoat and dug down into his pocket. He pulled out the canvas sack into which the deposit had been stuffed the night before, opened it, and started counting out twenty-dollar bills.

"Just a moment, sir," the salesman said in a startled voice. "Wouldn't it be simpler if—?"

"Who has a moment?" Uncle Zisha said. "And who needs it simpler? This is my nephew George. He's going home to New York. I don't want he should forget that for the first time in his life he's been in America. I want him to remember that there's more in America than that verkockte Fourth Street. I don't want he should bury himself in a hole just because my sister Tessie thinks that's a way to live. I want him to grow up understanding America is a big place, and a piece of it belongs to anybody who wants to take it. I want him to be something I never got a chance to be because I came to America too late. I want him to be like Judge Brandeis. All these things I want him to remember. If I drive him to the station in a car like this one in the window, maybe he'll remember better."

George felt the way the salesman looked. He couldn't decide whether Uncle Zisha was serious or joking.

"You mean, sir," the salesman said nervously, "you'd like to drive this car to the station right now?"

"What else?" Uncle Zisha said as he continued to count out bills from the canvas bag. "My nephew George has a train to catch."

"But sir," the salesman said. "We'll have to unhinge our front door, and there's no gas in the car, and—"

Uncle Zisha stopped counting out money. "A question, please," he said. "This car, here. You want to sell it?"

"Of course, sir. But—"

"So start with the door unhinging," Uncle Zisha said as he resumed peeling off twenty-dollar bills. "And go get some gas."

A half hour later, he and George were rolling down Pearl Street in the bright red car. George was confused. He sensed that a good deal of what Uncle Zisha had said to the salesman had actually been directed at him. But George didn't understand most of it. The part about Judge Brandeis was particularly baffling. Aside from the fact that Uncle Zisha had made it clear over and over again during the past two weeks that Judge Brandeis was his hero, George still did not know who the judge was. This was the first time he'd heard that Uncle Zisha had wanted to be like the judge, or that he wanted George to be like him. Most confusing of all was the fact that, having made all these baffling remarks to the salesman, Uncle Zisha had not added a word of clarification to George after they left the salesroom.

In fact, Uncle Zisha did not speak until they reached the station, and he had parked the car, and he had carried George's bag into the waiting train. After the suitcase was safely tucked away in the rack overhead, and the box lunch and George's cap were on the seat Uncle Zisha had chosen for him, the big man led George out to the platform.

"There's yet a few minutes to wait," Uncle Zisha said. "It's better to wait out here in the fresh clean air. The dirty air from Fourth Street you'll be breathing soon enough."

George would have preferred to wait in the train. He was afraid somebody would take his seat.

"These whole two weeks you were here," Uncle Zisha said. "It's funny you didn't get a letter from your friend, this Danny Schorr?"

For a moment George wasn't sure he had heard correctly. Then he saw the look on Uncle Zisha's face and George realized not only that he had heard correctly, but also how far he had come in the two weeks since he had climbed down from the train in this same station, and, up in his room after his first meal in Albany, had burst into sobs. Everything was different now. The terror was gone. He could think about Danny and Dora and what had happened in the Forest on Armistice Day without getting sick and beginning to sweat.

"Well, I don't know," George said. "Danny and I, we never wrote any letters to each other before."

"But before you were never away from Fourth Street," Uncle Zisha said. "So why should he write you letters?"

"I guess maybe Danny doesn't feel like writing letters," George said. "What happened in the Forest, it was pretty bad."

Effortlessly, without any hint of the nightmare that would have assailed him two weeks ago at the mere thought of what had happened, George heard himself telling Uncle Zisha all about it. After he described how Danny's father had been killed by the falling lumber and how Dora's arm had been crushed, George even pulled down his stocking and showed Uncle Zisha the small scars on his ankle where the heavy board had held him pinned to the Forest floor until help came. It did not occur to George until much later, when he was halfway to New York, that the explanation had been completely unnecessary, because Aunt Tessie must have written Uncle Zisha all about it. If she hadn't, how would Uncle Zisha have known about Danny?

"You like this Danny?" Uncle Zisha said.

George gave him a quick glance. Aunt Tessie had obviously written more than a description of what had happened on the dock on Armistice Day. Aunt Tessie had obviously told Uncle Zisha about Danny and Gerrity's saloon and what she thought of a Jewish boy who was friendly with shkutzim.

"He's my friend," George said.

Uncle Zisha's large, handsome face was expressionless. "A good friend?"

"Danny's the best friend I've got."

Uncle Zisha nodded. "Then you shouldn't be afraid to say so. Don't be like my sister Tessie. She's afraid."

The fact that George found this bit of information surprising, and didn't believe it, must have been clear on his face.

Uncle Zisha nodded firmly. "Nobody knows better than Zisha Hurst how afraid his sister Tessie is," the big man said. "She's afraid of the world. She's afraid of people. That's why she hides there in those two rooms on Fourth Street. That's why she never comes here to Albany to visit her own brother. That's why she hates your friend Danny for going with shkutzim. She's afraid to come out of her hole and look at the rest of America. She's afraid to go near people except they're exactly like she is." Uncle Zisha shook his head. "Don't be like my sister Tessie," he said. "Don't be afraid of the world. Don't be afraid of people. And you'll grow up to be like Judge Brandeis!"

The conductor called an unintelligible warning. Uncle Zisha's grave face broke into the crinkly pieces of his wonderful smile. He put his large, heavy hand on George's shoulder and they walked to the train step, side by side.

"The seven dollars and ninety-five cents that you got from the

Star bottles," Uncle Zisha said. "What are you going to do with it?"

George hesitated. He hadn't made any plans for the $7.95. He'd been thinking he would talk it over with Danny.

"I don't know," George said cautiously. "I mean I haven't thought about it."

"So think about maybe this," Uncle Zisha said. "College? Law school?" He must have seen that George didn't know what he was talking about, because the big man smiled and said, "To be like Judge Brandeis, the finest thing that anybody can be, a boy must go first to college and law school. College and law school, they cost money. This kind of money my sister Tessie doesn't have. You have already the beginning. Seven dollars and ninety-five cents. If you decide to spend that money to become like Judge Brandeis, then Zisha Hurst will pay the rest."

The big man stopped and waited. He looked the way he always looked, but George felt a difference. Uncle Zisha seemed tense. It was as though George's reply was very important to him.

"Thanks," George said.

It didn't seem like much of an answer, but it was more than enough for Uncle Zisha. The big man beamed. "The thanks they're all on my side," he said. "To do this will be for Zisha Hurst a pleasure."

The conductor called another warning. Uncle Zisha put a hand in his overcoat pocket, pulled out a flat package, and handed it to George. "A little present," he said. "To help you remember."

"Thanks," George said again.

He climbed up onto the train platform. Uncle Zisha put out his hand. George took it. They shook hands formally. Then, for a terrible moment, as he found he could not tug his hand free and he saw a sudden, unexpected gleam in Uncle Zisha's eyes, George thought the big man was going to cry. The moment passed, however, and as the train started to move, George realized how crazy it had been to have such a thought. Uncle Zisha was smiling as he walked along with the slowly moving train.

"Don't forget!" he called in his booming voice. "Don't forget—" He paused as though he couldn't decide what it was he wanted George not to forget, and then Uncle Zisha roared, "Don't forget anything!"

"I won't!" George called back, not quite knowing what he wasn't supposed to forget. Then, as Uncle Zisha took off his black Homburg and raised it in a salute, George remembered Mrs. Gerstenberger, and the small, painful feeling was suddenly back in his chest.

He went to his seat and sat down and opened the package Uncle Zisha had given him. It contained a picture of Judge Brandeis in a silver frame. George stared at it for a while, wondering what to do with it, and then he realized he was hungry. He put aside the picture of Judge Brandeis and picked up Mrs. Gerstenberger's lunch box. By the time he had it open, the painful feeling was gone. George had forgotten all about it.

He was thinking, as he bit into a fried chicken leg, what Danny's face would look like when George gave him the thirty-seven Oh Henrys.

8

Since George had never been away from home until he went to visit Uncle Zisha, it was not until he came back from Albany that he experienced for the first time in his life the series of shocks that add up to a homecoming.

The first one took place in Grand Central, where Aunt Tessie had come to meet him.

"So what's already with the eyes big like garbage-can covers?" she said. "I'm all of a sudden growing ice-cream cones out of my ears, maybe?"

George had forgotten how ugly she was. Then she smiled, and he forgot again.

"No," George said. "I was just remembering something Uncle Zisha said."

Aunt Tessie's smile disappeared. "It was about me?" Her voice was sharp. George nodded. Aunt Tessie said, "What did he say?"

"He was telling me about when he came to America and he got off the ship and you were waiting for him. In the whole world, Uncle Zisha said, there are only a few things that are better than that, better than to have somebody waiting for you when you get off a ship or a train, he meant, and he wasn't even sure, he said, that those few things *were* better."

Aunt Tessie's face got red, and for several minutes, from the way she hustled him across the railroad station to the waiting room, George thought she was sore. He had not wanted to make her sore. He had wanted merely to steer her away from what he knew was bound to come up next, her favorite subject: what a no-good bum Danny Schorr was, and how George would be much better off if he never went near that little shkutz lover again and made friends instead with like maybe a hungry snake or a wild Indian.

"What else did he have to say?" Aunt Tessie said when they were in the subway. "This brother of mine with the great big mouth?"

George was glad to see the trick had worked. He didn't want to have any arguments about Danny.

"Uncle Zisha said he wants to send me to law school," George said. "He wants me to become another Judge Brandeis."

"This is bad?" Aunt Tessie said.

"Who said it's bad?"

"All of a sudden you have a face long like a clothesline."

"He didn't tell me who Judge Brandeis is."

Aunt Tessie nodded. "If my brother Zisha in that factory of his he made ships instead of soda water, he'd be so busy picking out the fanciest paint, he'd forget to put in the engines. Let him pay for the law school, and me, I'll tell you who Judge Brandeis is."

She did, in elaborate detail, while the subway train carried them downtown. George was impressed and relieved. All the way from Albany he had been uneasy about Uncle Zisha's parting wish. If he'd wanted George to become another Babe Ruth or Jack Dempsey, that would have made sense. These, or rather they, were recognizable marks to shoot at. But Judge Brandeis was just a name. It could have belonged to some jerk Uncle Zisha was nuts about but nobody else had time for. How would it have looked to tell Danny and Dora or Miss Corcoran or anybody else that he wanted to grow up to be another Mr. Joe Schmuck? Now, with Aunt Tessie's explanation under his belt, George could stop worrying. In fact, as the subway train rattled him and Aunt Tessie along on the way home to Fourth Street, George began to feel proud that Uncle Zisha thought he had enough stuff on the ball to become another Judge Brandeis. He sensed vaguely that he was committing himself to an ambition that would absorb all his best efforts for the rest of his life, and the size of the undertaking frightened him a little, but it also made him feel safe. It was like living from day to day in different places from which you were tossed out every night and then, all at once, discovering that you had a permanent address. Now George knew what to say to people when they asked him what he intended to be when he grew up.

"Uncle Zisha's house," Aunt Tessie said suddenly. "It's big?"

George, who had been thinking about Danny and wondering how soon he could get to see him, was taken by surprise. "Pretty big," he said.

"What's by you pretty?" Aunt Tessie said.

"Well, it's a whole house."

"P.S. 188 is a whole house, too. How many floors?"

"Two."

"With the ground floor two?"

"No, there's two over the ground floor."

"For one man, he lives alone, a house with three floors he needs?"

"Uncle Zisha doesn't live alone."

Aunt Tessie gave George a quick glance. "So who lives with him, who?"

"Mrs. Gerstenberger."

Aunt Tessie made a gesture of annoyance. "This is the house-keeper, no?"

"Sure, but she lives in the house."

"Who else lives in the house?"

"Nobody."

"You're sure?"

"Sure I'm sure."

"The whole two weeks you were there, nobody else slept in the house?"

"Nobody."

"Only you and Uncle Zisha and this Mrs. Gerstenberger?"

"That's all."

The train stopped at Astor Place. Aunt Tessie and George got out. They waited for the Tenth Street crosstown and, when they were seated in the trolley car, Aunt Tessie stared thoughtfully for a long time at the boy in the yellow slicker in the Uneeda Biscuit ad.

"What time in Albany did you go to sleep at night?" she demanded abruptly.

"About ten o'clock," George said.

"Every night?"

"Pretty nearly."

"What's with the pretty nearly?"

"A couple of times, after we finished rolling pennies—"

"Rolling what?"

George explained how the hours after dinner were spent on Westerlo Street.

"So every night, after the rolling pennies, ten o'clock everybody went to sleep?"

"Except these two times, when we quit early, around eight o'clock."

"Why?"

"Uncle Zisha had to see somebody on business."

"Who?"

"How should I know?"

"Who else should know? I was in Albany? Or you?"

"I didn't see who it was," George said. "I went upstairs to my room, and this person, Uncle Zisha saw him downstairs in the living room."

"It was a him?"

"I guess so."

"Again with the guessing?"

"Well, Jesus, Aunt Tessie—"

"The Jesus you could leave in Albany. Here you talk plain English."

"All I'm trying to tell you is, I didn't see who it was."

"It could have been, then, a woman?"

George blinked up at the Uneeda Biscuit ad in astonishment. The thought had never occurred to him before. "What would Uncle Zisha want with a woman?" he said.

"Me you're asking?"

George shook his head. "It couldn't have been a woman."

"Why not?"

"Because Uncle Zisha said it was somebody he had to see on business."

"Some business. After supper, nine o'clock at night, with everybody quick go upstairs out of the way!"

"Mrs. Gerstenberger wasn't out of the way. She sleeps downstairs."

"And Uncle Zisha, where does he sleep?"

"Downstairs."

Aunt Tessie pursed her lips. She didn't unpurse them until the trolley car dropped her and George at the corner of Tenth Street and Avenue C. They started walking down toward Fourth.

"Where downstairs?" Aunt Tessie said suddenly.

"Where downstairs what?"

"Mrs. Gerstenberger. Where does she sleep?"

"Downstairs in the back. She has a big room behind the kitchen."

"It's far from Uncle Zisha's room?"

"Not too far."

Aunt Tessie walked along in silence for a while. She seemed to be counting the cracks in the sidewalk as they passed over them. "What does she look like?" she said finally. "Mrs. Gerstenberger?"

George described Uncle Zisha's housekeeper.

"And the cooking?"

George described that, too.

"He likes her?"

George didn't know what to say. This was another thought that had never entered his mind before.

"What's so hard to answer?" Aunt Tessie said irritably. "You know what it means to like someone. He likes her or he doesn't?"

"He makes her sit at the other end of the table."

"When you're eating?"

"No, when we're rolling pennies."

George described the evening ritual and the places all the parties to it had occupied while performing it. Aunt Tessie listened attentively, with a small frown, and finally shook her head.

"It doesn't mean nothing," she said gloomily. "He could like her like candy and still at the table make her sit far away just to fool you."

"What would he want to fool me about?"

"Never mind," Aunt Tessie said.

George didn't get a chance to mind because, just then, they turned the corner into Fourth Street and he had his second shock.

"What's the matter with you?" Aunt Tessie said as he stopped short.

George didn't know how to tell her. East Fourth Street seemed to have shrunk. Two weeks ago, when he left for Albany, it had been a broad highway. Now it was a narrow alley.

"I was just looking around."

"Look around tomorrow," Aunt Tessie said. "Today, it's already late, we need a bag of coal."

George was glad to hear it. He didn't want Aunt Tessie keeping him in the house with a lot of questions about how he felt and what had happened in Albany. George wanted to find Danny. Going for a bag of coal would give him the chance.

"I better hurry," he said.

When they came into the store, he stopped again. The two rooms looked so small that George couldn't believe he and Aunt Tessie actually lived in them.

"What's the matter?" she said again.

"Nothing," George said.

He was thinking of his room on the second floor of Uncle Zisha's big house on the hill.

"If it's nothing then you don't have to stand in the middle of the room like a lamppost," Aunt Tessie said. "Take off the clothes. In your good suit you don't go to get coal."

She opened his suitcase and started to unpack it. George began to take off his good suit.

"Just because Uncle Zisha has a whole house, with big rooms, and everything it's fancy-shmancy," Aunt Tessie said, "it doesn't mean it's better than Fourth Street."

George could feel his face get hot. "I didn't say—"

"I know you didn't say," Aunt Tessie said. "But I know what you're thinking. Everybody thinks like that when they come home from some place. In a little while, a few hours, a day, by tomorrow night, these rooms they won't look like egg boxes, and Fourth Street it'll be just as big again like it was when you went away." She shot him a glance out of the corner of her eye. "Even your Aunt Tessie by tomorrow she'll look all right again!" She kissed him quickly and then pushed him toward the door. "So if we're not going to freeze tomorrow, the coal we'll have to get today."

A few minutes later, down in the cellar, dragging out the beat-up old baby carriage in which he brought the coal from the dock, George suddenly began to think it was funny that Aunt Tessie had not even mentioned Danny. It was possible that she'd forgotten, but George doubted it. Aunt Tessie didn't forget things. Not things like her hatred for Danny Schorr. George figured he'd better quit fooling around and get on the ball. He pulled the carriage up into the back yard, left it near the cellar entrance, ran up the stone steps to the fifth floor, and knocked on the door.

A fat woman with a mole on her chin opened it. "What?" she said.

George had never seen her before. "Where's Danny?"

"What Danny?" she said. "There's no Danny here."

"Schorr," George said. "Danny Schorr."

The woman's face cleared. "Oh, *Schorr*," she said. "They don't live here no more. Mr. Schorr was killed. An accident on the dock. Here is now Sternshus. Last week we moved in."

George was only vaguely aware that there was some connection between the shocks he had already experienced since meeting Aunt Tessie in Grand Central and the shock he felt now. There was no vagueness about the extent of the shock. He felt the wallop all the way down in his toes. It had not occurred to him until this moment that, with the death of Mr. Schorr, Danny could not continue living in the same rooms on the fifth floor. Why hadn't he thought of it before? Where were his brains? You couldn't live in a place unless you had the money to pay the rent.

"Where does he live now?" George said.

"Who?" the woman said.

"Danny."

The woman's fat face creased with sudden anger. "Go ask the shkutzim over there by that Gerrity's!"

She slammed the door. Feeling uneasy, as though he were walking into an ambush, George went back down to the yard and got the baby carriage. Something was up. Something lousy. He shoved the carriage out to Lewis Street, crossed over, and moved down the dock. When he reached the gate that separated the Forest from O'Brien Coal he passed Doodoo Kashkewitz, shoving a bag of coal up toward Lewis.

"Look who's back," Doodoo said. "Kid Schmutz."

"In your hat and over your ears," George said, without stopping.

"Seen your boy friend yet?" Doodoo called. George didn't turn. He kept right on going. To hell with this Doodoo bastard, he thought. This Doodoo bastard's voice came after him. "Take a look in Gerrity's," he yelled. "You shkutz-loving son of a bitch! You and him both!"

George didn't have to take a look in Gerrity's. A few minutes later, after George had bought his sack of coal and was shoving it back up toward Lewis, Danny suddenly stepped out of Gerrity's side door, directly in front of George. There was something about

Danny that made George stop short, the way he'd stopped short in Grand Central when he first clapped eyes on Aunt Tessie. It was another one of those shocks that were part of coming home. Danny looked much taller than George remembered him.

"Hi," Danny said. "When'd you get back?"

"A few minutes ago," George said, and then, because he didn't want Danny to think he hadn't tried to find him immediately, he said, "I had to go get coal."

"Yeah," Danny said, and without warning he added sharply, "What the hell you looking at?"

George wasn't sure. He'd known Danny ever since the day Aunt Tessie had brought him to Fourth Street from the Henry Isaacs Orphan Asylum. The fact that they had been born on exactly the same day had always seemed to George more than a coincidence. It had made him think of Danny almost as his twin brother. For six years Danny had been as much a part of his life as Aunt Tessie herself. Yet now, two short weeks after George had last seen him, Danny could have been a total stranger. He seemed to have grown not only taller but more clearly defined. It was as though up to now he had been a cardboard cutout with fuzzy edges and, while George had been away, somebody had taken a pair of scissors and trimmed away the fuzz.

"Nothing," George said. "It's just I'm glad to see you."

What he saw was a bright, strong, clean-cut face with restless brown eyes that were in constant motion, twisting right and left, like a flashlight beam probing for something, the location of which the owner wasn't quite sure. Danny suddenly reminded George of the stove in the kitchen when Aunt Tessie got the fire going good. Danny seemed to be glowing. You could almost feel it. You could also feel yourself being drawn toward it, the way a carpet tack is drawn toward a magnet. George's heart jumped. For the first time in the six years of his friendship with Danny he understood something of its nature. It was a matter of pride. He had something other people didn't have. He had the friendship of this extraordinary creature.

"You bring me anything?" Danny said.

For a few moments, as George dug down into the baby carriage and groped for the paper bag, he couldn't swallow. Danny may have grown taller. Maybe he looked different. But one thing was still the same: he hadn't forgotten who his best friend was. Danny had expected George to bring him something. It made George choke up.

Then his throat cleared and he handed over the bag of Oh Henrys. Danny opened the bag.

"Holy Christ!" he said. "How many?"

"Thirty-seven," George said.

Danny's head came up. "All for me?" George nodded. Danny laughed and said again, "Holy Christ!"

He pulled an Oh Henry from the bag, stripped away the wrapper, and took a huge bite. The way he did it made George's mouth water. He thought for sure Danny would offer him one of those Oh Henrys, and for a couple of minutes, while Danny chewed away happily, George could scarcely stand it. His stomach kept making grinding noises. But Danny didn't offer him one of the Oh Henrys.

"I went upstairs first," George said. "The fifth floor. I didn't know you moved. Where you living, Danny?"

Danny jerked his head behind him. George glanced at Gerrity's side door, started to look back at Danny, then realized what Danny's curt nod might mean. No wonder the fat woman with the mole on her chin had been angry. No wonder Doodoo Kashkewitz had yelled curses. No wonder Aunt Tessie had not said a word about her favorite subject. She'd preferred to have George learn the terrible truth for himself.

"What the hell you want?" Danny said. "I should go better over to Henry Isaacs?" He punched the words out, as though he expected a fight.

George took a step backward. "I didn't say anything," he said.

"No, but everybody else on this God-damn block is saying it," Danny said. "Your Aunt Tessie, too. Well, they can all go drop dead. I'm not going over to live in no orphan asylum. Mike Gerrity give me a room, I take it. You got any objections?"

Objections wasn't exactly the word. It was bad enough to pick up nickels and dimes by running errands for shkutzim. But living with them, actually *living* with them, right there in the same house, sleeping in the same beds, eating their food—

George shook his head. He couldn't quite grasp the enormity of the horror. "No, I got no objections," he said slowly. He was trying to reconcile the horror with the way he felt about Danny. "I don't blame anybody doesn't want to go live in Henry Isaacs. I lived there. It stinks. Anything is better than—" He paused. He didn't really believe that. He was saying it only because he loved Danny. No matter what the reason, though, it was better not to say things like that. God might hear you and come along and kick the tail off you. George started again. "I hope you like the Oh Henrys," he said. "The way I got them, Uncle Zisha has this factory, see. Soda water, and his bottles they're not like this other company, Star. So every day, when the men bring back the—"

"Tell me later," Danny said. "I gotta go get something for Mike."

George stood there, watching his friend hurry up Fourth Street toward Avenue D, pleased because Danny had liked the Oh Henrys, worried because he could see that by living with the shkutzim in Gerrity's, Danny was placing a strain on their friendship that was bound to cause trouble in the future, yet not really caring too much. The future could take care of itself. What mattered right now was that he was back with Danny.

"Hello, George."

He turned, and had another shock. Dora Dienst looked different, too.

"Hello," he said.

"I'm a cripple," Dora said.

"Cut it out."

"You don't believe me? Look."

Dora lifted her left arm.

"What about it?" George said.

"I can't straighten it out." Dora lifted her right arm to show him the difference. "This one, it's a little crooked. I came home from the hospital yesterday. They said I'll never be able to straighten it out. They said I'll be a cripple till I die."

She sounded proud. For a few moments George envied her. He could see her showing the slightly crooked arm to other people, and he could see them staring in amazement, and he wished he had something like that, something that would make him stand out from other people, the way Danny stood out and the way that from now on Dora was going to stand out. Then George realized the slight crookedness of Dora's left arm was not what had made him think she looked different. It was the way she held her body, bent forward slightly from the waist, with the shoulders hunched, as though she had a pain somewhere inside and she was holding herself together around it. With her little pointed chin and her slightly slanted eyes, the curious posture made her look like a Chinese doll cowering from a blow that might come from any direction.

"I saw you talking to Danny," Dora said.

"Yeah," George said. He wondered if she had seen him give Danny the Oh Henrys. Maybe he should have divided them in half, eighteen for Danny and nineteen for Dora, or nineteen for Danny and eighteen for Dora. He should have brought something from Albany for Dora, too. "Danny said he had to go get something for Mike Gerrity."

"I don't want you should ever talk to him again," Dora said.

George blinked. "Talk to who?"

"You know who," Dora said, and all of a sudden it was like those lantern slides Miss Corcoran showed once in a while about La Salle and the Discovery of the Mississippi. Everything changed with a click. All of a sudden Dora's nice, smooth face was twisted with hate. Her braids shook as she said, "Don't ever go near him again. You hear?"

The sick feeling he had thought he'd left behind him in Albany was suddenly back in George's stomach. Nothing ever stayed good, the way you wanted it. Everything always changed, the way you hated it.

"Listen," he said. "Danny can't help it. He's gotta live some place. He doesn't want to go live in Henry Isaacs. Orphan asylums stink. I know. If Mike Gerrity wants to give Danny a room—"

"It isn't Mike Gerrity."

George stared at her.

"I don't care if Danny wants to live with the shkutzim," Dora said. "What I care about, the reason I don't want you should ever speak to him again, he made me a cripple. Look!" She held out her left arm. "He did it!" she screamed. "That rotten Danny Schorr! He did it! He did it! It's his fault!"

The sick feeling began to spread inside George like a drop of ink on a blotter. Nothing ever stayed good, and it didn't help to try to keep it from going bad, but you still had to try.

"No, it isn't," he said. "It's not Danny's fault. It's my fault. I was the one told you to go up on that lumber stack. I was the one sent you up there to keep an eye on the—"

"It's Danny's fault! Danny's fault! Danny's fault!" Dora closed her eyes and hit the air with her fists and stamped on the sidewalk as she shouted, "He was the one said let's trail Old Man Saydl! He was the one sent us into the Forest! He was the one went to get

the shkutzim to fight Doodoo and the soldiers! It's his fault I'm a
cripple! It's his fault, his fault, his fault!"

George stood there, holding the handle of the baby carriage,
letting her wild words pour over him, wondering if he was really
going to be sick, and not caring very much. His mind kept going
around in a circle, asking stupidly why it had to be like this? Why
couldn't it be the way it had always been? The way it had been before
Armistice Day? Him and Danny and Dora? A few arguments once in
a while, sure. Dora talking back to Danny now and then. Even
George once in a while asking how come. But nothing serious.
Always the three of them. Always friends. Why couldn't it be like
that?

"Dora, listen," George said. It didn't do any good to try, but
just the same you had to. Maybe, if you tried hard enough, you
found a way. He shoved back the sick feeling and he made his voice
sound nice and easy. "Dora, I brought you something from Albany."

She stopped screaming. It was like a bad rain, great big drops
hammering down, and somebody had turned it off like a faucet.
Dora looked at him suspiciously. She wiped the corner of her mouth
with the back of her hand. "What?" she said.

George took out the money he had earned in Albany by carrying
Star bottles down the hill to Mrs. Dougherty's ice-cream parlor.
"Here."

He handed over the five-dollar bill and the two singles and the
coins. He had not planned it this way. He didn't want to give the
money to Dora. But George didn't see that there was anything else
he could do. No matter what Dora said about Danny, George knew
better. He knew who had sent Dora to the top of the lumber pile
on Armistice Day. He knew who was responsible for her crooked
arm.

"How much is it?" Dora said.

"Seven dollars and ninety-five cents."

She counted it carefully. "It's all for me?"

George nodded.

"The whole thing?" she said.

"The whole thing," George said.

Dora smiled. The sick feeling, laced tight around George's
stomach like the fingers of a clenched fist, began to lose its grip.

He had found a way.

9

It was not a very good way.

For one thing, it was only temporary. As soon as the excitement generated by receiving $7.95 all in a lump wore off, Dora went right back to hating Danny. For another, it did nothing to ease George's own feeling of guilt. Even while Dora was beaming because she held in her hands more money than she had ever before possessed, and as a result of such beaming she had for the moment forgotten that she hated Danny, George was unable to forget.

The only one who seemed to be able to do that was Danny himself.

In the days when he had been in and out of Gerrity's all day long, he had never cared what the people of Fourth Street thought of him for associating with shkutzim. Now that he was actually living in Gerrity's, and the scandal was so much worse, Danny seemed to care even less. He was equally indifferent to the fact that Dora hated him. George could not understand this.

There was nothing secret about Dora's hatred. She talked about it constantly. Not to Danny, of course, but to anybody who would listen. Many people did. Nobody on Fourth Street, with the exception of George, could forgive Danny for living with the Gerritys. They enjoyed hearing a pretty little girl like Dora say aloud the things about the young shkutz lover that they were themselves afraid to say except in private, because saying them involved criticism of Mike Gerrity, who had a violent temper and would just as soon punch a Jew's head off as take another slug of whiskey. Dora did not limit herself to name-calling. When she saw Danny coming along the street, she would very ostentatiously move to the other side. Once, when she passed Danny in front of Gordon's candy stand, George saw Dora spit on the sidewalk. Danny didn't even turn around.

Danny's indifference made Dora hate him even more, which meant that George suffered more because, loving Danny and feeling responsible for Dora, George was caught in the middle. Danny didn't give a damn if he saw George talking to Dora. But if Dora saw George with Danny, she screamed bloody murder. George worried about it for a while, then decided maybe he could solve the problem by getting Danny to be nice to Dora.

The suggestion seemed to annoy Danny. "What the hell do I want to be nice to her for?" he said.

"It might help," George said.

"Help what?"

"The way she feels about you."

"Listen, pyoick. She hates me because she thinks I made her a cripple."

"That's crazy. I was the one sent her up that lumber stack. I've explained that to her."

"Yeah?" Danny said. "How much good did it do?"

"Well—"

"Well my ass. What she believes she believes. I could be nice to her from now to Yom Kippur and it wouldn't make any difference. Somebody wants to believe something, they believe it. You try to stop them, you're just wasting your time. She makes a pain in the neck out of herself, why don't you just tell her to drop dead?"

It would have made things a lot simpler, of course. But George couldn't do it. Ever since he had come home from Albany, Dora had made it plain that she regarded him as her protector. It was a role George did not mind or even see how he could avoid filling. There was something about the slender girl with the dark braids and the pointed chin, something about the way she held her body, as though shielding her damaged left arm from the eyes of the world, that gave George a feeling of discomfort. He had done this to her. He was responsible for what she had become. He couldn't tell her to drop dead.

"Dora's okay," he said.

"Okay for what?" Danny said.

The tone of his voice made George angry. "God damn it," he said. "It's not so long ago, when you were cooking up one of your deals, you were damn glad to have Dora come along and help. Even on Armistice Day, she was good enough for a lookout."

"Was is right," Danny said coolly. "But she ain't good enough any more. Now she's just another tomato with a gimpy arm and a big trap. You want to waste your time listening to her bellyache, go ahead. Me, I haven't got any time to waste."

This seemed to be true enough. George seldom saw Danny any more except in school. Prohibition had changed the nature of

Mike Gerrity's business, and while George wasn't too sure about the exact details of the change, he did know that it kept Danny hopping. Danny never hung around the school yard after classes any more to play basketball or cook up one of his deals. Every day, as soon as the three o'clock bell rang, Danny beat it back to the saloon. All his afternoons as well as his Saturdays and Sundays were spent carrying small packages wrapped in brown paper down to the barges moored at the dock or uptown to destinations, according to people who claimed to have seen Danny with their own eyes, as far west as First Avenue.

Dora said he was carrying booze for Mike Gerrity, and one of these days the cops would nab him, and that would be the end of Mr. Danny Schorr, the dirty little shkutz lover.

Aunt Tessie agreed. "Only one thing worries me," she said. "Where will they find a prison strong enough to hold the little momser, where?"

Aunt Tessie added one of the few smiles she ever allowed to escape beyond range of her beloved George. As soon as she'd learned how Dora's feelings for Danny had changed, Aunt Tessie had become very fond of the girl from the doll store across the stoop.

"They won't need such a strong prison," Dora said contemptuously. "Mr. Danny Schorr is not as tough as he thinks. It's just he's got all those shkutzim behind him, that's why he thinks he's so great. You wait, though. You just wait. The minute the cops grab him, all the shkutzim in the world won't be able to help him. It'll be the end."

The end, however, seemed to take its own sweet time about arriving. It had certainly not arrived on the day during George's last year in high school when Danny's life took the abrupt and surprising turn that neither Dora and Aunt Tessie who detested him, nor George who loved him, had anticipated.

It was the day after Fott Fromkin broke the centigrade thermometer in Mr. Gaspari's chemistry class.

Fott's real name was Melvin, but all his classmates, among whom were numbered friends as well as enemies, called him Fott because the only other human being named Melvin about whom they had previously heard was Melvin Ott, the Giants' centerfielder, and since it was perfectly obvious that you couldn't nickname a guy Ott, the next step was even more obvious: Melvin became Fott.

It did not improve his personality.

Franklin Pierce High School on Thirteenth Street was proud of its scholastic standards, which were high, and its democratic tradition, which was highly advertised. It was one of the oldest high schools in the city. Having opened its doors before the turn of the century, at a time when boys seeking a free secondary school education were limited in the number of places they could choose from, Franklin Pierce High attracted at once not only very bright but poor boys who could not afford private schools, but also the sons of parents who, even though they could pay tuition at a private school, believed it would have a salutary effect on their offspring to rub elbows several hours a day for four years with boys whose share of worldly goods was somewhat smaller than theirs.

George Hurst had never seen any statistics that might have proved or disproved the truth of this theory. By the time he was old enough to go to high school, only boys whose share of worldly goods was at least respectable had any choice about where they would obtain their secondary school education. Boys like George went where the Board of Education sent them. He considered himself lucky to be sent to Franklin Pierce.

So did Aunt Tessie and Uncle Zisha. A boy who graduated from Franklin Pierce with respectable marks would probably have no trouble with college and had a good chance to get into a decent law school, and any boy who was going to become another Brandeis had better get into a decent law school.

Fott Fromkin felt differently about being sent to Franklin Pierce High.

Fott Fromkin, whose father was a wealthy stockbroker, lived on Central Park West in something he called a duplex. George did not know what a duplex was, and he was too ashamed of his ignorance to ask, but he did know, because Fott never grew tired of telling everybody, that the elder Mr. Fromkin's son and heir was interested in only two subjects: jazz and nookie.

Neither of these could, of course, be explored with any degree of thoroughness in an all-male high school the faculty of which was dedicated to maintaining a scholastic standard that was, or at least was reputed to be, the highest in the city. But Fott tried.

When he wasn't complaining bitterly about his lousy son of a bitch of a father, who should have sent him to Phillips Exeter or Andover, the way the fathers of all his friends on Central Park

West had sent *their* sons, Fott was telling dirty stories or humming something hot by Duke Ellington. Since he was a fat boy with many pimples, small intelligence, large adenoids, and almost no memory, he did neither of these things well. Duke Ellington, however, is impervious to anything save deliberate sabotage, and dirty stories have been sure-fire for quite some time. Fott, therefore, never lacked for an audience. He had one the day Mr. Gaspari was setting up the nitrous oxide experiment at the front of the lab.

The lab was a large room on the top floor with twenty-four stone-topped tables arranged in four rows of six each. Four boys worked at each table. Mr. Gaspari worked alone at his table up front until the day's experiment was ready for demonstration. In theory, while Mr. Gaspari was setting up an experiment, his students were supposed to be studying the relevant material in their text-books. In practice, a great many other things went on, all the way from surreptitious games of stud poker to gaping at the physiological improbabilities in Fott Fromkin's stories.

"After she finishes taking out her glass eye and unhooking her false arm, this dame happens to notice a guy is watching her from the upper berth across the aisle of the train," Fott was saying in a low voice. "So she grabs the blankets and pulls them up to her chin and she says to the guy across the other side of the train, she snaps at him, real sore, 'What do *you* want?' The guy, he grins and says, 'You know what I want; hand it over!' "

Fott waited for his laugh, and it came. Perhaps it wasn't as loud as he expected. Or perhaps he was seized unexpectedly by an impulse to widen his horizons. Whatever the reason, this much was certain because George saw it happen: Fott put his finger to his lips, tiptoed down the side of the lab, sidled up to Mr. Gaspari's table and, as the chemistry teacher turned away to pick up a pair of test tube clamps, Fott snatched the centigrade thermometer.

Grinning happily, every pimple alight with the easily aroused pleasure of the simple-minded, he started back up the aisle, holding the thermometer aloft as though it were a flagpole. It almost could have been. It was eighteen inches long and as thick as a broomstick. These dimensions, plus the fact that halfway up the aisle he passed a boy who was bent over his textbook in an attitude of deep concentration, proved too much for Fott.

Grinning gleefully for his audience, and pointing at the buttocks of his engrossed classmate, Fott Fromkin began to snap the large glass tube in the air in a crude but recognizable imitation of a doctor shaking down a thermometer before inserting it for a reading. The response from his audience was so enthusiastic that Fott, obviously giddy with this unexpected success in a field he had never before explored, began to snap the thermometer in swifter and wider arcs. This proved to be a mistake. On one of its more violent descents, the end of the eighteen-inch glass tube touched the edge of the slate-top lab table on Fott's left. The contact was almost inaudible. The effect was astonishing.

The large room, which a moment before had been steeped in an almost total silence, was suddenly alive with a series of startled screams. Astonished, George saw smears of blood begin to appear on the faces of at least three boys near him. Several others were shouting as they probed scalps and other exposed parts of their bodies for what it took George a few moments to realize were possible wounds caused by bits of flying thermometer. And Mr. Gaspari, a mild little man with thick eyeglasses who always moved with painstaking slowness, was coming up the aisle on the double.

In the center of all this excitement, like the motionless hub of a rapidly spinning wheel, stood Fott, his fat, stupid face set in a look of dazed incredulity, as he stared at the six inches of shattered thermometer that still remained in his hand. He looked somewhat like a clown who, fighting what he thought was a mock duel which he was under the impression he was winning, suddenly wakes up to the fact that he is actually fighting for his life and his sword has been broken off at the hilt.

"For God's sake, Melvin!" Mr. Gaspari said. "What the hell do you think you're doing?"

"I—I—I—" Fott gasped.

Mr. Gaspari pulled himself together. A rapid survey of the damage caused by Fott's initial effort in the field of pantomime was reassuring. The cuts suffered by his classmates were minor. The thermometer, however, was quite clearly beyond repair. Mr. Gaspari may not have known what went on behind his back while he was setting up an experiment, but he knew that willful destruction of Board of Education property could not be treated lightly.

"Melvin," he said, "I want to talk to your father. You will bring him to school tomorrow. Is that clear?"

Fott nodded dumbly. The next day, when the chemistry class assembled in Mr. Gaspari's lab, George watched eagerly, along with the rest of the class, for Fott's father to show up. He never did.

"Melvin, I ordered you to bring your father here today," Mr.

Gaspari said severely when Fott came in alone. "Where is he?"

Fott sent a quick glance across his shoulder to make sure everybody was listening. He wore the look of moronic pleasure that always appeared on his fat face when he was about to deliver the punch line of one of his dirty jokes.

"In Campbell's Funeral Parlor over on Madison Avenue," he said in a loud, clear voice. "My father shot himself in his office down on Wall Street at five o'clock last night!"

Mr. Gaspari was stunned, but all George could think about was what Danny and Dora would say when he brought the thrilling news home to Fourth Street. He didn't often have tidbits as good as a suicide with which to lace together the gap that had appeared between their lives and his when the three of them graduated from P.S. 188. It was a gap that had taken George by surprise.

He had never paid attention to the belief so widely held on Fourth Street that the only reason Mike Gerrity had allowed Danny to remain in P.S. 188 was that the saloonkeeper knew he would have been in trouble with the city authorities if he'd taken Danny out of school before he completed the eighth grade, and the one thing a man in Mike Gerrity's business did not want was trouble with any kind of authorities. George had assumed that Danny liked school. He was astonished when he learned that Danny had no intention of going on from P.S. 188 to Franklin Pierce, but not nearly so astonished as Danny was when he learned about George's assumption.

"High school?" Danny said as though George had suggested that they try walking on water. "What the hell do I want to go to high school for?"

"If you want to be a lawyer, you have to go to college," George said. "And if you want to go to college, you have to go to high school first."

"*You're* the one wants to be a lawyer," Danny said. "Me, what I want, they can't teach me anything about it from books."

Dora had been equally emphatic. "What are they going to teach me in high school?" she said to George. "How to straighten out my crooked arm?"

George hated it when she talked about her arm. "You could learn bookkeeping or stenography," he said. "You could become a private secretary."

He was quoting Mr. Dunn, the P.S. 188 principal, who had told the members of the graduating class about the advantages to be derived from continuing their education by going on to high school.

"Some private secretary," Dora said bitterly. "With an arm like a corkscrew. You go to high school. You're going to be another Judge Brandeis. Me, I'll go help Frannie and Ida stick hair on Papa's dolls."

At first it used to make George feel uncomfortable to see her, when he came home from school, sitting beside her sisters in the store across the stoop, smearing the hot glue on the naked little doll heads and combing the tight little curls down into neat little wigs. It didn't seem right that he should spend his days with books and the simple odd jobs involved in helping Aunt Tessie, while this slender girl spent hers in a factory. Oddly enough, however, Dora didn't seem to mind. She didn't seem to mind anything, including the constant criticism of Frannie and Ida, who said her work was so sloppy that everything she did had to be done over again by them. It was as though the odd way she had of holding her body, with the shoulders hunched forward to shield her crooked arm, shielded her also from what went on around her.

She liked to have George stop in after school, or when he finished delivering a pressed dress or suit for Aunt Tessie, and tell her what had happened to him during the day. He enjoyed doing it, because he always enjoyed being near her, but even though she listened with apparent interest, George had the feeling that she didn't really hear what he was saying. It was as though she had built an invisible wall around herself and, while it was important to her that the wall should be neither scaled nor breached, it was equally important to her to pretend that the wall did not exist. Several times, when his account of something that had happened in school struck her for some reason as particularly interesting, Dora seemed to come out from behind the wall, her eyes flashing and her voice rising with quick interest, the way they used to before the Armistice Day accident in the Forest. These moments were for George so pleasant that he tried to repeat them as often as he could. This was not easy, because he never really knew what it was in each instance that had appealed to Dora strongly enough to cut through her lethargy.

The day that Fott Fromkin's father committed suicide, however, George had no such doubts. He knew he was bringing home a story that would top anything Dora had ever heard before. Unfortunately, George never got a chance to tell it to her.

Coming around the corner from Avenue D into Fourth Street, he saw Danny Schorr moving up the street toward him. This was an unexpected break. As a rule, he didn't get a chance to see Danny until after supper, when George had finished his homework and Danny had finished all his errands for Mike Gerrity. This way he would be able to tell Danny about Fott Fromkin's father before he told Dora. George quickened his pace. So did Danny. They met in front of the open lot next to Forman's grocery.

"Boy," George said, "have I got something to tell you!"

"Later," Danny said. "C'mere a minute."

He took George by the arm and pulled him into the empty lot. It was used by the O'Brien Coal Company as a parking area for wagons. From the way Danny moved him around one of the wagons, so that they were partially concealed from the street, it suddenly occurred to George that this meeting with Danny was no accident.

"You been waiting for me?" George said.

Danny nodded. "I need some help."

"Anything, Danny."

"You mean that?"

"Cut it out," George said. "You know I mean it."

Danny nodded again. "I was just kidding," he said. "Sure I know it."

"Then tell me what you want."

"I want to move in with you."

"In with me? You mean to *live*?"

"That's right."

"With me and Aunt *Tessie*?"

"What are you screaming about?"

"I'm not screaming. I'm just—"

"Just what?"

George gave himself a moment. It didn't help. The whole thing still seemed crazy. "I don't know," he said finally. "I don't understand what—?"

"Mike Gerrity was shot and killed last night some place uptown."

"Oh."

"Oh ain't enough. I need a yes or no. Which is it?"

"It's not up to me, Danny."

"You can make her do anything you want."

"Are you kidding?"

"I need a place to live. I'm not kidding."

"We only got the two small rooms."

"I could sleep in the store."

"She hates you, Danny."

"You can make her do anything you want."

"Danny, nobody makes Aunt Tessie do anything she doesn't want."

"You just said you were my friend."

"Sure I am. But what you're asking—"

"If you weren't my friend, I wouldn't be asking."

George stood there, wanting desperately to prove his friendship, and feeling helpless because he knew it was impossible to give Danny the proof he wanted. "I'll tell you what," he said at last.

"You'll fix it up with her?"

It was amazing that Danny, who was so smart about everything else, was apparently not smart enough to grasp the simple fact that nobody fixed things up with Aunt Tessie.

"Let's go talk to her," George said.

He tried to sound confident even though he knew it was hopeless, which only made him feel worse because trying to sound confident was in this case no better than lying, and he had never before lied to Danny. Just the same, George didn't see what else he could do. He couldn't let Danny think he wasn't even trying.

"So now, instead of carrying it out of the house," Aunt Tessie said coldly to George when he opened the front door and came in with Danny, "you're bringing garbage in?"

She was sitting in her rocking chair in the window, pulling the basting out of a yellow skirt.

"Don't get sore until you hear what it's all about," George said.

"I'm not getting sore, I'm getting up," Aunt Tessie said, doing precisely that. "And your shkutz-loving friend, he's getting out."

She stepped around Danny as though he were something one of the O'Brien Coal Company horses had just dropped in her path, and she started for the back of the store.

"Wait."

She stopped and turned, obviously surprised. So was George. He had never heard Danny sound like that.

"I know what you think of me," he said, talking to Aunt Tessie, but keeping his eyes fixed on the floor. "I'm not saying I blame you. But I didn't come here to argue about that. What I came here for, I'm in trouble, and I need help, and I came to my best friend to get it. Look at it this way. If your own George feels about me the way he does, maybe I'm not as bad as you figure me to be."

The expression on Aunt Tessie's face did not change, but George could tell from the slight narrowing of her eyes that a completely new thought had been planted in her mind.

"What kind of trouble?"

She sounded exactly as she had sounded a few moments earlier, when she had ordered Danny out of the store, but the mere fact that she had asked the question was astonishing. To George, at any rate. Danny didn't seem to find it astonishing. Danny continued to scowl down at his hands as, in a low voice, he told Aunt Tessie the nature of his trouble.

"Nobody told you to go live with shkutzim," Aunt Tessie said when he finished. "You went yourself. Because you liked it. If you like it, they must be your friends. So now, because one of them gets killed, all of a sudden they're not your friends? What kind of friends is this?"

"Mike—Mr. Gerrity, he was my friend," Danny said quietly. "The rest of them, they never liked me. Now, now that Mike's dead, they—they—" He paused, and he drew a deep breath, as though he needed all the strength he could muster for what he had to say next. "They kicked me out," Danny Schorr said.

It was like hearing Mr. Gaspari admit publicly that he didn't know how to set up an experiment in the chemistry lab. Even Aunt Tessie, who didn't know Mr. Gaspari, knew what it must have cost Danny to make this confession. George could see the muscles in her jaw ripple. For several moments the silence in the store was almost physically painful.

Danny broke it. "If I don't get a place to sleep," he said. "If the cops or somebody else, they come after me and I can't say where I live—" He paused, and he shrugged. The gesture of helplessness was even more shocking than the admission that the Gerritys had thrown him out. "They'll send me to Henry Isaacs," Danny Schorr said. "Or some place worse."

He raised his head. The brown, restless eyes looked directly into Aunt Tessie's. All at once George could hear his own heartbeats and the alarm clock ticking out in the kitchen. They seemed to be racing one another. George held his breath. Something extraordinary was happening. He didn't know what it was, but he knew it had something to do with that feeling Danny brought into a room, the feeling that reminded George of a carpet tack being drawn toward a magnet.

Aunt Tessie cleared her throat. "If I give you a place to live," she said, "you'll give me something back?"

"Anything you want," Danny said.

"I want from you a promise," Aunt Tessie said. "You'll never, never, never again, as long as you live, you'll never go again live with shkutzim."

"I promise," Danny said.

Aunt Tessie turned to George. "Go get blankets," she said. "We'll make a bed here in the back of the store."

10

Danny slept in it for three weeks. It took the surviving members of the Gerrity family that long to realize they couldn't get along without him.

As soon as they did, Mike Gerrity, Jr., who had lost an arm in the war, walked across the street to see Danny. He walked across the street, but he didn't come into Aunt Tessie's store. Even Mike Gerrity, Jr., who according to Danny was a dumb ox, had enough brains not to do that.

The incident took place shortly before noon, so that George, who was in school, did not see it. Dora Dienst saw it, however. This was fortunate, because Aunt Tessie, who had also seen it, refused to discuss the matter, and George wanted very much to know what had happened. Dora told him.

"I was sitting here, working, when all of a sudden I saw the side door, there—" Dora nodded toward the saloon across the street. "It opened, and instead of some drunken shkutz, out comes the big war hero, so right away I knew something was wrong."

George could understand that. Like the other members of his family, Mike Gerrity, Jr., rarely came out into the open. It was

generally believed on Fourth Street that this was due to the fact that
he was rarely sober enough to walk.

"He wasn't exactly drunk, but he wasn't *not* drunk, either,"
Dora said. "He walked crooked coming across the gutter, so I got up
and went over to the window for a better look, and I saw he'd stopped
in front of your Aunt Tessie's store, and he was calling Danny's
name. He called a long time, and after a while Danny came out and
asked what he wanted. Mother and I want you to come back, he
said. Isn't that nice, Danny said, and he spit across the big war
hero's head, out in the gutter. You know what you and your mother
can do, Danny said, and he turned to go back in, but Mike grabbed
Danny with his one hand and he said listen. Danny shook the hand
off and you know the way he gets when he's mad? His face tight and
his lips thin and his voice like it was hurting his throat to get the
words out?"

George nodded. He knew.

"Danny said you put your hand on me again, you dirty rotten
drunk, and I'll beat your brains out, you got one arm or not, you
hear? The big war hero heard all right," Dora said. "But he didn't
do anything about it. He just said he was sorry and he stood there,
holding himself up by the garbage can, and first I thought what's
Danny doing standing there? The way he talked, calling names and
all, and telling Mike and his mother to drop dead, why didn't he
turn around and beat it? You know why?"

"Why?" George said.

Dora smiled contemptuously. "Because he didn't *want* to go in,"
she said. "All that talk, drop dead, go to hell, you put your hand
on me again I'll beat your brains out, all that, it was just talk. What
Danny wanted, the dirty little shkutz lover, he wanted the big war
hero to come crawling, that's what. So he could bargain with him."

"Bargain about what?" George said.

"Danny said okay, I'll come back, but first we get a few things
straight. Mike said sure, anything, like Danny had given him a great
big present, and then Danny told him. He said from now on he
wanted Mike's room up on the second floor, not the old room he
used to have, and he wanted the couch moved into his room from
the parlor on the first floor, and he wanted nobody interfering with
what he did, because he was going to run the business his own way,
the way Mike's father taught him, or he wasn't going to run it at
all. The way he sounded when he was saying it, honest, even though

he was talking to a shkutz, it made my blood boil just to hear him. Anybody else, they would have spit in his eye and told him to go to hell, but the big war hero, that drunken shkutz, he was so glad the great Danny Schorr was coming back, he almost got down on the sidewalk and kissed his shoes. Honest to God," Dora said bitterly, "I wanted to vomit."

"That's all?" George said.

"It's not enough? He walked back across the street with the big war hero so fast, he didn't even have time to say good-bye to your Aunt Tessie."

George didn't believe this. He attributed the statement to Dora's hatred of Danny and to the fact that, when she'd learned Aunt Tessie had taken him in, Dora was so furious that for almost a week she had refused to speak to George or Aunt Tessie. When George learned that Dora had told the truth, he was upset enough to wait out in front of the store for almost two hours, until he finally saw Danny coming down the street. George went to meet him.

"I know, I know, I know," Danny said, holding up his hand like a traffic cop. "You went to all that trouble, you got your Aunt Tessie to take me in, and now I—"

"You're wrong," George said. "I didn't get Aunt Tessie to take you in. She did it herself."

Danny looked puzzled. "What's the diff?" he said.

"You don't owe me explanations or thanks or anything else, because I'm your friend," George said. "But Aunt Tessie, she's not your friend."

Danny scowled and slowly scratched the side of his jaw as he stared at George. He was obviously trying to get something straight in his mind.

"What the hell—?" he began slowly, and then he paused to think some more. Suddenly he snapped his fingers and grinned. "You mean it'll make you feel better if I go to see her?"

"That's right," George said.

"Then what are we waiting for?" Danny said. He took George by the arm. "Let's go."

Aunt Tessie was working in the rocking chair in the window when they came in. She looked up once, then dropped her eyes back to her work.

"I guess I left kind of in a hurry," Danny said. "I didn't get a chance to say good-bye."

"Good-bye," Aunt Tessie said without looking up.

Danny smiled. He was making a special effort, George could see, to be nice. "I appreciate what you did for me," Danny said.

"I didn't do nothing," Aunt Tessie said, her eyes fixed on the seam she was sewing.

Danny's smile grew a little wider. He was really turning on the charm. "I want to thank you for—"

"There's nothing to thank me."

"I was in trouble," Danny said. "I needed help. You took me in here and—"

"I didn't do it because you were in trouble," Aunt Tessie said. "I didn't do it because you needed help." She looked up from her work. "I did it because I thought there was a chance to save a Jewish soul. I was wrong." She pushed herself up out of the rocking chair. Her small, dark face was set. "Nobody can save you." She sounded like a judge pronouncing sentence. "There's nothing left to save," Aunt Tessie said. "Only by the shkutzim you're still a living person. By me, you're already dead."

Danny's thin, dark face went white. He opened his mouth to say something, then changed his mind. He turned on his heel and walked out of the store, slamming the door behind him.

He never mentioned the incident. Neither did Aunt Tessie. This made things a lot simpler for George. It was as though, now that she considered Danny to be dead, Aunt Tessie no longer considered George's friendship for him to be a troubling matter. How could a dead person do you any harm? George could think of a number of answers to that, but he did not make them to Aunt Tessie. He was content to let well enough alone. This involved no more than accepting Aunt Tessie's pretense that Danny Schorr no longer existed. She never mentioned his name. Not even on the day after George graduated from Franklin Pierce High School and he told Aunt Tessie he was going downtown to hunt for a job with Danny Schorr.

"Be careful when you cross the gutters," she said. "Look both ways."

The fact that she didn't say more, George realized much later, may not have been due entirely to Aunt Tessie's scrupulous refusal to utter Danny Schorr's name. It may have been due also to her embarrassment over the fact that George had to go out and look for a job.

Ever since his visit to Albany, when he was still in Miss Corcoran's class in P.S. 188, it had been taken for granted in the Hurst household that, when George graduated from Franklin Pierce, he would be sent first to college and then to law school by Uncle Zisha. For years every letter from Albany had contained some reference to this long-range plan. In the middle of George's last year at Franklin Pierce, however, these references became less frequent and finally stopped. For some reason that all his courses in economics never made quite clear to George, the bottom had fallen out of Uncle Zisha's soda-bottling business in Albany. Root beer and cream soda, it seemed, were a luxury that, as the nation's prosperity waned, people felt they could do without. They could do without Uncle Zisha's brand, at any rate. For months before George's graduation there had been hints of trouble. Aunt Tessie's reactions to them were mixed.

She did not like the news that, because business had fallen off so badly, Uncle Zisha had been forced to fire several drivers and had taken on some of the delivery work himself. "He's too fat and too old to shlep around those big cases full of bottles," she said with a worried scowl. "He's been living too good for too many years to all of a sudden stop eating and start working."

The news that Uncle Zisha had been forced to let Mrs. Gerstenberger go, however, caused Aunt Tessie to nod with satisfaction. "The house, if he has to clean for himself, in no time it'll look like pigs were living in it. But if he has to cook for himself, he won't eat so much." Aunt Tessie gave George a short glance. "And to throw out of the house a woman that he's not married to, this it'll never hurt him with God, believe me!"

What did hurt, if not with God then at least with Aunt Tessie, was the realization, as George's graduation from Franklin Pierce drew near, that, if he was going to become another Judge Brandeis, his college and law school tuition would have to be paid not by Uncle Zisha but by George himself. This did not bother him. All the boys and girls on Fourth Street, from Dora Dienst who had gone into her father's doll factory at thirteen to Doodoo Kashkewitz who started shoeing horses in the blacksmith shop across the street when George started intermediate algebra at Franklin Pierce, were expected to make some contribution to the income of their families, as soon as they were old enough to get their working papers. What did bother George was the fact that Danny Schorr had to go out and look for work, too.

Even though George was not altogether sure about the nature

of the Gerrity family business, which, like everybody else on Fourth
Street, he assumed involved some form of bootlegging, he had been
quite sure, again like everybody else on Fourth Street, that it was
prosperous. George had assumed further that Danny, who had gone
back to live in the saloon under his own stiff terms, was getting
his share of this prosperity. Nevertheless, a couple of weeks before
George graduated from Franklin Pierce, Danny told him one day
through a troubled frown that, unless he wanted to break himself
of the habit of eating regularly, he guessed he'd better go out and get
himself a job pretty soon.

"Last week we took in eight bucks," Danny said.

"Uncle Zisha's got his troubles up in Albany, too," George said.

"He's up in Albany," Danny said. "I'm down here."

"What kind of job you going to look for?"

"Christ knows."

"I've got to get me a job right after graduation or I don't go
to college in the fall," George said. "I've been reading the papers
every day."

"You see anything good," Danny said, "let me know."

What George saw every day for almost two weeks, in the middle
of the New York *World* want-ad section, was a square block of type
several times larger than any of the surrounding advertisements:

WANTED! WANTED! WANTED!
Young Men 17-20
Office Work
Good Pay
No Experience Necessary
Opportunities For Advancement
Apply in Person Only
ALLIED EMPLOYMENT AGENCY
20 CHURCH STREET

George showed the advertisement to Danny, who agreed that
it looked like a good bet. The morning after George's graduation,
they took the Avenue B trolley down to Park Row and walked across
to Church Street. There was a sign on the door of the Allied Employment Agency that said, "We open at 9:00 A.M." The only reason
George and Danny, who arrived at eight-fifteen, knew what was
printed on the sign was that George, who was a head taller than
Danny, was several inches taller than any of the other boys milling

around in front of the door. There were at least two hundred of them.

They couldn't seem to stand still. They prowled around in small circles, eying one another suspiciously, not exactly shoving but constantly pressing forward, maneuvering with shoulders and elbows, jockeying for positions closest to the door. When the door finally opened, they poured in like coal rattling down a chute. What they poured into was a large, square, unadorned room that, for some reason, reminded George of pictures he had seen of Spanish bull rings.

It was divided in half by a wooden rail behind which, at identical desks, sat half a dozen young men who could have been clothing dummies plucked from the window of Metzger's Men's Shop on Avenue B. Their suits didn't seem to have any creases at the elbows, and their faces were as smooth as the outside of a honeydew melon, and they sat bent over their desks, never raising their heads to glance toward the mob at the other side of the rail. It was as though they had been placed in those sitting positions by a window dresser. George found them a little disturbing. He felt he had seen them before, and even though he knew this was impossible, he couldn't shake off the additional feeling that he had been tipped off by somebody to watch out for these men. Four other young men, who looked exactly like the first six except for the fact that these four were in motion, faced the crowd of boys from behind the rail and shoved white cards into their clutching hands.

"Fill in all questions, return the cards, and wait until your name is called," these four young men chanted in a monotonous singsong that apparently involved only their vocal cords and their lips. The upper parts of their faces didn't move. "Fill in all questions, return the cards, and wait until your name is called."

As the filled-in cards were returned to the four young men at the rail, they passed them in small batches to the six clothing dummies at the desks. These creaseless wonders examined each card carefully, then passed them back one at a time to the four young men at the rail. As the young men at the rail called out the names, the boys came up out of the crowd. Nobody came up slowly and nobody came up looking as unworried as he was obviously trying to look. Standing at one side with Danny after they had turned in their cards, George saw that one of two things happened next. The boy whose name was called was either given his card and allowed to pass

with it through a gate in the wooden rail to take a seat beside one
of the six desks, in which case he began to look even more worried,
or, after listening to something one of the four young men at the rail
said, the boy turned without his card and walked out, looking a little
sick.

"What goes on?" George whispered.

"As soon as I find out," Danny said, "I'll send you a telegram."

He had the look on his face, eyes narrowed, upper teeth nibbling
slowly at the corner of his lower lip, that George knew as well as he
knew his own address. Danny was casing the situation.

"Schorr?" the voice at the rail sang out. "Daniel Schorr?"

"If I come back rich," Danny said out of the corner of his
mouth, "I'll buy you an Eskimo Pie."

He came back sooner than he expected, without his card, but
George didn't get a chance to ask what had happened because just
then his own name was called. Before he could do too much about
trying to arrange his face in an unworried look, George was at the
rail, facing the young man who had called his name.

"Sorry," the young man said. "We're all full up." He dropped
George's card into a wastebasket, looked at another card and, across
George's head, sang out, "Anderson? Eugene Anderson?"

The pain didn't catch up with George until he was out in the
hall, and then his first instinct was to find Danny. Looking around
quickly, what George saw instead were a half dozen faces that, as
the pain increased but the shock began to wear off, George realized
looked a lot the way he was sure his own face looked at the moment.

"Son of a bitches!"

George turned. A boy with red hair was moving past him, on
the way to the street door, with a boy in a brown suit.

"They don't want Jews, why the hell don't they say so in the
ad?" the boy with red hair said sullenly. "Make a guy spend carfare
coming all the way downtown for nothing, the bastards."

George stood there, paying no attention to the boys jostling
him on either side, staring at the receding red-headed figure, beginning to grasp the meaning of what had happened, and feeling like a
bottle filling slowly with something unfamiliar and dangerous. Things
he hadn't thought about for years were suddenly racing through his
mind, banging against each other, shooting off blinding sparks that
held him as though in a trance: phrases Uncle Zisha had used about
Judge Brandeis and the Land of Opportunity; Aunt Tessie's warn-

ings about shkutzim. All at once George understood why, as soon as he'd seen the clothing dummies behind the desks inside the agency, he'd had the feeling they were familiar. They wore different clothes, and they were not driving O'Brien coal wagons or loading Forrester lumber barges, but they looked exactly like the shkutzim who hung around Gerrity's saloon.

The red-headed figure at the end of the corridor disappeared through the street door. George came out of his trance. Breathing through his mouth, feeling his tongue go dry and sour, he ran down the corridor to the door. He caught up with the red-headed boy on the sidewalk. "What you just said. Why they threw us out. It's because we're Jews?"

The red-headed boy looked at him in surprise, turned to his companion in the brown suit, then swung back to George. "Why do you think it's because?" he said. "They don't like the way you part your hair?"

He took his friend's arm and walked off down the street. George turned, went back into the building, and hurried up the corridor to the Allied Employment Agency door. When he came in, the four young men at the rail were still calling out names. George was aware, as he pushed through the crowd, that boys were staring at him. He paid no attention to them. It was as though he had been entered by forces stronger than himself in a race against time. He had to finish what he had been chosen to do before the dangerous feeling flooding up inside him poured over the edge. When he reached the young man who had thrown his card into the waste-basket, George could hear his own breath coming in short, hard gasps. He leaned across the rail, grabbed the wastebasket, pushed the cards around, found the one with his name on it, and pulled it out.

George shoved the card under the nose of the young man at the other side of the rail. "Why did you throw this out?"

The young man looked surprised. "We're full up," he said. He glanced at the card in his hand and, across George's head, sang out, "Talmadge? Edward Talmadge?"

"If you're full up," George said, "how come you're calling Talmadge?"

"Step away from the rail, please."

"If you're full up," George said again, "how come you're calling Talmadge?"

"Get out of here before I have you thrown out."

"Why don't you answer my question? If you're full up, how come you're calling Talmadge?"

The face that up to now had been as smooth as the outside of a honeydew melon was suddenly a mass of small, angry creases.

"Listen, you little kike, if you don't get the hell out of here before—"

That was as far as he got. George's fist, digging deep into the belly at the other side of the wooden gate, smoothed away all the angry creases. The suddenly pop-eyed face came all the way forward, as though its owner were a pocketknife with an open blade that had suddenly started to snap shut. Any further attempt at completing the threat, even if the speaker had possessed the wind with which to make it, was eliminated by the inverted wastebasket. Showering cards like gigantic snowflakes, George brought the basket down with a hard thump as though the head in front of him were a fountain pen and he was ramming home the cap.

This hastily executed series of movements, each one separate, distinct, and clear in George's mind, was followed by a period of confusion during which he was aware of hands pulling at him and voices shouting around him, but George couldn't seem to bring them into focus. He didn't even try. It was as though he had punched open a hole inside himself, and the dangerous flood that had brought him to the level of violence was easing away. He allowed himself to be carried along until suddenly he realized the voices were all gone. All, that is, except one.

"Jesus," Danny Schorr was saying. "What the hella you think you're doing?"

George blinked at him and then looked around. He was out in what seemed to be a deserted alley, and Danny was holding him upright against a brick wall. George was grateful for the support. His knees felt weak.

"I—I—" George closed his eyes and shook his head. "I guess I flew off the handle."

"Boy," Danny said. "You took the handle with you."

George opened his eyes. Danny was looking at him curiously. George felt he'd better explain.

"First, I didn't know what happened. Then, when I—" He paused and said, "You know why they threw our cards away? You know why they told us they were full up?"

"Sure."

George blinked again. "You knew it when we came down here?"

"What kind of a shvantz do you think I am?" Danny said. "If I knew it when we came down here, would I come to begin with? When we came down here all I knew was I wanted a job. When I found out they weren't giving any to heebs, I look around for you, and what do I find? You're starting a God-damn riot." Danny released George and bent down to slap dust from his pants. "If I hadn't hustled you the hell out of there, you know where you'd be now? In the clink, boy. Those bastards don't fool around. They sent for the cops."

George saw that something was wrong. Danny, who was usually so quick at sizing things up, seemed to have muffed this completely.

"Forget about the cops," George said impatiently. "I'm talking about—"

Danny stopped dusting his knees. "If you have to be dumb," he said, "try not to be *that* dumb. People who forget about cops end up in places where the cops can forget about *them*."

"That's not what I mean," George said. "I mean those bastards in there, throwing guys out just because we're Jews, they have no right—"

"What the hell has right got to do with it?"

George looked at Danny in astonishment. "You mean you're not sore?"

"Sure I'm sore," Danny said irritably. "If I'd known they didn't take Jews, I'd've been prepared to handle it. This way, not prepared, coming down here, the whole thing was just a great big God-damn waste of time."

"That's all you're sore about? That they wasted your time?"

Danny's eyes narrowed and his upper teeth began to nibble at the corner of his lower lip. He stared at George for several moments. Then his face cleared, the way it always did when he had something figured out, and Danny grinned. "Georgie, boy," he said. "What else do you want me to be sore about?"

Again, in his mind, George ran through some of those things Uncle Zisha had said years ago about Judge Brandeis and the Land of Opportunity. Only a little while ago, in the corridor of the Allied Employment Agency, there had been enough power in those remembered phrases to make George haul off and belt a total stranger. Now, in the light of Danny's grin, the phrases suddenly seemed embarrassing.

"I don't want you to be sore about anything," George said uncomfortably. "It's just that, I don't know, getting roosted out on my tail like that, just because I'm a Jew, it burned me up."

"What's that got to do with the price of Indian nuts?" Danny said. George didn't answer. "Every place you go there's bastards they don't like heebs. Most of them, they can drop dead. Who needs them? But the other ones, the guys they got the jobs to hand out, you go around letting these stupid jerks burn you up just because they don't like the shape of your beak, where the hell you going to get the dough to pay for your Oh Henrys?"

George didn't know how to answer that. Any more than the people of Fourth Street who had tried to get Danny's father to stop Danny from running errands for Mike Gerrity had known how to answer Mr. Schorr when the house painter asked them if they planned to make him another Rockefeller.

The grin slid away from Danny's face. "You got to keep your eye on the ball," he said. "Belting guys because they don't like Jews, that's okay if you want to be a hero. But before you do any belting you better make up your mind what you want." Danny paused, and the bright, restless brown eyes seemed to grow a little brighter. "What do you want, kid?" he said quietly. "You want a job? Or you want to be a hero?"

What George wanted all of a sudden was a hole to crawl into. He dropped his glance. He was ashamed of what he had just done in the Allied Employment Agency. He felt grateful to Danny for straightening him out. He wondered why anybody as smart as Danny Schorr bothered to be friends with somebody as dumb as George Hurst.

"Sure I want a job," he muttered. "But—"

"When you want a job, it's the guy who's got the job to give that calls the buts." Danny grinned and poked George gently with his fist. "Come on, Dempsey," he said. "Let's get going."

"Where to?" George said.

"A place where they got what we want," Danny said.

11

The fact that the place proved to be the home office of L. L. Parker Stores, Inc., did not strike George as amazing until months later, when he came to know something about the origin of the policies by which the large organization was run. On the day when he and Danny Schorr were turned away by the Allied Employment Agency, George had never even heard of L. L. Parker Stores, Inc.

This was not surprising.

The L. L. Parker Stores, which were spread across the face of America like acne, functioned most successfully in towns with a population under 5,000. There were those who attributed this success to a belief that the incidence of gullibility varies in direct proportion to the size of a community. Or, as an embittered rival once put it: "Big town, small boobs; small town, big boobs."

Ludwig Leo Pauker, the once penniless German immigrant who founded the company, explained it somewhat differently at the eightieth birthday dinner given in his honor by the five sons and seventeen grandsons who had followed him into the highly prosperous business.

"Soon after I came to this country I learned an important lesson," the old man said, according to a stenographic record of his speech that was circulated surreptitiously for years by disgruntled employees. "You buy something for one dollar, you sell it for two dollars, maybe you make a profit and maybe you don't. Depends on how much of that second dollar you have to pay out for overhead. But you buy something for one dollar and you sell it for twenty dollars, and even a lousy businessman can make a profit, regardless of overhead. There are only two problems: where do you find damn fools willing to pay twenty dollars for something that cost you only one dollar, and how do you get them to pay it?"

The answer to the first question proved to be: stick to communities too small to support many stores, thus narrowing the purchaser's range of choice. The answer to the second question was even simpler: make the purchaser overlook the fact that he is paying twenty dollars for something that cost you only one.

"A girl sees a hat in a window and she wants it," continued the stenographic transcript of the multimillionaire octagenarian's birthday remarks. "The hat has a price tag on it that says twenty dollars, but the girl has in her pocket only three dollars. You say to the girl: forget the twenty-dollar price tag; give me the three dollars and you take the hat. Her eyes get big as pickle barrels and she says: you mean it? To prove you mean it, you take the hat out of the window, and you give it to her, and she gives you her three dollars. While she's trying the hat on, you say: the other seventeen dollars you can forget; just remember only one thing: for the next seventeen weeks, every payday, you come in and give me another dollar. That's all. Just one dollar every payday. That's not a lot, is it? A dollar a week. You'll never even notice it. And in the meantime, you've got this beautiful hat to wear! The girl isn't even listening. She's trying on the hat. And you? How do you stand? Well, even if she doesn't come in for the full seventeen weeks. Even if she gets tired or she runs out of money or she moves away after only five or six weeks. What then? Well, before she walked out of the store she already gave you three dollars for a hat that cost you only one dollar. A normal profit of two hundred per cent you already have in your pocket. From then on, every week that girl comes in with her dollar on payday, you are soaking up pure gravy!"

Young Ludwig Leo Pauker's next discovery was that, in certain parts of his adopted country, his German name was a handicap. A man who has no qualms about charging a shop girl twenty dollars for a hat that cost him one dollar is hardly likely to develop qualms over the matter of his name. Ludwig Leo Pauker became L. L. Parker, and the results were so gratifying that, before long, another problem arose, namely, where to find enough one-dollar hats.

The answer was the home of the millinery industry: New York. There, in a three-story building on Fifteenth Street near Sixth Avenue, L. L. Parker in 1906 set up the central buying office and bookkeeping department of the national chain bearing his name that then consisted of a mere seventy-six stores.

Before too many years had gone by, the process of soaking up pure gravy had swollen the chain to more than eight hundred stores selling jewelry and athletic equipment as well as complete lines of men's and women's apparel, and the expanding administrative machinery of the home office had engulfed a dozen of the original three-story building's neighbors on Fifteenth Street. So many of the founder's descendants were now taking an active part in the operation of the huge business, that the old man was free to devote himself exclusively to the formulation of its policies.

Some of these were demonstrably shrewd. For example, it was an L. L. Parker rule never to bring suit against a defaulting customer unless he ceased making weekly payments before the net profit to the company on his purchase amounted to less than eight hundred per cent.

"If you sue too many people the word begins to get around that you are a heartless organization to do business with, people become frightened, and they start going to your competitors for their hats and shoes and wrist watches," said the founder's memorandum to the staff on this subject. "Besides, eight hundred per cent is not a profit to be ashamed of."

Some of L. L.'s other policies were clearly the result of predilections the old man had brought with him from his native land. Several months before the day when George Hurst punched the young man in the Allied Employment Agency down on Church Street, old L. L. Parker up on Fifteenth Street had subjected his company's Employment Application Blank, which had remained unchanged since it was first printed in 1906, to a single revision.

The query RELIGIOUS AFFILIATION?, which on the old blank had been sandwiched carelessly between HOBBIES? and COLOR OF EYES? near the bottom of the sheet, was moved up to the top, immediately below the applicant's name, where it appeared in red ink.

Staring at the two boldly printed words which stood out from the rest of the page like a neon sign in a dark cellar, George hesitated. All the way uptown from Church Street, listening to Danny's advice on how to handle the situation, it had seemed sensible and simple. Things always seemed sensible and simple when Danny explained them. Sometimes, though, when you got beyond range of his voice, when you were all alone and the moment came to do what Danny had advised, it seemed not so simple after all. An elbow dug into George's ribs.

He moved his head to the right. Danny, bent over his own application blank in the next chair, pointed to the two red words and gave George a quick wink. George shoved the moment of doubt into a corner of his mind and winked back. Carefully, with the fountain pen Uncle Zisha had sent from Albany as a graduation present, George wrote in after the red inked query RELIGIOUS AFFILIATION? the single word: LUTHERAN.

He did it without conviction. There were in the L. L. Parker home office almost a thousand employees. The turnover of help was large and rapid. The staff of the Personnel Office, one man and two women with flat, hard, coldly appraising faces, must have at one time or another run across every trick in the book. In spite of Danny's assurances, George didn't see how they could be fooled by a dodge as simple as this. He was certain it wouldn't work. Ten minutes later his respect for Danny Schorr, which had always been high, took a marked leap upward.

"When can you start work?" the older of the two women was asking as she looked up from George Hurst's application blank.

"Right away," he said.

"Be here tomorrow at eight."

Aunt Tessie was pleased by the news that he had landed a job so quickly. George did not spoil her pleasure by telling her that, in order to get it, he had lied about his religion, or that Danny Schorr had landed a job in the same place.

"How much is the pay?" Aunt Tessie said.

"Twelve dollars," George said.

Aunt Tessie's eyebrows went up. "They're starting you off in the president's job?"

"I imagine the president of L. L. Parker Stores gets a little more than twelve bucks a week."

"Bucks you can talk out in the street with your friends. Here in the house you'll talk English. What do you have to do for this twelve dollars a week?"

"I don't know yet. All I know is I'm in the Mail Department."

"You know something else," Aunt Tessie said. "Now you know, if you behave yourself and you don't get into trouble, the money to pay for night school you won't have to go looking for with candles."

"I won't get into trouble."

"God should only be listening and believe you. The first day you get paid we'll open for you a bank account. By the end of the summer, when night school starts, Judge Brandeis should watch out or you'll have soon his job, too."

"I've got a long way to go before Judge Brandeis starts worrying."

"The longest way is the shortest way if you don't stop to look in every store window." Aunt Tessie stopped to look around her own store. "Maybe in the back here, by the pressing machine, we could put a desk?"

"What for?"

"To make potato lottkiss. Listen to a question! From a boy just graduated from high school yet. What does a person use a desk for, for what? In high school, to study there on the table in the kitchen, all right. But now soon you're starting college, and then it'll be law school. For college and for law school a table in the kitchen, no. We'll get a desk, and we'll put it here in the back with a good light, and by the end of the summer, when night school starts, you'll be ready with a place to study."

It didn't work out that way. Two weeks later, before Aunt Tessie had found a desk that met her ideas of what was appropriate for George, Uncle Zisha collapsed while carrying a case of bottles from his truck into a candy store. The telegram sent by his doctor urged Aunt Tessie to come to Albany at once.

"All his life, that brother of mine, everything he always did at the wrong time," she said angrily as she slapped things into the cardboard suitcase George had used so many years ago on his own visit to Albany. "A grown-up man, nearly sixty years old already, he's still doing it! This is a time to go to Albany? Now? In the middle of the summer? It's hot? You just got a job? I'm busy with looking for a desk?"

"Uncle Zisha can't help the time when he gets sick," George said. "I'm sure he didn't plan it this way."

"Who planned it, then?" Aunt Tessie snapped. "Me? You? The President? It's somebody else's fault, maybe, that for forty years he's been eating like a pig with eight eyes and four stomachs? Who's there to blame if a whole night long, when other people they're sleeping, he's running around with God knows who, drinking and worse yet than drinking? From this he expects to be healthy? Because of his eating and drinking and running around, I have to go shlep myself to Albany in the middle of the summer?"

George, who was accustomed to her sharp tongue, was disturbed by the way Aunt Tessie sounded. There was something in her voice that went beyond sharpness. It was as though a beautifully honed knife was being used clumsily as an axe.

"You want me to go instead?" George said.

"And lose the job you just got? What kind of brains is that?"

"We work only half a day on Saturday. I could get a train in the afternoon and be up there that night, and then come back Sunday."

Aunt Tessie hesitated. Watching her face, from which the anger had peeled away while she considered George's suggestion, he suddenly understood what was wrong. Aunt Tessie had never been away from Fourth Street. She had never been anywhere since she had come to America. Aunt Tessie, who George had thought was afraid of nothing but the common cold, was scared stiff by the prospect of leaving the nest in which she had been holed up all these years.

"Listen," George said, wanting to turn away, wishing he had not seen her like this, and knowing instinctively, with a twinge of sadness he could not explain, that because he had seen her like this, some strands of whatever it was that tied them together had been cut. "I could go to the drug store right now and call Grand Central and find out—"

"No," Aunt Tessie said. The anger came sliding back across her face like a mask. "If you go, he'll make a great big tzimiss about how sick he is. But me, his own sister, me he can't fool!"

He didn't even try. Uncle Zisha was so weak, Aunt Tessie reported when she got back from Albany ten days later, that the doctor had refused to allow him to sit up in his hospital bed.

"Work he'll never do again," Aunt Tessie said. "Even to walk again they're not sure he'll be able to. Like a baby he is. In the hospital now, it's nurses. When he goes home, somebody will have to be there every minute to take care of him."

"Who?" George said.

Aunt Tessie scowled at the knife as she cut slices from the loaf of bread on the kitchen table. "I don't know," she said.

"How about Mrs. Gerstenberger? Any chance of getting her back?"

Aunt Tessie shook her head. "I tried," she said. "Mrs. Gerstenberger is dead."

George could suddenly smell the fried chicken the stout German woman had put in his lunch box the day he left Albany years ago. Forced all at once to face the fact that the years he had already lived could never be lived again, sensing with uneasiness the speed with which those that still lay ahead were bearing down on him, George had a moment of terror for the passage of time.

"There must be somebody else," he said.

"There's thousands of somebody elses," Aunt Tessie said. "For thirty dollars a week."

"Oh," George said.

"All these years, in the letters he writes from Albany, he's a millionaire," Aunt Tessie said bitterly. "Now, in the hospital, all of a sudden what he has, he's got the house there on Westerlo Street, and from the business, it doesn't even belong to him any more, he has a few dollars a week to eat, and it won't be gold fish he'll be able to eat, either. This is all of a sudden what's left from the millionaire."

"Jesus," George said.

"In the street, with your friends, it's Jesus. Here, in the house, it's English, please."

"All I meant, if Uncle Zisha is that sick and he hasn't got the dough—"

"Dough you can leave outside with the Jesus. In here it's money."

"Without money to pay for somebody, who's going to take care of him?"

"Who is it that does things without money, who?"

George's forkful of stuffed veal stopped on its way to his mouth. "You're going back to Albany?"

"You could show me a way maybe how I could take care of Uncle Zisha from here on Fourth Street?"

"How long are you going to stay?"

"A minute ago, when I said the doctors told me he'll never be able to work again, they said for the rest of his life he'll need somebody to take care of him like a baby, where were your ears?"

The forkful of stuffed veal completed its journey to George's mouth. He chewed in silence for a while. Then he pushed aside his plate and stood up.

"Where you going?" Aunt Tessie said.

"Out."

"Out where?"

"Just out."

He went through the store and stopped on the stoop, staring across the street at Gerrity's. There was no sign of life behind the windows which had been painted black with the coming of Prohibition, but George knew Danny was in there somewhere. Every night, when they came home from their work in the L. L. Parker mailroom, Danny disappeared into the former saloon and did not come out again until it was time for him and George to go to work the next morning. George didn't know what went on inside Gerrity's these days, and he never asked, but he suspected it was not good. The rumor on Fourth Street was that Danny had his hands full with Mike

Junior, who was supposed to be blind drunk most of the time, and Mrs. Gerrity, who was slowly being paralyzed by arthritis. Nobody on the block felt sorry for either the Gerritys or Danny. On the contrary. There was a general feeling of satisfaction. The wicked, it was felt, were finally getting what they deserved.

George wondered sometimes why Danny continued to stay in the red brick house across the street. Now that Danny had a job and was earning good money, he could afford to live anywhere he chose. There were plenty of good rooms for rent near the L. L. Parker offices, all the way from University Place to Seventh Avenue. Every day, when George and Danny went to work, they saw the VACANCY signs. George wished at the moment that Danny didn't live with the Gerritys. If George waited until morning he would see Danny when they went to work or, if George missed him on the way, he would see Danny in the L. L. Parker mailroom. But George didn't feel like waiting. The news Aunt Tessie had brought back from Albany was upsetting. He didn't know what to think about it. He wanted to talk with Danny. He stood there, hesitating, weighing his desire to see Danny against his nameless fear of the house across the street in which he had never set foot, and suddenly George became aware that he was not alone. He turned.

Dora was watching him from the doorway of the doll store. "Aunt Tessie is back?"

"Yeah," George said. "She got home this afternoon."

"I thought so," Dora said. "I could smell cooking."

George came down the stoop and around toward Dora. She stood in the shadows of the darkened store, her thin shoulders bent forward, her bad arm turned away from him. Deep in the back of the store, in the lighted rooms behind the doll factory, Dora's crazy sister Ida was practicing her scales.

"I got tired of listening to her sing," Dora said. "If you can call it singing. I came out to get some air. I saw you standing there. I—" Dora paused, and she looked up at him, and she said quietly, "What's the matter, George?"

"We have to move to Albany."

Dora's hand came up to her mouth as though she had been slapped. "You and Aunt Tessie?"

George nodded.

"You're joking," Dora said.

"I wish I was."

"Why do you have to move?"

George told her.

"Why can't she go alone?"

Astonished, George said, "Aunt Tessie?" Dora nodded. George said, "Quit kidding."

"Who's kidding?"

"Aunt Tessie can't go alone."

"She just did."

"That was for only ten days. Just to see what's what. But this is for good. Uncle Zisha can't work or move or anything. Somebody has to take care of him. She'll have to live there."

"Why do you have to live there with her?"

The answer was so obvious that it made the question seem silly, and yet George couldn't put the answer into words. "It's not I have to live there with her or I don't have to live there with her," he said. "It's just I can't let Aunt Tessie go up there alone."

"What about night school? What about becoming another Judge Brandeis?"

"There's night schools in Albany. I can study up there."

"Sure you can," Dora said. "You can do anything. Why shouldn't you? There's nothing wrong with you."

George didn't realize until he saw her body begin to shake that she was crying. "Dora, for Christ's sake."

"Shut up."

"Dora, listen."

"Leave me alone."

She turned away, resting her forehead against the door, and George watched helplessly as Dora sobbed in the shadows of the doorway until she began to choke. In the back of the store Ida switched from scales to "Apple Blossom Time," screaming the song out into the summer night as though the words were being wrung from her by torture. George reached out awkwardly and put his hand on Dora's shoulder.

She squirmed away. "Don't touch me."

"Dora, listen."

"To what?" she said bitterly. "The fine time you're going to have in Albany? The wonderful things you're going to do there? Go ahead. Tell me again. Rub it in. It doesn't matter what you say to me. I'm just a cripple. I don't matter."

"Dora, please. Please listen. I—"

She turned, and suddenly she was leaning against him, sobbing into his shirt, shaking so hard that he had to put his arm around her to keep his balance.

"You're the only friend I have," she said brokenly, getting the words out in spurts, between gasps for air, so that the choppy phrases emerged like short, muffled screams. "Ida and Frannie, they're always yelling at me, I'm a slob, I don't do the work right, I don't earn even my meals and a place to sleep. Ma and Pa, they hate me because I'm a cripple. Everybody hates a cripple. You're the only one ever talks to me. If you go away, I won't have anybody. I'll be all alone."

George had never realized how thin she was. It was like holding a handful of bones. He could feel the sharp little shoulder blades under his outspread hand, moving with her sobs like the wings of an injured bird.

"No," George said, and he paused, the breath catching in his throat, surprised by something else: her hair smelled fresh and sweet, like Aunt Tessie's honey cake. "Dora, listen," George said. "You won't be alone," he whispered. "I promise."

In the long silence that followed he found himself wishing Ida would stop screaming that damned song. He had to think of a good way to break the news to Aunt Tessie that he was not going to Albany with her.

12

There were no good ways. George found that out three weeks later, the night before Aunt Tessie's departure.

"The train they say it leaves eleven o'clock tomorrow morning," she said. "But these shkutzim that run the railroads, who can trust them? We'll be smart, you and me. Tomorrow morning, in Grand Central, we'll be there half past ten, maybe even a little earlier. We'll make sure they don't leave us behind."

George stared at her. Was it possible that she hadn't heard a word he'd said during the past three weeks? Or was she merely pretending she hadn't heard?

"They'll leave one of us behind," George said. "I'm not going to Albany."

"It's too much to shlep our suitcases from here to the Tenth Street car and then in the subway," Aunt Tessie said, as though he had not spoken. "We'll call up by the drug store they should send a taxi."

"That's a good idea," George said. "Because I won't be able to help you take your stuff to Grand Central. I'll be working."

Aunt Tessie straightened up. They were standing among the racks and machines and chairs in the dismantled tailor shop. They had been examining the tags Mr. Noftooleh, the second-hand furniture dealer from Avenue C, had placed on the equipment after the weeks of haggling over price with Aunt Tessie had finally ended in a compromise late that afternoon, shortly before George came home from his job in the L. L. Parker mailroom.

"You'll be working?" Aunt Tessie said slowly, as though he had announced that he would be slaughtering hogs. "Tomorrow morning you'll be working?"

"I work every morning. I've got a job. You know that."

"But tomorrow morning we're going to Albany," Aunt Tessie said, even more slowly. "To live with Uncle Zisha."

"You're going to Albany to live with Uncle Zisha," George said. "Not me."

He spoke with great care, keeping his eyes fixed on her face, as though they were approaching each other from different ends of a tight rope and he was afraid that the slightest deviation, the faintest increase in the decibels of sound he was uttering would destroy their precariously maintained balance.

"I've been telling you for three weeks," George said. "I'm not going to live in Albany. I rented a room today on University Place. I'm staying here in New York."

There were several moments of silence, and then Aunt Tessie's thin body seemed to move slightly inside the long black alpaca dress she had worn ever since he had known her. It was as though somewhere in the machinery that kept her going the gears had been shifted.

"I never should have gone to Houston Street to get you," she said. "I should have left you there where I found you, by Henry Isaacs."

"You don't mean that," George said. "You're only saying it because you're angry."

"How do you want I should say it? With laughing?"

"I don't want you to say anything. All I want you to do is understand."

"You want I should understand? And you? You understand maybe? What it means to be all your life skinny like a needle and crooked-looking like a burned lottke? So people, instead of coming to touch you, to talk, to like you, the minute they see you they pick up their feet and they run? You understand maybe what it means to sit and to watch, that's all, just to sit and watch while other women they get married and they have children, and you, what you have, you have inside where other people have a full heart, by you it's like an empty pocketbook? You know maybe what it means when you're already no spring chicken, you go to Henry Isaacs, you see a little boy, you take him home, and inside here, where it's an empty pocketbook, all of a sudden it's full? All of a sudden, no matter what it says in the mirror, you're no more skinny like a needle, you're no more crooked-looking? Because all of a sudden you have what other women have? You understand maybe what it means to have this for fourteen years, for fourteen years to be like other people, and then in a one, two, three, with a handful words, all of a sudden the whole thing is nothing, it's again inside like an empty pocketbook? This you understand, maybe?"

If she would only scream, George thought. If she would only wave her arms or look hysterical. But she didn't scream, and she didn't wave her arms, and she didn't look hysterical. She stood up ramrod straight, the black-sheathed pipestem arms folded across her narrow little chest, her voice flat and calm, her words unhurried and evenly spaced, as though she were dictating a telegram over the phone, and it was a long, long time, or so it seemed, before the swelling in George's throat eased enough to allow him to speak.

"I'm not dying or going to Europe," he said, feeling helpless in the face of her strength, admiring a courage that could let her open her heart and yet never for a moment diminish the pride that held her together and kept her untouched, safe from the erosion of pity. "Albany is only a few hours away," George said. "I'll be coming up all the time to visit you."

"Me you'll come to visit, but Mr. Danny Schorr, with him you'll stay here to live."

Astonished, George said, "Danny? What's Danny got to do with it?"

"From the beginning, from the first day you saw him fourteen years ago, anything he wanted he could do with you." A touch of bitterness rose to the surface of the flat, calm voice. "The only thing I never knew, the only thing it never walked into my head, was that the day would come when he would take you away from me."

"He's not taking me away from you. It's not because of Danny that I'm staying in New York."

"Words you can put in my ears, but they won't change what I see with my eyes."

"I don't care what you see," George said angrily, furious with her for not being furious, for denying him with her self-control the relief he might have obtained from meeting rage with rage. "You're not seeing it right."

"No?" she said.

"No," George said. "It's not because of Danny that I'm staying in New York."

The thin lips twisted in a small, mocking smile. "So because of who is it, then?" Aunt Tessie said. "Who?"

George started to tell her, but all at once he could feel again the sharp little shoulder blades that were like the wings of a wounded bird under his outspread hand, and he could smell again the hair that reminded him of Aunt Tessie's honey cake fresh from the oven, and he couldn't get the words out.

There was no way to explain about that.

13

F. (for Friedrich) F. (for Feuer) Shumacher, head of the L. L. Parker mailroom, was fond of saying that his department was to the large organization what gasoline is to the Cadillac. He said it every morning at eight-fifteen.

"Most people look at a Cadillac and all they see is a great big shiny car," he said. "They never stop to think that without gasoline, the stuff they can't see at all, that great big shiny car would be about as useful as a statue in the park. The same with us. Most people look at L. L. Parker Stores and all they see is a live-wire organization that stretches clear across the country from Maine to California, from Washington to Florida, from the Canadian to the Mexican border.

They never stop to think that without this mailroom here on Fifteenth Street, something they don't even know exists, the L. L. Parker Stores would stop functioning in twenty-four hours."

This was an exaggeration, of course, but not by very much. With more than eight hundred stores sending in daily sales reports, requests for merchandise, and a dozen or more other types of communications standardized by efficiency experts to insure the smoothest possible relationship between the brain center of a commercial octopus and its outlying tentacles, the four small basement rooms on Fifteenth Street, through which every scrap of this paper stream had to flow, could very easily have become a serious bottleneck.

The fact that the L. L. Parker mailroom was not a bottleneck could be attributed entirely to the unique personality and special talents of Friedrich Feuer Shumacher, who was known to his staff, when they were addressing him directly, as Eff Eff, or, when they were talking about him among themselves, as Fart Face.

It did not require a particularly active imagination to figure out how the nickname had come into being.

F. F. Shumacher was a tall, thin man in his early sixties, with neatly combed snow-white hair, sallow, spotted skin that looked like used flypaper, false teeth so badly fitted that they clacked when he talked, a cackling laugh that would not have been out of place in a barnyard, and the fussy mannerisms of a nervous old lady trying to get through a subway turnstile during the rush hour while carrying half a dozen greased cantaloupes.

Every morning at eight o'clock he gathered all sixteen members of his staff around two ping-pong tables placed side by side in the largest of the department's four rooms. Standing four abreast on all sides of the large square they looked a good deal like players in a gambling casino gathered around an outsize roulette table. Mr. Shumacher, circling happily on the outskirts of the square, dumping across the shoulders of his staff scoops of mail from the sacks that had been brought over from the post office, looked like a demented farmer flinging feed to a brood of chickens he had trained to consume, like pigs, food from a common trough. At eight-fifteen, satisfied that the staff was snatching the mail at a good rate of speed from the common pile in the middle of the ping-pong tables and sorting it nicely, Eff Eff would emit a series of gleeful preparatory cackles and launch into the speech that explained why his department was to the large organization what gasoline is to the Cadillac.

By the time he had been on the job several weeks, George Hurst was good and sick of this comparison. It took him a little longer to lose his admiration for the ping-pong tables, which were Eff Eff's brainchild. Until he gave birth to it, the L. L. Parker mail had been sorted for almost three decades on various pieces of furniture scattered without plan throughout the four rooms. When Eff Eff took over the department, this arrangement bothered him. Not because it was inefficient but because it seemed to him unfriendly to have his staff spread out all over the place. His instincts being those of a mother hen, Eff Eff liked to have his entire brood under his benevolent glance at all times. The two ping-pong tables accomplished this purpose beautifully.

Their other accomplishment, though completely unintentional, was what kept the mailroom from becoming a bottleneck: working as one group in full view of the head of the department, instead of several groups spread through four rooms, the mailroom staff, from the very first day the new system went into operation, clipped twenty minutes from the best time ever before recorded for the morning sorting chore.

So many congratulations on this accomplishment poured in from department heads all over the organization, that Eff Eff, as delighted as a parent whose children have brought good report cards home from school, decided to reward his official family. He eliminated the staggered lunch hour that had been in operation for years, arranged with a catering company to deliver box lunches to the mailroom, and insisted that the whole staff lunch together every day, in a happy group, around the ping-pong tables that had been and continued to be the field of their triumph.

If there were any employees who were somewhat less than enthusiastic about this arrangement, seeing some virtues in the old system under which they had been free to go out for the midday meal and thus remove themselves for an hour from Eff Eff's relentless clacking chatter about the delights of sorting mail and whisking it to all corners of the home office in record time, they had enough sense to keep their traps shut.

George had not realized, during his first days on the job, that the communal lunch was compulsory. He had been so busy learning the routine that, when the caterer's man came around at eleven-thirty with the lunch boxes, he bought one without giving it a second thought, and, a half hour later, when Mr. Shumacher and the other employees began to pull chairs up to the ping-pong tables, George had pulled one up for himself. A few days later, when he had mastered the rather primitive routine of the job and was free to think about other matters, the communal lunch hour began to give him a swift pain in the neck.

The trouble was that Mr. Shumacher fancied himself as a Jewish dialect comedian.

Ordinarily, George did not mind jokes about Jews any more than he minded jokes about Republicans or channel swimmers. He had grown accustomed in high school, through Fott Fromkin and other members of the school of raconteurs to which Fott belonged, to the traditional anecdote that rested solidly on those three stock characters: Mike the Harp, Tony the Wop, and Izzy the Heeb. George had told his share of these jokes. But he had always told them to other Jewish boys, and while not all the jokes he'd heard had been told exclusively by Jews, George had never heard them under circumstances that were quite the same as those that existed around the ping-pong tables presided over by Mr. Shumacher: at that relentlessly festive board George Hurst traveled—or, more accurately perhaps, squirmed— under false colors.

From the moment he had written the word "Lutheran" on his employment application, George had never been free from the knowledge that he was living a lie. The lie did not bother him too much. Aunt Tessie had managed through the years to impress on him the general proposition that honesty was the best policy, even though the evidence of his own eyes indicated quite clearly that this was not always so, but George had long ago grasped the fact that telling a lie was not the equivalent of signing a death warrant. It was probably better not to lie, but, if you had to do it, you did it. Having done it, instead of counting on God to come along and strike you dead, you could actually count more heavily on His not even being aware of your existence. There was, therefore, no point in crying or even thinking about any one particular lie. Danny Schorr's hard-headed clarification of the issue continued to impress George as sound. You had to decide what you wanted and then keep your eye on the ball until you got it or, once you got it, for as long as you wanted to hold onto it.

What George wanted was this job in the L. L. Parker mailroom. Without it, or a job at least as good, he could not continue to live and study in New York, and so far as he could see from the want ads, no other jobs of any kind were available at this time. In order to continue living and studying in New York, George was willing, five days a week from eight in the morning until six at night and half a day on Saturday, to live the pretense that he was not a Jew. He did not find it a very difficult thing to do. Except during lunch hour.

When Mr. Shumacher, seated with his happy staff around the ping-pong tables, embarked on one of his stories, George could feel the skin on the side of his jaw begin to crawl and the food go dry in his mouth. In a few moments, when Eff Eff reached the punch line, his staff would explode into roars of appreciative laughter. George could not join them. He didn't understand why. In an organization run by policies drawn from the mind of a man like L. L. Parker, references somewhat less than complimentary to Jews were not rare in the day's work. George could and did dismiss these with a mental shrug. Or, when the remark was made to him directly, he even could and often did reply with a neutral phrase that, while it kept George's conscience clear, left with the person to whom it was addressed the impression that George shared his point of view.

Why, then, when Mr. Shumacher told one of his lousy jokes, couldn't George guffaw with the rest? What was the gap that separated this particular act of hypocrisy from the others he performed so easily? George didn't know. He knew only that he found it impossible to laugh at Eff Eff's stories. As a result George knew also that before long his failure to appreciate the boss's humor would be noticed. It was easy enough to imagine the chain of events that would follow: puzzlement would lead to suspicion, suspicion to investigation, and investigation to firing.

George could not afford to allow that to happen.

Even if he could get another job fairly soon, which the want-ad sections made it plain was highly unlikely, being out of work for no matter how short a period would mean serious trouble. Four of the twelve dollars George earned each week went to his landlady. Out of the remaining eight he had to pay for his food, buy his clothes, and take care of his tuition at Washington Square College. Every week was a race against insolvency. The fact that thus far he had been winning it, was no assurance that he would continue to do so. He had absolutely no cushion to fall back on, and the only two people from whom he could even imagine trying to borrow, should an emergency arise, were in worse financial shape than he was: Aunt Tessie's last letter from Albany had reported that Uncle Zisha, in order to meet his medical bills, had been forced to put a second mortgage on the Westerlo Street house; and Danny, who rarely talked about his relationship with the Gerritys, had several times during the past few weeks surprised George by remarking bitterly that he was getting sick and tired of sweating his ass off in the L. L. Parker mailroom to keep Mike Junior in booze and Mike's old lady in medicine.

For this reason George admired and envied the way Danny was able, when Mr. Shumacher delivered one of his punch lines, to laugh as hard as the others gathered around the ping-pong tables. Danny knew what he wanted, just as George did. The difference was that Danny was able to get it without tying himself up in knots. If, in order to hold onto his job, he had to laugh at Eff Eff's jokes, Danny laughed. George wished he could do the same. Sitting there with a mouthful of sandwich growing tasteless and then sour on his tongue, looking around at the grinning faces of Mr. Shumacher and his staff, George was reminded of the shkutzim who used to go in and out of Gerrity's saloon when he was a kid, and of the way he used to feel about the enemy stronghold across the street. Danny had never been afraid of that stronghold. Danny's lack of fear was paying off now. Eff Eff and his staff were to Danny just another bunch of shkutzim, like the coal-wagon drivers and lumber bargemen Danny had known all his life on East Fourth Street, and if there was anything Danny Schorr knew, he knew how to handle shkutzim.

George, who didn't, decided after several uncomfortable weeks at the ping-pong tables that the only solution to his problem was to go away from there. Three days later he learned he had made a mistake.

"Oh, George," Mr. Shumacher called when George came back to the mailroom at one o'clock. "Could I see you a moment?"

George went over to the roll-top desk where Eff Eff fooled around with papers when he wasn't supervising the sorting of mail or telling funny stories about Jews.

"Yes, sir?" George said.

"We've missed you at lunch."

There was a note in the old boob's gentle voice that went off in George's head like a fire alarm.

"I've been going out to eat," George said.

"So I've noticed," Mr. Shumacher said. "Don't you like to eat lunch with us?"

"It isn't that, sir."

"What is it, George?"

"Well—"

"You can speak up and be honest with me, George."

"Well, I can't afford those box lunches."

While this was not, of course, the real reason, the statement was true enough. According to the budget George had worked out for himself as soon as Aunt Tessie went to Albany and he was on his own, he could spend sixty-five cents a day on food. His breakfast, which consisted of two rolls and a glass of milk, cost him ten cents in Stewart's Cafeteria diagonally across the street from his rooming house on University Place. At six-thirty in the same cafeteria, before he went to his first class after finishing his day's work in the L. L. Parker mailroom, George could get for thirty-five cents a meat or fish dish with two vegetables and bread and butter, a nickel dessert, and another glass of milk. This left him with twenty cents for the middle of the day. The box lunches eaten around the mailroom ping-pong tables cost thirty-five cents. As a result, during the time he had attended Mr. Shumacher's luncheon parties, George had been forced to omit dessert and a beverage from his evening meals. He didn't like to antagonize his boss. But he didn't like going to bed feeling hungry, either.

"You mean to say, George, you can't afford thirty-five cents to join your colleagues for the period of relaxation to which we all look forward from the moment we begin our excellent work at eight in the morning and from which we all draw the invigorating juices that recharge our batteries and enable us to sustain the same high pitch of excellence for the balance of the day?"

Oy gevollt, George thought. "It isn't that, Mr. Shumacher," he said.

"You mean there's another reason?"

"Well—"

"Are you trying to say, George, that when you just said you have been going out to lunch because you couldn't afford to eat with your colleagues, you were not telling me the truth?"

"No, sir."

"Then what *are* you trying to say?"

"Nothing, sir."

The skin that looked like spotted flypaper drew together around Mr. Shumacher's lips like the neck of a sack narrowing down when the drawstring is pulled. It reminded George of the malicious smile that appeared on Mr. Forman's puss when the Fourth Street grocer was getting ready to let go with a real mean one about Aunt Tessie.

All bastards, whether shkutzim or heebs, apparently looked the same way when they were doing what came naturally.

"In other words, then, George, you really had no intention of, how shall I put it, yes, no intention of boycotting our lunch parties here in the mailroom?"

"No, sir."

"It was merely an oversight?"

"Yes, sir."

"From now on we can count on you to join us around the ping-pong tables every day at noon?"

"Yes, sir."

"Good. I'm very pleased, George. I'm sure the rest of our staff will be pleased, too."

At least one member of it was, anyway. That night, when George left the office, he found Danny waiting for him on the sidewalk.

"What did Eff Eff have you on the mat for?" he said as they started off side by side toward Fifth Avenue.

George told him.

"I been meaning to ask you myself how come you weren't around for lunch the last couple of days."

There was no point in telling him the real reason. Danny, who understood pretty damn near everything, would not understand what George himself didn't understand: why he couldn't laugh at Mr. Shumacher's jokes.

"It's those lousy box lunches," George said instead. "Those ham sandwiches. Pieces of cardboard with a shmeer of pink paint in between. An orange or an apple big as a walnut, and a hunk of pie, stick it in your eye and you'd never even feel it. Thirty-five cents down the drain, my insides are grinding, and half the dough for my supper is shot. Over on Sixth Avenue, or a little further down on Fourteenth Street, near Third, for twenty cents I get a knish and a couple of hot dogs and a glass of milk, and I've got something holding the sides of my stomach apart. Anyway, I did have, these last three days," George said sourly. "Tomorrow I go back to those crummy lunch boxes."

"And those crummy jokes."

Surprised, George gave Danny a quick glance. He was walking along with his hands in his pockets, scowling at the ground and kicking his heels down hard with each step, as though the sidewalk was in some way responsible for the black mood that had suddenly closed in on him. George was reminded of the way Danny used to look on

Fourth Street when he had to wait for somebody, shifting his weight impatiently from foot to foot, kicking the sidewalk, peering up and down the street, his thin, wiry body hopping around like spit on a hot stove. That was the thing about Danny. He couldn't wait. He was like one of those horses that pulled the O'Brien Coal wagons when the shkutz on the driver's seat was holding him in tight with the reins. You could see that horse pulling like crazy to bust out. You could see Danny doing the same. You could feel it. And you knew that whatever it was, some day it was going to give. It had to. Nothing could hold Danny forever.

"I thought you liked Eff Eff's jokes," George said.

"You're sure picking up some bright thoughts these days."

"I've got plenty of reason," George said. "Every time the old bastard gets to one of his punch lines, you look like you're trying to bust a gut."

Danny made a growling sound of disgust somewhere deep in his throat. He spit into the gutter. "If you want to hold onto your job in that dump, that's the way you'd better sound, too."

"Beginning tomorrow," George said dryly, "I'm going to try."

Danny punched his left fist into his right palm in a sudden explosion of impatience. "God damn it," he said. "God damn it. God *damn* it." He banged his palm again. "If only I didn't have that dead-head drunk and his old lady on my hands!"

He didn't seem to be talking to George. He was apparently cutting into a talk he'd been having with himself below the surface of the conversation he'd been carrying on with George. It was obviously the same running conversation out of which, during the past weeks, had come the seemingly irrelevant remarks that he was tired of working in the L. L. Parker mailroom to keep Mike Gerrity, Jr., in booze and Mrs. Gerrity in medicine. It occurred to George that maybe those remarks had not been so irrelevant. If paying thirty-five cents for a box lunch was a strain on George's budget, maybe it was worse for Danny. Danny didn't have to pay tuition at Washington Square College or rent for a room on University Place. But he did have to support, or for some reason felt he had to support, Mike Gerrity, Jr., and Mrs. Gerrity. For the first time in all the years they had known each other, George suddenly felt it was all right to raise the forbidden subject.

"Why don't you quit having them on your hands?" he said. "Why don't you just walk out of there?"

"I can't," Danny said.

"Why not?"

"I said I can't."

"And I said why not?"

"I just can't, that's all."

To George, who was not accustomed to seeing his cocky, self-confident friend in a defeated mood, it was not all.

"Look," he said warming to his idea. It had popped into his head unexpectedly but now, in the light of the opportunity it presented to be helpful to the despondent Danny, it seemed bright with sudden promise. "You could move in with me," George said. "It's a pretty big room. In addition to the bed, I've got this studio couch. You could have whichever one you wanted to sleep on, and we could split the rent in half. That way, not only would I be saving two bucks a week, which believe me I could sure use, but you wouldn't have to be shelling out for the Gerritys. Aside from your half of the rent, you'd have all the rest of the salary for yourself. With that much of an edge, sort of pooling our dough that way, we could even maybe take a chance, knock off for a day once in a while and go look for better jobs. Any kind of a break, and you wouldn't have to do any more laughing at Eff Eff."

"Yeah, and I could start laughing at myself."

George, stopped short in the middle of painting his glowing portrait of their common future, blinked as though he had come out of a dark room into the sunlight.

"What kind of a putz melamed do you think I am?" Danny said. "All these years, the time and work and everything else I invested in that drunken shmiggeggie and his old lady, I should walk out on the whole thing now and let somebody else move in?"

His thin, handsome face had lost its uncertainty. The brown eyes were crackling with restless light, as though they were mirrors picking up reflections from a pinwheel. The lips were pulled over to one side in the tight little half-smile through which, when he was going good, Danny Schorr's words emerged like slugs of metal type dropping crisply into waiting slots.

"All I was trying to do," George said, "I was just trying to help."

"Here's how you do your helping," Danny said. "You start laughing it up over those lunch boxes like all the rest of us around that ping-pong table so Shumacher won't get suspicious and start asking questions and maybe find out you're no more a Lutheran than I'm Benny Leonard. Because once he finds that out, he'll start on everybody else with Lutheran on their application blanks, which means me, and while no job that pays twelve bucks a week is my idea of heaven, until I get ready to tell him where he can stick it, I need that job and I want to hold onto it. Understand?"

What George did not understand was Danny's reference to the time and work he had invested in Gerrity's. A few months later, when George was down on Fourth Street visiting Dora Dienst one Sunday, he found out.

Neither George nor Dora had ever discussed these Sunday visits. They came about so naturally that George never even thought about them. If he had, his whole life would have been different.

For a while after Aunt Tessie went to Albany he was busy getting himself settled into his room on University Place, his job on Fifteenth Street, and his night classes on Washington Square. Then, one day, he was all settled, and with the shock of an unexpected physical blow he came up against an emotion that was completely new to him: loneliness.

All the days of his life up to now there had been no piece of any twenty-four-hour period when George was not in one way or another relating to someone he cared about or who cared about him. If it wasn't Danny sending him a message by tin can down the back-yard wall about an important meeting in Forman's, or Dora waiting in the doll store for him to bring her a juicy anecdote about his day at Franklin Pierce High, it was Aunt Tessie bawling him out for getting the sleeves of his sweater wet. Even when he was asleep George slept with the unconscious but reassuring knowledge that Aunt Tessie was ten feet away, in the bed near the kitchen stove, and Danny was in his room across the street in Gerrity's, and Dora was asleep somewhere back of the doll store at the other side of the stoop.

When Aunt Tessie went to Albany and George moved to University Place, all that changed. He still saw Danny every day, but seeing him in the mailroom at L. L. Parker was not the same as seeing him on Fourth Street. And late at night, when George got back to his room after classes, he was suddenly aware of the distance that separated him from Aunt Tessie and Danny and Dora. The awareness hurt. It was like carrying around a lump in your chest. George tried for a while to push the lump away by working hard in school and by writing long letters to Aunt Tessie, but he didn't succeed in pushing it very far. The most helpful thing, what sustained him most, was the knowledge that he had a goal.

Staring at the silver-framed picture of Judge Brandeis on the table near his bed, George didn't mind being lonely. Or he could pretend for a while that he didn't mind. He could kid himself into believing you had to feel this way if you were working toward something big. He didn't understand how the ambition had taken such fierce hold, how the desire of Uncle Zisha, a man George had seen only once for a couple of weeks a dozen years ago, had been transplanted intact, but George was grateful that it had been transplanted. He knew what he wanted. He knew where he was going. If the process of getting there meant feeling cut off and alone, that was all right with him.

It was all right for a while. Then one day when the pain came crowding back at him so powerfully that it was almost unbearable, George suddenly realized the next day was Sunday. He didn't have to go to work. He had no classes. He had a book report to write for English, and ten pages from *Le Livre De Mon Ami* to translate for his French class, and four chapters in his economics textbook to digest for an oral quiz the following night, but George figured the hell with it. The next morning he got up early and walked across town to see the Diensts.

They were all in the store, working hard on a rush order, but after they had asked a lot of questions about how he liked his job and what was he learning in night school and what did he hear from Aunt Tessie, Mrs. Dienst suddenly announced that they were all caught up with their work, and there were too many people in the store, anyway, so why didn't George and Dora go out for a walk?

"Better watch where you're walking," Ida said, and she grinned as she rolled her eyes crazily. "This street ends in a river, you know."

"You, you better know to watch the long tongue," Mrs. Dienst snapped, and then, to George and Dora, "Go, children, go."

They went down to the river and sat on the dock, where they watched the barges go by as they talked. At any rate, George talked. Dora just sat there, idly tearing splinters out of the weathered wood and dropping them into the river. It was like those afternoons when George used to come back from Franklin Pierce and drop into the doll store. Dora seemed to be listening with interest, but George had the feeling that she didn't really hear what he was saying. She sat hunched forward, shielding her crooked arm with the curve of her body, watching the ripples spread out from the splinters she tossed down into the water. The invisible wall she had built around herself after the Armistice Day accident was still there. George could feel it, forcing him to respect her unspoken desire to keep the world at a distance, but he could feel something else, too. He could feel the lump of loneliness in his chest ease away as he talked. He would have preferred to have Dora come out from behind the invisible wall, from the secret place she had built for herself and in which she felt safe, but the fact that she didn't was not important. What was important was the way talking to her made him feel. So George went right on talking.

Late that night, after he'd had supper with the Diensts in the kitchen behind the doll store and he was back in his room on University Place working on *Le Livre De Mon Ami*, George tried to remember what he had talked to Dora about, but he couldn't. He couldn't remember a damn thing. He felt better than he'd felt for a long time, though, and when he finished his work and climbed into bed and pulled out the light, he was already looking forward to next Sunday.

It was very much like the preceding Sunday, which proved to be not much different from all the Sundays that followed. The only change was dictated by the weather. If it rained or snowed or was too cold for sitting on the dock, George and Dora sat in the doll store with the other members of the Dienst family, and George talked while they worked on a rush order. There was always a rush order. George didn't like talking to the group as much as he liked talking to Dora alone. Not because Dora's sisters and parents were bored by what George had to say. On the contrary. They were a much better audience, especially Mr. and Mrs. Dienst and fat Frannie, who watched George's face as he talked and kept nodding their heads as though to urge him on. When he paused, Frannie always said eagerly, "Say some more, George!" and Mrs. Dienst would hand him an apple or a banana as though bribing him to continue. George continued, because he was beginning to discover that he enjoyed talking to a group, but he still wished it wasn't raining or snowing so that he and Dora could go out to the dock where he could talk to her alone. He didn't know why. It was just better out on the dock with Dora.

It also proved to be more revealing. One Sunday, when they were sitting in the sun and George was telling her how many pre-law credits he would have to pile up at Washington Square College before he could enter law school, and how many more years this would take, it suddenly seemed to him that he could hear voices.

George stopped and listened. "Sounds like somebody singing," he said.

"If you can call it singing," Dora said.

The bitterness in her voice reminded George of something. For several moments he didn't know what it was. Then he remembered the night in the darkened doorway of the doll store when, as he told Dora he was not going to Albany with Aunt Tessie, Ida's voice from somewhere in the back had been screaming "Apple Blossom Time" across their heads.

"Sounds like Ida," George said.

"Why shouldn't it sound like Ida?" Dora said. George looked at her in puzzlement, and Dora said, "Come on."

She led him from the dock to the gate that separated Forrester Box & Lumber from O'Brien Coal, and into the Forest. Years had passed since George had been in the Forest. For several uneasy moments, as he followed Dora down a long aisle, between the lumber stacks that led from the river toward Lewis Street, he was caught up in the remembered horror of Armistice Day. George looked quickly at Dora. If her thoughts were anywhere near the subject that filled his own, it did not show on her face. As they approached the fence that marked the end of the Forest and the beginning of Gerrity's back yard, the voice George had heard on the dock grew louder. When they reached the fence, Dora stopped. So did George. He looked across the fence, at the rear of the red-brick house, then at Dora, and back at the house. There didn't seem to be any doubt about it. From somewhere inside Gerrity's the voice of Ida Dienst, to the accompaniment of what sounded like a piano, was screaming "Apple Blossom Time." George turned back to Dora.

"That's Ida," he said. Dora nodded. George said, "What's she doing in there?"

"She calls it singing."

Somehow this didn't seem to be enough of an answer. "Who's in there with her?"

Dora shrugged. "How should I know? I've never been inside the place."

Something in her manner suggested a clue. "But Ida has?" George said.

"These last few weeks, more than a month already, she's been in there every night and all day Sunday."

"Doing what?"

"Can't you hear her?"

"Why is she doing it?"

"She says she's practicing."

"Practicing for what?"

Dora shrugged again. "Why don't you ask Mr. Danny Shorr? That rotten little shkutz lover is your friend, not mine."

George asked him the next day, in the L. L. Parker washroom.

Danny laughed. "You look like you think I'm putting the boots to her."

"That's not what I said."

Danny laughed again. "It's what you're thinking. I can tell by your puss. Well, you can quit thinking. When I want a piece of shtipp, I don't have to go looking for it around a dog like Ida Dienst."

"Then what's she doing there, singing in Gerrity's?"

"Come on down Thursday night and I'll show you."

"I've got classes Thursday night."

"Skip them for once and maybe you'll learn something they don't put into books."

"I can't do that. They allow you only a certain number of cuts. I have to save them for when I'm sick."

"What time do you get out?"

"A quarter to ten."

"That's time enough," Danny said. "If you come right down." He pulled a couple of paper towels from the holder over the basin, started punching his hands dry, then stopped. "Will you be there?"

George dipped down to splash water on his face. He did it carefully, taking a long time about it. When he straightened up, Danny was still standing there motionless, holding the wad of paper towels like a pitcher caught by the camera in the act of pulling back his arm for the throw.

"How about it?" Danny said. "Will you be there?"

"I don't know," George said as he pulled a towel from the holder. "When I get out of class I'm pretty bushed, and I've got all this homework to get ready for the next night."

Danny grinned and put his arm across George's shoulder.

"Your Aunt Tessie is all the way up there in Albany," he said. "I promise not to write and squeal to her."

"For Christ's sake," George said. "Aunt Tessie has nothing to do with it."

"No?"

"No."

Danny drew him slowly close in the bend of his elbow, so that they looked like a couple of wrestlers locked in a straining grip, until they were nose to nose. "Now say no," Danny said.

George twisted himself free. Danny straightened up, let out a bellow of laughter, and hurled the wadded paper towels across the washroom. "Honest to God," he said. "I swear to you we haven't boiled a heeb for supper since last Tuesday. I promise you'll be as safe as when you're listening to one of Shumacher's jokes. How about it?"

"Well—" George said. Then he caught a glimpse of Danny's face in the mirror over the basin, and he started to laugh, too. How the hell could anybody say no to Danny? "Sure," George said, "I'll be there."

"You just saying that to get out of this can?" Danny said. "Or is it a promise?"

"It's a promise," George said.

He wished, as he walked down Fourth Street toward the Lewis Street corner on Thursday night, that he could retract the promise. His curiosity about what Danny had cooked up was strong. As strong as it used to be when they were kids and the tin can would come banging gently down the back-yard wall carrying one of Danny's messages. Just as when they were kids, however, the mere thought of Gerrity's was enough to make George uncomfortable. Tonight he was dealing with more than thoughts. Tonight, knowing he had promised to meet Danny inside Gerrity's, George knew also that he was more than uncomfortable. He was scared.

It was silly. It was stupid. Considering that he was going to be twenty years old on his next birthday, George knew it was even shocking. What the hell was there to be scared of? A dirty old red brick building? The fact that it had once been a crummy saloon and, since Prohibition came in, had been functioning as an even crummier speakeasy? The old woman crippled by arthritis whose husband used to own it? Her one-armed lush of a son? The bargemen and wagon drivers to whom they sold their cheap rotgut?

George's intelligence told him that none of these was anything or anybody to be afraid of. Especially since Danny had them all in the palm of his hand. But in that place to which George's intelligence refused to penetrate, deep down where it clearly did not matter how sensible were the arguments he presented to himself, the thought of actually setting foot in Gerrity's evoked the same feelings that had hit him years ago, on the day Aunt Tessie first brought him to Fourth Street from the Henry Isaacs Orphan Asylum and, drawing him close as she stared across the street, she had uttered the single, terrifying word: shkutzim!

Two of them, George saw as he reached the Lewis Street corner, were just going in. He stood at the curb for a few moments, looking across the dark street at the closed door through which the shkutzim had disappeared, wondering if it might not be a good idea to stop in at the doll store and ask Dora to go with him. He didn't wonder very long. Considering the way Dora hated Danny, few ideas could be dumber. Besides, Danny's opinion of Dora was even lower than her opinion of him. On top of all that, Dora had not been invited. Telling himself to quit stalling, George stepped from the curb, crossed the street, and knocked on the black wooden door.

While he waited he noticed in the light from the lamppost behind him that the door was freshly painted, and he heard the murmur of voices behind it. The door slid open about four or five inches. Through the gap, along with the voices, came the sharp smell of cigarette smoke mixed with alcohol. Nothing happened for several moments. George couldn't see anything in the narrow gap, but he had the feeling he was being looked over by someone inside.

"Yeah?" a man's voice said finally.

"Danny Shorr told me to come over."

"What's your name?"

George told him.

The door slammed shut. There was the sound of a chain bolt being pulled free and then the door jerked open. "Come on in."

George came into what looked like a small, dark closet perhaps six feet square. Behind him the door was shoved shut. One wall of the closet began to sway crazily, as though it had been punched back by a muffled giant fist. Light from somewhere beyond the wall poured in. George saw that the closet was actually a set of long black curtains hung around the street door to form a crude vestibule. He saw also that the man who had let him in was Mike Gerrity, Jr. George had never been this close to him before. He found he couldn't take his eyes from Mike's left jacket sleeve. It was pinned up at the elbow.

"Danny said to let him know as soon as you showed," Mike said. "Come on."

There was something about the way he pronounced Danny's name that brought George's glance away from the pinned-up sleeve. Looking directly into Mike's face, George had a moment of shock. Like everybody else on Fourth Street, he knew that Mike had been twenty-two when he lost his arm at Château-Thierry. He couldn't, therefore, have been more than thirty-five now. But the man who had opened the door looked almost as old as Mr. Shumacher. Not because he had white hair. Mike's hair was the color of spit-out tobacco juice. But his skin was dirty and spotty, like Eff Eff's. His eyes had the runny blue look of raw egg-white. He kept pulling his lower lip up to his teeth and then letting it drop away again, as though he kept forgetting that the gums were red-hot. He moved jerkily and slowly, with pauses between each movement, like a clockwork toy that had to be wound up for each step. Forgetting that a few moments ago, on the other side of the door, he had been scared, George was surprised to find he felt sorry for this poor bastard. It was one thing to hear a guy was a lush. It was another thing to see and smell him. Mike smelled like a turned-over kerosene lamp.

"You better come on," he said. His words sounded like dice with worn-away edges rolling out on a padded table top. They had no crispness. "I don't want Danny to get sore," he mumbled. "Come on."

He pulled aside the curtain and held it for George to precede him. George had another shock. *Is this all?* he was suddenly asking himself. *Is this all?*

For years George had carried in his mind a picture that showed the inside of Gerrity's. The picture was vague at the edges, which kept moving back and forth endlessly, like surf, but in the center the picture was clear enough: a tangled mass of dirty men in work pants and flannel shirts, with vicious faces, packed together in a writhing mass like angleworms in a tin can, holding glasses and slobbering whiskey down their unshaved chins as they crawled all over one another, spitting on the sawdust-covered floor and screaming curses at the Jews who lived in the buildings all around them.

What George actually saw through the curtain Mike Gerrity, Jr., held aside for him was a room about the size of Mr. Forman's grocery store. The black wooden floor, like the street door, was freshly painted and the walls were hung with cheaply framed pictures, most of them obviously cut from newspapers and magazines, of Eddie Cantor, Marilyn Miller, Rudolph Valentino and other well-known entertainers. At one side, to the left of the curtain, there was a bar with a mirror behind it. Facing the bar from the other side of the room, near a door that apparently led to the rest of the house, was a small upright piano in front of which sat an old woman in a black shawl playing soft, tinkly music. Like the half-dozen tables on the floor and the chairs set around the tables, none of which matched, the piano had also recently received a fresh coat of black paint. The paint did not conceal the nicks and scars which indicated that, if the furniture in the room had not come from Mr. Noftooleh's on Avenue C, it had obviously been supplied by some other second-hand dealer who specialized in equally beat-up merchandise. Perhaps a dozen men and women were seated at the tables in groups of two and three. They were neatly dressed, and they either sat quietly, listening to the music, or they spoke to each other in whispers, as though they did not want to be rude to the old woman at the piano. They did not seem particularly interested in the glasses on the tables in front of them.

George tried, as he stared at the room in front of him, to synchronize what he was seeing with the picture of Gerrity's interior he had been carrying in his mind for so many years. He couldn't. It was like steeling yourself at a fraternity initiation to take a puff on what you are sure is an exploding cigar and then finding, when you put it to your lips, that the cigar is made of chocolate.

"What do you think of it?"

George turned. Danny had come up beside him. He was wearing a dark blue suit George had never seen before and he was grinning. George, who had been with him all day in the L. L. Parker mailroom, found himself looking at Danny as though he were seeing a stranger. In a way he was. He had never seen Danny look like this. He reminded George of the men in newspaper photographs of commencement exercises at which the awards are about to be handed out to the honor men. Even without reading the captions, just by looking at the row of faces, you could tell which one was going to get the top prize. Whatever prizes were being handed out tonight, George could tell from looking at his friend's face that Danny knew he had it in the bag. For the first time in all the years George had known him, Danny didn't look impatient.

"I don't know," George said, which was true enough. "What is it?"

Danny's grin changed to a look of annoyance. "For Christ's sake, what does it look like?"

A number of answers came to George's mind. "You'd get sore if I told you," he said. "I'd better let you tell me."

"It's a night club," Danny said.

George had never been in a night club. He took another look at this one. "Do they all look like this?"

"It's not what they look like that counts. It's what you got to offer the customers."

"What have you got to offer yours?"

The grin came back to Danny's face. "Wait and see, boy," he said. "Wait and see."

He lifted his hand and snapped his fingers. George, taken by surprise, ducked and turned. He saw Mike Junior, whose presence he had forgotten, drop the curtain and come forward. His movements were no quicker than they had been when he opened the door for George. Mike obviously couldn't move more quickly. He could try, however. That was even more obvious. All you had to do was look at his face. George, looking at it, wished he hadn't. Mike Junior, straining to respond swiftly to Danny's signal, reminded him of a dog trying to please its master, not to earn a pat but to avoid a kick.

"Get Mr. Hurst a drink," Danny said.

"Okay," Mike said.

"Okay what?"

"Okay, sir."

"I told you to watch that in front of the customers. We're trying to get a little class into the joint."

"Yes, sir."

Mike moved away toward the bar. Watching him go, Danny's lips twisted in the small, tight smile George had known since he was three. "All these years I been keeping him in booze, I finally figured out a way to get some of it back. What are you looking at?"

"The piano player," George said. "I just recognized her."

Danny seemed pleased by the statement. It was as though, by recognizing Mrs. Gerrity, George had recognized at the same time some talent of Danny's of which he was proud but that had hitherto escaped George's notice.

"She's not much good to the Yankee outfield, but she can still

move her hands. All these years I been pouring medicines into her,
I finally figured out a way to get some of it back from her, too. Try
this one, boy."

Danny pulled out a chair from one of the empty tables. George
sat down. Danny took the chair facing him. Mike brought a glass
and set it in front of George.

"Would you like one, too?" he said to Danny and, after a slight
pause, he added, "Sir?"

"No," Danny said. "Keep up the good work and I'll have you
giving a memory course in your spare time."

George hoped Mike wouldn't laugh. He didn't. Not exactly. He
merely tried. Which made it worse. Before it became unbearable,
however, he went back to the bar.

George moved the glass in a small circle on the painted table
top. "What is it?" he said.

Danny grinned. "Imported Scotch."

"No, I mean no kidding."

"These clucks in here are paying a buck a shot for it. You call
that kidding?"

"I'd still like to know what it is before I put it in my stomach."

"It's the same stuff I used to lug down to the barges for Mike
Senior when Prohibition first came in. Go ahead, try it. It's no worse
than the crappy Passover wine you and Aunt Tessie used to make."

George took a sip. Danny was wrong. It was a great deal worse.
George set down his glass and nodded toward the people at the
tables. "Where do they come from?" He knew damn well they
hadn't come off the lumber barges or the coal wagons.

"Uptown," Danny said. "First Avenue, Second Avenue, some
from around Third. Mostly Polacks. Can't you tell by their kissers?
I used to deliver to them for Mike Senior. After Mike got himself
knocked off, I tried to hold onto their business, but the son of a
bitches, they figured with Mike out of the way they didn't have to
pay. They'd take the stuff when I delivered, but when it came to
handing over the dough, they'd say next time, kid, and pretty soon
with most of them there wasn't any next time. That's what put
me in that God-damn L. L. Parker mailroom laughing my head off
at Shumacher's jokes for twelve bucks a week."

Danny paused, and he looked grimly around the room, moving
his head slowly from table to table, and then the grim look eased away
and became the twisted little smile.

"All these years I've been sorting that lousy mail and laughing at those crummy jokes I've been kicking my brain around, trying to figure a way to get back at these bastards." Danny paused again and he laughed quietly. "I finally figured it," he said. "I started dropping in on these shmohawks after work, sort of renewing old friendships, telling them what I was cooking up, and inviting them to the opening night. I could have used a couple dozen more for an opening night, but what the hell, all I want is to get started. These boobs go away satisfied tonight, they'll bring their buddies, and the buddies they'll bring other buddies. At a buck a shot, it won't be long before I've got back from these bastards every dime they held out on me after Mike kicked off, and then if you want to hear something real good, you stick around and listen the day I tell Eff Eff what he can do with his job."

For a few moments, as Danny contemplated that happy day in the near future, George could feel the glow that used to remind him of Aunt Tessie's stove on a bad winter day. Feeling himself drawn as always to the glow, George this time felt something new: a twinge of jealousy. Why should Danny have so much of it? Why should everything be so easy for him? Why wasn't it spread around a little? Why, to put it bluntly, when it was being handed out, didn't George Hurst get some of it handed to him?

"Danny," he said. "What's Ida Dienst got to do with all this?"

Danny brought his smile back from the day when he would be telling Mr. Shumacher what he could do with his job and dropped it to his wrist watch. Danny looked up, still smiling. "You want to do me a favor?"

"Couldn't I first have an answer to my question?"

"You do me the favor and the answer comes with it."

"Okay," George said.

"Hop across the street to the doll store and come back with Ida," Danny said. "She'll be waiting for me to come and get her."

George hesitated. He didn't like Ida Dienst and she didn't like him. "Couldn't you just answer my question without making me take a workout?"

"Go ahead," Danny said. "She won't bite. I got her trained."

George shrugged and stood up. "Whatever you say."

"Don't come in the side door," Danny said. "Come in the front." He nodded toward the door near the piano. "I'll meet you out there in the hall."

"Okay," George said.

Danny snapped his fingers. Mike Junior came out from behind the bar, crossed the room in front of George, and let him out into the street through the door behind the black curtains. He was surprised, as he crossed to the doll store, to see lights in the front windows. George was even more surprised, when he knocked on the door, to see Frannie come running out of the back rooms. She opened the door and, for several moments, she was clearly too astounded to talk.

"It's George!" she said finally, as though she were identifying him for an audience of slow-witted strangers. "George Hurst!"

"What are you looking at me like that for?" he said.

"I thought you were Doctor Sugarman."

"Doctor Sugarman?"

Frannie nodded. "For Ida," she said.

"For Ida?"

Frannie nodded again. "She's sick. A little while ago, a half hour maybe, all of a sudden she got hot like fire up here, her head, and she started to vomit. Dora ran to the drug store and called Dr. Sugarman. He said he'd come right away. We're waiting. When we heard knocking—"

Frannie paused and her fat, pleasant face creased with perplexity as she stared at the door on which the knocking that should have been done by Dr. Sugarman had, instead, produced George.

"George," she said. "What are you doing here?"

He started to explain, then remembered that his explanation would be carried into the rooms back of the store where Dora, who hated Danny, was waiting with the rest of her family for the arrival of Dr. Sugarman. It seemed best to skip the explanations. For the time being, anyway.

"I hope Ida feels better," George said quickly. "I've got to run now."

He did, across the street to Gerrity's front door, which opened as soon as he knocked. Danny, standing in the hall with his hand on the doorknob, stared past George, out into the street, as the expectant smile disappeared from his face.

"Ida," Danny said, and then, sharply, "Where's Ida?"

"She's sick."

"Sick?"

"That's what Frannie told me. They're waiting for Dr. Sugarman. Frannie said right after supper Ida got—"

"She can't be sick!"

Danny didn't usually say stupid things. George looked at him more closely. All of a sudden Danny no longer looked like the guy in the commencement exercises picture who is going to win the top prize. All of a sudden Danny looked like hell.

"She is," George said. "Frannie says—"

"Nuts to what Frannie says! Ida can't be sick!"

"Why the hell not? Anybody can be sick. Frannie says right after supper Ida got—"

"Because she's supposed to sing here tonight, that's why she can't be sick! Why the hell you think I been rehearsing her for weeks? What the hell you think I been telling these slobs in there? They should come pay a buck a slug and watch a game of pisha paysha? I told them I got a hot new singer! I told them they'd get a floor show!"

He shoved past George and disappeared into the street. The door banged shut behind him. George stood there for several moments, wondering what to do. Then he became aware of the soft, tinkly music and he moved toward it. He came into the big room through the door beside the piano. Several people looked up at him. Mrs. Gerrity was not one of them. The old woman with the black shawl sat straight and stiff, her eyes fixed on the sheet music, her body motionless except for her hands. She didn't seem to be interested in what they were doing or even aware that they were doing anything. Her hands seemed to be moving along the keys without any direction from her.

George crossed to the table where his drink was still standing. He sat down and looked around. He couldn't see any change in the room, but George could feel that there had been a change. Things were not the same as when he'd walked out a few minutes ago. It was as though the customers had learned somehow that the entertainment they had been promised, the show for which they had been waiting so patiently, had been canceled and they were trying to decide what to do about it. George didn't doubt that what they might do about it could be ugly. Maybe this room didn't look like the picture of it he had been carrying around in his head for years, but the people in it were still shkutzim. George didn't like the feeling of restlessness in the air.

"Ladies and gentlemen!"

George, furtively examining a party of three tough-looking customers on his right, turned toward the familiar voice. Danny had come in through the door near the piano. He was standing next to Mrs. Gerrity. He had one hand in the air, as though he were signaling to a taxi, and he was smiling at the people in the room. George had to hand it to him. Danny Schorr certainly knew how to take it. He didn't look like a man who was about to announce the collapse of a plan on which he had been counting so heavily. George, who knew what Danny's charm could do, wondered if it would be strong enough to handle this bunch of goons when they heard there would be no show.

"I have already told each and every one of you in person," Danny said, "when you arrived here tonight, what a pleasure it is to have you with us and how grateful I am for your display of confidence in coming to the opening of our little club. I have also told you that I had arranged for your pleasure and entertainment a really rare and special treat, the sort of thing that happens only once in most people's lifetime, the opportunity to help discover a new and great star. And so, without further introduction," Danny said as he turned toward the door beside the piano, "I want you to meet one of the biggest and brightest and greatest stars of tomorrow, the one, the only, the incomparable—Miss Dora Dienst!"

For quite some time, a period that could have been moments and might have been minutes, George was too stunned to put things into any sort of sequence. Later, when he tried, he wasn't at all sure he succeeded.

As Dora came through the door and Danny led her to the piano, George remembered wondering stupidly where she had got that red dress, and how Danny, whom she hated, had managed to get her to come across the street and take Ida's place. George remembered these and a dozen other questions racing through his head in all directions, like a bag of spilled marbles. But the thing he remembered most clearly, what brought those first minutes of confusion to an abrupt end, the thing he would never forget was the moment when Dora turned.

She had stopped on the exact spot Danny vacated, a little to the left of Mrs. Gerrity and three or four feet in front of the piano. Between the flaming red dress and the blue-black hair, her delicate face with the small pointed chin was chalk-white. Looking out gravely at the audience, her body turned at right angles toward the room so that her crooked arm was concealed, she waited, absolutely motionless, until the piano reached her opening phrase. Then, without effort, as though she were resuming a quiet conversation that had been interrupted by the roar of a passing train, Dora began to sing "Apple Blossom Time."

The song, which to George had always meant crazy Ida screaming in the summer night, suddenly seemed completely new. It was as though what he was hearing was not a song at all. The slender girl at the front of the room was telling her lover when she would come to him, using words that had never been used before, making them up as she went along, and George was suddenly remembering again the delicate pressure of the sharp little shoulder blades under his outspread palm and the fresh honey-cake smell of the blue-black hair. The lump of loneliness, which months ago he had managed to push aside, was suddenly back in his chest, making it difficult for him to breathe, and he was wondering stupidly why he had never before noticed how beautiful Dora was, when he saw it happen.

Easily, in a smooth flow of movement, like a doll mounted on a pivot, Dora began to turn toward the people in the room. George, who did not yet understand what was happening, understood clearly that it was crucial.

When she finally stood full-face to the audience, and her arms came up slowly with the final bars of the song, George had a moment of shock. This was not the girl who had come into the room a few minutes ago. Dora seemed to have changed completely.

Then, as her outspread arms seemed to lift the long sweet final note and hold it aloft, George understood what had happened. Dora's left arm, like her right, looked perfectly straight.

She had not changed. Dora had merely come out at last from behind the invisible wall she had built around herself all those years ago after the Armistice Day accident in the Forest.

14

There were times, during the weeks that followed, when George found himself wishing she had not come out so far.

Now that he knew he loved her, and in his desperate awkwardness was hunting ways to tell Dora how he felt, there were all at once very few opportunities. George, who for years had been the only person with whom Dora Dienst would go out for a walk, suddenly couldn't seem to arrange to be alone with her. He even had to wait until the morning after Dora made her first astonishing appearance in front of an audience before he could learn how it had come about. He cornered Danny in the L. L. Parker washroom and asked him.

"Search me," Danny said with a grin. "I was just as surprised as you were. When I sent you across the street to get Ida, and you came back and said she was sick, I was so God-damn mad, all those Polacks in there waiting for a floor show, what I had in mind when I went steaming across the street, I thought maybe Ida was stalling. Stage fright or something like that, the last minute. You know how broads are. I figured I'd bawl hell out of her, give her a pep talk, something like that, anything to get her on her feet. Or if that didn't work, believe me, kid, the way I felt, I'd've dragged her back across the street by the hair. The minute I walked in that doll store, though, I knew I was cooked. Sugarman was there, poking thermometers into her from both ends, and Mr. and Mrs. Dienst and that pig Frannie, they had looks on their squashes from here to here. You could see everybody was already figuring in their heads how much the funeral would set them back. All the attention they gave me, I could've been another couple of square feet of oilcloth on the floor, so I turned around and started to walk out, figuring what the hell does a guy do now?

"I'm halfway through the store when I see Dora standing there by the door, waiting for me. Jesus, I thought, that's all I need. On top of everything else, this tomato, the way she hates me, she sees I'm in a real deep hole, all I need is to have her come along and pee on me. Just open your yap, I thought to myself, you just let me hear even the beginning of a razzberry out of you, you gimpy bitch, I thought, and I'll let you have it right in the teeth. I wasn't kidding, either. The way I felt that minute, I'd've given her a shot in the mouth if she had two crippled arms, not one. Matter of fact, I was all ready to let her have it just for the hell of it, when I reach the door and instead of a razzberry Dora asks me if she could go across with me and sing instead of Ida. I mean real nice she asked. Just like that. Like I'm talking to you now. Let her come sing instead of Ida, she says, and just in case there's any chance for a mistake about how she's asking, she says please.

"It takes me a few seconds to sort of shift my gears, from wanting to belt her one, I mean, and then I figure she's kidding. But hell no. Kidding? She starts begging! First I think she's gone off her rocker a little, and I say since when did you become a singer? You can't sing. But she says she can sing better than Ida, which between me and you, you don't have to be very good to be able to do because this dog Ida, Jesus, she stinks on ice and when you take her off the ice the ice stinks, but she's so crazy to get to be a singer, and what the hell, she was doing it for free, and besides, for these dumb Polacks I had lined up, even a dog like Ida Dienst is too good for those son of a bitches.

"So I take another look at Dora, and one thing I have to admit right away, when it comes to looks she's got it over that sister of hers like a tent, so I said you can't sing in front of people in a night club in a dirty old smock you got it all gooked up with glue and hunks of doll hair. That's a night club I'm trying to start across the street there, I said, not a home for beat-up old sewer workers. So you know what she does? Right there in the store, right by that front door, she peels off that smock, and underneath, what she's got on underneath, she's wearing Ida's red dress! The one Ida made for herself to wear at the opening! Can you beat that? Her own sister, she's out there on her can in bed, flat, the doctor is still there, she could maybe be getting ready to croak or something, and this Dora, she's already copped her dress! A dame that can do that, I figure, a dame like that, I say to myself, you take a chance on, boy. Besides, what else could I do? Marilyn Miller and Ruth Etting and Helen Morgan, those broads, they weren't exactly standing outside breaking down the door screaming take me. It was either take Dora or go back across the street and face those Polacks with nothing, so I took Dora." Danny laughed. "Like they say, the rest is history, because you were there."

George, who had no way of knowing at that time what Danny had in mind for Dora, sensed in his friend's laugh a complication of the problem with which he had been wrestling since the night before: how was he going to tell Dora what he had learned about his feelings for her?

"What about Ida?" George said.

"How do you mean what about Ida?"

"This flu she's got, it can't last forever. A few days, a week, whenever she gets better, she'll still want to come across the street and sing, won't she?"

"In my place it's what I want not what anybody else wants that goes up on the scoreboard," Danny said. He looked thoughtfully at the wad of paper towels with which he had been blotting his hands dry. "You know, it's funny," Danny said in a tone of wonder. "She's been right there. Dora, I mean. All these years since that lousy accident she's been right there, across the street, in that God-damn doll store, shmeering glue and combing hair and—" Danny paused, leaving the tone of wonder high in the air, and then suddenly, as though he had finally removed the wrappings from a wonderful present about which when it was handed to him he had been suspicious, he smiled at George and said, "It's like old times again, isn't it?"

It was and it wasn't.

It was like old times to have Dora talking to Danny, and Danny including Dora in his plans, and both of them telling George all about it. The old triumvirate was back in business.

It was not at all like old times, however, for George to feel left out of those plans.

The first Sunday after the opening of Danny's club, when George walked down to the river for his regular weekly visit, he was told by Mrs. Dienst that Dora was across the street in Gerrity's.

"What's she doing there?" George said.

It was eleven o'clock in the morning.

"Practicing," Mrs. Dienst said.

It had not occurred to George that Dora would need or want to practice. "When will she be back?"

"Who knows?" Mrs. Dienst said. "Why don't you go over and take a look? She'll be glad to see you."

Mrs. Dienst was wrong.

Gerrity's side door, when George knocked, was opened by Mike Junior. "What do you want?" he said. George told him "Wait," Mike said. He closed the door. A couple of minutes later, when he reopened it, he said, "Danny says no visitors during rehearsal."

George felt his stomach tighten with annoyance. "What does Dora say?" he said. Mike Junior's gray, spotted, puffy face did not change. The dead, watery blue, egg-white eyes reflected neither comprehension nor interest. "Miss Dienst," George said irritably. "The girl who's rehearsing. Go back and ask her if I can come in and listen."

Mike closed the door again. A minute later he pulled it open again. "She says go over and wait in the doll store," he said. "She'll be there in a little while."

She wasn't. George sat in the doll store for hours, watching the Diensts work on the inevitable rush order, listening to their accounts of Ida's progress toward recovery from her attack of flu, eating the fruit Mrs. Dienst kept handing him, and hearing fat Frannie say over and over again, "George, say some more!" He tried, but he couldn't seem to do it. For once there was no fun in talking to this group of friendly, eager listeners. While he was trying to repeat a passage from one of Aunt Tessie's recent letters in which she described some aspect of her life in Albany with Uncle Zisha, or while he was reconstructing something that had happened during the past week in school or in the L. L. Parker offices, George found his mind was across the street, in Gerrity's. At three o'clock he couldn't stand it any longer.

"Tell Dora I'm sorry," he said, trying to sound calm and casual as he stood up. "I have to go."

"You waited already so long," Mrs. Dienst said, "wait another few minutes. Take a banana. She'll show up."

George took a banana and waited another few minutes but Dora did not show up.

"I have to go," George said again, angry at himself because, in spite of the effort he was putting into controlling himself, he could hear the slight quiver in his voice. "I've got a lot of schoolwork to do."

By the time he reached Avenue C he regretted his decision, and then, when he knew he couldn't turn back, he was furious with himself. He spent the afternoon lying on the bed in his room, feeling miserable. He didn't get any of his schoolwork done. He didn't sleep well that night. In the morning his head hurt, the pain in his chest was almost unbearable, and he cut himself while shaving. He decided grimly he would not mention his visit to Danny. George stuck to his decision until the middle of the afternoon, when he came into the L. L. Parker washroom and found Danny in front of the mirror, combing his hair and whistling "Apple Blossom Time."

"What the hell are you so God-damn cheerful about?" George said.

Danny stopped whistling and gave him a long look. "I'm making up the dialogue I'm going to use when I tell Shumacher what he can do with this job. I figure that ought to be in a couple of weeks, as soon as the club really gets rolling. What the hell are you so God-damn sore about?"

"I'm not sore," George said.

"Try saying it without screaming and maybe I'll believe you."

"What the hell do I care if you believe me or not?"

"Look at him!" Danny said with a grin, addressing his own reflection in the mirror. "Sunny Jim!"

"All right, you're such a wise guy, I'd like to know one thing: what's the idea all the God-damn rehearsing?"

For a long moment, still staring into the mirror, Danny looked startled. Then, all at once, he seemed to fall apart. He doubled up, holding onto the porcelain basin with both hands, as his body shook with helpless laughter.

"Oh, my God!" he gasped finally. There was another long spell of laughter, not quite so violent this time, and then Danny pulled himself together. "I'm sorry, kid," he said. "I didn't realize—I mean I forgot—" He stopped and shook his head, as though to fling away the laughter that was trying to close in on him again. "Look, we were rehearsing a couple of new routines," he said. "I forgot about the time. Dora, too. I mean I didn't realize until this minute that you must have been waiting all afternoon yesterday. I just remembered Mike Junior coming in and saying you were outside. It's not I didn't want you in there. It's Dora. She's still new at this. She freezes if somebody is around when she's rehearsing. Later, when she's got the song, it's all right no matter who's around. But until she's got it cold, she can't work with strangers listening."

George wanted to say coldly that he had never before thought of himself as a stranger so far as Dora was concerned, but he already regretted the outburst that had brought him so close to the dangerous edge of revelation. He couldn't tell anybody how he felt about Dora. Certainly not until he told Dora herself. If he didn't want to run the risk of revealing more, he'd better get a grip on himself.

"Sure," he said casually. "That's all right. I understand. Besides, I had a lot of schoolwork to do yesterday, anyway. How's everything going?"

"Great," Danny said. "This Dora, I'm telling you, she's got real stuff. The way she's improving, she keeps going at this rate, I'll have another Ruth Etting on my hands, no kidding. Why don't you come down tonight after class and have yourself another listen?"

Every nerve in his body was suddenly screaming, urging George to accept. "Thanks, but I can't," he heard himself saying. "I'm still way behind in my schoolwork."

All through the evening meal in Stewart's which he scarcely touched and the lectures that night which he did not hear, George kept asking himself helplessly, bitterly why he had refused Danny's invitation. No answer came to him. After his last class he had to fight with himself to keep his feet from turning toward the river instead of toward University Place. He won, and after he was alone in his room with the pain in his chest, George wondered stupidly why he had fought so hard for a victory he did not want. He came up with no answer to that one, either.

"I'll wait till Sunday," he said to himself. "That's only six days. Five and a half, really. I'll wait till Sunday."

The period of waiting seemed terribly important. It would enable him to see Dora without owing anything to anybody for the privilege. He always saw Dora on Sundays. This would be just another of his regular visits. It would look like that, anyway. And by forcing himself to wait until Sunday, by making himself live through this time of trial, whatever it was he would suffer while waiting would be counterbalanced by the reward God would surely bestow on him for proving he could take it. And George had no doubts about the form the reward would take: a way of conveying to Dora the fact that George loved her. George didn't know how to do this. But now he didn't have to worry. It was in God's hands.

"I won't do anything until Sunday," George told himself. "I'll see her on Sunday."

On Sunday, when he got to Fourth Street, he learned that Dora was again in Gerrity's, rehearsing with Danny. She was still there when, late in the afternoon, George could no longer stand Ida Dienst's malicious wisecracks. On the surface they dealt with Ida's opinion of Danny and her own sister who, Ida felt, had conspired to do her dirt when Ida was sick and helpless. George sensed, however, that Ida suspected what had happened to him. Her sarcastic remarks kept circling closer and closer to the pain he was finding it more and more difficult to conceal. Even though it almost killed him to leave without seeing Dora, George felt it was better to do that than risk being taunted openly by someone like Ida. He wouldn't have known how to handle that.

Another thing he didn't know how to handle was a second week of waiting. His pact with God had been dissolved by his failure to see Dora on Sunday. George would have been glad to extend it until the following Sunday, but he knew on Monday morning that he couldn't live that long without seeing Dora. His only hope was that Danny would invite him again to come down to Gerrity's after classes. Even though all day Monday he threw out hints so broad that, when he thought about them later, they made George blush, Danny didn't come through with an invitation. Later, of course, George realized that Danny had other things on his mind. At the time, however, George was incapable of thinking about anything but what was on his own mind. It drove him, finally, to Fourth Street without an invitation.

"Wait," Mike Junior said when he opened the door to George's knock on Monday night. A few moments later he came back and took down the chain bolt. "Come in."

Coming in, George could hear the tinkly music and, a moment after that, Dora's voice. He stopped just inside the black curtains, his heart hammering crazily, his eyes riveted on the delicate chalk-white face. He did not know what Dora was singing. He did not hear the words. He knew only that he wanted to take her in his arms. Then her own arms came up to hold the final note, and George realized Dora had been singing "Apple Blossom Time."

Her arms came down and the music stopped and George realized something else: there was no applause.

He looked around angrily, furious with an audience that could remain silent in the face of such a moving performance, and George saw with astonishment that there was no audience. Aside from Mrs. Gerrity at the piano, and Mike Junior behind the bar, and Dora threading her way toward him among the tables, the room was empty.

"I thought you were sore at me," Dora said when she reached him.

"Sore at you?" In view of the agony through which he had been living for the past ten days, her statement was so preposterous that George did not realize, until he heard the echoes of his own startled voice, that Dora had no way of knowing about his agony. Trying for a more reasonable tone, he said, "Why should I be sore at you?"

"I haven't seen you since the night we opened."

"Whose fault is that? I've been down every Sunday, regular, but you've been here all day rehearsing."

"See? You *are* sore."

"Wouldn't you be?"

"Not if I knew what you were doing is important to you."

"This is important to you?"

"Would I do it to an empty room if it wasn't?"

George looked around the room again. Mrs. Gerrity sat stiff and motionless at the piano, her head bowed, her eyes fixed on the keys, her hands folded in her lap. Mike Junior sat behind the bar, breathing through his open mouth, staring stupidly across the room at the black curtains that shielded the door. They could have been a couple of wax figures in a model for a stage set of one of those Russian plays about pimps, prostitutes, thieves, and drunkards gathered in a flophouse on Christmas Eve. They gave George the creeps.

He brought his glance back to Dora. "Why is it empty?" he said.

Dora's lips curved in a small, sarcastic smile. "No customers."

"I guess I walked into that. I mean why aren't there any customers?"

"Danny says the word of mouth hasn't spread yet."

"How long does it take for word of mouth to spread?"

Dora shrugged. "I don't know."

George was puzzled. He had been assuming from Danny's enthusiasm that the club was a success. He could still hear the familiar cocky note in Danny's voice as he told George in the L. L. Parker washroom that he was making up the dialogue he planned to use when he told Mr. Shumacher what the mailroom head could do with his job.

"What about the people who were here two weeks ago?" George said. "On opening night?"

Dora shrugged again. "Danny says they'll come back."

"Have any of them been back?"

Dora hesitated, gave George a quick glance, then put her hand on his arm. "Let's have a drink." She led him to a table near the wall and signaled to the bar. Mike Junior came over with two glasses.

"Thanks," George said. Mike didn't answer. He went back to the bar. Dora took a sip from her glass. George said, "You like this stuff?"

She wrinkled her nose. "It's something to do between songs."

"Dora."

"What?"

"Why do you sing to an empty room?"

"You sound as though you're talking to someone belongs in the booby hatch."

"I don't mean it that way."

"What way do you mean it?"

"It seems a little screwy."

"Why is it any screwier than going to college at night?"

"I don't see the comparison."

"You like going to school at night? You enjoy studying to be another Judge Brandeis? Or you hate it?"

"If I hated it, I wouldn't do it."

"If I hated singing, I wouldn't do it, either." Dora set down her glass. "George, look." She stretched out her left arm, holding it parallel with the table top, in a gesture that reminded George of priests he had seen in the movies performing an act of benediction. "How does it look?" Dora said. "Does it look straight, George?"

"Perfectly straight."

"You're a liar, George."

"Dora, listen."

She shook her head. "That's all right. I don't mind your lying. Not any more, anyway. I minded for years, but now, all of a sudden, I don't mind at all. It's not straight, and it doesn't look straight, and it never will be, but that doesn't matter. What matters is that it *feels* straight." Dora lowered her arm and took another long sip from her glass. "You don't know what I'm talking about."

"No," George said.

"All these years, ever since that day in the Forest," Dora said, "I thought I was no damn good. I thought people were always looking at me, whispering behind my back, calling me a cripple. Even in the store, my own mother and father, my sisters, they said I wasn't any good, I didn't do the work right, they had to do everything over that I touched. I guess they did, too. I *wasn't* any damn good. I was far behind everybody else, and I didn't see any way I could ever catch up. Then, ten days ago, I got up there in front of this room—"

Dora paused and nodded toward the piano and, for several moments, she stared at Mrs. Gerrity's back. Then she shrugged and took another pull at her glass.

"You hear people clapping their hands," Dora said. "It hits you all of a sudden they're clapping for you, and that minute, that second you realize you're not all the way behind everybody else.

You realize you're as good as they are and even better. If they're clapping for you, you *have* to be better. If they're clapping for you, who cares if your arm is a little crooked?" She raised her arm again and looked at the slightly bent elbow. "As long as they keep clapping," Dora said, "your arm is as straight as anybody else's."

George stared down into his untouched drink. He didn't dare look around the room in which there was nobody to clap for this girl who made his heart ache.

"Where's Danny?" he said.

"Out," Dora said quietly. "Trying to find customers who will come and clap for Dora Dienst."

There was a sharp knock on the outside door. It sounded like a signal.

"I guess he's found a couple," George said.

He watched Mike Junior make his way across the room. George heard the door open. He heard it catch against the chain bolt and then slam shut. He heard the chain bolt rattle free and, after the pause while the door was pulled wide, he heard the second slam and the rattle as Mike Junior replaced the chain bolt. The black curtains billowed and Danny came in. He was scowling and nibbling nervously at his lower lip. George knew that look. He had seen it the day Mike Senior was killed, the day Danny asked George to get Aunt Tessie to give him a place to sleep. It was the look that meant Danny was in trouble.

Then the restless eyes stopped on the table where George and Dora were sitting, and the look disappeared. Danny came across the room with a smile.

"Glad you dropped in," Danny said. "I was just thinking about you and figuring I'd have to wait until I saw you on the job tomorrow morning before I could talk to you."

"About what?" George said.

"Your landlady," Danny said. "Mrs. Bristol."

"No, Shissle," George said. "Mrs. Shissle."

15

Rhoda Shissle, who owned the brownstone rooming house in which George occupied one of the two "top-floor backs," was the widow of a tugboat captain. For thirty-three years she had lived with her husband aboard various vessels that worked in and around New York Harbor. When George became one of her fourteen tenants, Mrs. Shissle had been living alone for almost a dozen years in the quite spacious three-room apartment that formed the basement of her house on University Place. Nevertheless, she had never lost the habits of neatness, and the passion for utilizing every square inch of space, that she had been forced to learn as a matter of necessity during the years when she had been housekeeping for two in a twelve-by-eight-foot cabin that almost never sat level and was only rarely motionless.

As a result, when George told her he was expecting some packages by mail and asked her if she would be good enough to keep them in her apartment until he came home from school at night, because he was afraid they might be stolen if left lying around too long in the downstairs hall, Mrs. Shissle reacted as though he had asked her to stable a couple of trotting horses in her kitchen until he could arrange more appropriate accommodations.

"What kind of packages?" she asked nervously.

"Just packages," George said.

"Could you give me any idea of their size?"

"Well, not too big, I don't think. Say about this wide, maybe. Or even smaller."

"I wish you'd be more specific, Mr. Hurst."

"I don't see how I can be. I mean, I haven't seen them yet."

"But you know what's going to be in them, don't you?"

"Only in a general way."

Mrs. Shissle's face, which was plump, clean-looking, and waxen, like pork sausage, took on a puzzled look. George didn't blame her. He was somewhat puzzled himself, even though for a different reason.

"We're just not doing the business," Danny had said the night before at the table in Gerrity's. "It can't be because we're not giving the customers what they want. Our imported Scotch at a buck a throw is no worse than the panther piss they get in any uptown trap for three and four bucks a shot, and Dora's singing is so much better than most of the stuff they hear uptown that it's not even funny. That means the answer to why we're not doing the business must be something else, and after kicking the old brain around for a week I've come up with the answer." Danny had waved his hand to take in the room. "It's our plant. We put it together in a hurry with thirty-eight cents' worth of second-hand crap from Noftooleh's on Avenue C, and it looks it. Even if we were giving the booze away for free, and even if Dora was another Ruth Etting, which you can take it from me she's going to be, we'd never pull in the business as long as we're trying to pull it into a dump looks like this. Which means what we've got to do is brighten this place up a little, give it some class, and then the customers will come pouring down on us like rain. You agree?"

George wasn't sure that he did. He knew absolutely nothing about night clubs and even less about the people who frequented them. From what he read about both in the papers, however, some things seemed fairly obvious. George had noticed, for example, that the night clubs in which visiting foreign dignitaries like the Prince of Wales were entertained, home-grown celebrities like Tommy Manville met their future wives, and gangsters like Dutch Schultz were riddled with bullets, did not seem to be located on dirty little river-front streets that ended in docks to which coal and lumber barges were moored. The night clubs that were mentioned regularly in the papers, which George assumed were the night clubs that did good business, all seemed to be located in or near the theatrical district. He doubted that, by brightening up Gerrity's, the Prince of Wales and Tommy Manville and the as yet unpunctured equivalent of Dutch Schultz could be induced to forsake Times Square for Fourth Street.

"Well," George said, "I don't know."

"You don't have to," Danny said. "It's enough that I know. All you have to do is talk to your landlady."

"My landlady?"

"This Mrs. Shissle you pay rent to."

"What do you want me to talk to her about?"

"Some new stuff I'm ordering for this joint. I don't want it delivered here. During the day, when I'm on the job over at L. L. Parker, these two prize packages I leave behind me every morning, one of them can't move anything but her fingers across a bunch of piano keys, and the other one when I'm not looking he's as stiff as the

Brooklyn Bridge in the middle of January. I can't trust either one of them, especially with stuff that's breakable. If you talk to your land-lady, and she doesn't mind my having the stuff sent to your place, she could hold it for you till you get home from school and then you could bring it down here. What do you think?"

George didn't dare tell him. What he thought, as his heart began to race, was that Danny had just provided him with a solution to the problem that had been driving him crazy for ten days: how to get to see Dora more often.

"What kind of stuff are you ordering?" George said, trying to keep his voice steady. "I mean, how will it come? By truck or express or what? Mrs. Shissle is pretty fussy. She'll want to know."

"It'll be mostly ash trays and drinking glasses and pictures for up on the walls and maybe a few small mirrors. Stuff like that. Nothing very big, and I'm ordering it all from a couple of mail-order houses in Chicago and Philadelphia, because they're a hell of a lot cheaper than any of the stores I've been pricing stuff here in New York, so it'll all be coming parcel post. I don't know how they wrap things, because I've never bought from a mail-order house before, but shipping like that, parcel post, I don't guess any of the packages should be too heavy to handle."

"How many packages will there be?"

"So far I only ordered a couple dozen ash trays to see what the merchandise is like. You know, you look at something in a catalogue, it's fourteen-carat gold. It comes and you open the box, it's garbage. If these ash trays are okay, I'll order some more stuff." Danny laughed. "It'll mean maybe like a few trips for you," he said. "I hope you don't mind?"

George didn't mind at all. After the first trial shipment of ash trays, which Danny apparently found satisfactory, the packages from Chicago and Philadelphia began to arrive in groups of three and four. George started holding out on Danny in order to increase the number of trips to Fourth Street. He would take the packages from Mrs. Shissle's apartment in the basement, store them in his room on the top floor, and carry them down to Fourth Street one at a time. As a result, he was able to see Dora three and four times a week for almost two months. This did a great deal to ease the pain he felt when he was away from her. It did absolutely nothing, however, to solve the problem of how to tell Dora he loved her: George never saw Dora alone.

Not because business was so good that she was constantly besieged by customers. In spite of the ash trays and pictures and mirrors that came from the mail-order houses, which Danny put up on the walls and spread around the room until it did look much more gay and attractive, business continued to be terrible. There were rarely any customers in the place when George arrived. Mrs. Gerrity, however, was always at the piano, and Mike Junior was always behind the bar. They never paid any attention to George but, so long as they were in the room, he found it impossible to talk to Dora about anything personal. When Danny was present, it was impossible to talk about almost anything except the fortune he expected to make as soon as the word of mouth began to spread and the real big spenders started coming down to Fourth Street. When he wasn't wondering helplessly how he would ever get to tell Dora he loved her, George wondered nervously if his friend Danny Schorr could be slipping. It didn't seem possible that Danny, who for so many years had always been able to see things before George even knew there was anything to look at, should be completely blind to what seemed embarrassingly obvious to George: the club didn't have a prayer.

George was beginning to think it might be his duty as a friend to point this out to Danny, even if it meant having Danny come down on him with both feet, when he received the letter from the Post Office Department.

Years later, when he was a practicing accountant with a number of clients who seemed firmly convinced that the Collector of Internal Revenue employed several staff members for the exclusive purpose of carrying on a war of nerves against them, George realized that his reaction on finding in his letter box the innocent-looking envelope from the Post Office Department was not unlike the reactions of his clients when they found in the morning mail an envelope from the Bureau of Internal Revenue: George almost fainted.

He didn't know why. There was certainly nothing very ominous about the cheap brownish paper, the sloppily typed address in which his name was misspelled "Huerst," or the Gothic type in the upper left-hand corner that read: "Post Office Department, New York, N. Y." Perhaps it was the fact that there was no stamp on the envelope, implying by its absence that the sender operated on a level above and beyond the laws under which ordinary people were forced to function, and thus summoning up unclear but terrifying images of secret interrogations, diabolically ingenious torture chambers, and grim-visaged firing squads marching out at dawn into remote prison yards from which no innocent victim's frenzied screams for help would ever be heard.

Whatever the reason, George Hurst's hand shook so badly that he had to make three attempts before he managed to thumb open the back flap.

He drew out a piece of paper even rougher and cheaper than the envelope. It was a mimeographed form letter on the blank spaces of which enough words had been filled in, obviously by the same careless or inexpert hand responsible for the misspelling on the envelope, to convey the fact that a Mr. R. Sapina, Postal Inspector, would like the recipient to drop in at Room 347 of the General Post Office Building on Eighth Avenue and Thirty-first Street any time between the hours of 10:00 A.M. and noon or 1:30 and 4:30 P.M. "at your earliest convenience."

Since George was due in the L. L. Parker mailroom from 8:00 A.M. to 6:00 P.M., he obviously had no earliest convenience that could possibly fit in with the stipulation. For several minutes after he left Rhoda Shissle's rooming house and started walking to work it seemed to George that this excused him from complying with Mr. R. Sapina's request.

They wanted him to show up between ten and noon or one-thirty and four-thirty? Well, it so happened he had a job that made it impossible for him to show up at those times. Unless they wanted him to get fired, of course, and if they wanted him to get fired just so he could keep their lousy appointment, why, they could go to hell, that's what they could do. He wasn't losing his job for any postal inspector. So nuts to him and that was that.

By the time he reached Fifteenth Street, the brain that had been frozen by unreasonable terror on University Place had begun to thaw out somewhat, and George realized that this approach was not very sound. The Post Office was a branch of the government. If the government wanted to see you, and you didn't show up, they had plenty of ways to make sure you did. The sensible thing to do was avoid reaching the stage where they had to resort to these ways. It was obvious that George would have to ask Mr. Schumacher for some time off.

Hanging up his coat in the closet outside the washroom, George wondered worriedly whether he should invent an excuse for wanting the time off or whether he should simply show the letter to Mr. Shumacher. A couple of minutes later, when he took up his position at the ping-pong tables and Eff Eff started his demented flinging of mail across the shoulders of his staff, George decided against showing the letter to his boss. Common sense told him that, until he learned what this was all about, it was wisest to say nothing to somebody as crazy as Mr. Shumacher. Looking around at the staff to catch Danny's eye and signal that he'd like to see him a little later in the washroom, George saw with astonishment that Danny was not there.

George had been at Gerrity's the night before. Danny had looked a little depressed, which was understandable enough since there had not been a single customer in the place all night, but he had not looked sick. It was possible, of course, that something had hit him later, after George left, the way the flu had hit Ida Dienst the night the club opened. Somehow, though, George doubted it. Not because Danny never got sick. Lots of people who never got sick folded up fast when the flu hit them. What made George doubt it was that suddenly, as he stood at the ping-pong tables working steadily and swiftly, he found himself wondering if there could be any connection between Danny's absence and the puzzling letter from Mr. R. Sapina.

Before he had a chance to explore this thought, George saw Mr. Shumacher watching him from the other side of the ping-pong tables. Then Eff Eff hurled another fistful of letters onto the table, cackled crazily, and launched into his regular morning comparison between the relationship of gasoline to the Cadillac and the L. L. Parker mailroom to the huge organization. George wondered if he had actually seen Eff Eff watching him, or was it just his imagination? He didn't know, of course, but George realized suddenly that neither Mr. Schumacher nor any member of his staff had commented on Danny's absence. This was so unusual that George decided something was definitely up.

"Excuse me," he said to Mr. Shumacher when he came back after delivering his share of the morning mail to the various departments. "Could I see you a minute, sir?"

"Certainly, George." Eff Eff led him to the roll-top desk in the corner and said with a smile, "What's on your mind?"

"I was wondering if I could have a couple of hours off this afternoon, sir?"

"Off?"

"Yes, sir."

"You mean to leave the office?"

"Yes, sir."

"That's a little unusual, George."

"Yes, sir, I know it is."

"Would it be, ah, how shall I put it, would it be prying, George, to ask how you intend to spend these couple of hours?"

"I want to see a doctor."

"George, are you sick?"

"No, sir."

"I'm sure you'll excuse an old man's obtuseness, George. If you're not sick, why do you want to see a doctor?"

"I've got this pain, sir."

"Where?"

"Right here."

"Here?"

"No, a little further over, sir."

"Does it hurt, badly?"

"Not badly, sir. But I've had it a long time, and I think I'd better get it looked at before it gets worse."

"You have an appointment with this doctor?"

"No, sir. I didn't want to make an appointment until I got your permission to go see him, sir."

"If you have no appointment, George, how do you know he'll see you this afternoon?"

"He doesn't really work by appointments, sir. You come to his office and you wait. First come first served, sort of."

"But you did use the word appointment, George."

"Yes, sir. Just a sort of figure of speech, you might say, sir. What I meant was I'd like to have a couple of hours off to go to his office and wait."

"Does he have office hours in the morning, too?"

"I don't know, sir."

"Most doctors who work that way, without appointments, they usually have two periods of office hours every day, one in the morning and one in the afternoon. Did you know that, George?"

"No, sir."

"Well, it's true, and they usually run from ten to noon in the morning and one-thirty to four-thirty in the afternoon. If this pain has been bothering you for as long as you say it has, I don't think you ought to wait until this afternoon, George. I think you ought to take care of it at once." Mr. Shumacher looked at his wrist watch. "It's only nine-thirty," he said. "That gives you a full half hour. If you leave right now, George, you'll probably get there in plenty of time to be the first patient."

"Thank you, sir."

"Not at all, George, and I do hope it's nothing serious."

He was crossing Twenty-eighth Street, walking quickly up Eighth Avenue toward the huge, dirty gray building that faced the back of Penn Station, when George remembered that the hours during which Eff Eff had said doctors who worked without appointments saw their patients coincided exactly with the hours during which Mr. R. Sapina had said in his letter he would be available to see George. The next thing he remembered was the way Mr. Shumacher's face had kept twitching all during their talk, and George suddenly realized what that meant: Eff Eff had been trying to suppress one of his malicious *I know a secret* smiles!

George's step faltered. A wave of panic swept over him. He wanted to turn and run, away from this meeting with Mr. R. Sapina which Eff Eff seemed to know something about. What saved him was the unexpected image of Uncle Zisha.

It rose up, without any sort of warning, from the Eighth Avenue pavement. All at once George Hurst was once again nine years old, and he was standing on the railroad platform in Albany, and the tall, handsome man in the black fedora and the expensive overcoat was telling him not to be afraid. What Uncle Zisha had told him not to be afraid of, as George recalled it, had nothing to do with what was happening to him now, but the recollection did the trick.

It drove back the panic, and it carried George from Twenty-eighth to Thirty-first Street, into the dirty gray building, and up to Room 327, on the glass door of which he tapped.

"Yes?"

George opened the door. There were four desks in the room but only one man. He was seated in front of the desk nearest the window, his swivel chair tipped back, his feet up on the green blotter, both hands cupped around the bowl of a pipe.

"I'm looking for Mr. Sapina?"

"That's me," the man said. "Come in."

Coming in, George was certain Mr. Sapina could hear the beating of his heart. "I received this letter—?"

"I know."

Mr. Sapina nodded toward a chair beside his desk but did not reach for the letter. George continued to hold it out for another moment or two and then, feeling foolish, he sat down and put the letter in his pocket. Mr. Sapina didn't move his feet from the desk. He puffed quietly on his pipe and stared at George. He did it pleasantly enough, but without any particular interest, as though while waiting for a bus he had been joined on the street corner by a total stranger to whom his only obligation was to avoid jostling while they both waited. The silence in the room kept piling up like steam pressure in a boiler until George couldn't stand it any longer.

"I received this letter," he said again.

"I know."

George suddenly had the feeling that Mr. Sapina had been sitting there waiting for him, then decided that this didn't make much sense. How could Mr. Sapina be expecting him when George himself had not known until a half hour ago that he was coming here this morning?

"Have any trouble getting here, George?"

"No, sir. I just—"

George stopped. How did Mr. Sapina know his name was George? He hadn't even glanced at the letter George had put back in his pocket. He couldn't have seen the typewritten name on it.

"You just what, George?"

"I just told my boss I had to go out for a while."

"That's all?"

"Yes, sir."

"Sounds like a nice boss."

Again George started to say "Yes, sir," and then he remembered the image of Uncle Zisha, and George began to feel something new: anger. He had done nothing wrong. Why should he be afraid of Mr. Sapina or anybody else? What right did Mr. Sapina have to talk to him like this?

"Would you mind telling me, sir, why you wanted to see me?"

Perhaps Mr. Sapina sensed the change in George's voice. Or perhaps he had been too long in one position and he felt cramped. At any rate, Mr. Sapina moved. Not much. A couple of inches at most. A mere shrug, really. But it did something to the arrangement of sunlight falling through the window across his shoulders, and

George saw with surprise that Mr. Sapina had a small, closely cropped mustache.

"You've been buying a lot of stuff by mail," Mr. Sapina said.

"Stuff by mail?" George said. Then he remembered the packages for Danny that had been arriving steadily for almost two months, and all at once it was as though a great big weight had been removed from his shoulders. Why couldn't Mr. Sapina have said in his letter it was Danny's packages he was interested in? Why did the dumb son of a bitch have to be so mysterious about it and, as a result, put George through the hell he'd been suffering ever since he'd taken the damn letter out of his mailbox three hours ago? "Yes, that's right," George said. "What about it?"

If Mr. Sapina heard the belligerent note in George's voice, it was not reflected in his own voice. "Since last March seventh," he said, reading from a sheet of paper that had suddenly and a trifle mysteriously appeared in his hand, "you've bought close to four hundred dollars' worth of stuff from Pittman, Seeps & Croker out in Chicago and from Tapling-Koch in Philadelphia. Is that right?"

"I guess so."

"You guess so, George? Don't you know?"

"I don't know the amount."

"Any reason why you don't know the amount, George?"

"There's a very good reason."

"You mind telling me what it is, George?"

"I'll be glad to. As soon as you tell me why you sent for me in the first place, and what right you have to ask me all these questions?"

"Why, I'll also be glad to," Mr. Sapina said. "You see, George, all this stuff you've been buying has been paid for with stamps."

"With stamps?"

"Why, yes, George. Didn't you know that?" Mr. Sapina waited and then, as though he hadn't really expected an answer but had paused only because he did not want to seem rude, he said, "You see, George, whenever a big mail-order house like Pittman, Seeps & Croker or Tapling-Koch starts receiving large quantities of stamps in payment for merchandise, and especially when those large quantities of stamps start coming in from a single source, they get a little suspicious. Not because they can't use the stamps, or because they think the stamps are counterfeit, but because they know from many years of experience in the mail-order business that there's always a good chance the stamps might have been stolen from some place. So what they do, George, these mail-order houses report it in a routine way to the Post Office Department, and the Post Office Department in a routine way assigns an inspector to the case, and the inspector starts looking into it. In a routine way, George."

This time, when Mr. Sapina paused, he filled the gap of time by relighting his pipe. He did it with total absorption, as though no other activity in all the world could possibly have so much interest for him. George, who suspected in a vague way that he was probably suffering from shock, this being the only explanation he could imagine for the fact that he had as yet felt no reaction to Mr. Sapina's revelation, blushed as he recalled that only moments ago he had thought of this highly intelligent, admirably self-controlled man as a dumb son of a bitch.

"The funny thing about these routine things, George, is the funny things they turn up," Mr. Sapina was suddenly saying to the bowl of his well-fired pipe. "I don't mean the fact that the four hundred dollars' worth of stamps that went to pay for the stuff you've been buying came out of the L. L. Parker mailroom. That's standard, George. Think about it for a moment and you'll see why, George. Where would anybody put their hands on four hundred dollars' worth of stamps except in a place where so many thousands of dollars' worth of stamps are used in the normal course of business that four hundred dollars' worth is a drop in the bucket that would hardly be missed? So there's nothing funny about that part of it, George. The part of it that's very funny, though, the part that's about as funny as anything I've ever run into, George, is the stuff you've been buying." Mr. Sapina, again without any visible movement to explain how it happened to be back in his hand, was consulting the sheet of paper. "Four hundred dollars' worth of ash trays, highball glasses, framed views of Venice and the Swiss Alps, wall mirrors, and scatter rugs. Tell me," Mr. Sapina said. "What would a young man living in one room on University Place want with all that stuff, George?"

George scarcely heard the question. Halfway through it the shock had begun to wear off. It went fast, so that by the time Mr. Sapina finished the question, George had begun to react. He started to get up.

For the first time since George had come into the room Mr. Sapina looked surprised. "Where are you going?"

George, who in his mind was already halfway there, stopped short. "Sorry," he said, and dropped back into the chair. "I'm afraid I didn't hear what you said, sir."

Mr. Sapina gave him a long look across the bowl of his pipe. "George," he said. "Do you understand that sending stolen postage stamps through the mails in payment for merchandise is a federal offense?"

"Yes, sir."

Again Mr. Sapina looked surprised. "You do understand that?"

"Of course I understand it."

George hadn't meant to sound impatient, even though he was, because now that he knew what he had to do he wanted to get started doing it. He saw with regret that Mr. Sapina had noticed the impatience. Having noticed it, Mr. Sapina would undoubtedly now waste more of George's time by asking a whole flock of additional questions.

"In that case," Mr. Sapina said. "I mean if you do understand it, George, then you probably also understand that the consequences can be pretty unpleasant?"

"Yes, sir."

"Then I think you'd better answer my question."

"What question, sir?"

"Where's the stuff, George?"

"What stuff, sir?"

"One thing let's cut out of this talk, George, and that's the jokes. You know what stuff. The stuff you've been buying by mail. We know it's not in your room. That's been searched. Mrs. Shissle doesn't know where the stuff is. We'd like you to tell us, George. Where is it?"

"I can't answer that, sir."

"You mean you won't?"

"I mean I can't."

Mr. Sapina looked thoughtfully into the bowl of his pipe. "You mean you can't answer now?"

George, surprised that the older man should have grasped this, gave him a quick glance. "That's right, sir."

"But you will be able to answer it some time in the future?"

"That's right, sir."

"How far in the future?"

"A few hours," George said.

Mr. Sapina touched his mustache with the stem of his pipe in a curious little gesture of dismissal. "I'll be waiting right here, George," he said.

16

There are no available records to indicate how long it would take a crow to fly from the northwest corner of Thirty-first Street and Eighth Avenue to the northeast corner of Lewis and Fourth Streets. A taxi should be able to do it in anything from twenty minutes to a half hour, depending on traffic. George Hurst, who was not a crow and could not afford a taxi, had to depend on a combination of the I.R.T. subway, the Fourteenth Street crosstown trolley car, and his feet.

He left Mr. Sapina's office at 10:05 A.M. He knocked on Gerrity's side door at 11:20. Danny Schorr, who answered the knock, uttered a grunt of surprise, shoved the door shut to ease the chain bolt, slipped it free, and pulled the door wide.

"What the hell are you doing here?" Danny said.

"That's just what I was going to ask you," George said.

"I mean the job," Danny said. "Shumacher. You're supposed to be working."

"So are you."

Danny gave him a sharp glance. "I decided to take the day off."

"Why?"

"Fix the joint up a little," Danny said. "Come on in." He continued to talk as George followed him in. "I thought if we put the piano over here, against this wall, and we got the bar over this side, customers coming in, the first thing they'd see, instead of that lousy piano, they'd see a nice, clean—" Danny stopped and turned to face George. "All right, let's have it," he said. "What's on your mind, kid?"

George pulled out the letter from the Post Office Department and handed it over. Even if Danny had not taken so long to study the few lines, George would have known he was doing a lot more than reading: Danny's teeth were nibbling the left corner of his lower lip.

"When did you get this?" he said finally.

"It was in my letter box when I came down to go to work this morning."

"What are you going to do about it?"

"I've already done it."

"Done what?"

"What it says in that letter."

"You've gone to *see* this guy?"

"I've just come from his office."

"You great big horse's ass!" Danny crumpled the letter and hurled the wad of paper across the room. "You God-damn stupid son of a bitch!"

"Is that all you've got to say, Danny?"

"I'm just getting started, you putz melamed! Why the hell didn't you come and ask me before you went to see that bastard?"

"You weren't around for me to ask. Besides, what difference would that have made?"

"What difference would that have made? You ask what difference would that have made? What are you trying to do? Hang up a record for how dumb can one guy be? The difference it would have made, you great big frigging meat-head, instead of me standing here now trying to figure out what the government is going to do, all I'd have to worry about is what *you're* going to do!"

"You still have to worry about that."

Danny, who had spun away in his rage, stopped short and turned back. The skin seemed to tighten on his thin, handsome face as the jaw came forward a fraction of an inch. "Say that again," he said.

"You still have to worry about what I'm going to do," George said clearly, as clearly as he could make the words come out through what was happening inside him.

"I see," Danny said. George guessed he did. They didn't come any smarter than Danny Schorr. "Tell me a few things," he said. "Like for instance to begin with what this Mr. Saperino told you?"

"Sapina," George said. "He said all those packages that have been arriving for me, the stuff I've been bringing down here for you, Mr. Sapina said it was all paid for by postage stamps that were stolen from the L. L. Parker mailroom."

"So?"

That did it. The single, short, uninflected syllable was the turning point. Until it was uttered, George suddenly realized, he had been hoping that Danny, who had always been able to explain everything, would be able to explain this, too. Now George knew not only that his hopes had been vain. He knew also that a tie had been cut. It was like that moment years ago when he had suddenly understood, as Aunt Tessie angrily flung clothes into the suitcase she was taking to Albany, that she was not annoyed because Uncle Zisha had suffered a stroke at a time inconvenient to her, but was actually terrified at the prospect of leaving the nest she had built for herself on Fourth Street.

Up to now—until the moment when Danny said, "So?"—he had always been George Hurst's friend. He could do wrong, and he had done plenty, but what he did had never touched the core of their friendship. Or so it had seemed to George. Now, with a word, Danny had done something Aunt Tessie had never been able to do. He had revealed himself as Aunt Tessie had always seen him: a smooth operator to whom friendship was a tool, to be used the way a safecracker uses nitroglycerine, for getting what he wanted. George, who found the sight unpleasant, was nevertheless aware of a sense of relief. It was like learning that a pensioner, who for years has been a drain on your meager income, has finally died. George Hurst no longer had to worry about Danny Schorr.

"So it's like this," George said quietly. "Mr. Sapina told me the government knows, because they searched my room, that I don't have the stuff that's been bought with those stolen stamps. What the government wants to know from me, what Mr. Sapina asked, is who does have the stuff."

"And what did you tell him?"

"Nothing," George said. "Not yet."

The skin that was stretched so tight across Danny's face eased slightly as the outthrust jaw relaxed. "That's my boy," Danny said with a smile.

"No," George said. "Not any more."

"How's that again?"

"I said I'm not your boy," George said. "Not any more."

The corners of Danny's eyes crinkled. "You know, George, all the years we've known each other, there are times when I honest to Christ don't know what the hell you're talking about."

"This won't be one of them," George said. "This is one time I'm making it all clear. Four hundred dollars' worth of stamps have been stolen from the L. L. Parker mailroom. The government thinks I did it. You and I know better, Danny." He turned and started for the door.

Danny caught his arm and pulled him back. "Where you going?"

"Thirty-first Street and Eighth Avenue, Post Office Building, Room 347," George said. "Mr. Sapina is waiting for an answer."

"You're all of a sudden so God-damn high and mighty, why don't you turn your collar around backwards and make like a priest?"

"Let go my arm, Danny."

"What's all the rush? This Sapina won't run away. I want to talk to you."

"I don't want to listen."

"Why not? You think you're so much better than I am?"

"I'm not a crook."

"No? How about that Lutheran gag when you signed your application over at L. L. Parker?"

"I did that to get a job. I have to eat."

"How about me? Don't I have to eat? How can I get this club on its feet if I don't have some dough to buy furnishings? All right, so I copped four hundred bucks' worth of stamps. So what? Who gets hurt? L. L. Parker Stores? This is something you gotta run go get a tourniquet for? Where's the blood? That outfit has millions. What's four hundred bucks to them? Nothing. To me it makes the difference between staying a lousy mail clerk at twelve bucks a week, and climbing up out of the gutter and making something of myself."

"It's still stealing."

"So is your taking that salary every week when you know God-damn well if you hadn't put down that lie on your application blank they'd never give you the job. You're stealing to stay in college so you can become some day another Judge Brandeis. Me, I'm stealing to stay in business down here so I can become some day another Ziegfeld. What's the difference?"

"If you don't understand it, I can't explain it to you."

"Maybe you can't explain it because you don't understand it, either."

"I understand this," George said. "The government wants to

know where the stuff is. They know I know. If I don't tell them, I'll end up in jail. I'm not ending up in jail for something somebody else did."

"Who's asking you to end up in jail?"

"You are."

"You're hearing things that nobody said, George. I'm not asking you to go to jail."

"What are you asking, Danny?"

"Give me twenty-four hours. Less than that. Tomorrow morning. Don't go back to this Sapina with your answer until tomorrow morning. That's all I'm asking, George."

"What good will that do you?"

"I got a guy interested in the club. He's a pretty big operator uptown. He's been down a few times. He's listened to Dora sing. He likes the setup. He made an offer for a half interest in the place plus Dora's contract. He's coming down tonight to hear what I have to say. That's why I didn't go to work this morning. I wanted to spend the day fixing up the joint, make it look nice. When this guy shows tonight, I'm going to take his offer. I'm going to say okay, half the joint is yours. With what I get for it, the four hundred bucks I copped from L. L. Parker is taken care of. You go ahead tomorrow morning and tell this Sapina anything you want. The government comes after me, I'll say sure, I took the stamps. I needed them. Here's four hundred bucks to make it all square. They don't want to make it all square? They want to get tough? This guy I'm telling you about, this partner I'm taking in tonight, he knows how to put on the squeeze in the right places so they'll have to make it all square. If you go to Sapina now, if you tell the government what happened before I get a chance to close my deal tonight, the deal won't get closed. If I get arrested, this guy will figure all he has to do is sit tight and the joint will fall in his lap without his having to shell out a dime. You want that to happen, you want to fix me good, okay, beat it up to the Post Office Building now and go into your squealing act. You want to help out a friend, a guy you've known all your life, all you have to do is wait till tomorrow morning."

"How do I know you're not lying?"

"I can tell you he's not."

George turned. Dora was coming across the room toward them.

He had seen her the night before. But his heart leaped as though he had been away from her for weeks.

"Hi," he said, but that sounded foolish. George cleared his throat and tried for a crisp, businesslike tone. "Dora," he said. "What do you know about this?"

"Everything."

"About the stamps?"

"Yes."

"Why didn't you tell me?"

"You wouldn't have let us use your address. It was better you shouldn't know anything about it."

"Better for whom?" George said bitterly.

"Me," Dora said.

With the softly spoken word she reached him and put her hand on his arm. It was as though she had pressed a button. The feelings with which he had been struggling for months, ever since the night he had first heard her sing, were suddenly straining at the barriers he had so carefully built around them. The long suppressed desire to tell her how he felt, to share the bittersweet secret with which he had been living, came pouring to the surface.

"Dora," he said, his voice shaking. "Dora, I—"

"Please listen to me," she said, as though he had not spoken. "I've told you what singing means to me. How it evens things off. How it makes me forget I'm a cripple. How it doesn't matter when I hear people clapping for me that my arm is crooked. I want to keep on hearing it. I've got to keep hearing it. I can't go back to being a cripple again. I'd rather be dead than go back. If this deal falls through, I'm finished. I'll never get another chance. That's why I didn't tell you about the stamps. I couldn't take a chance on your saying no. Now it's all right to tell you. Because everything worked out. Exactly as Danny planned it. Nothing can go wrong now, George, unless you go to that man in the Post Office this afternoon. If you do that—" Dora paused, and she came a step closer, and with her came the smell of honey cake fresh from the oven. "George," she said, "I know you won't do that. You'll give me those few hours. George, you'll wait until tomorrow morning, won't you?"

For several moments he couldn't speak. All the words that had rushed to his lips, the flood of confession that had been released by the touch of her hand, all that had to be forced back and penned up again, like so many sheep that had come bounding out of a corral because somebody had opened the gate by mistake, and new words had to be found. He had trouble finding them.

"George," she said, "I want you to wait until tomorrow morning."

He turned to look quickly around the room, not quite knowing why, and then he realized he was alone with Dora, and he wondered vaguely when Danny had disappeared.

"George," Dora said, her voice rising slightly, as though to recapture his wandering attention. "George, please," she said. "I want—"

George blew out his breath in a soft, tired sigh. "All right," he said.

17

George left Gerrity's a few minutes before noon. Instinctively, without thinking about where he was going, he started for the place where at this hour of the day he belonged: the L. L. Parker mailroom. When he turned into Fifteenth Street from Fifth Avenue, he suddenly came up out of his troubled thoughts about the events of the morning to ask himself if the L. L. Parker mailroom was a sensible place for him to be at the moment.

Mr. Shumacher obviously knew about the theft of the stamps. Mr. Sapina had made that pretty clear. What was all at once even more clear was the fact that, so far as Eff Eff knew, George was the thief. Until that was straightened out, he didn't see how he could face his boss, and George had just promised Dora that he would not straighten it out until tomorrow morning.

He turned, walked back to Fifth Avenue, and started for University Place. The most sensible thing to do was spend the afternoon in his room.

Halfway there, this suddenly started looking somewhat less than sensible. According to Mr. Sapina, George's room had been searched. This couldn't have been done without the co-operation of Mrs. Shissle, and George knew his landlady well enough to be certain she wouldn't have co-operated until the reason for the search

had been explained to her. Mrs. Shissle, therefore, like Mr. Shumacher, also thought George was a thief. Until he was free to tell
her the truth, George didn't see how he could face his landlady
any more easily than he could face his boss.

George turned again, walked over to the Automat on Fourteenth
Street, bought himself a chopped egg sandwich and a glass of milk,
and tried to think as he ate. He didn't realize how poor his thinking
was until, a half hour later, he had almost reached the Washington
Square College library in which he had decided to spend the afternoon catching up on his French. For the third time in a little more
than an hour George stopped in the street.

He had told Mr. Sapina shortly after ten o'clock that he would
be back in a few hours with the information the postal inspector
wanted. A few hours had already gone by. Before many more of
them went by, Mr. Sapina would surely conclude that George had
no intention of keeping his promise. Mr. Sapina had not hesitated
to have George's room searched. It seemed reasonable to assume
he would not hesitate to ask the police to find George and bring
him in.

George had no very clear ideas about how the police proceeded
with the job of finding someone. His common sense told him, however, that the first thing they would do is check the places where
the man for whom they were looking normally spent his time. These,
in George's case, were three: the L. L. Parker mailroom, Mrs.
Shissle's rooming house, and Washington Square College. George
had decided to avoid the first two as a matter of pride. He saw now
that, if he was going to keep his promise to Dora, he would have
to avoid the third as a matter of necessity.

For a while, as he stood there in the street, hesitating, George
wondered if it might not be a good idea to go back to the Post Office
Building, or perhaps call Mr. Sapina on the telephone, tell the
postal inspector he would need a little more time to obtain the
information, and promise faithfully to bring it in the following
morning. This solution, however, while tempting, raised another
problem. Mr. Sapina, who had so amply demonstrated he was not
a dumb son of a bitch, would surely be smart enough to ask the
question that George himself would have asked: Why?

All Mr. Sapina wanted was the name of the person in whose
possession the government would find the merchandise that had
been paid for with the stolen postage stamps. Why couldn't George

give Mr. Sapina the name right now? Why did he have to wait until tomorrow morning?

George didn't see how he could answer that. It involved a confused mixture of events and emotions, beginning years ago with a small girl's terrified scream for help, running through the pressure of her shoulder blades against an outstretched palm, the smell of her hair, the sound of her voice raised in song toward the waiting applause that brought her cringing body up proud and straight, and ending only an hour ago with a flood of revelation cut short before it could find its way into words, events and emotions that, under the circumstances, Mr. Sapina might very well consider his business, but which George knew he would sooner die than reveal. He had promised Dora he would not go to see Mr. Sapina until tomorrow morning. He would keep that promise if it meant hiding out overnight from every cop in town.

George pulled out his money and counted it: $1.87. His next pay check was due on Saturday. Today being Wednesday, the $1.87 would have to last him three days. It was enough for a man who was accustomed to spending sixty-five cents a day on food. It might not be enough for a man who had to spend the next twenty-four hours as a fugitive.

George killed the first hour by walking uptown to the Public Library on Forty-second Street. He didn't realize this was a mistake until, seeing an old woman with a pretzel basket on the library steps, everything inside him started to growl. He bought two pretzels for a nickel, washed them down with a long drink from the water fountain in Bryant Park, and decided to avoid physical exercise which stimulated the appetite. He tried sitting on a bench in the sun, but this left him free to think about Dora, and soon the pain was worse than hunger. He went into the library, took down a book at random, found a chair, and forced himself to concentrate. After a while he realized he was counting the words rather than reading them. He put the book back on the shelf, left the library, and walked up Forty-second Street.

Between Seventh and Eighth Avenues he saw a movie marquee advertising a triple feature. The pictures were all very old, but the admission price was only twenty cents. George went in. He sat through the whole show twice. He tried to force himself to sit through it a third time, but the dialogue began to get away from him. The mouths on the screen moved, and he read the subtitles with grim concentration, but they made no sense. George thought he was going crazy. When he came out into the street, it was night. His head ached and his stomach was grinding again, but the clock on the Paramount Building showed twenty minutes after ten. It gave him a sense of accomplishment, as though he were a mountain climber who had put behind him a considerable portion of a steep ascent.

George walked down to the Automat near Fifth Avenue and had four nickel portions of macaroni and cheese, two rolls and butter, and a glass of milk. It was a few minutes before eleven when he walked into Grand Central. He moved around for a while, cruising back and forth from the train gates to the Lexington Avenue doors, passing through the waiting room a few times, covering the lower level twice, picking up discarded newspapers, but mainly keeping his eye on the corner seats in the waiting room. They looked the most promising because of the deep recess at the point where the benches turned at right angles. That, of course, was why they were all taken. At eleven-thirty George finally spotted one that was unoccupied. He dropped into it, jockeying himself back and forth until he was comfortable, and then opened one of the newspapers wide. He held it up in front of him, as though he were near-sighted. If there were any cops roaming the station, hunting vagrants who were getting ready to spend the night, he wanted to look like a man absorbed in his newspaper while waiting for a train. Gradually George allowed the paper to come closer and closer until it was resting on his face like a tent. It didn't block out all the light, but it did cut most of the glare. Besides, he was dog-tired.

When he woke up, his back and one leg hurt quite badly, but the clock on the wall showed a few minutes short of six. Only four more hours to go.

George went down to the washroom, scrubbed his face and hands, combed his hair, and straightened his clothes. He wished he had a razor, and for a while he considered going over to Woolworth's and picking one up for a dime, but his bankroll was down to $1.32 and, besides, there would be plenty of time to shave when it was all over.

He went upstairs to Thompson's, had his usual breakfast of rolls and a glass of milk, which reduced his cash to $1.22, then returned to the waiting room. It was now almost seven o'clock and the place was beginning to come alive. It was still too early, however, to pick up anything but yesterday's papers. It took ten minutes of prowling back and forth before George managed to find a *Daily News*. He carried it to the waiting room, sat down on a bench, and read everything in the paper from first page to last, including the advertisements, the recipes, the beauty hints, and the obituaries.

At eight forty-five he left Grand Central, walking as slowly as he dared without attracting attention, stopping frequently to examine the contents of store windows and, when he was sure nobody was watching, crossing and recrossing gutters twice. Even so, it was only nine-thirty when he reached the Post Office Building on Eighth Avenue and Thirty-first Street. For a few moments George thought of going across the street to Penn Station. It was not as complicated as Grand Central, but there was enough to see in it to kill a half hour. George decided against it, however. He'd had a bellyful of railroad stations for one day.

He turned into the Post Office Building, went up to Room 327, and knocked on the door. There was no answer. George knocked again. Still no answer. He tried the knob. It turned and the door gave under the pressure of his hand. George looked in. The room was empty. George went across to Mr. Sapina's desk, sat down in the chair he had occupied the day before, and settled himself to wait.

The pain in his back and his leg was gone. After a while he became aware that, bit by bit, the tempo of his breathing was increasing. Surprised, he realized that he was beginning to feel wonderful. Then, when he understood why, the surprise vanished and only pleasure remained: he was about to do something for Dora.

Promptly at ten o'clock the door opened and Mr. Sapina came in. When he saw George he stopped short in the doorway and slowly took the pipe from his mouth.

George stood up. "Good morning, sir."

"You're late, George."

"I've been here since nine-thirty."

"That's not what I mean, George."

"Yes, sir."

Mr. Sapina put the pipe back between his teeth and came into the room, and then George saw the other man. He was shorter than Mr. Sapina, with a square, unreal face, like that of the man in the Steeplechase ads. He wore a black derby that seemed to be part of his head. He followed Mr. Sapina into the room, closed the door carefully, and stood with his back to it. Mr. Sapina crossed to his desk and sat down without removing the topcoat from his shoulders, the hat from his head, or the pipe from his mouth. He tipped back the swivel chair, put his feet up on the green desk blotter, and lifted the corner of his upper lip away from the pipe-stem to release a long, sharp jet of smoke that reminded George of the steam whistle on a river tug blasting off.

"We've been looking for you, George."

"I'm sorry, sir."

"I don't think you are."

It was true enough. He had kept his promise. He had given Dora the few hours she wanted. George didn't feel sorry. He felt great.

"I mean I'm sorry if I caused you any trouble, sir."

"I get paid for this kind of trouble, George. I don't mind it. What I mind is when I think I've got something figured out and then it turns out I'm wrong." Mr. Sapina took the pipe from his mouth and scowled thoughtfully at the bowl. "Somebody stole four hundred dollars' worth of stamps from the L. L. Parker mailroom and used it to buy stuff that was shipped to your home address. There was no reason to believe you were not the thief. No reason, that is, until you walked in here yesterday. As soon as I took a look at you, after five minutes of talking to you, George, I figured you had nothing to do with it. This wasn't just a hunch on my part. There were two pieces of evidence to back up my conclusion. One, we'd compared the handwriting and signature on the application blank you filled out at L. L. Parker when you got the job, we compared it with the handwriting and signature on the orders that went to Pittman, Seeps & Croker in Chicago and Tapling-Koch in Philadelphia for the stuff that was bought with the stolen stamps, and the handwritings were not the same. Somebody had filled out those orders in your name, George, and had signed them for you. Our second piece of evidence was the fact that, when we searched your room, we couldn't find the stuff. These two pieces of evidence were not necessarily conclusive. You might have used a front man, somebody who filled out the order for you and to whom you turned over the merchandise when it arrived. I tossed this idea out for two other reasons. One, if you were the thief and you were using a front man, it would make more sense for you to use his signature and his address. Second and most important, George, what I just said: you.

Five minutes after you walked in here yesterday, I was convinced that it was the other way around. I was certain somebody had been using you as a front man and, what's more important, I was positive you hadn't known anything about it until I told you about it yesterday.

"Anyway, that's the way I had it figured. That's why, when you refused to tell me where the merchandise is, when you said you'd come back in a couple of hours with the information, I said all right. I figured you were sore at this somebody who had used you as a front man without your knowledge. I figured you wanted to tell him what you thought of him, or maybe even paste him one on the nose, before you turned him in. That's the way I figured it because that's the way I think I would have reacted if somebody had done it to me. That's why I let you walk out of here yesterday without bothering to put a tail on you. I believed you, George. I believed you'd be back in a couple of hours with the information."

Mr. Sapina, using the stem of his pipe as a lever, shoved up his hat an inch or two on his forehead, and pulled a book of matches from his topcoat pocket. "What happened, George?"

"I brought you the information you wanted, sir."

"That's not what I'm asking, George."

Mr. Sapina waited, as though he expected George to say something at this point, but George let him wait. He felt a little sorry for Mr. Sapina. He was even aware of a sense of regret for having disappointed this man who had apparently trusted him and whom George, to his mild surprise, found he rather liked. But the sorrow for Mr. Sapina, like the mild surprise, was as nothing by comparison with the way George felt about having given Dora what she wanted. It was a warm, secret feeling inside him that nothing could touch.

"I waited until four-thirty," Mr. Sapina said. "I knew you knew from the letter I'd sent you that I was in this office every day until that time. When you didn't show by four-thirty, George, I assumed I'd made a mistake in letting you go. I went out to find you. All I found was that you didn't go back to your job yesterday afternoon, you cut your classes last night, and you didn't sleep in your room. I was just about to make arrangements"—Mr. Sapina's pipe, moving with the head into which it was stuck, pointed for a moment at the man with the square face leaning against the closed door—"for a more thorough search, when I find you waiting for me here in my office. Why, George?"

"I brought you the information you wanted, sir."

"Is that all you have to say?"

"Yes, sir."

"Would you say a little more if I asked questions?"

"If I have the answers, yes, sir."

"Did you steal those stamps, George?"

"No, sir."

"Did you know they were being stolen?"

"No, sir."

"Did you send for the merchandise?"

"No, sir."

"Did you know the merchandise was being sent for?"

"Yes, sir."

"Can you make that a little more clear, George?"

"Yes, sir."

He explained what had happened. He omitted only one thing: all references to Dora.

When George finished, Mr. Sapina took the pipe from his mouth. "This Daniel Schorr, this so-called friend of yours," the postal inspector said. "Did you have to wait a long time last night until he showed up?"

For several moments George did not understand. Then he saw the slight twinkle in Mr. Sapina's eye and George saw also how the postal inspector was filling in the blank spaces. Mr. Sapina assumed that George had spent the night waiting in Gerrity's for a show-down with Danny. It seemed sensible at the moment to let the postal inspector hold onto that assumption. George said nothing.

The twinkle in Mr. Sapina's eye worked its way down to his lips. "Did you belt him a good one?" the postal inspector said with a smile.

Silence, which George had always heard was golden, was now demonstrating that it could also play the role usually reserved for actions: it was speaking louder than words. George decided to let it go right on doing the work. If he was going to succeed in keeping Dora out of it, anything further he said would have to be a lie, and no lie he invented could be an improvement on what Mr. Sapina had supplied for himself. George looked modestly down at his hands.

Mr. Sapina chuckled. "Okay," he said as he dropped his feet

from the desk to the floor and stood up. "Let's go have a talk with your friend Mr. Schorr."

They went in a long black car with a Police Department shield clamped to its license plate and driven by the man in the black derby hat. He parked it directly in front of Gerrity's side door and followed George and Mr. Sapina across the sidewalk.

Mike Junior answered George's knock. "What do you want?"

"These men want to see Danny."

"He's not here."

"You better open up."

"Nobody's here."

Mike Junior started to shove the door closed. The man in the derby hat, who had driven the black car across town with a lumbering care that seemed to indicate a cautious nature and a muscle-bound frame, now demonstrated that the way a man performs behind a steering wheel is not the most reliable key either to his character or his reflexes. The man in the derby moved George aside, got his arm through the narrow gap of open door, grabbed Mike Junior by the front of his shirt, and dragged Mike's startled face up against the chain bolt, all in a single, smooth, effortless flow of motion.

Across his shoulder Mr. Sapina spoke quietly. "Better open up, son," he said.

Mike opened up and stepped backwards through the black curtains into the room. The man in the derby hat and Mr. Sapina looked around with interest. The postal inspector picked up an ash tray, set it down, walked to the wall for a look at a framed view of Notre Dame, and straightened his tie in a small oval mirror.

"This the stuff?" he said.

"Yes, sir," George said. He turned to Mike Junior. "Better get Danny. These men want to talk to him."

"I told you Danny's not here."

"Where is he?"

"I don't know."

The man in the derby hat came forward. Mr. Sapina stopped him by touching the stem of his pipe to the man's arm.

"When did you see Mr. Schorr last?" the postal inspector asked.

The watery blue, egg-white, lifeless eyes showed no sign of recognition.

"He means Danny," George said to Mike Junior. "When did you see Danny last?"

"Not since yesterday."

"What time yesterday?"

"Right after you left."

Neither Mr. Sapina nor the man in the derby hat knew that George had left a few minutes before noon. George could tell, as the warning bell went off in his head, that the postal inspector and the policeman saw nothing significant in Mike's statement.

"Where did he go?" Mr. Sapina said.

"I don't know," Mike Junior said.

"When do you expect him back?"

"He's not coming back."

"He tell you that?"

"He didn't have to."

"How do you know he's not coming back?"

"He took my mother's two suitcases with him."

Mr. Sapina swung around to George. "He say anything to you about going somewhere?"

"No," George said. "He said—"

"Wait down here," Mr. Sapina said. The man in the derby hat fell in beside him as the postal inspector started for the door that led to the hall. "We'll take a look upstairs."

Wondering desperately why he should be frightened, trying to keep ahead of the puzzling fear that seemed to be racing up from behind to engulf him, George became aware all at once that he and Mike Junior were not alone in the room. He turned. Mrs. Gerrity had come in. She was moving toward them in an awkward, jerky manner, as though each step was painful, and her hands were clenched tightly around the ends of the black shawl. She looked a little the way Old Man Saydl looked when he used to drag himself through the streets with his tin cup, except that Old Man Saydl's face had never looked the way Mrs. Gerrity's face looked now. She was grinning.

"You can tell me where Danny is," George said. "I won't tell anybody. Where is he?"

Mrs. Gerrity's grin swung from George to her son. For a long moment Mike stared at George in silence. Then the grayish, puffy face seemed to fall apart. A moment or two went by before George realized what he was seeing was a smile and what he was hearing was a laugh. Mike took two staggering steps forward, toward his mother, as though seeking her support. They met and, hand in hand, staggered backward, toward the bar, each with a free hand upraised, as though feeling for support in the dark. When they found it, they clung together, holding themselves upright against the polished wood, and laughed until they choked.

"He'll get it now!" Mike gasped. "After all these years, the son of a bitch, he'll get it now!"

"The dirty little kike!" Mrs. Gerrity managed to say. "Now he's started with cops, now they'll both get it!"

The word "both" straightened it all out. George knew, as he started to run toward the black curtains, what it was that had frightened him when Mike Junior said the last time he'd seen Danny was right after George left the day before. He even knew, though he kept hoping he was wrong, what he would find when he got across the street.

Ida Dienst was alone in the doll store. "What the hella *you* want?" she said. "The gold fillings maybe out of Papa's teeth?"

"Where's Dora?"

"Go ask your friend Danny."

"Where is he?"

"Go ask Dora."

George walked up to the workbench, grabbed her by the shoulders, and dragged Ida Dienst to her feet with a short, hard pull that made her head snap. "Where is she?" George said again.

Ida's lips spread wide in the beginnings of a snarl, and then she seemed to see him for the first time. A puzzled look crossed her face.

"You kidding?" she said. "You don't know what happened?"

"Where's Dora?" George said. His voice was shaking.

"Stop breaking my arms," Ida said. "I don't know. Nobody knows. All we know is she's gone and her clothes are gone and Danny's gone, too."

"Where?"

"As far as they can get on three hundred dollars, I guess. That's how much there was in Papa's box, the money he was saving for this month's bills. They cleaned it out. Every cent. You mind letting me go now?"

George dropped his arms. He turned and started back toward the door. Now that it was too late, he could see it all clearly. There had been no deal on the fire to sell a half interest in the club. Danny

had made that up, on the spur of the moment, when George showed
him Mr. Sapina's letter and Danny realized he was trapped. Danny
had made that up, the way he had been making things up for years,
to gain time for his getaway.

It hurt to be used like that. It hurt worse to know Dora had
lied to him. She had tricked him into giving them the time to make
their getaway. George could feel the beginning of the pain, and he
knew it would get worse, but at the moment it was not yet unbearable, because at the moment George could not yet accept the fact
that he had lost her. He was still free, therefore, if only for a few
minutes, to choose among the pains Danny and Dora had left
behind for him.

It was not a difficult choice to make. What hurt most was
losing the wonderful feeling George had earned by his night as a
fugitive, the feeling that came with knowing he had done something for Dora. It turned out that he had not done it for Dora at all.

At the end of their friendship, as from the very beginning, it
was Danny who profited.

18

Twenty years later, hurrying through Grand Central toward the 5:25
that carried him home to Danville every evening, George Hurst could
see as he glanced hastily at the copy of *Worldweek* he'd bought on
his way into the station that he had underestimated the size
of the profit. The caption under the cover picture of Danny read:

HOTEL TYCOON SHAW
"The easiest million is the first!"

It had been a rough day. The problem Mr. Kashkin had dumped
in George's lap in the morning, after becoming unexpectedly complicated by his lunch with Nick Perrini, had been forgotten temporarily
in the flood of memories released by his visit to Miss Corcoran.
George saw now, as he pushed along to the train with the crowd
of commuters, that it was going to be difficult to keep the problem
from becoming further complicated by bitterness: he had known

for years that Danny Schorr had made his pile; it had not occurred to George until this moment that the pile was actually a mountain.

He wished he'd had enough sense on this Friday preceding the Fourth of July week end to try for an earlier train. The normal stream of commuters was thickened considerably by an outpouring of holiday travelers whose suitcases, tennis rackets, and golf bags were complicating the normal maneuverings for position by the men and women who made this trip every day. Of these, George after four years as a commuter was no slouch when it came to getting a seat. He managed to snag one far enough ahead of the bar car to minimize the number of interruptions that could be expected from those commuters who liked to start the day's drinking early, settled down with his copy of *Worldweek,* and opened the magazine to the cover story. George read:

THE DECENT MAN. *A handsome man of medium height, with a lean, strong face, alert brown eyes, and a magnetic manner, wearing a beautifully cut double-breasted blue pin stripe that had been made by Hawks of #1 Savile Row, walked into the barber shop of the Beverly Hills Hotel in Beverly Hills, California, followed by his chauffeur. He had not made an appointment by telephone; nor had he, like so many of the movie colony's upper echelon executives and stars, sent the chauffeur over to bring one of the barbers back to his mansion on swank Roxbury Drive's 900-block.*

"Mr. Shaw," Barber Matty Marushak tells his cronies, "comes in and takes his chances like anybody else."

Today nobody was ahead of Daniel Shaw. He slipped out of his jacket and vest, disposed of them on the line of hooks in the wall facing the mirrors and five chairs, hunched himself into a cashmere sweater held up for him by his chauffeur, and dropped into Matty Marushak's chair.

"Do you mind closing that door?" he said.

Shaw, who will be forty years old on July 2nd, is beginning to worry about drafts. He lay back in the chair, a sheet wrapped around his muscular athlete's frame, for his customary haircut and shampoo. Then he began to assault the barber with queries: "How is business?" and "What do your customers say about the stock market?" Then: "Is there much talk about a dip in box office revenues?" and "How do you think the Dodgers will do?"

Matty Marushak, who picks up as much important Beverly Hills talk as Hedda Hopper and Louella Parsons, came through with a concise briefing: business was good; the stock market would hold; box office reports for the first quarter of the year were down everywhere except in the Deep South; the Dodgers didn't have a prayer.

His thick black hair clipped, shampooed, and meticulously dried, Shaw gave Marushak a $10 bill for the $4.50 job, slipped back into his vest and jacket, and pointed for the next stop on his morning round.

"So long, Mr. Shaw," said the barber.

"So long, Matty," said the man who is known to his friends and associates as B.O.F. (Ball of Fire), the youthful tycoon who, in less than ten years, has placed himself so securely astride the middle echelon of America's hotel industry that he has been called by Walter Winchell "the poor man's Conrad Hilton."

The next point on his morning itinerary was the Heloise Harper Hood Home for unwed mothers in downtown Los Angeles, where Shaw left with Mrs. Dorothy T. Hagues, the Home's director, 200 sheets from his hotel chain's enormous linen closet and his personal check for $5,000. Shaw, who dislikes publicity, is rarely photographed, and would find it much easier to have his chauffeur deliver the sheets and the U.S. mail carry his check, insists on making all his many charitable contributions in person.

"If you're helping someone, you ought to take a look at the people you're helping," he says. "Money is only money. It's the human element that counts."

THE CROWDED AGENDA. *His tasks downtown completed, Daniel Shaw was driven back to The Nook, his 37-room Tudor home in which, as he does six days a week, except when he is traveling, he tackled a sheaf of papers at his kneehole desk in his small office to the right of the front door. Although he is publicly known as the proprietor of the largest privately owned hotel chain in the world, Shaw's main interest is good works.*

Without fanfare, he is building a small public beach on the old Kriewald estate near Sheepshead Bay in Brooklyn; acquiring more land for what he hopes will be the first Little League Stadium on Chicago's South Side; paying the hospital bills for the stepmother of a Japanese gardener who once worked on his Beverly Hills grounds; making plans for the removal of the ugly "shigs" (burst sewer pipes) left by last year's hurricane on the outskirts of West Haven, Conn.; making good the perennial deficit of the Fresno Marine Library; en-

couraging the Mount Hood Improvement Society to keep its ski runs in good shape and to provide plenty of parking space. He is on the phone endlessly to acquaintances and business associates, asking questions about various items on his crowded agenda in his soft, unobtrusive, beautifully modulated voice: "What will the whole thing cost? How much are the others putting up? How much can they accumulate without my contribution?"

LONG ON ACTS. At first glance the vigorous, youngish man in The Nook seems an unlikely candidate for the role of American business hero and philanthropist. Not because in appearance he looks so much more like one of the movie stars who are his neighbors in Beverly Hills and for whom, to his considerable embarrassment, Daniel Shaw is frequently mistaken by gawking tourists. He is retiring to the point of timidity. His shyness causes him almost physical pain. He finds it an agony to address even his most intimate friends by their given names.

"It amazes me how you can do it," he remarked recently when a couple of old friends were Tom-and-Bill-ing one another. "I wish I was built like that."

His neighbors in Beverly Hills, however, admire and like Daniel Shaw built the way he is.

"There's a lot of Yankee in Danny Shaw," cinemogul Sam Goldwyn said recently. "He's short on talk, but long on acts."

Daniel Shaw, as anyone who reads the gossip columns must know, is worth in the neighborhood of $50 million. He also, as everyone who reads any section of America's newspapers knows, made every penny of it himself.

"It's no great accomplishment," he said recently. "I don't know why people make such a fuss about people who make large sums of money. It's been my experience that once you make some, making more is practically automatic, and getting started making it is not as difficult as some people would like to have other people think. The first million is the easiest."

What differentiates Daniel Shaw from other millionaires is not the size of his bank account, but his attitude toward it.

"I don't know what being born with money does to a man," he said to friends at one of the small dinner parties that are almost his only form of recreation. "But I can tell you what being born without money does to a man: it makes him want to put his hands on some of it. When he does, that's when you can begin to measure him. Be-

cause the only question about money is what you do with it. It can be used for evil purposes, or it can be an instrumentality for constructive social living."

THE COMPULSION TO IMMORTALITY. *It is because Daniel Shaw has at forty dedicated himself to a life of socially constructive giving that he is entitled to be considered a genuine American hero, just as surely as any general who ever won an American victory on a battlefield, or any statesman who ever ran up a score for U.S. diplomacy. This compulsion to serve his fellow man is the direct result of lonely, frugal, and often discouraging years of seeking what Shaw calls "a direction in which to live." Most people, he believes, live like vegetables. "They just grow, and then one day they get picked and cooked, and that's that. There's nothing to show they were ever around," Shaw says. "I'd like to feel, when I go, that I've left something behind that will not only be a mark that I was there, but will also be useful to the people who come after me. If that's a form of immortality, then I guess you can say I want to be immortal."*

THE SUNNY, CLOUDLESS TIME. *Daniel Shaw was born on New York's lower East Side on July 2, 1909, the only son of an ascetic, saintly house painter and a gentle seamstress who died when the boy was five years old. Faintly, then with mounting excitement, his earliest ambitions and pleasures were intertwined with his father: father reading aloud from the Bible after the day's work; father walking the rain-soaked streets of the lower East Side to sit up all night with a sick friend; father taking his son to Tompkins Square Park on Sunday and teaching Daniel how to pitch a curve.*

"That," says Shaw, "was the sunny, cloudless time."

The rains came on Armistice Day, 1918, when the elder Shaw, in an attempt to save the lives of two gentle old German ladies who were about to be lynched by a mob drunk on cheap whiskey and an excess of misplaced patriotism, was himself killed in a brutal accident on the East Fourth Street dock.

"It was like having a light go out," Shaw says now. For a while, in the terrible darkness of orphanhood, the boy thought of suicide. Then, in an act of kindness he has never forgotten and that has in large measure influenced his life, young Shaw was taken into the household of a kindly Irishman named Mike Gerrity, who with the help of his wife and son earned a precarious living by selling coffee and sandwiches to the bargemen who brought lumber and coal to the

*storage yards on the Fourth Street dock that jutted out into the East
River.*

The Gerritys, as pious and puritanical as Shaw's own beloved
father, were teetotalers. Without any feeling of oddity, young Shaw,
not yet nine, signed a pledge to abstain for the duration of his life
from "coffee, tea, tobacco, profanity and the consumption of any
alcoholic beverages," a pledge he has kept. As the boy grew older, the
extraordinary Mike Gerrity taught him the meaning of how to earn
and how to pay out. Day after day young Daniel worked along with
Mr. and Mrs. Gerrity and their son Mike, Jr., carrying coffee and
sandwiches down to the bargemen for pennies, entering his earnings in
a meticulously kept ledger. When Mr. Gerrity died unexpectedly,
Daniel Shaw left school to give all his time to helping the widow and
her son who had literally taken him in off the streets when he was
nine. A couple of years later Mrs. Gerrity died of the arthritis that
had been crippling her slowly for a decade, and Mike Junior followed
her to her grave within six months. The Depression was just beginning
to take its strangling hold on the American economy, and Daniel
Shaw, not yet old enough to vote, was once again all alone in the
world.

"HE TRAVELS FASTEST." Loneliness, which is not generally considered a desirable state, has its advantages. "It gives you time to
think," Shaw says. Up to then, he had thought only about the Gerritys, trying with his devotion and hard work to repay them for their
kindness to him. Now, with nobody to think about but himself, the
penniless young man started to think about what he wanted from life.
First, of course, he wanted to eat, and fate arranged this by a happy
accident. Trudging home from the Brooklyn cemetery where he had
just seen Mike Gerrity, Jr., buried, young Shaw passed a small Bowery
hotel. There was a hand-lettered sign in the window: "Boy Wanted."
Shaw went in and asked for the job. The owner looked at the muscular
young man and shook his head.

"You're not a boy," he said. "The job pays only four dollars a
week."

"That's four dollars a week more than I'm earning now," said
young Shaw. "And I can do anything a boy can do."

He did it for three years, at the end of which time, when the
proprietor died and left the place to his young employee, Shaw had
mastered the basic elements of the hotel business and had started on
the career that has carried him to his present position of financial

eminence. If he has achieved success more rapidly than most, Shaw attributes it to luck, to the principles of thrift and decency implanted in him by the beloved Gerritys, and to the fact that fate has made him a lone wolf. As a result, he has been able to work harder and longer than other men.

"It's like what Kipling said in the poem," Shaw says. "He travels fastest who travels alone."

THE GLORIOUS TIME. He says it with a smile, but it would be an obtuse listener who did not sense the heartbreak behind the gently spoken words. Daniel Shaw, handsome, magnetic, and wealthy, seems to have everything. But while he never complains, it is no secret that he knows he does not have the one thing without which life remains an arid desert: the gift of requited love has been denied him.

Somewhere in his early years there was a girl. Shaw never speaks about her, but from the bits and pieces of gossip and hearsay that always foam up around the famous like spindrift, a tantalizing, shadowy picture emerges: a slender, dark-haired girl with the delicate face of a Chinese doll and the glorious voice of a Lily Pons, moving wraith-like and lovely through those early years on the lower East Side, capturing the heart of a lonely youngster and then, before the picture can come into focus, before the girl and her relationship to Daniel Shaw can be grasped, she is gone.

That she left a void which no other woman has ever been able to fill in his life, there is no doubt. That she was tremendously important to Shaw in those crucial formative years that followed the death of the Gerritys, there can be even less doubt. That she was responsible for turning him into those channels of selfless devotion to his fellow man that are now Daniel Shaw's main preoccupation, seems fairly certain. That she brightened what was for most other people a time of darkness can be guessed from the way Daniel Shaw still talks about the Depression years.

Making one of his rare public appearances to address the graduating class at UCLA last week, he said: "There is no secret to success. It is merely a matter of wanting it. I say to you young people on whom the future of this country rests, I say to you from the bottom of my heart: never lose your enthusiasm, always keep cool, and the world is yours. I learned that lesson during the Depression. Most people who lived through those years talk about them with hatred. I don't think it makes much sense to hate a period of time any more than it makes sense to hate the weather. The Depression was a fact that those of us *who grew up in it had to cope with. As a young man starting out in the world, I would have preferred, of course, to cope with a more pleasant fact, with a time of prosperity. But the choice wasn't mine, and that's the point I want to make. I had to work with what was handed to me, and what was handed to me was a depression. Instead of throwing up my hands, I rolled up my sleeves. Instead of finding the Depression a time of despair, I found it a time of opportunity. It was tough, but it was also exciting. It was a little the way I imagine Valley Forge was, a time of trial for the whole nation, a time from which we all emerged better and stronger than when we went in. It was the glorious time."*

19

Not for George Hurst. For him it was as glorious as a toothache.

The horror began a couple of hours after he learned that Danny and Dora had run away together. Mr. Sapina took the news with surprising calm. The postal inspector asked George to accompany him back to his office, where he busied himself at a typewriter, sending large blasts of pipe smoke toward the ceiling as he pecked away with two fingers. When he finished, Mr. Sapina pulled the sheets from the machine and handed them to George.

"What I've written there is an account of your relationship to this stamp theft," he said. "What you told me, what we just found out down on Fourth Street, the whole works. Read it over."

George did so.

"Is that the way it happened?" Mr. Sapina asked.

The words were different from the ones George had used, but the facts were accurate.

"Yes, sir," he said.

"In that case, sign here." The postal inspector handed George a fountain pen. "All three copies."

George signed all three copies and handed back the fountain pen.

"I'm not a policeman in the strictly technical sense," Mr. Sapina said. "I'm not interested in hanging up a score. None of us in the Department is. Our job is to help see to it that the post office functions as smoothly and efficiently as possible. When people steal stamps and use them as money to buy merchandise, the functions of the post office are being perverted. That's why we try to stop them. If the only way to stop them means sending them to jail, we go to the Attorney General and ask his department to send the stamp stealers to jail."

He paused to light his pipe.

"Are you going to go after Danny and send him to jail?" George asked.

"Do you care?"

Their eyes met across the match flame.

"Yes, sir," George said.

"Do you mean yes, sir, you care whether we send Daniel Schorr to jail or yes, sir, you care whether we send this girl Dora Dienst to jail with him?"

"Could she be sent to jail with him?"

"If anybody really wanted to do it, yes. A man interested in hanging up a score can do anything."

"Dora had nothing to do with this."

"How do you know?"

"She told me."

"She told you she didn't know all those ash trays and drinking glasses and pictures and mirrors were arriving in Gerrity's."

"She didn't know they were being paid for with stolen stamps."

Mr. Sapina shook out the match flame. "Perhaps not," he said.

"It's true, sir. Dora didn't know."

"As I said, perhaps not."

"I give you my word, sir."

"You gave me your word yesterday that you would be back in this office in a few hours."

"That was different, sir."

"It certainly was. If I hadn't taken your word, if I had insisted you tell me right then and there where the stuff was located, your pal Danny and this girl Dora would not have had almost twenty-four hours in which to make their getaway."

"That's not why I did it, sir," George said.

"I know that." Mr. Sapina picked up the three copies of the statement George had signed. "That's why I omitted from this report the fact that you showed up with the information this morning instead of yesterday afternoon as you promised." The postal inspector jogged the pages into alignment and dropped them on the desk. "As a rule, the Department doesn't care about people's motives. Neither do I, as a rule. I'm breaking the rule in this case because what I said earlier this morning, how I don't like it when I think I've got something figured out and then it turns out I was wrong, well, I've finally got this one figured out. I know why you did it, George. I've got a son just about your age. He might have done the same thing. As a matter of fact, if he had, I think I'd be proud of him. But that wouldn't mean what he did was bright. It would mean only that he was too young to know any better. Am I making myself clear?"

George didn't answer. Mr. Sapina went to work on his pipe again. When he had it firing properly he looked at the curled black head of the match as though he were an art expert who had just been led to a newly discovered Titian and asked to say whether or not it was genuine.

"The trouble with being young, George, as you will discover when you no longer are, is that you don't know how things are going to be," the postal inspector said. "You have no reservoir of experience to look back on and use as a yardstick. You get the idea that you can make a million dollars by, let's say, all right, let's take a preposterous example, by swimming the Atlantic Ocean. An older man, a man who has done some swimming in the past, he knows it can't be done. He's tried it, or he's tried something like it, and he's failed. So he doesn't try it again, or he doesn't try it to begin with. A young person hasn't had time to try it or to try anything like it. He hasn't lived long enough to try a lot of things, among them swimming the Atlantic Ocean. So he doesn't know it's impossible. He doesn't know he's going to fail. So he just walks right out into the water and starts swimming, and pretty soon somebody has to drop whatever he's doing to go out and save him. You might say that what I'm dropping right now, George, is the work the government pays me to do. Am I making myself any clearer?"

Again George did not answer. Mr. Sapina gently hissed out a long stream of smoke, cut it in half with a slow, deliberate, downward chop of his hand, and narrowed his eyes to examine the sudden whirling confusion of blue-gray eddies.

"I didn't know when you came in here yesterday, George, that a girl was involved," he said. "Now that I do know, I'd like to point something out to you that I hope, if my son were in your shoes, somebody would drop his work long enough to point out to him.

It's simply this: what's done is done, George. It can't be undone. What still lies ahead, what's going to be done in the future, that's what counts from here on in. All things considered, you've been pretty lucky. I'm convinced you're not a thief. I'm certain you were an innocent victim in this thing. I'm turning in a report to that effect. So far as the government is concerned, you're in the clear. It's all over. Finished. A closed book. When a girl is involved, though, there's always the chance that the closed book will get opened again. If it ever does, George, let somebody else write the next chapter. This girl isn't worth your time."

George found his voice. It sounded as though it had been lying out in the rain for a long time. "You don't know her," he said.

"I know what she did," Mr. Sapina said. "She did it for three hundred dollars. Leaving aside the fact that she stole it from her own father, it's a pretty low price for anybody to set on themselves. Any questions?"

"Yes, sir."

"Shoot."

"What's going to happen to her?"

"She'll end up in the gutter."

"That's not my question."

"Ask it again, George."

"What's going to happen to her because of this stamp thing?"

"So far as the government is concerned, nothing. I think your ex-friend Mr. Schorr has learned that it's not smart to fool with a branch of the federal government. We'll keep an eye open for him. If there's a recurrence of this L. L. Parker thing, we'll open something else for him: a nice comfortable cell in a federal penitentiary. If Miss Dora Dienst has anything to do with the recurrence, there will be a cell for her, too. Anything else, George?"

"No, sir."

"In that case—" Mr. Sapina stood up and, unexpectedly, he put out his hand. "So long, George. Believe it or not, it was nice meeting you."

George took the outstretched hand. "Thank you, sir."

"I won't be a hypocrite and say there's nothing to thank me for," Mr. Sapina said. "Neither will I be a jerk and ask you to give me the thanks I've earned. I'll settle for this: try to remember what I said, so that some time in the future, when you're no longer sore

at me, when you can think more clearly than I know you're thinking now, it might do you some good. Okay?"

"Yes, sir."

"One more thing. You don't have to worry about going back
to your job, or to your classes, or to your room. We didn't tell anybody down at Washington Square College why we were looking
for you last night, so you're in the clear there, and as soon as you
walk out of here I'll call your landlady and Mr. Shumacher. I'm
certain everything will be all right."

Mr. Sapina probably would have been less certain if he had
known something about the principles by which the L. L. Parker
Stores were run.

When George came into the mailroom, Mr. Shumacher
beckoned him to the roll-top desk in the corner. "I just had a telephone call from Mr. Sapina."

"Yes, sir. He told me he would call you, sir."

"I'm very glad to learn you're not a thief, George."

Mr. Shumacher did not look glad. The old man's clawlike
fingers of his left hand were picking nervously at the corner of a
sheet of paper on his desk, as though he were a bank teller trying
to count a stack of money and he couldn't get the riffling process
started, and he seemed to be having more trouble than usual with
his false teeth. He kept drawing his lips taut, as though to force
back the plates that were trying to work their way out of his mouth.

"If you'll excuse me, sir," George said, "I'll hang up my coat
and get to work."

"Would you mind waiting just one minute, George?"

"Of course not, sir."

"There are a couple of questions I'd like to ask."

"I'm sure Mr. Sapina will be glad to tell you anything else
you want to know, sir."

"I doubt that Mr. Sapina can answer these questions," Mr.
Shumacher said. "George, would you mind telling me what church
you attend?"

Here it comes, George thought. "Beg pardon, sir?" he said.

Mr. Shumacher lifted the sheet of paper at the corner of which
he had been picking. "You say here on your application blank,
George, the blank you signed when you applied for your job with
us, you say you're a Lutheran, George. I'd like to know the name
of the church you attend."

George knew the answer: the First Lutheran Church on Avenue B between Eighth and Ninth Streets. He even knew, if that question should come next, the name of the pastor: Dr. Thomas Hinzpeter. Danny Schorr was thorough. He had provided for everything. All at once, however, the things Danny had provided seemed distasteful. Even if he could have been certain it would save his job, George knew he would not use the life savers Danny had fashioned and left behind. Besides, George knew from the look on Mr. Shumacher's face that nothing could save his job.

"I can't tell you the name of the church I attend."

Mr. Shumacher's spotted flypaper skin stretched taut on his cheekbones as his eyebrows went up in a burlesqued exaggeration of amazement. "You can't?" he said. "Why not, George?"

"I don't attend church," George said.

He was aware of a small, sick feeling deep down in his stomach, and he knew it would get worse. At the moment, however, it did not bother him. It was like knowing on Friday, as the week end is about to start, that a debt would have to be paid on Monday. The debt was real enough, but before it had to be faced there was the fun of the intervening two days to live through. The sense of imminent fun was stronger than the small sick feeling. It was sending through George a charge of exhilaration not unlike that which a long-time spy might experience when permitted at last to assume his real identity. Everything inside George was suddenly jumping. He was about to be canned, but he was also about to tell this son of a bitch what he thought of him. George found it difficult to keep a straight face.

"You don't attend church?" Mr. Shumacher said.

"No, sir."

"Because you're not religious?"

"That's not the reason."

"Because you don't have the time?"

"I have plenty of time."

"Then why not, George?"

"I don't belong there, sir."

"But George, every decent Christian belongs in church."

"I'm not a Christian," George said. "Decent or otherwise."

Eff Eff scowled irritably. George almost laughed out loud. It wasn't going the way the old bastard had expected it to go. He'd had the script all worked out in his mind, and George was not sticking to the script.

"What are you, George?"

"I'm a Jew."

The creases of irritation smoothed away. Mr. Shumacher smiled gently. The performance had come back to the prepared script.

"Then you're also a liar, George, aren't you?"

"I guess you could say that, sir."

"You guess, George? What else can I say, George? You wrote on your application blank you're a Lutheran. Here. See for yourself. It's your own handwriting, isn't it?"

"That's right."

"And now you tell me you're not a Lutheran. What else can I say except that you're a liar, George."

"You can say what's on your mind."

"Yes," Mr. Shumacher said. "Yes, I can say that." He smiled sweetly. "You don't have to bother taking off your coat. Just stop at the cashier's window on your way out and pick up your last pay check."

"May I ask a question?"

"If you think it will do you any good."

George didn't see how it could do him any harm. "Are you firing me because I'm a liar?"

"What other reason could there be?"

"The reason why I wrote that lie on my application blank."

"I don't understand you, I'm afraid."

"You don't look afraid to me, Mr. Shumacher."

He looked as though he'd just come into an unexpected inheritance. "Why don't you just tell me the reason you wrote that lie on your application blank?"

"I needed a job," George said. "I was told it was an L. L. Parker policy not to hire Jews."

"Who told you that?"

"Word gets around."

"I can't help that."

"Can you deny it?"

"We hired you and your friend Daniel Schorr."

"Because we lied about our religion."

The spotted skin drew together around the crinkled lips in the sort of smile John D. Rockefeller, Sr., used to flash when he handed out a dime in front of the press photographers.

"You're merely proving, George, how wise we would be to adopt such a policy. Not that we have, mind you. Or ever will. I'm merely talking theoretically. Look at it yourself, George. The L. L. Parker Stores have never hired a Jew before you and your friend Daniel Schorr came along. Then we go ahead and hire two, and what happens? One of them turns out to be a crook and both turn out to be liars. Under the circumstances, George, would you hire any more Jews?"

"Under the circumstances, Mr. Shumacher, there's only one thing I can do."

"What's that, George."

"Watch."

George took the application blank from Eff Eff, tore it slowly and carefully into small bits, and then, before the startled old man could turn or duck, George grabbed him by the back of the neck and shoved the wad of paper scraps into his mouth. Walking out, George could hear Mr. Shumacher spitting scraps of paper, gasping for breath, and trying simultaneously to shout for help and scream obscenities about Jews. George didn't care. The lie he had been living ever since he had signed the application blank was over.

His contact with the principles by which the L. L. Parker Stores were run, however, was not. The cashier, George found when he got to the barred window on the first floor, had a small lesson in arithmetic waiting for him.

"We work a five and a half day week," he said to George through the bronze grille. "Your salary is twelve dollars a week. Five and a half days, or eleven half days, divided into twelve comes to $1.09 per half day or $2.18 per full day. You worked only three days this week, Monday, Tuesday, and Wednesday, which means we owe you three times $2.18 or $6.54." He shoved a piece of paper under the grille. "Sign here, please." George signed. The cashier pulled the paper back and pushed forward another piece of paper. "This is your final check."

He turned and walked away from the grille, taking the first two steps very fast, as though afraid George might reach in through the bars to grab him. George had other things on his mind. Walking out with the check for $6.54, he was adding the figure to the $1.22 in cash he had in his pocket. The result was sobering: he had $7.76 to keep him going until he found another job.

A half hour later he had only $3.76.

Coming into his rooming house on University Place, George met Mrs. Shissle in the downstairs hall.

"Oh, Mr. Hurst!" she said. "I've been so worried about you, but I just had a call from Mr. Sapina, and he said it was all a big mistake. Somebody had used your name and address without your—"

"It's all straightened out."

"Yes, I know. Mr. Sapina told me. Isn't it awful? I mean the things people do. When he first came to see me, Mr. Sapina I mean, a few weeks ago when he came and told me what he wanted, honestly, Mr. Hurst, I was so shocked—"

"Can you cash this, Mrs. Shissle?"

"What is it?"

"A check."

She took the slip of paper and examined it as though she were standing on a snow-white rug and he had just pulled the check dripping wet from a vat full of black ink.

"Well," she said, hesitating, and then her waxen, pork sausage face brightened. "I can't give you the full amount, but I can give you the difference."

"The difference?"

"Your rent is due tomorrow," Mrs. Shissle said. "If I deduct that four dollars from this, I can give you the difference in cash. Will that be all right?"

Few things at the moment could have been more all wrong. But George didn't see what he could do about it. He had brought out the check to change the subject. If Mrs. Shissle had changed it in a direction he would have preferred to avoid, that was his tough luck. He owed her the money.

"Sure," George said.

He wrote his name across the back of the check, took the $2.54 Mrs. Shissle counted out of the purse she kept tucked in the top of her tightly rolled stocking, and went up to his room. He put Mrs. Shissle's $2.54 and his original $1.22 in a small pile on the dresser. He turned several times while shaving to look at the $3.76. It was not a very reassuring sight. Not to a man who had put nothing into his stomach since the rolls and milk George had eaten in Grand Central at seven in the morning and, as a result, knew that before he could even begin to plan a sensible program for making his available funds last, the fund would have to be reduced by the price of an immediate meal.

It cost twenty cents in a stand-up restaurant on Fourteenth Street. After two hot dogs, a knish, and a glass of milk, George felt so much better that, in a sudden wave of confidence, he invested three cents in a copy of the *Evening World*. He took it and his remaining $3.53 back to his room where, for the balance of the afternoon, he studied the want-ad pages and worked out a plan of campaign.

He began by eliminating as hopeless all the downtown employment agencies, including those whose ads did not say "Christians Only." What George had learned the day he punched the young man in the Allied Employment Agency on Church Street had been confirmed by the gossip he had heard from fellow employees in the L. L. Parker mailroom: a Jew didn't have a chance at a white-collar job south of Canal Street.

George also eliminated all the specific listings, ads placed by employers with a single vacancy to fill, that called for personal appearances. The odds were too great against his being able to get to any of them before a mob of other applicants showed up, and George didn't want to waste too much of his small bankroll on fares.

The likeliest prospects fell into two groups: jobs that could be applied for by mail, and the Sixth Avenue agencies. The latter were within walking distance of University Place, and the former eliminated one of George's major problems: his shyness.

The word sounded a trifle silly in the ears of a man who, on his first visit to an employment agency had punched a clerk and, on leaving his first job, had shoved a wad of paper scraps down the throat of his boss. Silly or not, it was true. Not, however, when he was writing a letter. After he finished making up a list of the Sixth Avenue agencies he planned to visit the next day, George wrote seventeen applications for specific jobs that no reader in his right mind would have said had been composed by a shy man. George didn't want the readers of his letters to think he was a shy man. He wanted them to think he was the man for the job.

By the time he had disposed of the letters in the branch post office on the balcony of Hearn's Department Store on Fourteenth Street, George's bankroll had been reduced by the cost of seventeen two-cent stamps to $3.19, and it was time to go to school. Composing the letters had raised his spirits enough to make George hesitate only briefly before buying his usual thirty-cent dinner in Stewart's. He went to his first class with a delicious lump of hot goulash in his stomach, a feeling of confidence in his heart, and $2.89 in his pocket.

The next morning, after the breakfast of rolls and milk that cut his funds to $2.79, George set out for Sixth Avenue. By two-thirty, when he dropped wearily onto a bench in Bryant Park, George knew he was in trouble. He had visited every agency on his list, had received not a single nibble, and was convinced that unless he ate something at once he would faint. The conviction told his growling stomach that he was certainly entitled to his regular twenty-cent lunch, but a voice George refused stubbornly to identify as fear insisted on hammering through to him a number of hard facts: it was Saturday afternoon; the employment agencies and all business offices would be closed the next day; even if one or more of the glowing letters he had sent out last night should draw a response, he could not possibly receive it through the mails earlier than Monday morning; if he continued to spend his usual sixty-five cents a day on his usual three meals, he would find himself on Monday morning starting the new week with exactly $1.49 to his name. The margin seemed much too narrow.

At that moment, trudging through Bryant Park with her basket, came the old woman from whom on Thursday afternoon, when he was hiding out from Mr. Sapina, George had bought two pretzels on the steps of the Public Library. He bought two more, reducing his bankroll to $2.74, and ate them very slowly, making every bite count. They did for his hunger what a light summer shower might do for a raging forest fire, but they gave George an idea. He followed the old lady, bought ten pretzels from her, stuffed them into his pockets, and went back to his room.

He spent the week end in bed, eating two pretzels for his Saturday dinner, two for each of his three Sunday meals, and the last two for breakfast on Monday morning. George felt a trifle shaky when he came down the stairs a few minutes after eight o'clock, but he also felt pretty confident. The letters that had seemed merely good when he had written them on Friday now seemed irresistible. George didn't see how any employer could fail to ask the writer, at the very least, to come and see him.

Opening his mailbox, he wondered what he would do if he

received a reply to every letter he had sent. The most sensible thing
to do, George supposed, would be to study each reply and try to
arrange them in some sort of order, ranging from most to least
promising. Otherwise he might be tempted to take the first job that
was offered to him. This would be silly. Any one of the sixteen
others, which in his haste he had not given himself the time to
explore, might be better than that first one.

There was a single letter in George's box. It was from Aunt
Tessie in Albany. She wrote in Yiddish:

Dear George:

*Uncle Zisha and I are in the best of health, thank God, and
hope to hear the same from you. This will have to be a short letter
because Uncle Zisha had another stroke last night. The doctor says
he must not move even to go to the toilet, but you know how stubborn he is. I have to keep an eye on him every minute, just like a
little baby. He is now sleeping, thank God, so I have a few minutes
to write you this short letter. You know Mr. Brohmfin? You don't
know him, but I've written to you about him. Mr. Brohmfin is the
man who bought Uncle Zisha's business. He has been paying Uncle
Zisha $40 a week from the business. It's not a fortune, but it's enough
to live on for two people like Uncle Zisha and me. Last week Mr.
Brohmfin went bankrupt and the $40 a week stopped coming. That's
why Uncle Zisha had another stroke. He says no, but I know better.
To have $40 a week, and then to have nothing, it could give even
an elephant a stroke. The lawyer says maybe when the bankruptcy
is all settled Uncle Zisha will get something, but $40 a week, the
way he got from Mr. Brohmfin, this he'll never get. Never again.
I'm looking around to take in a few nice roomers and I'm starting to
do a little sewing for a few people. Why not? We must eat, and
this is a big house, with a lot of empty rooms, and I made my living
for forty years, thank God, by sewing, so I can do it again. Don't
worry about us. I just wanted you to know about Mr. Brohmfin. We
will be all right, thank God. You have not written to us for nearly
two weeks. Is something the matter, God forbid? Write a letter,
please. We are waiting. Your aunt*

Tessie

George stood there for a while, staring at Aunt Tessie's letter,
trying to stop his knees from shaking. He had not realized until this

moment that lying in a hidden corner of his mind, like an emergency bank account on which he could draw, had been the belief that if worst came to worst he could always write to Albany for help. All at once George could hear the warning voice of terror screaming in his head, but he couldn't stop himself. George walked out of the hallway and across the street to Stewart's. He did it the way a drunkard, after a long period of denial, goes toward a bottle. He put away two bowls of oatmeal, scrambled eggs with hashed brown potatoes, two orders of toast and butter, and three glasses of milk. He ate quickly, wolfing the food with his head down, as though he was ashamed of what he was doing. He was.

When it was all over, when he had paid for the food and left the cafeteria and counted his money and found he had exactly $1.94 left, George was too ashamed to go back to his room. He was afraid he would meet Mrs. Shissle in the hall and, somehow, his landlady would know what he had done. He kept right on walking, past the rooming house, moving uptown. After a while the food began to take effect and he felt better. He turned toward Sixth Avenue and started working his way systematically up and down the street, stopping in at every employment agency, including the ones he had visited on Saturday. By three o'clock he was exactly where he had been on Saturday at the same hour: on a bench in Bryant Park, hungry, having raised not the faintest hope of a job, and in his pocket the handful of coins that added up to $1.94.

Nothing changed very much for forty-eight hours except the handful of coins. The pretzel lady kept him going until Wednesday when, an hour before his first class, George lost control again. This second orgy was less expensive. Limiting himself to heavy hot nickel knishes in the stand-up restaurant on Fourteenth Street, George was able to stop his knees from shaking for twenty-five cents. He woke up Thursday morning with $1.44 and an idea.

It was the direct result of a dream in which he had been sitting at a table loaded with fruit, stuffing himself with bananas, oranges, peaches, pears, and plums. Coming out of the dream, George suddenly remembered the fruit Mrs. Dienst used to force on him in the doll store. Why didn't he walk down to Fourth Street right now and call on the Diensts? No matter what crazy Ida thought or said, George had not been responsible for what Dora had done. Mr. and Mrs. Dienst and fat Frannie knew that. If they didn't, he ought to explain it to them. They would believe him. They had always been friendly to him. George could say he had dropped in to see if they had heard anything about Dora. As soon as they started to talk, Mrs. Dienst was bound to offer him some fruit.

The prospect of sinking his teeth into a banana or an orange made George's stomach growl. He got out of bed, shaved carefully, put on one of his last three clean shirts, and walked across to Fourth Street. The final half-block, from the empty lot near Forman's to the Lewis Street corner, the smell of fresh fruit was so strong that George had to hold onto himself to keep from breaking into a run. When he came to the doll store he stopped short. His stomach, which had been growling in happy anticipation, seemed to fall away inside him. The door was locked.

George climbed the two steps and peered in the window. The workbenches, the chairs, the oven in which the doll hair was baked into curls and the glue heated, the racks on which the finished heads were stuck to dry, everything was gone. The store had been stripped.

George went around the corner to Mrs. Gordon's candy stand. "What happened to the Diensts?" he said.

Mrs. Gordon shrugged. "What should happen to a nice Jewish family the daughter steals money from her own father to run away with a shkutz lover?"

"They moved away?"

"If it was your daughter, maybe? If it happened to you? You could stay here where you always lived and hold up your head, maybe?"

"Where did they move?"

Mrs. Gordon shrugged again. "Who knows?"

Nobody on Fourth Street apparently, as George found out after asking a number of other people. His disappointment was so great that he could not resist buying three bananas for a nickel from a pushcart peddler on Avenue C. They kept him going until late afternoon when, after several hours of visiting employment agencies, he went back to his rooming house to check his mailbox and found the first reply to the seventeen letters he had sent out the previous Friday. It was from a manufacturer of labels on Vesey Street who wrote that he was interested in George's letter, but added that he had neglected to say in the ad that the young man he wanted in his office must be able to write shorthand and use a typewriter. Unless Mr. Hurst was a touch typist who could take dictation at the rate of at least one hundred and twenty words a minute, there was no point in calling for a personal interview.

There were two more replies the following morning. One was from a firm of exterminators on Forty-second Street that wanted a clean-cut door to door salesman, the other from a chain of dry cleaners that needed an office assistant with a pleasant voice to call customers and remind them that the firm's truck called at specified times and would they please have their things ready to be picked up.

George decided to answer the exterminators' letter first, because it was closest. He reached the Forty-second Street office at a quarter to nine. The job had already been filled. The office of the dry cleaning chain was on 125th Street. George had ninety-four cents left. The trip uptown and back would cost ten cents. It seemed more sensible to risk half that amount on a phone call. The decision was sound, since it turned out that this job had also been filled, but it reduced George's bankroll to eighty-nine cents.

He spent sixty-five of these the next day on subway fares, answering three ads in the *World* that led to nothing, and a plate of spaghetti in the stand-up restaurant on Fourteenth Street before he went to class. The next morning, which was Saturday, George realized the situation had entered a new phase: his rent was due.

Up to now his problem had been to keep himself from starving, and his supply of clean laundry from running out, until he landed a job. Now, or in a few hours, he would be faced with an additional problem: where to sleep while he continued his hunt for work.

Not because George believed Mrs. Shissle would throw him out of his room if he failed, as he had never before failed, to pay his rent promptly. As a matter of fact, George was pretty sure he could stall his landlady for a few days or even longer. All he had to do was tell her frankly that he was out of work and broke, and ask her to carry him until he found a job.

That was all he had to do, and it was impossible. George Hurst knew he could no more ask Mrs. Shissle to wait for her rent than he could go out into the street and beg for his food. It was stupid. It was the kind of pride he would have criticized in somebody else. It was also, however, a hard fact.

Facing up to it, George saw that the problem was not nearly so difficult as it looked. He had not told Mrs. Shissle about being fired from the L. L. Parker mailroom. If his comings and goings during the past desperate week had struck her as different from the schedule he had previously maintained, Mrs. Shissle had said nothing. Most landladies say nothing, so long as their rents are paid. This afternoon, however, if George came home and did not hand over the four dollars he had given her every Saturday afternoon since he had come to live in her house, Mrs. Shissle would have the right to ask how come. George did not doubt that she would exercise the right. The trick, therefore, was not to come home this afternoon. He would steer clear of Mrs. Shissle until Monday, by which time George felt sure something would break for him.

Drawing on the experience he had gained ten days before, when he had spent the night in Grand Central, George slipped his razor, a comb, and a toothbrush into his pocket. He walked out of the house a few minutes after eight, looking pretty much as he always did when he went to work. George did not realize until late in the afternoon that he had walked into a nightmare.

It started on what had become his favorite bench in Bryant Park. After six fruitless hours of tramping from employment agency to employment agency, George had dropped onto the bench for a rest. He saw the pretzel lady approaching and put his hand into his pocket for a nickel. It wasn't there. The shock was so great that, for several moments, he felt numb. Then he jumped up and poked his hand all the way down into the pocket. It was empty.

George had started the day with twenty-four cents. Ten had gone for two rolls and a glass of milk in Stewart's right after he left the house. The remaining fourteen cents, two nickels and four pennies, had been in the forefront of his mind all day. What had happened to them? A moment later his feverishly poking hand provided the answer: a hole in the pocket.

For a while, as the pretzel lady passed him and moved on through the park, George thought desperately of retracing his steps, going back to every agency he had visited during the day, in the hope of finding the lost coins. He actually started across the park towards Sixth Avenue before he realized the hopelessness of such a hunt. He stopped, torn between despair at the realization that he was literally penniless and the beginnings of fear for the foolish way it was making him act.

Don't panic, he told himself fiercely. If you panic, you're finished. Go back to that bench and sit down and give yourself time to think.

George went back to the bench and sat down. He remembered

that clearly and he remembered starting to shiver with cold. He remembered other things clearly, but he was never very sure about their chronology, because time and events suddenly started to run together in his mind, like pancakes poured too close to one another on a griddle.

He remembered, for example, finding himself late Saturday afternoon in Macy's grocery department, but George couldn't remember how he got there or what made him go to the department store. He moved around slowly, from counter to counter, thoughtfully studying the labels on imported hams and jars of caviar, like a gourmet hunting the ingredients for a rare dinner, but always coming back to the tray of free samples on the cheese counter. By five-thirty, when the crowd began to thin out, George had eaten so much cheese that he left the store with a slight feeling of nausea.

He spent the night on a bench in the Grand Central waiting room. He didn't sleep very well. His stomach kept struggling with its load of Macy's cheese samples. In the morning, George scraped together enough soap scraps in the men's washroom to work up an adequate shaving lather, and then used what was left as toothpaste. It tasted pretty awful, but it made his mouth feel fresh and clean.

The problem of getting something to eat was complicated by the fact that it was Sunday. Macy's was closed. The Automat, however, was open. George managed to pick up several scraps of toast from used plates and, by pouring an inch of sugar into a glass of water he made a slightly sickening but surprisingly nourishing drink. He spent the day touring the phone booths in Grand Central and in the neighboring drug stores, hoping to find something in the returned coin boxes. He found nothing. At five-thirty he stole two apples from the vendor on the corner of Forty-third and Lexington. It was surprisingly easy. Most apple vendors watched their small stocks as though they were rubies. So did this man. He fancied himself as something of a wit, however, and George noticed that every ten or fifteen minutes this vendor would turn away from his apple stand to lean against the lamppost and write with a piece of black crayon on a scrap of cardboard a joke about President Hoover or the Wickersham Commission, which he would then thumbtack to the side of his apple box in the hope of attracting customers. George, after watching him for some time, snatched the two apples while the vendor was in the middle of a hot one about Vice-President Dawes and his famous underslung bulldog pipe. From then on George knew that, when every other source failed him, he could always put his hands on an apple. It seemed wise, however, not to hang around the area where he had put his hands on the first ones, so he spent Sunday night in Penn Station. The benches were as comfortable as those in Grand Central, but the washroom smelled worse, and in the morning he couldn't find enough soap scraps to make a decent lather. George nicked himself twice while shaving.

At noon, wandering through the Garment Center, it suddenly occurred to him that he could not remember what, where, or if he'd had breakfast. George tried for several moments to force himself to remember, feeling vaguely that the effort was extremely important. He was not successful, however, and the effort was painful, so he let it go. With it George could feel a great many other things going, leaving him with a sense of lightness and freedom that was not unpleasant. From then on, nothing that happened seemed completely bad. Not even when his socks began to rot.

George had seen many men shave in the Grand Central and Penn Station washrooms, and he had seen many more asleep in the waiting rooms, but George had never seen anybody washing socks in either place. He was afraid that, if he washed his, he would attract so much attention that he would from then on lose the protective coloration of anonymity. On Wednesday, or perhaps it was Thursday, he stripped off the filthy socks, threw them away, and from then on wore his shoes on bare feet.

That night a man with a lisp tried to pick him up in Penn Station. George was so hungry, and the man was so pleasant, that it never occurred to George to wonder why a total stranger would invite him to dinner. They were seated side by side in a booth in an Italian restaurant on Seventh Avenue, with plates of hot minestrone steaming in front of them, when George suddenly felt the man's hand on his thigh and he got the idea. With regret, wishing he had got the idea a few minutes later, after the delicious soup was in his stomach, George tipped his plate sharply to the left. The minestrone poured over the edge of the table into the stranger's lap. He let out a scream. His hand left George's thigh and George left the restaurant.

He was so upset by this incident, mainly because he couldn't get the rich smell of the uneaten minestrone out of his nostrils, that George almost turned his back on the incident that saved him. The next morning, while he was sitting in the Grand Central waiting room, breakfasting on the apple he had just stolen from the joke-smith around the corner, a middle-aged man in a gray hat and a fly-front topcoat sat down beside George.

"Pardon me," the man said. "Would you like to earn fifty dollars?"

George looked him over. "Doing what?"

The man explained.

"Go on," George said. "Beat it."

"Sixty dollars."

"Now, look, buddy."

"I'm not your buddy," the man said. "I'm a doctor. I'm making you a business proposition."

"I said beat it."

"Seventy-five dollars?"

The improbable figure managed to cut through the haze in which George had been living for five days. Seventy-five dollars was more than six weeks' salary in the L. L. Parker mailroom.

"What do I have to do?" George said.

"Submit to a physical examination first."

"Where?"

"My office is around the corner, on Park Avenue."

George thought fast and decided to be smarter than he had been the night before. "I'll go on one condition."

"What's that?" the man said.

"I'd like some breakfast first."

The man stood up. "Let's go."

He led George to the Oyster Bar downstairs and sipped a cup of black coffee while George worked his way through two glasses of orange juice, ham and eggs, buckwheat cakes with butter, syrup, and sausages, and a quart of milk.

"For someone with your healthy appetite," the man said dryly, "I can almost dispense with the physical examination."

"That's all right with me," George said.

"I'm afraid it wouldn't be all right with my patient," the man said. "Shall we go?"

They went out to Park Avenue, walked down to Fortieth Street, turned left, and stopped in front of a remodeled brownstone. George was surprised to see that the man in the fly-front topcoat was opening the door of what actually did appear to be a doctor's office. The office of several doctors, in fact. On the wall near the door was a row of eight bronze shingles on which all the names were followed by the letters M.D. George wondered which name belonged to the man who had just bought his breakfast. The man seemed to guess what was going through George's mind.

"I won't ask your name," he said as he took off his coat. "Please don't ask mine."

"Why not?"

"Are you married?"

"No," George said.

"If you were, you might understand more readily. These things are extremely delicate for all concerned. For the husband who not unnaturally suffers from a feeling of inadequacy, and for the wife who feels an understandable embarrassment. It's best that all the parties involved remain total strangers to each other. Roll up your sleeve, please."

George rolled up his sleeve. A half hour later the doctor put down his instruments and tapped George on the shoulder.

"You'll do, young man." He opened the drawer of his desk, pulled out a small package, and said, "Hurry back here as quickly as you can."

"Hurry back?" George said. "Where am I supposed to do this?"

"In Grand Central," the doctor said, and then he added dryly, "The washroom, that is."

"Why can't I use your washroom?"

"In case I am ever asked, I want to be able to say with complete honesty that only the medical aspects of the operation were performed in my office. All clear?"

"Except for one thing," George said.

"What's that?"

"Could I have a small advance on that seventy-five dollars?"

"How small?"

"Ten cents."

"Certainly." The doctor pulled a dime from his pocket and handed it over. "May I ask why you want that?"

"I've never done this before," George said, trying for and succeeding in capturing something of the doctor's dry tone. "I think I'd better use a pay washroom."

The doctor nodded gravely. "Yes," he said. "I think you'd better."

Twenty minutes later, when he walked out of the doctor's office a second time, George carried with him an envelope containing three twenties, a ten, and a five, all brand-new. Twenty minutes after that, when he opened his mailbox on University Place, George found six replies to the letters he had sent out two weeks before. After explaining to Mrs. Shissle that he had been away visiting his sick uncle in Albany, and paying the landlady his back rent, George took the six letters up to his room and tried to study them carefully. He was too tired, however, to do anything sensible about them that day. He took a hot bath and, for the first time in a week, he lay down on a bed. He slept almost completely around the clock.

In the morning, after studying the six letters again, he decided to answer the one from Malvin Gewirtz & Company. It was written on engraved stationery.

20

Neither Malvin Gewirtz, who founded the firm that bore his name, nor Roland Brodsky, the partner who later assumed its active management, ever thought of their enterprise as an educational institution. Yet it seemed to George Hurst that, during his first six months as a junior accountant on the Gewirtz staff, he picked up more useful knowledge than he had managed to acquire during his eight years in P.S. 188, four years at Franklin Pierce High, and three years at Washington Square College.

Like any good curriculum, the one offered by Malvin Gewirtz & Company was sufficiently varied to provide an intelligent student with more than a working knowledge of the trade by which he had decided to earn his living. It gave him a glimpse of the world beyond his immediate horizon.

George's first glimpse supplied him with a realistic grasp of the elementary principles of economics that proved indelible. After Mr. Brodsky told George he was hired, a few minutes before sending him down to Astor Place with Mr. Rapf to audit the books of Perrini Brothers, Mr. Brodsky asked George how much salary he wanted.

"Twenty dollars," George said.

He said it with his heart not quite in his mouth but sufficiently close to it to make the words emerge with a noticeable gulp. Twenty dollars a week was eight dollars, or 66-2/3 per cent, more than he had been paid at L. L. Parker. On twelve dollars a week George had just managed to get by. On twenty he could live like a king. George didn't really know how kings lived, of course. With twenty dollars coming in every week, however, he was sure he would have so much of everything he wanted out of life that any king with brains would envy him.

Mr. Brodsky, a good-looking man who wore rimless octagon-shaped glasses and smoked Murad cigarettes, nodded shortly. "We'll see," he said.

George supposed Mr. Brodsky meant he wanted to see how his new employee shaped up before he settled the question of his salary. This seemed fair enough. George threw himself into his work with a zeal that caused Mr. Rapf, during George's third day on the job, to make an observation.

"The way to measure a good accountant is by how accurate he is, not by how hard he slams the ledgers down on the desk. Why don't you relax, son?"

George tried to relax, but he couldn't. Not until he found out how much he was going to be paid. On Saturday, when Mr. Brodsky handed him his first pay envelope, George took it out to the wash-room, went into one of the booths, locked the door, opened the envelope, and held his breath as he counted the contents. A ten, a five, and four singles. George blew out his breath. There seemed to be some mistake. He counted the money again. It still came to nineteen dollars. If there was a mistake, it clearly was not his. George wondered if it might be Mr. Brodsky's. Had the boss, intending to put twenty dollars into the envelope, by accident put in only nineteen? This didn't seem very likely. If Mr. Brodsky had intended to put twenty dollars into the envelope, surely he would have done it in the simplest way, namely, by putting in two tens. On the other hand, was it very likely that Mr. Brodsky could consider his new employee worth nineteen dollars a week but not twenty? How did he figure a difference so narrow?

George was too shy to put these questions directly to his new boss. Since he had on deposit in a brand-new savings bank account fifty of the seventy-five dollars he had been paid by the nameless doctor on Fortieth Street, George decided he could afford to wait another week to find out what Mr. Brodsky's intentions were. The following Saturday, when he opened his second pay envelope and counted the contents, it became clear that Mr. Brodsky's intentions were to pay George nineteen dollars a week.

George was pleased by the amount. It enabled him to eat better than he had eaten during the L. L. Parker days, and it gave him a feeling of confidence about his ability to pay the law school fees that would start as soon as he completed piling up his pre-law credits at Washington Square College: every Saturday, after Mrs. Shissle received her four dollars, four more went into George's savings bank account.

Nevertheless, the nineteen-dollar salary puzzled George. It seemed to him there was something significant in the difference between the twenty dollars he had asked for and the nineteen Mr. Brodsky had decided to pay him. Unable to work out the significance for himself, George decided one day, when he and Mr. Rapf were having lunch at a hot-dog stand on Sixth Avenue, to ask the senior. Mr. Rapf was clearly pleased by the question. He smiled at George, so that his buck teeth came into full view, and his tall, slightly stooped figure bowed up and down several times, as though he were a diver testing the high board before taking off on a half-gainer.

"You have placed your finger on an important economic fact," he said. "Namely and to wit: if you want to get rich, don't work for a service organization. A manufacturer of anything, whether it's locomotives or paper clips, earns profits. A service organization, whether it's a bunch of lawyers, doctors, or accountants, earns fees. You go to work for a manufacturer of locomotives, and you ask for twenty a week, you'll either get it or he'll say I'm looking for ten dollar a week employees. He won't chisel you down to nineteen. A dollar isn't that important to him. Labor is only one item in the cost of manufacturing his product. He can always make up that dollar by manipulating a number of other variables that go into the computation of his profit: he can put in a cheaper kind of raw material, he can wrap it in a less expensive package, he can even boost his sales price. But with an accountant or a lawyer or a doctor, labor is the main thing that goes into the service he sells. Labor or brains, to be more accurate. Your brains, my brains, the brains of the entire staff.

"An accountant or a doctor or a lawyer has only his overhead to manipulate: his office rent, telephone bill, stuff like that, and then that biggest item, his employees' salaries. Auditing fees, like fees for yanking tonsils or keeping pickpockets out of jail, depend on what the patient or client can afford to pay. You can never be sure what a client or a patient who hasn't come into your office yet is going to be able to pay. But you can be damn sure what you have to pay your employees, because they get paid every week, clients or no clients. The way to keep your head above water, therefore, is to pay them as little as possible. You asked for twenty. Brodsky gives you nineteen. You think it's funny. After all, what's a buck? Well, son, your buck adds up to fifty-two bucks a year. Brodsky has forty-two men on the staff. Forty-two times fifty-two, figure it out, you're learning to become an accountant, is $2,184 that Brodsky saves himself each year. Provided he nicks each staff member for only one buck, that is. You're a junior. Semi-seniors, who get more, he nicks for more than a buck. Seniors like me, who get paid the most, we get nicked the most. That is why Malvin Gewirtz, who is only sixty-one years old, is retired today in the Florida sunshine; Roland Brodsky, who is exactly my age, lives on Central Park West and smokes Murads; and you and I, who are much finer characters, naturally, than either of our bosses and even more naturally have much more brains, here we are, eating hot dogs for lunch on Sixth Avenue. Have I answered your question, son?"

"Yes, sir," George said. "Thank you."

"The pleasure is mine," Mr. Rapf said. "Helping the young to improve themselves has always been a hobby with me. Any little nuggets of advice or information I can toss your way, just speak up, son."

The next opportunity presented itself two weeks later. These nuggets dealt, not with economics, but with the social amenities, and in order to get them it was not necessary for George to do the speaking up.

"How would you like a short trip out of town?" Mr. Rapf asked one morning.

"How short?" George said.

"Two days. Maybe three."

"I go to school at night. I wouldn't like to cut my classes."

"You have classes Saturday and Sunday?"

"No. Just Monday to Friday."

"When's your last class on Friday?"

"Nine o'clock," George said. "I'm finished by a quarter to ten."

"We could take the sleeper at eleven Friday night and be back late Monday afternoon in plenty of time for you to get to your classes. Does it interest you?"

"Yes, sir."

"Stop with the sir. You're not in the army. Here's the deal. We've got this client down in Baltimore. Shlansky, Gaylord & Karp. Shirt manufacturers. We don't do a regular audit. Just check their royalty statements to this Starchless Collar Corporation up in Canada, the dough they have to pay out every month for using S.C.C.'s patents. Takes about a day and a half, two days. They like it done over the week end so it doesn't interfere with the work of their regular bookkeeping staff. Brodsky lets me take anybody I want. If you'd like to come along, I'll ask for you."

"Thanks," George said. "I'd like that very much."

He liked every moment of it until Saturday night when, having spent all day in the Shlansky, Gaylord & Karp offices and then eaten a huge sea food dinner in Miller's on the expense account, George and Mr. Rapf retired to their double room in the Lord Baltimore Hotel.

Mr. Rapf, who had seemed preoccupied during dinner, stopped undoing the knot in his tie and turned to George. "Son," he said. "Are you a very sensitive type?"

"I don't know," George said. "I don't think so. Why?"

"Well, I'd like to pass along a couple of those nuggets of advice I mentioned a few weeks ago, but if they're going to hurt your feelings, the hell with it."

"What kind of advice?"

"Advice that will help bring you up out of the bush leagues into the majors."

"I guess I'd better hear it, then."

"Okay, son."

Mr. Rapf walked across to the dresser and picked up the neatly folded paper bag George had borrowed from Mrs. Shissle and in which he had carried down to Baltimore his three clean shirts, three pairs of clean socks, razor, and toothbrush.

"Gypsies carry their belongings in paper bags," Mr. Rapf said. "Accountants use suitcases. Not that a paper bag doesn't serve the purpose. It's just that you get on a train, like last night, you get Pullman porters looking at you. Hotels, you walk in the way we walked into this one this morning, you get desk clerks and bellhops looking at you. Pullman porters and hotel desk clerks and bellhops are not clients. The way they look at you doesn't matter, maybe. Except that if anybody is going to look at you, it's better they should do it with respect rather than with a sneer. Next week, you get your salary, you go over to Macy's or Gimbels or some luggage shop maybe on Sixth Avenue, and you invest a few bucks in a nice little suitcase. Something like mine over there. It won't break you, and it'll help to make you. Are you still listening?"

"Yes, sir."

"What's with the sir?"

"I mean yes, Mr. Rapf."

"Then stop looking like that."

"I'm sorry."

"Forget it. I know it's embarrassing to hear these things, but it's better you should be embarrassed by me now, a guy I haven't any ax to grind, than by some son of a bitch later, he's out to get your scalp, when he embarrasses you he'll do it when and where it'll hurt the most. You game for another nugget?"

"Yes, sir. I mean Mr. Rapf."

"When you go out to buy yourself that suitcase, pick up a couple of pairs of pajamas at the same time. Farmers sleep in their under-wear, George. Not accountants."

"Anything else?"

"That's all for tonight, son."

It was not, however, all for the trip. The next day, which was Sunday, George was standing in the deserted Shlansky, Gaylord & Karp factory, staring around the huge room, when Mr. Rapf came out of the office to look for him.

"If we're going to get back to New York tomorrow, we better dig in and knock off some of this work," the senior said. "You walked out of the office ten minutes ago. What are you doing?"

"Looking for the can."

Mr. Rapf's buck teeth came into full view. "Here comes another one of those nuggets," he said through the smile that George was be-ginning to like. "Toilets you'll never find out in the middle of the factory floor. Those things always get built up against a wall."

George laughed, and Mr. Rapf laughed with him as he put his arm across George's shoulder, and whatever sting still remained from the night before was suddenly gone. George was not surprised. One of the most important things he had learned as a Malvin Gewirtz employee had not come to him in the form of one of Mr. Rapf's nuggets. It had come to him one night as he was walking home from his last class and he suddenly realized that, for the first time since Dora had run away with Danny, the dull ache in his chest was gone. George was so surprised that he stopped right there on the street to examine the extraordinary sensation.

The examination revealed what he had suspected but for weeks had refused to explore: the extent to which he had been hurt by what Danny and Dora had done. George had known for a long time that he loved her. Not until she was gone did he realize how much. Some instinct had warned him that, like a soldier under fire who has been hit, the only way to handle the wound was to pretend it didn't exist, to keep on going. Even during the nightmarish week when, without a penny in his pocket, he had managed somehow to remain alive on the pavements of New York, George had forced himself not to think about Dora. In this way the pain that might have been unbearable had been reduced to a dull ache that could be disregarded, like a bruise that hurts only when it is touched. Now, standing on University Place late at night, aware all at once that even the dull ache was gone, George was also aware of the reason for its disappearance: the atmosphere of Malvin Gewirtz & Company.

It was not unlike the atmosphere Mr. Shumacher had tried to create in the L. L. Parker mailroom, except in reverse. The forty-two staff members of Malvin Gewirtz & Company were all Jews.

Working with them was for George a good deal like being back on East Fourth Street with Aunt Tessie. He didn't have to lie about what he was. He didn't have to pretend to be something else. He didn't have to explain anything. Everybody knew. He could go through his days as he had gone through them on East Fourth Street: without hunching over the handlebars and sneaking nervous looks back across his shoulder.

He saw now that Aunt Tessie had been sound in warning him, when he first arrived on Fourth Street as a boy of three, against having anything to do with the shkutzim across the street, just as she had been sound to criticize and distrust Danny Schorr, first for being friendly and then for living with the Gerritys. Time, George saw now, had proved her right on both counts: a man who could consort with the enemy could do anything, as Danny had demonstrated by what he ended up doing to his best friend; and a man who wanted peace of mind had to stay with his own kind.

Having achieved it with surprising speed in the completely Jewish atmosphere of Malvin Gewirtz & Company, George was free to absorb Mr. Rapf's lessons in what the senior called The Range, Uses, and Possibilities of the Expense Account. These, in hands as skillful as Mr. Rapf's, would have been impressive under any auspices. Under those peculiar to Malvin Gewirtz & Company, the results were astonishing.

The firm's regular clients ranged all the way from a garter belt manufacturer like Perrini Brothers on Astor Place to a shirt manufacturer like Shlansky, Gaylord & Karp in Baltimore. When members of the Malvin Gewirtz staff visited these clients they were reimbursed for their expenses. These, in the case of a client like Perrini Brothers, amounted to ten cents in subway fares, a sum with which even an expense-account expert as accomplished as Mr. Rapf could do very little. In the case of a client like Shlansky, Gaylord & Karp, where the expenses for which the visiting auditors were reimbursed included not only the fare to and from Baltimore but also hotel bills and the cost of meals, even a crude expense-account manipulator could manage to make a small profit, and Mr. Rapf was far from crude. It was, however, in the more colorful field of bankruptcy work, to which the Malvin Gewirtz & Company staff devoted at least half its time, that Mr. Rapf demonstrated what, when the conditions are right, a man of talent can accomplish.

Whenever Malvin Gewirtz & Company was retained by the Receiver in Bankruptcy to audit the books and records of an insolvent company, the payment for services rendered was always on a "fee plus" basis. The word "plus," George learned, was subject to as many interpretations as a politician's promise.

To the Receiver in Bankruptcy it meant normal expenses incurred during the course of an audit: taxi and subway fares, telephone calls, meals consumed by the auditing staff when they worked at night. To Mr. Brodsky it meant an opportunity to demonstrate that he was something more than a penny pincher who, when a man asked for twenty dollars a week, paid him nineteen: since the expenses did not come out of his pocket, Mr. Brodsky didn't ask too many questions about what the expense money had been spent on. To Mr. Rapf, who as one of the firm's six seniors was responsible for making up approximately one sixth of its expense accounts, the word "plus" was a challenge. George never saw him meet it more spectacularly than on the Sunday night when the Gaylor Karken figures were completed.

It was strongly suspected by the Irving Trust Company, the Receiver in Bankruptcy by whom Malvin Gewirtz & Company was retained to audit Mr. Karken's records, that the leather merchant had been milking his business for some time with the deliberate intention of defrauding his creditors. A week after Mr. Rapf, George Hurst, and two other members of the Gewirtz staff started on the audit, a private detective hired by one of Karken's larger creditors reported that the leather merchant had booked passage on a ship sailing for England three days later. The Receiver immediately asked Mr. Brodsky if it would be possible to complete the audit within twenty-four hours so that, in the event that the figures indicated fraud had indeed been practiced, a warrant for Gaylor Karken's arrest could be sworn out before he sailed. Completing the audit so rapidly, Mr. Brodsky informed the Receiver, would mean working his staff night and day through the week end, which in turn would mean additional expense. Never mind the expense, said the Receiver. Mr. Brodsky, who never did, ordered Mr. Rapf to have the figures on his desk by nine o'clock Monday morning.

On Sunday night, at 11:20 P.M., the buck-toothed senior leaned back in his chair in the Gaylor Karken office on Twenty-third Street, dropped his pencil on the sheet of analysis paper on which for almost an hour he had been working in complete silence, and emitted a long, delicious, gently growling groan.

"Well, that does it."

"By it," said Herman Lustgarten, "do you mean Mr. Gaylor Karken's skin?"

Lustgarten was a semi-senior, a small, round man in his midthirties who was generally regarded as one of the best accountants on the Gewirtz staff even though a tendency to get badly rattled under pressure had thus far prevented him from passing the C.P.A. examinations, which he had been taking and flunking regularly for the past nine years.

"I do," said Mr. Rapf. "We've got this leather merchant's hide nailed to the wall, if Murph will allow that joke to stay in the ball park?"

"Why not? It's late at night," said Clint Lasky.

He was called Murph because he had a small button nose with a sharp upward tilt that, in the eyes of the members of the Gewirtz staff, made him look like an Irishman. Before coming to Malvin Gewirtz & Company as a semi-senior accountant, Murph Lasky had spent several of his twenty-eight summers working in carnivals around Providence, Rhode Island, where he had been born. As a result, he was considered an authority on humor, music, women, and other matters pertaining to show business.

"How much did he take the creditors for?" asked Herman Lustgarten.

"One hundred sixty-two thousand four hundred thirty-eight dollars," said Mr. Rapf and then, with a quick glance at the sheet of analysis paper, he added, "And twelve cents."

"You're getting pretty good on the double take," said Murph Lasky.

"Is that what you call it?" said Mr. Rapf.

"Not in professional circles," said Murph. "But here, a bunch of accountants all alone in a leather place late Sunday night, we've been working our tails off for the glory of Roland Brodsky and his partner toasting himself in the Florida sunshine Malvin Gewirtz, we're bushed, here what you just did, Mr. Rapf, we won't be fussy, we'll be real charitable and we'll call it a double take."

"Thank you," said Mr. Rapf. He stretched both arms up straight toward the ceiling, waving them from side to side as though he were signaling to somebody in the distance, and he yawned luxuriously. "This has been one son of a bitch of a job," he said. "I think we have earned ourselves a little treat."

"On the expense account?" said Murph.

"What else?" said Mr. Rapf.

"What kind of a treat?" said Herman Lustgarten.

"What kind would you suggest?" said Mr. Rapf.

"It's too late to eat another dinner," said Herman Lustgarten.

"Too late and too dull," said Mr. Rapf. "We had ourselves a good dinner at eight o'clock on the expense account. It is now eleven-twenty."

"How deep can we go?" said Herman Lustgarten.

"An annuity for life I can't fix up for you," said Mr. Rapf. "But anything reasonable, on an expense account like this one, I think I can bury it."

"There's a pair of fleece-lined gloves I saw the other day in Macy's," Herman Lustgarten said. "It's getting pretty cold and my wife's been telling me I ought to fix myself up with a pair of gloves for the winter. Three ninety-five, these gloves. Any chance?"

"Sure, if that's what you want," Mr. Rapf said with a shrug.

"It doesn't seem very exciting to me, though. How about you, George?"

"If it's all the same to you, Mr. Rapf," George said, "I'd like mine in cash."

"The trouble with you, George, you've got a single-track mind," Mr. Rapf said. "All you can think about is that bank account where you're saving for law school. What I'm talking about is not fleece-lined gloves or fixing it so you can become another Clarence Darrow twenty minutes earlier. I'm talking about something else. This bastard Gaylor Karken has just nicked his creditors for one hundred sixty-two thousand four hundred thirty-eight dollars and twelve cents. We have caught him with his pants down and the flap of his B.V.D.'s unbuttoned. Tomorrow morning, when I put these figures on Roland Brodsky's desk, he will start swinging from the chandeliers and he'll call up the Irving Trust and say look what wonderful accountants we are. We sure are, and because we are, Roland Brodsky is going to get his fees jacked up in the future, but what are we going to get? Us four here in this room? A pair of fleece-lined gloves? A couple of inches closer to a law degree? This is a way to celebrate? Where's your imagination, for God's sake? We've earned the right to a treat. A treat is what I'm talking about. Don't any of you guys know what a treat is?"

There was a brief silence, during which George tried to think of something he wanted that would satisfy Mr. Rapf's ideas about a treat. It was not easy because George knew that part of the pleasure for Mr. Rapf depended on choosing something that everybody else would think could not possibly be buried in an expense account.

"How about twenty bucks a head?" Murph Lasky said. "Could you bury that much?"

"If it was interesting enough to challenge the efforts of a real expense account artist," Mr. Rapf said, "I could bury anything. What's on your mind, Murph?"

"There's this joint uptown," Murph said. "I've never been there, but I've been hearing about it lately from some of my show-business friends. Twenty bucks a throw, and they tell me it's worth every penny of it. Real choice stuff."

"Now you're beginning to interest me," Mr. Rapf said. "I've got the Irving Trust to pay for a lot of things in my day, things that if they knew what they were they'd have a hemorrhage down there in those mahogany offices, but this may set a new standard, Murph. A mark to shoot at for years. Where is this joint?"

"I don't know but I know how to find out," Murph Lasky said. "All I need is a phone."

"You got one right there on your desk," Mr. Rapf said. "Use it."

"You serious?" Murph said. "You're not kidding?"

"Does Admiral Byrd kid about ice?" Mr. Rapf said. "Or Johnny Weissmuller about water?"

"Because this isn't one of these two-dollar joints, the dames sitting around in their underwear waiting for customers to come in off the street," Murph Lasky said. "This is a call house. Every piece of gash is tailor-made. This Mrs. Hooper that runs it, every customer is a special order. She's got to arrange for the dames to show up. Once I pick up this phone and make the call, there's no kidding around."

"You pick up the phone and make the call," Mr. Rapf said.

Murph made several before he located the proper friend, and then he had to wait for the friend to call back and say he had talked to Mrs. Hooper before Murph could call himself. All this took time. George spent it trying hard to look like a man of the world to whom twenty-dollar call houses were a commonplace and, at the same time, trying harder not to give any outward sign that he was scared stiff.

"One moment," Murph Lasky said into the phone. He covered the mouthpiece with his hand and said to his three colleagues, "Dark meat or white?"

"Make mine white," Herman Lustgarten said. "All I need is to carry home to Brooklyn a souvenir from the Gaylor Karken audit, a dose."

"Grow up, will you?" Murph Lasky said. "These dames are all clean."

"Make it two and two and we can later on swap," Mr. Rapf said. "I've never had any dark meat."

"You pay for every ride in a joint like this," Murph Lasky said. "You swap, that'll be another twenty bucks."

"The Irving Trust has plenty of money," Mr. Rapf said.

"Two and two," Murph Lasky said into the phone. "We'll be there in a half hour, Mrs. Hooper."

George waited until they were in the street and the taxi for which Mr. Rapf had whistled was pulling in toward the curb before he found the courage to speak. "You guys mind if I duck out on this?" he said.

They stared at him as though he had announced his imminent departure for Albany to assassinate Governor Roosevelt.

"Duck out on what?" Murph Lasky said.

"The party," George said. "I'm pretty tired. I'd rather go to bed."

"Where do you think *we're* going?" Herman Lustgarten said. He was not accustomed to making jokes. This one had apparently taken him by surprise. "Hey," Herman said. "That's pretty good, no?"

"Not as good as George's," Murph Lasky said.

"I'm not joking," George said. "You guys go ahead without me."

"George," Murph Lasky said. "This place we're going, it's the Cadillac of cat houses."

"I know," George said. "I'm just not in the mood."

"How much mood does a guy have to have for twenty-dollar jab?" Herman Lustgarten said. "All paid for by the Irving Trust Company?"

"It doesn't matter who's paying," George said. "If you're not in the mood, you're not in the mood."

"George," Murph Lasky said. "Are you a virgin?"

"For Christ's sake!" George said. "Just because a guy doesn't feel like—!"

"George," Mr. Rapf said.

"What?"

"Here comes one of those nuggets."

"One of those what?" Murph Lasky said.

"George knows what I mean," Mr. Rapf said. "Don't you, George?"

"Yes, sir."

"Are you listening, George?"

"Yes, sir."

"We just knocked off a real good job," Mr. Rapf said. "The four of us together. We're going out to celebrate it, the four of us together. If one guy says count me out, it louses up the celebration for the other three. You want to louse things up for me and Murph and Herman?"

"Of course not. I'm just saying—"

"Listen to what I'm saying," Mr. Rapf said. "You know what a guy does when he's in Rome?"

"In Rome?"

"He does like the Romans do," Mr. Rapf said, and he pulled open the taxi door. "Let's go, George."

George went. When the taxi cut across Columbus Circle and turned into Central Park West, Mr. Rapf's teeth came into full view. "Well, well, well," he said with a grin. "We're getting into my part of town." A few minutes later, when the taxi crossed Seventy-second Street, the grin disappeared. "Jesus," Mr. Rapf said nervously, "we're getting into my neighborhood."

"Well," Murph Lasky said. "You won't have far to go when you're finished."

"This isn't anything to make jokes about!" Mr. Rapf snapped. "I got a wife and three kids living in a building six blocks from here."

"What am I supposed to do about that?" Murph Lasky said.

"I'll tell you what you can do," Mr. Rapf said, and he did.

"No," Murph Lasky said. "I'm counting on doing that to a twenty-dollar broad in a few minutes."

"Well, you'll have to do it without me," Mr. Rapf said. He told the driver to pull up to the curb, counted out some money, handed it to Murph Lasky, and said, "Have a good time, boys."

"What about you?" Murph Lasky said.

"I'm going home," Mr. Rapf said, and he started to get out of the cab.

Murph Lasky pulled him back. "What about those nuggets you were handing out to George down on Twenty-third Street?" Murph said. He stuck out his lips in an imitation of Mr. Rapf. "We just knocked off a real good job," he said. "The four of us together. We're going out to celebrate it, the four of us together. If one guy says count me out, it louses up the celebration for the other three. You want to louse things up for me and Herman and George?"

"It doesn't matter to me," George said quickly. "I didn't really want to come in the first place. I'm willing to—"

"I'm not," Murph Lasky said. "I'm doing like our senior told you to do. I'm pretending I'm in Rome."

There was a long silence. George hoped Mr. Rapf would not give in.

The taxi driver turned and slid back the glass. "What do you say, gentlemen?"

Murph nodded to Mr. Rapf. "We're waiting for this gentleman to say it."

The senior looked quickly at George, then dropped his glance.

"Sorry, boys," Mr. Rapf said quietly. "I'm getting out." He shook off Murph Lasky's hand, opened the door, and stepped out of the cab.

"Okay," Murph said to the driver. "You know the address."

"Wait," George said. "Why don't you and Herman go ahead without me?"

"Because I'm sick and tired of the arguments," Murph said. "We started this thing together. We're finishing it together. Unless you're scared or something."

"I'm not scared," George said.

"Then shut up and think about what's waiting for you when we get there."

Thinking about it, George found, consisted mainly of remembering some dirty pictures Danny Schorr had once showed him. Pretty soon he found sitting in the cab extremely uncomfortable, and when Murph paid off the driver and they went into the apartment house, George had trouble with his breathing. The elevator operator didn't seem to think there was anything odd about three strange men coming in from the street after midnight. Neither did the woman who answered the door of 18-D. She looked so much like Mrs. Gerstenberger, Uncle Zisha's old housekeeper up in Albany, that for a startled moment George wanted to turn and run. Then Mrs. Hooper opened her mouth and the resemblance disintegrated.

"Good evening, gentlemen," she said in a voice that sounded like thick, rusted spikes being pulled out of a waterlogged board. "Won't you come in?" They came into a small foyer where, after closing the door, locking it, and sliding a bolt as big as a Hershey bar into place over the knob, Mrs. Hooper said, "Which one of you gentlemen is the gentleman I talked on the phone to?"

"That's me," Murph said.

Mrs. Hooper, whose face had all of the deceased Mrs. Gerstenberger's beefiness and none of its sweetness, looked at Murph Lasky as though she were a wrestler about to lunge at an opponent. "You told me there would be four of you gentlemen!"

"That's right," Murph said. "But one guy conked out on us."

"That's too bad," Mrs. Hooper said. "I ordered four ladies for you gentlemen the way you told me on the phone to. Three of them are already here."

"Why don't you call up the fourth and tell her to skip it?" Murph said.

"Suppose you're Hattie Carnegie and I call up and order four dresses and then when I come in I say to you I want only three, why don't you skip the fourth? What are you supposed to do with that fourth dress if you're Hattie Carnegie and it's all cut and practically sewed? Is that your idea of how a gentleman does business? I called this fourth girl on the phone at your order and told her I had an assignment for her. She's on her way now. It's too late to stop her. How am I going to feel when she opens that door expecting to work and be paid and I say to her I'm sorry, the gentleman canceled the order?"

"Don't get excited," Murph said. "We ordered four, we'll take four. Let's get the show on the road." He turned to Herman and George. "You guys heard what Mrs. Hooper said. No matter where you think you are, you just remember you're in the Temple Emanu-El." He turned back to Mrs. Hooper. "Where are the ladies?"

"That will be eighty dollars, please," Mrs. Hooper said. Murph gave her four of the twenties Mr. Rapf had given him. Mrs. Hooper looked at the bills as though she suspected Murph had made them himself, then folded the money and tucked it down the front of her bright green dress. "This way, gentlemen."

She led them through a small living room, the walls of which were hung with cheaply framed scenes of the gardens at Versailles, into a long, narrow corridor with doors on both sides.

"The ladies are in there and there and there," Mrs. Hooper said, pointing to two doors on the right and one on the left. "When the fourth girl comes I'll have her wait in the living room. Okay?"

"Okay," Murph said. Mrs. Hooper went back into the living room and closed the door. "If it doesn't make any difference to you guys how we start," Murph said to George and Herman, "I don't give a damn, either."

"Did Rapf give you enough to pay in case we want to swap?" Herman said.

"He sure did," Murph said. "And so far as I'm concerned there's no in case about it."

"So what difference does it make where we start?" Herman said. "I'll take this one." He moved to the far door on the right.

"How about you?" Murph said.

"I don't care," George said. He considered it a triumph that he managed to get the words out. His knees felt as though they were hollow and somebody had filled them with hot soup. "It doesn't make any difference."

"Then you take this one," Murph said and, before George could duck, he opened the door on the left, pushed George through, and said, "Go to it, kid. Compliments of the Irving Trust!"

Murph pulled the door shut. George was in a small bedroom, about half the size of his own room on University Place. The pictures on the wall seemed to have come from the same set that had provided the decorations for the living room, but George couldn't see them very clearly because the only light came from a small lamp on a table beside a large double bed. The bulb in the lamp couldn't have been larger than twenty-five watts and the silk shade, which was dark green, had a neatly folded hand towel pinned around the edges. As a result, several moments went by before George's eyes were able to take in everything. When they did, he gulped so hard and so unexpectedly that he did not have time to muffle the small, foolish sound.

It seemed to offend the girl sitting on the far edge of the bed. She sat with her hands clasped around her crossed knees, her back rigid, her chin tilted upward and to the left, as though she were posing for an advertisement for ivory-tipped cigarettes that required her to reach toward the light her escort in impeccable tails held out during an intermission at the opera. George didn't know whether he had gulped because the girl's skin looked as black and shiny as patent leather or because she was wearing a brown fur coat that might have been mink and certainly looked expensive. He did know that her thick lips moved slightly, adding to her haughty glance a touch of unmistakable contempt, as though she knew she would not receive from this boorish source the apology she so clearly felt she deserved.

"Sorry," George said.

The girl did not answer or move. George wondered what he was supposed to do. They were separated by a distance of ten or twelve feet, including the width of a double bed, and he was still wearing his overcoat. George stood there, feeling the sweat gather in his armpits, while the look of contempt on the girl's face deepened.

"Hello," George said tentatively.

The girl did not answer. She waited another few minutes and then, as though she were being directed in slow motion by somebody beyond George's field of vision, she unclasped her hands, uncrossed her legs, rose from the bed, and slipped out of the fur coat. George gulped again. The girl was stark naked. Dangling the fur coat from one outstretched hand, like a manikin showing all the fine points of a dress to customers gathered in a showroom, she turned slowly, making a complete, leisurely circle, and then stopped, facing George.

"Well," he said.

The remark was obviously inadequate. The girl waited for more. George couldn't think of anything more to say. The girl shrugged, dropped the fur coat on the bed, dipped down to the floor, picked up a large purse, and opened it. She took several bulky objects from the purse, set it back on the floor, sat down on the edge of the bed, and began to arrange the objects on her naked thighs, as though she were setting a table. For several moments after he was certain the girl was doing what his eyes told him she was doing, George couldn't move. He watched the girl scoop lumps of peanut butter from the jar she had taken from her purse, smear the lumps daintily with her finger on the crackers she pulled from the small square box that had also come out of her purse, and munch them with disdainful elegance. George watched her consume four crackers. Then he fled.

"Oh," Mrs. Hooper said from her chair when George came into the living room. "You finished already?"

"Yes," George said, and then the surprise in her voice caught up with him and his face reddened. "I mean no. I'm just—"

"Wouldn't you like to try one of the other ladies?"

"No, I've got an appointment. I have to leave now."

"Who did you have?"

"What?"

"Was it the white lady or one of the colored ladies?"

"That doesn't have anything to do with—"

"Some men don't like colored ladies. I mean they think they do when they order them, but then when they're in the room with them they find out they don't. Why don't you wait until Rita is free? She's a lovely person. Not only white, but very well bred. A real lady. She comes from a very wealthy family in Sacramento. They own horses. She—"

"No, I—"

The front-door buzzer sounded. Mrs. Hooper put down the copy of *Esquire* she had been reading when George came in. "Get back in the bedroom," she said.

"I've got to leave," George said. "I have an appointment."

"You'll keep it after I find out who this is," Mrs. Hooper said as she got up. "It's probably the fourth girl you gentlemen ordered, but it might be somebody else, and anybody that runs a respectable place the way I do can't take any chances."

She grabbed George's arm, hustled him across the living room, opened the door to the long, narrow hall, shoved him in, and pulled the door shut. George stood there, panting slightly, angry with himself for having allowed Mrs. Hooper to push him around, and yet afraid to go back into the living room. Suppose it was a cop who had pressed the front-door buzzer? Suppose this was a raid?

Trying to hear what was going on in the living room, George heard something else. He turned. The door of the bedroom from which he had just fled was opening. George's heart leaped. He knew he couldn't face that haughty colored girl. Not again. He knew also that he couldn't go out into the living room or into the bedrooms where Herman Lustgarten and Murph Lasky were enjoying the treat the Irving Trust Company didn't know it was paying for. George looked around desperately, and saw the only way out. He stepped to the door of the fourth bedroom, opened it, slipped in, and pulled the door shut. Standing flat against it, his ear pressed to the wood, he could hear a sudden confusion of noises outside. The sounds seemed to be coming from the living room and moving up the hall. Wondering where they were going, George suddenly became aware that they had stopped outside his door. He recognized Mrs. Hooper's voice.

"He's in there," she said, and there was a curious sound that it took George a couple of moments to identify as a giggle. "I don't think he's ever been to the pump before and he's scared," Mrs. Hooper said. "Think you can handle him?"

"Why not?" another voice said.

It sounded vaguely familiar.

"Well, see what you can do," Mrs. Hooper said. "This looks like an expense-account crowd to me. There might be a little something extra in it for you."

"All right," the other voice said.

George was wondering why the voice sounded familiar, when he realized the knob in his hand was being turned from the outside. He released it and stepped back, telling himself fiercely there was no need to panic. What was he afraid of? A whore? Some tramp anybody could buy for twenty bucks? All he had to do was—

The angry, reassuring words stopped hurtling through his head. The door had opened and a girl was coming in. She wore a coat, and

a bandanna was tied around her head, and she was half turned away
from George as she pushed the door shut, but there was no mistaking
the way she held her body, with the shoulders hunched forward, as
though trying to shield herself from a blow that might come at any
moment. She could not see George's face, because the dim light
from the table beside the bed was behind him, but George could
see hers. He could see it clearly. Even before she spoke, while the
world froze around him in a moment of horror that he felt would
never end, George Hurst knew why the voice in the hall had sounded
familiar.

Turning to the man she thought was a stranger, cooing the words
with professional sweetness, Dora Dienst said, "Hello, there!"

21

Coming across the deserted cafeteria, carrying the tray with the cup
of coffee and the glass of milk, George had the feeling that he was
fighting something off and just managing to hold his own. It was
like one of those dreams in which he was trapped in a fortified room
completely surrounded by a nameless, numerous, relentless enemy,
and the only thing that sustained him, as the enemy battered on the
door and sawed at the window bars and drilled down through the
ceiling and tunneled up through the floor, was the knowledge that,
if he could just hold out a little longer, a few more minutes, a few
more seconds, he would be saved. By what? By whom? How? George
did not know, any more than he knew what it was he was holding
off. He knew only that, unless he did, he was lost.

"You sure this is all you want?" he said when he reached the
table. "A sandwich, maybe?"

"No, just coffee," Dora said. "Thanks."

She spoke carefully, the way he did, as though they were strangers
just met in a language class, using a foreign tongue so new to them
that they were afraid, unless they proceeded with the utmost caution,
they might inadvertently employ phrases with meanings that were
outrageously intimate.

"It's pretty late," George said. "Almost one in the morning.
You ought to have something to eat."

Why was he doing this? Why didn't he turn and run while he still had the chance?

"No," Dora said. "Just coffee, thanks."

He set the cup in front of her, put down the glass of milk, slid the tray to the end of the table, and sat down facing her. He moved the glass of milk around in a series of small circles, counting them as he did so, telling himself when the count reached a hundred he would get up and leave.

"You've started to smoke," he said.

"Yes," she said. "Would you like one?"

What he would like, he thought, was the guts to beat it without counting stupid circles.

"No, thanks. I tried it a few times, but it makes me cough."

"Maybe if you didn't inhale."

"I didn't, but I coughed anyway."

Seventeen, eighteen, nineteen, twenty.

"What brand did you smoke?"

"All kinds. Chesterfield, Lucky Strike, Old Gold. I even tried that new one. Barking Dogs. Because of the ad. Barking Dogs Never Bite. They all made me cough."

Twenty-one, twenty-two, twenty-three.

"They don't make me cough," Dora said. "I enjoy smoking. It's —" She paused, looked at him, dropped her glance to the cup of coffee, took a long, deep drag on the cigarette, and scowled at her fingers as with delicate precision she rolled the burning end along the rim of the saucer until the fragment of ash broke loose. "Will you get into trouble?"

What did she think he was in now?

"For what?" George said.

"Rushing me out of there like that," Dora said, addressing the coffee cup. "Your friends sounded angry."

No angrier than he was sounding to himself. Why had he got himself into this? Why hadn't he just left her up there and walked out alone?

"They're not my friends," he said. "We work in the same place. There's nothing for them to be sore about. They have three other girls." She looked up quickly. Their eyes met. The blood drained out of her face and her thin shoulders came forward slightly, as though trying to make a more effective shield against the inevitable blow. I don't care, George said to himself. I don't care how much it hurts her. I don't owe her anything. It's her or me. Relentlessly, sensing that it was the only way to hold off the nameless enemy pressing hard to overwhelm him, he said brutally, "How about you? Won't you get in trouble with Mrs. Hooper?"

The blow went home. The slender body seemed to shiver, and then Dora shrugged. "I guess so. I don't really know her very well. This is the first time I've ever —" She paused. Their eyes met again. Dora shook her head. "No," she said quietly. "That's a lie."

What wasn't?

"You don't have to explain," George said. "I'm not interested."

That made him an even bigger liar.

"You might be interested in this," Dora said. "Wherever he is, this minute, I hope Danny Schorr is dead. If he isn't, I hope he drops dead before I finish this cigarette."

She crushed it out with a short thrust so savage and sudden that it missed the saucer. Bits of fiery ash spread across the table top. George stamped them out with the heel of his hand. He tried to force the words back, but he couldn't.

"Where is Danny?" he said.

"I don't know and I don't want to know, unless it's his funeral and then I'd like to be invited just to be able to spit on the grave."

More lies, he thought. Don't listen.

"You sound pretty bloodthirsty about your dear old friend."

"Some friend he is," Dora said.

"The things you did for him very few people do for their enemies," George said.

"How about the things *you* did for Danny?"

There weren't going to be any more things. Not for anybody.

"I did them because he was my friend," George said. "Or so I used to think."

While he was still capable of thinking, he'd better stop making stupid circles on the table with this glass of milk and push himself out of this chair and go home.

"I told you years ago what he was. When we were still in public school, when he made me a cripple on Armistice Day and you went to visit your uncle in Albany, when you came back I told you what Danny Schorr was, but you wouldn't listen."

Why couldn't he do the same now?

"I listened a year ago," George said. "When you told me how

important it was for me not to go see that postal inspector until the next morning."

"You were crazy to listen."

He was crazy to be listening now.

"I found that out the next day."

"It took me a little longer," Dora said. Her hand shook as she lit another cigarette. "It's funny how stupid people can be. I knew from the beginning, all my life I knew Danny Schorr was no good. But he said he'd make me a star, and that's what I wanted more than anything in the world, so I closed my brain to what I knew. Never mind that you know he's no good, I told myself. You're a cripple. Nobody wants a cripple. Only when you're singing, only when people are clapping their hands for you, that's the only time you're not a cripple, that's the only time they want you, I told myself. And the only reason you're singing, the only reason people are clapping their hands for you is because of Danny. Suppose he's no good for the rest of the world, I said to myself, he's still good for you, isn't he?" Dora laughed bitterly. "You start listening when you tell yourself that kind of stuff, and you'll do anything. I ought to know. I did it all. I lied to you, the only real friend I ever had, I lied to you because Danny told me to. I stole from my own father because Danny told me to. I cut myself off from my whole family because Danny told me to. And I ended up working for Mrs. Hooper."

Why couldn't she let it alone? Why couldn't she shut up about it?

"Because Danny told you to?"

Dora shrugged again.

"He just as well might have. Six weeks after we ran away from Fourth Street, I learned an interesting thing about Danny. He's just as big a liar when he's talking to himself as when he's talking to anybody else. The reason I believed him when he said he'd make me a star was that I wanted to believe him. But the trouble was that Danny believed it, too. We went to a small hotel on West Forty-ninth Street, just off Broadway, and Danny said he'd have me singing in a big night club in a very short time. I believed him and Danny believed himself. Every day he went out to see people. A few times he brought me to people who wanted to hear me sing. Nothing ever happened. But Danny wasn't discouraged. Neither was I. You couldn't be discouraged listening to Danny. You had to believe him. Until the morning I woke up and found he was gone."

He was smarter than I am, George thought. Go, he told himself angrily, get up and go. But he sat there, pushing the glass around in small circles. Sixty-eight, sixty-nine, seventy.

"We'd used up the money I'd stolen from my father," Dora said. "And we owed I don't know how much at the hotel. The time had come for Danny to wake up to the fact that he'd been wrong, that he wasn't ever going to make me into a star. So he walked out and left me. It didn't do me much good to remind myself that I'd known deep down in my heart, from the very beginning, that this was what would have to happen, because I'd known from the very beginning that Danny was no good. It was too late to tell myself that. Danny was gone. I didn't have any money. I couldn't go back home, not after what I'd done. And I couldn't get a job. It wasn't only that there weren't many jobs around. I learned another thing I'd really known from the very beginning. I'm not much good at anything. In the store when Frannie and Ida used to yell at me because I got the hair on the dolls all wrong and everything I did they had to do all over again, I used to say it was because they hated me. Maybe they did. But I saw now that I'd been doing the work wrong, too. I don't know why. I just don't seem to be good at anything. The hotel kept bothering me about the bill, and pretty soon I ran out of lies.

"One night, I was sitting in the lobby of the Astor, I don't know why, or how I got there. I was just tired, I guess. I hadn't eaten anything all day and I felt if I didn't sit down I'd faint, so I went in and sat down. Pretty soon this girl came up to me. How she knew, I don't know, but she did, and she asked me if I'd like to make some money, and I— I—" Dora paused, and she scowled down at her coffee cup, and then she drew a deep breath. "No," she said. "Danny didn't tell me to, but I listened to what he did tell me, and look." She lifted her left arm, holding it out parallel with the table top. "I'm still the same cripple I was down on Fourth Street," Dora Dienst said as her voice broke. "Except now, in addition to being a cripple, I'm working for Mrs. Hooper."

For a long moment, as he watched the sobs seize her slender body, George tried to continue to fight back. Then, understanding at last what it was he had been holding off, George also understood that resistance was hopeless. What she had done and what she had made him suffer suddenly seemed unimportant. All at once he couldn't remember the details. All at once he knew why he had been

unable to leave the call house by himself, and why he had been unable
to get up and walk out of the cafeteria. All at once he knew he was
trapped, and he didn't care. The long months of pretending the pain
was gone, telling himself it was all over, that pretense was behind
him. The smell of honey cake fresh from the oven was again in his
nostrils.

"No, you're not," George said. He pushed aside the glass of
milk and stood up. "You're finished with Mrs. Hooper," he said.
"You're coming with me."

22

Dora came as far as University Place before it occurred to George
that Mrs. Shissle might be a problem.

"You mind if we take it sort of easy going into the house?" he
said. "It's pretty late and we don't want to wake anybody up."

"You don't have to worry," Dora said. "These last few months
I've gotten pretty good at sneaking in and out of places."

George took her arm and pulled her around to face him. "You
can park that kind of talk right here out on the sidewalk," he said.
"I don't want to hear any more of it. The last few months are over.
It's finished. I want you to forget it."

"How about you?" Dora said. "Will you forget it?"

"I've forgotten it already," George said. "It never happened."

"No, it never happened, but you have to sneak me into your
room like an animal."

"It's the middle of the night. I don't want to have to make any
explanations to my landlady until the morning."

"You think it'll sound better in the morning?"

"I know it will."

"What are you going to tell her?"

"Wait and see."

She waited until they got up to his room, which they managed
to reach without waking Mrs. Shissle, and then Dora asked again.

"I'll tell you in the morning," George said. "Here, you take the
bed. I'll sleep on the studio couch. There's a pair of clean pajamas

in that bottom bureau drawer. You can get undressed in the bathroom. What about your things? Clothes and stuff?"

"I don't have much. It's all in the room I've been sharing with Rita on Thirty-ninth Street."

"Rita?"

"The girl who picked me up in the Astor lobby a few months ago and introduced me to Mrs. Hooper."

"You can forget her, too. I'll go get your things. Give me the address in the morning and I'll do it during my lunch hour."

"George."

"What?"

"Why are you doing all this for me?"

"That's another thing I'm not telling you tonight."

In the morning, when she asked again, the strain of the night before had faded a little. Not much, but enough to make him feel it was all right to speak.

"What I'm going to tell Mrs. Shissle," George said, "I'm going to tell her you and I are getting married."

"You think she'll swallow that?"

"She'll have to, when we show her the marriage certificate."

"Where are you going to get it?"

"Where everybody else gets them," George said. "City Hall."

"But I don't think you can get a marriage certificate unless—" Dora paused and then, as though it had just dawned on her that he was serious, she sat up straight. "You *mean* it? It's not just a gag to fool your landlady so I can stay here until I find a job?"

"I mean it. It's not just a gag. I want you to marry me."

She looked at him for several moments, leaning forward slightly as though the light was poor and she wanted to get a better view of his face. When she was apparently satisfied that he was not joking, Dora sat back on the edge of the bed and shook her head. "No."

"Dora, listen."

She shook her head again. "No."

"Dora, I'm not doing this to fool a landlady or because I feel sorry for you. I'm doing it because—"

"I don't want to hear the because."

"I've been trying to tell it to you for a long time. Before you ran away with Danny. It's something that—"

"George, if you don't stop, I'm walking out of here."

The tone of her voice stung like a slap.

"You don't have to walk out," George said slowly. "All you have to do is answer a question."

"Not if it's the one I think you're going to ask."

"Why won't you marry me?"

"I can't."

"Why not?"

"I just can't, that's all."

"You can't even tell me why?"

"I'm not going to tell you."

"Don't you think I have a right to know?"

"As long as I stay here, yes. So I guess maybe I'd better not stay here." She stood up.

"Okay," he said. "I'm sorry." It was a funny word for the way he felt.

"You don't have to be sorry," Dora said. "It's your room."

"It's yours, too. For as long as you want it."

"What'll we tell your landlady?"

"I don't know."

"You'll have to know by the time you walk out of here to go to work."

"I'll think of something."

"Tell her I'm your sister," Dora said. "I just came to town from Albany and I'm staying with you until I find a job and can afford a room of my own."

George didn't know whether he was more surprised by the fact that Dora had thought up the explanation or the fact that Mrs. Shissle accepted it. He sometimes thought, during the next few weeks, that his landlady knew or suspected the truth but pretended to believe otherwise because she disliked trouble. In either case, George didn't think about it often. He had other things on his mind. They all dealt with Dora.

All day while he was on the job, and all evening as he sat through his classes, George dreamed of the moment when he would open the door of his room and take her in his arms. It remained a dream. He never touched her. He couldn't. The old barrier was back in place, the wall she had erected between herself and the world after the Armistice Day accident, the wall from behind which she had emerged the night she first faced an audience in Gerrity's. It worried George to see her slip away like that once more, but this time there was something reassuring about her retreat. If it made her inaccessible, it also made her inviolate. It was like having the consolation of knowing that, while you were forbidden to draw on a certain bank account, the rest of the world was denied the same privilege. So long as Dora remained behind that wall, George knew he could not touch her, but he knew also that nobody else could, either.

She spent her days reading the Broadway columns, studying the theatre notes and *Variety*, smoking cigarettes and occasionally nibbling at the food George brought home every night from the delicatessen on the corner. She never seemed to wear anything but a pink negligee that George had brought back with her few belongings from the room she had shared with Rita on Thirty-ninth Street. He wished Dora would throw the negligee away because it reminded him of her days at Mrs. Hooper's. He didn't dare suggest it, however, because it was the only negligee Dora owned, and to buy one for her would have meant dipping into the money he was accumulating in the bank for his law school tuition. He couldn't do that. Every penny counted. Dora seemed to be aware of this. She never stopped talking about what a drain she was on his finances, and how hard she was working at finding a job. Every night, when George came home from school, Dora would show him the want ads she had marked in the evening paper and intended to answer in person the next day. Somehow or other, though, the next day would be gone before she had even had a chance to get dressed.

"I guess I'm just a slob," she said one night when George came home. "Look at this place. Like the bottom of an ash can." She seized a small, loaded ash tray, dumped its contents into a larger one, grabbed an armful of scattered newspapers, looked around for a place to put them, and smiled ruefully. "Honest to God," she said, "I don't know why you put up with me."

"I can answer that," George said quietly.

"Don't," she said.

"Why not?"

"Give me a chance to start off even with you. You've been wonderful to me, George. I want to be wonderful back to you. I can't do it if I think maybe I'm doing it because I owe you for food and rent and cigarettes, everything, even these damn newspapers I've got messing up the place. You wouldn't want it like that, George. Would you?"

It didn't seem to matter how he wanted it. Somebody else always seemed to call the tune.

"No," he said.

Dora smiled. "Tell you what," she said. "I'm going to cut out this lying around all day. Honest I am. Tomorrow morning I'm getting up bright and early and I'm going out job hunting. I really mean that, George."

"All right," he said.

"No kidding around, either," she said. "I want you to wake me up the same time you get up. Is that a deal?"

"All right," he said.

Shortly after George woke her up the next morning, Dora discovered that all her stockings had runs in them.

"I can't go out for a job looking like a bum," she said.

"I could get you a new pair."

"George, would you?"

"Sure," he said. It would mean no lunches for a few days, but he didn't see how he could say no. He certainly couldn't tell Dora that the nineteen dollars a week on which he had been living comfortably until she moved in with him had been, during the past weeks, barely enough to cover their basic expenses. He said, "Where do I buy silk stockings?"

"Hearn's over on Fourteenth is okay," Dora said. "But they don't open till nine or maybe nine-thirty."

"Mr. Rapf and I are working on the Perrini Brothers audit. That's over on Astor Place. During my lunch hour I'll go over to Hearn's, buy the stockings, and drop them off here before I go back to work."

"That'll be perfect," Dora said.

It proved to be somewhat less than that. When George came into the room a few minutes before one o'clock, carrying the silk stockings, the air was thick with cigar smoke. For a moment, as he stood in the open doorway, George refused to believe it. Then, as a vein began to throb in his forehead, he saw the wiry, smiling figure get up from the chair, remove the cigar, and come forward with hand outstretched.

"Hi, kid," Danny Schorr said. "Long time no see."

George disregarded the outstretched hand. "Not long enough for me," he said.

Danny laughed. "For a nice, pleasant guy," he said, "I must say you know how to carry a grudge."

"If you don't get the hell out of here in five seconds flat," George said, "I'll show you something else I know how to carry: a son of a bitch named Schorr that I've just knocked cold." He stepped aside and held the door wide. "Go on," George said. "Beat it."

Danny took a long drag on the cigar, blew the smoke out, and cocked his head to one side. "Tell me, boy," he said. "What are you scared of?"

"Oh, for heaven's sake," Dora said from the studio couch. "Will you both stop acting silly? George isn't scared."

George, who knew better than that, was grateful for the interruption. "If anybody around here is acting silly," he said, "it's not me. I don't know why you even let this bastard in here. How can you sit in the same room with him? After what he did to you and your father, your whole family? After what he's made you live through these past few months?"

Danny turned to Dora. "What have I made you live through these past few months?"

She gave George a sullen glance. "Nothing," she said. "George is just sore about that postal inspector."

"What the hell's the matter with you?" he said to her. "You know what I'm sore about. Mrs. Hooper."

"Mrs. Hooper?" Danny said. "Who she?"

Dora pushed herself up from the studio couch, ran across the room, threw her arms around George, and pulled his head down. "Don't tell him!" she whispered fiercely in his ear. "I'd die if he knew! I'd die!"

George could hear her heart hammering against him. He could feel the small, sharp shoulder blades against his palm. He could smell her hair. And he could understand her not wanting Danny to know.

"She's a woman who caused Dora a lot of trouble after you walked out on her," George said carefully, speaking across Dora's head. "Now you better walk out again. For good."

"How about it?" Danny said. "You want me to walk out, Dora?"

She lifted her head from George's shoulder. He was astonished to see tears in her eyes.

"Let him stay," she said.

"*Stay? Him?* You crazy?"

"He came here to offer me a job."

"Him and his God-damn jobs. Look what happened the last time he gave you what he called a job."

"It's singing, George. It's a job singing."

"It was singing last time, too. Look where you ended up."

"I'm no good at anything else, George. I can't stay here forever, letting you support me."

"You're not going to stay here forever. You'll get a job. You said last night you'll get a job. I brought you a pair of silk stockings. All you have to do—"

She shook her head. "I'll never get a job. Not if I wear all the silk stockings in Hearn's. Except singing, George. That's all I'm good at. I have to take this job in Danny's new place."

"You don't have to do anything you don't want to do."

"George, I've got to work. Singing is the only kind of work I know, and Danny needs a singer in this new place."

The fear Danny had sensed at once underneath George's tough words, the fear Dora had dismissed as nonsense, moved in and took a tighter grip. Something was happening that George didn't understand. After what Danny had done to her, Dora couldn't be going back to him merely because he was offering her a job. It wasn't enough. Not for a girl who, only a few weeks ago, had wanted to spit on Danny Schorr's grave. There was something else. George wished he knew what it was. The vein in his head began to jump.

"What kind of new place?" he said, turning to Danny, trying to sound sarcastic in spite of the fear. It must have been lying in the back of his mind all these weeks. It had come to the surface as soon as he opened the door, warning him in the moment of shock that only Danny could take her away from him. George said, "Don't tell me you've found another bunch of suckers like the Gerritys."

Danny smiled. Even as George wanted to smash the smile away with his fist, he could feel its pull. The old charm was still there. The charm before which even Aunt Tessie had once forgotten what she knew to be true, and before which Dora was forgetting now.

"If all I had to tell you was I'd found another couple of Gerritys," Danny said, "I wouldn't be here. A guy who stands still is a guy moving backwards. The Gerritys were okay for a dumb kid on East Fourth Street. Do I look like a dumb kid on East Fourth Street to you, George?"

He held the cigar up as though it were a pennant, hooked a thumb into the armhole of his vest, and pirouetted in a burlesqued imitation of a model displaying a dress. He certainly looked prosperous. The brown suit with the hand-stitched lapels was no $22.50 number from Howard's. The thick-soled shoes with perforations across the toes had not come out of Thom Mc An. Even the cigar, which looked a little silly because it was too big for Danny's tight little face, was no twofer. George could tell by the band. Mr. Brodsky kept a box of them on his desk for important visitors.

"You look like something I don't want to see too much of," George said.

"It's a lucky thing I don't feel the same way about you," Danny said. "If I did, you wouldn't be there tonight."

"Be where?" George said, but in his heart he already knew. He could tell from the way Dora was pushing herself out of his arms.

"Dora's opening," Danny said. "She does her first number at eleven sharp. That'll give you plenty of time to get there after your last class."

"If you're standing around waiting for any expressions of gratitude, don't waste your time," George said. "I won't be there."

Danny shrugged. "Suit yourself, kid."

"I will," George said.

"No you won't," Dora said irritably. "I won't feel right if you're not there. You know that, George. Why are you making such a fuss? Why can't you let bygones be bygones?"

"You want me to answer that?"

Unexpectedly, she laughed and then put her finger on his lips. "No, of course not," Dora said. "What I want is for you to be at Danny's new place tonight."

23

It was, George saw at once, quite an improvement over Danny's old place.

For one thing, West Eleventh Street had a Greenwich Villagey air that seemed more appropriate as a night-club location than East Fourth Street had been. For another, there was a crude marquee over the front door on which not very straight but clearly legible yellow wooden letters spelled out the words CHEZ SHAW.

"What does the name mean?" George asked Dora when she admitted him to the grimy closet she called her dressing room.

"Can't you guess?"

"My Franklin Pierce High School French gets me through the first word," George said. "It's the Shaw that beats me."

"The Shaw is Danny."

"Danny?"

"Danny *Schorr.*"

"Oh," George said. "Schorr into Shaw. Like Leibowitz into LeBeau."

"Well, if you want to be nasty."

"I don't want to be nasty. Not when I'm with you."

"Quit that," Dora said. "What have you got there?"

He handed her the small package wrapped in newspaper. "Some day, when I'm dragging down fat fees for pleading the cause of Wall Street corporations before the Supreme Court, I'll make those orchids."

Dora looked up from the twenty-five-cent bunch of violets he had bought near the subway entrance on Sheridan Square. Astonished, George saw that, for the second time that day, there were tears in her eyes.

"What did I do wrong now?" he said.

"Nothing," Dora said. "You never do anything wrong. That's the trouble. If I had any brains—" She paused and shrugged helplessly. "But I haven't. Not even a hint of brains." Swiftly, before he knew it was happening, she had pulled his head down, kissed him, and thrust him toward the door. "Go on, scram," Dora said with a laugh. "Before I say something both of us will be sorry for."

"I won't be sorry."

The smile disappeared. "You don't know what you're talking about."

"I'm willing to listen to an explanation."

"Not now," Dora said. "I have to dress."

"When, then?"

"When, then? It sounds like a song lyric."

"Dora, quit it."

"*You* quit it. I have to get dressed."

"Is this gentleman annoying you?"

They both turned.

"No, of course not," Dora said, laughing at Danny in the doorway. "Look what George brought me."

With a graceful, darting gesture, Danny plucked one of the violets from the bunch she held out.

"George," he said, "if you'd been born thirty years ago you'd be drinking champagne every night out of the girls' slippers in Rector's." He started to put the violet in the lapel of his dinner jacket, then stopped and held the flower out to George. "May I?"

"If Dora doesn't object."

Danny held the flower out to Dora. "May I?"

"Oh, cut it out, you two," she said with a quick laugh. She grabbed their sleeves and, before George could duck, she had laced Danny's arm through his, and she was pushing them, arm in arm, toward the door. "Stop acting like a couple of dumbbells," she said as she thrust them out into the hall. "When I finish dressing," Dora said, "I expect you to be talking nice to each other again."

She pulled the door shut. Danny looked down at George's arm on his sleeve, then up at George. There wasn't much light in the hall, but there was enough to show Danny's brown eyes. They were twinkling.

"How about it?" he said. "Do you take orders from a woman?"

George stood there, feeling foolish as he tried to straighten out his emotions. It wasn't easy. The anger that had seemed right in his room that afternoon, and to which he felt he was entitled, seemed curiously unconvincing now. Neither did it seem right that, at the age of twenty-one and after all that had happened, his heart should suddenly be leaping with anticipation, the way it used to leap down on Fourth Street when the tin can came tapping against the window beside his bed and he knew Danny was sending him a message. George withdrew his arm slowly from Danny's, looking into the handsome face that Aunt Tessie had once said bitterly George Hurst would follow without hesitation or question to his death. It didn't seem right, after all that had happened, to know that what Aunt Tessie had said was true.

George drew a deep breath. "Danny," he said. "Why did you do it?"

The question obviously took Danny by surprise. He pulled a cigar from his pocket, stared at the band for a few moments, then replaced the cigar carefully in his pocket.

"I don't know," he said. "And that's the God's honest truth, George."

"You could have told me," George said, each word coming with difficulty, every syllable chipping away a piece of the pride that for so long had been all he'd had to lean on. Yet he was glad that at last he was opening it up, like an infection buried deep that he had known all along would some day have to be lanced. "There wasn't anything in the world I wouldn't have done for you," he said. "All you had to do was ask. You knew that."

Danny nodded. "I knew that."

"Then why did you do it?"

Danny shook his head. "I said I don't know. That's not really true. Sure I know. The only thing is, what good does it do to know if you can't stop yourself?"

"Stop yourself from what?"

"Believing what you want to believe. Down there in Gerrity's I believed I was going to make it. I really did. It sounds crazy now. When I think of what I was trying to do, start a club in a dirty little saloon on the waterfront, a club I expected uptown spenders to come to, when I think of that now, I realize I must have been crazy. It was impossible. It was stupid. It was nuts. Anything you want to call it, you're right, that's what it was. But I believed it. I believed it so hard, I was so sure I was going to make it, that I acted like I *had* made it. It's like telling yourself you're a millionaire when you haven't got a dime in the bank, and you believe your own words so much you go out buying Cadillacs and signing checks for them. It's crazy. But it's real. That's what's wrong. It was so real to me that I'd made it down there in Gerrity's, I believed it so much, that there wasn't anything I wouldn't do to make it *seem* real. Anything, George. Even screw a friend."

Danny caught the corner of his lower lip in his teeth. There was a short silence. "George," he said finally.

"What?"

"This last year, ever since I pulled that thing on you, I've been kicking myself around the block eight times a day. Like you said, I didn't have to do it. Nobody knows that better than I do. All it got me was I lost a friend. If what I just told you makes any sense, if you understand a little piece of what I've been trying to make you understand, that I didn't want to do it, if you understand that, then you'll understand this." Danny paused again. "George," he said. "I want that friend back."

He stood there waiting. The silence, George found, was unbearable. It was wonderful and unbearable. Then George started to laugh.

"You son of a bitch," he said, and the laughter went out of control, so that it could have been mistaken for a sob, but George didn't care. "You son of a bitch," he said happily. "If you knew the way I been feeling all this time. If you knew, you son of a bitch."

Danny started to laugh, too. He put his arms around George and pulled him close in a hard, awkward hug.

"Look who's calling who a son of a bitch," Danny said. "The way you talked to me this afternoon in your room there on University Place."

They laughed until the tears came. Then George wiped his eyes.

"I been meaning to ask," he said. "How the hell did you find me?"

Danny pulled the cigar from his pocket, and he placed it against the side of his nose, and he winked, and the laughter seized them again.

"You son of a bitch," George said. "You wonderful son of a bitch."

Then, all at once, the laughter stopped. It was as though they had been taking a shower together in a locker room, splashing and shoving and yelling cheerful insults at one another after a basketball game, and somebody had turned off the water. George felt exposed. Danny spoke first.

"One thing we might as well get straight," he said, and nodded toward the closed door of Dora's dressing room. "I never put a hand on her."

"I'm not asking you," George said.

"I'm telling you," Danny said. "There never was any boy-girl stuff, and there never will be. It was strictly business all the way, and it's going to continue like that. I needed a singer then, and I need one now. That's absolutely all there's to it. My word may not count for very much with you any more, and if it doesn't I'm the last guy to blame you, but on that one point, if I'm lying to you, I hope I drop dead before this place opens tonight."

He stuck out his hand. George took it.

"Thanks, Danny."

"Forget it. I've owed you that for a long time." He smiled suddenly. "Do me one favor, though, will you?"

"What?"

"If it's wedding bells you got on your mind," Danny said, "will you hold off just a few weeks, until I get this joint on its feet?"

George laughed. "You don't have to worry," he said. "She won't marry me."

"You're kidding."

"I wish I were."

"She must be out of her mind."

"I don't know about that. Nineteen bucks a week and four years of law school still ahead of me? I guess I'm not much of a catch."

"By the time you finish law school and you're ready to practice, I'll be able to throw you enough business to make you the biggest catch since the Prince of Wales. I'm going all the way, George. This joint is only the beginning."

"It looks like a nice place."

"*Now*, yeah. But you should have seen it when I first did. I don't know if you noticed when you came in, but it's a hotel. Not that it ever made the guys who own the Waldorf nervous, but when I first saw this dump that's how the putz who owned it made his living. Renting out rooms. I guess there's money in renting out rooms, otherwise why would people build places like the Waldorf, but this shmerg wasn't picking up enough of it to buy wax for his mustache. I tried to talk him into tearing out a couple of walls on the ground floor, because the location isn't bad, and I figured if we put together a few tables and got in a piano and a kid with a good set of pipes, hell, we could make a buck. But this shmohawk, he said no. Rooms he'd always rented out. Rooms he wanted to go right on renting out. I got so disgusted, I was just about ready to tell him what he could do with his rooms and take a powder, when what do you know? He drops dead one morning nice and neat, without even making a splash, and then I find out he left the joint to me. That was six weeks ago, and if you think I've been wasting time, come on upstairs."

George could see when they got there what Danny meant. By knocking out walls, concealing the windows behind black and red velvet draperies, and putting his grand piano on a low platform, he had managed to create a professional atmosphere that had been lacking in Gerrity's.

"How do you like it?" Danny said.

"It looks swell," George said.

"It's better than that," Danny said. "You're not a pro, so you don't know, but what you're seeing is a room that's going to make history in this town. I was just a dumb kid, still wet behind the ears, down in Gerrity's. Here, in this place, I'm telling you, George—" He paused, as though there were no words to describe how he felt, but words were not necessary. George knew what Danny meant. He could feel it, the way he used to be able to feel it down on Fourth Street: the terrible impatience that burned inside Danny Schorr. "This is it, George," he said. "In twenty minutes, when Dora comes out there and starts to sing, the ball is going to start rolling. It's going to keep on rolling, George, until I'm one of the biggest guys in this town. Nothing can stop it. Not any more. I can feel it in my bones. I'm on my way, George."

There was something about the tone of his voice that George found embarrassing, as though he had unexpectedly overheard an intimate conversation between husband and wife.

George cleared his throat. "Good luck," he said.

Danny seemed to come back to the present. "Thanks, kid," he said with a grin. "I'm glad you like it."

It was nothing like the elaborate establishments George was accustomed to seeing in the movies, but he could see that to people who frequented night clubs this room would be recognizable at once as a fragment of their stamping grounds. George still did not understand why people would want to stamp around in grounds of this nature, but his lack of comprehension clearly was not universal. There were fifty or more people at the tables in the room when George and Danny came to stand in the doorway, and at least one of them seemed to be overwhelmed by the atmosphere. He was waving both hands above his head in a way that reminded George of a child desperately scrubbing away frost from a window for a glimpse of a receding parade.

"Oh, Jesus," Danny said. "Wally Moon's here already."

"Who's he?"

"George, don't make jokes."

"I'll be glad to stop as soon as you tell me what's funny about asking who Wally Moon is."

"Don't you read the *Evening Eagle*?"

"I don't get a chance to read any of the evening papers."

"Try to fit in a chance tomorrow."

"Why?"

"It looks like Chez Shaw is going to be in it."

"He's a reporter?"

"What they call a saloon reporter. Wally Moon is the newest and hottest Broadway columnist in town. It took plenty of wangling, believe me, to get him to come down and cover this opening, but it was worth it. A good mention in his column and I'm in." He grinned suddenly. "You're feeling pretty good, aren't you?"

George grinned back at him. "Better than I've felt in a year."

Danny put his arm across George's shoulder. "Okay, then, boy, while you're feeling good, do me a favor, will you? I don't want this Moon jerk to think he's dealing with a small-potatoes guy. Let's go over and impress him. All that waving he's doing, he's signaling to me."

George followed Danny to Wally Moon's table.

"Hi, Wally," Danny said and, after he shook hands with the columnist, Danny bowed to the woman sitting beside him. "Nice to see you, Mrs. Moon. Glad you could get down for the opening. Wait till you hear this girl. Believe me, she's a honey."

"Honey is sweet," Mrs. Moon said. "Wally hates sweet singers."

Danny roared with laughter, poked George in the ribs, and nodded toward Mrs. Moon as though the thin woman had just dashed off the Mona Lisa and Danny wanted George to catch a glimpse of the canvas before the impatient attendants whisked it off to the Louvre.

"You want to watch out for Mrs. Moon," Danny said when he could control his voice. "She's murder with the cracks. Half of Wally's column, the stuff that's credited to Dotty Parker and Bob Benchley and George Kaufman, all those real big ones, it's all Mrs. Moon. Oh, excuse me. I want you folks to meet my lawyer, George Hurst."

"By his own petard," Mrs. Moon said.

"What?" Danny said.

"Try it again, Lena," her husband said.

"Hurst," Mrs. Moon said. "By his own petard."

The columnist scowled at the ceiling for several moments, then pulled out a small notebook. He scribbled something, looked at it for several moments, then shook his head.

"No, Lena," he said. "Too literary. For The Conning Tower, maybe. Not for my column."

Mrs. Moon shrugged. "So?" she said. "Every time I open my face it has to be the Twenty-third Psalm?"

Danny released another roar of laughter. "What did I tell you,

George?" He turned to the columnist. "You mind if George sits with you folks?"

"As long as he's got nothing contagious," Mrs. Moon said.

To describe Danny's next reaction as laughter would have been somewhat like describing Vesuvius as a firecracker. He apparently succeeded in remaining on his feet only by an effort of will that would have done credit to St. Anthony.

"Oh, God, how I wish I could stay and listen," he gasped. "But I have to go see how things are going. Have fun, folks. I'll join you later."

His shoulders heaved with barely controlled hilarity until he disappeared through a set of velvet curtains at the far side of the room.

"You been his lawyer long?" Mrs. Moon asked.

George jumped slightly in his chair. Mrs. Moon's voice had much in common with the whistle of a mule-skinner's whip.

"Not too long," George said.

Mrs. Moon turned to her husband. "Everything you ask about this Shaw you get the same answer," she said. "Not too long."

"A man's got to start some time," Wally Moon said.

"With this Shaw everything sounds like it started yesterday," his wife said.

"That's not quite accurate," George said.

The Moons turned their full attention on him, and at once George regretted his small effort to ease Danny's path with the press. Mrs. Moon was blond and her husband was dark. She was tall and Wally Moon was short. Yet they both looked alike. Not because of their sunken cheeks and long, thin jaws. Not because of the beady little eyes that rolled about in their gaunt heads like loose ball bearings. What made them look alike, George decided after several moments of puzzled examination, was their posture and the fact that they looked hungry. They sat with their heads thrust far forward. Their nostrils flared and their mouths hung open. They reminded George of savage dogs that were kept chained and half starved so that, when the time came to turn them loose, they would do a workmanlike job on their prey.

"What do you mean it's not accurate?" Mrs. Moon said.

"To say that everything with Danny started yesterday," George said. "He's had other places."

"Where?" Mrs. Moon said.

"Well—"

"Is that in New York?" Mrs. Moon said.

Her husband pulled out his notebook and scribbled busily.

"Don't credit that one to Dotty Parker," Mrs. Moon said.

"Why not?" Wally Moon said.

"You had her in the column three times this week."

"Who should I give it to?"

"Alec Woollcott."

"Check," said the columnist.

Mrs. Moon turned back to George. "You got money in this trap?"

"Well—" he said.

"When one of your wells comes in I'd like to be around with a bucket."

Her husband scribbled wildly. "Marc Connelly?" he said.

"Or Willie Maugham," his wife said. "That crack is good enough for either one of them." She swung her hungry glance back to George. "You know anything about this Dora Dienst?"

"What sort of things?"

"Your client didn't put this joint together with cigar-store coupons. It cost dough. Mr. Shaw's got all that dough riding on an unknown card: Dora Dienst. How come?"

"He obviously thinks she's a good bet."

"I never heard of her," Mrs. Moon said.

"From now on," George said, "I guess you will."

"Mr. Hurst," Wally Moon said, "you mind shutting up? Here she comes."

She came bathed in a blue spotlight, moving slowly and gracefully, her face grave, her hands clasped in front of her. She stopped near the piano and waited, her eyes fixed on the floor, while the man at the keys ran through a few introductory bars. Watching her stand there with one shoulder thrust forward, so that her crooked arm was turned away from the audience, remembering the sound of her voice when she had tried to explain to him what it meant to her to sing in public, George could feel a lump of uneasiness forming slowly in his chest. He wanted her to succeed, to get what she wanted, but he knew that if she did he might lose her again. Suddenly, as he sat there watching her, the pain of those days after the opening night in Gerrity's, the days when he couldn't seem to find a moment in which to tell her how he felt, that pain was back. Then, as the introductory bars ended and Dora started to sing, the pain slipped away and with it went the lump of uneasiness.

She was singing "Apple Blossom Time," the song she had sung at the opening in Gerrity's, the song that was part of the moment when he first knew he loved her.

The moment came alive again, except that this time it was different because this time it was better. This time he was not listening to an inexperienced girl telling her lover when she would come to him. This time he was listening to a young woman pouring out her heart, a woman who knew the full value of every wasted moment that was not spent at her lover's side.

The change was for George so overwhelming that, when Dora began to turn full-face to the audience, and her arms came up slowly with the final bars of the song, he found himself holding his breath. It was as though she had been singing only to him.

Her outspread arms seemed to lift the long sweet final note and hold it aloft. The music stopped. Dora's arms came down. For several moments after he started clapping furiously, George didn't realize what was wrong. Then, astonished, he saw that his applause was arousing snickers and grins at nearby tables. He stopped clapping, feeling his face flush, and as he dropped his hands into his lap he realized something else: nobody was applauding.

George turned to Wally Moon. "What's the matter?"

"If you took stock in this joint instead of cash for your legal fee," the columnist's wife said, "I don't think you're going to have any wallpaper problems, Mr. Hurst." She stood up. "Credit that to Noel Coward," she said to her husband. "Let's go, Wally."

The columnist started to follow her. George grabbed his arm. "I asked what's the matter?"

"Can't you smell?" Wally Moon said. "Miss Dienst stinks."

George had hit him twice, and he was reaching down to pull him up from the floor so he could hit him again, when there was a neat, unbelievably sharp stab in the base of George's neck. He wondered stupidly if he had been clubbed with a whiskey bottle or a water carafe, decided it was the latter, then heard the crash of glass and silverware as a table went over somewhere on his left, and that was all he did hear. For a while, anyway.

24

When next he became aware of sounds, George couldn't identify them. Then, after a few moments of puzzled concentration, he understood why: the sounds were his own breathing.

Reconnoitering by moving nothing but his eyes, he saw that he was seated in a chair at the table he had shared with the Moons. His feet were up on the chair that had been occupied by the columnist's wife. Both chairs were set against the table in such a way that they formed a crude couch, and George was wedged into the couch in such a way that he could not fall off. Not unless he moved. He discovered this when, wondering why his head should be tipped forward at such an odd angle, George did try to move, and almost fell out of the chairs.

At the same time he almost lost the soggy wad of towel packed with cracked ice that had been resting between the back of his neck and the back of the chair. Pushing the towel gently back into place, George became aware that he was not alone in the room. A few moments later, after he was able to accept the fact that the dull throbbing was not going to tear the head from his shoulders and that the pain was actually subsiding, George had the curious feeling that he was trapped in a scene with which he should have been familiar. He couldn't understand why. If there was anything of which he was at the moment certain, it was that he had never lived through anything like this before. Yet the feeling of familiarity persisted. Determined to discover why, he moved his head cautiously, an inch at a time, to examine his surroundings.

Dora was seated at the other side of the table. She had not removed her make-up and she was still wearing the low-cut blue dress in which she had sung "Apple Blossom Time." Slowly, carefully, with scowling concentration, as though she were performing a religious rite, she was tearing matches from a book and arranging them on the table in a complicated pattern. She gave no sign that she knew George had come awake.

Neither did Danny.

He was sitting on the piano bench, at the other side of the room, with his back to the instrument. His elbows were up behind him, on the keys. His legs were thrust out stiff and straight, making of his slender body a sort of chute that ran from his feet up to the chin sunk on the bulge of his soiled shirt. The two halves of Danny's unbuttoned dinner coat hung down like black saddlebags on either side of the piano bench. His thumbs and forefingers were hooked behind the suspender buttons. Except for the remaining three fingers of each hand, which tapped up and down noiselessly on his black pants like the wings of trapped butterflies, Danny was absolutely motionless, his whole body sucked up in the act of total absorption by his own thoughts.

Then his lips moved in a short, bitter grimace, as though a twinge of pain had shot through his gums, and George knew why the scene seemed familiar.

It reminded him of a picture that used to hang on the wall behind Mr. Gaspari's desk in the chemistry lab at Franklin Pierce High. The picture showed Napoleon in his tent at Waterloo, surrounded by couriers and aides-de-camp and high-ranking officers, as the reports from the battlefield were being brought in.

In the picture Napoleon was wearing, not a dinner jacket, but some sort of uniform and, instead of a piano, it was a table strewn with maps against which he leaned. But he did it exactly as Danny was now doing it, and the same air of defeat that filled the picture now filled this room.

Oddly enough, there had been something very attractive about Napoleon in that picture, and it seemed to George that Danny Schorr had never looked more handsome than he did at this moment.

"Five G's," Danny said suddenly, in a low, thoughtful voice. "Five thousand bucks."

It was as though all this time Danny had been working out an arithmetic problem in his head and at last had come up with the answer, but he saw no cause for elation in the accomplishment because the problem was so simple that he should not have taken so long to work it out.

"You say something?" George said.

"Yep," Danny said. "Five thousand smackers."

George gave Dora a quick, puzzled glance. She had not looked up from her work with the matches.

"I mean, Danny, did you say it to me?" George said. "Or to Dora?"

Danny shifted the weight on his elbows. The piano uttered a low, surprisingly pretty moan.

"I said it to you, to Dora, to the world, to anybody who wants to listen, and to anybody who doesn't give a damn. Frankly, I don't see why anybody should, since the remark was being made by the biggest horse's ass in the Western Hemisphere." Danny shook his head pityingly and blew out his breath in a long tired sigh of disgust. "Some day, when you're a great big lawyer, George, maybe you'll get a law passed making it illegal for dopes as big as Danny Schorr to walk around loose."

George sent another puzzled glance at Dora. She had either not heard a word, or what was being said did not interest her. She continued to work on the arrangement of matches. George did not understand why she didn't look startled. He certainly was. Danny Schorr did not call himself names very often.

"Danny," George said, "I'm sorry."

"About what?"

George gestured toward the empty room. "Lousing up your opening."

Danny cocked his head to one side. "How do you figure you did that?"

"I had no business taking a sock at Wally Moon."

"Some day somebody was bound to make that his business."

"I'm sorry the guy who made it his business was me, and I'm even more sorry I did it tonight."

"I'm not. He was going to pan the ass off us anyway. Whether you socked him or not. I could tell from the cracks that bitch on roller skates he's married to was making before Dora even came out to sing. You're not around Broadway, so you don't know about these things, but I do. They're a team, those two. He writes it but she dictates it, and she had the shiv out for me the minute she walked into the joint. At least tomorrow, when I read what the little vontz says about Chez Shaw, I'll have the satisfaction of knowing the bastard is carrying around a shiner like a cantaloupe."

"If I hadn't socked him, it wouldn't have started a free-for-all and your customers would have stayed put."

"They wouldn't have stayed if Dora had sung twice as good as she did, and you can take it from me she sang better than good," Danny said. "I've heard Etting do that number maybe twenty times, and she never even came close to Dora tonight."

George looked at Dora. Even the compliment had not cracked the wall behind which she had retreated to play her game with the match sticks. It was as though she were in a trance. George decided the time had come to take her home. Delicately, avoiding abrupt movement, he lowered his feet from the chair and sat up. The throbbing, he was pleased to note, had almost disappeared.

"Danny," he said as he put the soggy lump of ice-packed towel on the table, "I don't know anything about night clubs but I do know your customers walked out tonight. If it wasn't because of Dora's singing, and it wasn't because of what I started, then why did they do it? There must be a reason."

"Damn right there's a reason," Danny said. "If you have brains, you see it the first time you get hit over the head with it. If you're a fourteen-carat boob, like your friend Danny Schorr, you don't see it the first time. You have to wait until you get hit over the head with it a second time. Don't look so puzzled, George. The reason is simple. They walked out tonight for the same reason they walked out of Gerrity's. You can't sell a diamond in a wooden setting. You've got to mount it in platinum." He waved his hand to take in the room. "Look at this dump. Why would anybody pay good money to come and sit in a joint that looks like this?"

It was possible, of course, George thought, that the crack on the head with the water carafe had thrown his mental equipment temporarily out of whack. He certainly wasn't making much sense out of what Danny was saying.

"But Danny," he said. "They did come. There were fifty or sixty people in this room when I walked in."

"Anybody will come any place once," Danny said. "All you have to do is spread the word around in the right places and do it the right way. The trick is to keep them coming back, but as long as I've got to show Dora in places that look like this, that's a trick I'll never pull off." He sent his glance around the room. "If I had five thousand bucks, though." He paused and looked up at the ceiling, his lips working silently, as though he were rechecking that problem in arithmetic. "Yeah," he said at last. "Five G's would do it. What do you think, George?"

George wished he knew. He couldn't believe the customers had walked out because Dora's singing had been so bad. He could still feel the things that had happened to him while he listened to her. It didn't seem possible that the other people in the room had not felt at least some part of what he had felt. On the other hand, Danny was equally certain they had not walked out because of the fight George had started. Why, then, had they walked out?

"I think maybe what's wrong is you're a little too far downtown," George said. "Or maybe this business of spreading the word around in the right places that you mentioned, maybe if you concentrated on that a little more before you opened—"

"That's not what I'm asking you," Danny said. "What I'm asking is do you think five thousand is enough?"

The feeling that he did not have a firm grip on the conversation grew stronger in George's mind.

"How the hell would I know a thing like that, Danny?"

"You work for a big firm of accountants. You ought to know something about the cost of fixtures."

"Malvin Gewirtz & Company doesn't have any night clubs for clients. I don't know the first damn thing about what it costs to fix one up."

"How about five thousand dollars, George? You know anything about where I can put my dukes on that kind of lettuce?"

George laughed. "You could always rob a bank."

Danny laughed with him. "Not me, boy. Not any more. I got close enough to the law on that L. L. Parker stamp deal to learn that that way is for dopes. The way I get this five G's has to be strictly on the up and up. Any suggestions for how I can raise it, George?"

If Danny had asked the question with a smile, George would have laughed again and not bothered to reply. But Danny had not asked it with a smile. He had spoken quietly, almost gravely, and he was now watching George, waiting calmly for an answer. George, who would have had trouble making suggestions about how to raise fifty dollars, couldn't think of one that involved five thousand.

"That's all that stands between Dora and stardom," Danny said. "Five lousy G's to turn this dump into a showcase worthy of her talents. Where do you think I can get the money, George?"

Before George could tell Danny to quit kidding, which seemed the only sensible reply he could make under the almost preposterous circumstances, Dora threw down her matches.

"Oh, stop it, Danny, for God's sakes!"

He turned toward her as though she were a stranger who had just come into the room. "Stop what?" he said.

"You know what!" she snapped. "I'm sick and tired of it!" She stood up. "Stop it!"

Danny shoved himself up from the piano bench. He buttoned his double-breasted dinner jacket as he came across the room. He stopped in front of Dora and, for several moments, they stared directly into each other's eyes. Finally, Danny broke the silence.

"Any time you really mean that," he said, "I'll be glad to find me another horse to put my money on."

He paused and waited for a reply. Dora didn't make one.

George cleared his throat. "It's late," he said. "We're all tired. Let's—"

"Nobody is as tired as I am," Danny said, still looking directly at Dora. "Of trying to do everything myself, without any help, not even from the people I'm doing it for. Well, what do you say? I'm waiting for an answer."

Dora dropped her glance. "I'm sorry," she said in a low voice.

Danny turned to George. "Better take her home, kid. She's bushed."

Neither of them spoke until they were back in the room on University Place.

"All right," George said as Dora sat down on the edge of the bed and scowled at her hands. "What was that all about?"

She looked up. "George, he's no good. He's no good!"

Astonished George saw that she was hammering her fists on her knees. He sat down beside her and put his arm around her shoulders.

"For God's sake," he said. "What is it?"

"You know what it is! It's Danny! He's no good, George! He's rotten! He's *rotten!*"

She shook so hard that he drew her close to try and calm her. "This afternoon, when I tried to throw him out of here, you begged me not to. Now you tell me—"

She hid her face in his shoulder. "Don't listen to what I tell you," she said, the words coming jerkily through her sobs. "Don't ever listen to what I tell you. It's not me talking. It's not what I want to say. It's Danny. It's what Danny wants me to say!"

"What does he want you to say now?"

Her small fists began to hammer his chest. "Don't you understand what I'm trying to tell you? Haven't you got eyes in your head? Or ears? Weren't you there tonight? Didn't you hear me? Don't you know why they walked out?"

"Danny says it's because—"

"God damn Danny! Him and his dirty, rotten lies! They walked out because I'm no good! Because I can't sing! Because they could tell what anybody with ears—!"

"I've got ears."

She stopped pounding his chest. Her head came up. The tears had sent the mascara down the sides of her face in two thin smears. They made her look more like a Chinese doll than ever.

"I heard what everybody else heard," George said. "Nobody walked out because of that."

She smudged the mascara streaks with two quick brushing movements of one hand. "You *liked* it?"

It was the wrong word for what had happened to him at Chez Shaw. It was no more appropriate for what was happening to him now. He felt helpless. "Dora, listen to me."

She shook her head impatiently. "I don't want to listen."

He was just as glad. The feel of her shoulder blades and the smell of her hair were making his knees shake. Soon he would be unable to handle it. He started to push himself up from the bed. She held on.

"George," she said. "George, you *liked* it?"

"How could I not like it? How could anybody not like it? Don't you know what you've got in your voice? Don't you know what it does to people?"

"Oh, God," she said with a happy sob as she pulled him down on the bed. "Oh, God, darling," Dora said as the shoulder strap of the blue dress broke. "What a fool I am!" she whispered as her lips probed greedily for his. "What a God-damn stupid fool!"

25

The fact that the next day was a Saturday seemed to George, who was in a mood for extravagant figures of speech, to add the final drop of happiness to a cup of joy that was already brimming over in an almost sloppy but undeniably delightful way. On Saturdays the Malvin Gewirtz & Company staff worked only until noon. This meant that unless he dropped dead, which George had no intention of doing, or there was a wreck on the subway, which he didn't believe God would be mean enough to let happen on this particular day, George would be separated from Dora for a mere four and

a half hours instead of the fourteen hours that on weekdays he had
to spend on the job and in his night classes.

"Don't you move," he said as he bent down over the bed at eight
o'clock to kiss her before going off to work. "I want you to be right
there when I get back at twelve-thirty."

Dora smiled lazily and reached up and pulled him down and
kissed him again, hard.

"Don't worry," she said. "I'll be here."

She wasn't. When George got back, promptly at twelve-thirty,
he found a note from Dora thumbtacked over the table he used as a
desk:

*Danny stopped in at eleven. He wants me to have some fittings for
a couple of new costumes. I don't know how long it will take but I
ought to be back by four or five.*

D.

*P.S. There's a special delivery letter for you on the table. Mrs. Shissle
brought it up a few minutes ago.*

George was so disappointed that, for several minutes, he didn't
even look at the letter. All morning he had been in a daze of happiness, reliving every moment of the night before and imagining every
moment of the afternoon to come. Finding the note on the wall was
like being slapped awake with a wet towel. He prowled impatiently
around the room, telling himself it was foolish to be angry. Danny had
no way of knowing how much George had been looking forward to
the next few hours, and Dora could hardly have told him without
embarrassing herself. Besides, she did work for Danny, and new
costumes were important to the job, so she couldn't refuse to go to
the fitting. Furthermore, four or five o'clock wasn't exactly next
year. It was just a few hours. He had waited so long for happiness,
now that he had finally achieved it, surely he could wait a little
longer. Wondering how he was going to fill in the time, George came
back to the table, idly picked up the special delivery letter, and saw
with astonishment that it was from Aunt Tessie. He tore it open and
read:

Dear George:
*Uncle Zisha and I are in the best of health and hope to hear the
same from you. Everything is fine here, thank God, and we hope*

*everything is fine with you. Please don't get excited or worried, but
we have some bad trouble. I can't tell you in a letter what it is. We
must see you right away. By right away I mean this Saturday or
Sunday the latest. Today is Friday and I'm sending this letter special
delivery so you'll have it tomorrow or Saturday. This is good because
you can come to Albany on Saturday and you can go home on Sunday. In this way you won't lose no time from the job. Uncle Zisha
says on Saturday there is a two o'clock train and a six o'clock train.
If you come on the two o'clock I'll have a nice hot supper for you
with kishke and tzimiss the way you like. If you come on the six
o'clock train you won't starve but the supper won't be hot. It's no
good to warm up kishke or tzimiss that you let get cold. It only tastes
dry and sour. Don't disappoint us. Without you we don't know what
to do. We will wait up for you. Hurry up. The trouble is very bad.
Take along a coat on the train. A person never knows where drafts
are coming from. Uncle Zisha is very happy you are coming. When
you hear the trouble you'll know why. Don't forget to take the coat.*

Aunt Tessie

George's mind had been so completely filled with thoughts of
Dora that, for several minutes after he read the letter, its significance
didn't really get through to him. Then, as the hastily scanned words
began to take on meaning, George read them again, slowly, and he
almost wished he hadn't, because he knew he could not disregard
them.

Aside from the common cold, only one thing had ever scared
Aunt Tessie: leaving the safe little nest she had made for herself on
East Fourth Street. Now, it was perfectly clear to George, something
else had frightened her. He could feel the terror behind the neatly
lettered Yiddish words as clearly as he could feel the sheet of paper
on which Aunt Tessie had written them.

Why, he thought with sudden anger, why did whatever it was
that had happened up in Albany have to happen on this particular
day? Why couldn't it have happened last Saturday, before Dora had
finally showed how much she loved him? Or why couldn't it have
happened next week, after he'd had time to adjust to his happiness and
tell Dora about his plans for the future? Why, on this of all days,
did—?

The angry questions stopped racing through his mind. Its natural
inclination to deal in orderly fashion with hard fact, rather than in
hysterical fashion with what might have been, told him that he was

wasting valuable time. The thing to do was find out what the trouble was. Perhaps, if he talked with Aunt Tessie on the telephone, the trip to Albany would not be necessary.

Twenty minutes later, in a phone booth in the corner drug store, George learned that it was impossible to talk with Aunt Tessie.

There was no telephone in the house on Westerlo Street. Mr. Brohmfin, the man to whom Uncle Zisha had turned over his bankrupt business, had apparently fared no better with it. At any rate, according to the long-distance operator, there was no listing in the Albany directory for anybody named Brohmfin, for anybody with a name even remotely like it, or for a soda bottling company on or anywhere near Westerlo Street. Even Mrs. Dougherty, the woman who had owned the ice-cream parlor at the foot of Westerlo Street in which George had once redeemed so many Star bottles first for nickels and then for Oh Henrys, failed him. There was, according to the long-distance operator, a Mrs. Dougherty on Westerlo Street, but she was a housewife whose husband worked for the gas company, she had never owned an ice-cream parlor, and she had her children to take care of and the supper to get ready, so she couldn't go running halfway across the city to call people to the telephone.

George hung up and looked at his watch. Not quite one o'clock. He could make the two o'clock train easily enough. But that would mean he'd miss Dora, who had said in her note that she wouldn't be back from the fittings before four or five o'clock. After what had happened last night, after the way he knew she now felt about him, he couldn't go off to Albany, even for a single day, without first seeing Dora. The two o'clock train was out. He would wait until Dora came home, explain about Aunt Tessie, and then catch the six o'clock train to Albany.

Maybe, he thought with sudden excitement, maybe Dora would even go with him? Why not? It would mean double fare, and now that he had piled up enough credits at Washington Square College and was about to enter law school every penny counted even more than it ever had. But it wasn't every day that the girl you've loved for a couple of years gets around to loving you back. A celebration was in order. Besides, Aunt Tessie had always liked Dora and Dora had always liked Aunt Tessie. They would be delighted to see each other again. Also, the train ride would give George a chance to discuss future plans with Dora. By the time they got to Albany, they might even have things settled enough to be able to announce to Aunt Tessie the date of their wedding.

Excited by these thoughts, George went back to his room to pack the overnight bag he had bought a few days after the nugget of advice that Mr. Rapf, during the Shlansky, Gaylord & Karp audit in Baltimore, had given him about the difference between the way gypsies carry their belongings and the way accountants carry theirs. Packing took exactly five minutes and meant that, even if Dora came home promptly at four, he had almost three hours to kill.

At two o'clock George was still mildly amused by what he was learning about how difficult this form of murder could prove to be. By three o'clock he had no fingernails left. At four o'clock the only reason he was not swinging from the chandelier was that the rooms in Mrs. Shissle's house contained no such equipment. By four-fifteen, even though Dora's note clearly said she might be as late as five o'clock, he was convinced she had been struck by a taxi or a bus and was lying in a pool of her own blood on some lonely sidewalk from which, unless he got to her at once, she would never again rise. George was actually on his way to the door with some vague notion about calling the police for help in finding her, when there was a sharp knock. He emitted a happy yelp, reached the door in a single bound, and hauled it open.

"Your sister just called," Mrs. Shissle said from the other side of the threshold.

Thrown completely off balance by the fact that he was not facing the expected Dora, George stared stupidly at his landlady for several moments. Then he remembered that Mrs. Shissle either believed or chose to believe the fiction he had passed on to her months ago, namely, that Dora was his sister.

"She called?" he said.

"On the telephone," Mrs. Shissle said. "Down in my apartment. She said—"

"Thanks a lot."

"Mr. Hurst, where are you going?"

George, who was halfway down the stairs to the floor below, stopped and turned. Mrs. Shissle's plump, waxen face was creased with puzzlement.

"To your apartment," George said. "To answer the phone. You said—?"

"I said she *called*. She's not on the phone now."

"Oh."

"She said to give you a message."

"What message?"

"I feel sort of foolish shouting it down the stairs."

"Sorry."

George came back up the stairs.

"She said to tell you the fittings took longer than she expected," Mrs. Shissle said. "She doesn't know exactly when she'll be home, but she's pretty sure it won't be before seven or eight o'clock, and you shouldn't wait."

"Wait?" George said. "Wait for what?"

"She didn't say," Mrs. Shissle said. "But I imagine she meant dinner."

"Oh," George said again, and then, seeing that Mrs. Shissle made no move to leave, he stepped around her and said, "Thanks."

"You're welcome, Mr. Hurst."

He went back into his room, closed the door, and stood with his back to it. After a while, when he was able to control his disappointment, he moved across to the table and sat down. He wrote Dora a note explaining that he was catching the six o'clock train to Albany and why, saying he was sorry he had missed her, and adding that he would be back the next day on the earliest train he could get. He thumbtacked the note on the wall over the table and stared at it for a while. It made him uncomfortable. It was cold and impersonal. It gave no hint of what was going on inside him. George took the note down and added a postscript.

I'm not sure that I made myself clear in what I said to you last night. I will try to do better when I see you tomorrow. In the meantime, however, I would like to say this: if the train I'm taking to Albany should be wrecked and I were killed, I'd be annoyed because it would mean I'd never see you again. But I can honestly say that I'd have no right to complain. I've had the best. No man can ever be happier than you made me last night. I intend to spend the rest of my life making you just as happy. I'm glad to be able to put that promise in writing. Don't go out in the street until I come back. Don't get hurt. Don't stop loving me. If you ever did, I'd want to die, and I probably would.

After that George felt much better. He took the subway to Grand Central, caught the six o'clock train, dozed most of the way, and arrived in Albany shortly before ten o'clock. By the time he got to the cab rank across the street from the station, all the taxis were gone. A porter passing by with a loaded luggage cart said more cabs would be along in a few minutes but, giving way to a sudden impulse, George decided to walk.

He had never forgotten the two weeks he had spent in Albany shortly after the Armistice Day disaster in the Forest. But he had not realized until now, a dozen years after that first visit, how much he had carried away from it. As soon as he had stepped out on the sidewalk in front of the railroad station, a whole flood of memories had suddenly come pouring down on him, memories that all at once he wanted to share with Dora.

If only she were here with him, if only she hadn't been delayed by those damned costume fittings, he could be taking her right now to the store on South Pearl Street out of which Uncle Zisha had driven the brand-new red Buick on the morning George went back to New York. He could be showing her the bank where he and Uncle Zisha had gone every day to make the deposit. He could be leading her up the hill to the big white house with the green shutters in which, surrounded by dozens of framed pictures of Judge Brandeis, his ambition to become a lawyer had been born. Above all, George could in a few minutes be introducing Dora to the tall, powerful, handsome man with the magnificent black beard and the booming laugh who towered over all those memories and gave them a dimension that made them seem, like Uncle Zisha himself, a little warmer, a little larger, a little more wonderfully bright and shiny than life itself ever managed to be.

George quickened his pace. He would bring Dora back with him as soon as possible. Maybe even next Saturday. To hell with the fare. That didn't matter. What mattered was for Dora to know what it felt like to turn into Westerlo Street and start the long climb up the steep hill at the top of which—

George stopped. Something was wrong. He turned and looked back. No, he had not made a mistake. The sign on the lamppost was clearly legible. This was Westerlo Street, all right. George turned again, to look up the hill toward the big white house with the green shutters, and the excitement drained away inside him.

The hill he had climbed so often, the hill that had been so steep a dozen years ago, was not a hill at all. It was just a gentle rise.

Uneasily, as though he had received a warning the meaning

of which was not clear, George approached what had once been to him a great white castle, so white that it used to hurt his eyes to look directly at it in the sunlight. He was in front of a shabby frame house clearly capable of causing pain only to the eyes of someone who couldn't stand broken shutters, splintered shingles, and flaking paint. The wide garden that Mrs. Gerstenberger had once tended so lovingly was now a narrow alley of grubby brown sod, in which nothing grew. Not even weeds. The wooden arch that spanned the driveway no longer said in large black and gold letters: "Hurst Soda Bottling Works, Inc." A small cardboard sign was nailed to the weather-beaten arch. On it appeared a single hand-lettered word: "Rooms."

Climbing the porch steps that badly needed mending, George was suddenly glad he had not brought Dora with him. He had wanted her to see Uncle Zisha's house as he remembered it, not as it was now. Through the feeling of sadness and disappointment that had closed in on him, George was grateful to Dora for being alive. The warmth of her body, the freshness of her lips, the delicate bones of her face, everything about her seemed all at once doubly precious. He knocked on the shabby door.

"So why couldn't you take the two o'clock train?" Aunt Tessie said as she opened it. "Now the tzimiss and the kishke, they're both cold!"

George could feel his spirits leap up with relief. There was nothing depressing about Aunt Tessie's voice. She could have been announcing to the world at large what she thought of Mr. Forman, that Hungarian crook who called himself a grocer.

"I had to work all afternoon," George said as he kissed her. "Besides, I'm not hungry."

"If you're not hungry, you're sick," Aunt Tessie said. "And you don't look sick to me, thank God."

"Neither do you," George said, and he added, "Thank God."

They stood there like that, in the open doorway, staring at each other, and George could feel the last of the uneasiness slide away. It had been foolish to be upset because what he remembered as a steep hill was a gentle rise, and a house that had once been white now needed paint. He should have known that nothing could change Aunt Tessie. She didn't seem to have aged at all during the three years since he had last seen her. If anything, in the neat black alpaca dress with the long sleeves and the little white collar that she had always worn on Fourth Street, she now looked younger. There was a brightness in her manner, a sort of peppery, pleased alertness that reminded George of the way Mr. Rapf looked when, after a series of dreary routine audits, he was suddenly assigned to a bankruptcy job that challenged all of his very considerable abilities. Up here in Albany, Aunt Tessie seemed finally to have come into her own.

"Tessie, it's George?"

The thin, high, querulous voice from the living room cut across George's soaring spirits like a cloud obscuring the sun.

"Who do you think it is?" Aunt Tessie shouted toward the living room doorway. "Jack the Ripper?"

Then she saw the look on George's face and she leaned close to him. "Uncle Zisha he's changed a lot," she whispered. "When you see him you shouldn't be surprised."

George wasn't. The word was hopelessly inadequate for what the sight of Uncle Zisha did to him. As soon as he stepped into the living room George understood why, at the foot of the street a few minutes ago, when he discovered that what he had remembered as a steep hill was actually a gentle rise, he had felt uneasy, as though he had received a warning the meaning of which was not clear. It was clear enough now. The tall, powerful, handsome man with the magnificent black beard and the booming laugh was gone. The Uncle Zisha lying on the old brown leather "lunch," his head propped up by a pillow and his legs wrapped in a shawl, was a bag of bones from which the loose skin hung in folds, like moss. George went across the room. There was something in the way Uncle Zisha followed him with his eyes that made George want to look away.

"You got so big!" Uncle Zisha said. "Look how tall! Look at the shoulders! George, a regular Jack Dempsey you grew up to be!"

The moist, lifeless feel of his hand was awful. The frightened look in his eyes was worse. But worst of all was the sound of his voice. It explained why George wanted to look away. Uncle Zisha was jealous, George realized with a feeling of horror. The emaciated old man on the couch was jealous of George's youth and health.

"You look fine," George said. "You look wonderful, Uncle Zisha."

"You mean it?" he said eagerly.

"What do you want he should say?" Aunt Tessie said. "You look terrible?"

A bitter look crossed the gray, worn-out, frightened face. "From this my sister Tessie today gets her pleasure," Uncle Zisha said in his uneven, shaky voice. "To see me like this, a nothing, a skeleton!"

"From living like a shamus in the synagogue you didn't become like this, a nothing, a skeleton!" Aunt Tessie retorted. "You live like a wild Indian, you eat like a pig and you drink like a fish and the nights instead of sleeping you're running around with blond bummerkes, so after fifty years such kind of living, you get what you deserve!"

The righteous tone in her voice was suddenly as meaningful and clear to George as one of Mr. Rapf's balance sheets. No wonder she seemed younger and brighter. No wonder there was a peppery, pleased alertness in her manner. No wonder Aunt Tessie looked as though up here in Albany she had at last come into her own. The wheel of virtue had come full circle. Life, which had thumbed its nose at her for so long, had finally proved her right. The way of the transgressor, which she had always insisted was hard, had sought out her own doorstep to demonstrate that it led to destruction: the broken transgressor had been delivered into her care.

"You're going to stand there a whole night telling George why today I'm sick?" Uncle Zisha said. "He just came from the train. He's hungry. Give him something to eat."

"By me he never yet starved before and he won't starve now," Aunt Tessie said. She turned to George. "While I'm in the kitchen, if he starts telling you how sick he is, don't listen. A whole day long, if you listen, that's all you hear."

"I don't mind listening," George said to Uncle Zisha after Aunt Tessie went out. "What does the doctor say?"

"Doctors," Uncle Zisha said with a sickly little smile. "They should drop dead, all of them. They take your money and they give you bottles and boxes with pills and medicines. To eat they give you celery because it stops the gas. To drink they give you milk because what else should a doctor tell you to drink? So a whole day long it's pills and celery and milk and more pills and you, you're just the same like before. A skeleton. A whole day on the lunch with pillows under the head and shawls on the feet, like a woman she just had a baby. Day in and day out it's the same thing until a person begins to think—" The thin, querulous voice stopped. Uncle Zisha moved his head up a few inches on the pillow. "George," he said, and he might have been pleading for alms. "You remember how Mrs. Gerstenberger used to cook? You remember how we used to eat?

George, you remember the factory? How I used to holler on the men? George, you remember the sack with pennies, how we used to roll them for the bank? George, you remember the red Buick, that salesman's face, when I said you want to sell it, so take out your door and go get some gas? George, you remember?"

"Remember what?" Aunt Tessie said, coming in with a tray. "How you used to be a millionaire? Remember better that in eight days, on the first of the month, we have a mortgage payment to make. Here, George, sit here. The soup eat first, it's hot, and don't forget with the bread."

"Thanks," George said, sitting down at the table from which, when it was in the dining room, he and Uncle Zisha had daily eaten three of Mrs. Gerstenberger's enormous meals. "I see you've moved the furniture around."

"You make from a house like this a rooming house, the only thing you don't move around is the cellar," Aunt Tessie said. "Uncle Zisha wanted you should sleep in your old room upstairs on the second floor, but it's now in there Mr. Singermann. He's a good tenant. I made for you a bed in the dining room, George."

"That's all right," George said. "I don't care where I sleep. How are you making out, Aunt Tessie?"

"It shouldn't get worse, we won't go bothering God with complaints," she said. "All the rooms we have full, thank God, and I got more sewing to do than I have time to finish. Take a bite bread, George. Don't eat without bread."

"Tessie with her bread," Uncle Zisha said. "For the whole world she has bread, but for her own brother it's only celery. George, you still have the silver picture?"

"On the table near my bed," George said. He nodded at the walls of the living room. They were hung with so many pictures of Judge Brandeis that he was reminded of a photographer's exhibit. "I see you've added a few new ones to your collection."

"It's not new ones," Aunt Tessie said. "From all over the house we had to move them in here. There's tenants they like to put up their own pictures."

"There's tenants they have where other people have brains they have dirty rags," Uncle Zisha said. "This Mr. Singermann you think he's such a big hoo-hah, Judge Brandeis on the wall he doesn't want, but a fat slob with cockeye eyes, *that* he likes on his wall!"

"The fat slob with cockeye eyes, it's Mr. Singermann's father," Aunt Tessie said. "George, how is it with the law school?"

"I registered last month. Classes start soon. No, thanks, Aunt Tessie. I don't really want any more."

"He doesn't really want any more! Listen to him! So what will I do with it, a good piece meat like that, if you don't eat it? Throw it out? Eat!"

"I can't, Aunt Tessie. Maybe I'll have some more later. What I want now is for you to tell me what this trouble is that you sent me the special delivery letter about."

As soon as he saw the expression on her face, George remembered the feeling of terror that had come through to him from the carefully lettered words she had written, and he regretted the impatience in his voice. He didn't want Aunt Tessie's feelings to be hurt. But his mind was suddenly flooded with the bright vision of Dora. He wanted to finish whatever it was he had been summoned here to do and get back to her.

"You remember, I suppose, your good friend Mr. Danny Schorr?"

It was the sarcasm in Aunt Tessie's voice as much as Danny's name that brought George's mind back from the bright vision of Dora to the shabby living room in Albany.

"What about Danny?" he said.

"He's becoming eppus a traveler," Aunt Tessie said. "He paid us here a visit on Thursday."

"*Danny?*"

"If you scream like that, it'll bring down Mr. Singermann, and the way that big mouth knows how to talk, it'll be next week till we get rid of him."

"Aunt Tessie, will you please cut out the jokes? You sent me a special delivery letter saying you're in some kind of bad trouble. What's it got to do with Danny?"

"He was here, George," Uncle Zisha said. "He came here Thursday and he—"

"Lay back on the lunch!" Aunt Tessie said sharply. "If you get excited, it'll be Dr. Hirsch again in the middle of the night! Five dollars before he even rings the bell, not counting the medicine!" She turned back to George. "I'm not making jokes," Aunt Tessie said. "Thursday, just before supper, he must have taken the two o'clock train from New York, there's a knock on the door, I go answer it, it's Mr. Danny Schorr."

George had the same feeling he'd had the night before in Chez Shaw when Danny was telling him about his plans to redecorate the place and he kept asking George if he thought five thousand dollars would be enough for the job. George had the feeling that this conversation, too, was getting away from him.

"Aunt Tessie, what was Danny doing up here in Albany?"

"He wanted five thousand dollars."

It was, all at once, like being trapped in a car hurtling downhill to certain disaster. George suddenly knew, as the terror closed in, how it was going to end. Every nerve in his body was screaming at him to leap free while there was still time, not to ask the questions that would weave the web of his own destruction, yet he couldn't stop himself.

"Why did Danny want five thousand dollars from you?"

"It's crazy!" Uncle Zisha's thin, high, querulous voice cut in. "Where are we going to get five thousand dollars? All we have left is this house, with on it already there's two mortgages. If we sell it, and the bank takes the mortgage money, maybe there's five thousand dollars left, but if we give it to this Danny, how will we live, Aunt Tessie and I? Without a house to rent rooms, how will we eat, Aunt Tessie and I?"

"Lay down!" Aunt Tessie ordered, pushing Uncle Zisha's head back on the pillow. "If you talk you'll get sick! Let me talk!" She turned to George. "First, like you, I thought it was a joke. But Danny Schorr that little shkutz lover, him I know from when he was still making in the pants. To come all the way to Albany to make jokes, this momser he doesn't do. So when he finished telling me and Uncle Zisha how he wants the five thousand dollars, instead of taking a broom and sweeping him out of the house like the dirt he is, I said only one thing. If we don't give you the five thousand dollars, I said, so then what?" Aunt Tessie paused. "So then, he said to me, there will be bad trouble for George."

The horror, George thought, was that he couldn't spare himself a single detail. Every one of them fell into place with frightening neatness, from the moment yesterday after lunch when he had walked into the room on University Place with the silk stockings for Dora and found her with Danny, to the moment this afternoon when Mrs. Shissle had come up to tell him Dora had called to say

the costume fittings would delay her until seven or eight o'clock
and he shouldn't wait for her. Of course she didn't want him to
wait for her. If George had waited, he would have missed the six
o'clock train to Albany, and Dora wouldn't have wanted him to do
that. Or rather, Danny wouldn't have wanted it, which amounted
to the same thing, since her every act, George now saw, had been
dictated by Danny.

"George," Aunt Tessie said sharply. "What are you thinking?"

He was thinking about the moment last night when Dora's lips
had hungrily sought his. George was wondering how Danny had
phrased the order covering that.

"Nothing," George said. "Nothing important."

"If you're still so blind you don't understand that little shkutz
lover," Aunt Tessie said angrily, "I'm not! When Danny Schorr
says there'll be trouble, you can be sure there'll be trouble!"

"George," Uncle Zisha said in his querulous, frightened voice.
"What are we going to do?"

George had a moment of envy for the worn-out old man on the
couch. Uncle Zisha was through. Before too long, whether or not
he stuck to his diet of celery and milk, Zisha Hurst would be out
of the race. But George Hurst was only twenty-one. The insurance
statistics said he had almost fifty years of life ahead of him. Now
that Dora was gone, now that he knew she had never been his, how
was he going to get through the next half century?

"You don't have to do anything," George said. "I'll take care
of it."

26

He started taking care of it the next day. As soon as he got off the
train in Grand Central, George went into a phone booth and called
Danny at Chez Shaw.

"If you're not too busy," George said, "I'd like to see you."

"Any guy that's too busy for his friends doesn't deserve to have
them."

If he failed in the night-club business, Danny could obviously
count on earning his living by writing footnotes to *Poor Richard's
Almanac.*

"Then it's all right if I come over in a little while?"

"Why should you come to see me?" Danny said. "I'll come over to see you."

"No," George said. "I want to come to your place."

"Why?"

Because he wanted to see Dora first and get that out of the way, but Danny didn't have to know this. Not yet, anyway.

"What I want to talk to you about involves business," George said. "I'd rather do that on your business premises."

"Okay, if that's the way you want it, kid," Danny said. "When will you be over?"

If he weren't so sure of himself, George thought grimly, Danny would have done a better job of concealing the impatience in his voice.

"I want to stop off in my room to take a shower and change my shirt," George said. "It's ten after five now. Why don't we say six sharp at Chez Shaw?"

"You've got a date, kid."

He had it, George discovered to his considerable annoyance when he opened the door, in his own room after all.

"Hi," Danny said cheerfully from the couch. "After you hung up, I decided it was only fair to save you the trip over to my place. After all," he said, nodding toward George's overnight bag, "you're the one who's been traveling, not me."

George wondered if it was Danny's impatience that had brought him here or whether his instincts, which were always a jump or two ahead of everybody else's, had told him it was probably smarter to get to George before George got to Dora.

"That's right," George said, putting down the overnight bag and closing the door. "I've been traveling."

To hell with wondering what Danny thought or wanted or planned. All that was finished and done with.

"Danny brought a bottle," Dora said from the sink, where she was running tap water into a couple of glasses. "I was just making drinks. I'll make one for you, George. You must be tired."

"Don't bother," George said. "I'm not all that tired."

Dora gave him a quick glance, but Danny didn't seem to sense anything wrong.

"Where you been, George?" he said pleasantly.

"Didn't Dora tell you?" George said. "Or have you got her

trained so she doesn't do any telling? She just listens to your orders and then carries them out?"

Danny, who was lying back on the couch, came up off his spine. "You don't sound to me, George, like a guy who's had a good trip."

"It was a waste of time. So was yours. You didn't have to go up to Albany on Thursday. You didn't have to feed me that line of bull Friday night. You didn't even have to tell Dora to do what she did. You wanted five thousand dollars? All you had to do was ask me, Danny. You'd have got exactly the same answer you're going to get now."

"What's that, George?"

"Go fuck yourself."

Danny's jaw came forward. The skin around his eyes tightened. He stood up. "George," he said. "There's a lady in the room."

"When did she come in? All I see is a whore. Since you're her pimp, there's something I want you to see. It's taken me eighteen years to learn it. I wouldn't want you to get any of the details wrong, so pay close attention. A long time ago, when Mike Gerrity got killed and you needed a place to sleep so the cops wouldn't pick you up, my Aunt Tessie took you in. When you broke your promise to her and walked out without even saying thanks, I told you it didn't matter what you did to me because I was your friend, but it mattered a hell of a lot what you did to Aunt Tessie because she wasn't your friend. I still felt that way two days ago, on Friday, even after what you did to me last year in that L. L. Parker stamp mess. Because Friday, standing there outside Dora's dressing room, the old magic was still working. I have a news flash for you, Danny. The magic stopped working last night up in Albany. There isn't a chance in the world that it'll ever work again. So you just take that bottle, and you get the hell out of here, and don't ever come back."

George walked to the door. He pulled it open and waited. Danny stared at him with a puzzled scowl on his face. He looked like an interpreter who has fallen so hopelessly far behind in his efforts to translate a rapid exchange that in his mind he is groping back toward the beginning of the conversation in the desperate hope of picking up some clue that will enable him to make sense of what he has missed.

"Let me get this straight," Danny said finally. "You mean I'm not getting the five grand?"

"Stop wasting any more of my time," George said. "Get out."

"You dumb bastard," Danny said, his voice rising. "You crazy stupid son of a bitch! Can't you see you'll get it back? With interest? Double and triple and maybe more? Don't you see it's the only thing holding me up? For Christ's sakes, George, use your head! I *need* this dough! If I don't get it, I'm stopped again! The way I was stopped last year! How often can a guy let himself get held up like this?" He came forward and grabbed George by the lapels. "I gotta get going! I gotta get going! God damn it, you boob, nobody's holding me up again! I'm getting that five G's if I have to—!"

Carefully, even though he was off balance, with a hard, downward chop of his fist, George split both Danny's lips. His grip on George's coat loosened. Staggering back with a surprised look on his face, his hand came up. He touched the blood that was beginning to flow freely, and looked down at the red smear on his fingers. Then, making a noise deep in his throat that was partly a growl of astonishment and partly a scream of rage, Danny came forward. This time George was in position. His right fist caught Danny squarely between the eyes. As he started to go down, George's left came up under Danny's chin. There was a faint, sharp, clean click. Danny's tooth hit the floor before Danny did. George reached down, took Danny by the collar and the seat of his pants, swung him slowly forward, then back, and forward again. At the end of the third swing George let go. Danny slithered out into the hall and came up against the far wall with a dull thump. George stepped to the table, picked up the bottle, carried it out into the hall, and dropped it on Danny's lap.

Danny's head rolled back against the wall. His eyes were beginning to puff. "I don't know how long you got to live," he panted. "But this much I can tell you: you'll live long enough to be sorry for this."

"A long time ago," George said, "I heard Aunt Tessie tell you that only by the shkutzim you were still alive. So far as she was concerned you were already dead. That goes for me, too."

He walked back into his room, saw Danny's tooth on the floor, kicked it out into the hall, and slammed the door shut.

Dora, who was sitting on the couch with her glass, drained it. "Now," she said, "I guess it's my turn."

George shook his head. He suddenly felt too tired even to talk. "You missed your turn," he said. "I was going to take care of you before I saw Danny, but he must have guessed that, so he came over and beat me to it."

"If there's anything you didn't want to say to me because Danny was here, I'm ready to listen now."

George shook his head again. None of it had happened the way he had planned it on the train coming down from Albany. The clean feeling was gone. The feeling that had been a part of his rage. His head hurt, and the place where his knuckles had broken Danny's tooth was beginning to throb, and he felt dirty.

"I don't have anything more to say," he said. He sat down heavily on the bed and bent over to undo the laces of his shoes. Suddenly he became aware of movement at the other side of the room. He looked up. "Where are you going?"

"Down to the drug store to give Rita a ring," Dora said. "If she can't take me in, I'm sure Mrs. Hooper will be able to arrange something."

"Oh, for Christ's sake," George said wearily. "Why don't you cut it out? If I haven't hit you up to now, I'm not likely to do it before morning. You can stay here tonight."

"What about after tonight?"

"I suggest you consult Danny in the morning about your future plans. He seems to have them pretty well in hand."

"In that case I guess you'll want this back." She held out a sheet of paper.

Surprised, George reached for it without thinking. It was the note he had written yesterday and thumbtacked on the wall before going off to catch the six o'clock train to Albany. "I guess you and Danny must have got quite a laugh out of this."

"Danny never saw it."

"How come?" George said. "Did you spend last night at Chez Shaw?"

She stared at him for a long moment, and then her hand came up to her mouth, the way it had come up that summer night when he told her in the darkened doorway of her father's doll store that he was going to live in Albany. She turned away and she buried her face in her hands and she started to cry. Desperately, like a fighter faced with a weapon he had not expected to have used against him, George tried swiftly to build a defense by remembering the things he had planned all the way down in the train from Albany to say to her. But he couldn't remember any of them. All he could remember was the way her lips had felt Friday night when she kissed him. Hating

himself, wishing there was some way he could stop, he came across
the room and took her in his arms.

"Why did you do it?" he said helplessly. "Why the hell did you
do it?"

"Because Danny told me to. Because I've never been able to say
no to him. I tried to warn you Friday night. I told you not to listen
to me. I told you it was Danny talking, not me, but you wouldn't
listen. I hate him. I hate him. I wish he was dead. But when he comes
into a room, when he comes near me, it's like—like—like being drunk.
I can't stop myself. I have to do what he says. It's always been like
that. These last few weeks, while I've been here with you, I thought
it was finished. I thought I was free. Then Friday morning, after you
went to work, when he showed up—" She shivered and her arms
tightened around him. "George, save me," she sobbed. "Please,
George, please save me!"

He made one last effort. But it wasn't any good. He wanted her
too much.

"I can't do it alone," George said. Her head came up. She looked
puzzled. "There's only one way," he said. "If we do it together."

"Together?"

"If you marry me," George said.

The puzzled look changed to disbelief. "You still want that?"

"Yes," George said.

The tears came up in her eyes. "I'll make it all up to you," she
said fiercely. "I'll be a good wife, George. I'll learn to cook and sew.
I'll learn to keep things neat. You'll be proud of me, George. You
wait and see. I'll make you happy, George. I promise."

27

She kept her promise. Or part of it, anyway.

Her attempts at cooking were abandoned after a week by mutual
consent, not because the results were inedible—a surprising number
of foods, George found, even when burned to a crisp are still technically edible—but because what ended up on their plates was so small
a fraction of the raw materials Dora bought in the market, that it
was cheaper to pay for tailor-made meals in Stewart's. The same

decision was reached about Dora's sewing after she infected her thumb by running a needle down to the bone while trying to replace a missing button on one of George's shirts. And even though she spent hours every day tidying up, when George came home after work the place always looked like a locker room between the halves of a big game.

But she did make him happy.

Even if she hadn't tried she would have succeeded in that merely by being there, and Dora did try. She seemed to be anxious to make up for the pain she had caused him in the past. She succeeded so well that there were times during the next few weeks when George found it difficult to believe the past had ever existed.

Occasionally when Dora said something bitter about Danny, there would be an incredible moment of blankness in George's mind before the once indelible image of his old friend would come back to him. It was as though his instincts, anxious to protect the happiness he had found at last, had ringed him with a ribbon of wasteland, the way men fighting a forest fire surround it with a fire of their own to create a cleared area across which the forest fire will be unable to move and within which it will be safely contained.

The extent to which the same thing had happened to Dora could be judged, George thought, by the fact that she seemed to have abandoned completely her ambition to become a singer.

She still spent most of her days lying around the room in her pink negligee, but she no longer seemed to have any interest in *Variety* or the gossip columns and, best of all, of course, she was lying around waiting for George. Everything and everybody seemed to be conspiring to make this the happiest period of his life.

For one thing, it was summer and George's law school classes were not scheduled to begin until the first week in October, so they were able to spend the long, warm nights together. Then, two weeks after he threw Danny Schorr out of his room, George was told by Mr. Brodsky that Malvin Gewirtz & Company was so pleased with his work that his salary was being raised to twenty-five dollars a week. This made their plans for the future such a concrete reality that George was tempted to write Aunt Tessie and tell her about them.

"What do you say?" he said to Dora the night he came home with the good news. "Shall I break it to the old folks in Albany?"

Dora smiled and shrugged. "If you like."

It was her invariable answer to every question he put to her. Her likes didn't matter. All that counted was what George wanted. Unfortunately, in this particular instance, George wasn't sure about what he wanted. He wanted Aunt Tessie to know of his happiness, but he didn't want the shrewd old lady in Albany to know that he and Dora had been living as husband and wife.

"On second thought," he said, "I guess it would be better to wait until we're actually married. We can write to her from Brigantine Beach."

This was the place near Atlantic City that, with the help of Mr. Rapf who through a friend provided them with a due bill, George and Dora had chosen for their honeymoon. His two-week vacation from Malvin Gewirtz & Company was supposed to start officially on the second Saturday in August. Thanks to Mr. Brodsky, however, who had told George he didn't have to come in that Saturday, they planned to get married late Friday afternoon.

"Maybe we can call Aunt Tessie long distance before we get on the train for Atlantic City," George said. "Right after the ceremony down in City Hall?"

"If you like," Dora said.

Then he remembered that there was no telephone in the house on Westerlo Street.

"I guess we'd better make it a telegram," George said.

"If you like."

He smiled and took her in his arms. "You know what I like?"

Dora laughed. "A girl begins to get the idea after a while."

"I thought up some new ideas during the day. Want to try them?"

"If you like."

George liked every moment of the next five weeks so much that he was almost sorry when his wedding day approached. Going over the plans with Dora one morning about a week before the big day, he felt a twinge of the sadness that is a part of all endings, even when they are merely the necessary prerequisites to brighter beginnings.

"Here are the train tickets," he said, laying them out neatly on the dresser. "Here's the marriage license, and here's the money for the two weeks at Brigantine. Any questions?"

Dora laughed. "Only a comment."

"Let's have it."

"For giving a girl a feeling of confidence," she said, "there's nothing like marrying someone efficient like an accountant."

"Since you don't have any questions," George said, "may I ask one?"

"If you like."

"Any regrets?"

She nodded gravely. "Yes, one."

"Shoot."

"I'm sorry for all the time I wasted, trying to be something I now know I don't have the talent to be. I'm sorry for the trouble and the suffering I caused by refusing to listen to what my heart told me long ago. I'm sorry I didn't have enough brains to love you from the beginning as much as I love you now."

"I'll feed you vitamins and keep you out of drafts so you'll live to a ripe old age and have plenty of time to catch up."

She laughed again and put her arms around him and pulled him close. "Now may I ask a question?"

"If you like," George said, and they both laughed.

"I don't mind your kidding me," Dora said. "I've really wanted it to be what you liked, all the way. Which brings me to my question. You remember that Sunday night? When you called me a whore?"

"For God's sake, is this the time to bring that up? I was sore. I was boiling. I was saying things that—"

"That happened to be true. Which is why I want to bring them up, if only for the last time. These past few weeks we've both been walking around the subject of Danny, not even mentioning his name, pretending he doesn't exist."

"So far as I'm concerned, he doesn't."

"I want it to be so far as we're both concerned," Dora said. "That Sunday night, when you threw him out, I told you how I hated him, how I always had, but how helpless I was when he showed up, how whatever he wanted me to do, no matter how much I hated it, I had to do it. Remember that?"

George nodded.

"You remember also, before you threw him out you said the old magic no longer worked and then you reminded him how Aunt Tessie once told him that only by the shkutzim he was still alive, by her he was already dead, and now the same went for you?"

George nodded again.

"This is what I wanted to tell you," Dora said. "After these last few weeks, it doesn't matter any more whether Danny shows up or not. The old magic doesn't work any more for me either. I'm finally in the same class with Aunt Tessie and with you. So far as I'm concerned, Danny Schorr is dead."

Three days later George was still so caught up in her words when he walked into the office that Miss Koenig, who served as the Malvin Gewirtz & Company telephone operator and receptionist, had to call to him twice before he heard her.

George stopped on his way across the reception room and came back to her switchboard. "Sorry," he said. "You want me?"

"I don't," Miss Koenig said. "But this guy does."

George took the message slip on which Miss Koenig had written:

Mr. D. S. Cathcart called at 5:30 last night. Wants you to call him this morning. Murray Hill 3700, Extension 692. Urgent.

The only Cathcart that George had ever heard about was the Dean of the John Marshall Law School in which George had registered and where he was to begin attending classes in October. He had never met Mr. Cathcart. He could not imagine why Mr. Cathcart should call him. George would have thought Mr. Cathcart, who presided over a student body that rarely numbered less than three thousand, was totally unaware of his existence. It was a little like receiving a telephone message from the President of the Pennsylvania Railroad just because he had bought a couple of tickets to Atlantic City for himself and Dora.

"May I have an outside wire?" George said to Miss Koenig.

She gave him a line on the reception-room phone. George dialed Orchard 3700.

"John Marshall Law School, good morning."

"Extension 692, please," George said.

"Dean Cathcart's office," a female voice said.

"My name is Hurst. I have a telephone message from Dean Cathcart. It says—"

"Who, please?"

"Hurst. George Hurst? Dean Cathcart called my office last night and left a message asking me—"

"Oh, yes, Mr. Hurst. I made the call for Dean Cathcart. I'm afraid he's not in yet."

"Could you tell me what he called me about?"

"No, I'm afraid I couldn't do that, Mr. Hurst, but the Dean said when you called back I was to ask if you could drop in to see him today?"

"Today?"

"Around three-thirty or four?"

"I've got a job. I can't leave when I want to. The only time I can —How about between twelve and one? My lunch hour?"

"Let me look." There was a pause. "Yes," the girl said after a few moments. "That seems all right. I don't see anything on the Dean's appointment calendar for twelve-thirty. I'll set you down for then, shall I?"

"All right," George said. "I'll be there."

The campus of the John Marshall Law School consisted of six floors in the Fortescue Building on East Forty-second Street. Since the remaining forty-three floors of the Fortescue Building were rented by the sort of tenants who could be found in almost any midtown Manhattan skyscraper, the location of the John Marshall Law School was the subject of quite a few jokes. Most of these dealt with the absence of lawns, which may be why they were not considered to be very good jokes, especially by the founders of the school. They had nothing against lawns. It was merely that their interests lay in another direction. They were interested in providing for people in and around New York City who wanted to study law, but were forced by economic circumstances to support themselves by working during the day, a first-rate school. In this the founders were so successful that, even though they had neglected to provide anything even resembling a lawn, for almost thirty years before George Hurst enrolled in the school John Marshall had ranked favorably with the most beautifully housed law schools in the country.

In the four decades of its existence, from John Marshall's un-ivy-covered halls had gone forth one Supreme Court justice; a governor of the state; two secretaries to Oliver Wendell Holmes; twenty-six members of various federal circuit courts of appeal; the author of the classic *Tischler on Torts*; the man who denied he had written the first draft of Clarence Darrow's summation in the Loeb-Leopold case; three mayors of New York City; a United States attorney general; the Mary D. Santos who, while waiting to be electrocuted for strangling her husband with a garter belt, composed in the Sing Sing death house the famous plea for a new trial that saved her life and caused two major revisions of the Penal Code; at least twelve men who, according to the Collector of Internal Revenue, had earned during the calendar year 1930 one million dollars or more by the practice of law; and a biographer of Lord Coke.

George was aware, as he hurried down the corridor of the Fortescue Building toward Dean Cathcart's office, that he secretly believed Dora was speaking no less than the truth when she had said proudly a couple of weeks ago that some day his own name would be added to this impressive roster. He could feel, as he opened the door of the Dean's outer office, an intensification of the thrill that shot through him whenever, in an idle moment, his glance happened to fall on the silver-framed picture of Judge Brandeis that Uncle Zisha had given him so many years ago. He belonged here. The law was in his blood. With Dora at his side, nothing could stop him from reaching hitherto unscaled heights in the great profession. Perhaps Dean Cathcart had sent for him because, merely from an examination of George's Washington Square College records, the head of the John Marshall Law School had sensed that his institution had once again been fortunate enough to enroll a student who was destined to add luster to the school's name, and he wanted to welcome George in person. It seemed singularly appropriate, to a man as happy as George was, that this should happen less than a week before his wedding day. He could just see Dora's face when he came home with this wonderful piece of news.

"Yes?"

"Dean Cathcart, please," George said to the girl at the desk. "I have a twelve-thirty appointment."

"Oh, you're Mr. Hurst?"

"That's right."

"Go right in. The Dean is waiting for you."

He was a tiny old man with an enormous bald head across which were carefully laid, like strips of bacon on a griddle, several thin strands of white hair combed up from the narrow fringe that still sprouted down around his ears. He wore a rumpled greenish tweed suit, a bow tie that looked like an inexpertly knotted black shoelace, and a troubled expression not at all appropriate to the face of a man about to greet with glowing pride a young genius whose natural talents it was to be his happy privilege to enhance and shape for the benefit of mankind.

"Mr. Hurst?"

"Yes, sir."

"Sit down, won't you?"

Sitting down in the chair beside the desk toward which the old man had nodded, George wondered with a sudden stab of uneasiness why Dean Cathcart should look troubled. He was turning over the papers in George's Washington Square College file. They showed that, in a class of almost seventeen hundred students, he had finished twelfth.

"Excellent, excellent," Dean Cathcart muttered, as though he were addressing himself. He looked up from the file with reluctance, as though he hated to turn from it to other matters. "Mr. Hurst, your records indicate clearly that you are precisely the sort of person we are most pleased to have enrolled at John Marshall."

The words fitted perfectly into the small fantasy George had built for himself about the purpose of this visit, but the tone in which the words had been uttered did not.

"Thank you, sir."

Dean Cathcart had sounded, George realized as his uneasiness mounted, exactly like Mr. Brodsky when he told a Malvin Gewirtz staff member that, even though his work was excellent, business conditions were such that it was simply impossible to give the man the raise in salary he so richly deserved.

"Yes, excellent, excellent," Dean Cathcart muttered again as, with an unmistakable gesture of regret, he closed the file. He looked at it for a long moment and then, with a brisk little shake of his huge head, he lifted his troubled glance to George's face. "Mr. Hurst," he said, "I have a most unpleasant duty to perform. I have been advised that you were involved sometime ago in the theft of a rather large sum in postage stamps from an organization known as L. L. Parker Stores, Inc."

He paused and waited. George waited with him, but for an entirely different reason. George wanted to make sure that, when he spoke, it would be to the point. And the point, he knew even in the moment of shock, was not that he had been a daydreaming fool to imagine the Dean had sent for him because he was so delighted to have a genius like George entering John Marshall Law School.

"I was not really involved, sir, except indirectly," he said. "My name and address were used by the real thief without my knowledge. If you will get in touch with a postal inspector named Sapina—"

"Before I called you at your office yesterday," Dean Cathcart said, "I had a long talk with Mr. Sapina."

"Didn't he explain—?"

"He did more than that," Dean Cathcart said. "Mr. Sapina allowed me to read his report on the entire affair."

Again the old man waited. This time, as the sweat began to gather on George's forehead, he wondered desperately what the Dean

was waiting for. George was innocent. Mr. Sapina had said so. The
report, which George had read, said so. What was this old man getting at?

"Sir?"

Dean Cathcart's fingers, which were absently fingering the black
string tie at his throat, leaped nervously. His troubled glance, which
had been roaming the room as though for help, came back to
George.

"Mr. Hurst?"

"I don't quite understand what—?"

"Oh, I'm sorry, I suppose I should have explained," the Dean
said, speaking with obvious relief, as though the opportunity for
making an explanation was a welcome postponement of the unpleasant necessity to face the issue, whatever the issue was. "In
order to become a member of the bar in this state, Mr. Hurst, or in
any other state for that matter, it is necessary for applicants to do
more than pass a series of written examinations designed to assess
their knowledge of the law. Applicants must also pass the scrutiny
of a character committee, a body of men set up to insure that only
individuals of the highest moral caliber are permitted to practice
the profession of which we are all so justly proud. This scrutiny,
in the case of most applicants, is more or less routine. In the case of
an applicant whose record contains something like the L. L. Parker
incident, the scrutiny is far from routine. It is, I must tell you, Mr.
Hurst, very severe indeed."

"What difference does that make, sir? As long as they have
access to Mr. Sapina's report? I'm sure he told you when you talked
to him yesterday that he was completely satisfied the whole thing
was a—"

"The character committe, I am afraid, will not be as easily
satisfied as Mr. Sapina."

"They'll have to be! If there's nothing more to the whole thing
than Mr. Sapina's report shows, how can they—?"

"*If* there is nothing more, Mr. Hurst."

"I beg your pardon?"

"I said *if* there is nothing more." The old man paused again,
but this time, after a couple of troubled moments, he seemed to
decide that there was no point in waiting. "You see, Mr. Hurst, the
source that brought this matter to my attention made it perfectly
clear that Mr. Sapina's report did not contain the entire story. I

was informed that a third person was involved. A young woman. Mr. Sapina, for reasons of his own, perhaps because he wanted to close the Post Office Department's files, seems to have been willing to omit from his report both the young woman and the role you played in shielding her from the law. I can assure you, Mr. Hurst, that the character committee will not be so accommodating. The burden will be upon you to convince them that no such young woman existed, and that you did not in fact shield anyone. I need hardly add that, if such a young woman did exist, your efforts to convince the character committee to the contrary would involve perjury, which would hardly improve matters." The old man paused once more and then, with obvious regret, as though he still could not abandon the wish that somebody else were uttering the words, Dean Cathcart said, "Your position, Mr. Hurst, is therefore this: no matter how excellent the scholastic record you turn in here at John Marshall during the next four years, and no matter how brilliantly you pass your bar examinations, the obstacle of the character committee will always remain. Unless and until you can eliminate that obstacle, I feel it is my duty to tell you, Mr. Hurst, that you will never be admitted to the practice of law in this or any other state."

He leaned forward, looking worried and helpful and annoyed with himself, like a parent who knows it is wrong to prompt a child at an examination yet cannot stifle the desire to help.

"Do you think you can eliminate that obstacle, Mr. Hurst?" George did not answer. Dean Cathcart's troubled face came forward a few more inches across the desk. "I don't want to pry into your private affairs," he said. "I don't want to ask if there was such a young woman. If there was, then—" The old man paused and shook his head irritably, as though annoyed with himself for choosing the wrong words. "What I am trying to say, Mr. Hurst, is that you need not, in fact you must not, take my word as final. It is merely an opinion. The fact that it is an informed opinion, based on years of experience in these matters, should not be conclusive. You can fight. The character committee will give you an opportunity to fight. There may be a set of extenuating circumstances that, when properly presented to the committee, will make the whole thing—what you did—will place the entire problem in a new light that won't seem so—so—" The old man's voice stopped. He leaned back. His fingers returned nervously to the bow tie, as though seeking help for what he wanted to say. "Mr. Hurst," he said finally. "If there is such a set of extenuating circumstances, and you refrain from presenting them to the committee, I can only conclude that you feel by telling the truth to the committee you would in some way cause injury to this young woman. Is that correct?"

George still did not answer. A touch of impatience came into Dean Cathcart's voice.

"Mr. Hurst," he said, "I must point out to you that if my conclusion is correct, then you must make a choice between your career and this young woman. You must balance one against the other. You must make a choice. Don't you see that?"

George saw it so clearly that he wanted to close his eyes, to turn away, to get up and run from what the kindly old man at the other side of the desk had inadvertently spelled out in huge, mocking letters. What George did not see, what he was unable to tell Dean Cathcart, was how he could face any group of men who had the right to ask questions that would open up the door he and Dora had closed forever. There was no way to go back through that door without retracing the steps that began with the day Dora disappeared from Fourth Street and the night George found her in Mrs. Hooper's apartment. Even if there had been a way, George knew he wouldn't have taken it. He couldn't. Not if he wanted to keep his date with Dora at City Hall three days from now. Since that was the only thing George did want, Dean Cathcart was wrong. George did not have a choice.

"Yes, sir," he said. "I see it."

Later, when he had time to think about his reactions, George understood why his next thoughts were for Uncle Zisha and Aunt Tessie. They had nothing but their ambitions for him. With those gone, what was left for them to look forward to? He, at least, had Dora.

"Are you sure?" Dean Cathcart said sharply.

"Yes, sir," George said. "Quite sure."

The old man scowled, hesitated, started to say something, stopped himself, and then shrugged.

"I take it, then, that you do not intend to assume the burden of appearing before the character committee and attempt to convince them that no such young woman existed and that you did not in fact shield anyone."

"That is correct, sir."

"I suppose you know best."

George knew only that he was helpless.

"What do you suggest I do, sir?"

"Unless you are willing to allow your interest in the study of law to remain forever academic," Dean Cathcart said, "I would recommend strongly that you withdraw your enrollment from this school."

"May I ask one more question?"

"Certainly."

"You spoke about a source that brought the L. L. Parker matter to your attention," George said. "Would you be good enough to identify the source for me?"

"Does that matter?"

"It matters a great deal, sir."

"A man named Daniel Shaw came to see me," Dean Cathcart said.

George nodded. At least that much was no surprise. By the time he was out in the street, he had already begun the process of adjustment. The ambition with which he had lived for so long was gone. But in three days Dora would still be his wife. Danny Schorr could get his revenge by taking away something Uncle Zisha had given George when he was a boy. But Danny could no longer take away Dora.

In the subway on his way back to work, George decided not to say anything to her about the visit with Dean Cathcart. In approximately seventy-two hours he and Dora would be married. In three days they would be starting on their honeymoon. He wasn't going to let Danny Schorr spoil that.

On Friday morning, just before he left the apartment for his last visit to the office, it suddenly occurred to George that Dora might have learned, somehow, what had happened at the interview with Dean Cathcart. She looked worried.

"I'll leave these things here on the dresser," George said casually as he laid out the train tickets, the marriage license, and the money for the two weeks at Brigantine. "My own bag is packed, and by the time I get back here at three o'clock to take you down to City Hall, I expect you'll be packed, too. Okay?" She nodded. "Unless there's something I've forgotten?" She didn't answer. George said, "Is there?"

Dora, who had been scowling at her foot as she pulled on a silk stocking, looked up. "What?"

"I said is there anything you can think of that I may have forgotten?"

She took a moment or two, as though to absorb the meaning of his words, then shook her head quickly. "No, not a thing."

"You sure?"

"Positive."

"You don't look positive. You look—"

Dora smiled quickly. "Cut it out," she said. "I'm just thinking."

George shoved the uneasy feeling out of his mind. "Keep your thoughts on the clock," he said with a grin. "I'll be back in five hours."

Mr. Brodsky, in whom George's marriage was bringing out a sentimental streak hitherto unsuspected by the Malvin Gewirtz & Company staff, arranged for him to be back in four.

"Okay, baby!" George said when he opened the door. "Next stop City Hall! Let's—"

The cheery words stopped in his throat. For a startled moment George thought of stepping back out into the hall to check the number on the door. He seemed to have come into the wrong room. Then he saw his bag on the floor near the dresser, the bag he had packed that morning, and he knew there was no mistake. He knew also, from the simple fact that Dora's bag was gone and even before he had time to take in all the details of the ransacked room, that he had been wrong about the things Danny Schorr could still take away from him.

George walked slowly across the floor, waiting for the pain to hit, stepping on shirts and towels and neckties that had been dragged out of drawers and thrown about like so much wastepaper, moving toward the table beside his bed. On it, face down, lay the picture of Judge Brandeis that Uncle Zisha had given him long ago. Without knowing why he was doing it, aware only that it seemed tremendously important, George picked up the picture and carried it with him to the dresser. Here, like a nurse arriving on the scene of a train wreck and beginning methodically to assess the damage, he bent down to take a close look.

The money he had laid out that morning for the two weeks at Brigantine was gone. The marriage license, however, was still there. So were the train tickets to Atlantic City. But both had been torn in half.

Trying to pick up the pieces, pretending he was unaware of the sick feeling that was beginning to flood up from his stomach into his throat, George became aware of the picture in his hand. Staring stupidly at the long-familiar face of Judge Brandeis, he wondered why all at once the picture looked so different. Then George saw that he was holding an unmounted photograph. The silver frame was gone.

Danny Schorr had never been one to leave anything of value behind.

28

"You know what I think?" Mr. Rapf said.

"Not yet," George said. "But I can see I'm not going to have to wait long to find out."

"You're going to have to wait a little longer than I planned when I invited you into this joint for lunch," Mr. Rapf said. "Here comes that joker who's carrying a torch for the chopped chicken liver."

The bald, emaciated, pasty-faced waiter arrived with the two plates of bean soup.

"That you'll enjoy it, this I'm sure," he said as he set the plates on the cracked white marble table top. "But here in Resnick's not to start with the chopped chicken liver, it's like calling Mrs. Resnick, she makes it herself, it's like calling her a dirty name."

"Give her our apologies," Mr. Rapf said. "We'll try the chopped chicken liver next time we come."

"Who can be sure in this world if he's got a next time?" the waiter said. "You could walk out of here after lunch and fall down dead from a heart attack or get hit by a truck. To die without once tasting Mrs. Resnick's chopped chicken liver, this is a way to live?"

"All right already, for God's sake, bring me some and leave us alone," Mr. Rapf said. "I'm trying to talk to my friend."

"Here in Resnick's, just to do a favor for a waiter," the waiter said haughtily, "I'm sorry, our chopped chicken liver we don't serve." He walked away.

"Jesus," Mr. Rapf said, picking up his spoon. "Where was I?"

"You were just about to tell me what you think," George said.

"That's right," Mr. Rapf said. He swallowed some soup and

shook his head admiringly. "You have to put up with a lot to get at it, but it's sure worth the trouble. This stuff is good. What I think, son, I think you're holding out on me."

"What have I got to hold out on you?"

"That's what I'm waiting to hear," Mr. Rapf said. "You're not the type guy to do something screwy without a damn good reason, and I haven't heard any kind of reason yet, damn good or otherwise."

"You consider it screwy for a guy to try to get ahead?"

"A guy who tries to get ahead by knocking himself out of the box, that I consider screwy."

"Whether or not I'm knocking myself out of the box," George said, "I guess we'll just have to wait and let time answer that one."

"Here's one I don't have to wait for anybody or anything to answer for me," Mr. Rapf said. "Up to a couple of days ago, the two years I've known you, you're a quiet, steady, reliable kid. You're so steady and reliable, especially with this thing you got about becoming a second Clarence Darrow, you drive a guy a little nuts just watching you. You don't smoke. You don't drink. You're offered a crack at a twenty-dollar piece of shtipp for free, you say could you have it in cash, please, so you can add it to your tuition money. You work so hard, and your work is so good, Roland Brodsky makes history by giving you a six-buck raise without anybody twisting his arm. In plain English, you're a nice clean-cut Jewish boy, with practically the whole Scout Law sticking out all over you like warts: trustworthy, loyal, helpful, friendly, courteous, kind, obedient, cheerful, thrifty, brave, clean, and reverent. Amen. And with all that, not a stuffy schmuck, either. In short, somebody any guy with brains would be proud to have for his own son. Up to three days ago, that is. Then, all of a sudden, three days ago, without warning, there's a change. The nice clean-cut Jewish boy I've known for two years shows up with a couple of guns on his hips. Stick 'em up, Em Gee and Company, I'm stealing this account."

"You've got it wrong," George said carefully. "I didn't steal the Perrini account. I happened to mention to Nick Perrini that I'd decided to quit my job with Malvin Gewirtz & Company and go into business for myself, and Nick said I could have the account. That's exactly the way it happened, and I resent the implication that I did anything wrong."

"You can resent it till Roland Brodsky starts handing out

diamond wrist watches like confetti on Forty-second Street and Broadway," Mr. Rapf said. "It doesn't change the facts. Malvin Gewirtz & Company had the Perrini Brothers account for eighteen years. Now, all of a sudden, you've got it. You don't want to call it stealing, you don't like my explanation you're acting this way because there's something you're holding out on me, okay, George, where would you like me to look for a better explanation?"

"In those nuggets of advice you make it a hobby to pass on to young people," George said. "When we first met, the day I got my second pay check, when I asked for twenty a week and Brodsky gave me nineteen and I asked you how come, you said it was a basic economic fact. If you want to get rich, you told me, don't work for a service organization. Look at Malvin Gewirtz, retired at sixty-one in the Florida sunshine, you said. Or look at Roland Brodsky, who is exactly your age and lives on Central Park West and smokes Murads, you told me. And then look at us, you and me, what are *we* doing? We're eating hot dogs for lunch on Sixth Avenue. Well, I looked where you told me to look, and I'm tired of eating hot dogs for lunch. I want some of what Malvin Gewirtz and Roland Brodsky have. I'm never going to get it by working for somebody else, so I've decided to go to work for myself."

Mr. Rapf put down his spoon. "Who you talking to, kid?"

"What?"

"I said who you talking to?" Mr. Rapf said quietly. "Because it's a cinch you're not talking to me."

George could feel his face grow hot. "I know what you're sore about," he snapped. "You've been working for Brodsky for twenty years and you'll be working for him another twenty, if not more, because you're too damn scared to go out on your own. Any guy that does go out on his own, especially if he's younger than you, you figure he's showing you up. Those nuggets of advice you're always handing out, why don't you take some of them yourself? You want to spend the rest of your life kissing Roland Brodsky's ass for a lousy weekly salary, okay, go to it. Not me. I'm not too yellow to take a crack at going it alone."

As soon as the words were out, George regretted them. Mr. Rapf's face was white as he stared down into his soup. His lips, thrust forward in the familiar effort to conceal his buck teeth, quivered slightly.

"There's some truth in what you say," the senior said in a low voice. "But there's a lot of other stuff in it, too."

"I'm sorry," George said. "I didn't mean—"

"For the part that's true you don't have to be sorry. And if you don't mean something, don't say it. Sure I'm scared to go out on my own. I got a wife and three kids. But that's doesn't mean I don't want to see somebody else get ahead. Especially it's somebody I like. Or thought I did."

"Listen—"

"Maybe I will, later. But first you listen. That big speech about how you're sick of eating hot dogs and you want a piece of what Malvin Gewirtz and Roland Brodsky have. I'm going to take a shot in the dark. When a kid as sensible as you starts acting screwy, there's usually a dame involved. That speech, you weren't talking to me. You were talking over my head, to somebody who's not even here in Resnick's eating bean soup and fighting off that bastard with the chopped chicken liver. It's some broad, that's who it is. Or the guy she's walked out on you for. Or maybe both. You think she did it because you're making a lousy twenty-five a week and you still got four years of law school ahead of you and a lot more years of eating canned beans before the caviar and the mink starts rolling in. So you're going to show her, or him, or both. You're going to get to that caviar and those minks before they do, or if he's got them to give her now, you're going to catch up with him fast. You'll show them, boy. You'll show them. You'll show them and the whole God-damn world, too. Right? How about it? Am I right?"

George didn't answer. If Mr. Rapf hadn't hit it right on the nose, he had come close enough.

"Okay," the senior said quietly. "You don't have to answer. You don't have to tell me who the girl is, or the guy, either. I don't want to know any of the details. But this much I want *you* to know: no matter what they taught you in plane geometry at Franklin Pierce High, the shortest distance between two points is not always a straight line. Some trips have to take the long, winding way around. One of those is where you were going. All the kidding I've given you about becoming a second Clarence Darrow or another Judge Brandeis doesn't change the fact that wanting to be like those men is a pretty big and a pretty wonderful thing. It's the kind of thing guys like me and Murph Lasky and Herman Lustgarten haven't got a prayer of becoming. You have. More than a prayer. You've got a damn good chance. No dame is worth chucking that away for. She wants minks? She prefers some other guy who can give them to her now? Let him have her. You're on the way to something better. By the time you get it, there'll be another dame, a better one. Can't you understand what I'm trying to tell you? It's not the lousy Perrini account you took away from Em Gee. It's quitting law school before you've even had a chance to attend a single class. That's what burns me. That's what I don't want you to do. God damn it, you snotty little squirt. What do I have to do, bust out crying? Don't just sit there staring into your soup. Open that kisser and tell me what I want to hear, that you're not chucking it, that when those law school classes start in October you'll be in the seat that all these years you've been saving up for."

For several terrible moments George struggled with the temptation to tell Mr. Rapf why it was impossible for him to say the words the senior wanted to hear. George knew he would probably never get a better chance to obtain some relief from the agony with which he had been living since Dora had walked out on him. He knew Mr. Rapf would listen with sympathy. He knew the mere act of telling it to Mr. Rapf would make him feel better. George knew it. And he knew also that it was impossible. Just as it had been impossible for him, when he was fired from the L. L. Parker mailroom, to ask Mrs. Shissle if she would mind waiting for her rent until he found another job. There were some things, George supposed, that common sense could lift across the senseless barrier of a stubborn, irrational pride. Sharing with anybody the knowledge of what Dora and Danny had done to him was not one of them.

"Sorry," George said, trying to sound indifferent because he couldn't risk sounding the way he felt, remembering all at once the night in the Lord Baltimore Hotel when Mr. Rapf had told him that accountants slept in pajamas, recalling in a sudden, confused rush a hundred other moments when the buck-toothed senior had demonstrated that he felt for George, who had never know his own father, what only a father can feel for a son. "Sorry," George said again, wondering helplessly why it had to be like this, why he couldn't say what was in his heart, knowing that with the single word he was losing something he had not realized until this moment he valued so highly: Mr. Rapf's friendship. "I've decided against becoming a lawyer," George said. "From here on in, I'm a member of your profession for keeps."

The words that rose to Mr. Rapf's lips did not have to be uttered. George could read them clearly in Mr. Rapf's eyes. Just the same, George was glad the arrival of the waiter prevented them from being spoken aloud.

"If you don't like bean soup," the waiter said, "so why do you order it, why?"

"Beat it," Mr. Rapf rapped out harshly, without looking at him.

The waiter jumped back. "Talk like this you can go make by Hitler in Germany," he said. "Not here in Resnick's in the U.S.A."

"I said beat it," Mr. Rapf said through his suddenly bared buck teeth, keeping his eyes fixed on George, "and don't come back to this table till I call you!"

The startled waiter sent a hurried glance from Mr. Rapf to George and back to Mr. Rapf, and then, moving with a nervous shuffle, he went away.

"To the kid I've known for two years I would have given my best wishes at a moment like this," Mr. Rapf said bitterly. "The wise guy I'm having lunch with now, he obviously doesn't need anybody's best wishes."

George was suddenly thinking of the day, more than a dozen years ago, when he was leaving Uncle Zisha's house for the trip back to New York and he was stopped in his tracks by the unexpected tears in Mrs. Gerstenberger's eyes. He wanted to reach out across the table and touch Mr. Rapf. Don't cut me off, he wanted to say. Don't turn your back on me. I'm not what you think I am. It's just that I can't tell you what's happened to me. Some day maybe I'll be able to. Now I can't. Now I can't even think about it. Please don't look like that. Please don't think what you're thinking. Please trust me. Believe in me. Be my friend. I don't have anybody else.

George did not reach out to touch Mr. Rapf. He couldn't do that, either. George cleared his throat.

"I don't know why you're taking this so hard," he said, trying for a light tone, knowing that to the list of reasons for hating Danny Schorr this moment would have to be added. "I'm just going into business for myself," he said. "It's not exactly the same as committing a crime, you know."

"That's right," Mr. Rapf said. "It's not exactly the same. But it's close enough. So close that I'm going to give you one more of those nuggets of advice. If you can stand it, that is."

"I can stand anything," George said.

"I'll bet you can," Mr. Rapf said with unmistakable contempt. "I'm surprised I never realized that about you before."

"Why don't you lay off the character analysis?" George said. "And just stick to the nugget of advice?"

"Here it is," Mr. Rapf said. "Sons of bitches are born, not made. You can't go out and study to be a louse. You've got to have it in you to start. So before you go much further with your new career as a bastard, my advice to you is to examine yourself pretty thoroughly and make sure you've got the raw materials, not just the desire."

He pulled some money from his pocket and put it on the table.

"That's for the bean soup neither one of us ate," Mr. Rapf said. He stood up. "It's a pretty small world, so the chances are that we'll be running into each other again."

The senior took his hat from the hook on the wall and, with hands that shook, set it on his head as though he were an archbishop lowering the crown into place at the climactic moment of a coronation.

"I'd like to make it prefectly clear right now that if and when we do meet," Mr. Rapf said in a voice that shook more noticeably than his hands, "so far as I'm concerned it'll be an accident."

III

III

29

The accident took place in 1939.

It was a cold day in February. George had just come out of a taxi into the lobby of the Woolworth Building, when he saw a tall, stooped figure moving toward him across the marble floor. There was something familiar about the way the upper half of the figure kept bobbing up and down, like the handle of a pump. Then George saw the lips thrust forward to cover the buck teeth and, at the same moment, Mr. Rapf saw George. He stopped short, hesitated, shifted the bundle of ledgers he was carrying to his other hand, and then took a hesitant step forward.

"Well," he said. "Well, for Christ's sake."

"Nice to see you, Mr. Rapf."

They shook hands awkwardly.

"Funniest God-damn thing," the senior said. "I was just thinking about you this morning."

"How come?"

"Didn't you see it in the papers?" Mr. Rapf said. "About Judge Brandeis retiring from the Supreme Court? Eighty-two years old?"

"Oh, that," George said. "Yes, I saw that."

"Made me think of you."

George didn't ask why. He just tried to think of something to say. He couldn't. Mr. Rapf seemed to be suffering from the same difficulty. A number of people hurrying by on both sides turned for a quick, surprised glance. George didn't blame them. He imagined he and Mr. Rapf looked pretty silly standing there like a couple of models in an advertisement for men's winter coats, holding a pose designed to show the many fine features of their garments while they waited for the photographer to click his shutter. Finally, George made an effort and broke the moment of embarrassment by which they were both trapped.

"I don't know what brings you this far downtown," he said. "But I'll bet it'll show up on somebody's expense account."

Mr. Rapf looked startled, as though George had violated the unwritten rules of a pact they had entered years ago and to which, until this moment, they had both adhered strictly. Then he saw George's grin and Mr. Rapf's teeth came into full view.

"You're not kidding," he said through his oddly appealing smile. "Remember Gaylor Karken?"

"The leather man? The one tried to sail to England before we finished the audit?"

"That's the boy," Mr. Rapf said. He lifted the bundle of ledgers a few inches and tapped them with his other hand. "They finally caught up with him. The Irving Trust started a turn-over action."

"My God," George said. "That guy went broke six years ago!"

"Seven," Mr. Rapf said. "But you know the Irving Trust. Like those cops in Canada. They always get their man. I don't know if Karken's got any of the loot left to turn over, but I've just been upstairs testifying for the Receiver, and even though I came downtown in the subway and that's the way I'm going back, on the expense account it's going to show up as Shlepping Ledgers from Thirty-fourth Street to Woolworth Building, Taxis Both Ways, Five Bucks."

George laughed. "Well," he said, "I'm glad to see at least one thing hasn't changed."

Mr. Rapf's smile disappeared. It was as though he had suddenly stepped out of the shadows into the light. His hair, George saw, was completely gray. The skin of his throat was loose and creased, like crumpled crepe paper. Mr. Rapf, who according to George's swift calculation couldn't have been much more than fifty, looked a dozen years older. Carefully, as though he were handling several paper cartons of eggs that were not very securely tied together, the senior set down the bundle of ledgers on the marble floor.

"Yeah," Mr. Rapf said, kneading the muscles of his carrying arm. "Yeah," he repeated in a low, tired voice. "That's one thing that hasn't changed."

"Hey, now, wait," George said. "I didn't mean—"

"I guess that's another thing that hasn't changed," Mr. Rapf said. "You're still saying things you don't mean."

"No," George said, hoping his smile would help. "What hasn't changed is you're still taking what I say the wrong way."

The smile didn't help.

"What's there to take wrong?" Mr. Rapf said. "I'm still just another jerk senior on the Malvin Gewirtz staff, kissing Roland Brodsky's ass for a few bucks a week and chiseling extra nickels and dimes on the expense account. But you?" Mr. Rapf paused and, very deliberately, as though he were spraying George with a hose, he looked him up and down. "You're getting to be quite a boy," Mr. Rapf said. "We've been hearing a lot about you up at the old shop." He reached out and fingered the lapel of George's coat. "Custom-made, huh?" He leaned close and took a long, noisy sniff. "I guess they don't carry that brand of after-shaving lotion in Woolworth's, eh?" He touched the briefcase in George's hand. "Where'd that come from? Mark Cross?"

"I don't know," George said, wishing he could break away without hurting Mr. Rapf's feelings. "It was a present."

"Who from?" Mr. Rapf said. "Bill Prager's daughter?"

"Now, listen—"

"I'd like to," Mr. Rapf said bitterly. "I might pick up a few hints on how to get ahead. Unfortunately, though, I can't stay and do any more listening. I'm just a salaried slob. If I don't get back to the office without wasting any more time, I might find out when I do show up that I haven't even got Roland Brodsky's ass to kiss any more." Mr. Rapf dipped down, picked up the bundle of ledgers, and cocked his head to one side, as though he wanted to get a good look at George from another angle. "Remember that last lunch we had?" he said. "In Resnick's?"

"I certainly do," George said.

"That final nugget of advice I gave you? Before you take off on a career as a bastard, better find out if you've got the talent for it or just the desire?"

"I remember that, too," George said, trying to hold onto his temper. "What about it?"

"From what your old pals up at Malvin Gewirtz & Company been hearing about your activities these last few years, especially in relation to one William Prager," Mr. Rapf said, "I guess you had the talent after all." He turned away.

George reached out, grabbed his arm, and pulled him back. "I don't know what you and my old pals have been hearing," he said carefully. "From the tone of your voice, though, especially in relation to Mr. Prager, I think you ought to know you've been hearing it wrong."

Mr. Rapf shook George's hand from his arm. "Maybe so," he said dryly. "Maybe so." He started to turn away again, then stopped himself. "Let me tell you something, kid," he said, speaking rapidly in a tense voice, as though, after a rambling debate in which he knew he should have done better, he had suddenly stumbled on the winning argument and he wanted to get it out before the timekeeper made him sit down. "In one way or another, to earn our three squares a day, we all have to lick boots. It may not look that way if you're doing it in a custom-made suit, carrying a forty-dollar briefcase, and smelling of imported toilet water, but that's what it is all the same: boot licking pure and simple. I'm not comparing Roland Brodsky's with the pair you're working on. I'm only saying this, kid, and you don't want to forget it," Mr. Rapf said savagely as he started moving away with his bundle of ledgers. "It's just a matter of luck that you've got your kisser planted up against a nice rich shiny pair like Mr. William Prager's."

"Twenty-two," George said to the elevator operator, wishing he could erase from his mind the image Mr. Rapf had evoked. It was the image of Danny Schorr, telling George on East Fourth Street twenty years ago why he didn't care what Dora Dienst said about him and why he'd be damned before he lifted a finger to be nice to her. People believed what they wanted to believe, Danny had said with that complete finality which, even at the age of nine, George had found so impressive. Dora wants to believe I made her a cripple, Danny had said. I could talk myself deaf and dumb and blue in the face trying to prove she's wrong, but she'd still go right on believing it. I'm not talking myself deaf and dumb and blue in the face for a dopey dame with a gimpy arm. Nuts to her.

Mr. Rapf, as well as George's other old pals up at Malvin Gewirtz & Company, obviously wanted to believe that George's success since he had gone into business for himself was due entirely to the fact that he had become one of William Prager's toadies. It wasn't true, of course, but that's what Mr. Rapf wanted to believe. George wished he could handle the situation the way Danny Schorr would have handled it. He couldn't. Even in his own mind George couldn't say nuts to Mr. Rapf.

"Twenty-two, sir," the elevator operator said.

Walking up the corridor from the elevator toward William Prager's suite of offices, George forgot all about Mr. Rapf. He was suddenly remembering, as George always did when he stepped out on the twenty-second floor of the Woolworth Building, how puzzled he had been on his first visit by the location of Prager's office. It was said in New York's more caustic real estate circles that the enormously wealthy broker owned more of Manhattan than the Indians had turned over to Peter Minuet for the legendary twenty-four dollars' worth of trinkets. And it was a fact George had heard from Prager's own lips that he did not own a square inch south of Twenty-third Street. It seemed odd, therefore, that Prager should choose to administer his huge holdings from a place so far downtown. After all, he could have had without even asking, since he owned them all, the choicest space available in any one of twenty-three of the finest office buildings in mid-town Manhattan. To disregard these in favor of setting up headquarters in the Woolworth Building struck George as being a good deal like deciding to run the British Empire from Miami. It probably could be done, but there was bound to be a great deal of waste motion. By the time he had made three or four trips to William Prager's office, George noticed a significant thing: the waste motion was all on his part. He began to understand something about William Prager: he liked not only to have people come to him; he also liked them to know when they got there that they had made something of a journey.

"Hello," Mrs. Zettel said when George came into the outer office. "I'll bet this is one day, Mr. Hurst, you wished you didn't have to come all the way downtown to a meeting."

She was a matronly woman of fifty, with complicated gray hair bound tightly in a black net, who looked out of place behind a switchboard. So did the rest of William Prager's many office employees. They reminded George of Hadassah members who, dressed for a committee meeting, have paused on their way out of the house to see that the roast in the oven is browning nicely. Most of them were middle-aged married women, related to William Prager either directly or by marriage, whose husbands did not earn enough to support their families.

"It sure is cold," George said. "Mr. Dworkin get here yet?"

"A few minutes ago," Mrs. Zettel said. "He's in with Mr. Prager now." George felt a twinge of irritation. He and Albert Dworkin, who had been William Prager's lawyer and right-hand man for thirty years, did not like each other. If Dworkin had got here first, he was bound to make some crack about George being late. "Mr. Hurst is here," Mrs. Zettel said into the phone. "All right." She pulled out the plug. "Mr. Prager said to go right in, Mr. Hurst."

"Hello, George," William Prager said from behind his desk. "Come sit here by the radiator. You look cold."

"Hello," George said. "It's pretty nippy out. Hello, Al."

"Hi, son," Albert Dworkin said and, after an ostentatious glance at his wrist watch, "Better late than never."

William Prager released one of his noncommittal chuckles. He must have known, even though George had never said a word to him about it, how George and Albert Dworkin felt about each other. And Prager, who was as quick and perceptive as anybody George had ever met, must have been aware that the reason Dworkin disliked George was that the lawyer was intensely jealous of anybody who might conceivably be a threat to his position as Prager's closest and most confidential adviser. Yet William Prager preferred to act as though George and Dworkin were very close friends. On top of that, even though he was careful not to take sides, Prager never failed to indicate that he was amused by the digs George and Dworkin were constantly taking at one another. Prager's attitude was not unlike that of a sultan who, in order to keep them at the top of their form and therefore in the best possible condition for his purposes, deliberately allows two members of his harem to think they are his favorites.

"I ran into someone down in the lobby as I came into the building," George said, directing his words at William Prager so that they wouldn't sound too much like what they were: a reply to Albert Dworkin's crack about his being late. "Man I used to work with when I was just a kid out of high school. He taught me pretty nearly everything I know. Wonderful guy. Hadn't seen him in I don't know how long. I couldn't just say hello and run."

"I know how that is," Albert Dworkin said. "There's this old geezer I clerked for when I first got out of law school. Marvelous man. Really marvelous. No matter how busy I am, I make it a point to have lunch with him a couple of times a year. You know how it is. You feel that way about somebody, I hate to let the relationship depend on my running into him by accident in an office building lobby."

William Prager chuckled again. He was a small, slender, extremely neat-looking man of sixty with a narrow, bald head that gleamed as though it were polished. He had a knife-thin hawklike nose on which a rimless pince-nez shivered constantly. His prissy little bud of a mouth was sunken above a pointed chin that curved upward, like the toe of an oriental slipper, as though trying to meet the downward sweep of his nose. He reminded George of a benevolent eagle in a Brook Brothers suit that had acquired a nervous habit hitherto unknown to ornithologists: Prager was constantly opening his mouth in a small, tightly controlled oval, as though he were about to blow a smoke ring, and running the beautifully manicured thumb and forefinger of one hand delicately down the corners, as though he were probing for some flaw in its pink perfection. When something really amused him, as Albert Dworkin's remark now clearly did, William Prager repeated the gesture twice. It was for him the equivalent of a belly laugh.

"I guess lawyers have a lot more time than accountants for lunches with their old teachers," George said as he put his folded overcoat on the window ledge, sat down in the chair at the other side of the desk, and opened the briefcase Rosemary Prager had given him for Christmas. "Either that, Al, or you've been concealing a sentimental streak that I must admit, during the five or six years we've known each other, I never would have suspected a tough businessman like you possessed."

George was pleased to note, as he pulled the papers out of his briefcase, that William Prager added two strokes of the lips to his chuckle. That evened things up with Dworkin.

"Tough businessman?" the lawyer said, his eyes spreading wide. "Me?" He turned to William Prager. "How do you like that, W. P.? You think I'm a tough guy?"

"Instead of exploring our characters, suppose we get down to business," George said. "You may be lunching with one of your old teachers, but I've got to be uptown at one o'clock to meet a client who thinks the Collector of Internal Revenue is carrying on a personal vendetta against him. May I start, W. P.?"

William Prager, who was chuckling and stroking the corners of his mouth, nodded without interrupting either activity.

"I closed the books of your father's firm, as I always do, as of

December 31st," George said, looking at the papers in his lap. "For the calendar year 1938, Leo Prager, Inc., showed a net loss of $34,-268.18. Since the net worth of the corporation as of December 31, 1937, was $32,149.29, this means that as of December 31, 1938, your father's company, W. P., was actually insolvent to the tune of $2,-118.89. Operations for the first month of 1939 were no more profitable than they have been for the past six years. In actual fact, operations for January resulted in a loss of $3,987.46. The company as of the end of last month was actually insolvent, therefore, to the extent of $6,106.35. The company has been losing approximately $36,000 a year for the past six years, or roughly $3,000 a month. There is no reason to believe the situation will change in 1939. So we can look to a loss of an additional $33,000, give or take a few hundred dollars, during the remaining eleven months of this year. I would say, therefore, that to wipe out the present insolvency of $6,106.35, and to keep the company on its feet for the balance of this year, will take an investment of fresh capital in the sum of $39,106.35 or, in round figures, $40,000.00."

George looked up. He had made this report, in almost the same words and using almost the same figures, five times before. The first time, which also happened to be the first time he had come to the Woolworth Building and met William Prager, George had looked up from his papers with a sinking feeling in his stomach. Leo Prager, Inc., was the second account he had picked up when he went into business for himself. He hadn't really picked it up, either. The account had been steered to him by Nick Perrini.

"It's not much of an account," Nick had said six years ago when he was urging George to take it on. "The damn thing pays only forty a month, and there isn't a Chinaman's chance that it'll ever pay more because the business is deader than Kelcey's nuts, but the old guy that runs it, Leo Prager, he's the father of this Bill Prager."

"The real estate man? *William* Prager?"

"That's right. He owns about half of New York City, including the loft building I got my factory in, which is how I know him and how I know about his old man's business and the trouble they have getting an accountant to take care of the old guy's books. The way I figure it, George, you're just starting out. Every dime counts. What the hell, forty a month is forty a month. Besides, you do a good job on the old man's books, it's bound to lead to other things with Bill Prager himself."

It hadn't. Five years ago, however, when George had come to William Prager's office for the first time to give the wealthy real estate broker a report on the state of his father's affairs, George didn't know that it would not lead to other things. He knew only that his first year in business had been rough, that he had managed to do little more than cover his expenses, and that unless he picked up some new business fast he might be forced before long to drop in on Roland Brodsky and ask if there was any chance of getting back his old job with Malvin Gewirtz & Company.

He didn't realize, until he finished reading that first report to William Prager and his lawyer, how much he had been counting on picking up that new business here in this Woolworth Building office. George did realize, as soon as he finished reading the report, how foolish he had been to entertain such hopes. The report was so dismal that he was sure the men listening to it would be too depressed to think of anything but their own dreary problems. It was with a feeling of shocked astonishment, therefore, that George had looked up to find both William Prager and his lawyer staring at him with the sort of pleasant but unconcentrated smiles that parents turn on children who have just recited a lesson to which the grownups have not listened very carefully.

After five years and five similar reports, George was no longer shocked or astonished. He was not shocked or astonished now. He knew what to expect.

"Well," Albert Dworkin said, as he had said five times before, "I guess that's not too bad, W. P., is it?"

"No, I guess not," William Prager said, as he had said five times before. "Draw the check, will you, Al?" He turned to George, smiled as he ran thumb and forefinger down the corners of his open mouth and, as he had done five times before, he said, "Thank you very much, George. That was a very clear and admirably presented picture of the situation. I am most grateful to you."

George started to thank him, as he had thanked William Prager five times before, and as he had done at this moment in the five previous meetings, George started to put the papers back in his briefcase. Then, before he was aware that he had come to a decision, the words stopped in his throat and his fingers stopped poking at the papers.

"If you don't mind my saying so," George said, "I don't think Al ought to draw that check."

The two men stared at him the way, five years ago, George had stared at them: in shocked astonishment. It was as though a neophyte, in the middle of helping two high priests with the performance of an ancient religious ceremony, had without warning injected a completely new and obscene variation into the ritual.

"I beg your pardon?" William Prager said.

For a moment George hesitated. Not to consider the consequences of what he was about to do, which were bound to be at least uncomfortable and might be disastrous, but to wonder why he was doing it. Later, when he had time to think it through, he saw it all clearly.

The accidental meeting with Mr. Rapf in the lobby had upset George more than he realized or cared to admit to himself. What Mr. Rapf and George's former pals up at Malvin Gewirtz & Company believed was not true. He had not succeeded in making a go of it on his own because he was handling the books of William Prager's many successful ventures. George knew very little more about William Prager's business affairs than Mr. Rapf did. The only direct business connection between George and William Prager was today exactly what it had been six years ago: the account of the real estate broker's father, Leo Prager, Inc., an account that still paid George what it had paid him then: forty dollars a month. That was the truth, and if Mr. Rapf or anybody else wanted to think different, that was all right with George Hurst.

At any rate, it had been all right down in the lobby. Up here in this office on the twenty-second floor, however, it was suddenly somewhat less than all right. Because up here in this office on the twenty-second floor George was suddenly intensely aware of a fact that, during the rest of the year, he was able to disregard: at least three quarters of the first-rate accounts George now had on his list, the clients whose lucrative fees enabled him to wear the custom-made overcoat and buy the imported after-shaving lotion for which Mr. Rapf professed to have so much contempt, had come to George Hurst because of William Prager.

Indirectly, true. But still because of.

Because George had met someone at Prager's house, or because someone he had met at Prager's house had said something to someone else, or because someone had heard that George went to Prager's house, or for any one of a dozen variations that, no matter how far afield they wandered, always came back to the same basic reason that could be expressed as follows: if this man Hurst is good enough to be William Prager's friend and handle the books of William Prager's father, then he's good enough to handle mine.

Yet what was wrong with that? The fact that William Prager liked George Hurst was admittedly a lucky break for George Hurst. But did the fact that George Hurst went to William Prager's house for dinner make George Hurst a toady?

Not down in the lobby of the Woolworth Building, it didn't.

Up here in this office on the twenty-second floor, however, George could suddenly hear much more clearly a good deal of what Mr. Rapf had said downstairs. "In one way or another, to earn our three squares a day, we all have to lick boots." How else, George Hurst was suddenly asking himself, could he describe this farce in which once a year he played his part with a completely straight face?

"I said, W. P.," George said carefully, "I don't think Al ought to draw that check."

"Aren't you stepping a little out of line, there?" Albert Dworkin said sharply. "Drawing the check, George, that's none of your business. Your business stops with presenting the figures."

"That's what I thought, too," George said. "That's what I thought these past five years. I don't think that any more, Al."

"Well, that's just too bad," Albert Dworkin snapped. "Because we're not interested in your thoughts. Only in your figures."

"Just a moment," William Prager said, and he paused to give the corners of his mouth an extra rub. "I'd like to hear what George has to say."

"It isn't much," George said. "As a professional man, however, I don't see how I can avoid saying it. I think, W. P., that you ought to liquidate your father's business."

"Oh, for Christ's sake," Albert Dworkin said irritably. "What do you think we are? Kids? We know what we're doing."

"Albert, please," Mr. Prager said, and he turned back to George. "Will you explain why you think that?"

George sent a quick, suspicious glance at the neat little man behind the desk. William Prager was no fool. He didn't need explanations for matters involving profit and loss.

"Isn't that pretty obvious, W. P.?"

Prager's pince-nez shivered crazily as he dipped his head in a short nod. "Perhaps it is," he said. "I would still like to hear you spell it out, George."

There was an odd little note of urgency in his voice, as though he felt he was about to hear a piece of information for which he had waited a long time.

"Six years ago, when I took on the account of Leo Prager, Inc.," George said, "I thought your father's company was having a bad time for the same reason so many other companies were having a bad time, namely, the country was in a depression. We're no longer in a depression, W. P., but your father's business continues to lose money. The reason seems to me so apparent that it embarrasses me to have to point it out to someone like yourself."

"Don't be embarrassed," William Prager said. "Just be clear."

"At one time your father may have been the biggest feather wholesaler in New York," George said. "I don't doubt it. But that was in the days when women wore feathers. They don't wear feathers any more, and I doubt very much that they're ever going to start again. All those tons of aigrettes and birds of paradise and what not that he's got stacked in his storerooms, it's almost fraudulent to give them a value as inventory on a balance sheet, even though the figure can be substantiated with bills that go back to 1901 and 1902 to prove what he paid for them. You and I know that the stuff is valueless, W. P. You and I know that weeks go by without a customer coming into the place. You and I know that there really is no business there. The fact that year in and year out the loss runs to almost exactly the same figure, three thousand a month, proves my point. That three thousand is overhead pure and simple: rent, telephone, electric light, salaries, and so on. As long as your father remains in business, he will lose three thousand dollars a month. Unless the landlord of his loft building raises his rent, or he gives his employees a raise in salary, in which case he will lose more. It's not a venture conducted for the purpose of profit. It's a pension fund for the people who eat up that three thousand dollars each month. I am not retained to audit the books of a charitable institution. I am retained to audit the books of a business venture. Leo Prager, Inc., has ceased to be that. For me to continue auditing its books for a fee under the conditions that now exist makes me a fool or a thief. I don't like to think of myself as either. I recommend that, instead of writing a check to cover the losses for this coming year, you liquidate the business at once."

There were several moments of silence during which Prager, keeping his glance fixed on George, stroked the corners of his mouth, and Albert Dworkin, keeping himself under control by a visible effort of will, stared at Prager as though waiting for the broker to leap across the desk and punch George in the nose.

"You understand, of course, George, do you not," William Prager said carefully, "that I don't write this check every year because I believe the women of America will one day go back to wearing aigrettes and birds of paradise and my father's concern will then become once again what it used to be, namely, a sound business venture."

George nodded. Now that he had spoken his piece, he felt a little foolish: the man for whose benefit he had spoken it was not present. Mr. Rapf was somewhere on the I.R.T. subway, shlepping the Gaymir Karken ledgers back to Thirty-fourth Street.

"Yes," George said. "I understand that."

"I write that check every year," William Prager said, "so that my father will continue to have a place of business to which he can go every day."

"I understand that, too," George said, wishing he had kept his big mouth shut.

"And if W. P.'s father doesn't have a place to go every day," Albert Dworkin burst out angrily, "it'll kill him, that's what it'll do! Do you understand that, too?"

George, who wished he could, saw no way of backing down now.

"Perfectly," he said.

The lawyer stared at him with disbelief, turned to William Prager as though he expected the broker to order George out of the office and then, seeing that William Prager was merely rocking himself gently back and forth in his swivel chair, Albert Dworkin turned back to George.

"And I'm the guy only a few minutes ago you were calling tough!" Dworkin said witheringly. "Why, you, you, you young wise guy, you haven't even got a heart, that's what you haven't got! W. P.'s father happens to be ninety-two years old! Did you know that, too, before you started making your wise guy recommendations?"

My God, George thought, how did I get into this?

"Figures are my business," he said.

Albert Dworkin blew out his breath in an explosion of frustrated rage. "Listen, W. P.! This—!"

"Not now," Prager said quietly. "At the moment I'm listening to George. Perhaps he will tell me something."

"Whatever you want to know," George said.

"Would you recommend this course of action even if you knew it would kill my father?"

Well, George thought, that ties it. Mr. Rapf and George's old pals up at Malvin Gewirtz & Company were hardly likely to hear any more stories about the friendship between George and William Prager.

"As a professional man," George said calmly, "I'd have to."

"Jesus Christ!" Albert Dworkin cried. "You ever hear such a cold-blooded son of a bitch of a thing in your life?"

"Shut up, Al," William Prager said. "One more question, George, if I may?"

"Of course."

"You realize that if I follow your recommendation and liquidate my father's business, you automatically lose a client?"

George thought he'd be lucky if that was all he did lose.

"I realize that," he said.

There was a long silence. William Prager broke it.

"It just occurred to me that there is still one more question, George."

"I'll be glad to answer it if I can."

"What are you doing for dinner tonight?"

George looked at the older man in astonishment. What was going on here? Albert Dworkin, to judge by the look on his face, obviously knew: W. P. had gone off his rocker.

"Nothing special," George said. "I was going to work late and then pick up Rosemary after the rehearsal."

William Prager nodded, sending the pince-nez into a wild, shivering dance. He didn't look like a man who had gone off his rocker. He looked like a man who, after waiting patiently at a traffic light for a long time, had finally received the signal to go ahead.

"You'll still be able to pick up Rosemary even if you come and dine with us," William Prager said. "I hope you can, George, because there's something of vital importance I want to discuss with you."

30

That night, as the elevator carried him up to the Prager apartment at Seventy-first Street and Park Avenue, George was aware of a sense of excitement. It was as though the final piece in a jigsaw puzzle at which he had worked for a long time was about to fall into place.

He had never understood his relationship to the Pragers. He had enjoyed it, and he had profited by it, but he had also been made uneasy and mystified by it. George had no doubt, from the way W. P. had sounded when he said at the meeting that morning in the Woolworth Building that there was something of vital importance he wanted to discuss with George at dinner that night, that the mystery was going to be solved at last.

The elevator stopped. George stepped out into the foyer dominated by the Rodin bronze of a brooding St. Joan, and pressed the buzzer. The door moved inward with a slow, massive grandeur that reminded George, as it always did, of a newsreel shot he had once seen of the raising of the portcullis at Windsor Castle.

"Good evening, sir," said Boland.

"Good evening," said George.

Handing his hat and coat to the butler, George wondered suddenly how much of his uneasiness about the Pragers was due to Boland. It was certainly not due to the fact that, until five years ago, George had never met anybody like the Pragers. When you were young, every time you met new people the odds were at least good that you had never met anyone like them. Before he went to work for Malvin Gewirtz & Company, for example, George had never met anybody like Roland Brodsky or Mr. Rapf or Herman Lustgarten or Murph Lasky. But none of these men had made him uneasy. Even though they were new to George, the way a kid whose family moved into the tenement down on East Fourth Street used to be new to him, there was something about all of them that George found reassuring. It was as though he were a baseball player, coming to bat for the first time in a game with a team he had never before played against, and he noticed that the pitcher delivered the ball with his eyes tightly closed. As a batter George would certainly find this interesting, and probably even startling, but there would be no reason to feel uneasy. After all, the man he was facing, though admittedly odd, was odd within a recognizable framework: he was a ball player.

The trouble with the Pragers, George found, was that while they looked like ball players, so to speak, they didn't make him feel as though he was in a ball park: it was a Jewish household but, when he was in it, George did not feel comfortable and at ease, the way he used to feel in the tailor shop with Aunt Tessie and, later, in the completely Jewish atmosphere of the Malvin Gewirtz & Company offices. Even though the Pragers were Jews, in their home George always felt the way he used to feel as a kid when, having forgotten for the moment his terror of the shkutzim, he found himself on the sidewalk in front of Gerrity's, or the way he felt later when he was forced as an employee in the L. L. Parker mailroom to listen to Mr. Shumacher's jokes about heebs. It didn't seem right to feel that way with people named Prager.

"Miss Rosemary asked me to give this to you when you arrived, sir."

"Thanks."

George took the envelope from the butler, slipped it into his pocket and, as he checked the knot of his black bow tie in the foyer mirror, he decided that very little of his uneasiness about the Pragers was due to Boland. Not because butlers had become old stuff to George. The Pragers were still the only people he knew who had, or could afford, a butler. It was simply that after five years of handing over his hat and coat to a man who managed, without moving a muscle in his face, to look as though he were receiving a bedpan just used by Typhoid Mary, that particular novelty about the Pragers had lost its capacity either to embarrass or impress George. This was not true of the rest of the household.

"Will you go down, sir?"

It was the only home George knew in which you went down rather than into the living room: the entrance to the Prager triplex was on the second floor.

George nodded to Boland, stepped out on the small landing of the circular stairway that had been shipped stone by stone from the bell tower of a fourteenth-century abbey on the Rhône, and saw with some surprise that there were already at least thirty people in the room at his feet. George had assumed, from the way W. P. had sounded in the morning when he had mentioned the matter of vital importance he wanted to discuss, that the matter was also confidential. But George could see, as his glance moved swiftly from group to group in the room below, that this was going to be what he had come to identify as one of the Pragers' Ball Rolling dinners.

Until he met the Pragers the word dinner had always been associated in George Hurst's mind exclusively with food.

On East Fourth Street it had meant the large meal Aunt Tessie served at noon on Saturdays and Sundays as opposed to the rest of the week, when the big meal of the day was served in the evening and identified by Aunt Tessie as "sopper." On University Place, during the happiest time of his life, dinner was what he and Dora ate in Stewart's after he came home from work and before he went to his classes at Washington Square College. During the lonely year after Dora disappeared on what was to have been their wedding day, and before he met the Pragers, dinner for George had been some inexpensive combination of meat and vegetables consumed hurriedly any time after sundown in whatever cafeteria happened to be nearest at the moment when it occurred to him that maybe he was feeling more depressed than usual because he had put nothing into his stomach for seven or eight hours.

In the triplex at Seventy-first and Park, George learned that his notions about the meaning of the word dinner before he met the Pragers were not unlike the notions held by cartographers about the shape of the world before Columbus sailed west. There was a lot more to it than the consumption of food.

Most of what there was to it had been spread out, during the past five years, for George's inspection. Or so he had thought until this moment. It had not occurred to him before that W. P. would want to discuss a confidential matter at a Ball Rolling dinner.

Confidential matters were usually discussed at Gloves Off dinners, gatherings of no more than ten or twelve at which people connected in one way or another with a Prager project that was either not going well, or going so well that new thinking was required to bring out all its potentialities, were given an opportunity to state their views with complete frankness. Ball Rolling dinners were large affairs at which all sorts of people who might be useful to a Prager project that was still in the planning stage were gathered together with the intention of isolating from the herd those best qualified to set the project in motion.

Staring down at the herd, which was broken up into small groups, each one serviced by a uniformed maid who hovered efficiently on the outskirts and kept its members supplied with drinks and hors d'oeuvres, George saw that Mrs. Prager was waving to him. She was standing near the caviar tray, under the Grant Wood portrait of herself. George waved back and started down the steps toward her. It was not a simple journey.

The group at the foot of the stairs, which seemed to consist entirely of martini drinkers, was gathered around a gaunt woman with fiery eyes who worked for a French news syndicate and held her glass pressed to one breast with both hands, as though it were a bouquet of flowers, while she hurled at her spellbound audience the harsh, raking phrases of what sounded to George like an accusation.

"Consider the pattern," she said. "Open your eyes and consider the pattern. First, there is your Clarence Streit, in public and for at once, now, to happen immediately, he advocates a merger of the Scandinavian and the North Atlantic democracies for a common self-defense. On January the four, your President Roosevelt speaks to your Congress. It is his annual message. What does he stress, your President? Revise the Neutrality Act of 1937, he stresses. And the next day. Again. January the five. To Congress your President Roosevelt sends his budget message, and what is on it? For national defense he requests in dollars $1,319,588,000. Two days later. January the seven. In California. Your Governor Olson, to Thomas J. Mooney, after twenty-three years in prison, he grants a pardon. Why? Do you not see the pattern? To divert the liberal clamor of your nation from Free This Tom Mooney to Help Us Prepare for War. That is the pattern. It is clear and obvious. The cry sounds through the land. Listen and you will hear it. Help Us Prepare for War!"

George edged his way around the group and ran into Leonard Prager, W. P.'s younger brother. He was carrying two highballs.

"Hello, George," he said. "Here, take one of these. You look parched."

"Hello, Leonard. It's that bloodthirsty French dame. Just listening to her, I could feel myself being ordered out by a tough top sergeant on a long hike in the broiling sun wearing a heavy winter uniform and no water for miles around."

"For an accountant you certainly have a vivid imagination. All that woman brought to my mind was that for a nation that's supposed to be famous for its nookie, the French certainly choose some dreary specimens to export. Here, have one of these."

"Thanks, but I'd better not deprive whoever it is you're carrying it to. I'll pick one up in a minute. I was just going over to say hello to your sister-in-law.

"You should learn to conceal your anxieties a little better. My brother and his wife are pretty demanding, but they're not unreasonable. You won't get a demerit for being tardy."

George could feel his face flush. Of all the Pragers, Leonard was the one who made him feel most uncomfortable. He was an extremely thin man of forty with a mean smile and a waspish tongue who taught English literature at City College. Rosemary Prager said the trouble with her uncle Leonard was that he was jealous of her father, and even though George could see how a man living on a college instructor's salary might be resentful of an older brother as rich as William Prager, somehow George didn't think that was the whole story. He wasn't particularly interested in the rest of the story. When George found himself near Leonard Prager he always wanted to get away. It was not always easy.

"You know something, Leonard?"

"If I don't, it's amply plain from your flushed face that the gap is about to be filled."

"You're just about the rudest son of a bitch I've ever met."

Leonard Prager's eyes twinkled. "I don't doubt it," he said. He leaned close, jerked his head toward a group behind him, and winked as he added, "That's the boy to keep your eye on, George. The one with the warts."

George gave Leonard a quick, sharp glance. He had suspected on a number of occasions in the past that Leonard knew of, and was amused by, George's uneasiness about his relationship to the Pragers. Did Leonard also know about the matter of vital importance W. P. planned to discuss with George? His mocking smile certainly seemed to indicate that he knew something.

"Leonard—"

"What?"

George hesitated. He couldn't ask Leonard about the missing piece in the jigsaw puzzle of his relationship to the Pragers. It was up to W. P. to supply that.

"This dinner," George said. "What are we getting the ball rolling for tonight?"

Leonard laughed and winked. "Keep your eye on the boy with the warts," he said.

He moved off around a maid with a tray of highballs. She caught

George's eye, smiled, and brought the tray up to him. George took a glass, thanked her, and gave her a chance to swing the tray to one side. Then he slipped through the gap and paused outside the group around the man with the warts.

He had four of them, arranged in a neat little square on one cheekbone, so that they looked like what Aunt Tessie used to call a beauty mark. It was difficult to say whether this added to or detracted from his appearance. Since the issue was in doubt, however, George thought the man with the warts would have been better advised not to wear a mauve dinner jacket with a wine-red bow tie. Taken in combination with the theatrically placed warts, and the sweeping gestures he was making with his empty highball glass as he denounced American journalism, the jacket and the tie made him look a good deal like a circus ringmaster in his cups, or teetering on the brink of them, telling the owners of the show why he could not give a performance that night.

"I've worked for them all," he said. "In every capacity from copy boy up to managing editor. In every state of the union from California to Maine. No matter what their politics, how large their circulation, or whether they come out every day or once a week, I tell you they're all the same: pious frauds, mouthing a lot of empty words on their editorial pages and mastheads about freedom of the press, and knuckling under shamefully and abjectly and disgustingly every minute of the day to the God-damn advertisers. Until the newspapers of this country are freed from the strangling clutch of advertising, the people of this country will continue to be denied the blessings and privileges of a truly free press."

George took a sip from his glass and decided Leonard Prager had given him a bum steer. It was not the first one. Leonard knew a lot about what motivated Iago and how Milton felt when he was dictating *Il Penseroso*, but, as his niece Rosemary had long ago pointed out to George, when it came to business matters Leonard didn't know his rear end from a hot rock. George had attended quite a few Ball Rolling dinners in the Prager triplex during the past five years, and he had seen W. P. put his money on many an odd ball, but the man with the warts did not look like anyone who was going to get the Prager nod. Mrs. Prager, George saw, was waving to him again. He thought of Leonard's remark about demerits, had a moment of shame, then figured Leonard could drop dead, and waved back to his hostess. George added a smile, gestured to indicate that he was coming as fast as he could, and edged his way around the group for whom the man with the warts was demolishing the American press. George emerged into a cleared space behind another group standing in front of the Dali painting of Rosemary in the dress she had worn at her graduation from Ethical Culture. A good-looking blonde in a strapless gown was staring meditatively at the portrait as she sipped from a squat glass of straight bourbon.

"This Dali," she said. "I suppose if you pay him enough he'll paint anybody's picture."

"For Christ's sake, Polly, will you watch it?" a man next to her said sharply. "I just saw W. P. go by."

"So what?" the blonde said. "Surely it's no news to Mr. William Prager that his only child ain't exactly no Norma Shearer."

"If it is," the man said, "I don't want him learning it from you."

George decided to linger for a moment. Anybody who was that worried about W. P. overhearing an unflattering remark about Rosemary was probably more than just polite. This might be the boy to watch. After doing it for several moments, George learned only that the boy he was watching was a magazine photographer who had just come back from covering the opening of the Golden Gate Exposition in San Francisco, an event by which he had been singularly unimpressed.

"They're going to lose their shirts," he said. "You wait and see."

"If I have to do any of my waiting in this room," the blonde said, "I want sun glasses. Why anybody who looks the way these Pragers look would want to hang so many pictures of themselves where they and the rest of the world can stare at them all the time is one thing that beats me."

"If you don't button up your big trap," the man said, "that's not the only thing that's going to beat you."

"Instead of threatening a poor defenseless girl, why don't you answer my question?" the blonde said. "Just look at the walls of this skating rink. Twenty thousand bucks' worth of Mama Prager in black satin. Thirty thousand bucks' worth of daughter Rosemary with a high school diploma. Forty thousand more of Mama in yellow taffeta. Another forty thousand of Rosemary graduating from Bennington. Fifty thousand bucks' worth of Papa Prager, first in a sack suit and then, over there, that one, the Picasso, another fifty thousand if not more, wearing what?"

"How should I know?" the man said. "I'm still stuck in his Blue Period."

"I guess these Pragers must be stuck on themselves," the blonde said.

It was a guess that George remembered, as he moved off toward the caviar tray, he had made himself shortly after he met the Pragers. They may not have been the handsomest people he had ever seen, but they were far from the ugliest, and there was certainly nothing wrong with having your portrait painted, especially if you could afford it. Yet there did seem to be something wrong about having it done so often and then hanging all the end products in the most public room of your house. It was as though Uncle Zisha, instead of covering his walls in Albany with pictures of Judge Brandeis, had covered them with photographs of himself.

"George!" Mrs. Prager said as he reached the caviar tray. "How nice that you could come!"

It was the sort of remark that made George uneasy. Mrs. Prager, who wore a three-hundred-dollar Bergdorf gown, could have been the twin sister of Mrs. Gordon, the shapeless fat woman who used to own the candy stand around the corner from Aunt Tessie's store.

"Hello," George said, taking Mrs. Prager's hand. It was a little like grasping a pineapple. Mrs. Prager's diamonds, unlike their owner, were tall. "It's nice of you to have me."

"Don't be silly," Mrs. Prager said. "You know there isn't anybody in the world we enjoy having more than we enjoy having you."

It was true enough. George didn't doubt, after five years of hearing them, that Mrs. Prager's words expressed something she honestly felt. It was one of the things that contributed to his uneasiness about the Pragers. What could he possibly mean to them or do for them, he had asked himself on his first visit, when he still did not own a dinner jacket, that would make him so welcome a guest in this wealthy household? After five years he still didn't know. But he knew that he was going to find out at last.

"Have you met Mr. Watchman?"

"Who?" George said.

"Wallace Watchman," Mrs. Prager said. "The guest of honor. William thought it would be nice to have a dinner for him and sort of, you know, start the ball rolling on his project. William is very anxious for you to meet Mr. Watchman. He was just here a moment ago looking for you. I said for heaven's sake, William, give him a chance to get here. George isn't like some of those other boys Rosemary wastes her time with. Nothing to do all day except lunch at the Stork Club. George runs a busy office, I said. Give him a chance to get home and take a shower."

"I guess maybe I'd better go find Mr. Prager," George said. "Have some caviar first."

George didn't like caviar. It tasted like the lox Mr. Forman used to sell at half price down on Fourth Street after it had been lying around on his counter so long that the edges had gone black. But George couldn't tell that to Mrs. Prager. She always made a fuss about the caviar. The other hors d'oeuvres were left to the kitchen staff and the efficient maids, but Mrs. Prager always handled the caviar herself. That was why, at all Prager dinner parties, whether Gloves Off or Ball Rolling, Mrs. Prager never stirred from the caviar tray until Boland announced that dinner was ready and the time came to move into the dining room. There was something touching about the way her stout body bent over the tray and her thick fingers fussed with the tiny silver implements. It was a ritual that obviously provided her with more than the simple satisfaction of seeing that her guests were well fed. It was almost as though, in putting together the dexterously arranged mounds of black beads, chopped onion, grated egg yolk, and sour cream on tiny slivers of toast, she was able to demonstrate most satisfactorily the unique power that wealth had brought her. Thus, George supposed, in the house of the Borgia, while minor poisons were left in the perfectly adequate hands of subordinates, when it came to a potion intended for royalty, Lucrezia herself did the brewing.

"There," Mrs. Prager said with a smile as she handed over the loaded piece of toast. "I've made you a really beautiful one."

George took it and looked at her the way he had looked at Leonard. Did she know what it was W. P. planned to discuss with him? Was she aware that the missing piece in the jigsaw puzzle of George's relationship to the Pragers was about to fall into place? She certainly seemed to be treating the piece of toast as though it was a birthday cake.

"Take it with you," she said. "It'll keep you from starving while you're trying to find W. P. in this mob."

"Thanks," George said.

Threading his way carefully back around the groups in the living

room, he looked about furtively for a place where he could dispose of
the caviar without being seen. He didn't find one. Coming out into the
small marble hall under the circular stairway, George saw that the
gooey mess was beginning to slide off the toast onto his fingers. He
decided to duck into Rosemary's bathroom and drop the caviar down
the drain. For a moment after he opened the door he thought he
had made a mistake. This was not surprising. The Prager triplex
was so large and complicated that George had learned long ago
never to set out for a bathroom without first memorizing the location of a number of doors and pieces of hall furniture that could
serve as guideposts on the way back. He had assumed that only
someone who knew the apartment fairly well would find his way
unassisted to Rosemary's bathroom instead of the powder rooms
reserved for guests. Then George saw that the stranger buttoning
his coat was not a total stranger. It was the man with the warts. As
he bent over the black marble basin and twisted the gold scarab
marked HOT, he looked up into the mirror and said, "Is this thing
real?"

"So I've been told," George said. "Fourteen carat."

The man caressed the golden beetle for a couple of thoughtful
moments. He seemed to be trying to work something out in his
mind. "You been here before?" he said finally.

"Once or twice," George said.

"Is it always like this?"

"Like what?"

The man made a gesture with his wet hands, a series of impatient, flapping movements. "A real Rodin in the vestibule," he
said. "Picassos in the living room. Caviar by the ton. Solid-gold
bathroom fixtures. I mean, Jesus Christ. You know what I mean?"

George thought he did, but it didn't seem the appropriate
moment to say so. He felt like the man with the blonde in the strapless gown out in the living room. This was the night when the
mystery of his relationship to the Pragers was going to be solved
by something W. P. wanted to discuss with him. This was no time
to make indiscreet remarks to total strangers who might carry them
back to the wrong ears.

"None of those things are new," George said carefully. "The
Rodin and the paintings and the toilet fixtures were all here on
my previous visits."

"That's not what I mean," the man with the warts said. He

flipped open the folds of a tiny, lace-edged hand towel. "I mean all the Jews I ever met before, they were different. Haven't you felt that?"

For a startled moment George refused to believe what the question so clearly implied: the man with the warts obviously assumed that George, like himself, was not a Jew.

"Felt what?" George said.

Again the man made the impatient, flapping gesture that seemed to take in the entire triplex. "There's so much dough around, it's all so God-damn rich, it sort of insulates the Jewishness," he said. "I mean, Christ, it's like being in the house of a Rockefeller or a Vanderbilt. What hits you first is the money, not the religion."

George stared at the man in astonishment. His mind had been geared to expecting from this evening the solution to the mystery of his relationship with the Pragers. It had not occurred to him he would also find out what it was about them that for five years had been making him uneasy. He had certainly not expected to find it out from a stranger.

"I see what you mean," George said.

No wonder, even though it was a Jewish household, being in the Prager triplex had always reminded him of the way the shkutzim in Gerrity's used to make him feel.

"I guess what it gets down to is this," the man with the warts said. "Jews without money or with some money are Jews, but Jews with real big money are just rich people." He tossed the crumpled towel into a receptacle that looked like a miniature Taj Mahal and may or may not have been made of solid gold. "By the way, my name is Watchman," he said, holding out his hand. "Wallace Watchman."

"Oh," George said. So Leonard Prager had been right after all about the boy to watch. "Mine's Hurst," he said, taking the other man's hand. "George Hurst."

Watchman's eyebrows went up. "No kid?" he said. "Bill Prager's been telling me a lot about you."

"In connection with what?"

"I understand our host doesn't like to have people jump the gun on him," Wallace Watchman said. "I'd better let W. P. tell you all about it himself."

31

It was almost ten o'clock before he got around to it.

"Let's go into the study," W. P. said to George as they were leaving the dining room behind the gaunt woman who worked for the French news syndicate. "Boland can bring us some brandy there."

Toward the end of a Ball Rolling dinner, when the guests broke up into small groups, Boland covered so much terrain with the brandy decanter that George often thought it would have been simpler for him to carry it in a small keg around his neck, like a St. Bernard.

"Thank you," W. P. said, taking the large glass from the butler and settling back in the huge red leather chair beside the fireplace. "George?"

"None for me," George said. "Thanks."

As a rule, even though he didn't like brandy any better than he liked caviar, when W. P. took him to the study for a talk, George usually had some. Tonight, on his way to the study, George had done some fast thinking and decided to break the rule. Not merely because he was anxious to have a clear head for this particular talk, but also because he sensed there was an advantage to be gained from continuing the streak of unorthodox behavior he had started that morning at the meeting in the Woolworth Building.

"In that case, Boland, that will be all," W. P. said. The butler bowed and left the room, moving backward as noiselessly as a caterpillar on butter. George took the chair facing W. P. He settled himself into it in a way that would show he was relaxed but not too relaxed. W. P. liked his guests to be comfortable, especially when they were summoned to the study for a talk, but he didn't like them to look as though they were having a massage. "That's another thing I've noticed about you," he said. "You don't drink much, George."

Since there was no mistaking the tone of approval in which this remark had been uttered, George felt he had a right to congratulate himself on his decision about the brandy.

"Oh, I don't know," George said. This was a lie, of course, but it was clearly the remark that was appropriate. "Can I fix that light for you, sir?"

"No, no," W. P. said with a gentle wave of the brandy glass, as he continued to squint up at the ceiling. It depicted the Seven Ages of Man and had been cut from four slabs of California redwood by a team of six Swiss woodcarvers who had been brought over secretly from Zurich by Mrs. Prager the year she decided to surprise her husband by redecorating his study for Christmas. "The light doesn't bother me," W. P. said. "What I'm smiling about, I was just thinking about Albert Dworkin's face this morning, that's all."

"I didn't mean to upset him or sound as tough as Al seems to think I sounded," George said. "I'd like to add now what I'm afraid I didn't get a chance to say at the meeting in your office this morning: there was nothing personal about my recommending that you liquidate your father's business, W. P. It just seemed to me it was high time somebody stated the plain, hard, unvarnished truth."

"High time indeed." W. P. brought his glance down from the ceiling. "I've been waiting five years to hear it, George, and I'd just about begun to give up hope."

George, who had enough self-control not to look startled even when he was, decided that this time it was probably wise not only to register surprise but to overdo it a little. W. P.'s chuckle was his reward.

"Sir?" George said.

The pince-nez danced as the knife-thin nose dipped down into the brandy fumes.

"Five years ago, George, when I was looking for an accountant to audit the books of my father's feather business and Nick Perrini recommended you, I was favorably impressed. I liked the way you looked. I liked the way you talked. I liked your sensible approach to business matters. Best of all, I liked your background."

This time there was no need for George to simulate astonishment.

W. P. chuckled again. "Surprises you, doesn't it?"

"Sort of," George said. "Yes." He hoped his astonishment concealed his sudden uneasiness.

"When I like someone," W. P. said, "I don't as a rule let it go at registering a generalized pleasant effect, the sort of thing one gets from looking at the ceiling of this room, for example, or sniffing the fumes from this glass. With people I like, I want more than a vague favorable impression. People are not like brandy. They're not a painting or a carving. They're flesh and blood. When I like one of them, I want to know what it is that makes me like that particular person. I want documentation. I make it a point to do a bit of investigating. I did that in your case, George, and I found out."

George dropped his glance to his hands in a manner that he hoped would look like modesty. His heart was suddenly racing in a lop-sided, plunging roll, like a horse with a broken leg forced brutally into a gallop. Had W. P. found out about Dora and Danny? Had he learned about the L. L. Parker stamp robbery? Had his investigations led him to Eff Eff Shumacher and Mr. Sapina and Dean Cathcart?

For half a dozen years, ever since the day Danny and Dora had stripped his room before dropping out of his life, George had kept all his feelings about them bound in a tight bundle shoved into a far corner of his mind, the way a frontiersman stored his food by hanging it from a high rafter so that while he slept it could not be reached by marauding animals. Now, all at once, sitting across the fireplace from this neat little rich man chuckling to himself, George could feel the tightly wrapped bundle burst open. His mind, which he had been so anxious to keep clear for this talk that he had refused even a sip of brandy, was suddenly a haze of painful recollections, as though the bundle that had burst open in his head was a pillow and each feather, floating about with such deceptive grace, was actually a jagged piece of lacerating metal.

"I beg your pardon?" George said.

W.P.'s fingers stroked the corners of his open mouth. "I asked if you remember the first time we invited you here to dinner."

George made an effort to force the whirling, painful thoughts back into their container. He tried for and succeeded in releasing a boyishly embarrassed smile. "I certainly do."

In the corner of the invitation had been written the two words: "Black Tie." George, who had never before received a formal invitation to dinner, had thought about this one for a while and then decided the puzzling words meant that the Pragers were mourning the death of a relative. With the dark blue suit in which he went out on dates at night, he had worn his black knitted tie.

"I liked the way you behaved," W. P. said. "I liked the fact that you didn't apologize for being the only man who was not wearing a dinner coat, and I liked even better the fact that between that first visit and the next time you came here you had gone out and bought yourself a dinner coat. I like people who don't have to be told about things. I like people who learn for themselves. It's one of the reasons I've always liked Albert Dworkin. He was born and raised practically around the corner from you. On Avenue C."

George sent a quick glance toward the neat little figure in the red leather chair. W. P. was stroking the corners of his mouth again.

"But that would have been a long time before—?"

"Oh, yes," W. P. said. "I've known Albert for almost thirty years, and he was not a child when we met. I didn't mean to imply that you and he are contemporaries. Albert must have left the Lower East Side years before you were born. All I meant was that from the moment I met you, George, I sensed in you the same qualities that had drawn me to Albert Dworkin a quarter of a century ago, and as soon as I completed my investigations, I was sure I was right."

The pince-nez went into the little dancing act as W. P.'s nose went down into the brandy fumes, and George decided to take a chance.

"You make it sound like you put the F.B.I. on my trail," he said with a small laugh. "I mean the word investigations."

"There have been times during the past five years when I've thought very seriously of putting something like the F.B.I. on your trail," W. P. said. "I was getting sort of desperate, George."

"Desperate?"

"Impatient. Desperate. Choose your own word. When I say investigations I mean I did some simple checking with Nick Perrini, who had introduced you to me in the first place, and I learned you were an East Side boy. That was enough for me. I've seen enough East Side boys to know what they're made of. They're all the same. They're put together out of a bundle of unsatisfied appetites and they're impatient to satisfy them. They're hungry and they can't wait to eat. They'll do anything to get to the table ahead of everybody else. They usually do. Impatience always spells success." W. P. smiled. "Am I describing anybody you know?"

"Yes," George said. He had never heard a better description of Danny Schorr.

"Anything wrong with my portrait?" W. P. asked.

"Nothing that I can think of," George said. It was hardly the moment to point out that the portrait did not apply to him.

"Neither could I," William Prager said. "I've found another Albert Dworkin, I said to myself five years ago when I met you. Albert is not an old man. Far from it. But he's getting on. Before too long I'll need somebody else to fill the role he's handled so beautifully for thirty years. You seemed the ideal choice, George. I didn't want to press things. After all, there was no rush. I thought I'd just let you go along handling my father's account, while I kept an eye on you, until the right moment came along. I waited and I waited, but nothing seemed to happen. A little while ago I used the words impatient and desperate. Perhaps the second one is an exaggeration, but not by too much. The moment just didn't seem to come."

"What moment?"

"The moment when I expected you to show what you were made of," William Prager said. "You took a long time getting to it, George, but when you did, it was well worth waiting for. The fact that it almost threw Albert Dworkin into an apoplectic fit proves my point." W. P. paused to stroke the corners of his mouth, then re-leased one of his chuckles. "I hope you won't mind if I don't act on your suggestion about liquidating my father's business. That's his particular toy and I see no reason why he shouldn't be allowed to go right on playing with it. The fact that you made the suggestion, however, is what counts. So far as I am concerned, I mean. If you don't mind my putting it bluntly, George, by making that suggestion about my father as you did this morning, to my face, you finally demonstrated that you do have that touch of ruthlessness which every East Side boy I've ever known has possessed and which I consider an absolute essential to the successful conduct of the sort of business ventures to which I give so much of my time."

W. P. paused. George was sorry that he had. The pause gave him time to think, and all at once George Hurst didn't like his thoughts. They were circling around Mr. Rapf and the words the buck-toothed senior had flung at him so bitterly in the lobby of the Woolworth Building that morning.

"I'm terribly sorry, W. P."

The beautifully manicured fingers stopped stroking the corners of the round, pink mouth. "For what, George?"

"I wasn't trying to act ruthless."

"Then what were you trying to do?"

I was trying to prove, George wanted to say, to a man who was not in the room, a man who might have been my father, that I was not the boot licker he'd just accused me of being.

"I was just trying to point out the facts," George said.

"You succeeded," W. P. said. "Not many people can. The capacity to point out facts is a form of ruthlessness so unique that I have learned to place an extremely high value on it."

W. P. smiled. George suddenly remembered the way the neat little millionaire had looked in his office that morning when Prager had asked George to come to dinner: like a man who, after waiting patiently at a traffic light for a long time, had finally received the signal to go ahead.

"Thank you, sir," George said.

He didn't know what he was thanking W. P. for, but George didn't doubt that he was about to find out. His relationship to the Pragers, which had puzzled him for five years, had just turned a corner.

"George, what do you think of Wallace Watchman?"

It was not the question George had been expecting. Five years of dealing with clients, however, had taught him how to handle unexpected questions. George squinted up across W. P.'s head as though the answer he sought was lettered on the hand-carved ceiling but, because he had left his reading glasses at home, he could not quite make out the words.

"Wallace Watchman," he said thoughtfully. "Wallace Watchman."

"The man across the table from you at dinner," W. P. said. "With the warts on his face."

George wasn't sure. He thought Mr. Watchman was a boob who had picked up enough glib jargon about the decadence of American journalism to sound impressive in a group composed of other boobs who had not yet picked up quite as much jargon as he had. On the other hand, no man who had put his finger on the reason why Jews like the Pragers made George feel as though he was in the presence of shkutzim like the Gerritys could be completely stupid. There was only one way to play this.

"Considering those warts and the shape of his face," George said, "I think Mr. Watchman makes a big mistake by wearing a mauve dinner jacket and a wine-red bow tie."

The chuckle that escaped from the neat little figure at the other side of the fireplace almost shook the dancing pince-nez loose.

"You may be right," W. P. said. "But I wouldn't tell that to Wallace when you start dealing with him."

"Am I going to start dealing with him?"

"As of tomorrow."

"May I ask, sir, in what connection?"

"Rosemary will give you the details."

"Rosemary?"

William Prager's fingers, stroking the corners of his mouth, stopped moving.

"Didn't Boland give you a note when you came in?"

For a stunned moment, as his hand went to the pocket in which he had thrust the envelope almost three hours ago, George had the feeling that by a silly oversight he had ruined five years of hard work. The feeling was followed at once by a wave of relief, as though he had escaped a degrading trap on the edge of which for a long time he had been indecisively teetering. In the background he could actually hear Mr. Rapf's admiring voice, grudgingly withdrawing the accusation that George was an ass kisser. Then the moment ended, and common sense came to the rescue. Common sense plus five years of dealing with clients who asked unexpected questions.

"Oh, the envelope," George said, smiling easily as he drew it from his pocket in such a way that W. P. could not see the flap was still sealed. As he turned the smile up a couple of notches to recover whatever ground he may have lost by his oversight, George was aware that he should have been a little more troubled by the fact that he was now able to say to himself what that morning, in the lobby of the Woolworth Building, he had thought only Danny Schorr would have been able to say: *nuts to Mr. Rapf.* "Yes, of course," George said. "The note."

William Prager's face cleared. "Then I'll just leave all the rest to Rosemary," he said.

32

Rosemary Prager had a theory, which she advanced to George shortly after they met, that if Madame Curie had been endowed with a better sense of organization she could have discovered radium in half the time.

"One thing I'll say for my daughter," Mrs. Prager had once confided to George. "Rosemary doesn't lack self-confidence."

"If Napoleon had taken Rosemary along with him to Moscow,"
William Prager had confided to George on another occasion, "I don't
say he would have won the war, but I do say his entire army would
have come home by Pullman."

In view of all this, it seemed to George two things about Rosemary Prager were surprising: one, that she was so attractive, and two,
that she should be so devoted to the theatre.

By attractive George did not mean beautiful. His ideas of beauty
were still conditioned by his feelings about Dora Dienst, and Rosemary had none of that dark, almost oriental fragility the mere thought
of which could still make him ache with longing. Also, aside from
Aunt Tessie, George had always disliked bossy, efficient women.
What took the curse off Rosemary's aggressiveness was that she could
laugh at herself for it. And when Rosemary Prager laughed, something pleasant happened in the entire area to which the sound
penetrated.

While her figure was not exactly exciting, she could send a golf
ball two hundred and fifty yards with an easy grace that was not
unpleasing to watch. It was true that her jaw, an obvious inheritance
from W. P., was unfortunate, but her blue-black hair, parted severely
in the middle, reminded George enough of Dora to make that count
in Rosemary's favor, and her wide gray eyes were alive and arresting.

And George supposed a perfectly good case could be made for
her devotion to the theatre. His own feeling that the case was not
good enough was based on the fact that Rosemary's talents were
organizational. These, while useful in any enterprise, limited her in
the theatre to a peripheral role. In view of what he was fairly certain
Rosemary was capable of doing, this seemed to George as wasteful as
limiting Babe Ruth to swatting houseflies.

"I agree," W. P. had replied when George made this observation
one evening in the triplex study as they waited for Rosemary, who
had called to say she would be late for dinner because Nikita Loewenthal, the director of The Living Theatre, had asked her to check
audience reaction during his afternoon lecture on Brecht at The
New School. "But everybody has to find their feet in their own way,
George. I think Rosemary senses her potentialities but she doesn't
yet know how far they will take her. In the theatre, which has always
been a family passion anyway, she can find out. When she does,"
W. P. had added with one of the chuckles that set the pince-nez

dancing like a speedometer needle, "I'm afraid we'd all better take to the hills."

George wondered, as he emerged into Park Avenue from the Ball Rolling dinner for Wallace Watchman, if taking to the hills would make him half as nervous as taking a taxi to meet Rosemary was making him now. Why couldn't W. P. have outlined the details of George's role in the new Wallace Watchman project while they were both seated comfortably in front of the fireplace in the study upstairs? Why did he have to send George chasing halfway across town at this hour of the night, like a player in a scavenger hunt tracking down a clue?

The answer, George supposed, was in some way connected with the reason why William Prager had his office all the way downtown in the Woolworth Building: a man who liked people when they came to see him to know that they had made something of a journey probably was equally fond of making sure that those to whom he was generous had occasion to remember the moment of generosity. The rich, George was beginning to grasp, while often free with their money, were never really easy about handing it out.

"Taxi, sir?" the doorman asked.

"Yes, please," George said.

Settling back on the scuffed leather seat, George drew from his pocket the envelope Boland had given him before dinner, pulled out the piece of heavy, perfumed paper, and reread Rosemary's note:

George, darling:

Sorry I won't be able to see you at the Watchman dinner tonight. I wanted very much to be there, but everything fell apart this afternoon during the rehearsal of the denunciation scene—not the one in Act II where the girl first sees the face at the window; I mean the big one, the scene in Act III where the boy tells his father he knew about the incest since the day before Easter—and Nikita hit the walls as well as the roof. I don't blame him, poor lamb. He's spent more time rehearsing this one scene than the rest of the play, and the whole damn shooting-match hinges on this scene. Unless it's right we'll look like fools next Wednesday night in Boston. So Nikita's keeping the entire cast for a night rehearsal and I have to stand by. I called Dad and explained, since I knew how much he was counting on my being there tonight, and he said it was okay. He'll talk to you right after dinner, and then you can

*come to the theatre for our talk. Don't come before eleven. Nikita
will be talking to the cast at ten, but he detests lectures, so that
part of it won't take long, and then I'll be free. I've alerted Sig at
the stage entrance that you're coming, and Boland promises to slip
this into your hot little hand the moment you show your handsome
face at the apartment, so all is under control. I wish I could say as
much for the play. Jesus, and Jesus again. What a rotten break.
Poor Nikita. Oh, well, c'est la vie, or c'est le théâtre, or something.
Eleven o'clock. Don't be late. I have loads to tell you. Love,*

R.

The taxi stopped. The driver turned. "You say the Jefferson?"
"That's right," George said.
"This is it."
George slipped the note back into his pocket, paid the driver,
and stepped out. West Forty-seventh Street looked crowded both
at the Broadway and Sixth Avenue ends, but the sidewalk in front
of the Jefferson Theatre was deserted. No lights showed. The lobby
doors were locked. The gate that barred the alley to the stage entrance was hooked back. On the gate, George noticed as he walked
into the alley, was a new poster. It read:

OPENS THURSDAY MARCH 19

The Living Theatre, Inc.
In association with
Sarah Sichel Spitzer and Clyde Koenig
Present
The High Hand
A New Play
Adapted from the Spanish of
José de Montenaga
By Everett Clarke O'Brien and Carlton Messinger
Directed by
NIKITA LOEWENTHAL

The members of the cast and the other credits were massed in
a block of smaller type at the bottom. George supposed he should
pause to read it. Rosemary was frequently annoyed by what she

called his lack of interest in the theatre. He glanced at his watch. It showed a minute or two after eleven. George decided to read the poster some other time. The old man in the broken swivel chair looked up from his paper when George came in.

"Hello, Sig."

The affability in George's voice got him nowhere. He hadn't expected it to.

"What do you want?"

"Miss Prager is expecting me," George said.

The old man looked at him with open hostility. George didn't blame him. Sig had spent almost all of his seventy years in the theatre. With him, as with Rosemary and her associates, the theatre was not a form of entertainment. It was a way of life. Sig had known a long time ago, the moment he first clapped eyes on him, that George was not a member of the club. Sig resented the fact that Rosemary, who was one of the anointed, should have anything to do with somebody who was such an obvious interloper.

"What's your name?"

"Hurst," George said, without annoyance. Sig knew his name. "Miss Prager said she told you I was coming."

Sig jerked his head grudgingly toward the door behind him. "Don't make any noise," he said. "Mr. Loewenthal is talking."

He must have been doing it for a long time, George guessed when he finally emerged from the backstage labyrinth into the corridor that spilled him out into the rear of the orchestra. Nikita Loewenthal sounded hoarse.

"Until you do understand it," he was saying, "the scene won't stand up. It will continue to lie there, a pointless, empty, meaningless bundle of words on a page. And you can't begin to understand it from the top. True comprehension must come from the bottom. You must think your way into the scene, from the inside, from the heart."

George looked around the darkened theatre. Only the footlights were on. They held the small, slightly bowed figure in the sweatshirt standing alone on the empty stage in a pitiless glare that George would have thought was painful. Nikita Loewenthal couldn't have shared this view, since the lighting arrangements were under his control. So, George saw, were the twenty or thirty people huddled in the first three rows. It was clear even from the side view George was able to get of their upturned faces that they were not merely hanging but practically chinning themselves on every one of Nikita's words.

"George!"

He turned quickly. Rosemary was tiptoeing toward him up the outside aisle.

"What's up?" he said.

"There's a trick break in the light front," she whispered in George's ear. "Just where you were standing, in the center aisle, you can see it from the stage. Anybody standing up when he's talking, it drives Nikita crazy."

There seemed to be some truth in the statement. The little man on the stage, George saw as Rosemary led him around to the aisle on the right, had bowed his head, like a charging buffalo in a Frederic Remington painting, and was wagging it violently from side to side.

"Not a participant," Nikita Loewenthal was saying. "That is the whole frightening point. Juan is only a child. He should be reacting to life, living it to the full, participating in it as only a child can. But he doesn't participate. He can't. He is incapable of living because he is numbed by the shock he suffered the day before Easter when he learned about the incest. He has become a spectator. That is the horror of the scene. A child of eight reduced to the role of a spectator of life."

Rosemary pointed to the two aisle seats in the last row. George stood aside for her to go first.

"No, you," she whispered. "I want to be on the aisle in case anything happens."

"What's going to happen?" George said.

"Who knows?" Rosemary said. "What a mess!"

George sat down. Rosemary slid into the aisle seat and flung the mink coat back from her shoulders.

"How's it going?" George asked.

"Not bad," Rosemary said. "Considering."

George was about to ask considering what, then stopped himself. That wasn't what he was here for.

"You sure it's all right?" he said instead. "For us to talk like this?"

"Who's going to stop us?"

Who, indeed? The Living Theatre would not live very long if William Prager's generous subsidy checks stopped coming in.

"All I meant," George said, "I don't want to disturb Mr. Loewenthal."

"We won't as long as we keep our voices down. Nikita's slightly deaf. Didn't I ever tell you that?"

"No."

"That's funny. I was sure I had. It's one of the most exciting things about him. I mean that he can continue to direct with so much drive and energy when he can't really hear a good deal of what's being said. It happened during a production of *The Infernal Machine*. Cocteau isn't easy to do, and this was way back in the days of The Subway Theatre, before Nikita was very well known, so that they almost literally had no money to work with. That didn't stop Nikita, though. He thought up this wonderful piece of business for *The Infernal Machine*. At the beginning, when the chorus tells the story, he wanted thunder in the background, but thunder costs money, even in those days with The Subway Theatre, so Nikita dressed all his chorus as drum majors, the whole bunch of them, and he got some old milk cans and he had them bang away at the milk cans while they told the story. With broomsticks. They just banged away, and it had a tremendous effect. People still talk about that production of *The Infernal Machine*. Nikita even got a letter from Cocteau, but he's never been able to hear very well since then. I'll ask him to show it to you some day. What did you think of what Dad told you?"

"He didn't really tell me very much."

"What did he tell you?"

"He said he'd been waiting five years for me to prove I had the ruthlessness all East Side boys were born with and that he considers essential to the successful handling of the kind of large business affairs in which he's interested, and finally, today in his office, I proved I had what it took, and you would tell me the details."

He could tell she was laughing even before he turned to look at her. The air suddenly seemed full of a very pleasant vibration. When he did turn, George realized that Rosemary was not laughing at him or at what he had said. Following her glance he saw that the figure on the stage had dropped to all fours and was hopping about stiffly, like a dog with its legs bound in splints that was being prodded by a sadistic tormentor.

"Pretend it is not a boy," Nikita Loewenthal was saying. "Let us go to a lower order of animal life in our quest for comprehension.

Let us pretend the playwright had in mind not a child of eight who viewed this horrible and numbing act on the day before Easter, but a sheep. I am a sheep. I have been out in the cold. It is freezing. My legs are stiff, as this boy's brain is stiff. All I want to do is lie down and die, as all this child wants to do is embrace oblivion. The last thing in the world I as a frozen sheep want at this moment is to face the meaning of the dreadful scene I witnessed six weeks ago. But I cannot lie down. I cannot sleep. I cannot embrace oblivion because look, here is my shepherd, as in the actual scene there is the child's father, prodding, poking, stabbing, forcing me from the role of bystander to that of participant. Do you follow me?"

The rapt faces in the front rows nodded, a single, slow, synchronized, almost catatonic bob of comprehension.

"God," Rosemary breathed. "Isn't he unbelievable?"

"He sure is," George said.

"What else did Dad say?"

"He said I'd better not be late getting to the theatre or you'd chew my ear off."

"George, do you feel that way about me, too?"

"What way?"

"That I'm bossy and, oh, you know, dominating?"

"It seems to me that everybody I've had anything to do with today, from Albert Dworkin in your father's office this morning to you right here and now, has insisted on my giving them an analysis of their character before they get to the point. I'm not a gypsy tearoom. I'm an accountant. What difference does it make whether I think you're bossy and dominating?"

"It happens to make a tremendous amount of difference," Rosemary said. "It's extremely important for us to know how we feel about each other if we're going to work together."

"Work together on what?"

"On *Noon*."

"What's *Noon*?"

"This new magazine Wallace Watchman is starting and Dad is backing."

"Are these the details W. P. said you'd give me?"

"Yes. Wallace Watchman is starting a new news magazine."

"Like *Time* and *Newsweek* and that other one, whatever it's called?"

"*Worldweek*, yes. Wallace Watchman is starting one called *Noon* and Dad is putting up the money for it."

"With *Time* and *Newsweek* and *Worldweek* already in business, why should W. P. back anybody who wants to put out a new magazine that will be in direct competition with them?"

"Because *Noon* is going to be completely and entirely and excitingly different from all the rest."

"In what way?"

"*Noon* will accept no advertising."

"Oh," George said, wishing he could say something that would come closer to the response Rosemary so obviously expected, but he couldn't. It was clear, merely from the excitement in her eyes, that to Rosemary a magazine that accepted no advertising was on the same level, so far as the welfare of the human race was concerned, with the invention of the wheel. To George, however, who dealt daily with men engaged in the endless struggle to emerge from their affairs with a profit rather than a loss, starting a magazine that accepted no advertising seemed uncomfortably similar to manufacturing a piggy bank without a slot for inserting coins. "Well," he said, "I suppose W. P. knows what—"

"Oh, my God!"

Rosemary rose from her nest of mink like a bird at the snap of a twig. George watched in astonishment as she ran along the back of the theatre and disappeared through the door by which he had come in. He stood up, hesitated, started to follow her, hesitated again, then turned toward the stage. Nothing unusual seemed to be happening. The small figure in the sweatshirt held by the glare of the footlights was standing upright again.

"From our comprehension of the stiff-legged frozen sheep to our complete grasp of the child's mother image is but a single step," Nikita Loewenthal was saying. "Her image is glorified. It draws him with unbreakable cords of longing. This longing, this loneliness will follow him all his life. He will carry it to the grave. Understanding that, we are now ready to understand his emotions in this scene so many many years this side of the grave, when the child is only eight."

From the wings, moving on tiptoe, holding something outstretched in both hands, so that she looked like a religious figure in a painting bearing a chalice, came Rosemary. When she reached the center of the stage she stopped. Without turning to look at her,

Nikita Loewenthal reached out, took what George saw was a glass of water, drained it slowly, handed the glass back, and resumed his lecture. Rosemary retraced her steps, disappeared in the wings, and reappeared a few moments later at the back of the theatre.

"What was that all about?" George said as she sat down beside him and worked her hips back into the nest of mink. "You jumped up as though you'd been stabbed."

"Couldn't you see?" Rosemary said.

"See what?"

"He was so parched he was about to faint. I'm surprised none of those clucks down in the front row realized what was happening."

"How did you realize it?"

"By the lisp. When he's dying of thirst Nikita starts lisping. I suppose they're so absorbed in what he's telling them about the renunciation scene that they didn't notice it. But I noticed it because all I was doing was telling you about *Noon*."

"Tell me some more."

"There isn't really very much more to tell. Wallace Watchman is going to be editor. Leonard is slated for the job of dramatic reviewer."

"Your *uncle* Leonard? Leonard *Prager*?"

"That's right."

"What does Leonard know about dramatic criticism?"

"He's been telling those classes of his at City College for years that he knows more than anybody else. This will be his chance to prove it. The rest of the staff is still just a bunch of names, so I won't throw them at you now, but when I do I'm sure you'll be just as excited as I am."

"I still haven't heard one detail that I'm sure W. P. wanted you to fill me in on."

"What's that?"

"How do I fit in?"

"I was coming to that," Rosemary said. "You're going in as the financial man, the chief watchdog of the Prager millions, of which I don't think even Dad knows at this stage how many it's going to take to make *Noon* a going concern, and according to the charts Dad and I have been working on, your official title is Assistant to the Publisher. How do you like it?"

George didn't really know. He was remembering the sense of excitement he had felt earlier that evening when the elevator was carrying him up to dinner, the feeling that the missing piece in the jigsaw puzzle of his relationship to the Pragers was going to be supplied that night. Now that it had been supplied, he didn't doubt that the piece was big. What George suddenly found himself doubting was that this was the piece he had been waiting for.

"Assistant to the Publisher," he said. "It sounds pretty impressive. By the way, who's the publisher?"

"Me," said Rosemary Prager.

33

During the weeks that followed, while Rosemary was on the road with *The High Hand*, it became clear that she had spoken the truth when she said not even W. P. knew how many millions it would take to make *Noon* a going concern. Rosemary might have added that Wallace Watchman didn't know, either. Nor, it seemed to George, did he care.

"I don't want to sound like a penny-pinching bookkeeper," George said to W. P. across the brandy glasses in the triplex study one night after dinner when *The High Hand* was in Boston. "But do you have any idea what's been going on this last month, since you gave Wallace Watchman the go ahead on *Noon?*"

"Only vaguely," W. P. said. "It takes a long time for news to trickle all the way downtown to the Woolworth Building."

"Two floors in the Chaiken Building on Madison for editorial and executive offices, with options in the lease on two more floors. A printing contract with Tainter, Coe & Shaygitz out in Chicago that commits us to the extent of a million six by January first and could cost us three million, if all the penalty clauses are exercised. As for staff, I took a look late this afternoon at the list of—"

There was a tap on the door.

"Yes?" W. P. said.

Boland came in carrying a phone. "Miss Rosemary on the wire, sir. Calling from Boston."

"Thank you."

W. P. took the phone, kept it in his lap while the butler plugged it in, waited until Boland had left the room, then held the instrument out to George.

Startled, George took the phone. "Hello?" he said.

"Who's this?" Rosemary, at the other end, was apparently just as startled.

"It's me. George."

"I told that dope Boland I wanted to talk to Dad."

"Wait, I'll put him on."

"No, no. As long as I've got you, how are things going?"

"Okay, I guess. How's the play?"

"Awful. Nikita is in a sweat. They're not getting the renunciation scene. What do you mean, you guess?"

"I don't want to bother you with details. You've got enough on your hands with the play. Who's not getting the renunciation scene?"

"Everybody. The critics missed the point completely. Three of them said in their reviews that the boy's learning about the incest the day before Easter was deliberately sacrilegious, so we passed out audience reaction cards at last night's performance and today's matinee, and eight out of ten said they felt it had some kind of dirty meaning. Nikita's thrown the whole thing out and is starting from scratch. He's talking to the cast right now, which is why I've been able to sneak out to a phone. What do you mean you don't want to bother me with details? I'm publisher of the magazine, aren't I?"

"Sure, but this is mostly financial stuff. You wouldn't be interested."

"George, darling, if there's anything about *Noon* I'm not interested in, I don't deserve to be publisher. What's happening?"

"The Tainter, Coe & Shaygitz contract was signed today."

"What about the penalty clauses?"

"They're in, which is what I've been worrying about, because they mean if we don't start publication by December of 1941, which is closer than you think, we are stuck for—"

"We won't be stuck, because I'm going to have the first issue of *Noon* on the stands by that date if I have to write every word of it myself, so that's one thing you can stop worrying about. What about the Cost of Living Bureau?"

"I haven't had time to start worrying about it yet. It— Say, how did you know about that? Wallace brought it up for the first time at today's meeting."

"George, darling, where do you suppose Wallace got the idea to bring it up at today's meeting?"

"If you spend your time on the long-distance phone slipping ideas to Wallace Watchman, no wonder Nikita is having trouble with the renunciation scene."

"What was the point of my bothering you about it? It's an editorial idea. It has nothing to do with the business end."

"Doesn't it? What do you think that little editorial idea is going to cost? We've already got a staff big enough to turn out not a news magazine but two volumes of the Encyclopedia Britannica every week. This Cost of Living Bureau, if it gets set up the way Watchman outlined it at today's meeting, with legmen actually shopping for stuff in every part of the country, it could mean anywhere from four or five hundred to a thousand additional employees."

"So what?"

"Rosemary, the days of hiring staff members out of the Guatemalan jungles are over. Peonage and serfdom have vanished as American institutions. Remember Lincoln? He issued a proclamation. We now have labor unions, and my rough calculation at today's meeting, when Wallace dropped what I thought was *his* latest brain wave in our laps, was that this Cost of Living Bureau, which will be one page a week in the magazine, and not much of a reading page, either, just a bunch of comparative figures on the cost of carrots in Tulsa and what nylons are selling for in Maine, this little gem is going to set us back in salaries alone a minimum of seventy-five thousand dollars a week. You multiply seventy-five thousand by fifty-two weeks in the year and—"

"I think you're an absolute darling to worry about Daddy's seventy-five thousand multiplied by fifty-two."

"I'm not worrying about it because I'm an absolute darling. I'm worrying about it because in my official capacity as Assistant to the Publisher, for which I draw down a nice juicy fee, it is my duty—"

"I know all about your duties, darling, but this Cost of Living Bureau is an absolutely wonderful idea, precisely the sort of thing readers don't get in any other magazine, precisely the sort of thing we're starting *Noon* for, precisely the sort of thing Wallace Watchman is magnificent at. Why do you think I got Daddy to back this venture? So we could turn out a carbon copy of the magazines already on the stands? Now, here's what I want you to do."

"Yes, sir."

"So now I've hurt your feelings."

"No you haven't."

"Yes I have, and I'm sorry, but every time that accountant's mind of yours begins to show through the beautifully shaped head in which it's encased, I forget how good you are at kissing."

"Your father is here in the study with me."

"Well, if he thinks all we do when we go out is discuss Wallace Watchman's brain waves, it's time he learned different."

"It's pretty hard for a man in New York to go out with a girl who is struggling with Nikita Loewenthal's renunciation scene in Boston."

"Maybe things will ease up a little next week when we're in Philadelphia, in which case I'll run over to New York or you can come to Philly and we can sneak away and neck for a while."

"Rosemary!"

"Stop blushing. I know that extension in the study. Dad can't hear a thing even if he's sitting right on your neck, and I know damn well he's sitting at the other side of the fireplace inhaling brandy fumes and staring up at the Seven Ages of Man. Is there going to be a meeting tomorrow?"

"Two. General Implementation at eleven. Idea Round-Up at three-thirty."

"Wallace will undoubtedly move the Cost of Living Bureau to the General Implementation agenda, and when it comes up, George, I want you to lay off. Understand?"

"Yes, sir."

"You quit that."

"I'll put your father on."

"I don't have time. Nikita is calling me. Give him my love."

"All right."

"And George—"

"What?"

"Take some for yourself."

George hung up carefully. W. P. pulled his nose out of the brandy fumes.

"Sorry to have taken up all of Rosemary's time," George said. "She had to get back to the rehearsal. She sends you her love."

"Thank you," W. P. said. He tipped his head back and stared at the ceiling for a while as though he were following the progress of an insect across the intricately carved redwood. "You know," he said finally, "I didn't plan that phone call."

"Sir?"

"You were talking about matters in which I'm naturally interested, since my money is behind the venture, but it seemed to me they were matters that should have been more properly reserved for the ears of the person running the venture, namely, the publisher. When Boland came in and said the publisher was on the wire and wanted to speak to me, it suddenly occurred to me that here was an excellent opportunity to get something straightened out."

W. P. paused to dip his nose into the brandy fumes. The pince-nez danced crazily in the flickering light from the fireplace.

"From what you told me before Rosemary called, and from your conversation with her on the phone," W. P. said when his nose came free again, "I take it that you have some reservations about Wallace Watchman."

George hesitated, saw that the hesitation was in itself a derogatory comment, then found himself wondering uneasily if it was derogatory to him or to Wallace Watchman.

"Well, I must say I've never before met anybody like him."

"Would it perhaps be more accurate, George, to say that you've never before had anything to do with the planning of a magazine?"

"Yes, sir. That might be more accurate."

"Just the same, based purely on your experience in business matters, your reservations might be completely justified. Wallace Watchman may not be the right man to edit *Noon*. You may have spotted it early while everything is still in the planning phase, before too much damage has been done. If you're right, and he *is* the wrong man for the job, by acting on your discovery at once I would undoubtedly save myself a great deal of money. The only trouble is, George, that I don't care about the money. I care about Rosemary."

There was another pause while the neat little figure at the other side of the fireplace sought refreshment in the brandy fumes. What George sought, as he tried to put together the bits and pieces of the puzzling conversation, was a clue to William Prager's motives.

"A long time ago, in this very room, when you expressed surprise at Rosemary's passion for the theatre," W. P. said, "I told you that some day Rosemary would find her feet, and when she did we'd all better take to the hills. Do you remember that?"

"Yes, sir."

"I think she's on the verge of finding them. That's why I deliberately decided to activate the *Noon* project at a time when

Rosemary was immersed in *The High Hand* rehearsals. I wanted her to be pulled two ways. I wanted her old loyalty to the theatre to be forced into a fight with the excitement of this new venture. I don't believe in making it too easy for people to find their feet. If you rock the boat a little and they don't fall down, they'll stand up more steadily in the end. If they do stand up, that is. I'm pretty sure Rosemary will. When she does, I don't want to have to take to the hills. To prevent that, she's going to take some handling. I don't much relish the job. Frankly, I don't think I am capable of it."

There was another pause. This time W. P. didn't bother fooling with his prop. He seemed to have forgotten about the brandy glass he held cupped in both hands. Behind the shivering pince-nez his eyes, fixed on George, were slightly narrowed.

"That's why I called you in," W. P. said quietly. "Handling Rosemary should be a cinch for a boy from East Fourth Street."

34

Wallace Watchman's passion for meetings, George learned soon after he started attending them, could be traced to the editor's first job. After graduating from Harvard, Watchman, who came from a fairly wealthy Boston family with a long tradition of public service, spent two years as a volunteer worker in a Bowery mission. This experience left him with a firm conviction that almost any problem could be solved by gathering a number of people in a room and talking about it in a manner resembling a group of repentant sinners belting out a spiritual. As a result, the talk at the *Noon* meetings did not always make much sense to George, whose most persistent reaction was a wish that the meeting would end more quickly so he could leave the *Noon* offices and catch up with his work for other clients. He had noticed, however, that the swirling words had a tonic effect on Wallace Watchman. The editor had looked pale, spiritless, and exhausted when he came into the General Implementation meeting at eleven. Now, five minutes after the hour, as he explained how the smudgeless ink idea had come to him, he sounded like a man half his age who had just returned from a long, refreshing vacation.

"My mother will be celebrating her eightieth birthday next month," Watchman said. "She belongs to an older tradition. She doesn't think very much of this modern world we live in, and she thinks even less of the newspapers and magazines that are supposed to report it honestly and impartially. Just the same, she makes an effort to keep up with what's going on. She reads several newspapers every day, all the news magazines every week, and I don't know how many monthly publications. This past week end, when I was visiting her in Boston, I happened to remark that she made me feel ashamed because she did so much better a job of keeping in touch with the world than I did. Perhaps I do, she said, but I'm thinking of giving it up. Why? I asked, thinking she would say the news she kept up with was too depressing for an old woman, which I certainly would have understood, or that reading so many publications took too much of her waning strength. I'm thinking of giving it up, she said, because of the cheap ink those publications use. Whenever I finish reading a newspaper or a magazine I feel as though I've been making up a coal fire with my bare hands. Look at my fingers, she said, and I looked. They were smudged with printer's ink. If somebody would only print a newspaper or a magazine with ink that did not come off on my hands, my mother said, I would not only read every issue from first page to last, but I would urge all my friends to do the same."

Watchman paused, touched the four small warts on his cheek, and smiled at the people gathered around the conference table.

"Five minutes later," he said, "I was on the long-distance phone to Chicago. Do you want to take it from there, Mr. Shaygitz?"

He gestured to the printer, who had flown in from Chicago for this meeting.

"Yes, thank you, Mr. Watchman," the printer said. "I've already indicated in another connection how proud we are at Tainter, Coe & Shaygitz to be associated with the appearance of what we all feel confident will be a major American publication. I would like to say now that we are proud for another reason. We at Tainter, Coe & Shaygitz think of ourselves as more than printers. We think of ourselves as participants in the task of making communications for the American people simpler and easier. For years we at Tainter, Coe & Shaygitz have felt about printer's inks the way Mr. Watchman's mother feels about them, and for years our research department has been at work on the problem. By a happy coincidence, at the almost precise moment when Mr. Watchman's call came in the other day, our plans had moved out of the research phase into the realm of practical reality. A smudgeless printer's ink has ceased to be a dream."

Mr. Shaygitz pulled back the zipper of his bulging briefcase, plunged in his hand like a magician going after a rabbit in a top hat, and came up with a red-labeled tin about the size of a can of baked beans.

"Gentlemen," he said, placing the tin on the table, "TAKOSHAY, the first printer's ink guaranteed not to come off on the reader's fingers." He pulled the zipper shut. "Few things would give us at Tainter, Coe & Shaygitz greater pleasure than to launch TAKOSHAY simultaneously with the publication of *Noon*."

Mr. Shaygitz sat back in his chair. Wallace Watchman leaned forward in his. He touched the red tin with a forefinger, as though he were tapping a tuning fork. Tilting his head to one side, he smiled as though listening for the note. It seemed to be the right one. He straightened up abruptly and pointed to Nick Tomasino, the circulation manager who had been brought on from Philadelphia and added to the *Noon* staff the week before.

"Nick, please," Watchman said. "Spell it out for us circulation-wise."

Nick cleared his throat. "Well, circulation-wise, Chief," he said, and then he leaned forward and began to speak more rapidly. "From the standpoint of circulation, I mean, I'd say this. I can't guarantee I can go to American News or Curtis or any of the other big distributors, I can't put it in black and white, a written guarantee, just because I tell them we're getting out a magazine that the ink it don't come off on your fingers they'll double their orders. This, any guy tries to tell you he can guarantee that, you can tell him from me Nick Tomasino says he's either a God-damn liar or he's just plain stupid, because I been in this business for years and I'm telling you, it comes to circulation, these big jobbers, what they're looking for, they want a—"

"Nick," Wallace Watchman said. "The plus factors are what we're interested in."

Nick bobbed his head. "I'm coming to that," he said. "The plus factors is like this. We got a good book, the jobbers they want what we're selling, on top of that if I tell them we got a gimmick, too, we got this ink it don't come off on your hands, then you got something.

I mean *then* this ink gimmick, it could pay off, but like maybe even big."

Wallace Watchman lifted his hand to Al Kreitzberg, the advertising manager.

Al came in smoothly. "Speaking from the advertising point of view," he said, "I can say this without the slightest hesitation or fear of contradiction. Give me a handle like smudgeless ink and I can lift *Noon* to the top."

To the top of what, George wondered, but there was no time to ask. Wallace Watchman swung toward him.

"How about you, George?" the editor said. "What do you think?"

If there was not precisely a touch of deference in his voice, there was enough of a change in tone to indicate clearly what Watchman, like everybody else in the room, was aware of: George represented the man who was paying their salaries. William Prager had never set foot in this room. He didn't have to, however, as long as George did.

"It's hard to say at this stage," George said. He was keenly aware of his power. He was even more keenly aware that he enjoyed it. What he was most keenly aware of, however, was that the power had not been handed to him for his enjoyment. Not because he wanted to be fair to Wallace Watchman, but because he wanted to hold onto the power he enjoyed, George exercised it with care. He said quietly, "It sounds fine, but before I okay it, Wallace, I'd want to know a few more things about it."

"What sort of things, George?"

There was no anger in Watchman's voice. He was too shrewd an operator to give himself away like that. But his hand went to the warts on his cheek in an involuntary gesture of irritation. George understood how he felt. The group had turned in a beautiful performance. Together, responding to his leadership, they had made a series of lovely noises. Now this damn bookkeeper had to come along with his completely irrelevant unmusical questions.

"Well, for example," George said, "I'd want to know how much using this smudgeless ink will add to the cost of printing each copy."

"That's easy," Wallace Watchman said. "I'm sure Mr. Shaygitz can tell us that."

"So am I," George said as Mr. Shaygitz started pulling papers from his briefcase. "But I don't think this is the time or place for us to go into it. You've presented the idea, Wallace. Al and Nick have given us their views. I suggest that as a next step Mr. Shaygitz prepare a report on costs for me. Could you do that, Mr. Shaygitz?"

"Certainly, sir."

"If you'll send it along," George said, "I'll go over it with the production people and see how it shapes up. If we can afford to use SHAKOTAY—"

"TA-ko-SHAY," the printer said. "It's a combination of the first syllable of our three names. Tainter, Coe, and Shaygitz. TAKOSHAY."

"I'm sorry, TAKOSHAY," George said. "If the cost doesn't prove prohibitive, I assure you, Mr. Shaygitz, we'll give every consideration to the possibility of using it for printing *Noon*. In the meantime, on behalf of the publisher, who is unfortunately out of town just now, I want to thank you for giving us the benefit of your views on this interesting subject."

"Not at all, sir," said Mr. Shaygitz. "It was my pleasure."

"And I wish, Wallace, you would convey the publisher's thanks to your mother," George said. "For sparking you into this interesting

ll do that," Watchman said. "But I must say I'm disappointed, George. I was hoping we could close this smudgeless ink thing here and now."

"I'm afraid we can't," George said, and since there was no way to say a thing like that without underscoring the words with the cutting edge of authority, he smiled at Wallace Watchman and added, "But I have one piece of news for you that I think will take the sting out of your disappointment over TAKOSHAY."

"What's that, George?"

"Your idea for a Cost of Living Bureau. The one you raised at yesterday's meeting. I had a talk about it with the publisher last night—"

"Is she back in town?"

"No, I talked with her on the phone," George said. "We discussed the pros and cons and finally decided to give you a go-ahead on that. You can start staffing at once."

"That's swell, George. I knew she'd see it my way. She's—" Watchman paused, fingered his warts for a moment as he gave George a quick glance, then said, "I was sure you'd *both* see it my way. After all, it's a damned smart idea to give your readers—" The phone at his elbow cut him short. Watchman picked it up and said,

"Hello?" There was a pause. "Yes, he is. Just a moment." He held the phone out to George. "For you."

"Tell them to take a message, will you?" George said. "I don't want to hold up the meeting."

Watchman's hand, holding out the phone, did not drop. "It's Miss Prager," he said. "Calling from Boston."

George reached for the phone, realized it was a mistake, then realized it was too late to correct it. Everybody in the room was watching him. He took the phone.

"Hello?"

"George, darling, listen. I've got only a minute. Can you hear me?"

"Clearly."

"You sound so stiff and formal."

"I'm in a meeting."

"Good. You'll have something to tell them when I hang up. You know that Cost of Living Bureau thing you were peeing on last night?"

"What about it?"

"I've been thinking over what you said about spending five thousand dollars a week for one page that shows the pri carrots in Dallas, and I think you're right. It's not all that hot an idea. Tell Wallace I've changed my mind. It's out."

"But Rosemary—"

"I can't talk very long, darling. Nikita's got a new slant on the renunciation scene and he's working us to death. The Cost of Living Bureau thing is out."

"Yes, but—"

"There's another thing, however, that I want in. Wallace told me on the phone yesterday he's going to bring it up at today's meeting. Smudgeless ink. Did he?"

"Yes, but—"

"I think that's one of the best ideas we've come up with yet. Wallace said he'd have that printer from Chicago at the meeting. Shaygitz. Is he there?"

"Yes, he's—"

"Then we can really begin to cook on this smudgeless ink at once. Give him the go-ahead."

"Rosemary—"

"I must run, darling. Here comes Nikita."

For several moments George continued to hold the dead phone at his ear, as though he were still listening, but he was not sure the pretense was successful. The faces around the table were expressionless. Yet George could tell that they knew something had happened. He could even tell that they sensed what it was. He didn't have to guess how it made them feel. He could figure that out for himself.

"All right," he said into the dead phone when he felt he could trust his voice. "Good-bye," he said, keeping the anger throttled down tight in a corner of his mind, trying to sound casual. All things considered, especially the way his heart was going, he succeeded. There were limits to what a man would do for his three squares a day. Even if the three squares included caviar. Mr. William Prager could get himself another pratt boy. His daughter Rosemary had just given George Hurst her last order.

"Gentlemen," he said to the men around the table, and then the angry words he had not had the time or the courage to say on the phone stopped in his throat. It was as though he had been thrust back a dozen years, to the alley outside the Allied Employment Agency on Church Street, and he had just punched the young man who had torn up his application blank because they had no jobs for Jews. Clearly, as though his old friend were sitting at his elbow, George could hear the voice of Danny Schorr saying quietly, "What do you want, kid? You want a job? Or you want to be a hero? Make up your mind."

George let the rage slide away. When would he learn to keep his eye on the ball? When would he grow up enough to stop confusing issues? What was the point of getting angry? He knew what he wanted. He had made up his mind the night William Prager sent him downtown to the Jefferson Theatre to get the details from Rosemary.

"Gentlemen," George said to Wallace Watchman and the other men around the table. "Gentlemen," he repeated, accepting the moment of humiliation as part of the price he had to pay for what he wanted, "I'd like to add some corrections to my previous remarks."

35

The day *The High Hand* opened in New York, shortly after three o'clock in the afternoon or less than six hours before the curtain was scheduled to go up, Leonard Prager came into George's office.

"With whom are you dining tonight?"

"I have a tentative date with Rosemary."

"Tentative is hardly the word," Leonard said. "She'll be taking Nikita Loewenthal's temperature and feeding him aspirin until curtain time. She'll never get out for dinner. How about eating with me?"

George hesitated. His feelings about Leonard Prager had not changed. Concealing them, however, had become more complicated. His contacts with Leonard were no longer limited to occasional meetings at parties in W. P.'s triplex at Seventy-first and Park. As soon as *Noon* had gone into what Wallace Watchman called "rehearsal gear," meaning that while the magazine was not yet actually being published the staff was going through the motions of getting out an issue every week, Leonard Prager had quit his job at City College and assumed his duties as the *Noon* dramatic critic. He covered all the openings, wrote reviews, and came into the office every day to handle the details of his job as head of the magazine's drama department. George didn't know how well he handled them. Wallace Watchman seemed to be satisfied. What George did know was that having just down the hall a man you didn't like, but from whom you had to conceal your dislike, was a pain in the neck.

"I'll give Rosemary a ring and see what she says."

"I just gave her a ring," Leonard said. "She said it was okay for you to have dinner with me."

"This may come as news to you, Leonard, but I like to run my own life."

"I'd got the impression these last few months that you'd forgotten how."

"What's that remark supposed to mean?"

Leonard's thin lips twisted in a small, sardonic smile. "You know what it means, George. You're not stupid. Nobody who is stupid could have moved in on my brother and entrenched himself as solidly as you have. Of course, if you're afraid that by dining with me you'll be offending W. P. to the point where he might cut you out of his will, I withdraw the invitation."

"I'm not afraid of anything, Leonard, and I wasn't aware that what you had extended was an invitation."

"Well, it is, and since I don't like to see bright people utter stupid remarks, let me straighten you out on a rather important point. We're all afraid of something, George. I can tell you what I'm afraid of, and perhaps some day I will, since this is obviously neither the time nor the place. I can also tell you what you're afraid of, but this is not the time or the place for that, either. So why don't we both limit ourselves to the matter in hand? I've invited you to dine with me before we go to the opening. Yes or no?"

"Thank you very much. It will be a pleasure."

Leonard's reedy body dipped in a short, mocking bow. "I will do my best to make it so. Have you ever been to the Aqua Vit?"

"No."

"They have a rather good smorgasbord, and it's on Sixth Avenue, between Forty-sixth and Forty-seventh, just around the corner from the Jefferson Theatre, which makes it convenient for tonight. How about meeting me there in the bar at, what, seven-thirty okay?"

"That will be fine," George said.

He doubted it. Being needled by Leonard in the office was bad enough. George didn't look forward to a solid hour of it across a dinner table. His doubts seemed more than justified when, on coming into the bar of the Aqua Vit at seven-thirty, he found that Leonard was sitting with two girls. Leonard's sharp tongue was always sharpest in front of an audience.

"See?" Leonard said to the girls. "I told you he was prompt."

The girls laughed and Leonard performed the introductions. George didn't get the names and made no effort to correct the omission. He knew all about Leonard Prager's girls. He had met a dozen or more of them. Their names didn't matter. They were all shicksehs, because Leonard disliked Jewish women, and they were all much younger than Leonard because he met them when they came up to speak to him after one of the lectures on English literature he was invited to give quite frequently at the various women's colleges in and around New York. Leonard's girls were always interested in all the arts, passionate about at least one, full of bright although not necessarily intelligible talk about several, and attractive in a cold way that George found a little upsetting. He would have been similarly upset if, when he was a kid, he had found Mike Gerrity attractive.

"We're having martinis," Leonard said. "What about you?"

"Scotch and water," George said.

"Accountants always drink Scotch," Leonard said. "I've often wondered why. I suppose because it's associated in their minds with the Scotch passion for thrift. If you drink martinis you end up in the gutter, but if you drink Scotch your books will balance."

The girls laughed, which did not surprise George. Leonard Prager's girls always laughed at his jokes. Encouraged by their response, Leonard made a few more. George didn't hear most of them. He was watching the clock. At ten minutes to eight he began to shift about on his bar stool.

"The bookkeeper in the party is getting restless," Leonard said. "Okay, girls, I guess we'd better grab plates and start working our way around the herring display."

George felt a stab of irritation. He had assumed up to this moment that Leonard had run into the girls in the bar and, while he waited for George and the girls waited for their dates, Leonard had asked them to have a drink with him. Now, grasping the annoying fact that Leonard had apparently also invited these two girls to join him and George for dinner, George wondered how they would be able to shake them in time to get to the theatre before the curtain went up. Few things annoyed W. P. more than people who came late to a play. Especially on an opening night.

"I don't know about Leonard," George said. "He's a dramatic critic, so I suppose he doesn't have to see all of a play to understand it or enjoy it. But me, I'm just an accountant. If I'm not in my seat before the curtain rises, I never catch up with the plot."

The girls laughed. Not as loudly as they had laughed at Leonard's jokes, but that was all right with George. He didn't think enough of any shickseh to want to make an impression on her, and he thought even less of those who went out with Leonard Prager. When these two went off with their plates for a second crack at the smorgasbord, George put down his napkin.

"Thanks for the dinner, but do you mind if I run along?" he said. "It's almost eight-thirty."

"Relax," Leonard said. "The curtain isn't going up on this clambake until nine o'clock, and from what I know of *The High Hand* after reading the script and listening to Rosemary yak about it for almost a year, we wouldn't want to be unchivalrous enough to subject these two nice girls to it on an empty stomach. Give them a chance to put away a second helping of the smoked eel liver before we drag them to their dose of Spanish symbolism as interpreted by Nikita Loewenthal."

"You mean they're going to the *opening* with us?"

"Few things would please me more than to take them to something more thrilling, like, say, a visit to the Aquarium. But you may recall that I happen to be the dramatic critic for an exciting new magazine called *Noon* that has not yet appeared on the stands but is treating its staff as though it has already been what Mr. Wallace Watchman calls activated, and I must attend this gruesome spectacle. Purely in the line of duty, of course."

"Leonard, for Christ's sake, why didn't you tell me you were inviting a couple of—?"

"Steady, George. Let's not have a scene, shall we? Here come the girls."

He rose gallantly and waited while the girls, carrying heaped plates that looked like colored topographical maps of the Andes, worked their way back into their chairs. George, who was furious, didn't budge. How could he have been so dumb as to let himself get trapped by a mean little bastard like Leonard Prager?

"Would you girls mind disposing of those highly indigestible comestibles a bit more rapidly?" Leonard said. "In case I haven't already told you, Mr. Nikita Loewenthal and his Living Theatre are in business only because of the generosity of my brother, Mr. William Prager, and since the Pragers will be out in full force tonight, and Mr. Hurst is a big wheel in the Prager financial empire, he naturally doesn't want to offend the biggest wheel of all from whom all blessings flow by being late."

"It isn't that," George said.

"What is it, then?" Leonard said through his mocking smile. "A new passion for the theatre?"

"No, just an old passion for keeping appointments," George said. Both girls had stopped eating and were staring at him and Leonard. "You knew damn well when you came to my office this afternoon and invited me to dinner that I'm sitting with the Prager party and that I'm supposed to be escorting Rosemary."

"Oh, now, look," one of the girls said. "If we're in the way—"

"Nonsense," Leonard said.

"It doesn't seem to be nonsense to Mr. Hurst," the girl said. "It certainly isn't," George said. "I'm sorry, Miss—Miss—?" "Sherrod," she said.

"I'm sorry, Miss Sherrod, but—"

"You needn't complicate matters by lying about it," she said. "You're not sorry at all."

"You're wrong," George said, glaring at her. "I'm damned sorry that you allowed your friend Mr. Prager to put you in an embarrassing position."

"Mr. Prager doesn't put women in embarrassing positions," Leonard said. "Not attractive ones, anyway. Miss Sherrod happens to be my date for tonight. She also happens to have been at Bennington with Rosemary. When I called my niece early this afternoon to wish her luck for tonight and told her Mary Sherrod was going with me to the opening and she wanted me to pass along her best wishes, too, Rosemary asked me to do her a favor. There were still so many things to take care of, she said, what with keeping Nikita on his feet and the cast on their toes, that she wasn't going to be able to have dinner with you as she'd planned, and since she was going to have to be backstage all evening she wasn't even going to be able to sit with you. She didn't want you to feel foolish, sitting through the performance with an empty seat beside you, so she asked me if I could get a girl for you and then the four of us could sit together. I said I would be delighted to do that favor for my niece Rosemary and my friend George, and I called on Miss Sherrod for help, with which she was promptly forthcoming, saying her friend and roommate, who also happened to be at Bennington with Rosemary, would be glad to join us tonight." The sardonic smile dug deeper into Leonard Prager's face as, with one of the short, mocking bows that always infuriated George, he said to the other girl, "May I take another stab, Miss Bucknell, at introducing you to your date for tonight? It doesn't seem to have taken the first time. George Hurst, Eileen Bucknell. Eileen Bucknell, George Hurst."

"How do you do?" she said, and covered her mouth with both hands in a hopeless attempt to conceal a giggle.

"How do you do?" George said, feeling not only foolish but baffled and, all at once, a little uneasy. He had never been on a date with a shickseh. He turned to Leonard and said, "Why the hell couldn't you explain all that in the first place?"

"The first place was so jammed to the scuppers with your nervous comments about being late for the curtain, it was pretty hard to slip a word in edgewise or otherwise." Leonard glanced at his watch. "Now I think we really *had* better get to our seats."

They proved to be on the aisle in the fourth row, immediately in front of Albert Dworkin and his wife and W. P. and Mrs. Prager. Since George and Leonard and the two girls arrived just as the house lights were being dimmed, there was no time to do more than nod a hasty greeting to W. P. and Mrs. Prager. They nodded back pleasantly enough, but Albert Dworkin's eyebrows went up when he saw the girls and, just before George turned to sit down, he saw the lawyer lean toward W. P. and whisper something in his ear.

As a result, all during the first act, instead of taking in what was happening on the stage, George was working out in his mind the phrasing of the explanation he would make to W. P. during the intermission about how he happened to be with a strange girl at an opening he was supposed to attend with Rosemary. It was not an easy thing to phrase, because, while the facts were innocent enough, imbedding them in an explanation changed their tone so that, even in his own mind, George sounded like a man caught with his hand in the till trying to pretend he had been reaching for a shoehorn.

Even though he succeeded finally in working out an explanation that he thought would accomplish the neat trick of allaying W. P.'s suspicions while at the same time saving something of George's face for feeling the necessity to allay suspicion, he didn't get a chance to make it. By the time the lights went on and George had slipped out of his seat and turned, the Pragers were moving up the aisle in the center of a chattering group of Living Theatre well-wishers. The group grew larger in the lobby, where George found himself nailed to the wall by Eileen Bucknell, who had a great deal to say about the first act of *The High Hand* and apparently felt it necessary to accompany what she said with whooping screams of delight. She attracted quite a lot of attention.

On the way down the aisle to his seat for the second act, George tried to work his way next to W. P., but Albert Dworkin got there first. While pretending as the lights went down that he was listening to Miss Bucknell, George leaned back and tried to hear what Albert Dworkin was whispering in W. P.'s ear. He couldn't. As a result, George absorbed nothing of what happened onstage during the second act, but he managed to shorten and sharpen the explanation he had worked out for W. P. during the first act.

When the lights went up for the second intermission George was quicker about getting to his feet, but he was not quick enough. Leonard Prager got to W. P. ahead of him. George hoped, as a new and larger wave of Living Theatre members and friends closed in and cut him off, that Leonard would explain about the two girls. But George knew the hope was vain. Leonard, who was a bastard to begin with, was bound to be a trouble-making son of a bitch to the bitter end. He was not, however, stupid.

"In case you're worrying about any misinterpretation my brother might place on your showing up here tonight with a strange girl," Leonard said quietly to George as they moved back down the aisle to their seats, "I just explained the circumstances to W. P."

"Thanks," George said, and then, hearing the relief in his own voice, his face went hot. "I mean—"

"I know what you mean," Leonard said dryly. "I wanted to put your mind at ease so you could enjoy the third act. I hear it's the best."

For George, who had not heard a word of the first and second, it certainly proved to be the most interesting: immediately following the renunciation scene, he suddenly realized that he could, if he wanted to, sleep with Miss Bucknell.

He didn't know how he knew, any more than he had ever known the same thing in the past with other girls. It was not only the slight pressure of Miss Bucknell's knee against his; or her faint, almost inaudible yet highly significant intake of breath when, shifting his weight an inch or two on the uncomfortable seat, his elbow brushed hers; or the way, when something happened on the stage that touched or amused her, she turned with a quick, half-formed smile to share the moment with him. It was all of those things, plus many more George could neither define nor identify, that always added up to the same thing: an inner voice suddenly advising him that this particular chase was won.

He had won often enough not to be overwhelmed by the assurance that it was going to happen again. Never before having embarked on a chase that involved a shickseh, however, the assurance this time carried with it overtones that were distressing. Gently returning the pressure of Miss Bucknell's knee, George suddenly felt the way he used to feel in the L. L. Parker mailroom when Mr. Shumacher came to the punch line of one of his stories about heebs and, along with the rest of the staff, George let out a bellow of laughter.

Rosemary, however, had been on the road with *The High Hand* for several weeks. George had not slept with her or anybody else for a long time. And since the opening was to be followed by a huge party in the Prager triplex that would probably go on until the small hours, the chances of his sleeping with Rosemary that night were pretty slim.

In view of all this, George found it surprisingly easy to overlook the fact that Miss Bucknell was not Jewish. It was astonishing when you got right down to it, and George promptly did, how little difference there was between the feel of a Jewish girl's thigh and that of a shickseh. In a darkened theatre, at any rate.

George was grateful, when the play ended, for the curtain call as an institution. It gave him and Miss Bucknell a chance to pull themselves together. When he felt he had, George turned around to tell W. P. what a magnificent job he thought Nikita Loewenthal had done, and saw that the Pragers and the Dworkins, surrounded by a shoal of Living Theatre enthusiasts, were already at the top of the aisle. Somebody touched George's shoulder. He turned. Leonard Prager was grinning at him.

"Don't worry about it," Leonard said. "You can pick up all your loose ends when you get to the party."

"I wasn't thinking of loose ends," George said. "I was thinking I have to go backstage and say hello to Rosemary."

"No you don't," Leonard said. "When I talked to her on the phone this afternoon she said to tell you not to try to go backstage. It'll be a madhouse. Rosemary said to go right on to Seventy-first Street and she'll meet you at the party. Would you mind taking Eileen?"

"Who?" George said, and then, as Leonard and both girls burst into laughter, George blushed. "Sorry," he said to Miss Bucknell. "I'm not very good at names." To cover his embarrassment, he leaned across Eileen Bucknell and said, "What about Miss Sherrod?"

"You can call her Mary, and she's coming with me to the office," Leonard said. "I like to have a pretty girl pacing about impatiently while I write a review. It brings out the Max Beerbohm in me. When I finish the review, Mary and I will come along and join you at the party."

"What kind of a review are you going to write?" Eileen Bucknell said as they moved slowly up the aisle with the crowd. "I mean," and she released one of her whooping screams of laughter, "considering that it's your brother's money that got the show on, and your niece is Nikita Loewenthal's assistant."

"Neither of those factors would stop me from saying it stank if it did stink," Leonard said. "In point of fact, while a good deal of it is pure beeswax, especially the heavy-handed symbolism about the goats and making the kid play the whole second act with that stuffed bird hanging around his neck, the fact remains that there's a hell of a lot of writing with hair on it in this play. I mean real guts. Especially the renunciation scene in the third act, where I think Nikita has really done a superb job of making you feel the terror of the mother complex meeting the eerie sweetness of the child's fantasy about the Hershey bar. That's real theatre, kids."

"I thought it was a lot of silly nonsense."

Leonard stopped to stare at Mary Sherrod. So did George and Eileen Bucknell.

"I beg your pardon?" Leonard said. "What was that last remark, lass?"

"I said I thought the renunciation scene was a lot of silly nonsense," Miss Sherrod repeated, and George wondered with sudden surprise why he shouldn't have noticed earlier not only that she was blond but easily the most beautiful girl he had ever seen. "It all hinged on the boy recognizing his father. Well, for heaven's sake, Leonard, aside from the father and the boy, the only other things on that stage were the two goats, the stuffed bird, and the mother. Any kid who couldn't pick his father out of that crew ought to be locked up."

Since this was precisely what George had felt, but had lacked the courage to say, he wished his date had said it instead of Leonard's. What Leonard wished, George could see, was that Miss Mary Sherrod would keep her pretty mouth shut. He took her arm and steered her up the aisle as though he were rushing her to the edge of a cliff.

"See you later," Eileen called after them when they were all out in the street, but only Mary Sherrod waved back in reply. Leonard Prager didn't even turn. Eileen Bucknell released one of her whooping screams and said, "Did you ever see anybody so mad?"

"Not nearly as mad as I'm going to be if we don't find a cab," George said. "Let's try Sixth Avenue."

They tried it, and found one, and as soon as George had given the driver the address of the Prager triplex, Miss Bucknell slid into his arms. She kissed him with her mouth open and managed, by freeing one hand, to undo the top two buttons of her dress so that he could reach her breasts.

"Why do we have to go to this damn party?" she whispered after a while. "Don't you live some place?"

"We won't stay long," George said. "I just have to show my face to some people."

The first one who saw it was Boland.

"Good evening, sir," the butler said. "Miss Rosemary was asking for you."

George, who was halfway out of his coat, stopped moving. "Miss Rosemary is here?"

"Yes, sir."

It was not the slight change in the butler's voice that told George he was in trouble. It was what he had learned during the past five years about the way the Prager mind worked. He finished taking off his coat and handed it to Boland.

"What's up?" Eileen Bucknell said as George took her arm and steered her around the Rodin, across the foyer, and out onto the small landing of the circular stairway. "I mean, you look sort of funny all of a sudden."

"It must be that smorgasbord," George said. "I've never been much good with smoked herring and sweet meatballs."

"My God," Eileen said, looking down into the huge room. "Are they going to feed this whole mob?"

George didn't answer. He was raking the crowded room swiftly with his glance, hunting for the place where he would have to take his punishment. There was no way to avoid it. The best he could hope for was that it would not be too public. Mrs. Prager, at her familiar stand beside the caviar tray, saw him and waved. George waved back.

"Who's that?" Eileen said.

"The lady of the manor. She wants us to come have some caviar."

"Well, what's holding us up?"

It proved to be W. P., waiting at the foot of the stairs. It had been impossible to see him from the landing at the top. George did not doubt that W. P. knew this when he took up his station.

"I'd like you to meet a classmate of Rosemary's," George said. "Miss Bucknell, Mr. Prager."

"How do you do?" W. P. said with a courtly bow. "Do you mind, my dear, if I have a word with George in private?"

"Don't keep him too long," Eileen said. "Nobody as good-looking as that should be kept private."

W. P. turned without another word and headed for the study. Following him, George had a moment of relief. At least it was not going to be done in front of all the guests.

"I'll come right to the point," William Prager said as he closed the door and planted himself in front of the fire with his hands clasped behind him. He didn't even bother to set the stage by easing himself into the red leather chair or provide himself with a hand prop by pouring out some brandy. "I'm shocked by your conduct tonight."

So was George, but for an entirely different reason.

"May I ask why, sir?"

"If you really need a reply to that question you're hardly the man to whom I have turned over the management of an investment that will run to several million dollars. You have done the one thing that I find absolutely inexcusable. You have humiliated my family in public."

It was like being accused of insulting Pike's Peak.

"I don't see how," George said, trying not to sound as desperate as he felt. "But if I have, I assure you it was unintentional. Everything I did tonight was done in accordance with instructions from Rosemary as conveyed to me by your brother Leonard."

"I am not criticizing you for being misled by my brother Leonard. I have no doubt that he tricked you into taking that girl to the theatre with you. I'm even certain he lied to you and said it was not necessary to go backstage after the final curtain to find Rosemary. That is not the point. The point is not even that you should have learned by this time to distrust my brother, who is a malicious troublemaker, and act as your own intelligence dictates, not Leonard's. The point is that you failed in your responsibility to my family."

"I'm afraid I can only repeat that I don't understand how, sir."

"The seat that was reserved for Rosemary in that theatre should not have been occupied by anybody else. It should have remained empty all through the performance." William Prager paused, obviously waiting to see if George understood. He did: when Queen Victoria

found it impossible because she was indisposed to attend the opening of Parliament, Prince Albert did not ask a girl friend to accompany him so that he wouldn't feel lonely with an empty throne
beside him. "After the performance was over," William Prager continued, "Rosemary should have had an escort to take her home to
this party. Do you understand now?"

"Yes, sir."

"Are you saying that to bring to an end an extremely unpleasant
interlude, or do you really understand what I mean?"

"I really understand," George said.

He sure did. What he didn't understand was how he could have
forgotten it. The Pragers had the money to buy anything they wanted,
including George Hurst. They didn't quibble about price. They
merely insisted on getting full value for their money.

"In that case," W. P. said, and it was only when his probing
forefinger sent the pince-nez into a wild shivering dance on the
knife-thin nose that George realized the small, neat figure on the
hearth had been standing absolutely rigid. "In that case," William
Prager repeated, "I can assume without asking for your assurance
that it won't happen again."

36

The High Hand received only one favorable review. Since this appeared in *Noon*, a magazine that was merely going through the
motions of publication and was still unavailable to the public,
Leonard Prager's rave did nothing for the play at the box office. The
morning after *The High Hand* closed, Rosemary Prager moved into
the *Noon* offices and assumed her duties as publisher on a full-time
basis. A number of changes took place immediately.

The General Implementation meeting, for example, which had
always been held at eleven in the morning, was moved up to four-
thirty in the afternoon, and an extra secretary was added to the
personnel of the meeting so that the work of the girl who took notes
would not have to be interrupted when the phone rang. Unfortunately, the girl assigned to take calls at the meeting had been
hired only the day before, so that she was still shaky about the names
of the staff members.

"Miss Prayer?" she said uncertainly, holding a hand over the mouthpiece and staring at the faces gathered round the big table. "Is there a Miss Prayer in the room?"

"Prager, darling," Rosemary said from the head of the table. "That's one name you should try to remember. I own the place. Who is it?"

"A Mr. Loewenthal."

"Tell him I'm in a meeting. I'll call back when I'm free." Rosemary stubbed out her cigarette as though she were trying to drive it through the ash tray into the table. "My God," she said to the room at large. "You'd think I was four people. Well, I'm afraid Nikita Loewenthal's going to get somebody else to hold his hand from now on. I've done my last chore for the Living Theatre. I've got a magazine to run. Where was I, Wallace?"

"You were advocating the addition of a staff of roving artists," Watchman said. "To supplement the staff of photographers we already have."

"You mean artists like with brushes and paints?" Nick Tomasino said.

"Did you think maybe I meant concert artists?" Rosemary said. "This is a magazine. Not Carnegie Hall. Get up on your toes, Nick. A lot of stuff is happening. A circulation manager who misses too much of it isn't going to be much of a circulation manager."

Nick Tomasino's dark face grew darker. "Anything I miss, Miss Prager, it ain't worth looking at," he said. "All I meant, I never heard on a weekly news magazine a staff of artists with brushes and paints like this Rembrandt or something."

"You never heard of a weekly news magazine that accepts no advertising, either," Rosemary said. "*Noon* is a completely new kind of publication, and if Rembrandt were alive I'd break my back trying to hire him, because he's precisely the sort of artist I had in mind."

"Before we go into the personnel aspects," Wallace Watchman said, "I wonder if it might not be wise, Rosemary, for you to give us a little more of a spellout on the motivation behind the idea?"

"Here, look." Rosemary held up a copy of that morning's *New York Times*. "An American ship, *The City of Flint*, gets seized by a German raider and is taken to a neutral port, Murmansk. Big news, right? On the front page of every paper in the country, right? The subject of major stories in all the news magazines that will hit the stands this week, right? Including our practice copy of *Noon*, right?"

Wallace Watchman's hand darted nervously to the warts on his cheekbone. The editor, who was not a tall man, seemed to have shrunk several inches since Rosemary had moved into the office.

"Absolutely," he said. "The German seizure of *The City of Flint* is an event of major importance. A couple more like that and those dumb Germans will drive us into this war the way they did in 1917."

"So we have an event of major importance," Rosemary said. "An event that could drive this country to war. And where are the pictures?"

"I beg your pardon?" Wallace Watchman said.

"Where are the pictures of this tremendous event that might drive this country into a war?"

"Well, Rosemary, really," Watchman said. "The only people on the scene were the German raider and *The City of Flint*, and the scene was mid-ocean. You can hardly expect a staff of photographers from *Life* or even *Noon* to have been hanging about in a rowboat so they could be present at the appropriate moment and take pictures of the event."

"Precisely, Wallace. There *were* no photographers around to take pictures of the event, and if you stop and think about it for one split intelligent second, you'll realize that there are no photographers around at *most* tremendous news events. Photographers always get there later. And yet one picture, there's a Chinaman keeps saying in all those ads, is worth ten thousand words. If he's not kidding, and I for one believe him, what are we going to do about it?"

"Rosemary," Wallace Watchman said, and there was a touch of desperation in his voice, "I'm afraid I can't follow you."

"How about it, Al?" Rosemary said. "Do you follow me?"

Al Kreitzberg, who had been building a tent in front of his ash tray with two match-book covers and a gold pencil, looked up with the preoccupied half-smile and slightly narrowed eyes of an architect who had been called back to the workaday world from his recurring, glowing dream of The Perfect City.

"As I understand it, Rosemary," he said in the smooth, rolling voice that always reminded George of the way Aunt Tessie's sewing machine used to purr out in the store while he sat at the kitchen table after supper doing his homework, "there are events which we as a news magazine should be intensely interested in covering photo-graphically, but the very nature of the event makes such coverage impossible. This *City of Flint* thing today, for example. Or, to take other examples at random, a plane blowing up in mid-air while flying over the North Pole, or a submarine ramming into some undersea obstruction, say, an iceberg or a rock, and going to the bottom with all hands. Later, when some of the bodies or the wreck-age is recovered, it's possible to get pictures of those bodies and that wreckage, but it's absolutely impossible to get pictures of the moment when the accident took place, except maybe by a fluke. I mean, Rosemary, that's my understanding of it."

"I wish I could say whether that puts this meeting ahead or behind," Rosemary said dryly. She put a cigarette to her lips and Al Kreitzberg snapped a light across the table with a smile from which an uninformed observer, coming into the room at this moment, would have been justified in drawing the inference that Miss Prager had just given her advertising manager a raise in salary. "Thanks," Rosemary said. "I'm glad to see you're not completely useless, Al. Now, then. Since it's impossible to get pictures of the moment when most of these unexpected big events take place, I'm going to provide readers of *Noon* with the next best thing: an artist's recreation of the moment when the event took place. Does that clear up the motivation behind my idea, Wallace?"

"Yes, beautifully," he said, not quite as smoothly as Al Kreitz-berg, but smoothly enough. "You mean let's have a staff of artists who can take the stuff off the wires, use the facts as the AP or UP sends them out, and draw or paint a picture that gives the reader the effect he'd get if he saw a news photograph of the event."

"That's it," Rosemary said. "How does it strike you?"

"Right square between the eyes," Wallace Watchman said. "A real bull's-eye, Rosemary."

"Yeah, but listen," Nick Tomasino said. "Why do they have to be roving? These artists?"

The muted telephone bell tinkled. The new girl picked up the instrument. "Hello?" she said. "Who? Just a moment." She covered the mouthpiece with her hand. "Is there a Mr. Hurst in the room?"

"Yes," said George, who was sitting next to her. "Who is it?"

"Take a message," Rosemary said from the head of the table. "I'm trying to explain the word roving to Nick."

"I think maybe I'd better answer this," George said. "Ernest

Shaygitz promised to call me from Chicago with the final dope on the smudgeless ink figures."

"Okay, but keep your voice down," Rosemary said. "Now, Nick, please listen."

"Hello," George said into the phone.

"Mr. Hurst?"

"Yes?"

"Or would I be considered pushing if I said George?"

"Who is this?"

"Oh, so you don't recognize the voice?"

"I'm afraid I don't."

"Eileen Bucknell."

"Oh."

"That's not how you sounded when we were in that taxi."

"At the moment I'm in a meeting."

The loud whooping scream came stabbing across the wire. George winced.

"Is it as interesting as the taxi was?" Eileen Bucknell asked.

George looked down the table toward Rosemary. She was patting Nick Tomasino's arm soothingly and flailing away at him with a long, complicated explanation about how the staff artists would rove.

"As I said," George said into the phone, "I'm in a meeting."

"Lots of people around?"

"That's right."

"Can't talk?"

"Not much."

"I shouldn't, either."

"What?"

"Talk," Eileen Bucknell said. "I shouldn't ever talk to you again."

"Why not?"

"After the way you left me flat with a fistful of caviar that night at the Prager party?"

"I'm sorry. I was called away on business. I sent a message with Boland."

"Who?"

"The butler. Didn't he—?"

"Oh, him. Yes. But it wasn't the butler I'd been in the taxi with."

"I'm sorry."

"I know I shouldn't do this, but I'm going to give you another chance. Come have a drink tonight."

"I can't. I have a dinner date."

"Who's the lucky girl?"

"It's business actually."

The whooping scream came stabbing along the wire again.

"I'll bet it is," Eileen Bucknell said. "You can still come and have a drink before your dinner date."

"There won't be time. This meeting I'm in won't break up before six and then I've got to get home to dress."

"Where do you call home?"

"University Place."

"That's practically around the corner from us. We're on Twelfth Street between University and Fifth."

"Even so I don't think I have the time tonight."

"Well, I guess I've made it pretty clear how I feel, so I can only add that Mary will be disappointed, too."

"Who?"

"Mary Sherrod. My roommate. Don't tell me you've forgotten her, too."

"No, no, of course not. It's just that for a moment I—"

"It was actually Mary's idea to call you for a drink, but if you can't you can't."

"Well, now, look. Why don't I jot down the address, and could we leave it this way? If the meeting breaks early enough—"

It broke at five-thirty because this was one of the three afternoons a week that the Prager masseur showed up at the triplex, and Rosemary wanted to get to him before W. P. and her mother did, so she would be nice and relaxed by the time George came to pick her up for dinner.

In the cab going downtown George began to relive the scene with Miss Bucknell in the other cab. As a result, he was soon torn between the hope that the visit would result in the completion of a piece of unfinished business and the feeling that, because the girl involved was a shickseh, the visit was a mistake. This feeling became a conviction a moment after George rang the bell on Twelfth Street. The door was opened by Leonard Prager.

"Hey, Eileen," he shouted across his shoulder. "You win!"

Miss Bucknell came out of the kitchen with a cracked soup plate full of ice cubes, which she set next to a whiskey bottle and some glasses on a small drop-leaf table near the fireplace. Leonard Prager took a wallet from his hip pocket, pulled out a dollar bill, and handed it to Miss Bucknell with an elaborate flourish. She took the money and stuck the bill under the edge of a flower pot full of dead stalks on the mantelpiece.

"What's this all about?" George said.

"When Eileen told me you'd said you might drop in for a drink," Leonard Prager said, "I bet her a dollar you wouldn't."

"He said you never did anything unless you cleared it first with some member of the Prager family," Eileen Bucknell said, and when she recovered from the whooping scream of delight she added, "But I said not the Mr. Hurst I know!"

Leonard Prager sent his eyebrows up into the middle of his forehead like a clown registering astonishment. "Here, here!" he said. "Have I been missing something?"

"There are more things in heaven and earth and East Twelfth Street than are dreamed of in your philosophy about why Iago did it, Leonard old boy," Eileen Bucknell said, and she took George's hand. "Come away from this cynical dramatic critic and meet a nice guy." From a chintz-covered chair with holes in both arms rose a small, mousy-looking man with a sweet, shy smile and bushy black hair that hung down over his forehead like a mop. "George Hurst, Milton Schneider," Eileen said. They shook hands and murmured greetings and Eileen said, "Milton teaches fashion design at the Academy on Fifty-seventh Street, where Mary and I are both taking courses, which reminds me." She turned toward the kitchen and called, "Hey, Mary!"

She came in carrying a silver tray as large and as beautiful as the one from which Mrs. Prager doled out caviar up on Seventy-first Street. Clustered in the center, like the Fiji Islands on a map of the Pacific, were six saltines partially covered with a thin, sickly brown smear.

"Hello," she said. "I'm so glad you could come, Mr. Hurst. Won't you have one of these? They look awful, I know, but it's all I could find in the kitchen for hors d'oeuvres. Eileen leaves the shopping to me, and I always leave it to Eileen, with the result that we never seem to have anything edible in the house. You have one, too, Milton. Please don't stare at them like that. It's liver paste. The end of the liver paste, I should say. And Leonard, instead of smiling sarcastically at everything and everybody, why don't you make Mr. Hurst a drink?"

Leonard Prager's reply was an elaborate quotation from *Absalom and Achitophel*, to which nobody paid any attention, but he did make George a drink. While he was doing it, Mary Sherrod led George to another chintz-covered chair which was clearly in even worse shape than the one Milton Schneider was sitting in, but which Mary said was far more reliable.

Sitting in it and sipping his drink, George noticed that both girls were wearing tweed skirts, saddle shoes, cashmere sweaters, and short strings of pearls. George guessed this was probably the Bennington uniform, since Rosemary used to dress like that when George first met her and on occasion she still did. Except that the uniform did very little for Rosemary's lumpy figure, whereas what it did for these two girls thrust George's thoughts back again to his taxi ride with Miss Bucknell. This made it impossible for him to keep his mind on the conversation. It also made him acutely uncomfortable. After several minutes of squirming about in his chair, George began to feel annoyed. Not only at himself for accepting an invitation that he had suspected wasn't going to lead anywhere, but mainly at Miss Bucknell for extending it.

If she knew she was going to have a houseful of people sitting around with drinks and talking their heads off, why had she made all those suggestive cracks on the phone? George's anger at Miss Bucknell increased as a surreptitious glance at his watch told him that, if he was going to get to his apartment for a shower and a change of clothes and not be late in getting uptown to pick up Rosemary, he could stay only a few more minutes.

He spent them wondering suddenly if Miss Bucknell had been smarter than he thought. The suggestive telephone conversation might have been no more than a lure to get him down here. George couldn't imagine for what, since he found it inconceivable that a Gentile girl should want anything from him, and yet it took very little imagination to see that something peculiar was going on.

Here were these two shicksehs, living in this puzzling dump that was furnished partly with the sort of second-hand crap Mr. Noftooleh used to handle down on Avenue C and partly with things like that expensive silver tray that only places like Tiffany handled, serving beat-up liver paste and expensive Scotch, to whom? Three Jews!

From his experience with shkutzim, George could not bring himself to believe that the presence of men named George Hurst, Leonard Prager, and Milton Schneider in the apartment of a couple of Bennington girls named Eileen Bucknell and Mary Sherrod was an accident. Something was up.

George would never have said so aloud, because he was secretly ashamed of his reaction. Having dealt with shkutzim in business for years, George had learned how to appear perfectly relaxed with them on the surface. The inner man, however, was not so tractable a student. George could force his features to do his bidding. He couldn't do a thing with his nervous system. His intelligence told him that his suspicions were those of a child standing on a sidewalk in front of an East Fourth Street saloon. His heart told him the suspicions were justified. Something was definitely up.

In an effort to find out what it was before he had to leave, George took a long pull at his drink and forced himself to pay attention to the conversation. Astonished, he discovered that the other four people in the room were discussing Rosemary's plan to add a group of roving artists to the *Noon* staff.

"It's one of the most exciting ideas I've ever heard," Mary Sherrod said. "Personally, Mr. Hurst, I can't think of anything I'd love to do more."

"Me, too," Eileen Bucknell said, and the whooping scream of delight came through on schedule. "Nothing happens up at *Noon*, not even an office boy gets hired, without Mr. Hurst's okay. Isn't that right, Mr. Hurst? And by the way, why don't we stop this Mr. Hurst stuff and settle for nice plain simple George?"

Because I'm not as plain and simple as you think I am, George thought bitterly, but he didn't say it. He wouldn't give a couple of shicksehs the satisfaction of knowing how angry he was.

"No, I'm afraid that's not right, Miss Bucknell," he said carefully. He set down his drink and stood up. The anger was now all directed at himself. He should have known better than to believe that any shkutzim, male or female, would be interested in a Jew for anything but selfish reasons. "I pass on certain fiscal matters, and I may sign a few contracts with printers and so on, but I don't do any of the actual hiring. I'm sorry that you've wasted your good whiskey on the wrong man. I didn't mean to come down here under false colors. You should have told me what you wanted when you spoke to me on the phone. If you and Miss Sherrod want jobs on *Noon*,

I suggest you go directly to Miss Prager, your old college classmate, who happens to be the magazine's publisher."

The moment he saw Leonard Prager's lips twist in the sardonic smile, George knew something was wrong. He looked quickly at Eileen Bucknell. She was staring at him as though in acknowledging an introduction to her mother he had recited a dirty limerick. Milton Schneider clearly thought George had gone crazy. George, who was beginning to think so himself, turned even more quickly, almost desperately, toward the blond girl.

"But Mr. Hurst, didn't you know—?" Mary Sherrod started to say, then paused and swung toward Eileen. "Didn't you tell Mr. Hurst that—?"

"It never occurred to me. Being right there in the office, and according to Leonard running the place, I thought he'd be the first to know the minute it—!"

"Know what?" George said. "What are you talking about?"

Mary Sherrod looked at her glass with obvious embarrassment. "We didn't ask you to come here because we wanted something from you," she said quietly, and he was suddenly reminded of the way she had sounded after the opening of *The High Hand* when, in her sensible, calm voice, she had told Leonard Prager what she thought of the renunciation scene. "This was supposed to be a celebration drink, Mr. Hurst," she said. "Eileen and I and Mr. Schneider, all three of us were hired by Rosemary early this afternoon as *Noon*'s staff of roving artists."

36

"The silver tray was my mother's contribution and the drop-leaf table came from Eileen Bucknell's mother," Mary Sherrod said. "We didn't want the darn things. Now that we'd graduated from college, all we wanted was to get out of Bala Cynwyd and live in New York, to which our families naturally objected, so Eileen and I had to—"

"Why should it be natural for them to object?" George said.

Mary put down her fork and looked at him across the restaurant table. "Didn't your family object when you decided to leave home?" she said.

George thought of the summer night, years before, in the kitchen behind the tailor shop, when he broke the news to Aunt Tessie that he was not going with her to live in Albany. He tried to synchronize this recollection with a scene in a house in Bala Cynwyd in which Mary Sherrod was telling her parents she planned to live in New York, but George couldn't do it. He had no idea what a house in Bala Cynwyd looked like.

"That's right," he said. "They didn't like the idea at all."

It seemed safer to say "they" than to start the series of questions that would be the inevitable result of his mentioning Aunt Tessie. George didn't want to answer any questions. Aunt Tessie and East Fourth Street were difficult enough to handle in connection with people like the Pragers. To a Bennington girl from the Philadelphia Main Line they would be impossible. Besides, Aunt Tessie and East Fourth Street were none of Mary Sherrod's business.

"Parents never like the idea," she said. "It's just as natural for them to scream when children want to leave home as it is for the children to want to leave. Especially if the place you want to leave is Philadelphia, in which case the desire to get out is even more natural."

George took a forkful of minced turkey. Now that he was sitting across a table from this beautiful blond girl, he was not sure about why he had asked her to have dinner with him. For two days after his visit to the apartment on Twelfth Street he had felt uncomfortable about the way he had acted. Asking himself irritably what difference it made *how* he had acted to a couple of shicksehs did not, somehow, ease the discomfort. After hesitating for a few hours, and arguing with himself for a couple more, George finally decided on the third day that the only solution was to call Mary Sherrod and apologize. It was true that he had already apologized once, as soon as he had learned about his mistake, but somehow, perhaps because he'd had to leave almost immediately to keep his dinner date with Rosemary, that apology didn't seem to count. It had certainly done nothing to relieve his discomfort. Before he could act on his decision to call Miss Sherrod, however, George had run into her in the *Noon* reception room, which seemed the wrong place to repeat an apology that was three days old. Instead, before he had time to think about why he was doing it, George had invited her to dinner. Now that he'd had several hours to think about it, he was still puzzled by his motives. Spending an evening with a beautiful girl, even the most beautiful girl he had ever met, was not enough of an answer. Not for anyone who felt the way he did about shkutzim, male or female.

"Why is it more natural to want to leave Philadelphia than any other place?" he said.

"Have you ever been there?"

"Only on business," George said. "I have a client who manufactures shirts here in New York but has a good deal of his actual processing done by a contractor on Walnut Street. I go out to see him two or three times a year."

Mary shook her head. "That wouldn't give you the idea even remotely," she said. "Philadelphia is a city that has its enthusiasts, of course. All places do. But Philadelphia is the sort of place to which people become resigned, rather than attached, if you know what I mean."

George looked at her with renewed interest. It seemed to him he was doing that constantly, as though the light in which she sat kept changing so that, every few minutes, she looked slightly different.

"No," he said. "I don't think I do."

"Well, I suppose you'd really have to live in Philadelphia to understand," Mary said. "It's only an hour and a half from New York by train, but the difference in spiritual climate between the two cities is so enormous that it makes the trip the longest ninety-minute ride in history. Don't you like that stuff, whatever it is?"

"Not much," George said. "It's minced turkey, I think."

"Why don't you go back and get something you do like?"

"There's not much point. I don't really care for any kind of smorgasbord."

She looked at him in surprise. "Then why did you suggest we come here?"

"I don't know," George said, but this didn't sound very bright, so he looked quickly around the crowded restaurant, as though among the chattering diners he might find the answer to why he had taken Mary Sherrod to the Aqua Vit. He didn't find it. "I just thought—" George started to say as he turned back to Mary, but the thought refused to take shape, so he abandoned it. "Don't mind me," he said, trying a forkful of the spiced sausage. "Go on about Philadelphia."

"I certainly won't go on about Philadelphia," Mary said. "Any more than I'd expect you to go on about Sing Sing if that's where you'd made *your* escape from. I was merely trying to explain how, in that collection of slapped-together junk with which Eileen and I furnished our apartment out of a second-hand shop on Sixth Avenue, we happen to have that silver tray and that drop-leaf table, which are worth a dozen or more times the value of everything else in the apartment put together. I guess our parents feel that as long as we have something from home base near us while we're living in Sodom we won't go completely astray." She laughed suddenly, and it occurred to George that she did it better than Rosemary Prager. "What Winston Sherrod will think when he learns his daughter has taken a job on *Noon* is something I'd rather not hear."

"Why not?" George said. "And who is Winston Sherrod?"

"My father," Mary said. "And I'm sure he'll think anything edited by someone like Wallace Watchman is Communist inspired and financed by Moscow gold. His political and economic ideas all go back to Constantine, but he's really quite nice. When he's not sounding off, I mean. I'm sure if you saw him in Bala Cynwyd, out in the garden spraying the roses or in the house mixing a martini—"

"What's Bala Cynwyd like?"

"Oh, I don't know. Sweet, really. Except after you've been to Bennington, I guess. Why do you want to know?"

"Just curious," George said. "What kind of a house?"

"Just a house. Like thousands of other houses. No different from the one you were raised in, I'll bet."

"Don't bet," George said.

She looked at him curiously. "Why not?"

"It's a bad habit. Give me some details. I'm trying to form a mental picture of the place."

"You make it sound so important."

It was. Very important. Even though he couldn't think why.

"I'm curious," he said.

"Well, it's white mostly, with green shutters, and there's a gravel driveway on the south side, and out in back there's the garden, with Father's roses and Mother's herbs and a really lovely grape arbor—" Mary paused as though an unexpected thought had suddenly crossed her mind, and she said, "Have you ever seen Blue Concords on the vine?"

"No," George said, and all at once he knew why it had been very important to hear details. He had been hunting for something that he and this girl had in common, and he had found it: all at once he could see again the pushcart peddler from whom every autumn Aunt Tessie used to buy the two baskets of grapes with which each year she and George made the Passover wine. "No," he said again. "We didn't have grape arbors where I lived."

"Oh, well, it doesn't matter," Mary said, and then she paused, and she cocked her head to one side as she looked thoughtfully at her plate of smorgasbord. "No, I don't mean that," she said finally. "It's funny, I never thought much about that grape arbor before, but now that I don't live there any more—" She paused again and then, after a moment, she shrugged and smiled and said, "I'm sure you don't want to hear any more about grape arbors in Bala Cynwyd. I know I don't want to talk about them any more. I want to hear about you."

"About me it's mostly profit and loss statements and balance sheets and various other details about accountancy, none of which can possibly interest you."

"Do you want to bet?"

"I told you that's a bad habit."

"Not if you win."

"Miss Sherrod, I assure you—"

"You call Eileen Eileen."

He gave her a quick glance. It was hard to tell from her small, grave smile just how she meant that.

"Eileen asked me to," George said.

"I'm asking you to."

"All right, Mary."

"Thank you."

"You're welcome, and you don't have to pretend to a polite interest in anything like accountancy just because I'm buying you a plate of indigestible smorgasbord."

"Why are you so self-conscious about what you do for a living?"

"I'm not self-conscious. I merely feel—"

"That what you do to earn your living is somehow inferior to what other people do?"

"I didn't say that. I said—"

"What you said doesn't matter. It's what you implied. Would you feel less reticent about talking about what you do for a living if you earned it as a brain surgeon or an arctic explorer or a criminal lawyer?"

"You have to admit the opportunities for sparkling dinner table conversation would be greater."

"Why do I have to admit any such thing?" Mary said. "Do you know Ernie Mergenthaler?"

"The millionaire?"

"Yes."

"The boy who manufactures airplanes? He's in the columns all the time? Him and Toby Wing? Him and Greta Garbo? That guy?"

"Yes. Do you know him?"

"Of course not. How would I know a man like that? What about him?"

"I went out with him for a few weeks last year."

"You did?"

"Don't be so impressed. Ernie Mergenthaler goes out with more girls than Ziegfeld ever got around to glorifying."

"What's he doing in this conversation?"

"Helping me make a point. The first two or three times I went out with him I was thrilled. I was still at Bennington, my last year, and he was the most glamorous bachelor in America, if not the world. The fact that he'd dropped the movie star routine for a while and was off on a college girl kick didn't change the fact that there I was, on his diamond-studded arm, at first nights, in the Stork Club, all those places, including the columns. I was so thrilled, it wasn't until my fourth or fifth date with him that I realized I was bored stiff."

"As I understand Mr. Mergenthaler's tendencies from what the boys say—"

"I know what the boys say, and they're all wrong. Not that I enjoy being pawed in taxicabs so much that my feelings are hurt when I'm not, but I'm a member of the opposite sex, and when I'm out with a man whose emotional response to my presence is about the same as it would be if he were squiring a filet of flounder, I begin to have my suspicions and few of them are about myself. The truth about Ernie Mergenthaler, and it's the truth about all these glamour boys who live their sex lives out in public, because I've gone out with quite a few of them, is that they have absolutely no interest in women. If they had they wouldn't have time to be in the Stork Club and Winchell's column. They'd be in bed.

"During my fourth date with Ernie, when I found myself yawning in the middle of one of his dutiful and well-bred speeches about how my hair reminded him of the sun coming up over the Petit Trianon or some such damn fool thing like that, I cut him short and told him to tell me about airplanes. He blinked and said huh? I said you manufacture airplanes. You must do it awfully well or you wouldn't make the money you do make by doing it. Anybody who does anything awfully well should be able to say something interesting about it. I'd certainly much rather hear you make the attempt, I said, than listen to you tell me about the color of my hair. I know about the color of my hair, but I don't know a damned thing about manufacturing airplanes, so please tell me."

Mary paused, and she took a forkful of smoked trout, and then she giggled.

"He told me," she said. "I didn't get home until five in the morning, and I will admit my eardrums ached a bit, but I'd learned an awful lot and, for the first time since I'd been going out with Ernie Mergenthaler, I had a good time."

"Why did you stop going out with him?"

"There isn't all that much to tell about the manufacture of airplanes," Mary said, and she gigled again. "Ernie asked me to marry him, in case you're interested, but by the time he got around to it he was already repeating himself about wing spread and propellor shafts, so I knew Mr. Mergenthaler and I had run our course. But it was fun while it lasted because few things are more fun than learning something new. Have I made my point?"

"Yes," George said, "but you've also made me nervous."

"Why?"

"There may not be all that much to tell about balance sheets."

"I'll let you know when you begin repeating yourself," Mary said. "How about beginning with what you do for most clients and how that differs, if it does differ, from what you do for *Noon?*"

Two hours later, as he paused to take a soothing sip of water, George's hand suddenly shook so badly that he splashed the tablecloth.

"What's the matter?" Mary said.

George didn't answer. He couldn't tell this girl from the enemy camp that, for the first time in a dozen years, he had recaptured the feeling he used to get down on Fourth Street, after Aunt Tessie went to live in Albany, when he would come across town from Mrs. Shissle's rooming house on Sunday morning and, sitting on the dock with their legs dangling over the water, he would spend hours telling Dora everything that had happened to him during the week.

"I just realized why, even though I hate smorgasbord," George said, "I brought you here to the Aqua Vit for dinner."

"Why?" Mary asked.

"Because this is where we met, and I don't like the fact that it happened under the auspices of Leonard Prager," George said. "I wanted us to come back and start all over again on our own."

37

Gloves Off dinners in the Prager triplex frequently reminded George of a box of Crackerjacks: just as you rarely knew until you had eaten halfway down whether the prize concealed in the molasses-covered popcorn was a whistle or a water pistol, there were times at a Prager Gloves Off dinner when George was not certain until the dessert was served what subject the guests had been assembled to take their verbal gloves off about.

The dinner given on the day Fiorello La Guardia was elected mayor of New York for a third term was a case in point.

Only six people, the ideal number for a Gloves Off dinner, were present: W. P., Mrs. Prager, Rosemary, Wallace Watchman, Leonard Prager, and George. There was a feeling of impending excitement in the air. This was typical of all Gloves Off dinners. It was as though the guests had been assembled in the grandstand of a sports arena without being told whether they were going to witness a heavy-weight championship prizefight or the Davis Cup finals.

At first, as he chatted with Mrs. Prager before dinner, George thought this excitement was due to the fact that it was already clear from the early returns that La Guardia, who had been backed publicly and financially by W. P., was victorious.

Later, at table, with the lobster bisque, George decided the feeling of excitement was due to the witty way Leonard Prager compared the second act of *The Mikado* with the warning issued to the people of the United States the day before by Ambassador Joseph C. Grew that there was a strong possibility of an attack by Japan on our Pacific installations. Leonard certainly kept the table in stitches.

When the steak was served, however, George changed his mind. It seemed clear now, as Rosemary described the cover that Milton

Schneider had designed for next week's issue, that the excitement at this Gloves Off dinner could be traced directly to the fact that *Noon's* long practice period was almost over and the first issue to be released to the public was due on the stands during the second week in December.

With the crème brulé, which was pretty late in the game but not unheard of at a Gloves Off dinner, George was forced to shift ground again. There seemed little doubt, as Wallace Watchman outlined his theory about the relationship between crusades and newsstand circulation, that here at last was the real reason why they had been assembled here tonight.

"I don't claim to be another Horace Greeley," he said. "But I do claim to have learned a good deal from studying the career of that great journalistic genius, and one of the things I have learned is what sells magazines. It's controversy. Just plain controversy pure and simple. Or, to put it another and perhaps better way, it's crusades. We have the example of the famous muckrakers during the era of Teddy Roosevelt to look back on and guide us. They were busting trusts and they were exposing the filth and the rottenness of the Chicago stockyards, but they were also selling magazines, and I don't want anybody at this table to forget that."

"Wallace," Mrs. Prager said. "Take some more crème brulé."

"What?"

"The dessert," Rosemary said. "You're holding it up."

"Sorry." Watchman helped himself to some more crème brulé and the maid moved on around the table. "While I think crusades are important for any publication that wants to make an impression on the public, it seems to me they're especially important for *Noon,* and when you hear my reasoning I'm sure you'll agree with me. When we activated this project more than two years ago, when we moved it out of the discussion to the planning phase, the world was hardly living through a period of sweetness and light, but it was still technically at peace. For two years now, however, Europe has been at war, and with Germany sitting astride all of Europe, the eyes of this entire country, meaning the eyes of every potential newsstand buyer of *Noon,* are focused on what's going to happen next in the war. Will England be invaded and go under? Will the war spread to Asia? Will we become involved in the actual shooting? With questions as momentous as these facing the average American every day, I feel strongly that a new publication like *Noon,* to attract buyers, must feed them something more than the war news they are already getting from the other news magazines with which we will be in direct competition. I feel that the something more we can give them is a series of exciting crusades."

"Crusades against what?" Leonard Prager said.

"I was just coming to that," Wallace Watchman said.

"Could you come to it with the coffee?" W. P. said.

"Of course," Wallace Watchman said.

As they rose from the table, George had the uneasy feeling that the wind had shifted again. There had been something in W. P.'s voice, a touch of impatience, that had suddenly made George think perhaps Wallace Watchman's theory about the relationship between crusades and newsstand sales was not the subject of tonight's Gloves Off dinner after all. But if it was not, this meant they had reached the coffee without reaching the proper subject, and George could not remember this happening before.

W. P. came up beside him and spoke quietly in his ear. "Do you mind, George, if you and I have our coffee in the study?"

For a startled moment George was struck by the thought that perhaps he, George Hurst, was the subject of tonight's Gloves Off dinner. This seemed so preposterous, however, that George thrust the thought from his mind as abruptly as it had come.

"Not at all, sir."

He followed W. P. down the familiar trail that led past the Picassos and the Renoirs to the study. As soon as W. P. opened the door, George knew his preposterous thought was not preposterous at all. Rosemary was standing in front of the fireplace, sipping coffee.

"Oh," W. P. said in surprise. "I didn't know you were in here."

"I know you didn't," Rosemary said.

W. P. gave her a sharp glance. "I wonder if you'd mind having your coffee somewhere else?" he said. "I was planning to have a little gloves-off talk with George."

"I know you were," Rosemary said. "That's why I brought my coffee in here."

"I prefer not to have any witnesses to this talk," W. P. said.

"That's my preference, too," Rosemary said. "So would you mind leaving the room, Dad?"

W. P. made a nervous stab at the centerpiece of his pince-nez. "Rosemary, I don't want this to—"

"Look, Dad," she said. "I'm not a kid any more, carrying the aspirin bottle around for Nikita Loewenthal and the rest of those creeps in The Living Theatre. I'm a great big grown-up girl with a magazine of my own and several hundred employees who call me publisher. I've been standing on my own feet and doing my own talking for quite some time, and I don't intend to quit now. Any time you want to pull the rug out from under me at *Noon*, okay, you go ahead. It's your money. But this is something on which nobody is going to bat for me. Not even you. On this, Dad, I'm doing my own talking. So will you please beat it?"

W. P. opened his mouth, but whether he intended to do more than rub the corners of his lips it was hard to say. He certainly didn't utter another word. He turned on his heel and walked out. Rosemary stared at the door until it clicked shut. Then she took a final swallow of coffee, set the cup on the mantelpiece, and folded her arms across her ample but curiously sexless breasts.

"George," she said, "when are we getting married?"

"Whenever you say," he said.

She looked startled, then annoyed. George was reminded of the way Mr. Shumacher had looked years ago in the L. L. Parker mailroom on the day he confronted George with the lie about being a Lutheran that George had written on his application blank, and George had not dropped to the floor in a dead faint. The script was not going the way Rosemary Prager had expected it to go.

"Doesn't it strike you as being a subject on which you should be the one to do the saying?" she snapped.

"Why don't you cut the crap, Rosemary?"

"Don't talk to me that way!"

"How do you want me to talk to you?"

"The way you talk to—"

She stopped, and bit her lip, and for a horrible moment George thought she was going to cry. But she didn't. She shook her head, as though reprimanding herself for a moment of weakness, and then, with a short, sharp movement, Rosemary punched her right fist into her left palm, as though she were an inexperienced orator who had been taught a series of basic gestures in an inexpensive public-speaking school from which she had only recently graduated.

"God damn it," Rosemary said irritably, "I wish I could figure you out."

"What do you find so puzzling?"

"You're not like those other slobs. You're no Wallace Watchman or an Al Kreitzberg, and yet you let me push you around as much as they do."

"Why shouldn't I?" George said. "I'm getting more out of it than they are."

Her gray eyes blinked rapidly, as though she was not quite sure she had heard him correctly, and then the wonderful laugh came rumbling out of her lumpy body. "There are times when I get so fed up with you for being a doormat, I could grab you by the neck and shake you. Then you say something that makes me feel maybe I've picked the right guy after all."

"Maybe you have," George said.

"Wouldn't you have preferred it if you'd done the picking?"

"There's not much chance of that where a Prager is concerned," George said. "Besides, it isn't my preference that counts."

"No," Rosemary said with a nod, "that's true enough. If I hadn't picked you, we wouldn't be standing in front of this fireplace together."

"Or if W. P. hadn't picked me for you."

"You don't leave a girl much room for kidding herself, do you?"

"If I felt you wanted that kind of room," George said, "I'd provide that, too."

"You don't think I want it?"

"From Wallace Watchman and Al Kreitzberg, maybe. You're not marrying them. From me, no."

"Where did you learn so much about me?"

"In bed."

"George—"

"What?"

"Am I any good?"

"You're good enough."

"Is that the best you can say?"

"We're not at a General Implementation meeting in the Chaiken Building on Madison Avenue. We're having a gloves-off talk in your father's study on Seventy-first Street. If we leave the baloney downtown, Rosemary, I think this marriage will work."

She scowled up at the carved ceiling for a moment, in a way that reminded George of W. P., as though she were trying to decipher her lines from a card being flashed for her by a prompter. "Yes, I think it will, too," she said finally. "How about if we set the date for the second week in December? Right after the first issue hits the stands?"

"That sounds fine."

"Is that all you can say?"

"What have I left out?"

"You could say how you feel about marrying me."

"I think it's a pretty good deal for all concerned."

"This you call a romantic remark?"

"You're a handful, Rosemary, and we both know it. If we go into this with our eyes open, it'll work. If not, it'll fall flat on its face. What more can I say?"

"You could say you love me."

"That's another way I'm different from Wallace Watchman and Al Kreitzberg," George said. "I'm not going to lie to you."

"Never?"

"Never."

"Then there's one thing I want you to tell me," Rosemary Prager said. "It's a promise I want you to make."

"If I can," George said, "I will."

"You'll have to," she said. "This is what Dad dragged you in here to have a gloves-off talk about, except he should know me well enough by now to know I prefer to do my own dirty work."

"Okay, let's have it."

"I want you to promise, and so does Dad, that you'll stop seeing Mary Sherrod."

George hesitated. Not because they were asking the impossible, or even too much. At the prices they were paying, the Pragers were entitled to ask for as much as they wanted. George hesitated because it had not occurred to him until this moment that anybody knew about him and Mary.

"All right," he said. A deal was a deal. "I promise."

38

A great many employees, soon after they joined the *Noon* staff, remarked that it felt odd to be part of an organization where, because the magazine went to the printer late Saturday night, and came off the presses early Monday morning, Saturday and Sunday were considered regular working days, and Monday and Tuesday were treated as the week end. George did not find it odd. In his days with Malvin Gewirtz & Company he had helped Mr. Rapf with so many bankruptcy audits, almost every one of which had involved a race against the calendar, that working on Sundays had long ago become for him a commonplace. As a matter of fact, George enjoyed working on Sundays. He liked going uptown through the quiet streets, riding in the almost empty subway, going up in the elevator through what seemed a deserted Chaiken Building, and then stepping out into the noisy confusion of the *Noon* offices.

It was more noisy than usual on this particular Sunday because the first issue of *Noon* intended for public sale was supposed to have gone to press the night before but had been slightly delayed. By lunch time there was such a racket in the corridor outside his door that George, who had nothing to do with the editorial problems of locking up Vol. 1 No. 1., found it impossible to concentrate on the complicated cost breakdown for the calendar year 1941 with which he had been struggling for a week. He decided to take the papers downtown to his apartment, where he could work without interruption until it was time to pick up Rosemary for the party the Pragers were giving that night to celebrate the appearance of the first issue.

As he stepped with his briefcase out of the *Noon* reception room into the elevator, a voice shouted from somewhere behind him, "Hold it, please!"

The elevator operator stopped sliding the door shut and held it. There was a clatter of heels on the marble floor of the reception room. Carrying a large sketchbox, a shoulder purse, and a sheet of yellow paper, Mary Sherrod stepped into the car.

"Thanks," she said to the operator as he slid the door shut.

"Glad to oblige," the operator said.

Mary set the sketchbox down, hiked the strap of the shoulder purse up into a more secure position on her beaver coat, and saw George.

"Oh," she said and then, with the directness he could not help admiring even when it annoyed him, she added, "Where have you been?"

"Been?"

"I haven't seen you for almost a month. I thought you were out of town."

"Oh, no," George said. "I've been right here."

"In the office?"

"Every day."

"Then you've been avoiding me."

George could feel his face flush. "Don't be silly," he said.

Mary made an impatient gesture. "How I hate people who tell me not to be silly. Being silly is one of the things a person can no more help than he can help being short or tall. If I'm being silly, I don't like to be reminded of it by being told to stop. And if I'm not being silly, I resent people who can't answer my perfectly sensible remark making an attempt to dismiss it by calling it a silly one. Every day since I came to work on *Noon* I have seen you at one time or another, even if only for a moment in the corridor. For the entire past month, however, even though I've been in the office every day and you say you've been in the office every day, I have not seen you. It seems to me perfectly obvious that you've been avoiding me, and not at all silly for me to say so."

The elevator stopped. George dipped down to pick up her sketchbox, but Mary reached it first. They walked out through the empty lobby, moving side by side in silence, as though they were total strangers who had fallen into step by accident. George was embarrassed and confused, and angry with himself for being embarrassed and confused. He hoped that Mary was confused, too. He knew her well enough by this time, however, not to expect much help from that particular hope. Mary Sherrod got angry, but he had never yet seen her confused. As they stood on the sidewalk in the bright, warm winter sunshine, he knew the smartest thing to do was tip his hat, say he'd be seeing her around, and beat it. The knowledge did him no good. It had done him no good on that first day he went down to Twelfth Street, either. He stood there, wishing he'd remained in his office and trying to think of something safe to say.

"Where are you going?" he said.

"Downtown."

"Whereabouts downtown?"

"I'm not too sure," Mary said, scowling at the sheet of yellow paper. "I suppose a taxi driver would know."

"Let me take a look," George said.

She handed him the sheet of yellow paper. It was one of Wallace Watchman's assignment memoranda. It read:

To:—Milton Schneider
From:—Editor
Re:—Rotten Poultry Crusade

*It was decided at this morning's General Implementation meet-
ing that, following our lead-off Bootleg Sleeping Pill Crusade with
which we are going to hit the public in our first three issues, we're
going to take out after the purveyors of rotten poultry. Research
Dept. has upturned astonishing statistics on number chickens, ducks,
turkeys, etc., consumed this country daily, especially in large urban
areas like New York, plus fact fortunes being reaped annually by
unscrupulous vendors who bulk buy condemned birds, below par
standards set by Board of Health. Kneichbreit's Poultry, Inc., 364
East Fifth Street, Manhattan, one of largest vendors local area
believed be one of worst offenders. Under cover of pretense we plan
factual educational spread in near future issue, have had two reporters
and one photographer in Kneichbreit premises for more than ten
days. Facts unearthed indicate clearly this story potential circulation
blockbuster comparable Lincoln Steffens' famous crusade vs. coal
field child labor. Day Noon hits stands with explosive poultry story
all hell will undoubtedly break loose in Kneichbreit premises. Since
for obvious reasons won't be able have photographer on scene at
moment Kneichbreits first see Noon story, this ideal opportunity for
our staff roving artists to fill gap. Please assign earliest convenience
one your best artists go downtown make sketches members Kneichbreit clan and prepare imaginative impression their reaction at
moment in future when they see our story. Chaim Kneichbreit, head
of clan, been alerted one our artists coming soon, told sketches
wanted for favorable publicity purposes. All Kneichbreits co-opera-
tive. If artist keeps mum our real purpose, am certain will encounter
no difficulty. Please send best artist you have.*

W. W.

In the upper right-hand corner of the sheet, Milton Schneider
had written: "Mary: will you take this one? Eileen and I are going
to Baltimore on the Poisoned Oyster Bed story and won't be back
until Tuesday or Wednesday. I've checked with Kneichbreit on
phone, and everything W. W. says in this memo is substantially
correct. Use your own judgment, of course, but I would think the
family at work rather than statically in living quarters would be your
best bet. Good sketching. Milton."

The address of the Kneichbreit premises in the middle of the
memorandum was heavily underscored in red ink.

"I don't mean that I'm not sure about where Fifth Street is,"

Mary said. "I live on Twelfth, so that logically it should be seven blocks further south, but it doesn't seem to work that way in this town. I mean if you go south from where Eileen and I live, you're all right until you reach Eighth Street, but then things like Washington Square begin to happen, and what's a poor immigrant from Philadelphia supposed to do?"

"She can put herself in my hands," George said. He wasn't really breaking his promise to Rosemary. It wasn't as though he had made a date with Mary. He had run into her by accident. They were going in the same direction. It was only polite to give her a lift. Strictly speaking, since she was on an assignment for the magazine, what he was doing was in the line of duty. He signaled to a taxi. "I know exactly where this place is," George said. "I was born just around the corner."

"George Hurst, why didn't you ever tell me?"

The answer was that, as he began slowly to understand the combination of Bennington and Philadelphia, it seemed wise not to go into detail about the combination of East Fourth Street and the Pragers. George decided to skip this answer and settle for a safe one.

"You never asked me," he said as the taxi pulled up at the curb and he opened the door.

"Well, I'm asking you now," Mary said as they settled back and the cab started downtown. "I want to know what it's like to be born and raised around the corner from Kneichbreit's Poultry, Incorporated."

George told her. He told her about the orphan asylum, and Aunt Tessie, and the Forest. He told her about Doodoo Kashkewitz, and Mr. Forman's grocery store, and Miss Corcoran. He told her about Old Man Saydl, and Armistice Day, and Uncle Zisha. He told it like a professional soldier picking his way across a still smoking battlefield, observing everything with interest, yet never forgetting to tread carefully and keep a sharp lookout for unexploded mines. George did not tell her about Danny and Dora.

"It must have been wonderful," Mary said as the taxi stopped.

George looked at her suspiciously. The word rubbed him the wrong way. "What's wonderful about growing up in a slum?"

Mary made an impatient gesture. "Kids don't know what a slum is," she said. "All they know is when they're happy or unhappy. If I could swap my first dozen years in Bala Cynwyd with your first dozen years down here, why, I'd do it like a shot."

George helped her out of the cab and paid the driver. He looked around. East Fifth Street hadn't changed very much. The kids in the street were wearing blue jeans instead of knickers and zippered jackets instead of the kind of heavy sweaters Aunt Tessie used to knit for him. But the garbage cans were still standing out in front of the stoops, and they were still full, and the tenements still looked dirty, and the wind from the river still cut at your face and neck.

George turned up his coat collar and nodded toward the garbage cans. "You'd swap Bala Cynwyd for this?"

"This doesn't count," Mary said. "The fact that you had a happy childhood does."

For several moments George stood there, absolutely motionless, pretending he was peering down the street to the river, but he didn't see a thing. He should never have answered the question Mary had asked uptown. Trying to pick his way through the past hadn't worked. He should have known that in the process of telling Mary only part of the story he would have to relive the whole story himself. The editor could not pretend he had not read the parts he had cut away. Not to himself, at any rate. All at once George could hear Dora's voice again as she held the last sweet note of "Apple Blossom Time," and he could feel the pressure of her sharp little shoulder blades against his outspread palm, and the fragrance of her hair was so strong in his nostrils that he turned his head sharply, as though to escape the memory he had thought was dead.

"Oh, dear, they're probably still asleep."

"Who's asleep?"

"The Kneichbreits," Mary said. "It's only twelve-thirty."

"This isn't Bala Cynwyd," George said. "This is East Fifth Street. Come on."

They crossed the sidewalk to the double store front. On both windows, which were painted black, appeared a picture of a roast chicken as big as a lion cub under the bold, golden legend:

KNEICHBREIT'S POULTRY, INC.
"Eat Kosher and Live Longer"

George tried the door. It was locked. He rapped on the glass. From somewhere in the back came the sound of running feet. The door opened and a wide-eyed girl of ten or twelve looked out at them with her mouth open as though a knock on the door was as astonishing an event as the consequence of Aladdin's rubbing his lamp.

"We're from the magazine *Noon*," Mary said. "I wonder if you would mind telling your father—?"

"Linda, who is it?"

The small girl turned toward the voice behind her. "From the magazine again, Pa!" she screamed. "Two more!"

Heavy, quick footsteps came toward her from the rear. The door was pulled wide by a big round barrel of a man wearing a blood-spattered white butcher's smock.

"From a big important magazine you keep people waiting outside like they was holdupnicks?" he said in hurt amazement, as though the little girl had pulled a gun on the visitors, and he thrust her behind him with a playful but firm shove. "Come in, come in, come in," he said with a smile that seemed to slash his head from ear to ear as he pulled Mary and George into the store. "Welcome to Kneichbreit's Poultry. I know already who you are. On the telephone they told me any day you'll come to paint pictures. Me, I'm Chaim Kneichbreit. Over here," he said, dragging George and Mary into a part of the store where a stout woman and a thin young man with hornrimmed glasses, both wearing blood-stained smocks, were plucking feathers from a couple of dead chickens, "this is my wife Hannah, and this is my son Ira, already in his second year law school, some day maybe with God's help on the Supreme Court he'll be like Judge Frankfurter, but today, when it's not the nose in the books it's still the hands in the feathers to help Papa and Mama, and this is my Linda, her you already met, sweet like sugar and a good head, even if when it comes to opening a door for important people she's not so quick, she helps, too, except sometimes what she helps we have to do it all over again!"

The big man paused to rub the little girl's hair affectionately, then beamed at George and Mary.

"So now you know the whole story. Kneichbreit's Poultry it's a family business." He turned and clapped his hands like a conductor calling for the attention of the members of his orchestra. "So in a one, two, three let's finish already, then everybody upstairs to wash and put on clean clothes and we'll be ready for the pictures!"

"No, no," Mary said. "Stay exactly as you are. Don't stop. I want to sketch you at your work."

Mr. Kneichbreit looked dubious. "Like this?" he said, staring down at himself. "All over with blood?"

"Yes, please," Mary said. "We don't want to interrupt a thing."

"It's not interrupting, honest," Mr. Kneichbreit said. "It's just a rush order. A nothing. On Sunday, except it's a rush order, we never work."

George knew better. He had never met the Kneichbreits before, but he knew there was always a rush order. Just as there had always been a rush order in the doll store around the corner. As a matter of fact, in a few minutes, when Mary had set up her sketchbox, and the Kneichbreits had returned to their work, and George was seated at one side on the chicken crate Linda had carefully covered with a newspaper to protect his pants, George had the feeling that ten years had been rolled away. He was twenty again, living with Mrs. Shissle on University Place and working in the L. L. Parker mailroom and studying at Washington Square College, and he had walked across town to spend a few Sunday hours with the Diensts. He was sitting in the doll store where Ida and Fat Frannie and Dora helped their parents with the rush order and George read them excerpts from Aunt Tessie's latest letter from Albany while he ate the bananas and apples and pears Mrs. Dienst forced on him.

"You'll have maybe some fruit?" Mrs. Kneichbreit said.

"Thank you, no," Mary said. "I had a very late breakfast."

"So a little fruit, what could it hurt?" Mrs. Kneichbreit said. "We have in the kitchen from grapes to bananas, everything."

"You're very kind," Mary said. "But I don't think so, thanks."

"You're sure?" Mrs. Kneichbreit said. "If you don't eat it, we'll just have to throw it out."

"No, really," Mary said. "I—"

"I'd like some, thank you," George said, not because he was hungry but because his memories were suddenly unbearable. "If you don't mind?"

"Mind? To give a guest a piece fruit is something to mind? Linda, quick!" Mrs. Kneichbreit said. "In the kitchen!"

Linda ran out to the kitchen, leaving the door open, and George could suddenly hear music from a radio in the other room. For several moments, as the shapeless sounds fell into a pattern that began to seem familiar, he refused to believe it. Then the pattern took shape, and he recognized the song, and for several more moments he sat absolutely motionless, with his head bowed, as though unable to face the past which had come not only to mock but seemed determined to destroy him. Then, abruptly, the strains of "Apple Blossom Time" stopped dead, as though somebody had snapped off the radio. This was not true, however, because the silence was only momentary. It was followed by a man's voice, speaking what sounded like a commercial he had not had the time to learn properly. Linda came in with a cut-glass bowl full of fruit. She approached George shyly and held out the bowl.

"Thanks," he said, taking an apple.

"Take two, they're small like plums," Mrs. Kneichbreit said. "What's he so excited about, the man on the radio, Linda, darling?"

"I don't know," Linda said. "Something about the Japs. They're bombing Pearl Harbor. Should I—?"

"Of course!" Mrs. Kneichbreit said, waving her daughter toward Mary. "The lady, too!"

"Oh, well, yes, I think I will," Mary said, smiling at the little girl holding out the bowl of fruit. She put down her pencil, tipped her head to one side as though giving serious thought to the choice and said, "Let me see. The bananas look—" Mary's voice stopped, and she said sharply to Linda, "What did you say?"

The little girl took a step backward, as though she had been pushed, and an apple slid off the top of the heaped bowl. The apple rolled across the floor toward George. He dipped down to stop it, and then Linda's words caught up with him, too.

"The Japs?" he said. "What—?"

He fell back on the chicken crate as Ira Kneichbreit, coming around the plucking table fast, slipped on the floor strewn with feathers and grabbed at George's shoulder to steady himself. By the time George managed to get to his feet, Ira had disappeared into the kitchen. Following him, George rammed into Mary, who had come running around the table from the other side. They both staggered, and he reached out to keep her from falling. So did she. They were standing like that, locked in each other's arms, when Ira Kneichbreit reappeared in the kitchen doorway.

"My God!" he said. "It's true!"

Not until a few minutes later, when by twisting the dial back and forth they had succeeded in milking from the radio nothing more than several repetitions of the same short, electrifying bulletin, did George hear Mrs. Kneichbreit's sobs.

"Now they'll take him," she wailed, and since she stared helplessly at the floor as the tears rolled down her cheeks and the sobs shook her stout body, George did not realize for a moment that she was referring to her son. "A whole life you work and you sweat and you live only for one thing, they should become something, not a butcher with feathers like the father and the mother, and then comes a war and they take him to be a soldier."

"Ma, for Christ's sake!" Ira said. "Will you cut that out?"

"Cut it out, sure, go cut it out," the stout woman moaned in a hopeless monotone. "From law school they'll take him. In a uniform they'll stick him, and some place to be killed by the Japs they'll send him, and he says to the mother go cut it out."

"They're not sending me yet, or anybody else, either," Ira Kneichbreit said. "Besides, this flash may be a mistake."

"No," his father said firmly. "It's not a mistake." Everybody turned to look at him, as though into a meeting hopelessly confused by conflicting information had come the one man who possessed the true facts. "The war it's here," Mr. Kneichbreit said. "A long time it's coming, but now it's here. From now on it's no more studying. Law school is finished. Everything has to wait. First comes now the war. That's the thing now that must be finished first."

"Chaim!" his wife wailed. "Chaim, what are you saying?"

"What every Jew will say today," Mr. Kneichbreit said. "Thank God it'll now be the end. That's what I'm saying. No more pogroms. No more killing little children because they're Jews. It's finished. You hear me? It's finished. On Hitler today I wouldn't write an insurance policy even for a penny. It's America he started up with now. With America it'll be no more monkey business like with Czechoslovakia and with Austria and with France. So many people he killed, so now already he'll be dead, too. America will fix him. My America. My wonderful America. Thank God I have a good Jewish son to send!"

He put his enormous arms around the thin young man and pulled him close. Ira Kneichbreit swallowed hard and clutched at his horn-rimmed glasses to keep them from falling.

"George," Mary whispered. "You're hurting me."

He looked down. "Sorry," George said, easing the pressure. He could not remember taking her hand. "I didn't mean—"

"I know," she said. "I'll get my sketchbox. I think we'd better get back to the office."

She tried to pull her hand free, but he held on. For several long moments he looked down at the smooth white fingers.

"No," he said. "To hell with the office," George Hurst said. "Let's go some place where we can talk."

39

He heard the phone but the bell sounded strange, so he did nothing about it and after a moment it stopped ringing. Then somebody was shaking him and George opened his eyes.

"It's for you," Mary said.

Sitting up and reaching for the phone, his glance swung across the bedroom, through the open door, into the living room, where he saw the beautiful silver tray sitting on the drop-leaf table next to the mantelpiece with the flower pot full of dead stalks, and George realized where he was. His hand dropped back to the blanket.

"I'm not here."

"What?" Mary said, startled, and she pressed the mouthpiece to her shoulder.

"I'm not here."

"Oh," Mary said and then, as she understood, her face flushed and she giggled. "That wasn't very bright of me, was it?" She took the mouthpiece from her shoulder and said into it. "No, I haven't seen him. I have no idea where he is. Yes, of course. If I see or hear from him, I'll tell him. What? Yes, certainly I'm coming into the office." She hung up and, as she knotted the belt of her robe, Mary said in a puzzled voice, "That's funny."

"What is?" George said.

"Her asking me if I'm coming into the office."

"Who's her?"

"Rosemary's secretary. She said—"

"Was that Rosemary's secretary?"

"Yes. It seems you were due at a party at the Pragers last night, and when you didn't show up Rosemary tried to get you at your apartment. She's been trying ever since, and—" Mary stopped. She looked quickly at George. "If she told her secretary to call here," Mary said slowly, "Rosemary must think you and I—?"

"Suppose Rosemary does think. Do you care?"

Mary sat down on the bed, took his face in both hands, and kissed him hard. "If I may borrow one of Miss Prager's favorite phrases," she said, "Rosemary can drop dead."

"It is my guess that our publisher is just about ready to do that right now."

Mary giggled again. "I can't say I blame her. If you broke a date with me, I'd be jealous, too."

"Rosemary is not dropping dead this morning out of jealousy," George said. "That party last night was supposed to celebrate the appearance of Noon's first issue on the newsstands."

"My God!" Mary said. "I forgot all about that!"

"So did the Japanese High Command. Let's get dressed and over to the nearest newsstand."

The nearest newsstand was at the corner of Twelfth Street and University Place. The small crowd clustered around it kept shifting restlessly, like sand at the base of a pole in an unsteady wind. People kept buying papers, stepping aside, glancing at the headlines, then stepping back to glance worriedly at the headlines of the other papers, as though the news in these might be better or different. It wasn't. Just the same, it was at the newspapers that the restless crowd looked, and it was the newspapers they bought. Nobody looked at the shining copies of Noon piled high on the lower shelf of the newsstand. From the size of the stack it was pretty clear that nobody had bought a copy, either. George wasn't surprised. The front pages of the newspapers dealt with yesterday's sneak attack on Pearl Harbor and the special session of Congress called for later that day at which the President would ask for a declaration of war. The cover of Noon dealt with Wallace Watchman's Bootleg Sleeping Pill Crusade.

"Gee whiz," Mary said. "What a rotten break."

"For the country?" George said. "Or the Prager investment?" He led her away from the crowd around the newsstand. "Listen," he said. "You remember the things I said to you yesterday?"

"Every word."

"I'm not kidding."

"Neither am I," she said. "From the moment we left Kneichbreit's Poultry, Eye, En, See, until the moment you fell asleep. I have it all by heart. You wouldn't care to have me repeat it to you, would you?"

"Not now," George said. "What I'd like you to do is go back to the apartment and wait for me."

"Where are you going?"

"Uptown," George said. "I have to tie up a few loose ends."

Getting at them, he realized as he stepped into the elevator of the Chaiken Building, was not going to be as easy as he'd thought.

Leonard Prager, who had stepped into the car a moment ahead of him, grinned maliciously as the operator slid the door shut.

"You look worried," Leonard said. "I assure you there's absolutely no reason to be. In the son-in-law business, George, a candidate with your unusual qualifications is always given ample opportunity to mend whatever fences he may have accidentally knocked down."

"Shut up, Leonard. You're not killing me this morning."

"It is the common fate of the humorist. I have been reconciled to it for years. You don't have to find me funny. All you have to do is listen. If I shut up, you won't be able to do that."

"There's nothing you've got to say that I'm interested in."

"I'm not so sure about that," Leonard Prager said. "Just to take an example at random, I was at the party on Seventy-first Street last night. You were not. I can tell you what happened. Knowing what happened, instead of having to guess at it, puts you in a better position when you go in to apologize for your absence."

"If you don't keep your trap shut, Leonard, you're the one who's going to do the apologizing. Now cut it out."

"I see. Belligerent. Hit them before they can hit you. Throw them off balance. Put them on the defensive. Not a bad technique. It might even work. It all depends on what you've got to back it up with. Coming up with something plausible shouldn't be too difficult for a boy as fast on his feet as you are. 'You ask me why I didn't show up at the party? You want to know where I was? Protecting your investment, Mr. Prager, that's where I was. As soon as I heard the news about Pearl Harbor I realized we would look so silly that we might never recover from it if we appeared on the newsstands at a time like this with a cover story about bootleg sleeping pills. There was no time to go to parties. There was no time even to make phone calls. I grabbed a plane and flew out to Chicago at once to see if I could stop the presses. Unfortunately, I was too late. But that's where I was, W. P., and that's why I didn't get to the party, and that's why you couldn't reach me on the phone last night.'"

Leonard paused. His lips twisted in the sardonic smile. "It's not bad, George. As a matter of fact, it doesn't have to be very good. A man who is anxious to buy a certain husband for his daughter, and has settled all the details including purchase price, will accept any excuses to cover temporary lapses that occur between the time the deal is made and the time it is consummated. Your

position may be a little more shaky this morning than it was yesterday, but basically, George, you're still in solid. You don't have to be
afraid."

"I'm not afraid of anything, Leonard. I've told you that before."

"So you have, and what I've told you before is that we're all
afraid of something. What you're afraid of, George, is the world of
the Gentiles. Somewhere, God alone knows the precise location,
probably at your mother's knee, you've picked up and believe the
same notions about Gentiles that so many Gentiles have picked
up and believe about Jews. That they're creatures from another
world or another planet, with cloven feet and spiked tails and a
passion for drinking human blood. That they're your natural and
implacable enemy. That consorting with them is an act of treachery
to your faith and your people. Why, you should have seen your face
the night *The High Hand* opened and you walked into the Aqua
Vit and you found I had invited two shicksehs to dine with us.

"You're so terrified of the Gentile world that you'll do anything
under the sun to make a nice safe nest for yourself in the part of
the Jewish world that you think is completely safe from attack by
the Gentile enemy because it's so effectively camouflaged with money,
namely, the world of the rich Jew, specifically, the world of William
Prager. To insure your safe little nest in that world where you think
all your fear of Gentiles will be laid at rest, you'll take any amount
of indignity, and boy, can my niece Rosemary dish out indignity,
although I must confess my brother William is no slouch at it himself." Leonard Prager laughed. "The funny part about the whole
thing is that neither Rosemary nor W. P. understands any of this.
They think you're doing it for the money." Leonard put his hand
on George's shoulder in a fatherly way. "It's all right," he said. "I
won't tip them off. I've been enjoying the performance too much
for five years to want to see it stop now."

"That's damned generous of you."

"Not really," Leonard Prager said. "You see, I sympathize with
my brother's motives. If I had a daughter, George, I'd try to buy
you for her, too." He chuckled. "Even if it meant going to my brother
to borrow the money."

For a moment, as he stared at the thin, sardonic man facing
him across the elevator, George forgot his anger. He was suddenly
remembering another night, almost three years ago, in another
elevator, when, riding up to dinner in the triplex on Seventy-first

Street, he had been aware of a sense of excitement because he felt that the missing piece in the puzzle of his relationship to the Pragers was going to be supplied at last. It hadn't been. Not that night. It didn't seem possible that it was going to be supplied now. And yet the feeling was with George again, stronger than before. He hated to put the question to this man he detested, but George knew he would never have another chance. He had come here this morning not, as Leonard Prager thought, to mend fences but, as George had told Mary, to tie up loose ends.

"Leonard," he said. "Why would you go out and borrow the money to buy me for your daughter?"

"The same reason any good horse breeder would go to his bank to borrow the cost of Man o' War's stud fee. My brother wouldn't admit it, of course, but the Prager blood lines have been running a bit thin. A man who piles up a fortune as large as my brother William's doesn't like to think that when he's gone it will all be peed away by some boob grandchildren with nothing between their ears but a passion for sports cars and hot jazz. If you're going to found a dynasty you'd better make sure your offspring don't cross breed with weaklings. My brother William's way of making sure was to go down into the stockyards of the lower East Side and choose a tough young bull who—"

The elevator had stopped and the door was just sliding open when George shoved him. As a result, there was nothing to stop Leonard Prager. He went slithering on his back all the way across the polished marble floor of the reception room and, with his legs waving and his hands clutching air, disappeared behind the desk of the receptionist.

"Hey!" the elevator operator said. "What—?"

George didn't wait to hear the rest of his question. Neither did he turn to catch the ones the receptionist was suddenly calling in a high, frightened voice. George kept right on going, down the corridor, past the conference room, and into Rosemary's suite. He shoved the door open and stopped on the threshold.

He was not surprised to see Wallace Watchman and Nick Tomasino and Al Kreitzberg. Under the special circumstances created the day before by the Japanese High Command, the editors and circulation managers and advertising directors of a great many American publications were probably at this very moment conferring in the offices of their publishers. The only surprise to George was William Prager. So far as George knew, this was W. P.'s first visit to the *Noon* offices.

"Well," Wallace Watchman said. "Look who's here. I must say it's high time."

"Don't say anything else," George said. "Just get out."

"Hey, now, what—?"

"You heard me, Wallace. Beat it." George turned to the others. "You, too, Nick. Al. You can come back in a couple of minutes. What I have to say won't take long. It doesn't happen to concern you."

The three men turned toward Rosemary for instructions. She hesitated, glanced at her father, then turned back to the three men.

"Okay, boys," she said. "I'll call you in a few minutes."

They went out. There was a moment of silence, as though the three people left in the room wanted to adjust to the feeling of being alone together. W. P. moved first. He opened his mouth, rubbed the corners with thumb and forefinger, and tapped the nose piece of his pince-nez as though he were pressing the starting button of a machine that did his talking for him.

"George," he said, "where were you last night?"

"That's my private affair."

"Nobody who works for me has private affairs."

"That's what I came to tell you," George said. "I'm no longer working for you, W. P."

The neat little figure stiffened in the chair beside Rosemary's desk. "I hope you understand the consequences of what you're saying."

"If I didn't," George said, "I don't think you would have trusted me with an investment of this size in the first place."

"I was not referring only to my investment."

"Dad!" Rosemary said sharply. "I'll handle that part of it."

"No you won't," George said. "It's all handled, Rosemary. If you hadn't paid for that engagement ring yourself, I'd ask for it back. There won't be any wedding this week. Or any other week. I'm going, Rosemary. For good. The deal is off. I can't honestly say whether it's been nice knowing you or not. All I can say is that it was damned interesting. That goes for you, too, sir. Good-bye."

He turned and started for the door. Rosemary reached it first. Astonished, he saw that there were tears in her eyes.

"George," she said, and she sounded as though she was talking through a mouthful of taffy. "Why are you doing this?"

"I don't have time to explain," he said. "Even if I did, I don't think you'd understand."

"There's one thing you're going to have to answer."

"I don't have to answer anything any more, Rosemary."

"This one question you have to."

"Don't ask it."

"George, please."

"No."

"I've got to know if it's another girl."

"Get out of my way, Rosemary."

"Is it Mary Sherrod?"

"Rosemary, I've got to catch a train to Albany. You're holding me up."

She drew a deep breath, and she shuddered, as though a chill had run through her. The tears, George saw with relief, had vanished. In their place had come a hard, bright look of defiance. The moment of weakness was over. George was glad. He had what he'd come back here to get: his lost self-respect. Rosemary was entitled to have what mattered just as much to her: the last word.

"You can thank God you've got a tough little rear end," she said. "Because as far as I'm concerned you're out on it."

40

"Another piece kishke?"

"No, thanks," George said. "I'm stuffed, Aunt Tessie."

"That's what it is to be healthy," Uncle Zisha said with a sigh of envy from the brown leather couch on which he lay with his legs wrapped in a blanket and his head propped up by two pillows. "To have kishke on the plate, right there under your nose where you can smell it, and to say no, I had already enough, I'm stuffed!"

"You, in the days when you were healthy, you never once in your life said I had already enough, I'm stuffed!" Aunt Tessie said. "Your stomach was always as big as your eyes. You ate kishke not only for yourself but for a dozen other people. That's why now you eat only celery and we have bills from Dr. Hirsch they're bigger than the mortgage!"

"If you need any money," George said, "I can always—"

"What we need, we earn!" Aunt Tessie said sharply. "The rooms, in every one, thank God, we have a tenant, and the sewing, thank God again, I should only be able to do how much they bring me. Money we don't need. What we need is a letter once in a while. To see a face that it's in our heads and our hearts all the time. That's what we need, not money."

"I'm sorry," George said, wishing he had not felt it necessary to come up and do this in person. A letter would have been so much easier. "I've been pretty busy."

"President Roosevelt, he's busy, too," Aunt Tessie said. "But in the papers I see he has time to write his mother a letter, and every week, every two weeks, I see he goes to this Hyde Park to see her a little. So from New York to Albany it's further than from Washington to Hyde Park?"

"Stop already with hitting him over the head and calling him names!" Uncle Zisha said. "George hasn't been here for a long time. He comes for a visit, unexpected. He has to run back quick on the six o'clock train. We have him for only a few hours, so why can't we enjoy him those few hours? Why do we have to sit here calling him names?"

"Somebody here in this room heard me calling somebody names?" Aunt Tessie said. "I said only instead of money what we need here in Albany is not money, what we need is once in a while to hear from him a little good news, that's what I said."

"That's why I came," George said. "To bring you some good news."

The gaunt figure straightened up on the old couch. A faint glow appeared in the sickly yellow skin that hung loosely from the once fleshy face.

"George, you changed your mind!" Uncle Zisha said. "To law school you're going!"

"I'm afraid I'm too old for that," George said. "Besides, there's a war on. It's no time for men my age to start going to law school. Even assuming that the draft board would let me."

"The draft board!" Aunt Tessie said, and her hands stopped fussing with the plates on the table. She straightened up, and her fists went to her heart, and it was as though the tall, thin figure in the black dress had been frozen motionless by the touch of a magic wand. "They're taking you!"

"Not exactly," George said, and he laughed nervously, hoping to relieve the tension. "I'm giving myself to them before they get around to grabbing me. In that way it looks as though I'll be able to get a commission."

"Commission?" Aunt Tessie said, her small, dark, ugly face puckered with suspicion. "What's with this a commission?"

"An officer!" Uncle Zisha said. "Like in the Austrian army, when I was a boy, before I came to America, the fancy ones that they told Zisha Hurst go clean up after Franz Josef's horses!" The emaciated old man on the couch cackled with delight. "My George, an officer!"

"I'm not an officer yet," George said. "All I've done is apply for—"

"So what more do you have to do?" Uncle Zisha said disdainfully. "Mr. Singermann, that dope, the one lives upstairs in your old room and on his walls he didn't want the pictures from Judge Brandeis, this shlemiel he has a nephew, a nothing, Singermann told me yesterday they made him a lieutenant by the navy. So I ask you, plain talk. If they make Singermann's nephew a lieutenant, with Uncle Zisha's George less than a general it couldn't be!"

"I doubt it," George said, laughing again. "We want to win this war, you know."

"So how it's better to make sure we win than to make you a general?" Uncle Zisha said, and he laughed, too. "George, listen," he said. "You'll do me two favors?"

"Of course."

"Hitler, when you see him, you'll give him a punch in the nose for Uncle Zisha?"

"Consider it done."

"And the other thing, in the Austrian army, a bastard by the name Sergeant-Major Schepps. The three years I ate black bread for Franz Josef, this Schepps he was like what you call my boss, George."

"You want me to punch him in the nose, too?"

"No," Uncle Zisha said. "Him, this Sergeant-Major Schepps, him when you find him, George, I want you should pick out a dozen good horses, good heavy eaters I mean, and give this Schepps a broom, and stick him behind them!"

He fell back against the pillows, cackling gleefully. George laughed with him.

"This is the good news you came from New York to bring us?" Aunt Tessie said. "That in the army to be a soldier you're going?"

"No," George said. "That's only part of it."

"So what's the other part, what?"

"I'm getting married."

There was a moment of silence in the room, as though the magic wand had touched all of them, and then Aunt Tessie's ugly little face began to glow.

"George! To who? To who? Dora?"

"Dora? What ever gave you that idea?"

"But I always thought—?"

"I can't help what you always thought. Why the hell does it have to be Dora? I haven't even seen her in years. She could be dead for all I know."

"The hells you could leave in New York," Aunt Tessie said, and George regretted the outburst. He could see from her face that his anger had told her something was wrong. "Here, in Albany, by Uncle Zisha and me, it's plain talk," she said. "So now, without the hells, please, who is it, then?"

"You don't know her."

"Why didn't you bring her along with you so we *could* know her?"

"I wanted to, but Mary felt it would be—"

"Mary?"

"Yes, she felt it might be easier if—"

"What kind of a name is this, Mary?"

"Tessie, for God's sake!" Uncle Zisha said. "Let him talk!"

"I'm stopping him?" she said, but she did not take her eyes from George. "So talk," Aunt Tessie said quietly. "What kind of a name is this Mary?"

"It's just a name," George said, wishing he'd had the sense to do this by mail and knowing that sense had nothing to do with it. "Girls have all kinds of names."

"Not Jewish girls," Aunt Tessie said. "Jewish girls don't have names like Mary."

"Tessie!" The shock in Uncle Zisha's voice rang out like the crash of a large plate splattering on a stone floor. "Tessie, you're all of a sudden crazy?"

"If I am," she said, her eyes fixed grimly on George's face, "I want him to tell me."

"George, for God's sakes!" Uncle Zisha said irritably. "Tell her!"

"There isn't anything to tell," George said. "She's right. Mary is not a Jewish name."

Aunt Tessie stood there, her arms bent at the elbow, one hand gripping the wrist of the other, both hands pressed tight to her middle, as though only by this outward pressure could she keep herself from falling. Uncle Zisha, sitting up on the couch, stared in bewilderment from George to Aunt Tessie's stony face, creased tight and hard as a walnut, and then back to George.

"What, George, what?" the old man said. "Tell us."

"I'm getting married," George said, keeping his glance on Aunt Tessie, "to a girl named Mary Sherrod. She's not Jewish."

Long after his voice stopped, he could hear the hum of the carefully enunciated words. They filled the room slowly and steadily, like water rising around them, but nobody moved. Aunt Tessie, her eyes hot and bright, shining as though with fever, did not waver. Neither did George. To do it, to keep his glance from dropping, required more strength than he'd thought he had. Where it came from he did not know. He knew only that he had to have it, that this was one battle he could not lose. He had come here to fight it, knowing that the easy victory, sending the news in a letter, would have been not a victory but a postponement. She loved him and he loved her, but she had made him what he was. Her terrors had seeded his own. It was from her he had learned that the world was divided into Jews and shkutzim. It was she who had taught him to which world he belonged, and which world he must fear. The bonds that held them had been frayed long ago, when he learned how frightened she was to leave her nest on East Fourth Street, but fraying was not enough. Unless the bonds were cleanly cut, the marriage to Mary was doomed from the start. Sooner or later Aunt Tessie would begin drawing in the slack. Sooner or later Aunt Tessie would win, just as she had won over Uncle Zisha. George loved her, but he would rather be dead than spend his life on a brown leather couch, a prisoner of her righteous care. He could not let her win.

"All right," she said. The words emerged in a gasp, as though in the long silence she had been holding her breath, trying to lift an enormous weight from the floor to a table, and at last, still short of the goal, she had been forced to drop it back to the ground. "All right," Aunt Tessie said again, with a touch of impatience, as though it annoyed her that the enemy could not see she was waving a white handkerchief, but in the moment of victory George felt no elation. Something had gone wrong. Aunt Tessie refilled her lungs. The effort seemed to exhaust her, but it also made her seem much taller. "All right," she repeated. "One question."

"As many as you want," George said.

"More than one I won't need," Aunt Tessie said. "Tell me only this. What I say, what I ask, if I beg, no matter how I do it, it won't stop you?"

"No," George said.

She nodded, like a mathematician ticking off an expected minor point on the way to a larger calculation.

"So listen," she said. "Not only with your ears. With your heart, too."

"I'm listening," George said.

"If you marry this girl," Aunt Tessie said slowly, "I don't want to see you, I don't want to hear, nothing, never again. It'll be by me like twenty-eight years ago I never went to the Henry Isaacs Orphan Asylum to find you."

"Tessie!" Uncle Zisha said in a shocked voice, and he pushed himself up on the couch. "This is a way to talk?" She didn't answer. The old man turned to George. "Don't listen to her!" he said, his voice shaking. "She was always afraid. She was always hiding in corners from the world. She's still afraid. She's still hiding. Let her. Let her hide. You be different. Don't make a hole for yourself and creep into it. Don't make yourself a private ghetto. Do what your heart says, not your religion. To be a man is more important than to be a Jew. Without listening to your heart you'll never be a man. You like this girl? She likes you? It says in your heart I want to marry her? So marry her!"

"Thanks," George said. "I'm going to marry her."

"Then by me," Aunt Tessie said in a tight, hard voice, "by me you're no more a living person!"

"Tessie!" Uncle Zisha said angrily. "What kind of craziness is in you?"

"By me," Aunt Tessie continued, grinding out the words, keeping her feverish eyes fixed on George, "by me you're already dead!"

She turned, her thin body so straight that she might have been a marionette suspended from the ceiling by invisible strings, and she started for the door. Halfway there she seemed to stumble. She put out her hand, as though clawing for something to steady her, but there was nothing within reach. Even as he jumped up and started around the table toward her, George knew what it was that had gone wrong with his victory.

He had not realized, until this moment when he dropped to his knees beside what already looked like a bundle of lifeless black sticks, that in order to win he would have to destroy her.

41

Almost six months later, walking down Fifth Avenue from the club where he had lunched with Winston Sherrod, George found that the victory he had just won over Mary's father was running together in his mind with the earlier victory over Aunt Tessie.

The complications of getting out of civilian life and into uniform, plus the excitement of his first tour of duty in London, had helped insulate the sense of guilt with which he lived during the months that dragged by between the day she collapsed in Albany and the day, still refusing to speak George's name, Aunt Tessie finally died in a New York hospital bed.

Now, unexpectedly, he was shaken by the knowledge that she was irrevocably gone. It was as though, striding from a tent where he had arrogantly laid down the terms under which he would accept surrender from an enemy commander, he suddenly discovered that his own army had vanished.

Seized by a sense of loneliness as acute as a toothache, George jumped into a cab, rode down to Mary's apartment, and started talking before he had kicked the door shut behind him.

"You arrange the details," she said when he finished. "I'll go change my clothes."

George went to the phone and called Nick Perrini.

"Well, I'll be a son of a gun," Nick said. "I thought you were over in London making like a general?"

"I was, until yesterday."

"When am I going to see you?"

"Any time this afternoon you can stop work long enough to come be best man at my wedding."

"George, you kidding?"

"Nope."

"Well, I'll be a son of a gun!"

"You said that."

"What else can I say until I meet the lucky girl?"

"Shall we see what we can do about arranging that?"

"You tell me where and when, kid."

"That's why I'm calling you, Nick."

"You mean you want me to fix a place? Like in my house maybe?"

"Not exactly."

"George, talk English."

"There are complications, Nick."

"Remember me? I'm the boy makes his living manufacturing a product that helps people avoid complications. Shoot me yours, boy."

"We have no marriage license, Nick. We haven't had a Wassermann test. Those are the two prerequisites I can think of that we haven't got. If there are any others, we haven't got those, either."

"Anything else?"

"Yes. We don't want the ceremony performed by a rabbi or a priest or a minister. We want someone neutral so far as religion is concerned, and it's got to be done by six o'clock so we can catch a seven o'clock train from Penn Station because I'm due down in Washington for three days of conferences before I fly back to London and that's all the honeymoon we're going to get."

"Any more complications?"

"Aren't those enough?"

"Give me the number you're calling from," Nick said. "And stand by."

George stood by. A half hour later Nick Perrini called back.

"You're as good as hitched, kid," he said. "Both of you meet me in apartment 18-D, 360 Central Park West, at five-thirty. Got that?"

"Apartment 18-D, 360 Central Park West, five-thirty. Whose place is it?"

"Judge Fusanbucco. His home. He'll have a marriage license ready to be filled out. I'll have a doctor there to give you both the old Wassermann. Mrs. Fusanbucco and me, we'll be the witnesses."

"How am I ever going to thank you for this, Nick?"

"Come back from this damn war in one piece and start auditing my books again. The meathead I got now thinks double entry means a house with two foyers."

George went into the bedroom and told Mary.

"That gives us almost three hours," she said. "Do you think I could go and have my hair washed?"

"It looks clean as sunlight."

"I know, but it seems the right thing to do before getting married."

"In that case, you go get your hair washed. While you're doing it, I'll run over to my place, take a shower, put on my best uniform, and pack my bag. I'll meet you back here in forty minutes."

He didn't get back for three hours. But Mary never knew that. When she arrived at the hairdresser and found every operator was booked solid for the afternoon, Mary wanted to leave, but the owner of the shop urged her to wait for a possible cancellation. By the time she got back to her apartment, therefore, and found George pacing about nervously, Mary's hair looked beautiful but her mind was in a turmoil of fury, with the hairdresser for urging her to wait and rage at herself for listening to him: she and George were due at Judge Fusanbucco's apartment in exactly fifteen minutes!

Luck in finding a taxi and more luck with traffic lights helped get them to their wedding on time. It did not, however, give George a chance to explain that he had arrived back in Mary's apartment a minute or two before she did. As a result, she never asked George what had delayed him. If she had, their life together might have been different. Assuming, of course, that he would have given her a truthful answer. George didn't know whether he would have been able to do that. He did know he never had to tell Mary that, while she was on her way to the hairdresser and he came hurrying into his apartment house, he found Dora Dienst waiting for him in the lobby.

His first reaction was a desire to turn and run. Dora, however, had seen him. His next reaction, which frightened him, carried George across the lobby to the bench from which she rose.

"George," she said, "I'm in trouble."

He didn't doubt it. He had not seen her for almost eleven years but not even in a hundred, if he lived that long, was he likely to forget the conditions under which she turned to him.

"What kind of trouble?"

She looked nervously around the lobby. "I can't talk about it here."

"I can't talk about it any other place," George said. "I'm just running upstairs to pick up my bag. I've got to catch a train to Washington in half an hour."

The lie didn't help. He hadn't expected it to. Not because his voice lacked conviction. It didn't help because she hadn't heard it. She had never listened to what she didn't want to hear.

"You've got to help me, George."

No, I don't, said the voice inside his head. He knew it well. It was the voice that had screamed warnings at him a dozen years ago in the deserted cafeteria, the night he had dragged Dora out of Mrs. Hooper's apartment, telling him over and over again to get the hell out of there. He had not got the hell out of there, and the voice was screaming the same advice at him now.

"All right," George said, aware that he was sealing his fate, yet forcing himself to act out the pretense that he was in control of the situation. "You can come up for a minute."

"My!" Dora said when he opened the door and she stepped into the apartment. "You've sure come up in the world since the days of Mrs. Shissle!"

"It's not my place any more," he said, speaking crisply, moving toward the bedroom where his suitcase lay open on the bed, trying to get away from the odor of honey cake fresh from the oven. "I sublet it for six months while I was stationed in London," he said, beginning to throw shirts and socks into the suitcase. "I'm being sent back to London in a few days, and I don't know how long I'll be there. Probably till the war is over. So I'm letting my lease on this place go. It only runs till the end of this month, anyway."

He looked up from the suitcase. She was standing in the bedroom doorway, leaning against the jamb, nibbling at a knuckle as she watched him, her eyes wide and bright and frightened. It was like that summer evening so many years ago when he had started to tell her in the doorway of her father's doll store that he was going away with Aunt Tessie to live in Albany. For a moment all the other feelings dimmed out as rage blazed up. Rage and resentment. He had thought he was finished with it. He had earned the right to be finished with it. Yet here it was, so many years later, on his wedding day, as strong as ever.

"I've got that train to catch," he said, speaking savagely because he thought that might help keep his voice from shaking. "You better talk fast."

She talked fast, across the knuckle she kept rubbing nervously along her lower lip, the wide, frightened eyes following his every movement. She looked and sounded like a child who, after playing hooky from school for a few hours, comes home to beg forgiveness and finds that her house and her parents have mysteriously vanished.

She explained that it was not she who had run out on him. It was not she who had ransacked his room in Mrs. Shissle's rooming house. It was not she who had taken the money he had set aside for their wedding, and it was not she who had torn in half the tickets that were supposed to take them to Brigantine Beach for their honeymoon, and it was not she who had stripped the silver frame from the picture of Judge Brandeis. No. It was Danny. He had reappeared unexpectedly, the way he always did, and as always she had found herself helpless in his hands. The only difference between this time and the other time was that this time he had married her. She didn't know why, since he didn't love her and never had, but she supposed it had something to do with business. Danny was always getting her to sign papers, so that when people came after him for money he could say he didn't have any. It was all in his wife's name. Except that there never seemed to be much of it around.

They had spent the ten years in Chicago and San Francisco and New Orleans and a dozen other cities, in every one of which Danny had been sure if he just got the right kind of place, a room that had class in which Dora's voice sounded right, he would hit it big. He never seemed to find the right kind of place, though, and nine months ago they had come back to New York. They had lived in various hotels around Times Square for several months, moving whenever the management became unpleasant about the bill, until the credit managers' association finally made checking into another hotel impossible. Then Danny had rented a small apartment on East Forty-eighth Street. He went out every day on the mysterious errands that were part of his preparation for hitting it big, and sometimes he had to stay away for a couple of days because, he said, the people who were going to help him hit it big wanted him to come down to the country to discuss details. Dora didn't know what Danny meant by the country, and she never asked. Not even when he started staying away three and four days at a time. That was why it had not occurred to her, when he went away the last time, that he was going for good.

"I thought it was just another three or four day trip," Dora said. "The kind he'd been going away on for a long time. But that was three months ago, and last month the landlord started to get sore, and this morning he—he—" Her voice broke, and it was as though the invisible bond that had tied her to the door had broken with it. She came across the bedroom, tears bouncing down the thin, unbelievably delicate face that reminded him of a Chinese doll, and she put her head against his chest and said, "George, what am I going to do?"

He stood there, arms rigid at his sides, his breath coming in slow, hauling gasps that carried the fresh honey-cake smell to every nerve in his body, listening to the voice inside his head screaming: *It isn't fair; not after all these years; not on my wedding day; it isn't fair!* But the screaming didn't do any good. From the moment downstairs in the lobby when he did not turn and run he had known nothing would do any good. He was as helpless now as he had been all those years ago on that summer night in the darkened doorway of her father's store. His hands came up, and the delicate little shoulder blades fitted against his outspread palm, and as she twisted with him slowly toward the bed and their mouths locked, a sound broke from his throat that he would never forget and never stop hating. It was a sob of happiness.

With the sound still ringing in his ears, he managed to twist free, and get off the bed, and move to the far corner of the bedroom, but he carried the feeling of horror with him. He hadn't done it. He had managed to break away. But it was a technical victory. He knew in his heart he was just as guilty, standing there shaking in a corner of the room, as he would have been if he had remained on the bed. It was as though he had been running desperately for ten years, away from a pain against which his only protection was distance, and just as he had reached a haven, on the threshold of the only place where he would be safe, he had tripped and fallen and been overtaken by the enemy against whom he was powerless.

"George."

"What?"

"Can I come back to stay?" Dora said.

He had known it was going to be her next question. It had to be. He stood there, fighting the weight of helplessness, trying to think of an answer. He couldn't. In the lobby downstairs, out in the living room, even here in the bedroom while he was packing, he'd had an answer: Mary. He had thrown that answer away, however, when he took Dora back in his arms.

"Sure," he said wearily, talking to the floor, refusing to turn and look at her. "I don't know how to arrange it, since I'm in the army, I mean, and I have to go back to London in a few days, but I suppose—"

His voice stopped. Unexpectedly, without warning, his mind was suddenly flooded with the image of Aunt Tessie, lying broken on the floor of the shabby living room in Albany. The fierce pride that had burned in that tiny body, the sharp tongue with which she had kept the mocking world at bay, the love she had tended and watched over and kept hidden like a miser's secret hoard for him alone, all that was gone. He had wiped it out. He had destroyed it to save himself. If he allowed himself to go under again, if he didn't show up in Judge Fusanbucco's apartment on Central Park West at five-thirty, what had Aunt Tessie died for?

"George," Dora said again, in a small, pleading voice. "Can I come back to stay?"

"I don't know," he said. "It's not completely up to me any more. Uncle Sam has something to do with it. I've missed the three o'clock train to Washington. If I miss the six o'clock they'll throw me in the clink. Why don't we do this? Let me go over to this place where you live and get your things. By the time I get back I'll have something figured out."

She wrote out the address while he got dressed. He took a taxi to Forty-eighth Street, thinking hard all the way. He let himself into the apartment with the key she had given him and continued to think as he packed her things. He had two of her suitcases packed and was almost finished with the third when there was a knock on the door. It proved to be the landlord but, after George gave him a check for $180 to cover Dora's back rent, he caused no trouble. In the taxi that carried him and Dora's suitcases back to University Place, George finally worked out the answer.

"Here's what you're going to do," he said to Dora as he set down her bags and pulled out his checkbook and fountain pen. "You can stay here for a few days, until my lease is up, while you get yourself set to go out to Reno."

"Reno?"

"That's right," George said. He signed the check and tore it out of the book. "This ought to be enough to carry you until you get your divorce from Danny."

"Divorce from Danny?" She sounded as though he had suggested that the only solution to her problem was suicide.

"It seems the only sensible thing to do," George said. "You admit you hate him. You say he doesn't love you and never did. He married you just to use you as a pawn in his business dealings, and now he's walked out on you. The thing to do is cut yourself loose from him as soon as you can. I'm not rich, but I've got enough saved to help you do that."

"What about after?"

"I don't know about after. That's going to be up to you."

"But George." She swung around to look at the bed on which, even though he had broken away in time, she had won more than a technical victory, and then she turned back to him. "George," she said uneasily, as though she could not understand why the fruits of her triumph should be denied her, "I thought you and I—?"

"You thought wrong." He kept his voice flat and hard, even though his heart was pounding. "Don't ever try to see me again."

George was not displeased, as he dropped the check in her lap, to find he was able to handle this as well as a son of a bitch like Danny Schorr would have handled it. It was the least he could do for the memory of Aunt Tessie.

"We're finished, Dora," he said. "This is the end."

42

Seven years later, on the Friday morning before the Fourth of July week end, a total stranger named Maurice Kashkin had demonstrated in George Hurst's office that it was far from the end.

Eight hours after the demonstration, as George climbed down from the 5:25 to the Danville station along with a couple of hundred other commuters, he carried with him more than the copy of *Worldweek* containing the glowing cover story about Daniel Shaw that he had bought in Grand Central. George carried with him the uneasy feeling that the forces which had been converging on him all day, from the moment early in the morning when Miss Akst's surprising phone call had interrupted his shave, were walking along grimly a pace or two behind him, like invisible bill collectors who had been put off once too often and were now determined to stay with their man until he paid up.

The sense of being followed was so strong that George whipped around, as though trying to surprise his stalkers. He surprised Milton Schneider.

"Please!" Eileen Bucknell's husband said, jumping back nervously.

"Sorry," George said. "I thought somebody was following me."

"Certainly I was following you," Milton said. "I looked with care for you on the train, but achieved no success, and I had reached the conclusion that I would have to look elsewhere for my ride, when I saw you descending from the car ahead of mine, so I ran to catch up, whereupon you hurled yourself around upon me like Chingachgook when he overhears in the forest a twig snap."

"It's been one of those days," George said. "What's this about a ride?"

Milton stopped combing his long, unruly black hair with his bony fingers. "Eileen did not speak to you?"

"Eileen?"

"She telephoned me in my office in New York this morning," Milton said. "She said she had talked to you earlier in Dr. Rettig's office."

"Oh, yes, that's right. Before I caught the nine-fourteen. I was bringing d'Artagnan in because he's got this bad ear, and Rettig was talking to Eileen on the phone. Something about getting Polly Stiefel's neurotic Bismarck banged by your darling Peppy."

"The other way around," Milton Schneider said. "Our darling Peppy is the bitch. Polly Stiefel's neurotic Bismarck is the male. It is our Peppy who is to be, as you put it, banged."

"Well, either which way, I know it was a big deal in Weimariners."

"Yes, and Eileen informed me that she told you she would pick up Mary tonight at your house and take her to the Stiefel party, whereas you would give me a ride from the train to the school from which, after the Dandypops meeting is completed, you and I would proceed to the Stiefel party to join Eileen and Mary. Is that not correct?"

"It is," George said. Milton had come to America in 1937 and had been naturalized in 1942. He could hardly be called a Hungarian refugee any longer. Yet he still retained the refugee's preoccupation with precise details about all arrangements, as though he could never quite shake off the feeling that in an alien country even the most kindly disposed people, unless you pinned them down on every conceivable point, might disappoint you unintentionally because they spoke a different language. George said, "I've got my car parked in the south lot back of the fire house."

Walking toward it, he did not hear very much of Milton's even-tempered, soft-spoken, but devastating tirade against the current president of the Dandypops. George was thinking that of the approximately ninety-six-hour reprieve Mr. Kashkin had given him, eight hours were already gone. That left him with roughly eighty-four. What could he do with them? He couldn't use the time to change the facts. He couldn't wipe out the record. He couldn't undo what had been done. By Tuesday morning he would have to tell Mr. Kashkin what the man from Albany wanted to know. If he didn't, Mr. Kashkin and his diggers would find it out for themselves. In either case, the result would be the same: an explosion from which nothing of the life that George Hurst had made here in Danville with Mary during the past four years could possibly remain. What Mr. Kashkin's reprieve amounted to, in the final analysis, was the postponement of a brutal choice: did George want to light the fuse himself, or did he prefer to have it done by Mr. Kashkin?

"You are not listening to me," Milton Schneider said.

"Sorry," George said as he inched the car out of the parking lot into Railroad Avenue. "I was just thinking that every year, as soon as the summer visitors move in on this town, it becomes practically impossible to get your car out of a parking lot at train time in under a quarter of an hour. What were you saying?"

"I was saying that if the big mouth of Mr. Hoxter Monahan can be kept closed at least during part of this meeting, perhaps you and I can arrive at the Stiefels in time for a drink before the food is served," Milton said. "Speaking for myself, I am in need of one."

"I am in need of two and possibly three," George said. "And I intend to have them, regardless of how much Mr. Hoxter Monahan has to say or when Mrs. Polly Stiefel starts flogging her guests toward the food. My guess is that Hoxter is going to have a lot to say. When

I took the kids to camp this morning, Tim Keogh said Hoxter had some new plan for tomorrow's clambake."

"How an organization composed of such highly intelligent men as the membership of the Dandypops could have elected a man of this low caliber as its president is a mystery of the deepest kind," Milton said. "The school term has been finished for three weeks. The clambake, which was planned with care from the middle of April, takes place tomorrow. Yet Mr. Hoxter Monahan, our president, sees fit to call a meeting on July the first to change those plans. Observe him, if you will, please."

Turning the car from Railroad Avenue into the curved driveway in front of the Danville Elementary School, George observed Hoxter Monahan. The proprietor of The Sports Emporium and president of the Dandypops was standing at the top of the stone front steps, waving both arms like a traffic policeman who has gone crazy, and, to judge by the way his mouth was working, screaming some sort of instructions. It was impossible to hear him, however, because the driveway, which was not intended as a parking area, was nevertheless being turned into one by the arriving Dandypops. This process involved a great deal of gear grinding, motor roaring, and friendly but noisy exchange of advice from car to car. Taking some from the man on his left and some from the man on his right, George succeeded in edging his car into a sliver of space at the foot of the stone steps. As soon as he cut the motor, he realized that Hoxter Monahan was shouting at him.

"The prize pig," Milton said as they climbed out of the car, "seems to be addressing you."

George went up the stone steps. "Hi, Hoxter," he said. "What's all the hysteria about?"

"Ask Porky Haenigson," Hoxter Monahan said angrily. "He's called you three times since I got here."

"Me?"

"For Christ's sake, George, don't you think I know how to take a telephone message? Sure you."

"But—"

George was about to say he scarcely knew Porky Haenigson. So why should the restaurateur be calling him? But Hoxter Monahan was clearly not the man to say it to.

"Save the buts for Porky," the proprietor of The Sports Emporium snarled. "Just go call him and get it over with, will you? I'm trying to get this God-damn meeting started."

George pushed through the front door and went down the hall to the phone booth outside the principal's office from which Win and Jimmy occasionally called Mary at three o'clock on a school day to ask if they could skip the ride home on the bus because a friend had invited them to spend the afternoon at his house and would Mary mind driving over to pick them up later. George looked up Porky's restaurant in the phone book and dialed the number. A woman's voice came on the wire.

"Haenigson's Steak House, good evening."

"Mr. Haenigson, please."

"He's not here."

"He's not?"

"No, sir."

"But I was just told he called me a couple of minutes ago and asked me to call him right back?"

"Who is this?"

"Mr. Hurst. George Hurst."

"Oh, hello, Mr. Hurst. This is Mrs. Haenigson."

"Hello."

"Porky did try to get you, Mr. Hurst, but Hoxter Monahan said you hadn't arrived at the meeting yet, so finally Porky couldn't wait any longer. I mean, you know, he's bringing over coffee and sandwiches for the Dandypops, and he had it all poured in the big thermos, the five-gallon one we use on catered affairs, but Porky thinks it's sprung a leak somewhere, not a leak really, I mean it doesn't lose liquid, but it's been losing heat, and he didn't want to take a chance on all that coffee getting cold, so he thought he'd better get going. Porky's on his way to the school right now. He'll see you there in a little while, Mr. Hurst."

"Mrs. Haenigson—"

"Yes?"

"Do you happen to know what Mr. Haenigson wanted to talk to me about?"

"Well, yes, it's—" The voice at the other end of the phone paused, then resumed on a note that was clearly hostile. "I think maybe I better let Porky tell you about it himself, Mr. Hurst."

For several moments after she hung up, George remained in the phone booth, holding the dead phone, trying to control the hard, cold, numbing knot of fear that was suddenly working its way up from his stomach.

George had never set foot in Haenigson's Steak House. Until

he had been assigned in April to the Food Committee for the Dandypops clambake, George had never spoken a word to Porky Haenigson. Since April he had probably spoken a couple of dozen, but they had all dealt with arrangements for the Fourth of July clambake, and most of them had been no more than grunts of assent to the duties Porky, as chairman of the Food Committee, had asked George to assume at the affair. There was absolutely no reason he could think of why Porky Haenigson, who knew he was going to see George at this Dandypops meeting, anyway, should try three times within the half hour before the meeting started to reach him on the phone.

George could not forget, however, that after he hung up on Miss Akst in the morning, he had been unable to think of any reason why her phone call should have left him feeling troubled. Mr. Kashkin had supplied that reason soon enough. It seemed insane to think there could be any connection between the ultimatum Mr. Kashkin had dropped in George's lap that morning in New York and these puzzling phone calls Porky Haenigson had just made here in Danville. In the pit of his stomach, however, to which the things his intelligence told him did not penetrate, George knew there had to be a connection. He couldn't imagine what it was, but he knew it was not going to be good. The invisible bill collectors were closing in.

George put up the dead phone. Trying to disregard the icy knot in his stomach, as though it was a stain he had discovered on his coat after leaving the house and there was nothing he could do about it until he got back home, George left the phone booth, walked down the stairs to the basement, and paused in the doorway of the school cafeteria where the Dandypops held their meetings.

"George!"

He turned. Milton Schneider was signaling to him from a table just inside and to the right of the door. George tiptoed toward it. He sat down beside Milton, who leaned toward him.

"I thought it would be wise to remain as close to the door as possible," Milton whispered. "If it develops that the reason for calling this meeting is pure nonsense, which I strongly suspect it will demonstrate itself to be, we can escape without making ourselves conspicuous."

George nodded. It was also the best place in the room from which to reach Porky Haenigson, when he came in with the coffee and sandwiches, before anybody else reached him. George wondered, as he pretended to look around the room with interest so that Milton would not suspect he was upset, how long it would take Porky to get here. Mrs. Haenigson had said he'd just left. Haenigson's Steak House was on the Post Road, halfway between Danville and West-port. If the traffic wasn't too bad, a good driver should be able to make it in fifteen minutes. Say twenty at the outside. George glanced at his watch. Seven twenty-five. Assuming that Porky had left his restaurant at seven-twenty, that meant—

"George."

He came up out of his troubled thoughts. Milton was leaning close again.

"I have just had a notion," Milton whispered. "If we slipped out now we could reach the Stiefels in ample time to consume our drinks in comfort, and if there is anything of importance at this meeting that we might miss because of our absence, could we not learn it from Fritz Courtenay or Mitchell Hazelkorn? I see they are both here, and surely, since they are TV impresarios, which to Polly Stiefel automatically makes them distinguished members of the artistic world, they, too, have been invited to her party?"

"Let's give it a few minutes, anyway," George said. "I want—"

"For Christ's sake, you guys!" Hoxter Monahan bawled from the table up front. "Couldn't we have a little quiet so we can get through this spinach and onto the main reason I called this meet-ing?"

Half a hundred heads turned. Milton, his face flushing, sank back in his chair. "Pig," he muttered.

Hoxter Monahan turned back to the man sitting beside him at the front table. George knew the man was the club secretary. He did not, however, know the man's name. Very few of the Dandypops knew each other's names. They came from all of Danville's many social and economic levels. The only thing they had in common was an interest in this school, which was attended by their children, and this club dedicated to making the school a better place for their children. Long ago somebody had tried to solve the problem of identification by introducing a motion, which was seconded, passed, and acted upon, to provide members with lapel badges containing their names. Most members, however, came to Dandypops meet-ings directly from their commuting trains and, like George, always forgot before leaving the house in the morning to slip the identification badge into their pockets. Even the club secretary, George saw, was not wearing his badge.

"That's the end of the minutes, Hoxter," the secretary said. "If somebody will move—?"

"I move the minutes be accepted as read," Tim Keogh called from the middle of the room.

"Seconded," another voice said.

"All those in favor?" Hoxter Monahan said.

A long thundering "Aye!" swept through the room and echoed back from the monel metal steam table behind Hoxter.

"All those against?" he demanded. Not a sound. Hoxter nodded. "The minutes are accepted as read." He picked up a sheet of paper. "Now, if you guys don't mind, I'd like to get to the reason why I called this meeting. It's one of the most—"

"Hoxter."

He looked up irritably. "Yes?"

"As long as we're all here," said a voice from the left side of the room, "I wonder if I could take a minute just to read this letter from Sister Cordelia of St. Anthony's Academy in Bridgeport?"

"What about?" Hoxter said.

"The $250 scholarship this club provided for Lucy Pampini, the top-ranking student in last year's Danville graduating class, which helped make it possible for that brilliant but unfortunately not very prosperous youngster to pursue her studies at—"

"Jesus Christ!" Hoxter Monahan snapped. "Will you please save that stuff for our first meeting in the fall? We got a clambake to run tomorrow. I called this meeting for the specific purpose—"

"I know, and I don't want to waste time, Hoxter, but as chairman of the Scholarship Committee, I just happened to receive this letter from Sister Cordelia this morning, thanking the Dandypops for our generous help to Lucy Pampini, and I thought as long as we're all gathered here—"

"We're not gathered here to listen to regular club business," Hoxter Monahan said. "We're gathered here because I as president called this special meeting about tomorrow's clambake. So will you lay off, please?"

"If this is a special meeting at which no regular business is to be discussed, how come you had the secretary read the minutes?"

"Because, God damn it, you can't have a legal meeting, parliamentary procedure and all that, without opening with a reading of the minutes! Now, will you please table that letter until the fall and let's get going, for Christ's sake!"

George glanced at the door, then down at his watch. Twenty-eight minutes after. If his calculation was correct, Porky Haenigson should now be making the turn from the Post Road into—

"George."

He looked up. Milton was leaning close again.

"What?"

"The compulsion to consume alcohol is becoming in the presence of this pig almost overpowering. Let us skip the coop."

"Fly the coop," George said. Milton's English was good but fuzzy at the edges. "Let's just give it a few more minutes."

He turned back to the room. A man whose name George did not know but had been seeing on the Danville railroad platform for years was on his feet at a table in the middle of the room.

"I know this meeting is a special one, Hoxter," he was saying. "And I know it's supposed to deal with the clambake, and I know the clambake is important, but I know something that's more important: the morals of the kids of this town. When I saw that magazine, I said to my son, I said Kip, where did you get that magazine? Why, Pop, he said, I bought it at Tinsey's Smoke Shop on Locust Street. The next day being Saturday, and not having to go into New York that day, I made it a point to go down to Tinsey's Smoke Shop and have a look for myself. It was certainly educational, and if any of you fathers want to see what the children of this town are being sold right there on Locust Street, I recommend a short trip to Tinsey's. It's just plain smut, that's what it is. Cheap, rotten, dirty pornography and nothing else. Poisoning the minds and the morals of our children, that's what those disgusting magazines are doing, and I personally don't give a damn whether this is a special meeting or a regular meeting or any other kind of meeting. I say this is what the Dandypops was formed for. I say this is the proper business of this club. I say let's form a committee right here and now to look into this and see what we can do to stop a man like Cal Tinsey, under the pretense of he's running a respectable business, I say let's stop him from ruining the morals of our children!"

"Will you please for God's sake bring that up at our first meeting in the fall?" Hoxter Monahan said. "We've got a clambake coming up tomorrow. This meeting—"

"I'd rather postpone the clambake than postpone saving the morals of my children!"

"We can't postpone the clambake! We've sold sixteen hundred tickets at three and a half bucks each! That's fifty-six hundred dollars!"

"The morals of my kids are worth more than fifty-six *million* dollars!"

"Okay, Cheever, if that's the way you—"

"My name happens to be Wyckliffe!"

"Okay, Wyckliffe!" Hoxter bellowed. "I hereby appoint you a committee of one to look into the sale of smutty magazines in the town of Danville! You satisfied now?"

"No! Why should I be the only one to take on this responsibility? Why should it be a committee of one? Aren't the rest of the men in this club interested in what's happening to the morals of their children?"

George looked at his watch. Twenty-five minutes to eight. He glanced toward the door. His heart jumped. Out in the hall, to the left of the door, Porky Haenigson was setting down a large thermos jug.

George stood up and tiptoed out. "Hi, Porky," he said.

Porky Haenigson, who was trying to set an enormous paper bag on top of the thermos, gave him a pleasant but vague smile. "Hi."

"I called you back," George said. Porky, it seemed, had not heard him. In a louder voice, George said, "I just spoke to your wife."

Porky's face still looked blank. "My wife?"

"Yes," George said, trying to conceal his impatience. "I called you, and she answered, and she said—"

"You called me?"

"Yes, of course," George said irritably. What was the matter with this boob? "As soon as I got here from the train and Hoxter gave me your message."

"Oh!" Porky's face cleared. "You're George Hurst." He smiled apologetically. "This club, I know all the guys. Their faces, I mean. The names, though, sometimes—" He shook his head and laughed sheepishly. "And you're on my Food Committee for the clambake, yet. Isn't that something?"

"Yes, I know," George said, abandoning the effort to control his impatience. The icy lump of fear in his stomach was spreading. It seemed more important to control that. He couldn't manage both.

"Mrs. Haenigson said she knew what you'd called me about, but she thought you'd prefer to tell me yourself."

"Damn right," Porky said, and he sent a conspiratorial glance across his shoulder before he leaned toward George and said quietly, "It's this dame."

"What dame?"

"The one I hired to sing in my place over the Fourth of July week end. She arrived from New York late this afternoon, and first thing, she's not even got her bag open, she starts asking me I should call you on the telephone, George Hurst. I told her here, there's the phone book, look it up, call him yourself, whoever he is. I mean I wasn't thinking."

Porky sent another glance across his shoulder and then winked at George.

"The rush and all, getting ready for the week end, I mean, who has time to think about stuff like that? A couple of minutes later, though, I see how worried she looks, it begins to click. Not that this guy she wants me to call, this George Hurst, I don't mean I connected him with you, the face of the guy on my clambake committee. To me, the way she looks, busting a gut to get in touch with him, to me he's just a guy and she's a dame wants to get in touch with him, that's all, the way dames all over the world they have guys, they get to the town the guy lives, they want to get in touch with him. Especially there's some kind of trouble. So I make the call for her, and Mrs. Hurst, she says when she answers, she says you're in New York, and you're coming out on the 5:25. So I say politely thank you very much, I will call him again this evening, and when your missus says is there any message, I say no thank you, no message, I will call Mr. Hurst this evening. He won't be home this evening, your missus says. He's going to a Dandypops meeting direct from the train, she says, and then he's joining me at a friend's house for dinner. Okay, thank you very much, I say, I'll try him tomorrow, no message, because if this guy is a Dandypop, by God, I figure, I'm not getting a fellow club member into any jams, so I hang up nice and polite, and I tell all this to this dame, the one that's singing for me over the week end, and she acts like I just told her they were sending you up the river or something. Either she's got it for this guy but big, I think, or the trouble she's in it ain't small. One thing is sure: she can't wait. So I said being a commuter, it's even money he's just got off that train and he's arriving at the Dandypops meeting right now. I'll get him on the phone for you, I says, but I guess that parking jam down around the station must be getting worse, because by the time I figured you should've made it already to the school, Hoxter, he answers the phone, he says no, you're not there yet, which is to this dame like a red flag to a bull. She drives me crazy the next half hour, I'm trying to get these sandwiches and this coffee ready. She made me call two more times before I had to beat it over with this stuff, and even then, before she lets me go, she makes me promise I'll tell you the minute I see you and ask you to call her up right away." Porky Haenigson winked again. "Personally, I think you better, or this dame, the way she's busting to see you, I don't think I got the right to answer for the consequences."

It was a right, George thought grimly, that belonged only to him. "Thanks," he said.

"Forget it," Porky said, "which is by the way what I'm going to do, too. Now I've told you the facts, I mean now I've carried the message, as a fellow Dandypop I assure you I don't remember none of it. You and this dame, who she is, what she wants, you and her, so far as I'm concerned, it never happened. You'll notice," he said with a roguish smile, "I never even mentioned the girl's name, which in these situations I always figure is completely unnecessary, if you know what I mean."

George, who knew what Porky meant, wished he didn't.

"Thanks," George said. "I know her name."

43

He knew also that he had an immediate problem: how to get rid of Milton Schneider.

"You and that Porky in the hall, there," Milton said as George backed the car out of the school driveway. "What were you talking about?"

"Some changes he wants in the Food Committee arrangements for tomorrow," George said shortly. "Nothing important."

Maybe there was a connection between Mr. Kashkin's ultimatum and Porky Haenigson's message, and maybe there wasn't, but this much was certain: George had to get to Haenigson's Steak House before anybody made any more attempts to reach him on the phone.

"For something you call nothing important," Milton said, "I must say you took a long enough time discussing it."

"I wasn't discussing," George said. He swung the car into Railroad Avenue and headed for the Post Road. "I was listening. You know how Porky is, once he gets started."

He tried to keep the irritation out of his voice. It was not easy. For the first time since Miss Akst's morning phone call started weaving the net that had been closing in on him all day a course of action had presented itself. For the first time in a dozen troubled, uncertain hours George Hurst knew what he had to do. Until he got rid of Milton Schneider, however, he couldn't do it.

"I do not know how Porky is when he gets started or even when he gets stopped," Milton said. "I know only that an hour ago, when we arrived at the Dandypops meeting and I suggested we leave early, you said no, let us wait and hear what the prize pig Hoxter Monahan has to say. Before the opportunity to hear him could be achieved, however, you dash out into the hall for a conference with Mr. Porky Haenigson, as a result of which you decide to do precisely what I originally suggested, namely, leave the foolish meeting, except that you perform the act of leaving as though the police were in our hot pursuit."

"If I'm driving too fast for you," George said, "I'll be glad to stop and let you out."

"You think that would be an unwise thing?" Milton said. "It does not make very good sense to imperil one's life merely because you are in so wild a hurry to reach Polly Stiefel's party."

"I'm not in any hurry to reach any damn party."

"I am not deaf, George. It is not necessary to shout."

"I'm not shouting."

"Neither are you watching the road. In this country, as I learned soon after I came to it, it is customary to drive on the right."

George slammed on the brakes and pulled up to the side of Railroad Avenue. "Okay, Milton," he said. "You go hitch yourself a ride with somebody whose driving you find more congenial."

Milton did not move. For several moments, as he combed the long, untidy strands of black hair from his forehead with his bony fingers, he stared at George. "A thought crosses my mind," he said finally. "I think you are trying to get rid of me."

"I'm merely trying to comply with your request for safer transportation."

"I withdraw the request," Milton said. "Whatever it was Porky Haenigson had to say, it has clearly proved upsetting. You are not at this moment the even-tempered George Hurst I have known for so long. Besides, the arrangement for me to drive with you to the Stiefel party was made this morning by Eileen, and I do not like to upset Eileen's arrangements."

"Why not? You scared of her?"

"I am not scared. I am merely thoughtful."

"Would you be so damn thoughtful if you were married to a Jewish girl from the Bronx instead of a shickseh from the Philadelphia Main Line?"

"And you, my friend George, who are you married to? The daughter of the chief rabbi of Jerusalem, perhaps? People who live in glass houses should not make nasty remarks. You are with me in the same boat, my friend."

Not quite. Nobody named Mr. Kashkin had showed up unexpectedly to spring a leak in Milton Schneider's boat.

"At the moment we're in the same car," George said. "And you were making noises about getting out."

"I have changed my mind," Milton said. "You may proceed to the Stiefels'."

"On one condition," George said.

"What is that?"

"You keep your trap shut until we get there."

"In your present frame of mind I do not find conversation with you even remotely entertaining," Milton said. "To drive in silence will be a pleasure for me."

It was not a pleasure for George. The Stiefels lived on Hawthorn Hill, across the Danville line, between Westport and Wilton, in the opposite direction from Haenigson's Steak House. If there was any chance to save himself before Mr. Kashkin's ultimatum ran out, George knew the chance lay not on Hawthorn Hill but in Porky Haenigson's restaurant. Why, then, was he wasting precious time, chauffeuring Eileen Bucknell's Hungarian husband to a party George hadn't wanted to attend in the first place?

"Milton."

"What?"

"When we get to the Stiefels', you mind if I drop you at the front door?"

"It seems to me I would have occasion to mind only if you drop me at the back door."

"Don't be a wise guy, Milton. It doesn't sit well on you. What I meant was I'd like to drop you at the front door because I want to run back into Danville for a few minutes. Would you tell Mary I won't be long?"

"I will also tell her why you are running back into Danville. If you tell me first, that is."

"I'm not going to tell you first," George said. "I'm just going to drop you at the front door."

He might have done it, too, if Polly Stiefel's tastes as a hostess had not leaned toward quantity rather than quality. The approach to the Stiefel house, which sat deep in an expensive nest of lawns, hedges, and gardens, was along a gravel driveway that wound up like a child's drawing of a writhing snake from two massive stone gateposts on Hawthorn Hill Road. As soon as he turned his car in between the gateposts George knew that, for a man anxious to get some place else, he had made a mistake.

"The only person who isn't going to be there is Albert Schweitzer," Eileen Schneider had said that morning on the phone in Dr. Rettig's office, "and if I know Polly Stiefel it isn't because she didn't send the old boy an invitation."

It seemed to George, as he stepped on the brake to avoid crashing into the yellow Cadillac convertible in front of him, that Polly had not only sent the invitation but Albert Schweitzer had accepted it. The white-haired man sitting between the driver and the woman in blue on the front seat of the Cadillac certainly looked like Schweitzer. From the back, anyway.

"This vulgar monosyllable you have just muttered," Milton Schneider said. "What is the occasion for it, may I ask?"

"Shut up," George said.

He turned, looked behind him, and muttered the vulgar monosyllable again. It was too late to back out of the driveway. Another Cadillac had eased up to his rear bumper.

"Before I shut up," Milton said, "I would like to point out that it looks as though your plan to drop me at the front door and run back into Danville for your mysterious errand may not be placed into operation for some time. It is even conceivable that we will spend the

entire Fourth of July week end here on this driveway. I have not
seen such a traffic jam since as a child in Budapest my father took me
to the opening of *Liliom*. Long have I been baffled by Polly Stiefel's
conviction that in order for one of her parties to be a success it must
be as densely populated as the bleachers at Ebbets Field on a day
when a double header is being performed. Regard, if you will, the
trio on the front seat of the yellow locomotive ahead of us. The driver
is Sigmund Scheuer, owner and operator of the Danville Hardware
Company. Obviously an indispensable guest at a party given in honor
of a major literary figure like Ella K. Mason from the Hollywood
cultural front. The lady in blue is Ceil Scheuer, the good Sigmund's
consort, for whose presence, once you accept Sigmund, a reasonable
case may be made out. But the white-haired gentleman between them
is the good Sigmund's father, a patriarch of eighty-six summers who
is totally deaf, partially infirm, almost blind, and about everything
but the cost of lawn mowers unbelievably stupid. What contribution
does Polly think this ancient pig can make to the entertainment of
Ella K. Mason?"

"Milton, if you don't button your lip," George said, "I will
throttle you with my—"

"It will not be necessary," Milton said. "Here, I think, comes
succor."

It came in the form of Eddie Boissevain, a member of Danville's
six-man police force, who added to his modest income by working
during his free time as parking attendant at Danville parties. This
party seemed to be a little too much for him. Eddie looked hot and
his breath was coming fast. He managed a smile, however, as he
came up beside the car.

"Hi, Mr. Hurst," he said. "Hi, Mr. Schneider. Do you mind
leaving it right here and walking up to the house? We're pretty well
jammed up, and it may be ten or fifteen minutes before we get
squared away. Hate to keep you sitting here all that time. If you
don't mind, I mean?"

"Not at all," Milton Schneider said, opening the door on his
side. "Nothing is better for the digestion than a nice brisk hike
before dinner."

Eddie laughed nervously, bobbed his head, and ran down the
line to the next car. George, cursing Polly Stiefel's passion for stuffing
her parties like a Thanksgiving turkey, stepped out of the car on the
other side and saw Willie Pitt, who ran the local taxi service, pulling

his long black sedan to a stop at the foot of the jammed driveway. As Willie got out, came around, and opened the rear door for a couple of Polly's guests, George sent a quick glance across his shoulder. Milton Schneider, heading up toward the house, had his back turned. George made his decision. He ran down the driveway, passing Willie's fares on the way up, and reached the black sedan just as the taxi driver had slipped back behind the wheel.

"Willie," George said. "Have you got a fare?"

Willie turned. "Oh, hello, Mr. Hurst. No, sir. Just going back to the garage."

"Would you mind taking me down to Haenigson's on the Post Road?"

"Porky's? Sure. Hop in."

George hopped in and for the next few minutes, as Willie Pitt guided the cab in and out of the Post Road traffic, George tried to work out an approach to the problem that faced him. After a while, however, he was forced to abandon the effort. Until he learned whether there was a connection between Mr. Kashkin's ultimatum and Porky Haenigson's message, every approach was a blind alley. A huge trailer truck cut out in front of the taxi to pass another car, and George saw the red and green neon sign winking on and off over Haenigson's Steak House on his right. As Willie pulled into the parking area, George saw something else: since he had last been down this way, Porky Haenigson's business activities had expanded. To the left of the restaurant, spread in neat rows across a gentle rise overlooking the Post Road, were twenty or thirty small green and white cabins. Turning back for another glance at the neon sign, George saw that the word MOTEL had been added. Under the neon sign a canvas pennant was stretched between the cross pieces, at right angles to the entrance, so that the lettering could be read by people moving in both directions on the Post Road:

LIMITED ENGAGEMENT!
Fourth of July Week End Only!!
Direct from Triumphant National Tour!!!
Sensational Singing Star!!!!
DORA DIENST
Limited Engagement!
Fourth of July Week End Only!!

"Wait for you, Mr. Hurst?"

"Yes, if you can spare five or ten minutes," George said. "If not, I'll give you a ring when I'm finished, and you can come get me."

"I'll wait," Willie said.

George walked toward the entrance. It was, he saw, a double affair. A door on the left led to a long, low room with a counter and stools that looked like any one of a hundred other diners on the Post Road. A door on the right led to the more elaborate establishment that Porky called his Steak House. George decided to use the less conspicuous door on his left. As soon as he pushed through it, he realized the choice had been a mistake. Porky Haenigson was behind the counter, frying hamburgers for two truck drivers.

"Hi!" he called to George and then, with a wink, he nodded toward the other door. "The lady is doing her stuff right now."

The truck drivers turned on their stools and stared.

"Hi," George said, pretending to disregard the stares. "Thanks, Porky. I guess I'll—"

He allowed the sentence to disintegrate as he turned quickly and moved down the diner toward the other door. A man in a soiled white dinner jacket was standing just inside the door, holding an armful of spotted menus with frayed edges. He turned when George came in.

"Good evening, sir," he said. "How many?"

"Just one, and I don't want dinner," George said. "Isn't there a—? Oh, yes, I see it. Fine."

He moved off toward the bar before the man in the dinner jacket could make any more conversation. George kept his glance fixed carefully on the bartender as he moved, pretending he had not yet started to hear either the piano or the voice it was accompanying. The bartender, who didn't have to pretend, was listening so intently that he failed to notice the new customer. George slid up on a stool and turned to face the room.

It was not exactly jammed but, if this was a typical Friday night crowd, George could see how Porky Haenigson was able to afford the grand gesture of supplying Dandypops meetings with sandwiches and coffee free of charge. George could also see, from the fact that about half the people in the room were listening as hard as the bartender and the other half were chattering together as though unaware that a performer was working within earshot, that the mystery of Dora's voice remained unsolved.

He had never been able to reconcile what her voice had done to him on that first night so long ago in Gerrity's and what it had so clearly failed to do for the customers on whom Danny Schorr had been counting. Even granting that George's reaction had been special because it was through her voice that he had learned he loved her, the fact remained that there were enough other people who felt at least something of what he felt when Dora sang to have kept her working all these years. A three-day engagement in a glorified hamburger joint on the Post Road wasn't much, but it was still something for which a hard-headed businessman like Porky Haenigson was willing to pay out good money. What, George wondered, had Porky, who must have auditioned her before she was hired, heard in Dora's voice?

Then Dora's arms came up to hold the final note and, as always, George stopped wondering. Even now, after all these years and all that had happened, as she began to turn full-face to the audience so that her slightly crooked elbow came into view, George could feel the familiar tremor that always started in his loins and went tingling up through his whole body, like an electric shock in slow motion, numbing everything but the hunger that was as strong today as it had been on that first night in Gerrity's, leaving him helpless and also a little angry because the helplessness was not unpleasant.

"Some set of pipes, that dame, huh?"

George turned and saw that the bartender was Henry Praskin, the young son-in-law of Mr. Karp, owner of the Danville Music Room.

"Hello," George said. "What are you doing here?"

"Helping out with the Fourth of July week-end rush. We got another baby coming in September. These days, a guy wants to keep ahead of the diaper bills, he has to hold down more than one job. What'll it be, Mr. Hurst?"

"Scotch and water, please."

"Scotch and water, right. Ever hear this dame sing before?"

"Did you?"

Henry Praskin shook his head as he poured the Scotch. "Never even heard her name before, but I can tell you this. If that dame was a man, she wouldn't be working in dumps like this for coffee and cake. If that dame was a man she could walk into any synagogue in the world and take over as cantor. She's got that thing." Henry Praskin hummed several notes, keeping time with the whiskey bottle. "Like on Yom Kippur, when they hit the *Kol Nidre*. She's got that same thing. You know?"

Curiously enough, all at once George did know. All at once, after all these years, he knew it so thoroughly that he turned quickly on the bar stool, to see if the people who had been listening so intently were, like Henry Praskin and himself, Jews.

Now that the song was over, however, the thing that had divided the people in the room was over, too. Everybody was moving and talking. It was difficult to tell which of these flushed, laughing faces in this saloon on the Post Road had been bored and which had been held by a spell that went back to the days of Abraham and Isaac.

"Say, George."

He turned back to the bar. Porky Haenigson had come up beside him.

"I got a little note here," Porky said gravely and then, as he handed it over, he winked and added in a low voice, "If it's what I think it is, there's a short cut through that back door over there by the can."

George took the note. Porky winked again and walked away toward the man in the white dinner jacket at the door. George opened the note and read:

I don't go on again until nine—meet me in my cabin—number 16 —second aisle from the road—Dora

George shoved the note into his pocket, paid for his drink, nodded to Henry Praskin, and walked out through the door near the men's room. The motel section of Porky Haenigson's business seemed to be doing as well as his Steak House. There was a car parked in front of every cabin in the first aisle. The second aisle, when George reached it, looked less popular. There were twelve cabins but only four cars. George walked down to number sixteen. A light was on over the door. Before George could knock, the door opened. Dora, in a pink negligee that looked exactly like the one she used to wear on University Place, smiled out at him.

"My God," she said, "I thought you'd never show up."

"Why didn't you tell me you were coming to Danville?"

"I didn't know myself until this morning. I got back from Omaha last night, and this morning Hillie Burns called me at the Taft and said—"

"Hillie Burns?"

"My new agent."

"What happened to Denker?"

"That slob. Four years, and the best he can get me is two weeks in the supper room at the Hagensdorf Hotel in Omaha. I told him to drop dead and signed with Burns. He's been after me for a long time, and I've been wanting to go with him for almost a year. Not only because he's a real hustler. You ought to see some of the jobs he's gotten for girls I know they can't sing a tenth as good as I can. But also because Burns thinks I've got a voice that deserves something better than the Hagensdorf Hotel in Omaha, and frankly so do I. I told him on the phone last week when he called me in Omaha, I said Hillie, you want me? Okay, I'll make you a deal. You get me a job for the Fourth of July week end in Danville, Connecticut, and I'm yours forever after, and what do you know? I finished at the Hagensdorf Thursday night, I flew back yesterday, and this morning Hillie Burns calls me up at the Taft and he says pack your bag, Dora, you start work in Danville tonight. How's that for an agent?"

"He sounds wonderful," George said, and then, casually, as casually as he dared, "Why did you want to work in Danville over the Fourth of July week end?"

Dora's hand came up, in a gesture that was as old as his memory of her, the knuckles rubbing slowly across her lower lip.

"Well, for one thing, it's your birthday," she said, "and I thought it would be nice to—"

"A ten-cent card would have conveyed the sentiment," George said. "With less trouble."

"George," she said in a hurt voice, "except during the war when you were overseas, every other year since then, July second, your birthday, I've always tried—"

"I know you have, and it's very nice of you, Dora, but you just said for one thing, so there must be another reason this time. Would you mind telling me what—?"

His voice stopped as a station wagon with a Wisconsin license plate came easing up the aisle and parked in front of cabin number seventeen. The man at the wheel looked curiously at George and Dora. The woman beside the driver said something that made him grin. Dora took George's arm, pulled him into her cabin, and pushed the door shut.

"For what Mr. Haenigson is paying me," she said, "I don't

have to give a performance out in the open for his motel guests."
She looked anxiously up into his face. "George, you're not really
sore, are you?"

He drew a deep breath. He had never been able to hurt her.
Not since Armistice Day, 1918, in the Forest, when she became
his responsibility. Not even when his life was at stake.

"No, of course not," George said, and he managed a smile. "I
was only kidding."

The frightened look disappeared from her eyes. She put out her
hand and touched his arm, shyly, as though to nail down the fact of
his forgiveness, to remind him that, if he should start getting angry
with her again, he had no right to do so because, and he must not
forget it, he had confessed he had only been kidding; and then,
as though the brief contact had sent her thoughts in a direction she
wanted to avoid, she pulled her hand away quickly.

"Oh, God," she said with a small, helpless shiver, "Why didn't
I marry you? George, why? Why didn't I?"

He shook his head. It was the one thing he couldn't do for her.
He couldn't answer that question. No matter how often she asked it.

"I don't know," he said. "Even if I did, it's a little late to be
wondering about that. I haven't got much time, Dora. In order to
get over here I sneaked out on a dinner party where at this very
minute I'm supposed to be meeting my wife, and I've got a taxi
waiting to take me back, so you'd better get to the point. What's the
real reason for your coming here to Danville?"

"Danny," she said.

The atmosphere in the small room changed abruptly. Not because of the way she uttered the hated name, making it sound like
a curse. Dora always did that when she mentioned Danny. What
made the atmosphere change was the abrupt removal of doubt, as
though the room had been full of smoke and the door had been
opened to admit a strong cleansing draft of fresh air. What George
had suspected ever since he had come home to Danville was no
longer a suspicion: there was a connection between Porky Haenigson's telephone message and Mr. Kashkin's ultimatum.

"What about Danny?" George said.

"I want to divorce him."

The knot in George's stomach tightened slightly. It was as
though the invisible bill collectors had suddenly taken two or three

quick steps, coming up closer, narrowing the gap between themselves and their quarry.

"Now?" George said. "After all these years?"

"Yes, now."

Do it slowly, the voice inside George's head warned. Don't sound worried.

"I don't get this sudden change of policy," he said. "You wouldn't divorce him during the war, when I gave you the money to go to Reno. You've refused to do it since the war. Why now, all of a sudden—?"

"Because up to now that's what Danny wanted me to do," Dora said. "That's why he walked out on me. He thought if he walked out I'd have to divorce him, to get money out of him. But I'm just as smart as he is."

"Smart?" George said, making no effort to conceal the annoyance in his voice. "What's so smart about living the way you've been living these last few years? Working like a dog in dumps like this for nickels and dimes? While your legal husband owns practically half the state of California? If you were really smart, all you had to do was get a lawyer, which I've offered to do for you at least a hundred times, and you could have nailed Mr. Daniel Shaw for more money than either of us has ever seen."

"Yes," Dora said. "If that's the way I wanted to nail him."

The invisible bill collectors took several more quick steps.

"Isn't that what you want?" George said. "To make him pay through the nose?"

"No," she said. "I want to be the one to do the paying. I want to pay him back for what he did to me. I've waited almost eight years to find a way."

"And now you've found it."

George did not put it as a question. He didn't have to. He knew why the invisible bill collectors had taken those sudden quick steps. He had come here with the hope of finding a loophole in Mr. Kashkin's ultimatum. He had found, instead, that any possibility of escape was being sealed up from another direction.

"There were some California people at the Hagensdorf," Dora said. "Two men. One night, after I finished singing, they asked me to have a drink with them. I sat down and had a drink and they started talking, and pretty soon I found out they work for Danny. He's thinking of buying the Hagensdorf for his chain of hotels, and these men had come out to look it over for him, and after a couple more drinks they told me something else he's thinking." Dora paused. "Danny is thinking of running for the United States Senate from California." She paused again, and she laughed. A series of short, dry sounds, without mirth. "I can't wait for him to try it," she said quietly.

"I see," George said, wishing he didn't, speaking slowly, as though the smallest delay might help, but aware even as he stalled for time that he was accomplishing no more in this motel room now than he had accomplished that morning in his office when he put Mr. Kashkin off until Tuesday. "As soon as Danny does try it," George said. "When his campaign is announced or under way, when he's deep in the race—?"

"That's right," Dora said, and she laughed again. This time, however, she seemed to enjoy it. This time she sounded like a small girl who has discovered a long overlooked birthday present. "I'll wait for the right moment," she said. "When it comes, I'll get not only a juicy property settlement and a fat alimony check and all the trimmings, but Mr. Danny Shaw will also get his wagon fixed." She put her hand on George's arm and leaned close, as though they were in a crowd and she wanted to whisper something to him. "He's not going to be any United States senator, George," she said. "I'm going to see to that. We'll both see to it. You and me, George. After all these years of waiting, we'll both be able to pay him back. Won't that be a laugh, George?"

For Dora, yes. She had nothing to lose.

"Look," George said. "I can't stay and discuss it now. I've got that taxi waiting. Suppose we postpone this discussion until—"

"There's nothing to postpone or discuss," Dora said. "I've waited eight years for this chance. I know exactly what I want to do and how to do it. All I need is a little help from you. You've been offering it to me for years. Now I want to take it. I want you to get me the right lawyer," Dora said. "And I want you to lend me the money to pay him."

It was like asking the condemned man to pay for his own scaffold.

"You know I'll help you if I can," George said. "But I want to sit down and have a real talk about it first."

"I tell you there's nothing to talk about."

"There may be more to talk about than you think," George

said. "I don't want you to do anything until we've had a chance to look at it from every angle."

"When will that be?"

"I'll come back later tonight," George said. "After this dinner party is over."

44

Ten minutes later, when Willie Pitt dropped him at the Stiefels' front door, George could tell that this party was not going to be over for a long time. He could hear music from the back of the house, which opened onto a terrace that faced the Danville River. It was on this terrace that Polly usually broke into her abandoned Charleston when a party boiled up to a point that indicated it had gathered enough momentum to keep going into the small hours, and it was Charleston music George was hearing now.

He wondered, as he gave his hat to a maid in the hall, if Mary would be out on the terrace. She usually enjoyed Polly's performances. If Mary was not on the terrace, however, George might get stuck with somebody like Ceil Scheuer, in which case there was no telling how long it would be before he could break away and find Mary. Therefore, even though he didn't recognize this maid, who had obviously been hired to help the regular Stiefel servants for the night, George decided to try for some information before he took off on his own.

"Do you happen to know where Mrs. Hurst is?"

The maid, who was putting the hat in a closet turned quickly. "Hurst?" she said.

"Yes, my wife. I'd like to—"

"You are Mr. Hurst?"

"Yes. I wondered if you knew whether my wife is out on the terrace or—"

"Come this way, please."

"Thanks," George said, following her across the hall. "Where is she?"

The maid did not answer. She had obviously not heard the question. George wasn't surprised. In addition to the music from the terrace, quite a racket was coming from the dining room on his left where the buffet was set out. The maid stopped at the door of a small room that Hume Stiefel used as an office when he brought work home. The door was closed.

"Here?" George said, wondering what Mary was doing in there. "It's Mrs. Hurst I'm looking for."

"I was told when Mr. Hurst arrives to bring him to the study, sir."

She opened the door and held it wide. George stepped in. The maid pulled the door shut behind him. The handsome man in the chair behind Hume Stiefel's desk took the cigar from his mouth, stood up, came around the desk, and held out his hand.

"Hi, kid," Daniel Shaw said with a smile. "Long time no see."

George's first thought struck him as almost insanely irrelevant: this was the way Danny had greeted him, with those exact words, almost eighteen years ago, on the day George came back during his lunch hour to his room on University Place with the pair of silk stockings he had bought for Dora in Hearn's. George's second thought was a swift computation: he had not seen Danny since the Sunday following that meeting, the Sunday George came back from Albany after learning from Aunt Tessie and Uncle Zisha about Danny's attempt to blackmail five thousand dollars out of them. It seemed a little unreal that now, almost eighteen years later, in Hume Stiefel's study, the end of that meeting should suddenly be so clear and vivid in George's mind that he could almost hear the sound Danny had made when George hit him, and he could see Danny's body slithering across the floor and out the door into Mrs. Shissle's hall, and he could feel the pain in his knuckles from the second punch. George had disregarded Danny's outstretched hand when he came back into his life eighteen years ago. He disregarded it now.

"I see you've had that tooth replaced," he said.

Danny dropped his hand and laughed. "You can't expect a man in my position to go around looking like Huckleberry Finn." He took a deep drag on his cigar and cocked his head to one side. He stared at George curiously. "After all these years, kid, is that all you have to say?"

It was all, George realized with a feeling of surprise, he saw any point in saying. Many times, during the eighteen years that had gone by, he had imagined what he would say if he ever ran into Danny Schorr again. Now that it had happened, however, George couldn't remember the words he had rehearsed so often. If he had remembered the words, he realized now he wouldn't have used them. Words wouldn't bring back what Danny had taken out of his life any more than they would bring back the silver frame he had taken from Judge Brandeis' picture when he stripped George's room. George was aware that he did not even feel angry. This was so much more surprising that he forced himself to hunt for a reason, and after a moment or two he had it: too much time had gone by. Too many other things had happened. When the man facing him had been young he had altered the course of George Hurst's life as surely and irrevocably as an earthquake alters the course of a river, and yet the man who had become Daniel Shaw the hotel tycoon had no reality for George Hurst. He could have been an illustration in a history book, somebody who had once done something significant but was in no position to affect the lives of people walking the streets today.

"Yes, I guess that's all I've got to say," George said. "Except that I see you're wearing the same tie you wore when they took your picture for the cover of the current issue of *Worldweek*."

"Oh," Danny said, "so you read that?" He sounded pleased.

"Yes," George said, "I read it."

"Quite a job, didn't you think?"

"Job is the word," George said.

Danny laughed again. "You always had a sense of humor, kid. That's why I told Polly Stiefel to say this party was for someone named Ella K. Mason. I told her you'd get a laugh out of that."

"You mean there's no such person?"

"Not to my knowledge," Danny said. "You're looking at Polly's guest of honor right now."

"If Polly had announced the truth, that the party was for you, you were afraid I wouldn't show up?"

Danny shook his head. "I wasn't afraid," he said. "I knew you'd show up. Just as I know you're going to help me with the thing I came all the way from California to see you about."

Grudgingly, annoyed with himself for feeling it, George sensed the stirrings of an admiration mixed with envy that went back three and a half decades. The world, it suddenly occurred to him, must be as different a place to a man born with Danny's self-confidence as it undoubtedly was to a man born with the gift of clairvoyance.

"You mean you still think, after everything that's happened, you can get me to do things for you?"

"Why not?" Danny said. "I've known you ever since we were both this high. I've always thought of you as practically my twin brother. Blood is thicker than water."

"Then why did you bother with all this window dressing? Getting Polly Stiefel to give a party for you under a phony name? Hiding in Hume's study and getting a maid to lead me to it? Why didn't you call me up? Or write to me, the way you wrote to Miss Corcoran, the old schoolteacher, and I quote, who devoted her whole life to implanting and instilling and inculcating in men like you the important rules of morals and conduct by which you have lived your lives and achieved whatever success you have achieved, unquote?"

Danny gave him a sharp glance. "I see you keep in touch with the old girl."

"I see her once in a while. I happened to drop in on her this afternoon. She showed me those pages of beautiful poetry you sent her in the form of a letter."

"Do you think she'll—? I mean, if anybody comes to see her about me, do you think—?" Danny made a gesture with the cigar. "You know what I mean, kid. Do you think she'll give them—?"

"—exactly the same kind of honest, up-beat facts about the kind of kid you were as you will be giving those researchers from *Time* magazine and *Worldweek* magazine when they come to see her about the cover story on a typical retired schoolteacher that you're going to use your influence to get written about her, unquote again?"

Danny chuckled. "Boy, you sure read that letter, kid."

"I sure did," George said. "Edgar A. Guest never turned in a better performance. How about my question? Why didn't you come to see me direct, or call me, or write me one of those letters? Why did you have to fool around with Polly Stiefel?"

The smile on Danny's face changed slightly. "You won't believe this, of course," he said, staring at the end of his cigar as though he was puzzled by the way it was drawing. "But I'm not as brash as I used to be." He looked up quickly, like a small boy who has used a word about the meaning of which he is uncertain and as a result is afraid he might be laughed at. Danny's lean, handsome, tanned face flushed slightly. "I see you don't believe that," he said. "But it's true. Once you've made your pile, the way I have, you don't need brashness." He bore down on the word, as though defying

George to laugh at him for using it. "You need it when you're young," Danny said. "When you're hungry. When you're hacking your way up. That's the time you need everything you've got or can get. Once you've made it, though, once you don't have to hunch over the handlebars any more, once you've got time to think, you begin to think maybe this guy is still sore at me for something I did a long time ago, when I was hungry, when I was punching my way up. Maybe this guy doesn't understand that I wasn't doing it to him personally. Maybe this guy doesn't understand that I was doing it to the world, the world out of which I was hacking my bundle, and he just happened to be in the way. When you've got your bundle, and you begin thinking that way, for some of the things you want, instead of coming after them yourself, you use people like Polly Stiefel." He paused and then, almost shyly, Daniel Shaw said, "Does that make sense to you?"

"I'm the wrong guy to ask," George said.

He was the guy who had happened to be in Danny's way.

"You're the only guy I'm interested in asking," Danny said.

"For what?"

"A break."

"From me?"

Danny nodded. "I've got my bundle," he said. "Now I want the kind of thing that makes a bundle sweet. I've been asked to run for the United States Senate. I'm going to accept. I want that Senate seat, George."

"Why don't you take it?"

"I'm going to," Danny said. "But I've got to clear up a small obstacle first: the old L. L. Parker stamp mess. It isn't much, but when the opposition is looking to hang something on you, it could be enough. The whole thing is buried somewhere in the files. Nobody looks into dead files unless they get nudged. The only one who could nudge anybody toward this thing is you. You're the only one who knows about it that's still alive. Shumacher is dead. The postal inspector, Sapina, he's gone. Everybody. I've checked. Even Mrs. Shissle. You're the only one that's left, George. If you keep quiet, my next address is Washington, D. C. What do you say, George?"

What George wanted to say was: you're worrying about the wrong obstacle. It isn't the L. L. Parker stamp mess that Mr. Kashkin is interested in. What the man from Albany, and the men in California for whom he is working, want to know about is Dora.

But George didn't say a word. He couldn't. He was too busy trying to conceal his sudden excitement as he examined the implications of Danny's request.

The examination indicated clearly that this was one time when Danny, who always used to know everything before George did, was running second: he obviously did not yet know about Mr. Kashkin and his investigators.

If George told him, if Danny saw that the promise of silence he wanted from George meant nothing because it was only a matter of time before Mr. Kashkin and his diggers would reach the L. L. Parker stamp mess without any nudging from George or anybody else, then there was an excellent chance that Danny would change his mind about trying for that Senate seat. If this change of mind could be conveyed to Mr. Kashkin, then the ultimatum he had issued to George would cease to exist. With Danny out of the Senate race, Mr. Kashkin and the men who were thinking of backing Danny would not waste more of their good money on continuing the digging process that had stopped when they reached George.

He would not have to call the Waldorf on Tuesday morning with the answer to Mr. Kashkin's question. The life he had bulit with Mary and the children here in Danville would remain untouched. He would be as safe as he had been for almost eight full years. His life would return to the pleasant jogging pace that had been shattered a few minutes after seven this morning when Miss Akst's phone call had interrupted his shave.

George could feel the excitement mounting inside him, straining at the barriers he had placed around it to keep his mind free for thinking clearly. Running back swiftly over his hurried thoughts, he could see no flaw in the chain. The straining excitement was justified. So was the stalling for time that had seemed so pointless in his office that morning when he had insisted on putting Mr. Kashkin off until Tuesday. The loophole George had been hunting so desperately all day had appeared at last.

"I know why you're hesitating," Danny said. "I know what's going through your mind."

George came up out of the excitement churning inside him like a swimmer surfacing after a deep dive. He had been so intent on examining each link in the chain that had led him to the loophole that he had almost forgotten about Danny.

"You do?" he said in surprise.

"Sure," Danny said. "You're thinking why should you do this for me, for the guy who went to see the Dean of that law school and fixed it so you could never be another Judge Brandeis. I can answer that, George. Whatever I did to you years ago because you were the guy who happened to be in my way, I can make it up to you now. You're an accountant. I'm a pretty big bug, as you may have gathered. You do this for me, George, and I'll swing enough stuff your way to make you ten times as rich as you'd be if you graduated from every law school in the country and you had every one of those nine seats on the Supreme Court to stick around your own dining-room table. Isn't that a lot better than getting even? They say revenge is sweet, but I'll tell you something I've learned, kid. The guys who say it don't know what they're talking about. The truth about revenge is that it's unprofitable. Look at it this way, George. We're older. We'll both be forty tomorrow. All the stuff that happened when we were in knee pants, hell, it could have happened to a couple of guys named Joe. When you get older, George, you also get different. I'm not the guy I was on Fourth Street. Neither are you. I'm willing to forget that you once punched a tooth out of my head. Why shouldn't you be willing to forget your end of it, too?"

Because I'm not built like you, George wanted to say. Because the world is a different place for me than it is for you. Because there are things I'll never forget. Not as long as I live. No matter how hard I try or how much I'm paid to do it. But George didn't say any of that, even though every word of it was true. It was not the truth he wanted. It was the loophole.

"I think I'd better set you straight on something," George said. "Even if I gave you my promise, it wouldn't do you any good."

"I feel I'm a better judge of that than you are," Danny said.

"You wouldn't feel so sure if you knew—"

George's voice stopped. So did the excitement churning inside him. It was as though the chain that led him to the loophole had snapped, hurling him back into the fear with which he had been living all day.

"If I knew what?" Danny said.

Don't say it! the warning voice inside George's head screamed. Don't tell him. Not yet.

"If you knew what was really going on in my mind," George managed to say. "You see, Danny, you haven't changed as much as you think."

Danny smiled. "Neither have you," he said. "That's what I'm counting on."

"Don't count on it too much," George said, moving toward the door, forcing himself to do it casually. "I want to think this over."

He couldn't tell Danny about Mr. Kashkin until he got back to Dora.

"Don't think too long," Danny said. "I'm flying home Sunday morning. I'd like to take your promise back with me. Will you call here at the Stiefels' before then and give it to me?"

"I can't say yet," George said, pulling open the door. Unless he stopped Dora, it wouldn't make any difference what he promised. The invisible bill collectors would get their man. "If that's the way my thinking comes out," George said, "I'll call you."

45

All the way to Queen's Court Road, Mary sat in silence, staring straight ahead through the windshield, turning the ring on her left hand with short twists of thumb and forefinger, as though it were a toothpaste cap that refused to tighten. George drove as fast as he dared, hoping Mary would not notice that he was in a hurry, trying to work out in his mind a series of arguments that would carry conviction when he faced Dora in Haenigson's Steak House.

"You go on in the house and send Gordon out," Mary said as he turned the car into their driveway. "I'll pay him and drive him home."

George did not reply until he had taken the car to the top of the driveway, backed it around carefully, and driven down to the flag-stone walk that led to the front door. Then he said, "No, I'll drive Gordon home."

He reached across Mary, and opened the door on her side.

"I think I'd better drive him home," she said.

"There's nothing to think about," George said. "I'll drive Gordon home."

Mary gave the ring an extra twist. "I don't think you'd better," she said. "Not in your condition."

"There's nothing about my condition to prevent my driving a fifteen-year-old boy half a mile. Go on in and send Gordon out."

Mary did not move. "A half hour ago you said you were so tired and you thought you were coming down with something that you had to leave the Stiefel party immediately," she said. "If that's true, then you're in no condition to—"

"Let's not make an issue of this," George said. "I've always driven our sitters home. I'm driving this one home tonight."

Mary gave him a troubled glance, then opened the door and stepped out of the car. A couple of minutes later Gordon Rothchild came down the walk carrying his stamp album.

"Hi," George said, opening the door for him. "Get many pasted up tonight?"

"Hi, Mr. Hurst. Some." Gordon climbed in and pulled the door shut. "I hope you had a good time tonight, sir."

"Yes, fine, thanks," George said, easing the car back out into Queen's Court Road. "We came home early because I was tired. Had a long day in town, and then a Dandypops meeting about tomorrow's clambake before I went off to join Mrs. Hurst at this dinner party." Mrs. Rothchild was very fussy about the people for whom she allowed her son to sit. It was wise, George had found, to provide Gordon with a set of uncomplicated answers for the cross-examination to which his mother subjected him when he got home. "Boys okay?"

"Yes, sir," Gordon said. "Win complained of a sharp pain in his belly around eight o'clock, and for a while I wondered if I should call Mrs. Hurst at the Stiefels', but then Win said he'd had five hamburgers and four hot dogs at the Camp Shawmut cook-out today, not to mention pickles and relish and a lot of other stuff, so I figured that was probably it, just a stomach ache."

"It probably was."

"Yes, sir. Anyway, the pain went away after a while, so I decided not to disturb you at the Stiefels'."

"Jimmy all right?"

"Yes, sir, except he caught two steelies at camp this afternoon and he kept taking them out of the refrigerator and bringing them into the living room so he could have them near him while he watched TV, but I made him put them back because of the smell."

"Quite right. Anybody call?"

"Yes, sir. A woman called twice. Once at eight minutes after eight and the second time at either sixteen minutes after ten or eighteen minutes after. I'm sorry about not being more accurate, but this second call came in during one of the times I was making Jimmy put the steelies back in the refrigerator and things got sort of confused."

"That's all right, Gordon. This woman leave her name?"

"No, sir, but she said you'd know the name and you should call her at Haenigson's Steak House the minute you got in."

"Thanks," George said. He gave himself a couple of moments. "Did you tell Mrs. Hurst about the calls?"

"You mean just now?"

"Yes, when she came in the house."

"Yes, sir. She said to give the messages to you. I hope there's nothing wrong, sir?"

Several long moments went by before George realized that Gordon had repeated his question.

"No, no, nothing's wrong. It's just that—" George paused. A fifteen-year-old boy was hardly the proper person with whom to discuss whether it was more sensible to turn back at once and make some sort of explanation to Mary, or keep going to Haenigson's Steak House and try to save the loophole. Either way involved a risk. It seemed odd that, after eight years of marriage, he should be unable to decide which risk was greater. "Well, here we are," George said. "Did Mrs. Hurst pay you?"

"Yes, sir."

"Well, good night, then. My best to your mother, Gordon."

"Thank you, sir. Hope you have good weather for the clambake tomorrow. Good night, Mr. Hurst."

"Good night," George said.

He backed out, hesitated for another moment at the bottom of the Rothchild driveway, then turned the car toward Haenigson's.

46

"For God's sake," Hoxter Monahan said. "What do you think you're doing?"

George looked up from the trestle table. It was one of sixty that the members of the Grounds Committee, who had started work at seven-thirty that morning, hoped to have set up before the ticket holders began to arrive at five in the afternoon.

"I'm tying clams," George said.

He had been doing it since eight o'clock, dipping the clams up out of the buckets Porky Haenigson kept bringing in his pick-up truck, wrapping bunches of fifty in cheesecloth, and lugging the bundles across the beach to the fire pit where Dr. Henry Hubert, the bakemaster, buried them in the steaming seaweed.

"Who told you to do that?" Hoxter Monahan demanded.

"Porky Haenigson," George said carefully, telling himself to take it easy. Hoxter Monahan had nothing to do with Mr. Kashkin's ultimatum or Dora's stubbornness. Hoxter just happened to be the president of the Dandypops. "I'm on the Food Committee," George said. "Porky is chairman. I do what Porky tells me to do. Porky told me to wrap clams."

"If you stuck around when I call a special Dandypops meeting, instead of beating it before I even get a chance to explain the reason why I called the meeting, you'd know you're not on the Food Committee any more," Hoxter Monahan said. "I called that meeting last night because with sixteen hundred tickets sold for this clambake, Eddie Boissevain told me he and the two other cops assigned to handle the parking wouldn't be enough. Eddie said it'll take thirty men to handle a mob that size, not counting the work of taping out the parking field in advance. I had to cut all the committees in half and give those men to Eddie for the parking detail. You're one of the men I yanked from the Food Committee and gave to Eddie Boissevain, which is who you should be with right now, up there, by the bathhouses, helping tape out the parking lot, not down here tying clams. If you'd stick around when I call a special meeting, you'd know that."

"I'm sorry about walking out on your special meeting," George said, speaking even more carefully. "I stayed as long as I could. Then I had to go on to another engagement."

"If it's more important to you to show up at some party than to help get this clambake off the ground so we'll have some money in our treasury to buy baseball mitts for our kids in school, okay with me," Hoxter said. "I'm not running your life. One thing I *am* running, though, and that's this clambake, so you can quit tying those clams right now and beat it over to the parking field to help Eddie Boissevain."

George wiped his hands on a piece of cheesecloth and stood up. "You may be running this clambake, but you're not running me," he said. "I'm sorry if I've spent the last four hours tying clams instead of taping out the parking lot, but there's nothing I can do about that now. So long, Hoxter."

"Where you going?"

"Home."

"For Christ's sweet sake, George, is that a way to act? We have to get this thing rolling. We need all the help we can get."

"You've had all the help you're getting out of me until five o'clock this afternoon," George said. "It happens to be my birthday. My family is giving me a party. I'd like to be there. Do you mind?"

"Why does your birthday have to come the day I'm trying to run a clambake?"

"You seem to know all the answers, Hoxter. You take a crack at coming up with that one, too."

"What about tonight? Will you be here at five o'clock to help with the parking?"

"If I don't have another engagement," George said.

By the time he swung the car into Queen's Court Road, he had calmed down enough to forget Hoxter Monahan and remember what Mr. Ashorn, the jeweler on Scheuer Square, had told him yesterday morning about the way Win and Jimmy, accompanied by Mary, had chosen a Waterman pen and pencil set as his birthday present. Pulling into the driveway, George could see the cake he was certain Mary had baked, and he could see Win's fresh, round face, the blue eyes wide with anticipation, and Jimmy's small, neat face, the dark eyes glowing, as they watched George pull in his breath to blow out the forty candles. George could see it so clearly that, as he turned off the ignition key, he suddenly had trouble with his breathing, the way he did every morning when he came into the kitchen and he had his first chance of the day to catch a glimpse of his family all in a group: there was that funny little feeling in his heart.

"Hi!" he called as he came in the front door.

There was no answer. George walked through the hall, across the living room, and stopped on the dining-room threshold. There was no birthday cake on the table. It wasn't even set. The only thing on the table was the silver bowl Eileen and Milton Schneider had given George and Mary as a wedding present, and the fresh zinnias Mary had placed in it that morning from the small cutting garden she had planted on the south side of the grape arbor.

"Hey, Win!" George called, starting across the dining-room to the kitchen. "Jimmy!"

Mary appeared in the kitchen doorway. "They're not here," she said.

There was something in her voice that made George stop moving toward the kitchen. "Where are they?" he said.

"At the movies, with Carlotta Schneider," Mary said. "Milton called at eleven and said today's children's matinee at the Odeon included a revival of *Fantasia*, so I gave Win and Jimmy an early lunch, and Milton stopped by and picked them up."

She spoke quietly and clearly, without special emphasis on any particular word, as though she were reading off her grocery order on the phone to the clerk at the Danville Food Centre and she wanted to make sure there would be no errors.

"But it's my birthday," George said slowly. "The cake. The party. I thought the kids—"

"They left this for you," Mary said. She held out a small, rectangular package wrapped in yellow paper and tied with a green ribbon. Reaching for it, George realized the dining-room table was between them. "It's a Waterman fountain pen and pencil set," Mary said. "Win and Jimmy bought it at Mr. Ashorn's out of their allowance money. It's all the celebration I thought we'd better have today."

"Why?"

"I didn't want the kids in the house when I asked you a question."

"What question?"

"It was not quite twelve-thirty when you left here last night to drive Gordon home. The Rothchilds live half a mile up the road from here. It was almost three o'clock in the morning when you got back."

"You want to know where I was?"

Mary shook her head. "I know the answer to that question. While you were at the beach this morning helping with the clam-bake preparations, I had a phone call. I learned long ago, in those psychology classes at Bennington about which you've been making jokes all these years, how eager people are to convey malicious information about other people. I never realized until this morning how thorough they can be about details. I know exactly how much of those two and a half hours last night you spent at the bar in Porky Haenigson's Steak House and how much of that time you spent in cabin sixteen of Porky's Motel."

"The little rat."

"Who?"

"Henry Praskin. He's the one who called, isn't he?"

"Does that matter?"

The flash of anger went as quickly as it had come. George shook his head. "No, of course not."

"Now that we've got that out of the way, I'd like to ask my question." Mary paused, and for a moment George was reminded of the way, during their interview in the John Marshall Law School years ago, Dean Cathcart, after talking around the subject for some time, had paused before finally coming to the unpleasant point about the L. L. Parker stamp scandal. It was clear that Mary, like the old man who was now probably dead, wished she didn't have to come to the point, either. "George," she said finally. "Who is Dora Dienst?"

He drew a deep breath. "We'd better go into the living room and sit down."

"I'm perfectly comfortable where I am," Mary said.

She wasn't, of course. She was standing too straight for comfort, her hands jammed down so hard in the pockets of her apron that the shoulder strip, cutting deep into the flesh of her neck, was almost completely hidden.

"I think you ought to sit down."

Mary shook her head again. "Stop it," she said impatiently. "Just tell me."

George told her. He told her about the doll store, and Gerrity's, and the tin can he and Danny used for sending messages to each other. George told her about the accident in the Forest on Armistice Day, and the night Ida Dienst got sick and Dora came across the street to take her sister's place at Danny's first opening, and the way Danny got him into trouble with Mr. Shumacher in the L. L. Parker mailroom. George told her about Mr. Sapina, and the job at Malvin Gewirtz & Company, and how he met Dora again in Mrs. Hooper's apartment. George told her about the opening of Chez Shaw, and the interview with Dean Cathcart, and what Danny did to his room in Mrs. Shissle's house when he ran away with Dora. George told her about the day Dora came back, the day George and Mary were married in apartment 18-D at 360 Central Park West by Judge Fusanbucco, and George told her about yesterday's visit from Mr. Kashkin.

"It threw me into a panic," George said. "I'd kept Dora a secret from you all these years. I don't really know why. All I know is that ever since that day in the Forest when I sent her to the top of that lumber stack to act as lookout, I've felt responsible for her. She's not very smart about money, and she's not good enough as a singer to earn much of it, so I've helped her out now and then during these past years. Not much. Twenty or thirty dollars once in a while, to get something out of hock, or pay for a dress she needed to work in. A couple of times she's been in trouble with the tax department for not filing returns, and I helped straighten it out. That sort of thing. She's not in New York very often. Maybe two, three times a year. When she is, she calls me and I usually see her. I didn't know she was coming to Danville this week end until I got to the Dandypops meeting last night and Porky Haenigson gave me the message. When I found out why she'd showed up, it made me more panicky. Now it wasn't only because of Kashkin that you might find out about Dora. It was also because of Dora herself. I stalled her the way I'd stalled Kashkin, telling her not to do anything till we had a chance to talk it over. When I got to the Stiefels' and found Danny and he told me what he wanted, I thought I saw a way out. If I could get Dora not to sue him for divorce, and if I could get Danny not to run for senator—"

George paused and shook his head. "That's why I went back to Haenigson's after we got home last night," he said. "I spent those hours trying to argue Dora out of going ahead with the divorce. It didn't do any good. I should have known that from the start. I should have known—" He paused again and he said quietly, "I should have known better than to keep the whole thing a secret. I should have told you years ago, when it happened, on our wedding day."

His voice stopped. In the sudden silence, hearing the hammer strokes of his own heart, George found himself hating the dining-room table. If it was not between them. If he could have held her in his arms as he spoke. If he could take her in his arms now—

"George—"

"Yes?"

"Is that all there's to it?"

"Mary, for God's sake—"

She shook her head, scowling, as though her effort to get something straight in her mind was being thwarted by irrelevant sounds. "There's got to be more to it," she said slowly. "If that's all there was, if it was only what you told me just now, you would have told me about her long ago." Mary paused and waited. He did not speak. "George," she said. "You've slept with this girl?"

"I told you I did," he said. "I told you about the night she opened at Chez Shaw and then later, when we were living in my room on University Place, long before I met you—"

Mary's head made the same sharp movements of impatience. "I mean—" Her voice stopped. One hand came up out of the apron pocket to touch her lips. She looked shocked, as though she could not believe something that had just crossed her mind. "George," she said in a hushed voice. She might have been pleading with him. "George," she said. "That day when I went to get my hair washed and you went to pack your bag," Mary said, the words coming with an effort, as though she hated the sound of them. "The day she reappeared? Our wedding day? An hour before we were married? You and she—?"

George shook his head, hard and fast, as though the labored words, torn from her with painful slowness, had to be hurled back at once, stopped in their tracks like attacking soldiers coming up out of a trench, before they could gain the momentum that would destroy him. "No!" George said. "That's not true! Nothing happened!"

Mary's restless eyes, suddenly bright as though with fever, the way Aunt Tessies eyes had been bright the day he came to Albany to destroy her, searched his face, pleading. "George," she said. "That's the truth?"

"I swear to you! I swear to God—no, wait! By anything you choose! By Win and Jimmy, may they not live through this day if I'm lying, I swear to you absolutely nothing happened!"

Mary shook her head, impatiently, the feverish glow in her eyes growing brighter. "That's not what I mean," Mary said. "I'm not interested in legal details—did it happen in the eyes of the law. I don't mean that. George, I mean—"

Her words ground to a halt. Staring into her eyes, George Hurst could suddenly hear again the sound that had broken from his throat years ago as he and Dora, their mouths locked, twisted toward the bed in his apartment on University Place. Staring into Mary's eyes, hearing again the sob of happiness he could neither forget nor stop hating, George Hurst knew that, after eight years of concealment, Mary could hear it, too.

"Mary, listen," he said, but now it was his words that were labored. It was as though he had to drag them through the hopeless, impenetrable, smothering fact he had learned on his wedding day and with which he had lived for so long: the technical victory was meaningless. In his heart, where under careful guard he kept the core of the life he had built with Mary and Win and Jimmy, he knew he was guilty. It was plain from her eyes that Mary knew it, too.

"My God," she said, and the other hand came up out of her apron pocket and went to her lips, as though she thought perhaps with both hands she could keep the pain from pouring over. "My God," she said again and then, on a rising note of helplessness, "Why did you marry me?"

For a long, long moment George Hurst couldn't speak. The words Mary's father had thrown at him years ago across the luncheon table in Winston Sherrod's club were suddenly winking on and off in his mind, as though they were being spelled out in neon lights on Porky Haenigson's sign: *It's all very well for you youngsters to thumb your noses selfishly at the rest of the world, but the rest of the world has a way of catching up with you and having the last laugh.*

"I married you because I loved you," George Hurst said. "I've never stopped loving you. I love you now."

Mary shook her head. "No," she said. "Even if you believed that, even if I wanted to believe it, you couldn't do what you did on our wedding day—you couldn't *feel* like that, whether you did it or not—you couldn't, you couldn't, you couldn't! No, it couldn't be true. You never loved me. You—" She paused, and her eyes narrowed slightly, and she caught her lower lip in her teeth, as though she were trying to do a simple arithmetic problem in her head, something she had done over and over again on other occasions, but now the answer would not come to her. "And yet I could have sworn," Mary said, very slowly. "There were times when—" She paused again, obviously thinking about those times. "I couldn't have been wrong," she said finally, as though addressing herself. "I felt it," she said. "I never before felt it." Mary looked at him quickly. "That day in Kneichbreit's, that silly place where they—"

"Poultry."

"Yes," she said, nodding, her words coming faster. "Pearl Harbor Day. That day. Later, I mean. When we left that place. All the things you said to me—" She paused and looked at him pleadingly. "George, that day, you loved me that day, didn't you?"

"I've just told you. I loved you then. I love you now."

Mary shook her head, sharply. "No," she said, her voice firm. "It's a lie," Mary said. "You couldn't love me then, and do what you did an hour before we got married. It doesn't make sense."

"I didn't say it makes sense. I'm saying I couldn't help myself."

She looked puzzled. "You couldn't help yourself?" she said slowly, as though she wanted to make sure she had heard the words correctly. "I don't understand that."

"I can't explain it," George said. "I can only repeat that I couldn't help myself."

"Then you won't be able to help yourself the next time you see her. Tomorrow. The day after. Ten minutes from now." Mary shook her head. "Animals can't help themselves," she said. "Not human beings. If you love someone, the way I've loved you, the thought of some other person, some other man, why, it's—" She made a gesture of revulsion and then she stopped again, as though stunned by her own incredulity, and then she looked at him with sudden interest. "Years ago, when we first met, Leonard Prager told me it wasn't me you were interested in. He said it was Eileen. He said you and Eileen—"

"That bastard Leonard Prager, he'd say anything to cause trouble."

"Even the truth?"

"Mary, for Christ's sake!"

"It *is* the truth, isn't it?"

"Mary, will you quit this God-damn—!"

"Why should I? Because I'm striking close to home? Because I'm finding out after all these years what you really are? All these years, living here, fixing up the house, the children growing up, going to the train every morning, doing your chores, taking the clock to Mr. Ashorn to be fixed, d'Artagnan to the vet to have his ear looked at, dropping Win and Jimmy at camp every morning, picking up Carolina at the bus, all those things, and all that time, for eight years, deep down inside you've kept this secret, you've been living another life, a total stranger, a man I never suspected—"

"God damn it," George said, starting around the table toward her. "If you don't quit this stupid, crazy talk, I'll—"

Mary backed away, circling the table, keeping it between them. "Don't touch me," she said, her eyes wide, her breath coming fast. "Don't put your hands on me,—you—you—you—"

George stopped moving toward her. It was like that day so long ago when he was broke and sleeping in Grand Central and he did not realize until the minestrone was set before him why the man who had picked him up was paying for his dinner. George thought he was going to be sick.

"Go ahead," he said savagely. "Say it. You're all the same. Every damn one of you. From Mike Gerrity and Eff Eff Schumacher right straight up to the Sherrods of Philadelphia. Why don't you go ahead and say what you want to say? Why don't you call me a dirty kike?"

There was a pause. The look in Mary's eyes changed slightly. Her face did that extraordinary thing it always did when her mind, constantly on the alert for new facts, found one. Her face seemed to glow. This time, however, the light of discovery was streaked with horror, as though in the moment of revelation, hard on the heels of the newly uncovered fact, had come the shattering knowledge that what she had just learned would have been better left unlearned.

"You think—?" she began, her voice uneven, as though she were struggling to recover from the impact of the blow. "All these years you've been thinking that I—?" She paused again, and she shook her head angrily, but it was clear that the anger was directed at herself because, wanting desperately to remain calm for dealing with the horror, she could not make her shaking body do her bidding. "All these years," she managed to say, and the note of wonder, of disbelief, came through clearly, in spite of the horror and the way her body shook and the tears that were straining for release, "you've believed I could call you that? All these years you've believed I think of you not as someone I love but as a Jew?" She sucked in her breath and, with a sharp, involuntary shiver, she said, "That's what you've believed about me all these years?"

Fighting against the distraction, wishing he could erase the recollection so he would be free to handle what all at once was completely unmanageable, George was suddenly remembering clearly the agonizing moment, during his first visit to Mary's apartment on Twelfth Street, when he had discovered that she had asked Eileen Bucknell to invite him down for a drink, not because she was scheming to get something from him, but because Mary had wanted him to join her in celebrating the fact that she had that day joined the *Noon* staff. It had not occurred to him then, when he had known her for a matter of days, that a Gentile could want to spend time with a Jew except for ulterior motives. It was even more agonizing to learn now, when he had been married to her for almost eight years, that this Gentile had never thought of him as a Jew but as a human being.

"Listen," he said. "Mary, listen. I—"

"No, I won't listen," she said, shaking her head again, impatiently, as though, aware that her time was limited, she could not allow interruptions before she finished what she had to say. "Neither will I do what you want me to do. You'd like me to do it, wouldn't you? Because that would solve everything for you, wouldn't it? All I have to do is call you that dirty name, and then everything that happened, what you did on our wedding day, none of it would be your fault. All of it would be due to the fact that I hate Jews, like your Mr. Gerrity and that Mr. Shumacher. Well, I'm not going to give you that easy way out. I'm not going to let you hide what you've done, or what you think you've done, or the way you've thought about me for eight years, I'm not going to let you hide any of that behind a dirty name. Because I'm different from your Mr. Gerrity and that Mr. Shumacher and yes, my own father. I don't hate Jews. If I did, I never would have married one. But now, now, *now*. I'll tell you now what I do hate. *You!*"

With the final syllable, exploding on a note of hopelessness and desperation, went the last flimsy barriers that had managed to create the illusion of self-control. In the few numbed moments before the pain struck, while the room still hummed from the fierceness with which she had slammed the door behind her, George could hear the convulsive, tearing sobs that had accompanied her out of the room. He stood there, absolutely motionless, like a man caught in the debris of a train wreck who knows he must try to escape but finds himself too distracted by a distant, puzzling sound to make the effort to save himself. After several moments the sound ceased to be puzzling. George Hurst knew what it was. A mocking inner voice was telling him the long masquerade had finally ended. He could stop pretending he liked coffee. It was all right to cut down the grape arbor. He never again would have to name a son after a man he hated.

The lesson that cost Aunt Tessie's life had at last been learned.

IV

VI

47

"Surprise, surprise," Dr. Henry Hubert said as he stopped his car. "What are you doing here?"

Trying to find my way back, George wanted to say. Hunting for a crack in the door Mary slammed in my face several hours ago. But of course he couldn't say that to an outsider. Any more than he could say to Mary, who lay white-faced and silent on her bed behind the locked door on Queen's Court Road, I made a mistake; I didn't realize you were different from the other members of the enemy camp; excuse it, please.

"I'm doing the same thing these other Dandypops in this parking area are doing," George said. "Seeing to it that you visitors to our little clambake don't bang up your fenders."

He wondered, with a sudden wave of panic, what he would do if he couldn't find a way back. His mind had been churning all afternoon, plotting and planning, but it had turned up nothing that made sense. What was he going to do when this foolish clambake was over? Or even when all the cars were parked? Without Mary and the kids, how was he going to fill the time between now and eternity?

"That's not what I mean," Dr. Hubert said. "I thought you were on the Food Committee?"

"I was," George said. "But Hoxter Monahan didn't seem to like the way I tied clams, so he bumped me up here to the parking detail." I'll find a way, George thought. I've got to. Even if the only way is to break the door down. Now that it had been slammed in his face, he understood for the first time the true value of what lay behind it. A horn honked behind Dr. Hubert's car. "You better pull in up there to the right, Henry, next to that blue and white Chevvy," George said. "There's an impatient customer behind you."

Dr. Hubert's car moved on. Polly Stiefel's maroon Cadillac pulled up beside George.

"I don't know why I even bother to talk to you," she said.

"I'm sorry about last night," George said. "I really was too tired to stay longer."

"Yes, I'll bet you're sorry."

"This is no place to make book. Just pull it up there to the right, Polly, next to Dr. Hubert."

"I'll never make it without crashing into him. I'm the world's worst parker. Would you do it for me, George?"

"All right, move over."

"No, I'll hop out."

She did, leaving the door of the Cadillac open, and George slipped in behind the wheel. He nodded to Hume Stiefel without actually looking at the bathing-suit manufacturer at the far end of the wide front seat. George was thinking of the way he felt every morning when he came into the kitchen for his breakfast and he had his first chance of the day to catch a glimpse of his family all in a group. There was that funny little feeling in his heart. Not because the inner voice was asking, as it did every morning, "How did I do it? How did I get a wife like this and kids like these? How did it happen?" This time the funny little feeling was in his heart, because now that George Hurst knew the answer at last, he had to find a way to hold onto them. He eased the Cadillac up beside Dr. Hubert's car, pulled the brake tight, and turned off the ignition.

"Better leave the keys in the car, Hume. Just in case we have to move any of these—"

George's voice stopped. He was not talking to Hume Stiefel.

"I don't want to rush you," Daniel Shaw said from the far end of the seat. "But my plans have changed. I'm not staying until to-morrow. I had a call from the coast. Something's come up that makes it necessary for me to fly back tonight."

"The deal for buying the Hagensdorf Hotel in Omaha?"

Danny took the cigar out of his mouth with an abrupt little gesture of surprise. "How'd you know about that?"

"I heard it from an old client," George said dryly.

"Well, I'll be damned," Danny said. "I thought the Hagensdorf deal was so far under wraps that not even my own lawyers know all the details. What kind of client, kid? A hotel owner?"

"The nature of her business wouldn't interest you."

"A her, huh?" Danny laughed. "You know, kid, a respectable married man like you shouldn't have women clients. People might talk."

"Nobody ever talks about accountants."

"I know one guy who might."

"Who?"

"Me," Danny said. George turned to look at him. Danny took a long pull on the cigar, blew the smoke out the window, then examined the ash. "George," he said quietly, "I asked you last night to do me a favor. You said you'd think it over. I was willing to let you think, not only for old time's sake but also because I believed I had until tomorrow to sit around while you did your thinking. Now that I find I don't have until tomorrow, I'm afraid I have to shift gears, kid. I'm not asking you to keep quiet about the L. L. Parker stamp mess as a favor to me. I'm ordering you to keep quiet about it as a favor to yourself."

"It looks like living out there in all that sun has done something to your memory," George said. "I stopped taking orders from you a long time ago."

He shoved open the door of the car. Danny pulled him back.

"Don't force me to cause trouble," Danny said. "Maybe you didn't hear me so good. I gave you that order as a favor to yourself. You'll do it, kid, or else."

"Or else what?" George said.

"You'll keep quiet about the L. L. Parker thing," Danny said, "Or I'll see to it that your wife finds out you've been seeing Dora regularly ever since you got married."

"How do you know that?"

As soon as the words were out, George realized they were the wrong ones. Danny was grinning.

"I have old clients, too," he said dryly. "You'd be surprised what they tell me."

George wondered for a moment how best to phrase the surprise he had in store for Danny, and then he abandoned the effort. It wasn't worth the trouble. What Danny had said the night before was true enough. Revenge, which was so highly advertised as sweet, was actually a bore. It was Mary and the children he wanted. Not evening the old score with Danny. The time had come to get him out of the way.

"Danny, it doesn't make any difference whether I give you the promise you want or not," George said. "You're never going to get that Senate seat."

"Something else you heard from that old client?"

"Yes," George said. "Her name is Dora. She told me last night she's just waiting for the moment when you've accepted the nomination and your campaign is in high gear before she slaps you with a divorce suit that will raise a smell from coast to coast."

"And you believed her?"

George looked at Danny curiously. "Don't you?"

"Doing a thing like that could hurt a man," Danny said.

"The way I analyze it," George said, "I'd say that's exactly what Dora had in mind."

"Well, kid, I analyze it differently. I don't think Dora wants to hurt Daniel Shaw."

"Why not?"

"Would you do anything to hurt somebody you love?"

It was a strange question to be asked a few hours after what had happened on Queen's Court Road.

"We're not talking about me," George said. "We're talking about Dora. Every time I've seen her since that day in the Forest when her arm got hurt, she's told me how much she hates you."

Danny nodded. "Sure," he said sarcastically. "That's why she came across the street to help me out of a jam the night I was opening Gerrity's and her sister Ida conked out on me. That's why she helped me screw you on that Sapina deal. That's why she hopped in the sack with you on my orders the time I needed five grand and I thought the only way I could put my hands on it was by getting her to hook you. That's why, on the day she was supposed to become Mrs. George Hurst, she ran away and married me instead." Danny laughed. "Some hate, huh?" He shook his head. "I know how you used to feel about her, so that explains how you could be wrong about her in those days. But you're a big boy now, George. It's time you learned the facts of life. That dame was always crazy about me. All that stuff about how she hates me was just a cover-up because she knew I didn't give a damn about her."

"You married her."

Danny nodded. "And lived with her for years because I needed her," he said. "I'm not ashamed to admit it. She needed me, too. We went into it with our eyes open, because I needed a singer and she needed someone to make her a singer. I told her in advance I didn't love her. I warned her if the time came when the deal didn't work, I'd walk out. She said she didn't care. She married me. On her insistence. She was the one wanted the marriage license, not me. Without it, she said, it was no deal. I did it her way, and when the time came when the deal wasn't working, I asked for a divorce. She refused. I argued and argued and after a while I got tired of arguing. I just blew. I figured pretty soon she'd get the idea and divorce me. She never did. I haven't seen or heard from her in a long time, but the first years after I walked out, when I was just beginning to hit my stride, I offered her plenty if she'd give me a divorce. She said no. She didn't want any dough. She wanted me. You're never going to get me, I told her. She wouldn't listen, so I stopped talking and never went back.

"After a while I lost track of her. Lots of times, these last few years, ever since I made it really big, I thought she'd walk in on me and ask for her cut. Any other dame would. But not Dora Dienst. She never asked me for a dime, and she never will. You know why? Because she's tough. That delicate little kisser, like one of those dolls in her old man's store. That gimpy arm. Those big black eyes. You'd think she was made of glass. One touch and she'll break. Glass, huh? That dame is made of copper tubing. Wherever she is, she's outwaiting me. I'm going to have to come to her, she figures. Until that day, she'll live on bread and water. She'll eat stones. She'll hook some poor slob to support her while she's waiting, or she'll hook a dozen. She'll do anything. It doesn't matter what. You name it, she'll do it. Because she loves me and she thinks I'll come back to her some day. Well, I'm not coming back to her, wherever she is, but this much you can be sure of: wherever she is, it's Danny Shaw she's still carrying the torch for, and that's why she'll never sue for divorce while I'm in the middle of a political campaign or anything else. She'll just keep waiting, and so far as I'm concerned, kid, she can keep right on waiting. So let's just forget about Dora and stick to us. Do I get your promise, or don't I?"

George didn't answer. Not because he was still having trouble with words. All at once he was having trouble with his breathing. It was as though that illustration in the history book had stood up on the page and stepped out into the street. All at once Daniel Shaw the hotel tycoon was more real to George Hurst than Danny Schorr had ever been: the way back, the crack in the door Mary had slammed shut, had suddenly opened up.

"You've got all you're ever getting out of me," George said, and he shoved the door open. "I'm not giving you any more."

Danny pulled the cigar from his mouth as though he were taking a cork from a bottle. He slid across the seat. "Take my advice and don't do anything stupid," he said as George got out of the car. "You know I mean what I say," Danny called, his voice rising the way it used to rise on Fourth Street when some detail in one of the deals he had cooked up went wrong. "Use your head, kid," he shouted. "Before you do anything, you'd better think, and think hard!"

George tried to do some of it as he crossed the tape lines of the parking lot and pushed through the crowd to the place beyond the bathhouses where he had parked his own car. He heard Hoxter Monahan call to him as he got into the car, but George neither turned nor called back. He tried harder as he pulled away from the beach and drove up Dune Drive toward the Post Road, but he couldn't seem to get his mind in gear. Thinking and hoping didn't mix. Just the same, when he turned into the parking area in front of Haenigson's Steak House, he was still trying.

He jumped out of the car, ran toward the entrance with double doors, then stopped and glanced at his watch. A quarter to six. Even if Porky Haenigson supplied all his Fourth of July week-end cutomers with dinner music, it wasn't likely that any of them would be listening to it this early. George veered to the left, moved around the main building, and hurried down the second aisle to cabin number sixteen. In front of the door, with his hand raised to knock, he made one last attempt. It wasn't any good. This was one thing he couldn't think his way through. This was one thing he had to see for himself. He knocked on the door.

"Yes?"

"It's me."

The door opened.

"For heaven's sake!" Dora said. She was wearing the same pink negligee. "I thought you said yesterday you'd be working all night at that clambake?"

"I was," George said. "But I got to thinking about the talk we had last night and it occurred to me there was one angle we never got around to discussing."

"What's that?"

"Let's go inside," George said. "Before that man with the Wisconsin license plate in number seventeen starts clapping for an encore."

Dora stepped back into the cabin. George followed her in and closed the door. She picked up a glass from the litter of make-up jars and tubes on the cheap pine bureau top.

"Do you want a drink?" He shook his head. Dora said, "Mind if I finish this one?" George shook his head again. Dora sat down on the bed and crossed her legs. One bare ankle came free through the folds of the negligee. She swung it up and down slowly as she took a sip and said, "What's the angle we didn't get around to discussing?"

"What you're going to do after you get the divorce from Danny."

Dora laughed. "With the bundle I'll take from him, that won't be much of a problem," she said. "Don't worry."

"I can't help worrying," George said. "In fact, I'm so worried about it that I've decided to make it a condition of my helping you."

"A condition?" Dora said. "What do you mean, condition?"

"I'll get you the lawyer, and I'll pay him," George said. "On condition that you convince me I'm not wasting my time or my money."

A tremor of suspicion raced across Dora's face. It was as though, having agreed without thought to cash a small check for an old friend, it had just begun to dawn on her that she had been tricked into subjecting herself to a charge of forgery.

"How can I do that?" she said.

"By telling me the truth."

"But George, I've always told you the—" She paused, and she caught her lower lip in her teeth for a moment, and then she said, "George, I don't know why you're all of a sudden taking this attitude."

"It's simple enough," George said. "Danny wants that Senate seat pretty badly. Suppose, in the middle of his campaign, when you come out of left field to slap your divorce suit against him, suppose Danny says let's make a deal. Suppose he says no matter what you're asking for, no matter how much of a bundle you want, I'll give you more, I'll give you twice as much, I'll give you everything I've got, if instead of divorcing me, you come back and live with me?"

"Cut it out," Dora said harshly. "Quit it."

She turned away. George walked around the bed and faced her again.

"If you could have him back right now?" he said. "Would you take him?"

She didn't answer. George put his hand under Dora's chin and pushed her head up. His heart jumped the way it had jumped twenty minutes ago on the front seat of Polly Stiefel's Cadillac when the figure of Daniel Shaw had come up off the page of the history book and become a living man who had pointed out for George Hurst the way back he had been hunting all afternoon. The look in Dora's eyes was all the answer he needed. But it was not all the answer he wanted. After thirty years he was entitled to more.

"If you could have him back right now," George repeated. "Would you take him?"

Dora shook her chin free. She squeezed her eyes tight shut and put both fists to her mouth, as though fighting off an attack of dizziness. When she opened her eyes, she looked frightened.

"Danny doesn't want me back," she said.

"Not now, no. But in the middle of a campaign, when he can almost feel the leather of that Senate seat against his pants, when he'll do anything not to lose what he wants more than he wants money, at a time when it's a matter of political life and death for him to look respectable, to look like any other happily married man, at a time like that, no matter what he thinks of you or how he feels about you, even if he hates your guts," George said, putting it as brutally as he could so that, when she gave him her answer, there would be no doubt about its meaning, "at a time like that Danny might take you back." George paused. "Isn't that what you've been counting on?" he said quietly. "Isn't that what you've been waiting for? Isn't that why you've refused to divorce him all these years? Isn't that what you really had in mind when you finally asked me yesterday to get you a lawyer?" George paused again. Dora did not speak. "You don't want a divorce," George said. "You want what you've always wanted, from the very beginning, all the way back there when we were kids on East Fourth Street. You want Danny. That's all you want and that's all you've ever wanted. On any terms. Under any conditions. Danny. Just Danny. Isn't that right, Dora?"

Staring into her eyes, trying to disregard the beating of his own heart, George was suddenly shocked into remembering the way he had felt the day before in Resnick's, when Nick Perrini had asked what it would be like for his Violetta to live with all those Jews. George could see from the look in Dora's eyes that for her, too, the long masquerade was over. By closing her in, by leaving her with no escape hatch, by forcing her to a statement from which there could be no retraction, George had stripped away the wall she had built around herself after her arm was hurt in the Forest on Armistice Day and from behind which she could emerge only when she was singing to an audience. With the disappearance of the wall went the sense of responsibility she had imposed on him, the carefully nurtured belief that he must take care of her, a feeling he had mistaken for love. It was as though an impostor, a thief who had managed to live successfully for years by passing checks with a forged signature, had at last been caught. She was completely exposed. There was nothing left behind which she could hide. For Dora, as for him, the moment of truth had arrived.

"Yes, I want Danny," she said in a low voice, turning her head to one side, as though unable to face her own humiliation, and then her body moved in a slight, trembling shiver. She looked up. Their eyes met again. As though an important afterthought had just occurred to her, Dora nodded: two short, crisp bobs of her head. She seemed to be conceding his right to the ironical justice of hearing her say it again, with unmistakable clarity. Even more quietly, she said, "Under any conditions. On any terms. I want Danny."

George could feel the tension ease out of his arms and legs. His whole body seemed to sag. It was all over. He was free at last.

"You don't need any lawyers," he said, and he paused to look at her curiously, as though he had never seen her before. In a way, he never had. All these years, because he thought she hated Danny but was trapped by his power over her, George had felt responsible for her. Now that he knew she was not his responsibility, he was free to feel for her something entirely new: pity. She was trapped worse than he had ever been. "You don't need any lawyers," he repeated. "You don't even have to wait until the middle of Danny's campaign," George said quietly. "You can do this by yourself. Tuesday morning, when you get back to New York, call up a Mr. Maurice Kashkin at the Waldorf-Astoria. That's K, a, s, h, k, i, n, Kashkin. Just tell him who you are, and he'll deliver your devoted husband to you on a silver platter."

George turned and walked out. Dora did not call to him. If she had, he wouldn't have turned back. His responsibilities now lay in another direction. He hurried up the aisle of cabins to the double entrance between Porky Haenigson's two restaurants. The phone booth was empty. George decided to consider that a good omen. The decision seemed justified by the speed with which the long-distance operator put him through to the Waldorf, and the fact that Mr. Kashkin was in his room.

"I promised to call you at the Waldorf on Tuesday," George said. "I'm calling now to say that I'm afraid I'm going to have to break that promise."

Mr. Kashkin's voice rose sharply. "Does that mean, Mr. Hurst, that I'm not going to get the information I asked for?"

"It means you're not going to get it from me," George said. "I've arranged for somebody else to call you at the Waldorf on Tuesday."

"Will this somebody else be in a position to tell me whether Mrs. Daniel Shaw is alive or dead?"

"I'll let you judge that for yourself, Mr. Kashkin."

"I think it only fair to repeat now what I told you in your office yesterday, Mr. Hurst. If I do not get the information I want through you, I will have to instruct our investigators, who stopped digging when they got as far as you, to resume their digging."

"All right," George said. "You've repeated it."

"Digging, as I also told you yesterday, is a nasty business, Mr. Hurst. Once a man starts digging, there's no telling what he'll find."

"Then it should be a very rewarding activity for a man who enjoys surprises," George said. "You keep right on digging, Mr. Kashkin."

He hung up and walked out to his car. All the way up the Post Road he kept wondering what Mr. Kashkin's diggers would find first. Danny's role in the L. L. Parker stamp robbery? Or the fact that his wife had once earned twenty dollars a night by working for Mrs. Hooper? The sequence didn't matter. Either one would be enough to keep Daniel Shaw from changing his address to Washington, D.C.

Racing up the Post Road, George suddenly found himself wishing that Uncle Zisha was still alive. Not because the importance of keeping a man like Danny from becoming a legislator in the same country that had produced Judge Brandeis was something Uncle Zisha would have understood. George wished Uncle Zisha was alive because it was his lesson, and not Aunt Tessie's, that George had finally learned.

Don't hide, Uncle Zisha had said. Don't dig a hole, don't make a private ghetto for yourself and creep into it, the way Aunt Tessie did. Do what your heart tells you, not your religion. It's more important to be a man than a Jew, Uncle Zisha had said, and without listening to your heart you'll never be a man.

What Uncle Zisha had omitted from his lesson was the problem of acoustics. Listening to the heart was not easy. There were too many distracting sounds. It had taken George Hurst eight years to sort them out.

Turning the car into Queen's Court Road, where Mary and the children would just be sitting down to supper, he was reminded of the way he had felt all those years ago, when he was going to meet her for their first date. There was the same sense of excitement, the same feeling that he was standing on a threshold, that stretching before him lay a world of fulfillment to which all men were entitled but only a fortunate few achieved. He had not known then, of course, that he would achieve it. Now, years later, he didn't see how he could miss.

If Winston Sherrod's prediction had come true, if the world at which George Hurst had thumbed his nose had finally caught up with him, it was not—he knew, finally, as he inserted the key in the lock of his front door—because he had been barred from a few hotels in Florida but because with his own terrors he had barred himself from going to Mary as she had come to him, and as he was now free at last to go to her: with no strings attached.

ABOUT THE AUTHOR

JEROME WEIDMAN, novelist and short-story writer, was born in 1913 on New York City's Lower East Side where—between part-time jobs as a newsboy, Coney Island hot dog vendor, and operator in a necktie factory—he was educated in the public schools. He started to write at nineteen, while studying accountancy in the evening session at the College of the City of New York, and two years later was contributing short stories regularly to *The New Yorker*. He was studying law at New York University when, at the age of twenty-four, his first novel, *I Can Get It for You Wholesale*, was published in 1937. He quit law school at once to devote all his time to writing, and has been doing so ever since, except during the war when he served with the Office of War Information in this country and overseas. He has traveled extensively in America and the far corners of the world, from which he has brought back raw material for a dozen novels and approximately two hundred short stories, published in almost every magazine in the United States as well as in Canada, Europe, Australia and Asia. His books have been translated into eight languages. THE ENEMY CAMP, his sixteenth book, was written in Westport, Connecticut, where Mr. Weidman lives with his wife and two young sons.